ANTHONY TROLLOPE, the fourth of six surviving children, was born on 24 April 1815 in London. As he describes in his *Autobiography*, poverty and debt made his childhood acutely unhappy and disrupted his education: his school fees at Harrow and Winchester were frequently unpaid. His family attempted to restore their fortunes by going to America, leaving the young Anthony alone in England, but it was not until his mother, Frances, began to write that there was any improvement in the family's finances. Her success came too late for her husband, who died in exile in Belgium in 1835. Trollope was unable to afford a university education, and in 1834 he became a junior clerk in the Post Office. He achieved little until he was appointed Surveyor's Clerk in Ireland in 1841. There he worked hard, travelled widely, took up hunting and still found time for his literary career. He married Rose Heseltine, the daughter of a bank manager, in 1844; they had two sons, one of whom emigrated to Australia. Trollope frequently went abroad for the Post Office and did not settle in England again until 1859. He is still remembered as the inventor of the letter-box. In 1867 he resigned from the Post Office and became the editor of *St Paul's Magazine* for the next three years. He failed in his attempt to enter Parliament as a Liberal in 1868. Trollope took his place among London literary society and counted William Thackeray, George Eliot and G. H. Lewes among his friends. He died on 6 December 1882 as the result of a stroke.

Anthony Trollope wrote forty-seven novels and five volumes of short stories as well as travel books, biographies and collections of sketches. The Barsetshire series and the six Palliser or 'political' books were the first novel-sequences to be written in English. His works offer an unsurpassed portrait of the professional and landed classes of Victorian England. In his *Autobiography* (published posthumously in 1883) Trollope describes the self-discipline that enabled his prolific output: he would produce a given number of words per hour in the early morning, before work; he always wrote while travelling by rail or sea, and as soon as he finished one novel he began another. His efforts resulted in his becoming one of England's most successful and popular writers.

Marion Fay (1882) was first published simultaneously in the *Graphic* and in the *Illustrated Sydney News*. Shortly after starting the manuscript in 1879, Trollope laid it aside to write a biography of his friend, Thackeray. The novel draws on Trollope's early experiences as a clerk in the Post Office, as was recognized by a critic in the *Saturday Review* who noted: 'The various degrees in that office, from high to low, the dialogues between heads and subordinates, are all given with spirit, and are accepted by the reader as dealing with matter on which the writer is an authority.' The *Athenaeum* commented that 'in Mr Trollope's latest novel the reader will recognize with pleasure much of the brightness and lightness of touch which characterized his early work.'

MARION FAY

ANTHONY TROLLOPE

PENGUIN BOOKS

PENGUIN BOOKS

Published by the Penguin Group
Penguin Books Ltd, 27 Wrights Lane, London W8 5TZ, England
Penguin Books USA Inc., 375 Hudson Street, New York, New York 10014, USA
Penguin Books Australia Ltd, Ringwood, Victoria, Australia
Penguin Books Canada Ltd, 10 Alcorn Avenue, Toronto, Ontario, Canada M4V 3B2
Penguin Books (NZ) Ltd, 182–190 Wairau Road, Auckland 10, New Zealand

Penguin Books Ltd, Registered Offices: Harmondsworth, Middlesex, England

First published 1882
Published in Penguin Books 1993
1 3 5 7 9 10 8 6 4 2

Printed in England by Clays Ltd, St Ives plc

CONTENTS OF VOLUME I.

CONTENTS.

CONTENTS.

CONTENTS.

CONTENTS OF VOLUME II.

CONTENTS.

CONTENTS.

CONTENTS.

CHAPTER XX.

CHAPTER XXI.

CONTENTS OF VOLUME III.

CONTENTS.

CONTENTS.

CHAPTER XIII.

CHAPTER XIV.

CHAPTER XV.

CHAPTER XVI.

CHAPTER XVII.

CHAPTER XVIII.

CHAPTER XIX.

CONTENTS.

CHAPTER XX.

CHAPTER XXI.

VOLUME I

MARION FAY.

CHAPTER I.

THE MARQUIS OF KINGSBURY.

When Mr. Lionel Trafford went into Parliament for the Borough of Wednesbury as an advanced Radical, it nearly broke the heart of his uncle, the old Marquis of Kingsbury. Among Tories of his day the Marquis had been hyper-Tory,—as were his friends, the Duke of Newcastle, who thought that a man should be allowed to do what he liked with his own, and the Marquis of Londonderry, who, when some such falling-off in the family politics came near him, spoke with indignation of the family treasure which had been expended in defending the family seat. Wednesbury had never been the Marquis's own; but his nephew was so in a peculiar sense. His nephew was necessarily his heir,—the future Marquis, — and the old Marquis never again, politically, held up his head. He was an old man

when this occurred, and luckily for him he did not live
to see the worse things which came afterwards.

The Member for Wednesbury became Marquis and
owner of the large family property, but still he kept
his politics. He was a Radical Marquis, wedded to all
popular measures, not ashamed of his Charter days,
and still clamorous for further Parliamentary reform,
although it was regularly noted in Dod that the
Marquis of Kingsbury was supposed to have strong
influence in the Borough of Edgeware. It was so
strong that both he and his uncle had put in whom
they pleased. His uncle had declined to put him in
because of his renegade theories, but he revenged himself by giving the seat to a glib-mouthed tailor, who, to
tell the truth, had not done much credit to his choice.

But it came to pass that the shade of his uncle was
avenged, if it can be supposed that such feelings will
affect the eternal rest of a dead Marquis. There grew
up a young Lord Hampstead, the son and heir of the
Radical Marquis, promising in intelligence and satisfactory in externals, but very difficult to deal with as
to the use of his thoughts. They could not keep him
at· Harrow or at Oxford, because he not only rejected,
but would talk openly against, Christian doctrines; a
religious boy, but determined not to believe in revealed
mysteries. And at twenty-one he declared himself a
Republican,—explaining thereby that he disapproved
altogether of hereditary honours. He was quite as bad
to this Marquis as had been this Marquis to the other.

The tailor kept his seat because Lord Hampstead would not even condescend to sit for the family borough. He explained to his father that he had doubts about a Parliament of which one section was hereditary, but was sure that at present he was too young for it. There must surely have been gratification in this to the shade of the departed Marquis.

But there was worse than this,—infinitely worse. Lord Hampstead formed a close friendship with a young man, five years older than himself, who was but a clerk in the Post Office. In George Roden, as a man and a companion, there was no special fault to be found. There may be those who think that a Marquis's heir should look for his most intimate friend in a somewhat higher scale of social rank, and that he would more probably serve the purposes of his future life by associating with his equals;—that like to like in friendship is advantageous. The Marquis, his father, certainly thought so in spite of his Radicalism. But he might have been pardoned on the score of Roden's general good gifts, —might have been pardoned even though it were true, as supposed, that to Roden's strong convictions Lord Hampstead owed much of the ultra virus of his political convictions,—might have been pardoned had not there been worse again. At Hendon Hall, the Marquis's lovely suburban seat, the Post Office clerk was made acquainted with Lady Frances Trafford, and they became lovers.

The radicalism of a Marquis is apt to be tainted by

special considerations in regard to his own family. This Marquis, though he had his exoteric politics, had his esoteric feelings. With him, Liberal as he was, his own blood possessed a peculiar ichor. Though it might be well that men in the mass should be as nearly equal as possible, yet, looking at the state of possibilities and realities as existent, it was clear to him that a Marquis of Kingsbury had been placed on a pedestal. It might be that the state of things was matter for regret. In his grander moments he was certain that it was so. Why should there be a ploughboy unable to open his mouth because of his infirmity, and a Marquis with his own voice very resonant in the House of Lords, and a deputy voice dependent on him in the House of Commons? He had said so very frequently before his son, not knowing then what might be the effect of his own teaching. There had been a certain pride in his heart as he taught these lessons, wrong though it might be that there should be a Marquis and a ploughboy so far reversed by the injustice of Fate. There had been a comfort to him in feeling that Fate had made him the Marquis, and had made some one else the plough-boy. He knew what it was to be a Marquis down to the last inch of aristocratic admeasurement. He would fain that his children should have understood this also. But his lesson had gone deeper than he had intended, and great grief had come of it.

The Marquis had been first married to a lady alto-

gether unconnected with noble blood, but whose father
had held a position of remarkable ascendancy in the
House of Commons. He had never been a Cabinet
Minister, because he had persisted in thinking that he
could better serve his country by independence. He
had been possessed of wealth, and had filled a great
place in the social world. In marrying the only
daughter of this gentleman the Marquis of Kingsbury
had indulged his peculiar taste in regard to Liberalism,
and was at the same time held not to have derogated
from his rank. She had been a woman of great beauty
and of many intellectual gifts,—thoroughly imbued
with her father's views, but altogether free from feminine pedantry and that ambition which begrudges to
men the rewards of male labour. Had she lived, Lady
Frances might probably not have fallen in with the
Post Office clerk ; nevertheless, had she lived, she
would have known the Post Office clerk to be a worthy
gentleman.

But she had died when her son was about sixteen
and her daughter no more than fifteen. Two years
afterwards our Marquis had gone among the dukes, and
had found for himself another wife. Perhaps the freshness and edge of his political convictions had been
blunted by that gradual sinking down among the great
peers in general which was natural to his advanced
years. A man who has spouted at twenty-five becomes
tired of spouting at fifty, if nothing special has come
from his spouting. He had been glad when he married

Lady Clara Mountressor to think that circumstances as they had occurred at the last election would not make it necessary for him to deliver up the borough to the tailor on any further occasion. The tailor had been drunk at the hustings, and he ventured to hope that before six months were over Lord Hampstead would have so far rectified his frontiers as to be able to take a seat in the House of Commons.

Then very quickly there were born three little flaxen-haired boys,—who became at least flaxen-haired as they emerged from their cradles,—Lord Frederic, Lord Augustus, and Lord Gregory. That they must be brought up with ideas becoming the scions of a noble House there could be no doubt. Their mother was every inch a duke's daughter. But, alas, not one of them was likely to become Marquis of Kingsbury. Though born so absolutely in the purple they were but younger sons. This was a silent sorrow;—but when their half sister Lady Frances told their mother openly that she had plighted her troth to the Post Office clerk, that was a sorrow which did not admit of silence.

When Lord Hampstead had asked permission to bring his friend to the house there seemed to be no valid reason for refusing him. Low as he had descended amidst the depths of disreputable opinion, it was not supposed that even he would countenance anything so horrible as this. And was there not ground for security in the reticence and dignity of Lady Frances herself?

The idea never presented itself to the Marchioness. When she heard that the Post Office clerk was coming she was naturally disgusted. All Lord Hampstead's ideas, doings, and ways were disgusting to her. She was a woman full of high-bred courtesy, and had always been gracious to her son-in-law's friends,—but it had been with a cold grace. Her heart rejected them thoroughly,—as she did him, and, to tell the truth, Lady Frances also. Lady Frances had all her mother's dignity, all her mother's tranquil manner, but something more than her mother's advanced opinions. She, too, had her ideas that the world should gradually be taught to dispense with the distances which separate the dukes and the ploughboys,—gradually, but still with a progressive motion, always tending in that direction. This to her stepmother was disgusting.

The Post Office clerk had never before been received at Hendon Hall, though he had been introduced in London by Lord Hampstead to his sister. The Post Office clerk had indeed abstained from coming, having urged his own feelings with his friend as to certain unfitnesses. "A Marquis is as absurd to me as to you," he had said to Lord Hampstead, "but while there are Marquises they should be indulged,—particularly Marchionesses. An over-delicate skin is a nuisance; but if skins have been so trained as not to bear the free air, veils must be allowed for their protection. The object should be to train the skin, not to punish it abruptly. An unfortunate Sybarite

Marchioness ought to have her rose leaves. Now I am not a rose leaf." And so he had stayed away.

But the argument had been carried on between the friends, and the noble heir had at last prevailed. George Roden was not a rose leaf, but he was found at Hendon to have flowers of beautiful hues and with a sweet scent. Had he not been known to be a Post Office clerk,—could the Marchioness have been allowed to judge of him simply from his personal appearance,— he might have been taken to be as fine a rose leaf as any. He was a tall, fair, strongly-built young man, with short light hair, pleasant grey eyes, an aquiline nose, and small mouth. In his gait and form and face nothing was discernibly more appropriate to Post Office clerks than to the nobility at large. But he was a clerk, and he himself, as he himself declared, knew nothing of his own family,—remembered no relation but his mother.

It had come to pass that the house at Hendon had become specially the residence of Lord Hampstead, who would neither have lodgings of his own in London or make part of the family when it occupied Kingsbury House in Park Lane. He would sometimes go abroad, would sometimes appear for a week or two at Trafford Park, the grand seat in Yorkshire. But he preferred the place, half town half country, in the neighbourhood of London, and here George Roden came frequently backwards and forwards after the ice had been broken by a first visit. Sometimes the Marquis would be there, and with him his daughter,—rarely the Marchioness. Then came the time when Lady Frances declared boldly to her stepmother that she had pledged her troth to the Post Office clerk. That happened in June, when Parliament was sitting, and when the flowers at Hendon were at their best. The Marchioness came there for a day or two, and the Post Office clerk on that morning had left the house for his office work, not purposing to come back. Some words had been said which had caused annoyance, and he did not intend to return. When he had been gone about an hour Lady Frances revealed the truth.

Her brother at that time was two-and-twenty. She was a year younger. The clerk might perhaps be six years older than the young lady. Had he only been the eldest son of a Marquis, or Earl, or Viscount; had he been but an embryo Baron, he might have done very well. He was a well-spoken youth, yet with a certain modesty, such a one as might easily take the eye of a wished-for though ever so noble a mother-in-law. The little lords had learned to play with him, and it had come about that he was at his ease in the house. The very servants had seemed to forget that he was no more than a clerk, and that he went off by railway into town every morning that he might earn ten shillings by sitting for six hours at his desk. Even the Marchioness had almost trained herself to like him,—as one of those excrescences which are sometimes to be found in noble families, some governess, some chaplain or private

secretary, whom chance or merit has elevated in the
house, and who thus becomes a trusted friend. Then by
chance she heard the name "Frances" without the
prefix "Lady," and said a word in haughty anger. The
Post Office clerk packed up his portmanteau, and
Lady Frances told her story.

Lord Hampstead's name was John. He was the
Honourable John Trafford, called by courtesy Earl of
Hampstead. To the world at large he was Lord Hampstead,—to his friends in general he was Hampstead; to
his stepmother he was especially Hampstead,—as would
have been her own eldest son the moment he was born
had he been born to such good luck. To his father he
had become Hampstead lately. In early days there
had been some secret family agreement that in spite of
conventionalities he should be John among them. The
Marquis had latterly suggested that increasing years made
this foolish; but the son himself attributed the change
to step-maternal influences. But still he was John to
his sister, and John to some half-dozen sympathising
friends,—and among others to the Post Office clerk.

"He has not said a word to me," the sister replied
when she was taxed by her brother with seeming
partiality for their young visitor.

"But he will?"

"No girl will ever admit as much as that, John."

"But if he should?"

"No girl will have an answer ready for such a
suggestion."

" I know he will."

" If so, and if you have wishes to express, you should speak to him."

All this made the matter quite clear to her brother. A girl such as was his sister would not so receive a brother's notice as to a proposed overture of love from a Post Office clerk, unless she had brought herself to look at the possibility without abhorrence.

" Would it go against the grain with you, John ? " This was what the clerk said when he was interrogated by his friend.

" There would be difficulties."

" Very great difficulties,—difficulties even with you."

" I did not say so."

" They would come naturally. The last thing that a man can abandon of his social-idolatries is the sanctity of the women belonging to him."

" God forbid that I should give up anything of the sanctity of my sister."

" No; but the idolatry attached to it ! It is as well that even a nobleman's daughter should be married if she can find a nobleman or such like to her taste. There is no breach of sanctity in the love,—but so great a wound to the idolatry in the man ! Things have not changed so quickly that even you should be free from the feeling. Three hundred years ago, if the man could not be despatched out of the country or to the other world, the girl at least would be locked up. Three hundred years hence the girl and the man will

stand together on their own merits. Just in this period
of transition it is very hard for such a one as you to
free himself altogether from the old trammels."

"I make the endeavour."

"Most bravely. But, my dear fellow, let this individual thing stand separately, away from politics and
abstract ideas. I mean to ask your sister whether I can
have her heart, and, as far as her will goes, her hand.
If you are displeased I suppose we shall have to part,
—for a time. Let theories run ever so high, Love will
be stronger than them all." Lord Hampstead at this
moment gave no assurance of his good will; but when
it came to pass that his sister had given her assurance,
then he ranged himself on the side of his friend the
clerk.

So it came to pass that there was great trouble in the
household of the Marquis of Kingsbury. The family
went abroad before the end of July, on account of
the health of the children. So said the *Morning Post.*
Anxious friends inquired in vain what could have befallen those flaxen-haired young Herculeses. Why was
it necessary that they should be taken to the Saxon
Alps when the beauties and comforts of Trafford Park
were so much nearer and so superior? Lady Frances
was taken with them, and there were one or two noble
intimates among the world of fashion who heard some
passing whispers of the truth. When passing whispers
creep into the world of fashion they are heard far
and wide.

CHAPTER II.

LORD HAMPSTEAD.

LORD HAMPSTEAD, though he would not go into Parliament or belong to any London Club, or walk about the streets with a chimney-pot hat, or perform any of his public functions as a young nobleman should do, had, nevertheless, his own amusements and his own extravagances. In the matter of money he was placed outside his father's liberality,—who was himself inclined to be liberal enough,—by the fact that he had inherited a considerable portion of his maternal grandfather's fortune. It might almost be said truly of him that money was no object to him. It was not that he did not often talk about money and think about money. He was very prone to do so, saying that money was the most important factor in the world's justices and injustices. But he was so fortunately circumstanced as to be able to leave money out of his own personal consideration, never being driven by the want of it to deny himself anything, or tempted by a superabundance to expenditure which did not otherwise approve itself to

him. To give 10*s.* or 20*s.* a bottle for wine because
somebody pretended that it was very fine, or £300 for a
horse when one at a £100 would do his work for him,
was altogether below his philosophy. By his father's
lodge gate there ran an omnibus up to town which he
would often use, saying that an omnibus with company
was better than a private carriage with none. He was
wont to be angry with himself in that he employed a
fashionable tailor, declaring that he incurred unnecessary
expense merely to save himself the trouble of going
elsewhere. In this, however, it may be thought that
there was something of pretence, as he was no doubt
conscious of good looks, and aware probably that a
skilful tailor might add a grace.

In his amusements he affected two which are
especially expensive. He kept a yacht, in which he
was accustomed to absent himself in the summer and
autumn, and he had a small hunting establishment in
Northamptonshire. Of the former little need be said
here, as he spent his time on board much alone, or
with friends with whom we need not follow him ; but
it may be said that everything about the *Free Trader*
was done well,—for such was the name of the vessel.
Though he did not pay 10*s.* a bottle for his wine, he
paid the best price for sails and cordage, and hired
a competent skipper to look after himself and his
boat. His hunting was done very much in the same
way,—unless it be that in his yachting he was given
to be tranquil, and in his hunting he was very fond

of hard riding. At Gorse Hall, as his cottage was called, he had all comforts, we may perhaps say much of luxury, around him. It was indeed hardly more than a cottage, having been an old farm-house, and lately converted to its present purpose. There were no noble surroundings, no stately hall, no marble staircases, no costly salon. You entered by a passage which deserved no auguster name, on the right of which was the dining-room; on the left a larger chamber, always called the drawing-room because of the fashion of the name. Beyond that was a smaller retreat in which the owner kept his books. Leading up from the end of the passage there was a steep staircase, a remnant of the old farm-house, and above them five bed-rooms, so that his lordship was limited to the number of four guests. Behind this was the kitchen and the servants' rooms—sufficient, but not more than sufficient, for such a house. Here our young democrat kept half-a-dozen horses, all of them—as men around were used to declare—fit to go, although they were said to have been bought at not more than £100 each. It was supposed to be a crotchet on the part of Lord Hampstead to assert that cheap things were as good as dear, and there were some who believed that he did in truth care as much for his horses as other people. It was certainly a fact that he never would have but one out in a day, and he was wont to declare that Smith took out his second horse chiefly that Jones might know that he did so. Down here, at Gorse Hall, the Post Office clerk had often

been received as a visitor,—but not at Gorse Hall had
he ever seen Lady Frances.

This lord had peculiar ideas about hunting, in reference to sport in general. It was supposed of him, and
supposed truly, that no young man in England was
more devotedly attached to fox-hunting than he,—and
that in want of a fox he would ride after a stag, and in
want of a stag after a drag. If everything else failed
he would go home across the country, any friend
accompanying him, or else alone. Nevertheless, he
entertained a vehement hostility against all other
sports.

Of racing he declared that it had become simply a
way of making money, and of all ways the least profit-
able to the world and the most disreputable. He was
never seen on a racecourse. But his enemies declared
of him, that though he loved riding he was no judge of
an animal's pace, and that he was afraid to bet lest he
should lose his money.

Against shooting he was still louder. If there was
in his country any tradition, any custom, any law hateful to him, it was such as had reference to the preservation of game. The preservation of a fox, he said, stood
on a perfectly different basis. The fox was not preserved by law, and when preserved was used for the
advantage of all who chose to be present at the amusement. One man in one day would shoot fifty pheasants
which had eaten up the food of half-a-dozen human
beings. One fox afforded in one day amusement to two

hundred sportsmen, and was—or more generally was not—killed during the performance. And the fox during his beneficial life had eaten no corn, nor for the most part geese,—but chiefly rats and such like. What infinitesimal sum had the fox cost the country for every man who rushed after him? Then, what had been the cost of all those pheasants which one shooting cormorant crammed into his huge bag during one day's greedy sport?

But it was the public nature of the one amusement and the thoroughly private nature of the other which chiefly affected him. In the hunting-field the farmer's son, if he had a pony, or the butcher-boy out of the town, could come and take his part; and if the butcher-boy could go ahead and keep his place while the man with a red coat and pink boots and with two horses fell behind, the butcher-boy would have the best of it, and incur the displeasure of no one. And the laws, too, by which hunting is governed, if there be laws, are thoroughly democratic in their nature. They are not, he said, made by any Parliament, but are simply assented to on behalf of the common need. It was simply in compliance with opinion that the lands of all men are open to be ridden over by the men of the hunt. In compliance with opinion foxes are preserved. In compliance with opinion coverts are drawn by this or the other pack of hounds. The Legislature had not stepped in to defile the statute book by bye-laws made in favour of the amusements of the rich. If injury were

done, the ordinary laws of the country were open to the
injured party. Anything in hunting that had grown to
be beyond the reach of the law had become so by the
force of popular opinion.

All of this was reversed in shooting, from any partici-
pation in which the poor were debarred by enactments
made solely on behalf of the rich. Four or five men
in a couple of days would offer up hecatombs of
slaughtered animals, in doing which they could only
justify themselves by the fact that they were acting as
poultry-butchers for the supply of the markets of the
country. There was no excitement in it,—simply the
firing off of many guns with a rapidity which altogether
prevents that competition which is essential to the enjoyment of sport. Then our noble Republican would
quote Teufelsdröckh and the memorable epitaph of the
partridge-slayer. But it was on the popular and un-
popular elements of the two sports that he would most
strongly dilate, and on the iniquity of the game-laws
as applying to the more aristocratic of the two. It
was, however, asserted by the sporting world at large
that Hampstead could not hit a haystack.

As to fishing, he was almost equally violent, ground-
ing his objection on the tedium and cruelty incident to
the pursuit. The first was only a matter of taste, he
would allow. If a man could content himself and be
happy with an average of one fish to every three days'
fishing, that was the man's affair. He could only think
that in such case the man himself must be as cold-

blooded as the fish which he so seldom succeeded in
catching. As to the cruelty, he thought there could
be no doubt. When he heard that bishops and ladies
delighted themselves in hauling an unfortunate animal
about by the gills for more than an hour at a stretch, he
was inclined to regret the past piety of the Church and
the past tenderness of the sex. When he spoke in this
way the cruelty of fox-hunting was of course thrown in
his teeth. Did not the poor hunted quadrupeds, when
followed hither and thither by a pack of fox-hounds,
endure torments as sharp and as prolonged as those
inflicted on the fish? In answer to this Lord Hampstead was eloquent and argumentative. As far as we
could judge from Nature the condition of the two
animals during the process was very different. The
salmon with the hook in its throat was in a position
certainly not intended by Nature. The fox, using all
its gifts to avoid an enemy, was employed exactly as
Nature had enjoined. It would be as just to compare
a human being impaled alive on a stake with another
overburdened with his world's task. The overburdened
man might stumble and fall, and so perish. Things
would have been hard to him. But not, therefore,
could you compare his sufferings with the excruciating
agonies of the poor wretch who had been left to linger
and starve with an iron rod through his vitals. This
argument was thought to be crafty rather than cunning
by those who were fond of fishing. But he had another
on which, when he had blown off the steam of his

eloquence by his sensational description of a salmon
impaled by a bishop, he could depend with greater confidence. He would grant,—for the moment, though he
was by no means sure of the fact,—but for the moment
he would grant that the fox did not enjoy the hunt.
Let it be acknowledged—for the sake of the argument
— that he was tortured by the hounds rather than
elated by the triumphant success of his own manœuvres.
Lord Hampstead "ventured to say,"—this he would
put forward in the rationalistic tone with which he
was wont to prove the absurdity of hereditary honours,
—"that in the infliction of all pain the question as to
cruelty or no cruelty was one of relative value." Was it
"tanti ? " Who can doubt that for a certain maximum
of good a certain minimum of suffering may be inflicted
without slur to humanity ? In hunting, one fox was
made to finish his triumphant career, perhaps pre-
maturely, for the advantage of two hundred sportsmen.
"Ah, but only for their amusement ! " would interpose
some humanitarian averse equally to fishing and to
hunting. Then his lordship would arise indignantly
and would ask his opponent, whether what he called
amusement was not as beneficial, as essential, as necessary to the world as even such material good things as
bread and meat. Was poetry less valuable than the
multiplication table ? Man could exist no doubt without fox-hunting. So he could without butter, without
wine, or other so-called necessaries;—without ermine
tippets, for instance, the original God-invested wearer

of which had been doomed to lingering starvation and death when trapped amidst the snow, in order that one lady might be made fine by the agonies of a dozen little furry sufferers. It was all a case of "tanti," he said, and he said that the fox who had saved himself half-a-dozen times and then died nobly on behalf of those who had been instrumental in preserving an existence for him, ought not to complain of the lot which Fate had provided for him among the animals of the earth. It was said, however, in reference to this comparison between fishing and fox-hunting, that Lord Hampstead was altogether deficient in that skill and patience which is necessary for the landing of a salmon.

But men, though they laughed at him, still they liked him. He was good-humoured and kindly-hearted. He was liberal in more than his politics. He had, too, a knack of laughing at himself, and his own peculiarities, which went far to redeem them. That a young Earl, an embryo Marquis, the heir of such a house as that of Trafford, should preach a political doctrine which those who heard ignorantly called Communistic, was very dreadful; but the horror of it was mitigated when he declared that no doubt as he got old he should turn Tory like any other Radical. In this there seemed to be a covert allusion to his father. And then they could perceive that his " Communistic " principles did not prevent him from having a good eye to the value of land. He knew what he was about, as an owner of

property should do, and certainly rode to hounds as
well as any one of the boys of the period.

When the idea first presented itself to him that his
sister was on the way to fall in love with George Roden,
it has to be acknowledged that he was displeased. It
had not occurred to him that this peculiar breach would
be made on the protected sanctity of his own family.
When Roden had spoken to him of this sanctity as one
of the "social idolatries," he had not quite been able
to contradict him. He had wished to do so both in
defence of his own consistency, and also, if it were
possible, so as to maintain the sanctity. The "divinity"
which "does hedge a king," had been to him no more
than a social idolatry. The special respect in which
dukes and such like were held was the same. The
judge's ermine and the bishop's apron were idolatries.
Any outward honour, not earned by the deeds or words
of him so honoured, but coming from birth, wealth, or
from the doings of another, was an idolatry. Carrying
on his arguments, he could not admit the same thing
in reference to his sister ;—or rather, he would have to
admit it if he could not make another plea in defence
of the sanctity. His sister was very holy to him ;—but
that should be because of her nearness to him, because
of her sweetness, because of her own gifts, because as
her brother he was bound to be her especial knight till
she should have chosen some other special knight for
herself. But it should not be because she was the
daughter, granddaughter, and great-granddaughter of

dukes and marquises. It should not be because she
was Lady Frances Trafford. Had he himself been a
Post Office clerk, then would not this chosen friend
have been fit to love her ? There were unfitnesses, no
doubt, very common in this world, which should make
the very idea of love impossible to a woman,—unfitness
of character, of habits, of feelings, of education, unfitnesses as to inward personal nobility. He could not
say that there were any such which ought to separate
his sister and his friend. If it was to be that this
sweet sister should some day give her heart to a lover,
why not to George Roden as well as to another ? There
were no such unfitnesses as those of which he would
have thought in dealing with the lives of some other
girl and some other young man.

And yet he was, if not displeased, at any rate dis-
satisfied. There was something which grated against
either his taste, or his judgment,—or perhaps his
prejudices. He endeavoured to inquire into himself
fairly on this matter, and feared that he was yet the
victim of the prejudices of his order. He was wounded
in his pride to think that his sister should make
herself equal to a clerk in the Post Office. Though
he had often endeavoured, only too successfully, to
make her understand how little she had in truth
received from her high birth, yet he felt that she had
received something which should have made the proposal of such a marriage distasteful to her. A man
cannot rid himself of a prejudice because he knows

or believes it to be a prejudice. That the two, if they
continued to wish it, must become man and wife he
acknowledged to himself;—but he could not bring
himself not to be sorry that it should be so.

There were some words on the subject between himself and his father before the Marquis went abroad with
his family, which, though they did not reconcile him to
the match, lessened the dissatisfaction. His father was
angry with him, throwing the blame of this untoward
affair on his head, and he was always prone to resent
censure thrown by any of his family on his own peculiar
tenets. Thus it came to pass that in defending himself
he was driven to defend his sister also. The Marquis
had not been at Hendon when the revelation was first
made, but had heard it in the course of the day from his
wife. His Radical tendencies had done very little
towards reconciling him to such a proposal He had
never brought his theories home into his own person-
alities. To be a Radical peer in the House of Lords, and
to have sent a Radical tailor to the House of Commons,
had been enough, if not too much, to satisfy his own
political ideas. To himself and to his valet, to all
those immediately touching himself, he had always
been the Marquis of Kingsbury. And so also, in his
inner heart, the Marchioness was the Marchioness, and
Lady Frances Lady Frances. He had never gone
through any process of realizing his convictions as his
son had done. "Hampstead," he said, "can this possibly be true what your mother has told me?" This

took place at the house in Park Lane, to which the Marquis had summoned his son.

"Do you mean about Frances and George Roden?"

"Of course I mean that."

"I supposed you did, sir. I imagined that when you sent for me it was in regard to them. No doubt it is true."

"What is true? You speak as though you absolutely approved it."

"Then my voice has belied me, for I disapprove of it."

"You feel, I hope, how utterly impossible it is."

"Not that."

"Not that?"

"I cannot say that I think it to be impossible,—or even improbable. Knowing the two, as I do, I feel the probability to be on their side."

"That they—should be married?"

"That is what they intend. I never knew either of them to mean anything which did not sooner or later get itself accomplished."

"You'll have to learn it on this occasion. How on earth can it have been brought about?" Lord Hampstead shrugged his shoulders. "Somebody has been very much to blame."

"You mean me, sir?"

"Somebody has been very much to blame."

"Of course, you mean me. I cannot take any blame in the matter. In introducing George Roden to you, and to my mother, and to Frances, I brought you to the knowledge of a highly-educated and extremely well-mannered young man."

"Good God!"

"I did to my friend what every young man, I suppose, does to his. I should be ashamed of myself to associate with any one who was not a proper guest for my father's table. One does not calculate before that a young man and a young woman shall fall in love with each other."

"You see what has happened."

"It was extremely natural, no doubt,—though I had not anticipated it. As I told you, I am very sorry. It will cause many heartburns, and some unhappiness."

"Unhappiness! I should think so. I must go away, —in the middle of the Session."

"It will be worse for her, poor girl."

"It will be very bad for her," said the Marquis, speaking as though his mind were quite made up on that matter.

"But nobody, as far as I can see, has done anything wrong," continued Lord Hampstead. "When two young people get together whose tastes are similar, and opinions, — whose educations and habits of thought have been the same——"

"Habits the same!"

"Habits of thought, I said, sir."

"You would talk the hind legs off a dog," said the

Marquis, bouncing out of the room. It was not unusual with him, in the absolute privacy of his own circle, to revert to language which he would have felt to be unbecoming to him as Marquis of Kingsbury among ordinary people.

CHAPTER III.

THE MARCHIONESS.

THOUGH the departure of the Marquis was much hurried, there were other meetings between Hampstead and the family before the flitting was actually made.

"No doubt I will. I am quite with you there," the son said to the father, who had desired him to explain to the young man the impossibility of such a marriage. "I think it would be a misfortune to them both, which should be avoided,—if they can get over their present feelings."

"Feelings!"

"I suppose there are such feelings, sir?"

"Of course he is looking for position—and money."

"Not in the least. That might probably be the idea with some young nobleman who would wish to marry into his own class, and to improve his fortune at the same time. With such a one that would be fair enough. He would give and take. With George that would not be honest;—nor would such accusation be true. The position, as you call it, he would feel to be burdensome.

As to money, he does not know whether Frances has a shilling or not."

" Not a shilling,—unless I give it to her."

" He would not think of such a matter."

" Then he must be a very imprudent young man, and unfit to have a wife at all."

" I cannot admit that,—but suppose he is ? "

" And yet you think—— ? "

" I think, sir, that it is unfortunate. I have said so ever since I first heard it. I shall tell him exactly what I think. You will have Frances with you, and will of course express your own opinion."

The Marquis was far from satisfied with his son, but did not dare to go on further with the argument. In all such discussions he was wont to feel that his son was " talking the hind legs off a dog." His own ideas on concrete points were clear enough to him,—as this present idea that his daughter, Lady Frances Trafford, would outrage all propriety, all fitness,. all decency, if she were to give herself in marriage to George Roden, the Post Office clerk. But words were not plenty with him,—or, when plenty, not efficacious, —and he was prone to feel, when beaten in argument, that his opponent was taking an unfair advantage. Thus it was that he often thought, and sometimes said, that those who oppressed him with words would " talk the hind legs off a dog."

The Marchioness also expressed her opinion to Hampstead. She was a lady stronger than her husband ;—

stronger in this, that she never allowed herself to be worsted in any encounter. If words would not serve her occasion at the moment, her countenance would do so,—and if not that, her absence. She could be very eloquent with silence, and strike an adversary dumb by the way in which she would leave a room. She was a tall, handsome woman, with a sublime gait. —"Vera incessu patuit Dea." She had heard, if not the words, then some translation of the words, and had taken them to heart, and borne them with her as her secret motto. To be every inch an aristocrat, in look as in thought, was the object of her life. That such was her highest duty was quite fixed in her mind. It had pleased God to make her a Marchioness,—and should she derogate from God's wish? It had been her one misfortune that God should not also have made her the mother of a future Marquis. Her face, though handsome, was quite impassive, showing nothing of her sorrows or her joys; and her voice was equally under control. No one had ever imagined, not even her husband, that she felt acutely that one blow of fortune. Though Hampstead's politics had been to her abominable, treasonable, blasphemous, she treated him with an extreme courtesy. If there were anything that he wished about the house she would have it done for him. She would endeavour to interest herself about his hunting. And she would pay him a great respect,—to him most onerous,—as being second in all things to the Marquis. Though

a Republican blasphemous rebel,—so she thought of
him,—he was second to the Marquis. She would
fain have taught her little boys to respect him,—as
the future head of the family,—had he not been so
accustomed to romp with them, to pull them out
of their little beds, and toss them about in their
night-shirts, that they loved him much too well for
respect. It was in vain that their mother strove to
teach them to call him Hampstead.

Lady Frances had never been specially in her way,
but to Lady Frances the stepmother had been perhaps
harder than to the stepson, of whose presence as an
absolute block to her ambition she was well aware.
Lady Frances had no claim to a respect higher than
that which was due to her own children. Primogeni-
ture had done nothing for her. She was a Marquis's
daughter, but her mother had been only the offspring
of a commoner. There was perhaps something of
conscience in her feelings towards the two. As Lord
Hampstead was undoubtedly in her way, it occurred
to her to think that she should not on that account
be inimical to him. Lady Frances was not in her
way,—and therefore was open to depreciation and
dislike without wounds to her conscience ; and then,
though Hampstead was abominable because of his
Republicanism, his implied treason, and blasphemy,
yet he was entitled to some excuse as being a man.
These things were abominable no doubt in him, but
more pardonably abominable than they would be in a

woman. Lady Frances had never declared herself to
be a Republican or a disbeliever, much less a rebel,—
as, indeed, had neither Lord Hampstead. In the
presence of her stepmother she was generally silent
on matters of political or religious interest. But she
was supposed to sympathise with her brother, and was
known to be far from properly alive to aristocratic
interests. There was never quarrelling between the
two, but there was a lack of that friendship which may
subsist between a stepmother of thirty-eight and a
stepdaughter of twenty-one. Lady Frances was tall
and slender, with quiet speaking features, dark in
colour, with blue eyes, and hair nearly black. In
appearance she was the very opposite of her stepmother, moving quickly and achieving grace as she
did so, without a thought, by the natural beauty of
her motions. The dignity was there, but without a
thought given to it. Not even did the little lords,
her brothers, chuck their books and toys about with
less idea of demeanour. But the Marchioness never
arranged a scarf or buttoned a glove without feeling
that it was her duty to button her glove and arrange
her scarf as became the Marchioness of Kingsbury.

The stepmother wished no evil to Lady Frances,—
only that she should be married properly and taken out
of the way. Any stupid Earl or mercurial Viscount
would have done, so long as the blood and the money
had been there. Lady Frances had been felt to be
dangerous, and the hope was that the danger might be

got rid of by a proper marriage. But not by such a marriage as this !

When that accidental calling of the name was first heard and the following avowal made, the Marchioness declared her immediate feelings by a look. It was so that Arthur may have looked when he first heard that his Queen was sinful,—so that Cæsar must have felt when even Brutus struck him. For though Lady Frances had been known to be blind to her own greatness, still this,—this at any rate was not suspected. "You cannot mean it !" the Marchioness had at last said.

"I certainly mean it, mamma." Then the Marchioness, with one hand guarding her raiment, and with the other raised high above her shoulder, in an agony of supplication to those deities who arrange the fates of ducal houses, passed slowly out of the room. It was necessary that she should bethink herself before another word was spoken.

For some time after that very few. words passed between her and the sinner. A dead silence best befitted the occasion;—as, when a child soils her best frock, we put her in the corner with a scolding; but when she tells a fib we quell her little soul within her by a terrible quiescence. To be eloquently indignant without a word is within the compass of the thoughtfully stolid. It was thus that Lady Frances was at first treated by her stepmother. She was, however, at once taken up to London, subjected to the louder anger

of her father, and made to prepare for the Saxon Alps.
At first, indeed, her immediate destiny was not communicated to her. She was to be taken abroad;—and,
in so taking her, it was felt to be well to treat her as
the policeman does his prisoner, whom he thinks to be
the last person who need be informed as to the where-
abouts of the prison. It did leak out quickly, because
the Marquis had a castle or chateau of his own in
Saxony;—but that was only an accident.

The Marchioness still said little on the matter.—
unless in what she might say to her husband in the
secret recesses of marital discussion; but before she
departed she found it expedient to express herself
on one occasion to Lord Hampstead. "Hampstead,"
she said, "this is a terrible blow that has fallen
upon us."

"I was surprised myself. I do not know that I
should call it exactly a blow."

"Not a blow! But of course you mean that it will
come to nothing."

"What I meant was, that though I regard the
proposition as inexpedient——"

"Inexpedient!"

"Yes;—I think it inexpedient certainly; but there
is nothing in it that shocks me."

"Nothing that shocks you!"

"Marriage in itself is a good thing."

"Hampstead, do not talk to me in that way."

"But I think it is. If it be good for a young man

to marry it must be good for a young woman also. The one makes the other necessary."

"But not for such as your sister,—and him—together. You are speaking in that way simply to torment me."

"I can only speak as I think. I do agree that it would be inexpedient. She would to a certain extent lose the countenance of her friends——"

"Altogether!"

"Not altogether,—but to some extent. A certain class of people,—not the best worth knowing,—might be inclined to drop her. However foolish her own friends may be we owe something—even to their folly."

"Her friends are not foolish,—her proper friends."

"I quite agree with that; but then so many of them are improper."

"Hampstead!"

"I am afraid that I don't make myself quite clear. But never mind. It would be inexpedient. It would go against the grain with my father, who ought to be consulted."

"I should think so."

"I quite agree with you. A father ought to be consulted, even though a daughter be of age, so as to be enabled by law to do as she likes with herself. And then there would be money discomforts."

"She would not have a shilling."

"Not but what I should think it my duty to put that right if there were any real distress." Here spoke the heir, who was already in possession of much, and upon whom the whole property of the family was entailed. "Nevertheless if I can prevent it,—without quarrelling either with one or the other, without saying a hard word,—I shall do so."

"It will be your bounden duty."

"It is always a man's bounden duty to do what is right. The difficulty is in seeing the way." After this the Marchioness was silent. What she had gained by speaking was very little,—little or nothing. The nature of the opposition he proposed was almost as bad as a sanction, and the reasons he gave for agreeing with her were as hurtful to her feelings as though they had been advanced on the other side. Even the Marquis was not sufficiently struck with horror at the idea that a daughter of his should have condescended to listen to love from a Post Office clerk !

On the day before they started Hampstead was enabled to be alone with his sister for a few minutes. "What an absurdity it is," she said, laughing,—"this running away."

"It is what you must have expected."

"But not the less absurd. Of course I shall go. Just at the moment I have no alternative; as I should have none if they threatened to lock me up, till I got somebody to take my case in hand. But I am as free to do what I please with myself as is papa."

"He has got money."

"But he is not, therefore, to be a tyrant."

"Yes he is;—over an unmarried daughter who has

got none. We cannot but obey those on whom we
are dependent."

"What I mean is, that carrying me away can do no
good. You don't suppose, John, that I shall give him
up after having once brought myself to say the word !
It was very difficult to say;—but ten times harder
to be unsaid. I am quite determined,—and quite
satisfied."

" But they are not."

" As regards my father, I am very sorry. As to
mamma, she and I are so different in all our thinking
that I know beforehand that whatever I might do
would displease her. It cannot be helped. Whether
it be good or bad I cannot be made such as she is.
She came too late. You will not turn against me,
John ? "

" I rather think I shall

" John ! "

"I may rather say that I have. I do not think
your engagement to be wise."

" But it has been made," said she.

" And may be unmade."

" No;—unless by him."

" I shall tell him that it ought to be unmade,—for
the happiness of both of you."

" He will not believe you."

Then Lord Hampstead shrugged his shoulders, and
thus the conversation was finished.

It was now about the end of June, and the Marquis

felt it to be a grievance that he should be carried away
from the charm of political life in London. In the
horror of the first revelation he had yielded, but had
since began to feel that too much was being done in
withdrawing him from Parliament. The Conservatives
were now in; but during the last Liberal Government
he had consented so far to trammel himself with the
bonds of office as to become Privy Seal for the con-
cluding six months of its existence, and therefore felt
his own importance in a party point of view. But
having acceded to his wife he could not now go back,
and was sulky. On the evening before their departure
he was going to dine out with some of the party. His
wife's heart was too deep in the great family question
for any gaiety, and she intended to remain at home,—
and to look after the final packings-up for the little
lords.

"I really do not see why you should not have gone
without me," the Marquis said, poking his head out of
his dressing-room.

"Impossible," said the Marchioness.

"I don't see it at all."

"If he should appear on the scene ready to carry
her off, what should I have done ?"

Then the Marquis drew his head in again, and went
on with his dressing. What, indeed, could he do
himself if the man were to appear on the scene, and
if his daughter should declare herself willing to go
off with him ?

When the Marquis went to his dinner party the Marchioness dined with Lady Frances. There was no one else present but the two servants who waited on them, and hardly a word was spoken. The Marchioness felt that an awful silence was becoming in the situation. Lady Frances merely determined more strongly than ever that the situation should not last very long. She would go abroad now, but would let her father understand that the kind of life planned out for her was one that she could not endure. If she was supposed to have disgraced her position, let her be sent away.

As soon as the melancholy meal was over the two ladies separated, the Marchioness going up-stairs among her own children. A more careful, more affectionate, perhaps, I may say, a more idolatrous mother never lived. Every little want belonging to them,—for even little lords have wants,—was a care to her. To see them washed and put in and out of their duds was perhaps the greatest pleasure of her life. To her eyes they were pearls of aristocratic loveliness ; and, indeed, they were fine healthy bairns, clean-limbed, bright-eyed, with grand appetites, and never cross as long as they were allowed either to romp and make a noise, or else to sleep. Lord Frederic, the eldest, was already in words of two syllables, and sometimes had a bad time with them. Lord Augustus was the owner of great ivory letters of which he contrived to make playthings. Lord Gregory had not as yet been

introduced to any of the torments of education. There
was an old English clergyman attached to the family
who was supposed to be their tutor, but whose chief
duty consisted in finding conversation for the Marquis
when there was no one else to talk to him. There
was also a French governess and a Swiss maid. But
as they both learned English quicker than the children learned French, they were not serviceable for
the purpose at first intended. The Marchioness had
resolved that her children should talk three or four
languages as fluently as their own, and that they
should learn them without any of the agonies generally incident to tuition. In that she had not as yet
succeeded.

She seated herself for a few minutes among the
boxes and portmanteaus in the midst of which the
children were disporting themselves prior to their final
withdrawal to bed. No mother was ever so blessed,
—if only, if only! "Mamma," said Lord Frederic,
"where's Jack?" "Jack" absolutely was intended to
signify Lord Hampstead.

"Fred, did not I say that you should not call him
Jack?"

"He say he is Jack," declared Lord Augustus, rolling
up in between his mother's knees with an impetus
which would have upset her had she not been a strong
woman and accustomed to these attacks.

"That is only because he is good-natured, and likes
to play with you. You should call him Hampstead."

"Mamma, wasn't he christianed?" asked the eldest.

"Yes, of course he was christened, my dear," said the mother, sadly,—thinking how very much of the ceremony had been thrown away upon the unbelieving, godless young man. Then she superintended the putting to bed, thinking what a terrible bar to her happiness had been created by that first unfortunate marriage of her husband's. Oh, that she should be stepmother to a daughter who desired to fling herself into the arms of a clerk in the Post Office! And then that an "unchristianed," that an infidel, republican, un-English, heir should stand in the way of her darling boy! She had told herself a thousand times that the Devil was speaking to her when she had dared to wish that,—that Lord Hampstead was not there! She had put down the wish in her heart very often, telling herself that it came from the Devil. She had made a faint struggle to love the young man,—which had resulted in constrained civility. It would have been unnatural to her to love any but her own. Now she thought how glorious her Frederic would have been as Lord Hampstead,—and how infinitely better it would have been, how infinitely better it would be, for all the Traffords, for all the nobles of England, and for the country at large! But in thinking this she knew that she was a sinner, and she endeavoured to crush the sin. Was it not tantamount to wishing that her husband's son was—dead?

CHAPTER IV.

LADY FRANCES.

THERE is something so sad in the condition of a girl who is known to be in love, and has to undergo the process of being made ashamed of it by her friends, that one wonders that any young woman can bear it. Most young women cannot bear it, and either give up their love or say that they do. A young man who has got into debt, or been plucked,—or even when he has declared himself to be engaged to a penniless young lady, which is worse,—is supposed merely to have gone after his kind, and done what was to be expected of him. The mother never looks at him with that enduring anger by which she intends to wear out the daughter's constancy. The father frets and fumes, pays the debts, prepares the way for a new campaign, and merely shrugs his shoulders about the proposed marriage, which he regards simply as an impossibility. But the girl is held to have disgraced herself. Though it is expected of her, or at any rate hoped, that she will get married in due time, yet the falling in love with a man,

—which is, we must suppose, a preliminary step to marriage,—is a wickedness. Even among the ordinary Joneses and Browns of the world we see that it is so. When we are intimate enough with the Browns to be aware of Jane Brown's passion, we understand the father's manner and the mother's look. The very servants about the house are aware that she has given way to her feelings, and treat her accordingly. Her brothers are ashamed of her. Whereas she, if her brother be in love with Jemima Jones, applauds him, sympathizes with him, and encourages him.

There are heroines who live through it all, and are true to the end. There are many pseudo-heroines who intend to do so, but break down. The pseudo-heroine generally breaks down when young Smith,—not so very young,—has been taken in as a partner by Messrs. Smith and Walker, and comes in her way, in want of a wife. The persecution is, at any rate, so often efficacious as to make fathers and mothers feel it to be their duty to use it. It need not be said here how high above the ways of the Browns soared the ideas of the Marchioness of Kingsbury. But she felt that it would be her duty to resort to the measures which they would have adopted, and she was determined that the Marquis should do the same. A terrible evil, an incurable evil, had already been inflicted. Many people, alas, would know that Lady Frances had disgraced herself. She, the Marchioness, had been unable to keep the secret from her own sister, Lady Persiflage, and

Lady Persiflage would undoubtedly tell it to others. Her own lady's maid knew it. The Marquis himself was the most indiscreet of men. Hampstead would see no cause for secrecy. Roden would, of course, boast of it all through the Post Office. The letter-carriers who attended upon Park Lane would have talked the matter over with the footmen at the area gate. There could be no hope of secrecy. All the young marquises and unmarried earls would know that Lady Frances Trafford was in love with the "postman." But time, and care, and strict precaution might prevent the final misery of a marriage. Then, if the Marquis would be generous, some young Earl, or at least a Baron, might be induced to forget the "postman," and to take the noble lily, soiled, indeed, but made gracious by gilding. Her darlings must suffer. Any excess of money given would be at their cost. But anything would be better than a Post Office clerk for a brother-in-law.

Such were the views as to their future life with which the Marchioness intended to accompany her stepdaughter to their Saxon residence. The Marquis, with less of a fixed purpose, was inclined in the same way. "I quite agree that they should be separated;— quite," he said. "It mustn't be heard of;—certainly not; certainly not. Not a shilling,—unless she behaves herself properly. Of course she will have her fortune, but not to bestow it in such a manner as that."

His own idea was to see them all settled in the château, and then, if possible, to hurry back to London

before the season was quite at an end. His wife laid
strong injunctions on him as to absolute secrecy, having
forgotten, probably, that she herself had told the whole
story to Lady Persiflage. The Marquis quite agreed.
Secrecy was indispensable. As for him, was it likely
that he should speak of a matter so painful and so
near to his heart! Nevertheless he told it all to Mr.
Greenwood, the gentleman who acted as tutor, private
secretary, and chaplain in the house.

Lady Frances had her own ideas, as to this going
away and living abroad, very strongly developed in
her mind. They intended to persecute her till she
should change her purpose. She intended to persecute
them till they should change theirs. She knew herself
too well, she thought, to have any fear as to her own
persistency. That the Marchioness should persuade,
or even persecute, her out of an engagement to which
she had assented, she felt to be quite out of the
question. In her heart she despised the Marchioness,
—bearing with her till the time should come in which
she would be delivered from the nuisance of surveil-
lance under such a woman. In her father she trusted
much, knowing him to be affectionate, believing him
to be still opposed to those aristocratic dogmas which
were a religion to the Marchioness,—feeling probably
that in his very weakness she would find her best
strength. If her stepmother should in truth become
cruel, then her father would take her part against
his wife. There must be a period of discomfort,—

say, six months; and then would come the time in
which she would be able to say, " I have tried myself,
and know my own mind, and I intend to go home
and get myself married." She would take care that
her declaration to this effect should not come as a
sudden blow. The six months should be employed
in preparing for it. The Marchioness might be persistent in preaching her views during the six months,
but so would Lady Frances be persistent in preaching
hers.

She had not accepted the man's love when he had
offered it, without thinking much about it. The lesson
which she had heard in her earlier years from her
mother had sunk deep into her very soul,—much
more deeply than the teacher of those lessons had supposed. That teacher had never intended to inculcate
as a doctrine that rank is a mistake. No one had
thought more than she of the incentives provided by
rank to high duty. " Noblesse oblige." The lesson
had been engraved on her heart, and might have
been read in all the doings of her life. But she had
endeavoured to make it understood by her children
that they should not be over-quick to claim the
privileges of rank. Too many such would be showered
on them,—too many for their own welfare. Let them
never be greedy to take with outstretched hands those
good things of which Chance had provided for them so
much more than their fair share. Let them remember
that after all there was no virtue in having been born

a child to a Marquis. Let them remember how much
more it was to be a useful man, or a kind woman'. So
the lessons had been given,—and had gone for more
than had been intended. Then all the renown of
their father's old politics assisted,—the re-election of
the drunken tailor,—the jeerings of friends who were
high enough and near enough to dare to jeer,—the
convictions of childhood that it was a fine thing,
because peculiar for a Marquis and his belongings, to
be Radical;—and, added to this, there was contempt
for the specially noble graces of their stepmother.
Thus it was that Lord Hampstead was brought to his
present condition of thinking,—and Lady Frances.

Her convictions were quite as strong as his, though
they did not assume the same form. With a girl, at
an early age, all her outlookings into the world have
something to do with love and its consequences.
When a young man takes his leaning either towards
Liberalism or Conservatism he is not at all actuated
by any feeling as to how some possible future young
woman may think on the subject. But the girl, if
she entertains such ideas at all, dreams of them as
befitting the man whom she may some day hope to
love. Should she, a Protestant, become a Roman
Catholic and then a nun, she feels that in giving up
her hope for a man's love she is making the greatest
sacrifice in her power for the Saviour she is taking
to her heart. If she devotes herself to music, or
the pencil, or to languages, the effect which her

accomplishments may have on some beau ideal of man-
hood is present to her mind. From the very first she is
dressing herself unconsciously in the mirror of a man's
eyes. Quite unconsciously, all this had been present
to Lady Frances as month after month and year after
year she had formed her strong opinions. She had
thought of no man's love,—had thought but little of
loving any man,—but in her meditations as to the
weaknesses and vanity of rank there had always been
present that idea,—how would it be with her if such
a one should ask for her hand, such a one as she might
find among those of whom she dreamed as being more
noble than Dukes, even though they were numbered
among the world's proletaries? Then she had told
herself that if any such a one should come,—if at any
time any should be allowed by herself to come,—he
should be estimated by his merits, whether Duke or
proletary. With her mind in such a state she had of
course been prone to receive kindly the overtures of
her brother's friend.

What was there missing in him that a girl should
require? It was so that she had asked herself the
question. As far as manners were concerned, this
man was a gentleman. She was quite sure of that.
Whether proletary or not, there was nothing about him
to offend the taste of the best-born of ladies. That he
was better educated than any of the highly-bred young
men she saw around her, she was quite sure. He had
more to talk about than others. Of his birth and

family she knew nothing, but rather prided herself in
knowing nothing, because of that doctrine of hers that
a man is to be estimated only by what he is himself,
and not at all by what he may derive from others. Of
his personal appearance, which went far with her, she
was very proud. He was certainly a handsome young
man, and endowed with all outward gifts of manliness :
easy in his gait, but not mindful of it, with motions
of his body naturally graceful but never studied, with
his head erect, with a laugh in his eye, well-made as
to his hands and feet. Neither his intellect nor his
political convictions would have recommended a man
to her heart, unless there had been something in the
outside to please her eye, and from the first moment
in which she had met him he had never been afraid
of her,—had ventured when he disagreed from her
to laugh at her, and even to scold her. There is no
barrier in a girl's heart so strong against love as
the feeling that the man in question stands in awe
of her.

She had taken some time before she had given him
her answer, and had thought much of the perils before
her. She had known that she could not divest herself
of her rank. She had acknowledged to herself that,
whether it was for good or bad, a Marquis's daughter
could not be like another girl. She owed much to her
father, much to her brothers, something even to her
stepmother. But was the thing she proposed to do
of such a nature as to be regarded as an evil to her

family? She could see that there had been changes in the ways of the world during the last century,— changes continued from year to year. Rank was not so high as it used to be,—and in consequence those without rank not so low. The Queen's daughter had married a subject. Lords John and Lords Thomas were every day going into this and the other business. There were instances enough of ladies of title doing the very thing which she proposed to herself. Why should a Post Office clerk be lower than another?

Then came the great question, whether it behoved her to ask her father. Girls in general ask their mother, and send the lover to the father. She had no mother. She was quite sure that she would not leave her happiness in the hands of the present Marchioness. Were she to ask her father she knew that the matter would be at once settled against her. Her father was too much under the dominion of his wife to be allowed to have an opinion of his own on such a matter. So she declared to herself, and then determined that she would act on her own responsibility. She would accept the man, and then take the first opportunity of telling her stepmother what she had done. And so it was. It was only early on that morning that she had given her answer to George Roden,—and early on that morning she had summoned up her courage, and told her whole story.

The station to which she was taken was a large

German schloss, very comfortably arranged, with the mountain as a background and the River Elbe running close beneath its terraces, on which the Marquis had spent some money, and made it a residence to be envied by the eyes of all passers-by. It had been bought for its beauty in a freak, but had never been occupied for more than a week at a time till this occasion. Under other circumstances Lady Frances would have been as happy here as the day was long, and had often expressed a desire to be allowed to stay for a while at Königsgraaf. But now, though she made an attempt to regard their sojourn in the place as one of the natural events of their life, she could not shake off the idea of a prison. The Marchioness was determined that the idea of a prison should not be shaken off. In the first few days she said not a word about the objectionable lover, nor did the Marquis. That had been settled between them. But neither was anything said on any other subject. There was a sternness in every motion, and a grim silence seemed to preside in the château, except when the boys were present,—and an attempt was made to separate her from her brothers as much as possible, which she was more inclined to resent than any other ill usage which was adopted towards her. After about a fortnight it was announced that the Marquis was to return to London. He had received letters from "the party" which made it quite necessary that he should be there. When this was told to Lady Frances

not a word was said as to the probable duration of
their own stay at the château.

"Papa," she said, "you are going back to London?"

"Yes, my dear. My presence in town is imperatively
necessary."

"How long are we to stay here?"

"How long?"

"Yes, papa. I like Königsgraaf very much. I
always thought it the prettiest place I know. But I
do not like looking forward to staying here without
knowing when I am to go away."

"You had better ask your mamma, my dear."

"Mamma never says anything to me. It would be
no good my asking her. Papa, you ought to tell me
something before you go away."

"Tell you what?"

"Or let me tell you something."

"What do you want to tell me, Frances?" In
saying this he assumed his most angry tone and sternest
countenance,—which, however, were not very angry
or very stern, and had no effect in frightening his
daughter. He did not, in truth, wish to say a word
about the Post Office clerk before he made his escape,
and would have been very glad to frighten her enough
to make her silent had that been possible.

"Papa, I want you to know that it will do no good
shutting me up there."

"Nobody shuts you up."

"I mean here in Saxony. Of course I shall stay for

some time, but you cannot expect that I shall remain here always."

" Who has talked about always ? "

" I understand that I am brought here to be——out of Mr. Roden's way."

" I would rather not speak of that young man."

" But, papa,—if he is to be my husband——"

" He is not to be your husband."

" It will be so, papa, though I should be kept here ever so long. That is what I want you to understand. Having given my word,—and so much more than my word,—I certainly shall not go back from it. I can understand that you should carry me off here so as to try and wean me from it——"

" It is quite out of the question; impossible ! "

" No, papa. If he choose,—and I choose,—no one can prevent us." As she said this she looked him full in the face.

" Do you mean to say that you owe no obedience to your parents ? "

" To you, papa, of course I owe obedience,—to a certain extent. There does come a time, I suppose, in which a daughter may use her own judgment as to her own happiness."

" And disgrace all her family ? "

" I do not think that I shall disgrace mine. What I want you to understand, papa, is this,—that you will not ensure my obedience by keeping me here. I think I should be more likely to be submissive at home.

There is an idea in enforced control which is hardly
compatible with obedience. I don't suppose you will
lock me up."

"You have no right to talk to me in that way."

"I want to explain that our being here can do no
good. When you are gone mamma and I will only be
very unhappy together. She won't talk to me, and will
look at me as though I were a poor lost creature. I
don't think that I am a lost creature at all, but I shall
be just as much lost here as though I were at home
in England."

"When you come to talking you are as bad as your
brother," said the Marquis as he left her. Only that
the expression was considered to be unfit for female
ears, he would have accused her of "talking the hind
legs off a dog."

When he was gone the life at Königsgraaf became
very sombre indeed. Mr. George Roden's name was
never mentioned by either of the ladies. There was
the Post Office, no doubt, and the Post Office was at
first left open to her; but there soon came a time in
which she was deprived of this consolation. With such
a guardian as the Marchioness, it was not likely that
free correspondence should be left open to her.

CHAPTER V.

MRS. RODEN.

GEORGE RODEN, the Post Office clerk, lived with his mother at Holloway, about three miles from his office. There they occupied a small house which had been taken when their means were smaller even than at present;—for this had been done before the young man had made his way into the official elysium of St. Martin's-le Grand. This had been effected about five years since, during which time he had risen to an income of £170. As his mother had means of her own amounting to about double as much, and as her personal expenses were small, they were enabled to live in comfort. She was a lady of whom none around knew anything, but there had gone abroad a rumour among her neighbours that there was something of a mystery attached to her, and there existed a prevailing feeling that she was at any rate a well-born lady. Few people at Holloway knew either her or her son. But there were some who condescended to watch them, and to talk about them. It was ascertained that Mrs.

Roden usually went to church on Sunday morning, but
that her son never did so. It was known, too, that
a female friend called upon her regularly once a week ;
and it was noted in the annals of Holloway that this
female friend came always at three o'clock on a Monday.
Intelligent observers had become aware that the return
visit was made in the course of the week, but not
always made on one certain day ;—from which circumstances various surmises arose as to the means, where-
abouts, and character of the visitor. Mrs. Roden
always went in a cab. The lady, whose name was soon
known to be Mrs. Vincent, came in a brougham, which
for a time was supposed to be her own peculiar property. The man who drove it was so well arrayed as
to hat, cravat, and coat, as to leave an impression that
he must be a private servant ; but one feminine
observer, keener than others, saw the man on an
unfortunate day descend from his box at a public-house,
and knew at once that the trousers were the trousers
of a hired driver from a livery-stable. Nevertheless
it was manifest that Mrs. Vincent was better to do
in the world than Mrs. Roden, because she could afford
to hire a would-be private carriage ; and it was
imagined also that she was a lady accustomed to
remain at home of an afternoon, probably with the
object of receiving visitors, because Mrs. Roden made
her visits indifferently on Thursday, Friday, or Saturday. It was suggested also that Mrs. Vincent was no
friend to the young clerk, because it was well known

that he was never there when the lady came, and it was supposed that he never accompanied his mother on the return visits. He had, indeed, on one occasion been seen to get out of the cab with his mother at their own door, but it was strongly surmised that she had then picked him up at the Post Office. His official engagements might, indeed, have accounted for all this naturally; but the ladies of Holloway were well aware that the humanity of the Postmaster-General allowed a Saturday half-holiday to his otherwise overworked officials, and they were sure that so good a son as George Roden would occasionally have accompanied his mother, had there been no especial reason against it. From this further surmises arose. Some glance had fallen from the eye of the visitor lady, or perhaps some chance word had been heard from her lips, which created an opinion that she was religious. She probably objected to George Roden because he was anti-religious, or at any rate anti-church, meeting, or chapel-going. It had become quite decided at Holloway that Mrs. Vincent would not put up with the young clerk's infidelity. And it was believed that there had been "words" between the two ladies themselves on the subject of religion,— as to which probably there was no valid foundation, it being an ascertained fact that the two maids who were employed by Mrs. Roden were never known to tell anything of their mistress.

It was decided at Holloway that Mrs. Roden and

Mrs. Vincent were cousins. They were like enough in face and near enough in age to have been sisters; but old Mrs. Demijohn, of No. 10, Paradise Row, had declared that had George been a nephew his aunt would not have wearied in her endeavour to convert him. In such a case there would have been intimacy in spite of disapproval. But a first cousin once removed might be allowed to go to the Mischief in his own way. Mrs. Vincent was supposed to be the elder cousin,—perhaps three or four years the elder, —and to have therefore something of an authority, but not much. She was stouter, too, less careful to hide what grey hairs years might have produced, and showing manifestly by the nature of her bonnets and shawls that she despised the vanities of the world. Not but that she was always handsomely dressed, as Mrs. Demijohn was very well aware. Less than a hundred a year could not have clothed Mrs. Vincent, whereas Mrs. Roden, as all the world perceived, did not spend half the money. But who does not know that a lady may repudiate vanity in rich silks and cultivate the world in woollen stuffs, or even in calico? Nothing was more certain to Mrs. Demijohn than that Mrs. Vincent was severe, and that Mrs. Roden was soft and gentle. It was assumed also that the two ladies were widows, as no husband or sign of a husband had appeared on the scene. Mrs. Vincent showed manifestly from her deportment, as well as from her title, that she had been a married woman. As to Mrs. Roden, of course, there was no doubt.

In regard to all this the reader may take the settled opinions of Mrs. Demijohn and of Holloway as being nearly true. Riddles may be read very accurately by those who will give sufficient attention and ample time to the reading of them. They who will devote twelve hours a day to the unravelling of acrostics, may discover nearly all the enigmas of a weekly newspaper with a separate editor for such difficulties. Mrs. Demijohn had almost arrived at the facts. The two ladies were second cousins. Mrs. Vincent was a widow, was religious, was austere, was fairly well off, and had quarrelled altogether with her distant relative George of the Post Office. Mrs. Roden, though she went to church, was not so well given to religious observances as her cousin would have her. Hence words had come which Mrs. Roden had borne with equanimity, but had received without effect. Nevertheless the two women loved each other dearly, and it was a great part of the life of each of them that these weekly visits should be made. There was one great fact, as to which Mrs. Demijohn and Holloway were in the wrong. Mrs. Roden was not a widow.

It was not till the Kingsburys had left London that George told his mother of his engagement. She was well acquainted with his intimacy with Lord Hampstead, and knew that he had been staying at Hendon

Hall with the Kingsbury family. There had been no
reticence between the mother and son as to these
people, in regard to whom she had frequently cau-
tioned him that there was danger in such associations
with people moving altogether in a different sphere.
In answer to this the son had always declared that
he did not see the danger. He had not run after
Lord Hampstead. Circumstances had thrown them
together. They had originally met each other in a
small political debating society, and gradually friendship had grown. The lord had sought him, and not he
the lord. That, according to his own idea, had been
right. Difference in rank, difference in wealth, difference in social regard required as much as that. He,
when he had discovered who was the young man whom
he had met, stood off somewhat, and allowed the friendship to spring from the other side. He had been slow
to accept favour,—even at first to accept hospitality.
But whenever the ice had, as he said, been thoroughly
broken, then he thought that there was no reason why
they should not pull each other out of the cold water
together. As for danger, what was there to fear?
The Marchioness would not like it? Very probably.
The Marchioness was not very much to Hampstead,
and was nothing at all to him. The Marquis would
not really like it. Perhaps not. But in choosing a
friend a young man is not supposed to follow altogether
his father's likings,—much less need the chosen friend
follow them. But the Marquis, as George pointed out

to his mother, was hardly more like other marquises than the son was like other marquis's sons. There was a Radical strain in the family, as was made clear by that tailor who was still sitting for the borough of Edgeware. Mrs. Roden, however, though she lived so much alone, seeing hardly anything of the world except as Mrs Vincent might be supposed to represent the world, had learned that the feelings and political convictions of the Marquis were hardly what they had been before he had married his present wife. " You may be sure, George," she had said, "that like to like is as safe a motto for friendship as it is for love."

" Not a doubt, mother," he replied ; " but before you act upon it you must define ' like.' What makes two men like—or a man and a woman ? "

" Outside circumstances of the world more than anything else," she answered, boldly.

" I would fancy that the inside circumstances of the mind would have more to do with it." She shook her head at him, pleasantly, softly, and lovingly,—but still with a settled purpose of contradiction. " I have admitted all along," he continued, " that low birth——"

" I have said nothing of low birth ! " Here was a point on which there did not exist full confidence between the mother and son, but in regard to which the mother was always attempting to reassure the son, while he would assume something against himself which she would not allow to pass without an attempt of faint denial.

"That birth low by comparison," he continued, going on with his sentence, "should not take upon itself as much as may be allowed to nobility by descent is certain. Though the young prince may be superior in his gifts to the young shoeblack, and would best show his princeliness by cultivating the shoeblack, still the shoeblack should wait to be cultivated. The world has created a state of things in which the shoeblack cannot do otherwise without showing an arrogance and impudence by which he could achieve nothing."

"Which, too, would make him black his shoes very badly."

"No doubt. That will have to come to pass any way, because the nobler employments to which he will be raised by the appreciating prince will cause him to drop his shoes."

"Is Lord Hampstead to cause you to drop the Post Office?"

"Not at all. He is not a prince nor am I a shoeblack. Though we are far apart, we are not so far apart as to make such a change essential to our acquaintance. But I was saying—— I don't know what I was saying."

"You were defining what 'like' means. But people always get muddled when they attempt definitions," said the mother.

"Though it depends somewhat on externals, it has more to do with internals. That is what I mean. A man and woman might live together with most en-

during love, though one had been noble and wealthy
and the other poor and a nobody. But a thorough
brute and a human being of fine conditions can hardly
live together and love each other."

"That is true," she said. "That I fear is true."

"I hope it is true."

"It has often to be tried, generally to the great
detriment of the better nature."

All this, however, had been said before George Roden
had spoken a word to Lady Frances, and had referred
only to the friendship as it was growing between her
son and the young lord.

The young lord had come on various occasions to
the house at Holloway, and had there made himself
thoroughly pleasant to his friend's mother. Lord
Hampstead had a way of making himself pleasant in
which he never failed when he chose to exercise it.
And he did exercise it almost always,—always, indeed,
unless he was driven to be courteously disagreeable by
opposition to his own peculiar opinion. In shooting,
fishing, and other occupations not approved of, he
would fall into a line of argument, seemingly and indeed truly good-humoured, which was apt, however, to
be aggravating to his opponent. In this way he would
make himself thoroughly odious to his stepmother,
with whom he had not one sentiment in common.
In other respects his manners were invariably sweet,
with an assumption of intimacy which was not unbecoming; and thus he had greatly recommended

himself to Mrs. Roden. Who does not know the fashion
in which the normal young man conducts himself when
he is making a morning call? He has come there
because he means to be civil. He would not be there
unless he wished to make himself popular. He is
carrying out some recognized purpose of society. He
would fain be agreeable if it were possible. He would
enjoy the moment if he could. But it is clearly his
conviction that he is bound to get through a certain
amount of altogether uninteresting conversation, and
then to get himself out of the room with as little
awkwardness as may be. Unless there be a pretty
girl, and chance favour him with her special companionship, he does not for a moment suppose that any social
pleasure is to be enjoyed. That rational amusement
can be got out of talking to Mrs. Jones does not enter
into his mind. And yet Mrs. Jones is probably a fair
specimen of that general society in which every one
wishes to mingle. Society is to him generally made
up of several parts, each of which is a pain, though
the total is deemed to be desirable. The pretty girl
episode is no doubt an exception,—though that also
has its pains when matter for conversation does not
come readily, or when conversation, coming too readily,
is rebuked. The morning call may be regarded as
a period of unmitigated agony. Now it has to be
asserted on Lord Hampstead's behalf that he could
talk with almost any Mrs. Jones freely and pleasantly
while he remained, and take his departure without that

dislocating struggle which is too common. He would
make himself at ease, and discourse as though he had
known the lady all his life. There is nothing which a
woman likes so much as this, and by doing this Lord
Hampstead had done much, if not to overcome, at
any rate to quiet the sense of danger of which Mrs.
Roden had spoken.

But this refers to a time in which nothing was known
at Holloway as to Lady Frances. Very little had been
said of the family between the mother and son. Of the
Marquis George Roden had wished to think well, but
had hardly succeeded. Of the stepmother he had
never even wished to do so. She had from the first
been known to him as a woman thoroughly wedded
to aristocratic prejudices,— who regarded herself as
endowed with certain privileges which made her altogether superior to other human beings. Hampstead
himself could not even pretend to respect her. Of
her Roden had said very little to his mother, simply
speaking of her as the Marchioness, who was in no
way related to Hampstead. Of Lady Frances he had
simply said that there was a girl there endowed with
such a spirit, that of all girls of her class she must
surely be the best and noblest. Then his mother had
shuddered inwardly, thinking that here too there might
be possible danger; but she had shrunk from speaking
of the special danger even to her son.

" How has the visit gone ? " Mrs. Roden asked, when
her son had already been some hours in the house.

This was after that last visit to Hendon Hall, in which Lady Frances had promised to become his wife.

"Pretty well, taking it altogether."

"I know that something has disappointed you."

"No, indeed, nothing. I have been somewhat abashed."

"What have they said to you?" she asked.

"Very little but what was kind,—just one word at the last."

"Something, I know, has hurt you," said the mother.

"Lady Kingsbury has made me aware that she dislikes me thoroughly. It is very odd how one person can do that to another almost without a word spoken."

"I told you, George, that there would be danger in going there."

"There would be no danger in that if there were nothing more."

"What more is there then?"

"There would be no danger in that if Lady Kingsbury was simply Hampstead's stepmother."

"What more is she?"

"She is stepmother also to Lady Frances. Oh, mother!"

"George, what has happened?" she asked.

"I have asked Lady Frances to be my wife."

"Your wife?"

"And she has promised."

"Oh, George!"

"Yes, indeed, mother. Now you can perceive that

she indeed may be a danger. When I think of the power of tormenting her stepdaughter which may rest in her hands I can hardly forgive myself for doing as I have done."

"And the Marquis?" asked the mother.

"I know nothing as yet as to what his feelings may be. I have had no opportunity of speaking to him since the little occurrence took place. A word escaped me, an unthought-of word, which her ladyship overheard, and for which she rebuked me. Then I left the house."

"What word?"

"Just a common word of greeting, a word that would be common among dear friends, but which, coming from me to her, told all the story. I forgot the prefix which was due from such a one as I am to such as she is. I can understand with what horror I must henceforward be regarded by Lady Kingsbury."

"What will the Marquis say?"

"I shall be a horror to him also,—an unutterable horror. The idea of contact so vile will cure him at once of all his little Radical longings."

"And Hampstead?"

"Nothing, I think, can cure Hampstead of his convictions;—but even he is not well pleased."

"Has he quarrelled with you?"

"No, not that. He is too noble to quarrel on such offence. He is too noble even to take offence on such

a cause. But he refuses to believe that good will
come of it. And you, mother?"

"Oh, George, I doubt, I doubt."

"You will not congratulate me?"

"What am I to say? I fear more than I can hope."

"When I tell you that she is noble at all points,
noble in heart, noble in beauty, noble in that dignity
which a woman should always carry with her, that she
is as sweet a creature as God ever created to bless
a man with, will you not then congratulate me?"

"I would her birth were other than it is," said
the mother.

"I would have her altered in nothing," said the son.
"Her birth is the smallest thing about her, but such
as she is I would have her altered in nothing."

CHAPTER VI.

PARADISE ROW.

About a fortnight after George Roden's return to Holloway,—a fortnight passed by the mother in meditation as to her son's glorious but dangerous love, —Lord Hampstead called at No. 11, Paradise Row. Mrs. Roden lived at No. 11, and Mrs. Demijohn lived at No. 10, the house opposite. There had already been some discussion in Holloway about Lord Hampstead, but nothing had as yet been discovered. He might have been at the house on various previous occasions, but had come in so unpretending a manner as hardly to have done more than to cause himself to be regarded as a stranger in Holloway. He was known to be George's friend, because he had been first seen coming with George on a Saturday afternoon. He had also called on a Sunday and walked away, down the Row, with George. Mrs. Demijohn concluded that he was a brother clerk in the Post Office, and had expressed an opinion that "it did not signify," meaning thereby to imply that Holloway need not interest

itself about the stranger. A young Government clerk
would naturally have another young Government clerk
for his friend. Twice Lord Hampstead had come down
in an omnibus from Islington; on which occasion it
was remarked that as he did not come on Saturday
there must be something wrong. A clerk, with Saturday half-holidays, ought not to be away from his work
on Mondays and Tuesdays. Mrs. Duffer, who was
regarded in Paradise Row as being very inferior to
Mrs. Demijohn, suggested that the young man might'
perhaps, not be a Post Office clerk. This, however,
was ridiculed. Where should a Post Office clerk find
his friends except among Post Office clerks ? " Perhaps
he is coming after the widow," suggested Mrs. Duffer.
But this also was received with dissent. Mrs. Demijohn
declared that Post Office clerks knew better than to
marry widows with no more than two or three hundred
a year, and old enough to be their mothers. " But
why does he come on a Tuesday ? " asked Mrs. Duffer ;
" and why does he come alone ? " " Oh you dear old
Mrs. Duffer ! " said Clara Demijohn, the old lady's
niece, naturally thinking that it might not be unnatural that handsome young men should come to
Paradise Row.

All this, however, had been as nothing to what
occurred in the Row on the occasion which is now
about to be described.

" Aunt Jemima," exclaimed Clara Demijohn, looking
out of the window, " there's that young man come

again to Number Eleven, riding on horseback, with a groom behind to hold him!"

"Groom to hold him!" exclaimed Mrs. Demijohn, jumping, with all her rheumatism, quickly from her seat, and trotting to the window.

"You look if there aint,—with boots and breeches."

"It must be another," said Mrs. Demijohn, after a pause, during which she had been looking intently at the empty saddle of the horse which the groom was leading slowly up and down the Row.

"It's the same that came with young Roden that Saturday," said Clara; "only he hadn't been walking, and he looked nicer than ever."

"You can hire them all, horses and groom," said Mrs. Demijohn; "but he'd never make his money last till the end of the month if he went on in that way."

"They aint hired. They're his own," said Clara.

"How do you know, Miss?"

"By the colour of his boots, and the way he touched his hat, and because his gloves are clean. He aint a Post Office clerk at all, Aunt Jemima."

"I wonder whether he can be coming after the widow," said Mrs. Demijohn. After this Clara escaped out of the room, leaving her aunt fixed at the window. Such a sight as that groom and those two horses moving up and down together had never been seen in the Row before. Clara put on her hat and ran across hurriedly to Mrs. Duffer, who lived at No. 15, next door but one to Mrs. Roden. But she was altogether too late to communicate the news as news.

"I knew he wasn't a Post Office clerk," said Mrs. Duffer, who had seen Lord Hampstead ride up the street; "but who he is, or why, or wherefore, it' is beyond me to conjecture. But I never will give up my opinion again, talking to your aunt. I suppose she holds out still that he's a Post Office clerk."

"She thinks he might have hired them."

"Oh my! Hired them!"

"But did you ever see anything so noble as the way he got off his horse? As for hire, that's nonsense. He's been getting off that horse every day of his life." Thus it was that Paradise Row was awe-stricken by this last coming of George Roden's friend.

It was an odd thing to do,—this riding down to Holloway. No one else would have done it, either lord or Post Office clerk ;—with a hired horse or with private property. There was a hot July sunshine, and the roads across from Hendon Hall consisted chiefly of paved streets. But Lord Hampstead always did things as others would not do them. It was too far to walk in the midday sun, and therefore he rode. There would be no servant at Mrs. Roden's house to hold his horse, and therefore he brought one of his own. He did not see why a man on horseback should attract more attention at Holloway than at Hyde Park Corner. Had he guessed the effect which he and his

horse would have had in Paradise Row he would
have come by some other means.

Mrs. Roden at first received him with considerable
embarrassment,—which he probably observed, but in
speaking to her seemed not to observe. "Very hot,
indeed," he said ;—"too hot for riding, as I found soon
after I started. I suppose George has given up walking
for the present."

"He still walks home, I think."

"If he had declared his purpose of doing so, he'd
go on though he had sunstroke every afternoon."

"I hope he is not so obstinate as that, my lord."

"The most obstinate fellow I ever knew in my life!
Though the world were to come to an end, he'd let
it come rather than change his purpose. It's all
very well for a man to keep his purpose, but he may
overdo it."

"Has he been very determined lately in anything?"

"No ;—nothing particular. I haven't seen him for
the last week. I want him to come over and dine
with me at Hendon one of these days. I'm all alone
there." From this Mrs. Roden learnt that Lord
Hampstead at any rate did not intend to quarrel with
her son, and she learnt also that Lady Frances was
no longer staying at the Hall. "I can send him
home," continued the lord, "if he can manage to come
down by the railway or the omnibus."

"I will give him your message, my lord."

"Tell him I start on the 21st. My yacht is at

Cowes, and I shall go down there on that morning.
I shall be away Heaven knows how long;—probably
for a month. Vivian will be with me, and we mean
to bask away our time in the Norway and Iceland
seas, till he goes, like an idiot that he is, to his grouse-
shooting. I should like to see George before I start.
I said that I was all alone; but Vivian will be with
me. George has met him before, and as they didn't
cut each other's throats then I suppose they won't
now."

"I will tell him all that," said Mrs. Roden.

Then there was a pause for a moment, after which
Lord Hampstead went on in an altered voice. "Has
he said anything to you since he was at Hendon;—as
to my family, I mean?"

"He has told me something."

"I was sure he had. I should not have asked unless
I had been quite sure. I know that he would tell you
anything of that kind. Well?"

"What am I to say, Lord Hampstead?"

"What has he told you, Mrs. Roden?"

"He has spoken to me of your sister."

"But what has he said?"

"That he loves her."

"And that she loves him?"

"That he hopes so."

"He has said more than that, I take it. They have
engaged themselves to each other."

"So I understand."

" What do you think of it, Mrs. Roden ? "

" What can I think of it, Lord Hampstead ? I hardly dare to think of it at all."

" Was it wise ? "

" I suppose where love is concerned wisdom is not much considered."

" But people have to consider it. I hardly know how to think of it. To my idea it was not wise. And yet there is no one living whom I esteem so much as your son."

" You are very good, my lord."

" There is no goodness in it,—any more than in his liking for me. But I can indulge my fancy without doing harm to others. Lady Kingsbury thinks that I am an idiot because I do not live exclusively with counts and countesses ; but in declining to take her advice I do not injure her much. She can talk about me and my infatuations among her friends with a smile. She will not be tortured by any feeling of disgrace. So with my father. He has an idea that I am out-Heroding Herod, he having been Herod ;—but there is nothing bitter in it to him. Those fine young gentlemen, my brothers, who are the dearest little chicks in the world, five and six and seven years old, will be able to laugh pleasantly at their elder brother when they grow up, as they will do, among the other idle young swells of the nation. That their brother and George Roden should be always together will not even vex them. They may probably receive some benefit themselves, may achieve some diminution of the folly natural to their position, by their advantage in knowing him. In looking at it all round, as far as that goes, there is not only satisfaction to me, but a certain pride. I am doing no more than I have a right to do. Whatever counter-influence I may introduce among my own people, will be good and wholesome. Do you understand me, Mrs. Roden?"

"I think so;—very clearly. I should be dull, if I did not."

"But it becomes different when one's sister is concerned. I am thinking of the happiness of other people."

"She, I suppose, will think of her own."

"Not exclusively, I hope."

"No; not that I am sure. But a girl, when she loves——"

"Yes; that is all true. But a girl situated like Frances is bound not to,——not to sacrifice those with whom Fame and Fortune have connected her. I can speak plainly to you, Mrs. Roden, because you know what are my own opinions about many things."

"George has no sister, no girl belonging to him; but if he had, and you loved her, would you abstain from marrying her lest you should sacrifice your— connections?"

"The word has offended you?"

"Not in the least. It is a word true to the purpose in hand. I understand the sacrifice you mean. Lady

Kingsbury's feelings would be—sacrificed were her daughter,—even her stepdaughter,—to become my boy's husband. She supposes that her girl's birth is superior to my boy's."

"There are so many meanings to that word 'birth.'"

"I will take it all as you mean, Lord Hampstead, and will not be offended. My boy, as he is, is no match for your sister. Both Lord and Lady Kingsbury would think that there had been—a sacrifice. It might be that those little lords would not in future years be wont to talk at their club of their brother-in-law, the Post Office clerk, as they would of some earl or some duke with whom they might have become connected. Let us pass it by, and acknowledge that there would be—a sacrifice. So there will be should you marry below your degree. The sacrifice would be greater because it would be carried on to some future Marquis of Kingsbury. Would you practise such self-denial as that you demand from your sister?"

Lord Hampstead considered the matter a while, and then answered the question. "I do not think that the two cases would be quite analogous."

"Where is the difference?"

"There is something more delicate, more nice, requiring greater caution in the conduct of a girl than of a man."

"Quite so, Lord Hampstead. Where conduct is in question, the girl is bound to submit to stricter

laws. I may explain that by saying that the girl
is lost for ever who gives herself up to unlawful love,
—whereas, for the man, the way back to the world's
respect is only too easy, even should he, on that score,
have lost aught of the world's respect. The same
law runs through every act of a girl's life, as contrasted
with the acts of men. But in this act,—the act now
supposed of marrying a gentleman whom she loves,—
your sister would do nothing which should exclude
her from the respect of good men or the society of
well-ordered ladies. I do not say that the marriage
would be well-assorted. I do not recommend it.
Though my boy's heart is dearer to me than anything
else can be in the world, I can see that it may be fit
that his heart should be made to suffer. But when
you talk of the sacrifice which he and your sister are
called on to make, so that others should be delivered
from lesser sacrifices, I think you should ask what duty
would require from yourself. I do not think she would
sacrifice the noble blood of the Traffords more effect-
ually than you would by a similar marriage." As she
thus spoke she leant forward from her chair on the
table, and looked him full in the face. And he felt,
as she did so, that she was singularly handsome,
greatly gifted, a woman noble to the eye and to
the ear. She was pleading for her son,—and he
knew that. But she had condescended to use no mean
argument.

"If you will say that such a law is dominant among

your class, and that it is one to which you would submit yourself, I will not repudiate it. But you shall not induce me to consent to it, by even a false idea as to the softer delicacy of the sex. That softer delicacy, with its privileges and duties, shall be made to stand for what it is worth, and to occupy its real ground. If you use it for other mock purposes, then I will quarrel with you." It was thus that she had spoken, and he understood it all.

" I am not brought in question," he said slowly.

" Cannot you put it to yourself as though you were brought in question ? You will at any rate admit that my argument is just."

" I hardly know. I must think of it. Such a marriage on my part would not outrage my step-mother, as would that of my sister."

" Outrage ! You speak, Lord Hampstead, as though your mother would think that your sister would have disgraced herself as a woman ! "

" I am speaking of her feelings,—not of mine. It would be different were I to marry in the same degree."

" Would it ? Then I think that perhaps I had better counsel George not to go to Hendon Hall."

" My sister is not there. They are all in Germany."

" He had better not go where your sister will be thought of."

"I would not quarrel with your son for all the world."

"It will be better that you should. Do not suppose that I am pleading for him." That, however, was what he did suppose, and that was what she was doing. "I have told him already that I think that the prejudices will be too hard for him, and that he had better give it up before he adds to his own misery, and perhaps to hers. What I have said has not been in the way of pleading,—but only as showing the ground on which I think that such a marriage would be inexpedient. It is not that we, or our sister, are too bad or too low for such contact; but that you, on your side, are not as yet good enough or high enough."

"I will not dispute that with you, Mrs. Roden. But you will give him my message?"

"Yes; I will give him your message."

Then Lord Hampstead, having spent a full hour in the house, took his departure and rode away.

"Just an hour," said Clara Demijohn, who was still looking out of Mrs. Duffer's window. "What can they have been talking about?"

"I think he must be making up to the widow," said Mrs. Duffer, who was so lost in surprise as to be unable to suggest any new idea.

"He'd never have come with saddle horses to do that. She wouldn't be taken by a young man spending his money in that fashion. She'd like saving ways better. But they're his own horses, and his own man, and he's no more after the widow than he's after me," said Clara, laughing.

" I wish he were, my dear."

"There may be as good as him come yet, Mrs. Duffer. I don't think so much of their having horses and grooms. When they have these things they can't afford to have wives too,—and sometimes they can't afford to pay for either." Then, having seen the last of Lord Hampstead as he rode out of the Row, she went back to her mother's house.

But Mrs. Demijohn had been making use of her time while Clara and Mrs. Duffer had been wasting theirs in mere gazing and making vain surmises. As soon as she found herself alone the old woman got her bonnet and shawl, and going out slily into the Row, made her way down to the end of the street in the direction opposite to that in which the groom was at that moment walking the horses. There she escaped the eyes of her niece and of the neighbours, and was enabled to wait unseen till the man, in his walking, came down to the spot at which she was standing. "My young man," she said in her most winning voice, when the groom came near her.

" What is it, Mum ? "

" You'd like a glass of beer, wouldn't you ;—after walking up and down so long ? "

" No, I wouldn't, not just at present." He knew
VOL. I.   G

whom he served, and from whom it would become him
to take beer.

"I'd be happy to pay for a pint," said Mrs. Demijohn,
fingering a fourpenny bit so that he might see it.

"Thankye, Mum; no, I takes it reg'lar when I takes
it. I'm on dooty just at present."

"Your master's horses, I suppose?"

"Whose else, Mum? His lordship don't ride generally nobody's 'orses but his own."

Here was a success! And the fourpenny bit saved!
His lordship! "Of course not," said Mrs. Demijohn.
"Why should he?"

"Why, indeed, Mum?"

"Lord——; Lord——;—Lord who, is he?"

The groom poked up his hat, and scratched his head,
and bethought himself. A servant generally wishes
to do what honour he can to his master. This man
had no desire to gratify an inquisitive old woman, but
he thought it derogatory to his master and to himself
to seem to deny their joint name. "'Ampstead!" he
said, looking down very serenely on the lady, and then
moved on, not wasting another word.

"I knew all along they were something out of the
common way," said Mrs. Demijohn as soon as her niece
came in.

"You haven't found out who it is, aunt?"

"You've been with Mrs. Duffer, I suppose. You
two'd put your heads together for a week, and then
would know nothing." It was not till quite the last

thing at night that she told her secret. "He was a
peer! He was Lord 'Ampstead!"

"A peer!"

"He was Lord 'Ampstead, I tell you," said Mrs.
Demijohn.

"I don't believe there is such a lord," said Clara,
as she took herself up to bed.

CHAPTER VII.

THE POST OFFICE.

WHEN George Roden came home that evening the matter was discussed between him and his mother at great length. She was eager with him, if not to abandon his love, at any rate to understand how impossible it was that he should marry Lady Frances. She was very tender with him, full of feeling, full of compassion and sympathy; but she was persistent in declaring that no good could come from such an engagement. But he would not be deterred in the least from his resolution, nor would he accept it as possible that he should be turned from his object by the wishes of any person as long as Lady Frances was true to him. "You speak as if daughters were slaves," he said.

"So they are. So women must be;—slaves to the conventions of the world. A young woman can hardly run counter to her family on a question of marriage. She may be persistent enough to overcome objections, but that will be because the objections themselves are not strong enough to stand against her. But here the objections will be very strong."

"We will see, mother," he said. She who knew him well perceived that it would be vain to talk to him further.

"Oh, yes," he said, "I will go out to Hendon, perhaps on Sunday. That Mr. Vivian is a pleasant fellow, and as Hampstead does not wish to quarrel with me I certainly will not quarrel with him."

Roden was generally popular at his office, and had contrived to make his occupation there pleasant to himself and interesting; but he had his little troubles, as will happen to most men in all walks of life. His came to him chiefly from the ill-manners of a fellow-clerk who sat in the same room with him, and at the same desk. There were five who occupied the apartment, an elderly gentleman and four youngsters. The elderly gentleman was a quiet, civil, dull old man, who never made himself disagreeable, and was content to put up with the frivolities of youth, if they did not become too uproarious or antagonistic to discipline. When they did, he had but one word of rebuke. "Mr. Crocker, I will not have it." Beyond that he had never been known to go in the way either of reporting the misconduct of his subordinates to other superior powers, or in quarrelling with the young men himself. Even with Mr. Crocker, who no doubt was troublesome, he contrived to maintain terms of outward friendship. His name was Jerningham, and next to Mr. Jerningham in age came Mr. Crocker, by whose ill-timed witticisms our George Roden was not unfrequently made to suffer.

This had sometimes gone so far that Roden had contemplated the necessity of desiring Mr. Crocker to
assume that a bond of enmity had been established between them ;—or in other words, that they were not " to
speak " except on official subjects. But there had been
an air of importance about such a proceeding of which
Crocker hardly seemed to be worthy; and Roden had
abstained, putting off the evil hour from day to day,
but still conscious that he must do something to stop
vulgarities which were distasteful to him.

The two other young men, Mr. Bobbin and Mr.
Geraghty, who sat at a table·by themselves and were
the two junior clerks in that branch of the office, were
pleasant and good-humoured enough. They were both
young, and as yet not very useful to the Queen. They
were apt to come late to their office, and impatient
to leave it when the hour of four drew nigh. There
would sometimes come a storm through the Department, moved by an unseen but powerful and
unsatisfied Æolus, in which Bobbin and Geraghty
would be threatened to be blown into infinite space.
Minutes would be written and rumours spread about;
punishments would be inflicted, and it would be given
to be understood that now one and then the other
would certainly have to return to his disconsolate
family at the very next offence. There was a question at this very moment whether Geraghty, who
had come from the sister island about twelve months
since, should not be returned to King's County. No

doubt he had passed the Civil Service examiners with distinguished applause; but Æolus hated the young Crichtons who came to him with full marks, and had declared that Geraghty, though no doubt a linguist, a philosopher, and a mathematician, was not worth his salt as a Post Office clerk. But he, and Bobbin also, were protected by Mr. Jerningham, and were well liked by George Roden.

That Roden was intimate with Lord Hampstead had become known to his fellow-clerks. The knowledge of this association acted somewhat to his advantage and somewhat to his injury. His daily companions could not but feel a reflected honour in their own intimacy with the friend of the eldest son of a Marquis, and were anxious to stand well with one who lived in such high society. Such was natural;—but it was natural also that envy should show itself in ridicule, and that the lord should be thrown in the clerk's teeth when the clerk should be deemed to have given offence. Crocker, when it first became certain that Roden passed much of his time in company with a young lord, had been anxious enough to foregather with the fortunate youth who sat opposite to him; but Roden had not cared much for Crocker's society, and hence it had come to pass that Crocker had devoted himself to jeers and witticisms. Mr. Jerningham, who in his very soul respected a Marquis, and felt something of genuine awe for anything that touched the peerage, held his fortunate junior in unfeigned esteem from the

moment in which he became aware of the intimacy.
He did in truth think better of the clerk because the
clerk had known how to make himself a companion to
a lord. He did not want anything for himself. He
was too old and settled in life to be desirous of new
friendships. He was naturally conscientious, gentle,
and unassuming. But Roden rose in his estimation,
and Crocker fell, when he became assured that Roden
and Lord Hampstead were intimate friends, and that
Crocker had dared to jeer at the friendship. A lord
is like a new hat. The one on the arm the other on
the head are no evidences of mental superiority. But
yet they are taken, and not incorrectly taken, as
signs of merit. The increased esteem shown by Mr.
Jerningham for Roden should, I think, be taken
as showing Mr. Jerningham's good sense and general
appreciation.

The two lads were both on Roden's side. Roden
was not a rose, but he lived with a rose, and the lads
of course liked the scent of roses. They did not particularly like Crocker, though Crocker had a dash
about him which would sometimes win their flattery.
Crocker was brave and impudent and self-assuming.
They were not as yet sufficiently advanced in life to
be able to despise Crocker. Crocker imposed upon
them. But should there come anything of real war-
fare between Crocker and Roden, there could be no
doubt but that they would side with Lord Hampstead's
friend. Such was the state of the room at the Post

Office when Crocker entered it, on the morning of
Lord Hampstead's visit to Paradise Row.

Crocker was a little late He was often a little
late,—a fact of which Mr. Jerningham ought to have
taken more stringent notice than he did. Perhaps Mr.
Jerningham rather feared Crocker. Crocker had so
read Mr. Jerningham's character as to have become
aware that his senior was soft, and perhaps timid. He
had so far advanced in this reading as to have learned
to think that he could get the better of Mr. Jerningham by being loud and impudent. He had no
doubt hitherto been successful, but there were those
in the office who believed that the day might come
when Mr. Jerningham would rouse himself in his
wrath.

"Mr. Crocker, you are late," said Mr. Jerningham.

"Mr. Jerningham, I am late. I scorn false excuses.
Geraghty would say that his watch was wrong. Bobbin
would have eaten something that had disagreed with
him. Roden would have been detained by his friend,
Lord Hampstead." To this Roden made no reply even
by a look. "For me, I have to acknowledge that
I did not turn out when I was called. Of twenty
minutes I have deprived my country; but as my
country values so much of my time at only seven-
pence-halfpenny, it is hardly worth saying much
about it."

"You are frequently late."

"When the amount has come up to ten pound

I will send the Postmaster-General stamps to that amount." He was now standing at his desk, opposite to Roden, to whom he made a low bow. " Mr. George Roden," he said, " I hope that his lordship is quite well."

" The only lord with whom I am acquainted is quite well; but I do not know why you should trouble yourself about him."

" I think it becoming in one who takes the Queen's pay to show a becoming anxiety as to the Queen's aristocracy. I have the greatest respect for the Marquis of Kingsbury. Have not you, Mr. Jerningham ? "

" Certainly I have. But if you would go to your work instead of talking so much it would be better for everybody."

" I am at my work already. Do you think that I cannot work and talk at the same time ? Bobbin, my boy, if you would open that window, do you think it would hurt your complexion ? " Bobbin opened the window. " Paddy, where were you last night ? " Paddy was Mr. Geraghty.

" I was dining, then, with my sister's mother-in-law."

" What,—the O'Kelly, the great legislator and Home Ruler, whom his country so loves and Parliament so hates! I don't think any Home Ruler's relative ought to be allowed into the service. Do you, Mr. Jerningham ? "

" I think Mr. Geraghty, if he will only be a little

more careful, will do great credit to the service," said Mr. Jerningham.

"I hope that Æolus may think the same." Æolus was the name by which a certain pundit was known at the office;—a violent and imperious Secretary, but not in the main ill-natured. "Æolus, when last I heard of his opinion, seemed to have his doubts about poor Paddy." This was a disagreeable subject, and it was felt by them all that it might better be left in silence. From that time the work of the day was continued with no more than moderate interruptions till the hour of luncheon, when the usual attendant entered with the usual mutton-chops. "I wonder if Lord Hampstead has mutton-chops for luncheon?" asked Crocker.

"Why should he not?" asked Mr. Jerningham, foolishly.

"There must be some kind of gilded cutlet, upon which the higher members of the aristocracy regale themselves. I suppose, Roden, you must have seen his lordship at lunch."

"I dare say I have," said Roden, angrily. He knew that he was annoyed, and was angry with himself at his own annoyance.

"Are they golden or only gilded?" asked Crocker.

"I believe you mean to make yourself disagreeable," said the other.

"Quite the reverse. I mean to make myself agreeable;—only you have soared so high of late that ordinary conversation has no charms for you. Is there any reason why Lord Hampstead's lunch should not be mentioned?"

"Certainly there is," said Roden.

"Then, upon my life, I cannot see it. If you talked of my mid-day chop I should not take it amiss."

"I don't think a fellow should ever talk about another fellow's eating unless he knows the fellow." This came from Bobbin, who intended it well, meaning to fight the battle for Roden as well as he knew how.

"Most sapient Bobb," said Crocker, "you seem to be unaware that one young fellow, who is Roden, happens to be the peculiarly intimate friend of the other fellow, who is the Earl of Hampstead. Therefore the law, as so clearly laid down by yourself, has not been infringed. To return to our muttons, as the Frenchman says, what sort of lunch does his lordship eat?"

"You are determined to make yourself disagreeable," said Roden.

"I appeal to Mr. Jerningham whether I have said anything unbecoming."

"If you appeal to me, I think you have," said Mr. Jerningham.

"You have, at any rate, been so successful in doing it," continued Roden, "that I must ask you to hold your tongue about Lord Hampstead. It has not been by anything I have said that you have heard of my acquaintance with him. The joke is a bad one, and will become vulgar if repeated."

"Vulgar!" cried Crocker, pushing away his plate, and rising from his chair.

"I mean ungentlemanlike. I don't want to use hard words, but I will not allow myself to be annoyed."

"Hoity, toity," said Crocker, "here's a row because I made a chance allusion to a noble lord. I am to be called vulgar because I mentioned his name." Then he began to whistle.

"Mr. Crocker, I will not have it," said Mr. Jerningham, assuming his most angry tone. "You make more noise in the room than all the others put together."

"Nevertheless, I do wonder what Lord Hampstead has had for his lunch." This was the last shot, and after that the five gentlemen did in truth settle down to their afternoon's work.

When four o'clock came Mr. Jerningham with praiseworthy punctuality took his hat and departed. His wife and three unmarried daughters were waiting for him at Islington, and as he was always in his seat punctually at ten, he was justified in leaving it punctually at four. Crocker swaggered about the room for a minute or two with his hat on, desirous of showing that he was by no means affected by the rebukes which he had received. But he, too, soon went, not having summoned courage to recur to the name of Roden's noble friend. The two lads remained for the sake of saying a word of comfort to Roden, who still sat writing at his desk. "I thought it was very low form," said Bobbin; "Crocker going on like that."

" Crocker's a baist," said Geraghty.

"What was it to him what anybody eats for his lunch?" continued Bobbin.

"Only he likes to have a nobleman's name in his mouth," said Geraghty. "I think it's the hoighth of bad manners talking about anybody's friends unless you happen to know them yourself."

"I think it is," said Roden, looking up from his desk. "But I'll tell you what shows worse manners; —that is, a desire to annoy anybody. Crocker likes to be funny, and he thinks there is no fun so good as what he calls taking a rise. I don't know that I'm very fond of Crocker, but it may be as well that we should all think no more about it." Upon this the young men promised that they, at least, would think no more about it, and then took their departure. George Roden soon followed them, for it was not the practice of anybody in that department to remain at work long after four o'clock.

Roden as he walked home did think more of the little affair than it deserved,—more at least than he would acknowledge that it deserved. He was angry with himself for bearing it in mind, and yet he did bear it in mind. Could it be that a creature so insignificant as Crocker could annoy him by a mere word or two? But he was annoyed, and did not know how such annoyance could be made to cease. If the man

would continue to talk about Lord Hampstead there
was nothing by which he could be made to hold his
tongue. He could not be kicked, or beaten, or turned
out of the room. For any purpose of real assistance
Mr. Jerningham was useless. As to complaining to
the Æolus of the office that a certain clerk would talk
about Lord Hampstead, that of course was out of the
question. He had already used strong language, calling
the man vulgar and ungentlemanlike, but if a man
does not regard strong language what further can an
angry victim do to him ?

Then his thoughts passed on to his connexion with
the Marquis of Kingsbury's family generally. Had
he not done wrong, at any rate, done foolishly, in thus
moving himself out of his own sphere ? At the present
moment Lady Frances was nearer to him even than
Lord Hampstead,—was more important to him and
more in his thoughts. Was it not certain that he
would give rise to misery rather than to happiness
by what had occurred between him and Lady Frances ?
Was it not probable that he had embittered for her all
the life of the lady whom he loved ? He had assumed
an assured face and a confident smile while declaring
to his mother that no power on earth should stand
between him and his promised wife,—that she would
be able to walk out from her father's hall and marry
him as certainly as might the housemaid or the plough-
man's daughter go to her lover. But what would be
achieved by that if she were to walk out only to

encounter misery? The country was so constituted
that he and these Traffords were in truth of a different
race; as much so as the negro is different from the
white man. The Post Office clerk may, indeed,
possibly become a Duke; whereas the negro's skin
cannot be washed white. But while he and Lady
Frances were as they were, the distance between them
was so great that no approach could be made between
them without disruption. The world might be wrong
in this. To his thinking the world was wrong. But
while the facts existed they were too strong to be set
aside. He could do his duty to the world by struggling
to propagate his own opinions, so that the distance
might be a little lessened in his own time. He was
sure that the distance was being lessened, and with
this he thought that he ought to have been contented.
The jeering of such a one as Crocker was unimportant
though disagreeable, but it sufficed to show the feeling.
Such a friendship as his with Lord Hampstead had
appeared to Crocker to be ridiculous. Crocker would
not have seen the absurdity unless others had seen it
also. Even his own mother saw it. Here in England
it was accounted so foolish a thing that he, a Post
Office clerk, should be hand and glove with such a one
as Lord Hampstead, that even a Crocker could raise a
laugh against him! What would the world say when
it should have become known that he intended to lead
Lady Frances to the "hymeneal altar?" As he repeated the words to himself there was something

ridiculous even to himself in the idea that the hymeneal altar should ever be mentioned in reference to the adventures of such a person as George Roden, the Post Office clerk. Thinking of all this, he was not in a happy frame of mind when he reached his home in Paradise Row.

CHAPTER VIII.

MR. GREENWOOD.

RODEN spent a pleasant evening with his friend and his friend's friend at Hendon Hall before their departure for the yacht,—during which not a word was said or an allusion made to Lady Frances. The day was Sunday, July 20th. The weather was very hot, and the two young men were delighted at the idea of getting away to the cool breezes of the Northern Seas. Vivian also was a clerk in the public service, but he was a clerk very far removed in his position from that filled by George Roden. He was attached to the Foreign Office, and was Junior Private Secretary to Lord Persiflage, who was Secretary of State at that moment. Lord Persiflage and our Marquis had married sisters. Vivian was distantly related to the two ladies, and hence the young men had become friends. As Lord Hampstead and Roden had been drawn together by similarity of opinion, so had Lord Hampstead and Vivian by the reverse. Hampstead could always produce Vivian in proof that he was not, in truth, opposed to his

own order. Vivian was one who proclaimed his great
liking for things as he found them. It was a thousand
pities that any one should be hungry; but, for himself,
he liked truffles, ortolans, and all good things. If there
was any injustice in the world he was not responsible.
And if there was any injustice he had not been the
gainer, seeing that he was a younger brother. To him
all Hampstead's theories were sheer rhodomontade.
There was the world, and men had got to live in it as
best they might. He intended to do so, and as he
liked yachting and liked grouse-shooting, he was very
glad to have arranged with Lord Persiflage and his
brother Private Secretary, so as to be able to get out
of town for the next two months. He was member
of half-a-dozen clubs, could always go to his brother's
country house if nothing more inviting offered, dined
out in London four or five days a week, and considered
himself a thoroughly useful member of society in that
he condescended to write letters for Lord Persiflage.
He was pleasant in his manners to all men, and had
accommodated himself to Roden as well as though
Roden's office had also been in Downing Street instead
of the City.

"Yes, grouse," he said, after dinner. "If anything
better can be invented I'll go and do it. American
bears are a myth. You may get one in three years,
and, as far as I can hear, very poor fun it is when
you get it. Lions are a grind. Elephants are as big
as a hay-stack. Pig-sticking may be very well, but

H 2

you've got to go to India, and if you're a poor Foreign
Office clerk you haven't got either the time or the
money."

"You speak as though killing something were a
necessity," said Roden.

"So it is, unless somebody can invent something
better. I hate races, where a fellow has nothing to do
with himself when he can't afford to bet. I don't
mean to take to cards for the next ten years. I have
never been up in a balloon. Spooning is good fun,
but it comes to an end so soon one way or another.
Girls are so wide-awake that they won't spoon for
nothing. Upon the whole I don't see what a fellow is
to do unless he kills something."

"You won't have much to kill on board the yacht,"
said Roden.

"Fishing without end in Iceland and Norway! I
knew a man who killed a ton of trout out of an Iceland
lake. He had to pack himself up very closely in
tight-fitting nets, or the midges would have eaten
him. And the skin came off his nose and ears from
the sun. But he liked that rather than not, and he
killed his ton of trout."

"Who weighed them ? " asked Hampstead.

"How well you may know a Utilitarian by the
nature of his questions ! If a man doesn't kill his ton all
out, he can say he did, which is the next best thing to it."

"Are you taking close-packing nets with you ? "
Roden asked.

"Well, no. Hampstead would be too impatient.
And the *Free Trader* isn't big enough to bring away
the fish. But I don't mind betting a sovereign that
I kill something every day I'm out,—barring Sundays."

Not a word was said about Lady Frances, although
there were a few moments in which Roden and Lord
Hampstead were alone together. Roden had made
up his mind that he would ask no questions unless
the subject were mentioned, and did not even allude
to any of the family; but he learnt in the course of
the evening that the Marquis had come back from
Germany with the intention of attending to his
Parliamentary duties during the remainder of the
Session.

"He's going to turn us all out," said Vivian, "on the
County Franchise, I suppose."

"I'm afraid my father is not so keen about County
Franchise as he used to be, though I hope he will
be one of the few to support it in the House of
Lords if the House of Commons ever dares to
pass it."

In this way Roden learnt that the Marquis, who had
carried his daughter off to Saxony as soon as he had
heard of the engagement, had left his charge there and
had returned to London. As he went home that
evening he thought that it would be his duty to go to
Lord Kingsbury, and tell him, as from himself, that
which the father had as yet only learnt from his
daughter or from his wife. He was aware that it

behoves a man when he has won a girl's heart to go to
the father and ask permission to carry on his suit.
This duty he thought he was bound to perform, even
though the father were a person so high and mighty
as the Marquis of Kingsbury. Hitherto any such
going was out of his power. The Marquis had heard
the tidings, and had immediately caught his daughter
up and carried her off to Germany. It would have
been possible to write to him, but Roden had thought
that not in such a way should such a duty be performed. Now the Marquis had come back to London;
and though the operation would be painful the duty
seemed to be paramount. On the next day he informed
Mr. Jerningham that private business of importance
would take him to the West End, and asked leave
to absent himself. The morning had been passed in
the room at the Post Office with more than ordinary
silence. Crocker had been collecting himself for an
attack, but his courage had hitherto failed him. As
Roden put on his hat and opened the door he fired
a parting shot. "Remember me kindly to Lord
Hampstead," he said; "and tell him I hope he enjoyed
his cutlets."

Roden stood for a moment with the door in his hand,
thinking that he would turn upon the man and rebuke
his insolence, but at last determined that it would be
best to hold his peace.

He went direct to Park Lane, thinking that he would
probably find the Marquis before he left the house after

his luncheon. He had never been before at the town
mansion which was known as Kingsbury House, and
which possessed all the appanages of grandeur which
can be given to a London residence. As he knocked
at the door he acknowledged that he was struck with
a certain awe of which he was ashamed. Having said
so much to the daughter surely he should not be
afraid to speak to the father! But he felt that he
could have managed the matter much better had he
contrived to have the interview at Hendon Hall, which
was much less grand than Kingsbury House. Almost
as soon as he knocked the door was opened, and he
found himself with a powdered footman as well as
the porter. The powdered footman did not know
whether or no "my lord" was at home. He would
inquire. Would the gentleman sit down for a minute
or two? The gentleman did sit down, and waited
for what seemed to him to be more than half-an-hour.
The house must be very large indeed if it took the
man all this time to look for the Marquis. He was
beginning to think in what way he might best make
his escape,—as a man is apt to think when delays of
this kind prove too long for the patience,— but the man
returned, and with a cold unfriendly air bade Roden
to follow him. Roden was quite sure that some evil
was to happen, so cold and unfriendly was the manner
of the man; but still he followed, having now no means
of escape. The man had not said that the Marquis
would see him, had not even given any intimation

that the Marquis was in the house. It was as though he were being led away to execution for having had the impertinence to knock at the door. But still he followed. He was taken along a passage on the ground floor, past numerous doors, to what must have been the back of the house, and there was shown into a somewhat dingy room that was altogether surrounded by books. There he saw an old gentleman;—but the old gentleman was not the Marquis of Kingsbury.

"Ah, eh, oh," said the old gentleman. "You, I believe, are Mr. George Roden."

"That is my name. I had hoped to see Lord Kingsbury."

"Lord Kingsbury has thought it best for all parties that,—that,—that,——I should see you. That is, if anybody should see you. My name is Greenwood;— the Rev. Mr. Greenwood, I am his lordship's chaplain, and, if I may presume to say so, his most attached and sincere friend. I have had the honour of a very long connexion with his lordship, and have therefore been entrusted by him with this,—this,—this delicate duty, I had perhaps better call it." Mr. Greenwood was a stout, short man, about sixty years of age, with pendant cheeks, and pendant chin, with a few grey hairs brushed carefully over his head, with a good forehead and well-fashioned nose, who must have been good-looking when he was young, but that he was too short for manly beauty. Now, in advanced years, he had become lethargic and averse to exercise; and having grown to

be corpulent he had lost whatever he had possessed in
height by becoming broad, and looked to be a fat dwarf.
Still there would have been something pleasant in his
face but for an air of doubt and hesitation which
seemed almost to betray cowardice. At the present
moment he stood in the middle of the room rubbing his
hands together, and almost trembling as he explained
to George Roden who he was.

"I had certainly wished to see his lordship himself,"
said Roden.

"The Marquis has thought it better not, and I must
say that I agree with the Marquis." At the moment
Roden hardly knew how to go on with the business in
hand. "I believe I am justified in assuring you that
anything you would have said to the Marquis you may
say to me."

"Am I to understand that Lord Kingsbury refuses
to see me?"

"Well;—yes. At the present crisis he does refuse.
What can be gained?"

Roden did not as yet know how far he might go in
mentioning the name of Lady Frances to the clergyman, but was unwilling to leave the house without
some reference to the business he had in hand. He
was peculiarly averse to leaving an impression that
he was afraid to mention what he had done. "I
had to speak to his lordship about his daughter," he
said.

"I know; I know; Lady Frances! I have known

Lady Frances since she was a little child. I have the warmest regard for Lady Frances,—as I have also for Lord Hampstead,—and for the Marchioness, and for her three dear little boys, Lord Frederic, Lord Augustus, and Lord Gregory. I feel a natural hesitation in calling them my friends because I think that the difference in rank and station which it has pleased the Lord to institute should be maintained with all their privileges and all their honours. Though I have agreed with the Marquis through a long life in those political tenets by propagating which he has been ever anxious to improve the condition of the lower classes, I am not and have not been on that account less anxious to uphold by any small means which may be in my power those variations in rank, to which, I think, in conjunction with the Protestant religion, the welfare and high standing of this country are mainly to be āttributed. Having these feelings at my heart very strongly I do not wish, particularly on such an occasion as this, to seem by even a chance word to diminish the respect which I feel to be due to all the members of a family of a rank so exalted as that which belongs to the family of the Marquis of Kingsbury. Putting that aside for a moment, I perhaps may venture on this occasion; having had confided to me a task so delicate as the present, to declare my warm friendship for all who bear the honoured name of Trafford. I am at any rate entitled to declare myself so far a friend, that you may say anything on this delicate subject which you would think it necessary to say to the young lady's father. However inexpedient it may be that anything should be said at all, I have been instructed by his lordship to hear,— and to reply."

George Roden, while he was listening to this tedious sermon, was standing opposite to the preacher with his hat in his hand, having not yet had accorded to him the favour of a seat. During the preaching of the sermon the preacher had never ceased to shiver and shake, rubbing one fat little clammy hand slowly over the other, and apparently afraid to look his audience in the face. It seemed to Roden as though the words must have been learnt by heart, they came so glibly, with so much of unction and of earnestness, and were in their glibness so strongly opposed to the man's manner There had not been a single word spoken that had not been offensive to Roden. It seemed to him that they had been chosen because of their offence. In all those long-winded sentences about rank in which Mr. Greenwood had expressed his own humility and insufficiency for the position of friend in a family so exalted he had manifestly intended to signify the much more manifest insufficiency of his hearer to fill a place of higher honour even than that of friend. Had the words come at the spur of the moment, the man must, thought Roden, have great gifts for extempore preaching. He had thought the time in the hall to be long, but it had not been much for the communication of the Earl's wishes, and then for the preparation of all these words. It was necessary, however, that he must make his reply without any preparation.

"I have come," he said, " to tell Lord Kingsbury that I am in love with his daughter." At hearing this the fat little man held up both his hands in amazement,—although he had already made it clear that he was acquainted with all the circumstances. " And I should have been bound to add," said Roden, plucking up all his courage, " that the young lady is also in love with me."

" Oh,—oh,—oh ! " The hands went higher and higher as these interjections were made.

" Why not ?   Is not the truth the best ? "

" A young man, Mr. Roden, should never boast of a young lady's affection,—particularly of such a young lady ;—particularly when I cannot admit that it exists ; —particularly not in her father's house."

" Nobody should boast of anything, Mr. Greenwood. I speak of a fact which it is necessary that a father should know. If the lady denies the assertion I have done."

" It is a matter in which delicacy demands that no question shall be put to the young lady. After what has occurred, it is out of the question that your name should even be mentioned in the young lady's hearing."

" Why ?—I mean to marry her."

" Mean ! "—this word was shouted in the extremity

of Mr. Greenwood's horror. " Mr. Roden, it is my
duty to assure you that under no circumstances can
you ever see the young lady again."

" Who says so ? "

" The Marquis says so,—and the Marchioness,—and
her little brothers, who with their growing strength
will protect her from all harm."

" I hope their growing strength may not be wanted
for any such purpose. Should it be so I am sure they
will not be deficient as brothers. At present there
could not be much for them to do." Mr. Greenwood
shook his head. He was still standing, not having
moved an inch from the position in which he had
been placed when the door was opened. " I can
understand, Mr. Greenwood, that any further conversation on the subject between you and me must be quite
useless."

" Quite useless," said Mr. Greenwood.

" But it has been necessary for my honour, and for
my purpose, that Lord Kingsbury should know that I
had come to ask him for his daughter's hand. I had
not dared to expect that he would accept my proposal
graciously."

" No, no ; hardly that, Mr. Roden."

" But it was necessary that he should know my
purpose from myself. He will now, no doubt, do so.
He is, as I understand you, aware of my presence in
the house." Mr. Greenwood shook his head, as though
he would say that this was a matter he could not any

longer discuss. "If not, I must trouble his lordship with a letter."

"That will be unnecessary."

"He does know." Mr. Greenwood nodded his head. "And you will tell him why I have come?"

"The Marquis shall be made acquainted with the nature of the interview."

Roden then turned to leave the room, but was obliged to ask Mr. Greenwood to show him the way along the passages. This the clergyman did, tripping on, ahead, upon his toes, till he had delivered the intruder over to the hall porter. Having done so, he made as it were a valedictory bow, and tripped back to his own apartment. Then Roden left the house, thinking as he did so that there was certainly much to be done before he could be received there as a welcome son-in-law.

As he made his way back to Holloway he again considered it all. How could there be an end to this, —an end that would be satisfactory to himself and to the girl that he loved? The aversion expressed to him through the person of Mr. Greenwood was natural. It could not but be expected that such a one as the Marquis of Kingsbury should endeavour to keep his daughter out of the hands of such a suitor. If it were only in regard to money would it not be necessary for him to do so? Every possible barricade would be built up in his way. There would be nothing on his side except the girl's love for himself. Was

it to be expected that her love would have power to
conquer such obstacles as these? And if it were,
would she obtain her own happiness by clinging to
it? He was aware that in his present position no
duty was so incumbent on him as that of looking to
the happiness of the woman whom he wished to make
his wife.

CHAPTER IX.

AT KÖNIGSGRAAF.

VERY shortly after this there came a letter from
Lady Frances to Paradise Row,—the only letter which
Roden received from her during this period of his
courtship. A portion of the letter shall be given, from
which the reader will see that difficulties had arisen at
Königsgraaf as to their correspondence. He had
written twice. The first letter had in due course
reached the young lady's hands, having been brought
up from the village post-office in the usual manner,
and delivered to her without remark by her own maid.
When the second reached the Castle it fell into the
hands of the Marchioness. She had, indeed, taken
steps that it should fall into her hands. She was
aware that the first letter had come, and had been
shocked at the idea of such a correspondence. She
had received no direct authority from her husband
on the subject, but felt that it was incumbent on
herself to take strong steps. It must not be that
Lady Frances should receive love-letters from a Post

Office clerk! As regarded Lady Frances herself, the
Marchioness would have been willing enough that the
girl should be given over to a letter-carrier, if she could
be thus got rid of altogether,—so that the world should
not know that there was or had been a Lady Frances
But the fact was patent,—as was also that too, too-
sad truth of the existence of a brother older than
her own comely bairns. As the feeling of hatred
grew upon her, she continually declared to herself
that she would have been as gentle a stepmother as
ever loved another woman's children, had these two
known how to bear themselves like the son and daughter
of a Marquis. Seeing what they were,—and what
were her own children,—how these struggled to repudiate that rank which her own were born to adorn and
protect, was it not natural that she should hate them,
and profess that she should wish them to be out of
the way? They could not be made to get out of
the way, but Lady Frances might at any rate be
repressed. Therefore she determined to stop the
correspondence.

She did stop the second letter,—and told her daughter
that she had done so.

"Papa didn't say I wasn't to have my letters,"
pleaded Lady Frances.

"Your papa did not suppose for a moment that you
would submit to anything so indecent."

"It is not indecent."

"I shall make myself the judge of that. You are

now in my care. Your papa can do as he likes when
he comes back." There was a long altercation, but
it ended in victory on the part of the Marchioness.
The young lady, when she was told that, if necessary,
the postmistress in the village should be instructed
not to send on any letter addressed to George Roden,
believed in the potency of the threat. She felt sure
also that she would be unable to get at any letters
addressed to herself if the quasi-parental authority of
the Marchioness were used to prevent it. She yielded,
on the condition, however, that one letter should be
sent; and the Marchioness, not at all thinking that
her own instructions would have prevailed with the
post-mistress, yielded so far.

The tenderness of the letter readers can appreciate
and understand without seeing it expressed in words.
It was very tender, full of promises, and full of trust.
Then came the short passage in which her own
uncomfortable position was explained ;—

"You will understand that there has come one letter
which I have not been allowed to see. Whether
mamma has opened it I do not know, or whether she
has destroyed it. Though I have not seen it, I take it
as an assurance of your goodness and truth. But it
will be useless for you to write more till you hear from
me again; and I have promised that this, for the
present, shall be my last to you. The last and the
first ! I hope you will keep it till you have another, in
order that you may have something to tell you how well

I love you." As she sent it from her she did not know
how much of solace there was even in the writing of a
letter to him she loved, nor had she as yet felt how
great was the torment of remaining without palpable
notice from him she loved.

After the episode of the letter life at Königsgraaf
was very bitter and very dull. But few words were
spoken between the Marchioness and her stepdaughter,
and those were never friendly in their tone or kindly in
their nature. Even the children were taken out of
their sister's way as much as possible, so that their
morals should not be corrupted by evil communication.
When she complained of this to their mother the
Marchioness merely drew herself up and was silent.
Were it possible she would have altogether separated
her darlings from contact with their sister, not because
she thought that the darlings would in truth be injured,—as to which she had no fears at all, seeing that
the darlings were subject to her own influences,—but
in order that the punishment to Lady Frances might
be the more complete. The circumstances being such
as they were, there should be no family love, no
fraternal sports, no softnesses, no mercy. There must,
she thought, have come from the blood of that first
wife a stain of impurity which had made her children
altogether unfit for the rank to which they had unfortunately been born. This iniquity on the part of Lady
Frances, this disgrace which made her absolutely
tremble as she thought of it, this abominable affection

for an inferior creature, acerbated her feelings even
against Lord Hampstead. The two were altogether so
base as to make her think that they could not be intended by Divine Providence to stand permanently in
the way of the glory of the family. Something certainly would happen. It would turn out that they
were not truly the legitimate children of a real Marchioness. Some beautiful scheme of romance would
discover itself to save her and her darlings, and all the
Traffords and all the Montressors from the terrible
abomination with which they were threatened by these
interlopers. The idea dwelt in her mind till it became an almost fixed conviction that Lord Frederic
would live to become Lord Hampstead,—or probably
Lord Highgate, as there was a third title in the family,
and the name of Hampstead must for a time be held to
have been disgraced,—and in due course of happy time
Marquis of Kingsbury. Hitherto she had been accustomed to speak to her own babies of their elder brother
with something of that respect which was due to the
future head of the family ; but in these days she altered
her tone when they spoke to her of Jack, as they would
call him, and she, from herself, never mentioned his
name to them. " Is Fanny naughty ? " Lord Frederic
asked one day. To this she made no reply. " Is
Fanny very naughty ? " the boy persisted in asking.
To this she nodded her head solemnly. " What has
Fanny done, mamma ? " At this she shook her head
mysteriously. It may, therefore, be understood that

poor Lady Frances was sadly in want of comfort during
the sojourn at Königsgraaf.

About the end of August the Marquis returned.
He had hung on in London till the very last days of
the Session had been enjoyed, and had then pretended
that his presence had been absolutely required at
Trafford Park. To Trafford Park he went, and had
spent ten miserable days alone. Mr. Greenwood had
indeed gone with him; but the Marquis was a man
who was miserable unless surrounded by the comforts
of his family, and he led Mr. Greenwood such a life
that that worthy clergyman was very happy when he
was left altogether in solitude by his noble friend.
Then, in compliance with the promise which he had
absolutely made, and aware that it was his duty to
look after his wicked daughter, the Marquis returned
to Königsgraaf. Lady Frances was to him at this
period of his life a cause of unmitigated trouble. It
must not be supposed that his feelings were in any
way akin to those of the Marchioness as to either of
his elder children. Both of them were very dear to
him, and of both of them he was in some degree proud.
They were handsome, noble-looking, clever, and to
himself thoroughly well-behaved. He had seen what
trouble other elder sons could give their fathers, what
demands were made for increased allowances, what
disreputable pursuits were sometimes followed, what
quarrels there were, what differences, what want of
affection and want of respect! He was wise enough

to have perceived all this, and to be aware that he
was in some respects singularly blest. Hampstead
never asked him for a shilling. He was a liberal
man, and would willingly have given many shillings.
But still there was a comfort in having a son who
was quite contented in having his own income. No
doubt a time would come when those little lords would
want shillings. And Lady Frances had always been
particularly soft to him, diffusing over his life a sweet
taste of the memory of his first wife. Of the present
Marchioness he was fond enough, and was aware how
much she did for him to support his position. But
he was conscious ever of a prior existence in which
there had been higher thoughts, grander feelings, and
aspirations which were now wanting to him. Of these
something would come back in the moments which
he spent with his daughter; and in this way she was
very dear to him. But now there had come a trouble
which robbed his life of all its sweetness. He must go
back to the grandeur of his wife and reject the tenderness of his daughter. During these days at Trafford he
made himself very unpleasant to the devoted friend who
had always been so true to his interests.

When the battle about the correspondence was
explained to him by his wife, it, of course, became
necessary to him to give his orders to his daughter.
Such a matter could hardly be passed over in silence,—
though he probably might have done so had he not
been instigated to action by the Marchioness.

)

"Fanny," he said, "I have been shocked by these letters."

"I only wrote one, papa."

"Well, one. But two came."

"I only had one, papa."

"That made two. But there should have been no letter at all. Do you think it proper that a young lady should correspond with,—with,—a gentleman in opposition to the wishes of her father and mother?"

"I don't know, papa."

This seemed to him so weak that the Marquis took heart of grace, and made the oration which he felt that he as a father was bound to utter upon the entire question. For, after all, it was not the letters which were of importance, but the resolute feeling which had given birth to the letters. "My dear, this is a most unfortunate affair." He paused for a reply; but Lady Frances felt that the assertion was one to which at the present moment she could make no reply. "It is, you know, quite out of the question that you should marry a young man so altogether unfitted for you in point of station as this young man."

"But I shall, papa."

"Fanny, you can do no such thing."

"I certainly shall. It may be a very long time first; but I certainly shall,—unless I die."

"It is wicked of you, my dear, to talk of dying in that way."

"What I mean is, that however long I may live I shall consider myself engaged to Mr. Roden."

"He has behaved very, very badly. He has made his way into my house under a false pretence."

"He came as Hampstead's friend."

"It was very foolish of Hampstead to bring him,—very foolish,—a Post Office clerk."

"Mr. Vivian is a clerk in the Foreign Office. Why shouldn't one office be the same as another?"

"They are very different;—but Mr. Vivian wouldn't think of such a thing. He understands the nature of things, and knows his own position. There is a conceit about the other man."

"A man should be conceited, papa. Nobody will think well of him unless he thinks well of himself."

"He came to me in Park Lane."

"What! Mr. Roden?"

"Yes; he came. But I didn't see him. Mr. Greenwood saw him."

"What could Mr. Greenwood say to him?"

"Mr. Greenwood could tell him to leave the house, —and he did so. There was nothing more to tell him. Now, my dear, let there be no more about it. If you will put on your hat, we will go out and walk down to the village."

To this Lady Frances gave a ready assent. She was not at all disposed to quarrel with her father, or to take in bad part what he had said about her lover. She had not expected that things would go very easily. She had promised to herself constancy and final success; but she had not expected that in her case the course of true love could be made to run smooth. She was quite willing to return to a condition of good humour with her father, and,—not exactly to drop her lover for the moment,—but so to conduct herself as though he were not paramount in her thoughts. The cruelty of her stepmother had so weighed upon her that she found it to be quite a luxury to be allowed to walk with her father.

"I don't know that anything can be done," the Marquis said a few days afterwards to his wife. "It is one of those misfortunes which do happen now and again!"

"That such a one as your daughter should give herself up to a clerk in the Post Office!"

"What's the use of repeating that so often? I don't know that the Post Office is worse than anything else. Of course it can't be allowed;—and having said so, the best thing will be to go on just as though nothing had happened."

"And let her do just what she pleases?"

"Who's going to let her do anything? She said she wouldn't write, and she hasn't written. We must just take her back to Trafford, and let her forget him as soon as she can."

The Marchioness was by no means satisfied, though she did not know what measure of special severity to recommend. There was once a time,—a very good time, as Lady Kingsbury thought now,—in which a young lady could be locked up in a convent, or perhaps in a prison, or absolutely forced to marry some suitor whom her parents should find for her. But those comfortable days were past. In a prison Lady Frances was detained now; but it was a prison of which the Marchioness was forced to make herself the gaoler, and in which her darlings were made to be fellow-prisoners with their wicked sister. She herself was anxious to get back to Trafford and the comforts of her own home. The beauties of Königsgraaf were not lovely to her in her present frame of mind. But how would it be if Lady Frances should jump out of the window at Trafford and run away with George Roden? The windows at Königsgraaf were certainly much higher than those at Trafford.

They had made up their mind to return early in September, and the excitement of packing up had almost commenced among them when Lord Hampstead suddenly appeared on the scene. He had had enough of yachting, and had grown tired of books and gardening at Hendon. Something must be done before the hunting began, and so, without notice, he appeared one day at Königsgraaf. This was to the intense delight of his brothers, over whose doings he assumed a power which their mother was unable to withstand. They were made to gallop on ponies on which they had only walked before; they were bathed in the river, and taken to the top of the Castle, and shut up in the

dungeon after a fashion which was within the reach of
no one but Hampstead. Jack was Jack, and all was
delight, as far as the children were concerned; but the
Marchioness was not so well pleased with the arrival.
A few days after his coming a conversation arose as
to Lady Frances which Lady Kingsbury would have
avoided had it been possible, but it was forced upon
her by her stepson.

"I don't think that Fanny ought to be bullied," said
her stepson.

"Hampstead, I wish you would understand that I
do not understand strong language."

"Teased, tormented, and made wretched."

"If she be wretched she has brought it on herself."

"But she is not to be treated as though she had
disgraced herself."

"She has disgraced herself."

"I deny it. I will not hear such a word said of her
even by you." The Marchioness drew herself up as
though she had been insulted. "If there is to be such
a feeling about her in your house I must ask my father
to have her removed, and I will make a home for her.
I will not see her broken-hearted by cruel treatment.
I am sure that he would not wish it."

"You have no right to speak to me in this manner."

"I surely have a right to protect my sister, and I
will exercise it."

"You have brought most improperly a young man
into the house——"

"I have brought into the house a young man whom I am proud to call my friend."

"And now you mean to assist him in destroying your sister."

"You are very wrong to say so. They both know, Roden and my sister also, that I disapprove of this marriage. If Fanny were with me I should not think it right to ask Roden into the house. They would both understand that. But it does not follow that she should be cruelly used."

"No one has been cruel to her but she herself."

"It is easy enough to perceive what is going on. It will be much better that Fanny should remain with the family; but you may be sure of this,—that I will not see her tortured." Then he took himself off, and on the next day he had left Königsgraaf. It may be understood that the Marchioness was not reconciled to her radical stepson by such language as he had used to her. About a week afterwards the whole family returned to England and to Trafford.

CHAPTER X.

"NOBLESSE OBLIGE."

"I QUITE agree," said Hampstead, endeavouring to discuss the matter rationally with his sister, "that her ladyship should not be allowed to torment you."

"She does torment me. You cannot perceive what my life was at Königsgraaf! There is a kind of usage which would drive any girl to run away,—or to drown herself. I don't suppose a man can know what it is always to be frowned at. A man has his own friends, and can go anywhere. His spirits are not broken by being isolated. He would not even see half the things which a girl is made to feel. The very servants were encouraged to treat me badly. The boys were not allowed to come near me. I never heard a word that was not intended to be severe."

"I am sure it was bad."

"And it was not made better by the conviction that she has never cared for me. It is to suffer all the authority, but to enjoy none of the love of a mother. When papa came of course it was better; but even papa cannot make her change her ways. A man is comparatively so very little in the house. If it goes on it will drive me mad."

" Of course I'll stand to you."

" Oh, John, I am sure you will."

"But it isn't altogether easy to know how to set about it. If we were to keep house together at Hendon——" As he made this proposition a look of joy came over her face, and shone amidst her tears. "There would, of course, be a difficulty."

" What difficulty ?" She, however, knew well what would be the difficulty.

" George Roden would be too near to us."

" I should never see him unless you approved."

" I should not approve. That would be the difficulty. He would argue the matter with me, and I should have to tell him that I could not let him come to the house, except with my father's leave. That would be out of the question. And therefore, as I say, there would be a difficulty."

" I would never see him,—except with your sanction, —nor write to him,—nor receive letters from him. You are not to suppose that I would give him up. I shall never do that. I shall go on and wait. When a girl has once brought herself to tell a man that she loves him, according to my idea she cannot give him up. There are things which cannot be changed. I could have lived very well without thinking of him had I not encouraged myself to love him. But

I have done that, and now he must be everything to me."

" I am sorry that it should be so."

" It is so. But if you will take me to Hendon I will never see him till I have papa's leave. It is my duty to obey him,—but not her."

" I am not quite clear about that."

" She has rejected me as a daughter, and therefore I reject her as a mother. She would get rid of us both if she could."

" You should not attribute to her any such thoughts."

" If you saw her as often as I do you would know. She hates you almost as much as me,—though she cannot show it so easily."

" That she should hate my theories I can easily understand."

" You stand in her way."

" Of course I do. It is natural that a woman should wish to have the best for her own children. I have sometimes myself felt it to be a pity that Frederic should have an elder brother. Think what a gallant young Marquis he would make, while I am altogether out of my element."

" That is nonsense, John."

" I ought to have been a tailor. Tailors, I think, are generally the most ill-conditioned, sceptical, and patriotic of men. Had my natural propensities been sharpened by the difficulty of maintaining a wife and children upon seven and sixpence a day, I really think

I could have done something to make myself conspicuous. As it is, I am neither one thing nor another;
neither fish nor fowl nor good red herring. To the
mind devoted to marquises I can understand that I
should be a revolting being. I have no aptitudes for
aristocratic prettinesses. Her ladyship has three sons,
either of which would make a perfect marquis. How
is it possible that she should not think that I am
standing in her way?"

"But she knew of your existence when she married
papa."

"No doubt she did;—but that does not alter her
nature. I think I could find it in my heart to forgive
her, even though she attempted to poison me, so much
do I stand in her way. I have sometimes thought
that I ought to repudiate myself; give up my prospects, and call myself John Trafford—so as to make
way for her more lordly lordlings."

"That is nonsense, John."

"At any rate it is impossible. I could only do it
by blowing my brains out—which would not be in
accordance with my ideas of life. But you are not
in anybody's way. There is nothing to be got by
poisoning you. If she were to murder me there would
be something reasonable in it,—something that one
could pardon; but in torturing you she is instigated
by a vile ambition. She is afraid, lest her own
position should be tarnished by an inferior marriage
on your part. There would be something noble in

killing me for the sake of dear little Fred. She would be getting something for him who, of course, is most dear to her. But the other is the meanest vanity;— and I will not stand it."

This conversation took place early in October, when they had been some weeks at Trafford Park. Hampstead had come and gone, as was his wont, never remaining there above two or three days at a time. Lord Kingsbury, who was ill at ease, had run hither and thither about the country, looking after this or the other property, and staying for a day or two with this or the other friend. The Marchioness had declined to invite any friends to the house, declaring to her husband that the family was made unfit for gaiety by the wicked conduct of his eldest daughter. There was no attempt at shooting the pheasants, or even preparing to shoot them, so great was the general depression. Mr. Greenwood was there, and was thrown into very close intercourse with her ladyship. He fully sympathized with her ladyship. Although he had always agreed with the Marquis,— as he had not forgotten to tell George Roden during that interview in London,—in regard to his lordship's early political tenets, nevertheless his mind was so constituted that he was quite at one with her ladyship as to the digraceful horror of low associations for noble families. Not only did he sympathize as to the abomination of the Post Office clerk, but he sympathized also fully as to the positive unfitness which

Lord Hampstead displayed for that station in life to which he had been called. Mr. Greenwood would sigh and wheeze and groan when the future prospects of the House of Trafford were discussed between him and her ladyship. It might be, or it might not be, well, —so he kindly put it in talking to the Marchioness,— that a nobleman should indulge himself with liberal politics; but it was dreadful to think that the heir to a great title should condescend to opinions worthy of a radical tailor. For Mr. Greenwood agreed with Lord Hampstead about the tailor. Lord Hampstead seemed to him to be a matter simply for sorrow,—not for action. Nothing, he thought, could be done in regard to Lord Hampstead. Time,—time that destroys but which also cures so many things,—would no doubt have its effect; so that Lord Hampstead might in the fulness of years live to be as staunch a supporter of his class as any Duke or Marquis living. Or perhaps, —perhaps, it might be that the Lord would take him. Mr. Greenwood saw that this remark was more to the purpose, and at once went to work with the Peerage, and found a score of cases in which, within half-a-century, the second brother had risen to the title. It seemed, indeed, to be the case that a peculiar mortality attached itself to the eldest sons of Peers. This was comforting. But there was not in it so much ground for positive action as at the present moment existed in regard to Lady Frances. On this matter there was a complete unison of spirit between the two friends.

Mr. Greenwood had seen the objectionable young man, and could say how thoroughly objectionable he was at all points,—how vulgar, flippant, ignorant, impudent, exactly what a clerk in the Post Office might be expected to be. Any severity, according to Mr. Greenwood, would be justified in keeping the two young persons apart. Gradually Mr. Greenwood learnt to talk of the female young person with very little of that respect which he showed to other members of the family. In this way her ladyship came to regard Lady Frances as though she were not Lady Frances at all,—as though she were some distant Fanny Trafford, a girl of bad taste and evil conduct, who had unfortunately been brought into the family on grounds of mistaken charity.

Things had so gone on at Trafford, that Trafford had hardly been preferable to Königsgraaf. Indeed, at Königsgraaf there had been no Mr. Greenwood, and Mr. Greenwood had certainly added much to the annoy-ances which poor Lady Frances was made to bear. In this condition of things she had written to her brother, begging him to come to her. He had come, and thus had taken place the conversation which has been given above.

On the same day Hampstead saw his father and dis-cussed the matter with him;—that matter, and, as will

K 2

be seen, some others also. "What on earth do you wish me to do about her?" asked the Marquis.

"Let her come and live with me at Hendon. If you will let me have the house I will take all the rest upon myself."

"Keep an establishment of your own?"

"Why not? If I found I couldn't afford it I'd give up the hunting and stick to the yacht."

"It isn't about money," said the Marquis, shaking his head.

"Her ladyship never liked Hendon for herself."

"Nor is it about the house. You might have the house and welcome. But how can I give up my charge over your sister just when I know that she is disposed to do just what she ought not."

"She won't be a bit more likely to do it there than here," said the brother.

"He would be quite close to her."

"You may take this for granted, sir, that no two persons would be more thoroughly guided by a sense of duty than my sister and George Roden."

"Did she show her duty when she allowed herself to be engaged to a man like that without saying a word to any of her family."

"She told her ladyship as soon as it occurred."

"She should not have allowed it to have occurred at all. It is nonsense talking like that. You cannot mean to say that such a girl as your sister is entitled to do what she likes with herself without consulting any of her family,—even to accepting such a man as this for her lover."

"I hardly know," said Hampstead, thoughtfully.

"You ought to know. I know. Everybody knows. It is nonsense talking like that."

"I doubt whether people do know," said Hampstead. "She is twenty-one, and as far as the law goes might, I believe, walk out of the house, and marry any man she pleases to-morrow. You as her father have no authority over her whatever;"—here the indignant father jumped up from his chair; but his son went on with his speech, as though determined not to be interrupted,—"except what may come to you by her good feeling, or else from the fact that she is dependent on you for her maintenance."

"Good G—— !" shouted the Marquis.

"I think this is about the truth of it. Young ladies do subject themselves to the authority of their parents from feeling, from love, and from dependence; but, as far as I understand in the matter, they are not legally subject beyond a certain age."

"You'd talk the hind legs off a dog."

"I wish I could. But one may say a few words without being so eloquent as that. If such is the case I am not sure that Fanny has been morally wrong. She may have been foolish. I think she has been, because I feel that the marriage is not suitable for her."

"Noblesse oblige," said the Marquis, putting his hand upon his bosom.

"No doubt. Nobility, whatever may be its nature, imposes bonds on us. And if these bonds be not obeyed, then nobility ceases. But I deny that any nobility can bind us to any conduct which we believe to be wrong."

"Who has said that it does?"

"Nobility," continued the son, not regarding his father's question, "cannot bind me to do that which you or others think to be right, if I do not approve it myself."

"What on earth are you driving at?"

"You imply that because I belong to a certain order, —or my sister,—we are bound to those practices of life which that order regards with favour. This I deny both on her behalf and my own. I didn't make myself the eldest son of an English peer. I do acknowledge that as very much has been given to me in the way of education, of social advantages, and even of money, a higher line of conduct is justly demanded from me than from those who have been less gifted. So far, *noblesse oblige.* But before I undertake the duty thus imposed upon me, I must find out what is that higher line of conduct. Fanny should do the same. In marrying George Roden she would do better, according to your maxim, than in giving herself to some noodle of a lord who from first to last will have nothing to be proud of beyond his acres and his title."

The Marquis had been walking about the room impatiently, while his didactic son was struggling to ex-

plain his own theory as to those words *noblesse oblige*.
Nothing could so plainly express the feelings of the
Marquis on the occasion as that illustration of his as
to the dog's hind legs. But he was a little ashamed
of it, and did not dare to use it twice on the same occasion. He fretted and fumed, and would have stopped
Hampstead had it been possible; but Hampstead was
irrepressible when he had become warm on his own
themes, and his father knew that he must listen on to
the bitter end. "I won't have her go to Hendon at
all," he said, when his son had finished.

"Then you will understand little of her nature,—or
of mine. Roden will not come near her there. I can
hardly be sure that he will not do so here. Here
Fanny will feel that she is being treated as an enemy."

"You have no right to say so."

"There she will know that you have done much to
promote her happiness. I will give you my assurance
that she will neither see him nor write to him. She
has promised as much to me herself, and I can trust
her."

"Why should she be so anxious to leave her natural
home?"

"Because," said Hampstead boldly, "she has lost her
natural mother." The Marquis frowned awfully at
hearing this. "I have not a word to say against my
stepmother as to myself. I will not accuse her of anything as to Fanny,—except that they thoroughly misunderstand each other. You must see it yourself, sir."

The Marquis had seen it very thoroughly. "And Mr. Greenwood has taken upon himself to speak to her,— which was, I think, very impertinent."

"I never authorized him."

"But he did. Her ladyship no doubt authorized him. The end of it is that Fanny is watched. Of course she will not bear a continuation of such misery. Why should she? It will be better that she should come to me than be driven to go off with her lover."

Before the week was over the Marquis had yielded. Hendon Hall was to be given up altogether to Lord Hampstead, and his sister was to be allowed to live with him as the mistress of his house. She was to come in the course of next month, and remain there at any rate till the spring. There would be a difficulty about the hunting, no doubt, but that Hampstead if necessary was prepared to abandon for the season. He thought that perhaps he might be able to run down twice a week to the Vale of Aylesbury, going across from Hendon to the Willesden Junction. He would at any rate make his sister's comfort the first object of his life, and would take care that in doing so George Roden should be excluded altogether from the arrangement.

The Marchioness was paralyzed when she heard that Lady Frances was to be taken away,—to be taken into the direct neighbourhood of London and the Post Office. Very many words she said to her husband, and often the Marquis vacillated. But, when once the promise was given, Lady Frances was strong enough to demand its fulfilment. It was on this occasion that the Marchioness first allowed herself to speak to Mr. Greenwood with absolute disapproval of her husband. "To Hendon Hall!" said Mr. Greenwood, holding up his hands with surprise when the project was explained.

"Yes, indeed! It does seem to me to be the most, —most improper sort of thing to do."

"He can walk over there every day as soon as he has got rid of the letters." Mr. Greenwood probably thought that George Roden was sent about with the Post Office bags.

"Of course they will meet."

"I fear so, Lady Kingsbury."

"Hampstead will arrange that for them."

"No, no!" said the clergyman, as though he were bound on behalf of the family to repudiate an idea that was so damnatory to its honour.

"It is just what he will do. Why else should he want to have her there? With his ideas he would think it the best thing he could do utterly to degrade us all. He has no idea of the honour of his brothers. How should he, when he is so anxious to sacrifice his own sister? As for me, of course, he would do anything to break my heart. He knows that I am anxious for his father's name, and, therefore, he would disgrace me in any way that was possible. But that the Marquis should consent!"

"That is what I cannot understand," said Mr. Greenwood.

"There must be something in it, Mr. Greenwood, which they mean to keep from me."

"The Marquis can't intend to give her to that young man!"

"I don't understand it. I don't understand it at all," said the Marchioness. "He did seem so firm about it. As for the girl herself, I will never see her again after she has left my house in such a fashion. And, to tell the truth, I never wish to see Hampstead again. They are plotting against me; and if there is anything I hate it 'is a plot." In this way Mr. Greenwood and the Marchioness became bound together in their great disapproval of Lady Frances and her love.

CHAPTER XI.

LADY PERSIFLAGE.

HAMPSTEAD rushed up to Hendon almost without seeing his stepmother, intent on making preparations for his sister, and then, before October was over, rushed back to fetch her. He was very great at rushing, never begrudging himself any personal trouble in what he undertook to do. When he left the house he hardly spoke to her ladyship. When he took Lady Frances away he was of course bound to bid her adieu.

"I think," he said, "that Frances will be happy with me at Hendon."

"I have nothing to do with it,—literally nothing," said the Marchioness, with her sternest frown. "I wash my hands of the whole concern."

"I am sure you would be glad that she should be happy."

"It is impossible that any one should be happy who misconducts herself."

"That, I think, is true."

"It is certainly true, with misconduct such as this."

"I quite agree with what you said first. But the question remains as to what is misconduct. Now——"

"I will not hear you, Hampstead; not a word. You can persuade your father, I dare say, but you cannot persuade me. Fanny has divorced herself from my heart for ever."

"I am sorry for that."

"And I'm bound to say that you are doing the same. It is better in some cases to be plain."

"Oh—certainly; but not to be irrational."

"I am not irrational, and it is most improper for you to speak to me in that way."

"Well, good-bye. I have no doubt it will come right some of these days," said Hampstead, as he took his leave. Then he carried his sister off to Hendon.

Previous to this there had been a great deal of unpleasantness in the house. From the moment in which Lady Kingsbury had heard that her stepdaughter was to go to her brother she had refused even to speak to the unfortunate girl. As far as it was possible she put her husband also into Coventry. She held daily consultations with Mr. Greenwood, and spent most of her hours in embracing, coddling, and spoiling those three unfortunate young noblemen who were being so cruelly injured by their brother and sister. One of her keenest pangs was in seeing how boisterously the three bairns romped with "Jack" even after she had dismissed him from her own good graces as utterly unworthy of her regard. That night he positively brought Lord Gregory down into the drawing-room in his night-shirt, having dragged the little urchin out of his cot,—as one might do who was on peculiar terms of friendship with the mother. Lord Gregory was in Elysium, but the mother tore the child from the sinner's arms, and carried him back in anger to the nursery.

"Nothing does children so much good as disturbing them in their sleep," said Lord Hampstead, turning to his father; but the anger of the Marchioness was too serious a thing to allow of a joke.

"From this time forth for evermore she is no child of mine," said Lady Kingsbury the next morning to her husband, as soon as the carriage had taken the two sinners away from the door.

"It is very wrong to say that. She is your child, and must be your child."

"I have divorced her from my heart;—and also Lord Hampstead. How can it be otherwise, when they are both in rebellion against me? Now there will be this disgraceful marriage. Would you wish that I should receive the Post Office clerk here as my son-in-law?"

"There won't be any disgraceful marriage," said the Marquis. "At least, what I mean is, that it will be much less likely at Hendon than here."

"Less likely than here! Here it would have been impossible. There they will be all together."

"No such thing," said the Marquis. "Hampstead will see to that. And she too has promised me."

"Pshaw!" exclaimed the Marchioness.

"I won't have you say Pshaw to me when I tell you. Fanny always has kept her word to me, and I don't in the least doubt her. Had she remained here your treatment would have induced her to run away with him at the first word."

"Lord Kingsbury," said the offended lady, "I have always done my duty by the children of your first marriage as a mother should do. I have found them to be violent, and altogether unaware of the duties which their position should impose upon them. It was only yesterday that Lord Hampstead presumed to call me irrational. I have borne a great deal from them, and can bear no more. I wish you would have found some one better able to control their conduct." Then, with a stately step, she stalked out of the room. Under these circumstances, the house was not comfortable to any of the inhabitants.

As soon as her ladyship had reached her own apartments after this rough interview she seated herself at the table, and commenced a letter to her sister, Lady Persiflage, in which she proceeded to give a detailed account of all her troubles and sufferings. Lady Persiflage, who was by a year or two the younger of the two, filled a higher position in society than that of the Marchioness herself. She was the wife only of an Earl; but the Earl was a Knight of the Garter, Lord Lieutenant of his County, and at the present moment Secretary of State for the Home Department. The

Marquis had risen to no such honours as these. Lord
Persiflage was a peculiar man. Nobody quite knew of
what his great gifts consisted. But it was acknowledged
of him that he was an astute diplomat; that the honour
of England was safe in his hands; and that no more
perfect courtier ever gave advice to a well-satisfied
sovereign. He was beautiful to look at, with his soft
grey hair, his bright eyes, and well-cut features. He
was much of a dandy, and, though he was known to be
nearer seventy than sixty years of age, he maintained
an appearance of almost green juvenility. Active he
was not, nor learned, nor eloquent. But he knew how
to hold his own, and had held it for many years. He
had married his wife when she was very young, and
she had become, first a distinguished beauty, and then
a leader of fashion. Her sister, our Marchioness, had
been past thirty when she married, and had never been
quite so much in the world's eye as her sister, Lady
Persiflage. And Lady Persiflage was the mother of her
husband's heir. The young Lord Hautboy, her eldest
son, was now just of age. Lady Kingsbury looked
upon him as all that the heir to an earldom ought
to be. His mother, too, was proud of him, for he was
beautiful as a young Phœbus. The Earl, his father,
was not always as well pleased, because his son had
already achieved a knack of spending money. The
Persiflage estates were somewhat encumbered, and
there seemed to be a probability that Lord Hautboy
might create further trouble. Such was the family to

whom collectively the Marchioness looked for support in her unhappiness. The letter which she wrote to her sister on the present occasion was as follows;—

> "*Trafford Park,*
> "*Saturday, October 25th.*

"MY DEAR GERALDINE,—

"I take up my pen to write to you with a heart laden with trouble. Things have become so bad with me that I do not know where to turn myself unless you can give me comfort. I am beginning to feel how terrible it is to have undertaken the position of mother to another person's children. God knows I have endeavoured to do my duty. But it has all been in vain. Everything is over now. I have divided myself for ever from Hampstead and from Fanny. I have felt myself compelled to tell their father that I have divorced them from my heart; and I have told Lord Hampstead the same. You will understand how terrible must have been the occasion when I found myself compelled to take such a step as this.

"You know how dreadfully shocked I was when she first revealed to me the fact that she had promised to marry that Post Office clerk. The young man had actually the impudence to call on Lord Kingsbury in London, to offer himself as a son-in-law. Kingsbury very properly would not see him, but instructed Mr. Greenwood to do so. Mr. Greenwood has behaved very well in the matter, and is a great comfort to me. I hope we may be able to do something for him some day. A viler or more ill-conditioned young man he says that he never saw;—insolent, too, and talking as though he had as much right to ask for Fanny's hand as though he were one of the same class. As for that, she would deserve nothing better than to be married to such a man, were it not that all the world would know how closely she is connected with my own darling boys!

"Then we took her off to Königsgraaf; and such a time as I had with her! She would write letters to this wretch, and contrived to receive one. I did stop that, but you cannot conceive what a life she led me. Of course I have felt from the first that she would be divided from her brothers, because one never knows how early bad morals may be inculcated! Then her papa came, and Hampstead,—who in all this has encouraged his sister. The young man is his friend. After this who will say that any nobleman ought to call himself what they call a Liberal? Then we came home; and what do you think has happened? Hampstead has taken his sister to live with him at Hendon, next door, as you may say, to the Post Office clerk, where the young man has made himself thoroughly at home;—and Kingsbury has permitted it! Oh, Geraldine, that is the worst of it! Am I not justified in declaring that I have divorced them from my heart?

"You can hardly feel as I do, you, whose son fills so well that position which an eldest son ought to fill! Here am I with my darlings, not only under a shade, but with this disgrace before them which they will never be able altogether to get rid of. I can divorce Hampstead and his sister from my heart; but they will still be in some sort brother and sister to my poor boys. How am I to teach them to respect their elder brother, who I suppose must in course of time become Head of the House, when he is hand and glove with a dreadful young man such as that! Am I not justified in declaring that no communication shall be kept up between the two families? If she marries the man she will of course drop the name; but yet all the world will know because of the title. As for him, I am afraid that there is no hope;—although it is odd that the second son does so very often come to the title. If you look into it you will find that the second brother has almost a better chance than the elder,—although I am sure that nothing of the kind will ever happen to dear Hautboy. But he knows how to live in that state of life to which it has pleased God to call him! Do write to me at once, and tell me what I ought to do with a due regard to the position to which I have been called upon to fill in the world.

"Your most affectionate sister,
"CLARA KINGSBURY.

"P.S.—Do remember poor Mr. Greenwood if Lord Persiflage should know how to do something for a clergyman. He is getting old, and Kingsbury has never been able to do anything for him. I hope the Liberals never will be able to do anything for anybody. I don't think Mr. Greenwood would be fit for any duty, because he has been idle all his life, and is now fond of good living ; but a deanery would just suit him."

After the interval of a fortnight Lady Kingsbury received a reply from her sister which the reader may as well see at once.

" Castle Hautboy,
" November 9th.

" MY DEAR CLARA,—

"I don't know that there is anything further to be done about Fanny. As for divorcing her from your heart, I don't suppose that it amounts to much. I advise you to keep on good terms with Hampstead, because if anything were to happen, it is always well for the Dowager to be friends with the heir. If Fanny will marry the man she must. Lady Di Peacocke married Mr. Billyboy, who was a clerk in one of the offices. They made him Assistant Secretary, and they now live in Portugal Street and do very well. I see Lady Diana about everywhere. Mr. Billyboy can't keep a carriage for her, but that of course is her look-out.

"As to what you say about second sons succeeding,

L 2

don't think of it. It would get you into a bad frame
of mind, and make you hate the very person upon
whom you will probably have to depend for much of
your comfort.

"I think you should take things easier, and, above
all, do not trouble your husband. I am sure he could
make himself very unpleasant if he were driven too
far.   Persiflage has no clerical patronage whatever,
and would not interfere about Deans or Bishops for
all the world. I suppose he could appoint a Chaplain
to an Embassy, but your clergyman seems to be too
old and too idle for that.

"Your affectionate sister,

"GERALDINE PERSIFLAGE."

This letter brought very little comfort to the distracted Marchioness.   There was much in it so cold that
it offended her deeply, and for a moment prompted her
almost to divorce also Lady Persiflage from her heart.
Lady Persiflage seemed to think that Fanny should be
absolutely encouraged to marry the Post Office clerk,
because at some past period some Lady Diana, who at
the time was near fifty, had married a clerk also.   It
might be that a Lady Diana should have run away
with a groom, but would that be a reason why so
monstrous a crime should be repeated? And then
in this letter there was so absolute an absence of all
affectionate regard for her own children! She had
spoken with great love of Lord Hautboy; but then

Lord Hautboy was the acknowledged heir, whereas her own children were nobodies. In this there lay the sting. And then she felt herself to have been rebuked because she had hinted at the possibility of Lord Hampstead's departure for a better world. Lord Hampstead was mortal, as well as others. And why should not his death be contemplated, especially as it would confer so great a benefit on the world at large? Her sister's letter persuaded her of nothing. The divorce should remain as complete as ever. She would not condescend to think of any future advantages which might accrue to her from any intimacy with her stepson. Her dower had been regularly settled. Her duty was to her own children,—and secondly to her husband. If she could succeed in turning him against these two wicked elder children, then she would omit to do nothing which might render his life pleasant to him. Such were the resolutions which she formed on receipt of her sister's letter.

About this time Lord Kingsbury found it necessary to say a few words to Mr. Greenwood. There had not of late been much expression of kindness from the Marquis to the clergyman. Since their return from Germany his lordship had been either taciturn or cross. Mr. Greenwood took this very much to heart. For though he was most anxious to assure to himself the friendship of the Marchioness he did not at all wish to neglect the Marquis. It was in truth on the Marquis that he depended for everything that he had in the world. The Marquis could send him out of the house to-morrow,—and if this house were closed to him, none other, as far as he knew, would be open to him except the Union. He had lived delicately all his life, and luxuriously,—but fruitlessly as regarded the gathering of any honey for future wants. Whatever small scraps of preferment might have come in his way had been rejected as having been joined with too much of labour and too little of emolument. He had gone on hoping that so great a man as the Marquis would be able to do something for him,—thinking that he might at any rate fasten his patron closely to him by bonds of affection. This had been in days before the coming of the present Marchioness. At first she had not created any special difficulty for him. She did not at once attempt to overthrow the settled politics of the family, and Mr. Greenwood had been allowed to be blandly liberal. But during the last year or two, great management had been necessary. By degrees he had found it essential to fall into the conservative views of her ladyship,—which extended simply to the idea that the cream of the earth should be allowed to be the cream of the earth. It is difficult in the same house to adhere to two political doctrines, because the holders of each will require support at all general meetings. Gradually the Marchioness had become exigeant, and the Marquis was becoming aware that he was being thrown over. A feeling of anger was growing up in his mind which he did not himself analyze. When he heard that the clergyman had taken upon himself to lecture Lady Frances,—for it was thus he read the few words which his son had spoken to him,—he carried his anger with him for a day or two, till at last he found an opportunity of explaining himself to the culprit.

" Lady Frances will do very well where she is," said the Marquis, in answer to some expression of a wish as to his daughter's comfort.

" Oh, no doubt ! "

" I am not sure that I am fond of too much interference in such matters."

" Have I interfered, my lord ? "

" I do not mean to find any special fault on this occasion."

" I hope not, my lord."

" But you did speak to Lady Frances when I think it might have been as well that you should have held your tongue."

" I had been instructed to see that young man in London."

" Exactly ; — but not to say anything to Lady Frances."

" I had known her ladyship so many years ! "

" Do not drive me to say that you had known her too long."

Mr. Greenwood felt this to be very hard ;—for what he had said to Lady Frances he had in truth said under instruction. That last speech as to having perhaps known the young lady too long seemed to contain a

terrible threat. He was thus driven to fall back upon
his instructions. "Her ladyship seemed to think that
perhaps a word in season——"

The Marquis felt this to be cowardly, and was more
inclined to be angry with his old friend than if he had
stuck to that former plea of old friendship. "I ·will
not have interference in this house, and there's an end
of it. If I wish you to do anything for me I will tell
you. That is all. If you please nothing more shall be
said about it. The subject is disagreeable to me."

*   *   *   *   *   *

"Has the Marquis said anything about Lady Frances
since she went ?" the Marchioness asked the clergyman
the next morning. How was he to hold his balance
between them if he was to be questioned by both sides
in this way ? "I suppose he has mentioned her ?"

"He just mentioned the name one day."

"Well ?"

"I rather think that he does not wish to be interrogated about her ladyship."

"I dare say not. Is he anxious to have her back
again ?"

"That I cannot say, Lady Kingsbury. I should
think he must be."

"Of course I shall be desirous to ascertain the truth.
He has been so unreasonable that I hardly know how
to speak to him myself. I suppose he tells you !"

"I rather think his lordship will decline to speak
about her ladyship just at present."

"Of course it is necessary that I should know. Now that she has chosen to take herself off I shall not choose to live under the same roof with her again. If Lord Kingsbury speaks to you on the subject you should make him understand that." Poor Mr. Greenwood felt that there were thorny paths before him, in which it might be very difficult to guard his feet from pricks. Then he had to consider if there were to be two sides in the house, strongly opposed to each other, with which would it be best for him to take a part? The houses of the Marquis, with all their comforts, were open for him; but the influence of Lord Persiflage was very great, whereas that of the Marquis was next to nothing.

CHAPTER XII.

CASTLE HAUTBOY.

" YOU'D better ask the old Traffords down here for a few weeks. Hampstead won't shoot, but he can hunt with the Braeside harriers."

This was the answer made by Lord Persiflage to his wife when he was told by her of that divorce which had taken place at Trafford Park, and of the departure of Lady Frances for Hendon. Hampstead and Lady Frances were the old Traffords. Lord Persiflage, too, was a Conservative, but his politics were of a very different order from those entertained by his sister-in-law. He was, above all, a man of the world. He had been our Ambassador at St. Petersburg, and was now a Member of the Cabinet. He liked the good things of office, but had no idea of quarrelling with a Radical because he was a Radical. He cared very little as to the opinions of his guests, if they could make themselves either pleasant or useful. He looked upon his sister-in-law as an old fool, and had no idea of quarrelling with Hampstead for her sake. If the girl persisted in making a bad match she must take the consequences. No great harm would come,—except to her. As to the evil done to his " order," that did not affect Lord Persiflage at all. He did not expect his order to endure for ever. All orders become worn out in time, and effete. He had no abhorrence for anybody ; but he liked pleasant people ; he liked to treat everything as a joke ; and he liked the labours of his not un-laborious life to be minimised. Having given his orders about the old Traffords, as he called them in reference to the " darlings," he said nothing more on the subject. Lady Persiflage wrote a note to " Dear Fanny," conveying the invitation in three words, and received a reply to the effect that she and her brother would be at Castle Hautboy before the end of November. Hampstead would perhaps bring a couple of horses, but he would put them up at the livery stables at Penrith.

" How do you do, Hampstead," said Persiflage when he first met his guest before dinner on the day of the arrival. " You haven't got rid of everything yet ? "

This question was supposed to refer to Lord Hampstead's revolutionary tendencies. " Not quite so thoroughly as we hope to do soon."

" I always think it a great comfort that in our country the blackguards are so considerate. I must own that we do very little for them, and yet they never knock us over the head or shoot at us, as they do in Russia and Germany and France." Then he passed on, having said quite enough for one conversation.

"So you've gone off to Hendon to live with your brother?" said Lady Persiflage to her niece.

"Yes; indeed," said Lady Fanny, blushing at the implied allusion to her low-born lover which was contained in this question.

But Lady Persiflage had no idea of saying a word about the lover, or of making herself in any way unpleasant. "I dare say it will be very comfortable for you both," she said; "but we thought you might be a little lonely till you got used to it, and therefore asked you to come down for a week or two. The house is full of people, and you will be sure to find some one that you know." Not a word was said at Castle Hautboy as to those terrible things which had occurred in the Trafford family.

Young Vivian was there, half, as he said, for ornament, but partly for pleasure and partly for business. "He likes to have a private secretary with him," he said to Hampstead, "in order that people might think there is something to do. As a rule they never send anything down from the Foreign Office at this time of year. He always has a Foreign Minister or two in the house, or a few Secretaries of Legation, and that gives an air of business: Nothing would offend or surprise him so much as if one of them were to say a word about affairs. Nobody ever does, and therefore he is supposed to be the safest Foreign

Minister that we've had in Downing Street since old ——'s time."

"Well, Hautboy." "Well, Hampstead." Thus the two heirs greeted each other. "You'll come and shoot to-morrow?" asked the young host.

"I never shoot. I thought all the world knew that."

"The best cock-shooting in all England," said Hautboy. "But we shan't come to that for the next month."

"Cocks or hens, pheasants, grouse, or partridge, rabbits or hares, it's all one to me. I couldn't hit 'em if I would, and I wouldn't if I could."

"There is a great deal in the couldn't," said Hautboy. "As for hunting, those Braeside fellows go out two or three times a week. But it's a wretched sort of affair. They hunt hares or foxes just as they come, and they're always climbing up a ravine or tumbling down a precipice."

"I can climb and tumble as well as any one," said Hampstead. So that question as to the future amusement of the guest was settled.

But the glory of the house of Hauteville,—Hauteville was the Earl's family name,—at present shone most brightly in the person of the eldest daughter, Lady Amaldina. Lady Amaldina, who was as beautiful in colour, shape, and proportion as wax could make a Venus, was engaged to marry the eldest son of the Duke of Merioneth. The Marquis of Llwddythlw was a young man about forty years of age, of great promise, who had never been known to do a foolish thing in his life, and his father was one of those half-dozen happy noblemen, each of whom is ordinarily reported to be the richest man in England. Lady Amaldina was not unnaturally proud of her high destiny, and as the alliance had already been advertised in all the newspapers, she was not unwilling to talk about it. Lady Frances was not exactly a cousin, but stood in the place of a cousin, and therefore was regarded as a good listener for all the details which had to be repeated. It might be that Lady Amaldina took special joy in having such a listener, because Lady Frances herself had placed her own hopes so low. That story as to the Post Office clerk was known to everybody at Castle Hautboy. Lady Persiflage ridiculed the idea of keeping such things secret. Having so much to be proud of in regard to her own children, she thought that there should be no such secrets. If Fanny Trafford did intend to marry the Post Office clerk it would be better that all the world should know it beforehand. Lady Amaldina knew it, and was delighted at having a confidante whose views and prospects in life were so different from her own. " Of course, dear, you have heard what is going to happen to me," she said, smiling.

" I have heard of your engagement with the son of the Duke of Merioneth, the man with the terrible Welsh name."

"When you once know how to pronounce it it is the prettiest word that poetry ever produced!" Then Lady Amaldina did pronounce her future name;—but nothing serviceable would be done for the reader if an attempt were made to write the sound which she produced. "I am not sure but what it was the name which first won my heart. I can sign it now quite easily without a mistake."

"It won't be long, I suppose, before you will have to do so always?"

"An age, my dear! The Duke's affairs are of such a nature,—and Llwddythlw is so constantly engaged in business, that I don't suppose it will take place for the next ten years. What with settlements, and entails, and Parliament, and the rest of it, I shall be an old woman before I am,—led to the hymeneal altar."

"Ten years!" said Lady Fanny.

"Well, say ten months, which seems to be just as long."

"Isn't he in a hurry?"

"Oh, awfully; but what can he do, poor fellow? He is so placed that he cannot have his affairs arranged for him in half-an-hour, as other men can do. It is a great trouble having estates so large and interests so complicated! Now there is one thing I particularly want to ask you."

"What is it?"

"About being one of the bridesmaids."

" One can hardly answer for ten years hence."

" That is nonsense, of course. I am determined to
have no girl who has not a title. It isn't that I care
about that kind of thing in the least, but the Duke
does. And then I think the list will sound more
distinguished in the newspapers, if all the Christian
names are given with the Lady before them. There
are to be his three sisters, Lady Anne, Lady An-
toinette, and Lady Anatolia;—then my two sisters,
Lady Alphonsa and Lady Amelia. To be sure they
are very young."

" They may be old enough according to what you
say."

" Yes, indeed. And then there will be Lady
Arabella Portroyal, and Lady Augusta Gelashires. I
have got the list written out somewhere, and there
are to be just twenty."

" If the catalogue is finished there will hardly be
room for me."

" The Earl of Knocknacoppul's daughter has sent
me word that she must refuse, because her own
marriage will take place first. She would have put
it off, as she is only going to marry an Irish baronet,
and because she is dying to have her name down as
one of the bevy, but he says that if she delays any
longer he'll go on a shooting expedition to the Rocky
Mountains, and then perhaps he might never come
back. So there is a vacancy."

" I hardly like to make a promise so long beforehand.

Perhaps I might have a young man, and he might go off to the Rocky Mountains."

"That's just what made me not put down your name at first. Of course you know we've heard about Mr. Roden?"

"I didn't know," said Lady Frances, blushing.

"Oh dear, yes. Everybody knows it. And I think it such a brave thing to do,—if you're really attached to him!"

"I should never marry any man without being attached to him," said Lady Frances.

"That's of course! But I mean romantically attached. I don't pretend to that kind of thing with Llwddythlw. I don't think it necessary in a marriage of this kind. He is a great deal older than I am, and is bald. I suppose Mr. Roden is very, very handsome?"

"I have not thought much about that."

"I should have considered that one would want it for a marriage of that kind. I don't know whether after all it isn't the best thing to do. Romance is so delicious!"

"But then it's delicious to be a Duchess," said Lady Frances, with the slightest touch of irony.

"On, no doubt! One has to look at it all round, and then to form a judgment. It went a great way with papa, I know, Llwddythlw being such a good man of business. He has been in the Household, and the Queen will be sure to send a handsome present. I

expect to have the grandest show of wedding presents
that any girl has yet exhibited in England. Ever so
many people have asked mamma already as to what I
should like best. Mr. MacWhapple said out plain that
he would go to a hundred and fifty pounds. He is a
Scotch manufacturer, and has papa's interest in Wigton-
shire. I suppose you don't intend to do anything very
grand in that way."

" I suppose not, as I don't know any Scotch manu-
facturers. But my marriage, if I ever am married, is a
thing so much of the future that I haven't even begun
to think of my dress yet."

" I'll tell you a secret," said Lady Amaldina, whispering. " Mine is already made, and I've tried it on."

" You might get ever so much stouter in ten years,"
said Lady Frances.

" That of course was joking. But we did think the
marriage would come off last June, and as we were in
Paris in April the order was given. Don't you tell
anybody about that."

Then it was settled that the name of Lady Frances
should be put down on the list of bridesmaids, but
put down in a doubtful manner,—as is done with other
things of great importance.

A few days after Lord Hampstead's arrival a very
great dinner-party was given at the Castle, at which
all the county round was invited. Castle Hautboy is
situated near Pooly Bridge, just in the county of
Westmoreland, on an eminence, giving it a grand

prospect over Ulleswater, which is generally considered
to be one of the Cumberland Lakes. Therefore the
gentry from the two counties were invited as far round
as Penrith, Shap, Bampton, and Patterdale. The
Earl's property in that neighbourhood was scattered
about through the two counties, and was looked after
by a steward, or manager, who lived himself at Penrith,
and was supposed to be very efficacious in such duties.
His name was Crocker; and not only was he invited
to the dinner, but also his son, who happened at the
time to be enjoying the month's holiday which was
allowed to him by the authorities of the office in
London to which he was attached.

The reader may remember that a smart young man
of this name sat at the same desk with George Roden
at the General Post Office. Young Crocker was
specially delighted with the honour done him on this
occasion. He not only knew that his fellow clerk's
friend, Lord Hampstead, was at the Castle, and his
sister, Lady Frances, with him ; but he also knew that
George Roden was engaged to marry that noble lady !
Had he heard this before he left London, he would
probably have endeavoured to make some atonement
for his insolence to Roden ; for he was in truth filled
with a strong admiration for the man who had before
him the possibility of such high prospects. But the
news had only reached him since he had been in the
North. Now he thought that he might possibly find
an opportunity of making known to Lord Hampstead

M 2

his intimacy with Roden, and of possibly saying a word—just uttering a hint—as to that future event.

It was long before he could find himself near enough to Lord Hampstead to address him. He had even refused to return home with his father, who did not like being very late on the road, saying that he had got a lift into town in another conveyance. This he did, with the prospect of having to walk six miles into Penrith in his dress boots, solely with the object of saying a few words to Roden's friend. At last he was successful.

"We have had what I call an extremely pleasant evening, my lord." It was thus he commenced; and Hampstead, whose practice it was to be specially graceful to any one whom he chanced to meet but did not think to be a gentleman, replied very courteously that the evening had been pleasant.

"Quite a thing to remember," continued Crocker.

"Perhaps one remembers the unpleasant things the longest," said Hampstead, laughing.

"Oh, no, my lord, not that. I always forget the unpleasant. That's what I call philosophy." Then he broke away into the subject that was near his heart. "I wish our friend Roden had been here, my lord."

"Is he a friend of yours?"

"Oh dear, yes;—most intimate. We sit in the same room at the Post Office. And at the same desk,—as thick as thieves, as the saying is. We often have a crack about your lordship."

"I have a great esteem for George Roden. He and I are really friends. I know no one for whom I have a higher regard." This he said with an earnest voice, thinking himself bound to express his friendship more loudly than he would have done had the friend been in his own rank of life.

"That's just what I feel. Roden is a man that will rise."

"I hope so."

"He'll be sure to get something good before long. They'll make him a Surveyor, or Chief Clerk, or something of that kind. I'll back him to have £500 a year before any man in the office. There'll be a shindy about it, of course. There always is a shindy when a fellow is put up out of his turn. But he needn't care for that. They can laugh as win. Eh, my lord!"

"He would be the last to wish an injustice to be done for his own good."

"We've got to take that as it comes, my lord. I won't say but what I should like to go up at once to a senior class over other men's heads. There isn't a chance of that, because I'm independent, and the seniors don't like me. Old Jerningham is always down upon me just for that reason. You ask Roden, and he'll tell you the same thing,—my lord." Then came a momentary break in the conversation, and Lord Hampstead was seizing advantage of it to escape. But Crocker, who had taken enough wine to be bold,

saw the attempt, and intercepted it. He was desirous
of letting the lord know all that he knew. "Roden is
a happy dog, my lord."

"Happy, I hope, though not a dog," said Hampstead,
trusting that he could retreat gracefully behind the
joke.

"Ha, ha, ha! The dog only meant what a lucky
fellow he is. I have heard him speak in raptures of
what is in store for him."

"What!"

"There's no happiness like married happiness; is
there, my lord?"

"Upon my word, I can't say. Good night to
you."

"I hope you will come and see me and Roden at
the office some of these days."

"Good night, good night!" Then the man did go.
For a moment or two Lord Hampstead felt actually
angry with his friend. Could it be that Roden should
make so little of his sister's name as to talk about
her to the Post Office clerks,—to so mean a fellow as
this! And yet the man certainly knew the fact of
the existing engagement. Hampstead thought it
impossible that it should have travelled beyond the
limits of his own family. It was natural that Roden
should have told his mother; but unnatural,—so
Hampstead thought,—that his friend should have
made his sister a subject of conversation to any one
else. It was horrible to him that a stranger such as

that should have spoken to him about his sister at all. But surely it was not possible that Roden should have sinned after that fashion. He soon resolved that it was not possible. But how grievous a thing it was that a girl's name· should be made so common in the mouths of men !

After that he sauntered into the smoking-room, where were congregated the young men who were staying in the house. " That's a kind of thing that happens only once a year," said Hautboy, speaking to all the party; " but I cannot, for the life of me, see why it should happen at all."

" Your governor finds that it succeeds in the county," said one.

" He polishes off a whole heap at one go," said another.

"It does help to keep a party together," said a third.

" And enables a lot of people to talk of dining at Castle Hautboy without lying," said a fourth.

" But why should a lot of people be enabled to say that they'd dined here ? " asked Hautboy. " I like to see my friends at dinner. What did you think about it, Hampstead ? "

" It's all according to Hampstead's theories," said one.

" Only he'd have had the tinkers and the tailors too," said another.

" And wouldn't have had the ladies and gentlemen," said a third.

"I would have had the tailors and tinkers," said Hampstead, "and I would have had the ladies and gentlemen, too, if I could have got them to meet the tailors and tinkers;—but I would not have had that young man who got me out into the hall just now."

"Why,—that was Crocker, the Post Office clerk," said Hautboy. "Why shouldn't we have a Post Office clerk as well as some one else? Nevertheless, Crocker is a sad cad." In the mean time Crocker was walking home to Penrith in his dress boots.

CHAPTER XIII.

THE BRAESIDE HARRIERS.

THE Braeside Harriers can hardly be called a "crack" pack of hounds. Lord Hautboy had been right in saying that they were always scrambling through ravines, and that they hunted whatever they could find to hunt. Nevertheless, the men and the hounds were in earnest, and did accomplish a fair average of sport under difficult circumstances. No "Pegasus" or "Littlelegs," or "Pigskin," ever sent accounts of wondrous runs from Cumberland or Westmoreland to the sporting papers, in which the gentlemen who had asked the special Pigskin of the day to dinner were described as having been "in" at some "glorious finish" on their well-known horses Banker or Buff, —the horses named being generally those which the gentlemen wished to sell. The names of gorses and brooks had not become historic, as have those of Ranksborough and Whissendine. Trains were not run to suit this or the other meet. Gentlemen did not get out of fast drags with pretty little aprons tied

around their waists, like girls in a country house
coming down to breakfast. Not many perhaps wore
pink coats, and none pink tops. One horse would
suffice for one day's work. An old assistant huntsman
in an old red coat, with one boy mounted on a ragged
pony, served for an establishment. The whole thing
was despicable in the eyes of men from the Quorn
and Cottesmore. But there was some wonderful riding
and much constant sport with the Braeside Harriers,
and the country had given birth to certainly the best
hunting song in the language ;—

> Do you ken John Peel with his coat so gay ;
> Do you ken John Peel at the break of day ;
> Do you ken John Peel when he's far, far away
>   With his hounds and his horn in the morning.

Such as the Braeside Harriers were, Lord Hampstead
determined to make the experiment, and on a certain
morning had himself driven to Cronelloe Thorn, a
favourite meet halfway between Penrith and Keswick.

I hold that nothing is so likely to be permanently
prejudicial to the interest of hunting in the British Isles
as a certain flavour of tip-top fashion which has gradually enveloped it. There is a pretence of grandeur
about that and, alas, about other sports also, which is,
to my thinking, destructive of all sport itself. Men
will not shoot unless game is made to appear before
them in clouds. They will not fish unless the rivers be
exquisite. To row is nothing unless you can be known
as a national hero. Cricket requires appendages

which are troublesome and costly, and by which the minds of economical fathers are astounded. To play a game of hockey in accordance with the times you must have a specially trained pony and a gaudy dress. Racquets have given place to tennis because tennis is costly. In all these cases the fashion of the game is much more cherished than the game itself. But in nothing is this feeling so predominant as in hunting. For the management of a pack, as packs are managed now, a huntsman needs must be a great man himself, and three mounted subordinates are necessary, as at any rate for two of these servants a second horse is required. A hunt is nothing in the world unless it goes out four times a week at least. A run is nothing unless the pace be that of a steeplechase. Whether there be or be not a fox before the hounds is of little consequence to the great body of riders. A bold huntsman who can make a dash across country from one covert to another, and who can so train his hounds that they shall run as though game were before them, is supposed to have provided good sport. If a fox can be killed in covert afterwards so much the better for those who like to talk of their doings. Though the hounds brought no fox with them, it is of no matter. When a fox does run according to his nature he is reviled as a useless brute, because he will not go straight across country. But the worst of all is the attention given by men to things altogether outside the sport. Their coats and waistcoats, their boots and breeches, their little strings and pretty scarfs, their saddles and bridles, their dandy knick-knacks, and, above all, their flasks, are more to many men than aught else in the day's proceedings. I have known girls who have thought that their first appearance in the ball-room, when all was fresh, unstained, and perfect from the milliner's hand, was the one moment of rapture for the evening. I have sometimes felt the same of young sportsmen at a Leicestershire or Northamptonshire meet. It is not that they will not ride when the occasion comes. They are always ready enough to break their bones. There is no greater mistake than to suppose that dandyism is antagonistic to pluck. The fault is that men train themselves to care for nothing that is not as costly as unlimited expenditure can make it. Thus it comes about that the real love of sport is crushed under a desire for fashion. A man will be almost ashamed to confess that he hunts in Essex or Sussex, because the proper thing is to go down to the Shires. Grass, no doubt, is better than ploughed land to ride upon; but, taking together the virtues and vices of all hunting counties, I doubt whether better sport is not to be found in what I will venture to call the haunts of the clodpoles, than among the palmy pastures of the well-breeched beauties of Leicestershire.

Braeside Harriers though they were, a strong taste for foxes had lately grown up in the minds of men and in the noses of hounds. Blank days they did

not know, because a hare would serve the turn if
the nobler animal were not forthcoming; but ideas
of preserving had sprung up; steps were taken to
solace the minds of old women who had lost their
geese; and the Braeside Harriers, though they had
kept their name, were gradually losing their character. On this occasion the hounds were taken off
to draw a covert instead of going to a so-ho, as
regularly as though they were advertised among the
fox-hounds in *The Times*. It was soon known that
Lord Hampstead was Lord Hampstead, and he was
welcomed by the field. What matter that he was
a revolutionary Radical if he could ride to hounds?
At any rate, he was the son of a Marquis, and was
not left to that solitude which sometimes falls upon
a man who appears suddenly as a stranger among
strangers on a hunting morning. "I am glad to see
you out, my lord," said Mr. Amblethwaite, the Master.
"It isn't often that we get recruits from Castle
Hautboy."

"They think a good deal of shooting there."

"Yes; and they keep their horses in Northamptonshire. Lord Hautboy does his hunting there.
The Earl, I think, never comes out now."

"I dare say not. He has all the foreign nations
to look after."

"I suppose he has his hands pretty full," said
Mr. Amblethwaite. "I know I have mine just at
this time of the year. Where do you think these

hounds ran their fox to last Friday? We found
him outside of the Lowther Woods, near the village
of Clifton. They took him straight over Shap
Fell, and then turning sharp to the right, went all
along Hawes Wall and over High Street into
Troutbeck."

"That's all among the mountains," said Hampstead.

"Mountains! I should think so. I have to spend
half my time among the mountains."

"But you couldn't ride over High Street?"

"No, we couldn't ride; not there. But we had
to make our way round, some of us, and some of
them went on foot. Dick never lost sight of the
hounds the whole day." Dick was the boy who
rode the ragged pony. "When we found 'em there
he was with half the hounds around him, and the
fox's brush stuck in his cap."

"How did you get home that night?" asked
Hampstead.

"Home! I didn't get home at all. It was pitch
dark before we got the rest of the hounds together.
Some of them we didn't find till next day. I had
to go and sleep at Bowness, and thought myself
very lucky to get a bed. Then I had to ride home
next day over Kirkstone Fell. That's what I call
something like work for a man and horse.—There's
a fox in there, my lord, do you hear them?" Then
Mr. Amblethwaite bustled away to assist at the duty
of getting the fox to break.

"I'm glad to see that you're fond of this kind of thing, my lord," said a voice in Hampstead's ear, which, though he had only heard it once, he well remembered. It was Crocker, the guest at the dinner-party,—Crocker, the Post Office clerk.

"Yes," said Lord Hampstead, "I am very fond of this kind of thing. That fox has broken, I think, at the other side of the cover." Then he trotted off down a little lane between two loose-built walls, so narrow that there was no space for two men to ride abreast. His object at that moment was to escape Crocker rather than to look after the hounds.

They were in a wild country, not exactly on a mountain side, but among hills which not far off grew into mountains, where cultivation of the rudest kind was just beginning to effect its domination over human nature. There was a long spinney rather than a wood stretching down a bottom, through which a brook ran. It would now cease, and then renew itself, so that the trees, though not absolutely continuous, were nearly so for the distance of half a mile. The ground on each side was rough with big stones, and steep in some places as they went down the hill. But still it was such that horsemen could gallop on it. The fox made his way along the whole length, and then traversing, so as to avoid the hounds, ran a ring up the hillside, and back into the spinney again. Among the horsemen many declared that the brute must be killed unless he would make up his mind for a fair start. Mr. Amblethwaite was very busy, hunting the hounds himself, and intent rather on-killing the fox fairly than on the hopes of a run. Perhaps he was not desirous of sleeping out another night on the far side of Helvellyn. In this way the sportsmen galloped up and down the side of the wood till the feeling arose, as it does on such occasions, that it might be well for a man to stand still awhile and spare his horse, in regard to the future necessities of the day. Lord Hampstead did as others were doing, and in a moment Crocker was by his side. Crocker was riding an animal which his father was wont to drive about the country, but one well known in the annals of the Braeside Harriers. It was asserted of him that the fence was not made which he did not know how to creep over. Of jumping, such as jumping is supposed to be in the shires, he knew nothing. He was, too, a bad hand at galloping, but with a shambling, half cantering trot, which he had invented for himself, he could go along all day, not very quickly, but in such fashion as never to be left altogether behind. He was a flea-bitten horse, if my readers know what that is, — a flea-bitten roan, or white covered with small red spots. Horses of this colour are ugly to look at, but are very seldom bad animals. Such as he was, Crocker, who did not ride much when up in London, was very proud of him. Crocker was dressed in a green coat, which in a moment of extravagance he had had made for hunting, and in brown breeches, in which he delighted to display himself on all possible occasions. " My lord," he said, " you'd hardly think it, but I believe this horse to be the best hunter in Cumberland."

" Is he, indeed ? Some horse of course must be the best, and why not yours ? "

" There's nothing he can't do ;—nothing. His jump- ing is mi—raculous, and as for pace, you'd be quite surprised.—They're at him again now. What an echo they do make among the hills ! "

Indeed they did. Every now and then the Master would just touch his horn, giving a short blast, just half a note, and then the sound would come back, first from this rock and then from the other, and the hounds as they heard it would open as though encouraged by the music of the hills, and then their voices would be carried round the valley, and come back again and again from the steep places, and they would become louder and louder as though delighted with the effect of their own efforts. Though there should be no hunting, the concert was enough to repay a man for his trouble in coming there. " Yes," said Lord Hampstead, his disgust at the man having been quenched for the moment by the charm of the music, " it is a wonderful spot for echoes."

" It's what I call awfully nice. We don't have any- thing like that up at St. Martin's-le-Grand." Perhaps it may be necessary to explain that the Post Office in London stands in a spot bearing that poetic name.

"I don't remember any echoes there," said Lord Hampstead.

"No, indeed;—nor yet no hunting, nor yet no hounds; are there, my lord? All the same, it's not a bad sort of place!"

"A very respectable public establishment!" said Lord Hampstead.

"Just so, my lord; that's just what I always say. It ain't swell like Downing Street, but it's a deal more respectable than the Custom House."

"Is it? I didn't know."

"Oh yes. They all admit that. You ask Roden else." On hearing the name, Lord Hampstead began to move his horse, but Crocker was at his side and could not be shaken off. "Have you heard from him, my lord, since you have been down in these parts?"

"Not a word."

"I dare say he thinks more of writing to a correspondent of the fairer sex."

This was unbearable. Though the fox had again turned and gone up the valley,—a movement which seemed to threaten his instant death, and to preclude any hope of a run from that spot,—Hampstead felt himself compelled to escape, if he could. In his anger he touched his horse with his spur and galloped away among the rocks, as though his object was to assist Mr. Amblethwaite in his almost frantic efforts. But Crocker cared nothing for the stones. Where the

lord went, he went. Having made acquaintance with
a lord, he was not going to waste the blessing which
Providence had vouchsafed to him.

" He'll never leave that place alive, my lord."

" I dare say not." And again the persecuted nobleman rode on,—thinking that neither should Crocker, if
he could have his will.

" By the way, as we are talking of Roden——"

" I haven't been talking about him at all." Crocker
caught the tone of anger, and stared at his companion.
" I'd rather not talk about him."

" My lord! I hope there has been nothing like a
quarrel. For the lady's sake, I hope there's no misunderstanding ! "

" Mr. Crocker," he said very slowly, " it isn't customary——"

At that moment the fox broke, the hounds were
away, and Mr. Amblethwaite was seen rushing down
the hill-side, as though determined on breaking his
neck. Lord Hampstead rushed after him at a pace
which, for a time, defied Mr. Crocker. He became
thoroughly ashamed of himself in even attempting to
make the man understand that he was sinning against
good taste. He could not do so without some implied
mention of his sister, and to allude to his sister in
connection with such a man was a profanation. He
could only escape from the brute. Was this a punishment which he was doomed to bear for being—as his
stepmother was wont to say—untrue to his order ?

In the mean time the hounds went at a great pace
down the hill. Some of the old stagers, who knew the
country well, made a wide sweep round to the left,
whence by lanes and tracks, which were known to them,
they could make their way down to the road which
leads along Ulleswater to Patterdale. In doing this
they might probably not see the hounds again that
day,—but such are the charms of hunting in a hilly
country. They rode miles around, and though they did
again see the hounds, they did not see the hunt. To
have seen the hounds as they start, and to see them
again as they are clustering round the huntsman after
eating their fox, is a great deal to some men.

On this occasion it was Hampstead's lot—and
Crocker's—to do much more than that. Though they
had started down a steep valley,—down the side rather
of a gully,—they were not making their way out from
among the hills into the low country. The fox soon
went up again,—not back, but over an intervening spur
of a mountain towards the lake. The riding seemed
sometimes to Hampstead to be impossible. But Mr.
Amblethwaite did it, and he stuck to Mr. Amblethwaite.
It would have been all very well had not Crocker stuck
to him. If the old roan would only tumble among the
stones what an escape there would be! But the old
roan was true to his character, and, to give every one
his due, the Post Office clerk rode as well as the lord.
There was nearly an hour and a-half of it before the
hounds ran into their fox just as he was gaining an

earth among the bushes and hollies with which Airey
Force is surrounded. Then on the sloping meadow just
above the waterfall, the John Peel of the hunt dragged
out the fox from among the trees, and, having dismem-
bered him artistically, gave him to the hungry hounds.
Then it was that perhaps half-a-dozen diligent, but
cautious, huntsmen came up, and heard all those details
of the race which they were afterwards able to give, as
on their own authority, to others who had been as
cautious, but not so diligent, as themselves.

"One of the best things I ever saw in this country,"
said Crocker, who had never seen a hound in any other
country. At this moment he had ridden up alongside
of Hampstead on the way back to Penrith. The
Master and the hounds and Crocker must go all the
way. Hampstead would turn off at Pooley Bridge.
But still there were four miles, during which he would
be subjected to his tormentor.

"Yes, indeed. A very good thing, as I was saying,
Mr. Amblethwaite."

CHAPTER XIV.

COMING HOME FROM HUNTING.

LORD HAMPSTEAD had been discussing with Mr. Amblethwaite the difficult nature of hunting in such a county as Cumberland. The hounds were in the road before them with John Peel in the midst of them. Dick with the ragged pony was behind, looking after stragglers. Together with Lord Hampstead and the Master was a hard-riding, rough, weather-beaten half-gentleman, half-farmer, named Patterson, who lived a few miles beyond Penrith and was Amblethwaite's right hand in regard to hunting. Just as Crocker joined them the road had become narrow, and the young lord had fallen a little behind. Crocker had seized his opportunity;—but the lord also seized his, and thrust himself in between Mr. Patterson and the Master. "That's all true," said the Master. "Of course we don't presume to do the thing as you swells do it down in the Shires. We haven't the money, and we haven't the country, and we haven't the foxes. But I don't know whether for hunting we don't see as much of it as you do."

" Quite as much, if I may take to-day as a sample."

" Very ordinary;—wasn't it, Amblethwaite?" asked Patterson, who was quite determined to make the most of his own good things.

" It was not bad to-day. The hounds never left their scent after they found him. I think our hillsides carry the scent better than our grasses. If you want to ride, of course, it's rough. But if you like hunting, and don't mind a scramble, perhaps you may see it here as well as elsewhere."

" Better, a deal, from all I hear tell," said Patterson. " Did you ever hear any music like that in Leicestershire, my lord?"

" I don't know that ever I did," said Hampstead. " I enjoyed myself amazingly."

" I hope you'll come again," said the Master, " and that often."

" Certainly, if I remain here."

" I knew his lordship would like it," said Crocker, crowding in on a spot where it was possible for four to ride abreast. " I think it was quite extraordinary to see how a stranger like his lordship got over our country."

" Clever little 'orse his lordship's on," said Patterson.

" It's the man more than the beast, I think," said Crocker, trying to flatter.

" The best man in England," said Patterson, " can't ride to hounds without a tidy animal under him."

" Nor yet can't the best horse in England stick to

hounds without a good man on top of him," said the determined Crocker. Patterson grunted,—hating flattery,
and remembering that the man flattered was a lord.

Then the road became narrow again, and Hampstead fell a little behind. Crocker was alongside of
him in a moment. There seemed to be something
mean in running away from the man;—something
at any rate absurd in seeming to run away from him.
Hampstead was ashamed in allowing himself to be
so much annoyed by such a cause. He had already
snubbed the man, and the man might probably be
now silent on the one subject which was so peculiarly offensive. "I suppose," said he, beginning a
conversation which should show that he was willing
to discuss any general matter with Mr. Crocker,
"that the country north and west of Penrith is less
hilly than this?"

"Oh, yes, my lord; a delightful country to ride
over in some parts. Is Roden fond of following the
hounds, my lord?"

"I don't in the least know," said Hampstead, curtly.
Then he made another attempt. "These hounds
don't go as far north as Carlisle?"

"Oh, no, my lord; never more than eight or ten
miles from Penrith. They've another pack up in
that country; nothing like ours, but still they do
show sport. I should have thought now Roden
would have been just the man to ride to hounds,
—if he got the opportunity."

"I don't think he ever saw a hound in his life. I'm rather in a hurry, and I think I shall trot on."

"I'm in a hurry myself," said Crocker, "and I shall be happy to show your lordship the way. It isn't above a quarter of a mile's difference to me going by Pooley Bridge instead of Dallmaine."

"Pray don't do anything of the kind; I can find the road." Whereupon Hampstead shook hands cordially with the Master, bade Mr. Patterson good-bye with a kindly smile, and trotted on beyond the hounds as quickly as he could.

But Crocker was not to be shaken off. The flea-bitten roan was as good at the end of a day as he was at the beginning, and trotted on gallantly. When they had gone some quarter of a mile Hampstead acknowledged to himself that it was beyond his power to shake off his foe. By that time Crocker had made good his position close alongside of the lord, with his horse's head even with that of the other. "There is a word, my lord, I want to say to you." This Crocker muttered somewhat piteously, so that Hampstead's heart was for the moment softened towards him. He checked his horse and prepared himself to listen. "I hope I haven't given any offence. I can assure you, my lord, I haven't intended it. I have so much respect for your lordship that I wouldn't do it for the world."

What was he to do? He had been offended. He had intended to show that he was offended.

And yet he did not like to declare as much openly. His object had been to stop the man from talking, and to do so if possible without making any reference himself to the subject in question. Were he now to declare himself offended he could hardly do so without making some allusion to his sister. But he had determined that he would make no such allusion. Now as the man appealed to him, asking as it were forgiveness for some fault of which he was not himself conscious, it was impossible to refrain from making him some answer. " All right," he said ; " I'm sure you didn't mean anything. Let us drop it, and there will be an end of it."

" Oh, certainly ;—and I'm sure I'm very much obliged to your lordship. But I don't quite know what it is that ought to be dropped. As I am so intimate with Roden, sitting at the same desk with him every day of my life, it did seem natural to speak to your lordship about him."

This was true. As it had happened that Crocker, who as well as Roden was a Post Office Clerk, had appeared as a guest at Castle Hautboy, it had been natural that he should speak of his office companion to a man who was notoriously that companion's friend. Hampstead did not quite believe in the pretended intimacy, having heard Rodén declare that he had not as yet formed any peculiar friendship at the Office. He had too felt, unconsciously, that such a one as Roden ought not to be intimate with such a one as Crocker. But there was no cause of offence in this. " It was natural," he said.

" And then I was unhappy when I thought from what you said that there had been some quarrel."

" There has been no quarrel," said Hampstead.

"I am very glad indeed to hear that." He was beginning to touch again on a matter that should have been private. What was it to him whether or no there was a quarrel between Lord Hampstead and Roden. Hampstead therefore again rode on in silence.

"I should have been so very sorry that anything should have occurred to interfere with our friend's brilliant prospects." Lord Hampstead looked about to see whether there was any spot at which he could make his escape by jumping over a fence. On the right hand there was the lake rippling up on to the edge of the road, and on the left was a high stone wall, without any vestige of an aperture through it as far as the eye could reach. He was already making the pace as fast as he could, and was aware that no escape could be effected in that manner. He shook his head, and bit the handle of his whip, and looked straight away before him through his horse's ears. "You cannot think how proud I've been that a gentleman sitting at the same desk with myself should have been so fortunate in his matrimonial prospects. I think it an honour to the Post Office all round."

"Mr. Crocker," said Lord Hampstead, pulling up his horse suddenly, and standing still upon the spot, "if you will remain here for five minutes I will ride on; or if you will ride on I will remain here till you are out of sight. I must insist that one of these arrangements be made."

"My lord!"

"Which shall it be?"

"Now I have offended you again."

"Don't talk of offence, but just do as I bid you. I want to be alone."

"Is it about the matrimonial alliance?" demanded Crocker almost in tears. Thereupon Lord Hampstead turned his horse round and trotted back towards the hounds and horsemen, whom he heard on the road behind him. Crocker paused a moment, trying to discover by the light of his own intellect what might have been the cause of this singular conduct on the part of the young nobleman, and then, having failed to throw any light on the matter, he rode on homewards, immersed in deep thought. Hampstead, when he found himself again with his late companions, asked some idle questions as to the hunting arrangements of next week. That they were idle he was quite aware, having resolved that he would not willingly put himself into any position in which it might be probable that he should again meet that objectionable young man. But he went on with his questions, listening or not listening to Mr. Amblethwaite's answers,

till he parted company with his companions in the
neighbourhood of Pooley Bridge. Then he rode alone
to Hautboy Castle, with his mind much harassed by
what had occurred. It seemed to him to have been
almost proved that George Roden must have spoken
to this man of his intended marriage. In all that
the man had said he had suggested that the information had come direct from his fellow-clerk. He had
seemed to declare,—Hampstead thought that he had
declared,—that Roden had often discussed the marriage
with him. If so, how base must have been his friend's
conduct! How thoroughly must he have been mistaken in his friend's character! How egregiously
wrong must his sister have been in her estimate of
the man! For himself, as long as the question had
been simply one of his own intimacy with a companion whose outside position in the world had been
inferior to his own, he had been proud of what he
had done, and had answered those who had remon-
strated with him with a spirit showing that he despised
their practices quite as much as they could ridicule
his. He had explained to his father his own ideas of
friendship, and had been eager in showing that George
Roden's company was superior to most young men
of his own position. There had been Hautboy, and
Scatterdash, and Lord Plunge, and the young Earl of
Longoolds, all of them elder sons, whom he described
as young men without a serious thought in their
heads. What was it to him how Roden got his bread,

so long as he got it honestly? "The man's the man
for a' that." Thus he had defended himself and been
quite conscious that he was right. When Roden had
suddenly fallen in love with his sister, and his sister
had as suddenly fallen in love with Roden,—then he
had begun to doubt. A thing which was in itself
meritorious might become dangerous and objectionable
by reason of other things which it would bring in
its train. He felt for a time that associations which
were good for himself might not be so good for his
sister. There seemed to be a sanctity about her rank
which did not attach to his own. He had thought
that the Post Office clerk was as good as himself;
but he could not assure himself that he was as good
as the ladies of his family. Then he had begun to
reason with himself on this subject, as he did on all.
What was there different in a girl's nature that ought
to make her fastidious as to society which he felt
to be good enough for himself? In entertaining the
feeling which had been strong within him as to that
feminine sanctity, was he not giving way to one of
those empty prejudices of the world, in opposition to
which he had resolved to make a life-long fight? So
he had reasoned with himself; but his reason, though
it affected his conduct, did not reach his taste. It
irked him to think there should be this marriage,
though he was strong in his resolution to uphold his
sister,—and, if necessary, to defend her. He had not
given way as to the marriage. It had been settled

between himself and his sister and his father that there should be no meeting of the lovers at Hendon Hall. He did hope that the engagement might die away, though he was determined to cling to her even though she clung to her lover. This was his state of mind, when this hideous young man, who seemed to have been created with the object of showing him how low a creature a Post Office clerk could be, came across him, and almost convinced him that that other Post Office clerk had been boasting among his official associates of the favours of the high-born lady who had unfortunately become attached to him ! He would stick to his politics, to his Radical theories, to his old ideas about social matters generally; but he was almost tempted to declare to himself that women for the present ought to be regarded as exempt from those radical changes which would be good for men. For himself his " order " was a vanity and a delusion ; but for his sister it must still be held as containing some bonds. In this frame of mind he determined that he would return to Hendon Hall almost immediately. Further hope of hunting with the Braeside Harriers there was none ; and it was necessary for him to see Roden as soon as possible.

That evening at the Castle Lady Amaldina got hold of him, and asked him his advice as to her future duties as a married woman. Lady Amaldina was very fond of little confidences as to her future life, and had as yet found no opportunity of demanding the

sympathy of her cousin. Hampstead was not in truth
her cousin, but they called each other cousins,—or
were called so. None of the Hauteville family felt
any of that aversion to the Radicalism of the heir
to the marquisate which the Marchioness entertained.
Lady Amaldina delighted to be Amy to Lord Hampstead, and was very anxious to ask him his advice as to
Lord Llwddythlw.

"Of course you know all about my marriage, Hampstead?" she said.

"I don't know anything about it," Hampstead
replied.

"Oh, Hampstead; how ill-natured!"

"Nobody knows anything about it, because it hasn't
taken place."

"That is so like a Radical, to be so precise and
rational. My engagement then?"

"Yes; I've heard a great deal about that. We've
been talking about that for——how long shall I say?"

"Don't be disagreeable. Of course such a man as
Llwddythlw can't be married all in a hurry just like
anybody else."

"What a misfortune for him!"

"Why should it be a misfortune?"

"I should think it so if I were going to be married
to you."

"That's the prettiest thing I have ever heard you
say. At any rate he has got to put up with it, and
so have I. It is a bore, because people will talk about

nothing else. What do you think of Llwddythlw as a
public man ? "

"I haven't thought about it. I haven't any means
of thinking. I am so completely a private man myself,
that I know nothing of public men. I hope he's good
at going to sleep."

" Going to sleep ? "

"Otherwise it must be so dull, sitting so many
hours in the House of Commons. But he's been at
it a long time, and I dare say he's used to it."

" Isn't it well that a man in his position should have
a regard to his country ? "

" Every man ought to have a regard to his country ;
—but a stronger regard, if it be possible, to the world
at large."

Lady Amaldina stared at him, not knowing in
the least what he meant. "You are so droll," she
said. "You never, I think, think of the position you
were born to fill."

" Oh yes, I do. I'm a man, and I think a great deal
about it."

" But you've got to be Marquis of Kingsbury, and
Llwddythlw has got to be Duke of Merioneth. He
never forgets it for a moment."

" What a nuisance for him,—and for you."

" Why should it be a nuisance for me ? Cannot
a woman understand her duties as well as a man ? "

" Quite so, if she knows how to get a glimpse at
them."

"I do," said Lady Amaldina, earnestly. "I am always getting glimpses at them. I am quite aware of the functions which it will become me to perform when I am Llwddythlw's wife."

"Mother of his children?"

"I didn't mean that at all, Hampstead. That's all in the hands of the Almighty. But in becoming the future Duchess of Merioneth——"

"That's in the hands of the Almighty, too, isn't it?"

"No; yes. Of course everything is in God's hands."

"The children, the dukedom, and all the estates."

"I never knew any one so provoking," she exclaimed.

"One is at any rate as much as another."

"You don't a bit understand me," she said. "Of course if I go and get married, I do get married."

"And if you have children, you do have children. If you do,—and I hope you will,—I'm sure they'll be very pretty and well behaved. That will be your duty, and then you'll have to see that Llwddythlw has what he likes for dinner."

"I shall do nothing of the kind."

"Then he'll dine at the Club, or at the House of Commons. That's my idea of married life."

"Nothing beyond that? No community of soul?"

"Certainly not."

"No!"

"Because you believe in the Trinity, Llwddythlw won't go to heaven. If he were to take to gambling and drinking you wouldn't go to the other place."

"How can you be so horrid."

"That would be a community of souls,—as souls are understood. A community of interests I hope you will have, and, in order that you may, take care and look after his dinner." She could not make much more of her cousin in the way of confidence, but she did exact a promise from him, that he would be in attendance at her wedding.

A few days afterwards he returned to Hendon Park, leaving his sister to remain for a fortnight longer at Castle Hautboy.

CHAPTER XV.

MARION FAY AND HER FATHER.

"I saw him go in a full quarter of an hour since, and Marion Fay went in before. I feel quite sure that she knew that he was expected." Thus spoke Clara Demijohn to her mother.

"How could she have known it," asked Mrs. Duffer, who was present in Mrs. Demijohn's parlour, where the two younger women were standing with their faces close to the window, with their gloves on and best bonnets, ready for church.

"I am sure she did, because she had made herself smarter than ever with her new brown silk, and her new brown gloves, and her new brown hat,—sly little Quaker that she is. I can see when a girl has made herself up for some special occasion. She wouldn't have put on new gloves surely to go to church with Mrs. Roden."

"If you stay staring there any longer you'll both be late," said Mrs. Demijohn.

"Mrs. Roden hasn't gone yet," said Clara, lingering. It was Sunday morning, and the ladies at No. 10

were preparing for their devotions. Mrs. Demijohn herself never went to church, having some years since had a temporary attack of sciatica, which had provided her with a perpetual excuse for not leaving the house on a Sunday morning. She was always left at home with a volume of Blair's Sermons; but Clara, who was a clever girl, was well aware that more than half a page was never read. She was aware also that great progress was then made with the novel which happened to have last come into the house from the little circulating library round the corner. The ringing of the neighbouring church bell had come to its final tinkling, and Mrs. Duffer knew that she must start, or disgrace herself in the eyes of the pew-opener. "Come, my dear," she said; and away they went. As the door of No. 10 opened so did that of No. 11 opposite, and the four ladies, including Marion Fay, met in the road. "You have a visitor this morning," said Clara.

"Yes;—a friend of my son's."

"We know all about it," said Clara. "Don't you think he's a very fine-looking young man, Miss Fay?"

"Yes, I do," said Marion. "He is certainly a handsome young man."

"Beauty is but skin deep," said Mrs. Duffer.

"But still it goes a long way," said Clara, "particularly with high birth and noble rank."

"He is an excellent young man, as far as I know

him," said Mrs. Roden, thinking that she was called
upon to defend her son's friend.

Hampstead had returned home on the Saturday,
and had taken the earliest opportunity on the following
Sunday morning to go over to his friend at Holloway.
The distance was about six miles, and he had driven
over, sending the vehicle back with the intention
of walking home. He would get his friend to walk
with him, and then should take place that conversation which he feared would become excessively
unpleasant before it was finished. He was shown
up to the drawing-room of No. 11, and there he
found all alone a young woman whom he had never
seen before. This was Marion Fay, the daughter of
Zachary Fay, a Quaker, who lived at No. 17, Paradise
Row. "I had thought Mrs. Roden was here," he said.

"Mrs. Roden will be down directly. She is putting
her bonnet on to go to church."

"And Mr. Roden?" he asked. "He I suppose is
not going to church with her?"

"Ah, no; I wish he were. George Roden never
goes to church."

"Is he a friend of yours?"

"For his mother's sake I was speaking;—but why
not for his also? He is not specially my friend,
but I wish well to all men. He is not at home
at present, but I understood that he will be here
shortly."

"Do you always go to church?" he asked, ground-

ing his question not on any impertinent curiosity as
to her observance of her religious duties, but because
he had thought from her dress she must certainly
be a Quaker.

"I do usually go to your church on a Sunday."

"Nay," said he, "I have no right to claim it as
my church. I fear you must regard me also as a
heathen,—as you do George Roden."

"I am sorry for that, sir. It cannot be good
that any man should be a heathen when so much
Christian teaching is abroad. But men I think
allow themselves a freedom of thought from which
women in their timidity are apt to shrink. If so
it is surely good that we should be cowards?" Then
the door opened, and Mrs. Roden came into the room.

"George is gone," she said, "to call on a sick
friend, but he will be back immediately. He got
your letter yesterday evening, and he left word
that I was to tell you that he would be back by
eleven. Have you introduced yourself to my friend
Miss Fay?"

"I had not heard her name," he said smiling,
"but we had introduced ourselves."

"Marion Fay is my name," said the girl, "and
yours, I suppose is—Lord Hampstead."

"So now we may be supposed to know each other
for ever after," he replied, laughing; "—only I fear,
Mrs. Roden, that your friend will repudiate the
acquaintance because I do not go to church."

"I said not so, Lord Hampstead. The nearer we were to being friends,—if that were possible,—the more I should regret it." Then the two ladies started on their morning duty.

Lord Hampstead when he was alone immediately decided that he would like to have Marion Fay for a friend, and not the less so because she went to church. He felt that she had been right in saying that audacity in speculation on religious subjects was not becoming a young woman. As it was unfitting that his sister Lady Frances should marry a Post Office clerk, so would it have been unbecoming that Marion Fay should have been what she herself called a heathen. Surely of all the women on whom his eyes had ever rested she was,—he would not say to himself the most lovely,—but certainly the best worth looking at. The close brown bonnet and the little cap, and the well-made brown silk dress, and the brown gloves on her little hands, together made, to his eyes, as pleasing a female attire as a girl could well wear. Could it have been by accident that the graces of her form were so excellently shown? It had to be supposed that she, as a Quaker, was indifferent to outside feminine garniture. It is the theory of a Quaker that she should be so, and in every article she had adhered closely to Quaker rule. As far as he could see there was not a ribbon about her. There was no variety of colour. Her head-dress was as simple and close as any that could have been

worn by her grandmother. Hardly a margin of smooth
hair appeared between her cap and her forehead.
Her dress fitted close to her neck, and on her shoulders
she wore a tight-fitting shawl. The purpose in her
raiment had been Quaker all through. The exquisite
grace must have come altogether by accident,—just
because it had pleased nature to make her gracious!
As to all this there might perhaps be room for doubt.
Whether there had been design or not might possibly
afford scope for consideration. But that the grace
was there was a matter which required no consideration,
and admitted of no doubt.

As Marion Fay will have much to do with our story,
it will be well that some further description should
be given here of herself and of her condition in life.
Zachary Fay, her father, with whom she lived, was a
widower with no other living child. There had been
many others, who had all died, as had also their mother.
She had been a prey to consumption, but had lived
long enough to know that she had bequeathed the
fatal legacy to her offspring,—to all of them except to
Marion, who, when her mother died, had seemed to be
exempted from the terrible curse of the family. She
had then been old enough to receive her mother's last
instructions as to her father, who was then a broken-
hearted man struggling with difficulty against the
cruelty of Providence. Why should it have been that
God should thus afflict him,—him who had no other
pleasure in the world, no delights, but those which were

afforded to him by the love of his wife and children?
It was to be her duty to comfort him, to make up as
best she might by her tenderness for all that he had
lost and was losing. It was to be especially her duty to
soften his heart in all worldly matters, and to turn him
as far as possible to the love of heavenly things. It
was now two years since her mother's death, and in all
things she had endeavoured to perform the duties which
her mother had exacted from her.

But Zachary Fay was not a man whom it was easy to
turn hither and thither. He was a stern, hard, just
man, of whom it may probably be said that if a world
were altogether composed of such, the condition of such
a world would be much better than that of the world
we know;—for generosity is less efficacious towards
permanent good than justice, and tender speaking less
enduring in its beneficial results than truth. His
enemies, for he had enemies, said of him that he loved
money. It was no doubt true; for he that does not love
money must be an idiot. He was certainly a man who
liked to have what was his own, who would have been
irate with any one who had endeavoured to rob him
of his own, or had hindered him in his just endeavour
to increase his own. That which belonged to another
he did not covet,—unless it might be in the way of
earning it. Things had prospered with him, and he
was—for his condition in life—a rich man. But his
worldly prosperity had not for a moment succeeded in
lessening the asperity of the blow which had fallen upon

him. With all his sternness he was essentially a loving
man. To earn money he would say—or perhaps more
probably would only think—was the necessity imposed
upon man by the Fall of Adam ; but to have something
warm at his heart, something that should be infinitely
dearer to him than himself and all his possessions,—
that was what had been left of Divine Essence in a man
even after the Fall of Adam. Now the one living thing
left for him to love was his daughter Marion.

He was not a man whose wealth was of high order,
or his employment of great moment, or he would not
probably have been living at Holloway in Paradise Row.
He was and had now been for many years senior clerk
t) Messrs. Pogson and Littlebird, Commission Agents,
at the top of King's Court, Old Broad Street. By
Messrs. Pogson and Littlebird he was trusted with
everything, and had become so amalgamated with the
firm as to have achieved in the City almost the credit
of a merchant himself. There were some who thought
that Zachary Fay must surely be a partner in the
house, or he would not have been so well known or so
much respected among merchants themselves. But in
truth he was no more than senior clerk, with a salary
amounting to four hundred a year. Nor, though he was
anxious about his money, would he have dreamed of
asking for any increase of his stipend. It was for Messrs.
Pogson and Littlebird to say what his services were
worth. He would not on any account have lessened
his authority with them by becoming a suppliant for

increased payment. But for many years he had spent much less than his income, and had known how to use his City experiences in turning his savings to the best account. Thus, as regarded Paradise Row and its neighbourhood, Zachary Fay was a rich man.

He was now old, turned seventy, tall and thin, with long grey hair, with a slight stoop in his shoulders,— but otherwise hale as well as healthy. He went every day to his office, leaving his house with strict punctuality at half-past eight, and entering the door of the counting-house just as the clock struck nine. With equal accuracy he returned home at six, having dined in the middle of the day at an eating-house in the City. All this time was devoted to the interests of the firm, except for three hours on Thursday, during which he attended a meeting in a Quaker house of worship. On these occasions Marion always joined him, making a journey into the City for the purpose. She would fain have induced him also to accompany her on Sundays to the English Church. But to this he never would consent at her instance,—as he had refused to do so at the instance of his wife. He was he said a Quaker, and did not mean to be aught else than a Quaker. In truth, though he was very punctual at those Quaker meetings, he was not at heart a religious man. To go through certain formularies, Quaker though he was, was as sufficient to him as to many other votaries of Church ordinances. He had been brought up to attend Quaker meetings, and no doubt would continue to attend them as long as

his strength might suffice; but it may be presumed of
him without harsh judgment that the price of stocks
was often present to his mind during those tedious
hours in the meeting-house. In his language he always
complied with the strict tenets of his sect, "thou-ing"
and "thee-ing" all those whom he addressed; but he
had assented to an omission in this matter on the part
of his daughter, recognizing the fact that there could
be no falsehood in using a mode of language common to
all the world. "If a plural pronoun of ignoble sound,"
so he said, "were used commonly for the singular
because the singular was too grand and authoritative
for ordinary use, it was no doubt a pity that the
language should be so injured; but there could be no
untruth in such usage; and it was better that at any
rate the young should adhere to the manner of speech
which was common among those with whom they lived."
Thus Marion was saved from the "thees" and the
"thous," and escaped that touch of hypocrisy which
seems to permeate the now antiquated speeches of
Quakers. Zachary Fay in these latter years of his life
was never known to laugh or to joke; but, if circumstances were favourable, he would sometimes fall into
a quaint mode of conversation in which there was
something of drollery and something also of sarcasm;
but this was unfrequent, as Zachary was slow in making
new friends, and never conversed after this fashion with
the mere acquaintance of the hour.

Of Marion Fay's appearance something has already

been said; enough, perhaps,—not to impress any clear
idea of her figure on the mind's eye of a reader, for
that I regard as a feat beyond the power of any writer,
—but to enable the reader to form a conception of his
own. She was small of stature, it should be said,
with limbs exquisitely made. It was not the brilliance
of her eyes or the chiselled correctness of her features
which had struck Hampstead so forcibly as a certain
expression of earnest eloquence which pervaded her
whole form. And there was a fleeting brightness of
colour which went about her cheeks and forehead, and
ran around her mouth, which gave to her when she
was speaking a brilliance which was hardly to be
expected from the ordinary lines of her countenance.
Had you been asked, you would have said that she
was a brunette,—till she had been worked to some
excitement in talking. Then, I think, you would have
hardly ventured to describe her complexion by any
single word. Lord Hampstead, had he been asked
what he thought about her, as he sat waiting for his
friend, would have declared that some divinity of
grace had been the peculiar gift which had attracted
him. And yet that rapid change of colour had not
passed unobserved, as she told him that she was sorry
that he did not go to church.

Marion Fay's life in Paradise Row would have been
very lonely had she not become acquainted with Mrs.
Roden before her mother's death. Now hardly a day
passed but what she spent an hour with that lady.

They were, indeed, fast friends,—so much so that
Mrs. Vincent had also come to know Marion, and
approving of the girl's religious tendencies had invited
her to spend two or three days at Wimbledon. This
was impossible, because Marion would never leave her
father;—but she had once or twice gone over with
Mrs. Roden, when she made her weekly call, and had
certainly ingratiated herself with the austere lady.
Other society she had none, nor did she seem to desire
it. Clara Demijohn, seeing the intimacy which had
been struck up between Marion and Mrs. Roden,—as
to which she had her own little jealousies to endure,—
was quite sure that Marion was setting her cap at the
Post Office clerk, and had declared in confidence to
Mrs. Duffer that the girl was doing it in the most
brazen-faced manner. Clara had herself on more than
one occasion contrived to throw herself in the clerk's
way on his return homewards on dusky evenings,—
perhaps intent only on knowing what might be the
young man's intentions as to Marion Fay. The young
man had been courteous to her, but she had declared
to Mrs. Duffer that he was one of those stiff young
men who don't care for ladies' society. "These are
they," said Mrs. Duffer, "who marry the readiest and
make the best husbands." "Oh;—she'll go on sticking to him till she don't leave a stone unturned," said
Clara,—thereby implying that, as far as she was
concerned, she did not think it worth her while to
continue her attacks unless a young man would give

way to her at once. George had been asked more
than once to drink tea at No. 10, but had been asked
in vain. Clara, therefore, had declared quite loudly
that Marion had made an absolute prisoner of him,—
had bound him hand and foot,—would not let him
call his life his own. "She interrupts him constantly
as he comes from the office," she said to Mrs. Duffer;
"I call that downright unfeminine audacity." Yet she
knew that Mrs. Duffer knew that she had intercepted
the young man. Mrs. Duffer took it all in good part,
knowing very well how necessary it is that a young
woman should fight her own battle strenuously.

In the mean time Marion Fay and George Roden
were good friends. "He is engaged;—I must not
say to whom," Mrs. Roden had said to her young
friend. "It will, I fear, be a long, long, tedious affair.
You must not speak of it."

"If she be true to him, I hope he will be true
to her," said Marion, with true feminine excitement.

"I only fear that he will be too true."

" No, no ;—that cannot be. Even though he suffer
let him be true. You may be sure I will not mention
it,—to him, or to any one. I like him so well that
I do hope he may not suffer much." From that time
she found herself able to regard George Roden as a
real friend, and to talk to him as though there need
be no cause for dreading an intimacy. With an
engaged man a girl may suffer herself to be intimate.

CHAPTER XVI.

THE WALK BACK TO HENDON.

"I was here a little early," said Hampstead when his friend came in, "and I found your mother just going to church,—with a friend."

"Marion Fay."

"Yes, Miss Fay."

"She is the daughter of a Quaker who lives a few doors off. But though she is a Quaker she goes to church as well. I envy the tone of mind of those who are able to find a comfort in pouring themselves out in gratitude to the great Unknown God."

"I pour myself out in gratitude," said Hampstead; "but with me it is an affair of solitude."

"I doubt whether you ever hold yourself for two hours in commune with heavenly power and heavenly influence. Something more than gratitude is necessary. You must conceive that there is a duty,—by the non-performance of which you would encounter peril. Then comes the feeling of safety which always follows the performance of a duty. That I never can achieve. What did you think of Marion Fay?"

"She is a most lovely creature."

"Very pretty, is she not; particularly when speaking?"

"I never care for female beauty that does not display itself in action,—either speaking, moving, laughing, or perhaps only frowning," said Hampstead enthusiastically. "I was talking the other day to a sort of cousin of mine who has a reputation of being a remarkably handsome young woman. She had ever so much to say to me, and when I was in company with her a page in buttons kept coming into the room. He was a round-faced, high-cheeked, ugly boy; but I thought him so much better-looking than my cousin, because he opened his mouth when he spoke, and showed his eagerness by his eyes."

"Your cousin is complimented."

"She has made her market, so it does not signify. The Greeks seem to me to have regarded form without expression. I doubt whether Phidias would have done much with your Miss Fay. To my eyes she is the perfection of loveliness."

"She is not my Miss Fay. She is my mother's friend."

"Your mother is lucky. A woman without vanity, without jealousy, without envy——"

"Where will you find one?"

"Your mother. Such a woman as that can, I think, enjoy feminine loveliness almost as much as a man."

"I have often heard my mother speak of Marion's

good qualities, but not much of her loveliness. To
me her great charm is her voice. She speaks
musically."

" As one can fancy Melpomene did. Does she come
here often ? "

"Every day, I fancy;—but not generally when I
am here. Not but what she and I are great friends.
She will sometimes go with me into town on a Thursday morning, on her way to the meeting house."

" Lucky fellow !" Roden shrugged his shoulders as
though conscious that any luck of that kind must
come to him from another quarter, if it came at all.

" What does she talk about ? "

" Religion generally."

" And you ? "

" Anything else, if she will allow me. She would
wish to convert me. I am not at all anxious to
convert her, really believing that she is very well as
she is."

"Yes," said Hampstead; "that is the worst of
what we are apt to call advanced opinions. With
all my self-assurance I never dare to tamper with
the religious opinions of those who are younger or
weaker than myself. I feel that they at any rate
are safe if they are in earnest. No one, I think,
has ever been put in danger by believing Christ to
be a God."

"They none of them know what they believe," said
Roden; "nor do you or I. Men talk of belief as

though it were a settled thing. It is so but with few; and that only with those who lack imagination. What sort of a time did you have down at Castle Hautboy?"

"Oh,—I don't know,—pretty well. Everybody was very kind, and my sister likes it. The scenery is lovely. You can look up a long reach of Ulleswater from the Castle terrace, and there is Helvellyn in the distance. The house was full of people,—who despised me more than I did them."

"Which is saying a great deal, perhaps."

"There were some uncommon apes. One young lady, not very young, asked me what I meant to do with all the land in the world when I took it away from everybody. I told her that when it was all divided equally there would be a nice little estate even for all the daughters, and that in such circumstances all the sons would certainly get married. She acknowledged that such a result would be excellent, but she did not believe in it. A world in which the men should want to marry was beyond her comprehension. I went out hunting one day."

"The hunting I should suppose was not very good."

"But for one drawback it would have been very good indeed."

"The mountains, I should have thought, would be one drawback, and the lakes another."

"Not at all. I liked the mountains because of their echoes, and the lakes did not come in our way."

" Where was the fault ? "

" There came a man."

" Whom you disliked ? "

" Who was a bore."

" Could you not shut him up ? "

" No; nor shake him off. I did at last do that, but it was by turning round and riding backwards when we were coming home. I had just invited him to ride on while I stood still,—but he wouldn't."

" Did it come to that ? "

" Quite to that. I actually turned tail and ran away from him;—not as we ordinarily do in society when we sneak off under some pretence, leaving the pretender to think that he has made himself very pleasant; but with a full declaration of my opinion and intention."

" Who was he ? "

That was the question. Hampstead had come there on purpose to say who the man was,—and to talk about the man with great freedom. And he was determined to do so. But he preferred not to begin that which he intended to be a severe accusation against his friend till they were walking together, and he did not wish to leave the house without saying a word further about Marion Fay. It was his intention to dine all alone at Hendon Hall. How much nicer it would be if he could dine in Paradise Row with Marion Fay! He knew it was Mrs. Roden's custom to dine early, after church, on Sundays, so that the

two maidens who made up her establishment might
go out,—either to church or to their lovers, or perhaps
to both, as might best suit them.   He had dined there
once or twice already, eating the humble, but social,
leg of mutton of Holloway, in preference to the varied,
but solitary, banquet of Hendon.   He was of opinion
that really intimate acquaintance demanded the practice of social feeling.   To know a man very well, and
never to sit at table with him, was, according to his
views of life, altogether unsatisfactory.   Though the
leg of mutton might be cold, and have no other accom-
paniment but the common ill-boiled potato, yet it
would be better than any banquet prepared simply
for the purpose of eating.   He was gregarious, and
now felt a longing, of which he was almost ashamed,
to be admitted to the same pastures with Marion Fay.
There was not, however, the slightest reason for supposing that Marion Fay would dine at No. 11, even
were he asked to do so himself.   Nothing, in fact,
could be less probable, as Marion Fay never deserted
her father.   Nor did he like to give any hint to his
friend that he was desirous of further immediate
intimacy with Marion.   There would be an absurdity
in doing so which he did not dare to perpetrate.   Only
if he could have passed the morning in Paradise Row,
and then have walked home with Roden in the dark
evening, he could, he thought, have said what he had
to say very conveniently.

But it was impossible.   He sat silent for some

minute or two after Roden had asked the name of
the bore of the hunting field, and then answered him
by proposing that they should start together on their
walk towards Hendon. "I am all ready; but you
must tell me the name of this dreadful man."

"As soon as we have started I will. I have come
here on purpose to tell you."

"To tell me the name of the man you ran away
from in Cumberland?"

"Exactly that;—come along." And so they started,
more than an hour before the time at which Marion
Fay would return from church. "The man who
annoyed me so out hunting was an intimate friend
of yours."

"I have not an intimate friend in the world except
yourself."

"Not Marion Fay?"

"I meant among men. I do not suppose that
Marion Fay was out hunting in Cumberland."

"I should not have ran away from her, I think,
if she had. It was Mr. Crocker, of the General Post
Office."

"Crocker in Cumberland?"

"Certainly he was in Cumberland, unless some one
personated him. I met him dining at Castle Hautboy,
when he was kind enough to make himself known to
me, and again out hunting,—when he did more than
make himself known to me."

"I am surprised."

" Is he not away on leave ? "

" Oh, yes ;—he is away on leave. I do not doubt that it was he."

" Why should he not be in Cumberland,—when, as it happens, his father is land-steward or something of that sort to my uncle Persiflage ? "

" Because I did not know that he had any connection with Cumberland. Why not Cumberland, or West-moreland, or Northumberland, you may say ? Why not ?—or Yorkshire, or Lincolnshire, or Norfolk ? I certainly did not suppose that a Post Office clerk out on his holidays would be found hunting in any county."

" You have never heard of his flea-bitten horse ? "

" Not a word. I didn't know that he had ever sat upon a horse. And now will you let me know why you have called him my friend ? "

" Is he not so ? "

" By no means."

" Does he not sit at the same desk with you ? "

" Certainly he does."

" I think I should be friends with a man if I sat at the same desk with him."

" With Crocker even ? " asked Roden.

" Well ; he might be an exception."

" But if an exception to you, why not also an exception to me ? As it happens, Crocker has made himself disagreeable to me and instead of being my friend, he is,—I will not say my enemy, because I should

be making too much of him; but nearer to being
so than any one I know. Now, what is the meaning
of all this? Why did he trouble you especially
down in Cumberland? Why do you call him my
friend? And why do you wish to speak to me about
him?"

"He introduced himself to me, and told me that
he was your special friend."

"Then he lied."

"I should not have cared about that;—but he
did more."

"What more did he do?"

"I would have been courteous to him,—if only
because he sat at the same desk with you;—but——"

"But what?"

"There are things which are difficult to be told."

"If they have to be told, they had better be told,"
said Roden, almost angrily.

"Whether friend or not, he knew of——your
engagement with my sister."

"Impossible!"

"He told me of it," said Lord Hampstead impetuously, his tongue now at length loosed. "Told me
of it! He spoke of it again and again to my extreme
disgust. Though the thing had been fixed as Fate,
he should not have mentioned it."

"Certainly not."

"But he did nothing but tell me of your happiness, and good luck, and the rest of it. It was

impossible to stop him, so that I had to ride away
from him.   I bade him be silent,—as plainly as I
could without mentioning Fanny's name.   But it was
of no use."

"How did he know it?"

"You told him!"

"I!"

"So he said."   This was not strictly the case.
Crocker had so introduced the subject as to have
avoided the palpable lie of declaring that the tidings
had been absolutely given by Roden to himself.   But
he had not the less falsely intended to convey that
impression to Hampstead, and had conveyed it.   "He
gave me to understand that you were speaking about
it continually at your office."   Roden turned round and
looked at the other man, white with rage—as though
he could not allow himself to utter a word.   "It was
as I tell you.   He began it at the Castle, and afterwards continued it whenever he could get near me
when hunting."

"And you believed him?"

"When he repeated his story so often what was I
to do?"

"Knock him off his horse."

"And so be forced to speak of my sister to every
one in the hunt and in the county?   You do not feel
how much is due to a girl's name."

"I think I do.   I think that of all men I am the
most likely to feel what is due to the name of Lady

Frances Trafford. Of course I never mentioned it to
any one at the Post Office."

"From whom had he heard it?"

"How can I answer that? Probably through some
of your own family. It has made its way through
Lady Kingsbury to Castle Hautboy, and has then been
talked about. I am not responsible for that."

"Not for that certainly,—if it be so."

"Nor because such a one as he has lied. You
should not have believed it of me."

"I was bound to ask you."

"You were bound to tell me, but should not have
asked me. There are things which do not require
asking. What must I do with him?"

"Nothing. Nothing can be done. You could not
touch the subject without alluding to my sister. She
is coming back to Hendon in another week."

"She was there before, but I did not see her."

"Of course you did not see her. How should you?"

"Simply by going there."

"She would not have seen you." There came a
black frown over Roden's brow as he heard this. "It
has been understood between my father and Fanny and
myself that you should not come to Hendon while she
is living with me."

"Should not I have been a party to that agreement?"

"Hardly, I think. This agreement must have been
made whether you assented or not. On no other terms

would my father have permitted her to come. It was
most desirable that she should be separated from Lady
Kingsbury."

"Oh, yes."

"And therefore the agreement was advisable. I
would not have had her on any other terms."

"Why not?"

"Because I think that such visitings would have
been unwise. It is no use my blinking it to you. I
do not believe that the marriage is practicable."

"I do."

"As I don't, of course I cannot be a party to throwing
you together. Were you to persist in coming you
would only force me to find a home for her elsewhere."

"I have not disturbed you."

"You have not. Now I want you to promise me
that you will not. I have assured my father that it
shall be so. Will you say that you will neither come
to her at Hendon Hall, or write to her, while she is
staying with me?" He paused on the road for an
answer, but Roden walked on without making one, and
Hampstead was forced to accompany him. "Will you
promise me?"

"I will not promise. I will do nothing which may
possibly subject me to be called a liar. I have no wish
to knock at any door at which I do not think myself to
be welcome."

"You know how welcome you would be at mine, but
for her."

"It might be that I should find myself forced to endeavour to see her, and I will therefore make no promise. A man should fetter himself by no assurances of that kind as to his conduct. If a man be a drunkard, it may be well that he should bind himself by a vow against drinking. But he who can rule his own conduct should promise nothing. Good-day now. I must be back to dinner with my mother."

Then he took his leave somewhat abruptly, and returned. Hampstead went on to Hendon with his thoughts sometimes fixed on his sister, sometimes on Roden, whom he regarded as impracticable, sometimes on that horrid Crocker;—but more generally on Marion Fay, whom he resolved that he must see again, whatever might be the difficulties in his way.

CHAPTER XVII.

LORD HAMPSTEAD'S SCHEME.

DURING the following week Hampstead went down
to Gorse Hall, and hunted two or three days with
various packs of hounds within his reach, declaring
to himself that, after all, Leicestershire was better
than Cumberland, because he was known there, and
no one would dare to treat him as Crocker had done.
Never before had his democratic spirit received such
a shock,—or rather the remnant of that aristocratic
spirit which he had striven to quell by the wisdom
and humanity of democracy! That a stranger should
have dared to talk to him about one of the ladies of
his family! No man certainly would do so in Northamptonshire or Leicestershire. He could not quite
explain to himself the difference in the localities, but
he was quite sure that he was safe from anything
of that kind at Gorse Hall.

But he had other matters to think of as he galloped
about the country. How might he best manage to
see Marion Fay? His mind was set upon that;—or,
perhaps, more dangerously still, his heart. Had he

been asked before he would have said that there could
have been nothing more easy than for such a one
as he to make acquaintance with a young lady in
Paradise Row. But now, when he came to look at
it, he found that Marion Fay was environed with
fortifications and a *chevaux-de-frise* of difficulties which
were apparently impregnable. He could not call at
No. 17, and simply ask for Miss Fay. To do so he
must be a proficient in that impudence, the lack of
which created so many difficulties for him. He thought
of finding out the Quaker chapel in the City, and
there sitting out the whole proceeding,—unless desired
to leave the place,—with the Quixotic idea of returning to Holloway with her in an omnibus. As he
looked at this project all round, he became sure that
the joint journey in an omnibus would never be
achieved. Then he imagined that Mrs. Roden might
perhaps give him aid. But with what a face could
such a one as he ask such a one as Mrs. Roden to
assist him in such an enterprise? And yet, if anything were to be done, it must be done through Mrs.
Roden,—or, at any rate, through Mrs. Roden's house.
As to this too there was a new difficulty. He had
not actually quarrelled with George Roden, but the
two had parted on the road as though there were
some hitch in the cordiality of their friendship. He
had been rebuked for having believed what Crocker
had told him. He did acknowledge to himself that
he should not have believed it. Though Crocker's

lies had been monstrous, he should rather have supposed him to be guilty even of lies so monstrous, than
have suspected his friend of conduct that would certainly
have been base.   Even this added something to the
difficulties by which Marion Fay was surrounded.

Vivian was staying with him at Gorse Hall.   " I
shall go up to London to-morrow," he said, as the
two of them were riding home after hunting on the
Saturday,—the Saturday after the Sunday on which
Hampstead had been in Paradise Row.

" To-morrow is Sunday,—no day for travelling,"
said Vivian.   " The Fitzwilliams are at Lilford Cross
Roads on Monday,—draw back towards the kennels ;
—afternoon train up from Peterborough at 5·30 ;—
branch from Oundle to meet it, 4·50—have your
traps sent there.   It's all arranged by Providence.
On Monday evening I go to Gatcombe,—so that it
will all fit."

"You need not be disturbed.   A solitary Sunday
will enable you to write all your official correspondence
for the fortnight."

"That I should have done, even in your presence."

" I must be at home on Monday morning.   Give my
love to them all at Lilford Cross Roads.   I shall be
down again before long if my sister can spare me ;
—or perhaps I may induce her to come and rough
it here for a week or two."   He was as good as his
word, and travelled up to London, and thence across
to Hendon Hall, on the Sunday.

It might have been said that no young man could have had stronger inducements for clinging to his sport, or fewer reasons for abandoning it. His stables were full of horses; the weather was good; the hunting had been excellent; his friends were all around him; and he had nothing else to do. His sister intended to remain for yet another week at Castle Hautboy, and Hendon Hall of itself had certainly no special attractions at the end of November. But Marion Fay was on his mind, and he had arranged his scheme. His scheme, as far as he knew, would be as practicable on a Tuesday as on a Monday; but he was impatient, and for the nonce preferred Marion Fay, whom he probably would not find, to the foxes which would certainly be found in the neighbourhood of Lilford Cross Roads.

It was not much of a scheme after all. He would go over to Paradise Row, and call on Mrs. Roden. He would then explain to her what had taken place between him and George, and leave some sort of apology for the offended Post Office clerk. Then he would ask them both to come over and dine with him on some day before his sister's return. In what way Marion Fay's name might be introduced, or how she might be brought into the arrangement, he must leave to the chapter of accidents. On the Monday he left home at about two o'clock, and making a roundabout journey *via* Baker Street, King's Cross, and Islington, went down to Holloway by an omnibus.

He had become somewhat abashed and perplexed as to his visits to Paradise Row, having learned to entertain a notion that some of the people there looked at him. It was hard, he thought, that if he had a friend in that or any other street he should not be allowed to visit his friend without creating attention. He was not aware of the special existence of Mrs. Demijohn, or of Clara, or of Mrs. Duffer, nor did he know from what window exactly the eyes of curious inhabitants were fixed upon him. But he was conscious that an interest was taken in his comings and goings. As long as his acquaintance in the street was confined to the inhabitants of No. 11, this did not very much signify. Though the neighbours should become aware that he was intimate with Mrs. Roden or her son, he need not care much about that. But if he should succeed in adding Marion Fay to the number of his Holloway friends, then he thought inquisitive eyes might be an annoyance. It was on this account that he made his way down in an omnibus, and felt that there was something almost of hypocrisy in the soft, unpretending, and almost skulking manner in which he crept up Paradise Row, as though his walking there was really of no moment to any one. As he looked round after knocking at Mrs. Roden's door, he saw the figure of Clara Demijohn standing a little back from the parlour window of the house opposite.

"Mrs. Roden is at home," said the maid, "but there are friends with her." Nevertheless she showed the

young lord up to the drawing-room. There were
friends indeed. It was Mrs. Vincent's day for coming,
and she was in the room. That alone would not have
been much, but with the two elder ladies was seated
Marion Fay. So far at any rate Fortune had favoured
him. But now there was a difficulty in explaining
his purpose. He could not very well give his general
invitation,—general at any rate as regarded Marion
Fay,—before Mrs. Vincent.

Of course there was an introduction. Mrs. Vincent,
who had often heard Lord Hampstead's name, in
spite of her general severity, was open to the allurements of nobility. She was glad to meet the young
man, although she had strong reasons for believing
that he was not a tower of strength on matters of
Faith. Hampstead and Marion Fay shook hands as
though they were old friends, and then the conversation naturally fell upon George Roden.

"You didn't expect my son, I hope," said the
mother.

"Oh, dear no! I had a message to leave for him,
which will do just as well in a note."

This was to some extent unfortunate, because it
made both Mrs. Vincent and Marion feel that they
were in the way.

"I think I'll send Betsy down for the brougham,"
said the former. The brougham which brought Mrs.
Vincent was always in the habit of retiring round
the corner to the "Duchess of Edinburgh," where the

driver had succeeded in creating for himself quite an
intimacy.

"Pray do not stir, madam," said Hampstead, for
he had perceived from certain preparations made by
Miss Fay that she would find it necessary to follow
Mrs. Vincent out of the room. "I will write two
words for Roden, and that will tell him all I have
to say."

Then the elder ladies went back to the matter they
were discussing before Lord Hampstead had appeared.
"I was asking this young lady," said Mrs. Vincent,
"to come with me for two or three days down to
Brighton. It is absolutely the fact that she has never
seen Brighton."

As Mrs. Vincent went to Brighton twice annually,
for a month at the beginning of the winter and then
again for a fortnight in the spring, it seemed to her
a wonderful thing that any one living, even at Holloway,
should never have seen the place.

"I think it would be a very good thing," said Mrs.
Roden,—"if your father can spare you."

"I never leave my father," said Marion.

"Don't you think, my lord," said Mrs. Vincent,
"that she looks as though she wanted a change?"

Authorized by this, Lord Hampstead took the opportunity of gazing at Marion, and was convinced that
the young lady wanted no change at all. There was
certainly no room for improvement; but it occurred to
him on the spur of the moment that he, too, might

spend two or three days at Brighton, and that he might find his opportunities there easier than in Paradise Row. "Yes, indeed," he said, "a change is always good. I never like to stay long in one place myself."

"Some people must stay in one place," said Marion with a smile. "Father has to go to his business, and would be very uncomfortable if there were no one to give him his meals and sit at table with him."

"He could spare you for a day or two," said Mrs. Roden, who knew that it would be well for Marion that she should sometimes be out of London.

"I am sure that he would not begrudge you a short recreation like that," said Mrs. Vincent.

"He never begrudges me anything. We did go down to Cowes for a fortnight in April, though I am quite sure that papa himself would have preferred remaining at home all the time. He does not believe in the new-fangled idea of changing the air."

"Doesn't he?" said Mrs. Vincent. "I do, I know. Where I live, at Wimbledon, may be said to be more country than town; but if I were to remain all the year without moving, I should become so low and out of sorts, that I veritably believe they would have to bury me before the first year was over."

"Father says that when he was young it was only people of rank and fashion who went out of town regularly; and that folk lived as long then as they do now."

"I think people get used to living and dying according

to circumstances," said Hampstead. "Our ancestors
did a great many things which we regard as quite
fatal. They drank their water without filtering it,
and ate salt meat all the winter through. They did
very little in the washing way, and knew nothing of
ventilation. Yet they contrived to live." Marion Fay,
however, was obstinate, and declared her purpose of
declining Mrs. Vincent's kind invitation. There was a
good deal more said about it, because Hampstead
managed to make various propositions. "He was very
fond of the sea himself," he said, "and would take
them all round, including Mrs. Vincent and Mrs.
Roden, in his yacht, if not to Brighton, at any rate
to Cowes." December was not exactly the time for
yachting, and as Brighton could be reached in an hour
by railway, he was driven to abandon that proposition
with a little laughter at his own absurdity.

But it was all done with a gaiety and a kindness
which quite won Mrs. Vincent's heart. She stayed
considerably beyond her accustomed hour, to the
advantage of the proprietor of the "Duchess of Edinburgh," and at last sent Betsy down to the corner
in high good humour. "I declare, Lord Hampstead,"
she said, "I ought to charge you three-and-sixpence
before I go. I shall have to break into another hour,
because I have stayed talking to you. Pritchard never
lets me off if I am not back punctually by four."
Then she took her departure.

"You needn't go, Marion," said Mrs. Roden,—

"unless Lord Hampstead has something special to say to me." Lord Hampstead declared that he had nothing special to say, and Marion did not go.

"But I have something special to say," said Hampstead, when the elder lady was quite gone, "but Miss Fay may know it just as well as yourself. As we were walking to Hendon on Sunday a matter came up as to which George and I did not agree."

"There was no quarrel, I hope?" said the mother.

"Oh, dear, no;—but we weren't best pleased with each other. Therefore I want you both to come and dine with me one day this week. I shall be engaged on Saturday, but any day before that will do." Mrs. Roden put on a very serious look on receiving the proposition, having never before been invited to the house of her son's friend. Nor, for some years past, had she dined out with any acquaintance. And yet she could not think at the moment of any reason why she should not do so. "I was going to ask Miss Fay to come with you."

"Oh, quite impossible," said Marion. "It is very kind, my lord; but I never go out, do I, Mrs. Roden?"

"That seems to me a reason why you should begin. Of course, I understand about your father. But I should be delighted to make his acquaintance, if you would bring him."

"He rarely goes out, Lord Hampstead."

"Then he will have less power to plead that he

is engaged. What do you say, Mrs. Roden? It would give me the most unaffected pleasure. Like your father, Miss Fay, I, too, am unaccustomed to much going out, as you call it. I am as peculiar as he is. Let us acknowledge that we are all peculiar people, and that therefore there is the more reason why we should come together. Mrs. Roden, do not try to prevent an arrangement which will give me the greatest pleasure, and to which there cannot be any real objection. Why should not Mr. Fay make acquaintance with your son's friend? Which day would suit you best, Wednesday, Thursday, or Friday?"

At last it was settled that at any rate George Roden should dine at Hendon Hall on the Friday,—he being absent during the discussion,—and that time must be taken as to any further acceptance of the invitation. Mrs. Roden was inclined to think that it had best be regarded as impossible. She thought that she had made up her mind never to dine out again. Then there came across her mind a remembrance that her son was engaged to marry this young man's sister, and that it might be for his welfare that she should give way to these overtures of friendship. When her thoughts had travelled so far as this, she might have felt sure that the invitation would at last be accepted.

As to Marion Fay, the subject was allowed to drop without any further decision. She had said that it was impossible, and she said nothing more. That was the last dictum heard from her; but it was not repeated as would probably have been the case had she been quite sure that it was impossible. Mrs. Roden during the interview did not allude to that branch of the subject again. She was fluttered with what had already been said, a little angry with herself that she had so far yielded, a little perplexed at her own too evident confusion, a little frightened at Lord Hampstead's evident admiration of the girl. As to Marion, it must, of course, be left to her father,—as would the question as to the Quaker himself.

"I had better be going," said Marion Fay, who was also confused.

"So must I," said Hampstead. "I have to return round by London, and have ever so many things to do in Park Lane. The worst of having two or three houses is that one never knows where one's clothes are. Good-bye, Mrs. Roden. Mind, I depend upon you, and that I have set my heart upon it. You will let me walk with you as far as your door, Miss Fay?"

"It is only three doors off," said Marion, "and in the other direction." Nevertheless he did go with her to the house, though it was only three doors off. "Tell your father, with my compliments," he said, "that George Roden can show you the way over. If you can get a cab to bring you across I will send you back in the waggonette. For the matter of that, there is no reason on earth why it should not be sent for you."

"Oh, no, my lord. That is, I do not think it possible that we should come."

"Pray do, pray do, pray do," he said, as he took her hand when the door at No. 17 was opened. As he walked down the street he saw the figure still standing at the parlour window of No. 10.

On the same evening Clara Demijohn was closeted with Mrs. Duffer at her lodgings at No. 15. "Standing in the street, squeezing her hand!" said Mrs. Duffer, as though the very hairs of her head were made to stand on end by the tidings,—the moral hairs, that is, of her moral head. Her head, in the flesh, was ornamented by a front which must have prevented the actual standing on end of any hair that was left to her.

"I saw it! They came out together from No. 11 as loving as could be, and he walked up with her to their own house. Then he seized her hand and held it,—oh, for minutes !—in the street. There is nothing those Quaker girls won't allow themselves. They are so free with their Christian names, that, of course, they get into intimacies instantly. I never allow a young man to call me Clara without leave asked and given."

"I should think not."

"One can't be too particular about one's Christian name. They've been in there together, at No. 11, for two hours. What can that mean ? Old Mrs. Vincent was there, but she went away."

"I suppose she didn't like such doings."

"What can a lord be doing in such a place as that," asked Clara, "—coming so often, you know? And one that has to be a Markiss, which is much more than a lord. One thing is quite certain. It can't mean that he is going to marry Marion Fay?" With this assurance Clara Demijohn comforted herself as best she might.

CHAPTER XVIII.

HOW THEY LIVED AT TRAFFORD PARK.

THERE certainly was no justification for the ill-humour which Lady Kingsbury displayed to her husband because Hampstead and his sister had been invited down to Castle Hautboy. The Hautboy people were her own relations,—not her husband's. If Lady Persiflage had taken upon herself to think better of all the evil things done by the children of the first Marchioness, that was not the fault of the Marquis! But to her thinking this visit had been made in direct opposition to her wishes and her interests. Had it been possible she would have sent the naughty young lord and the naughty young lady altogether to Coventry, —as far as all aristocratic associations were concerned. This encouragement of them at Castle Hautboy was in direct contravention of her ideas. But poor Lord Kingsbury had had nothing to do with it. "They are not fit to go to such a house as Castle Hautboy," she said. The Marquis, who was sitting alone in his own morning room at Trafford, frowned angrily. But her ladyship, too, was very angry. "They have disgraced themselves, and Geraldine should not have received them."

There were two causes for displeasure in this. In the first place the Marquis could not endure that such hard things should be said of his elder children. Then, by the very nature of the accusation made, there was a certain special honour paid to the Hauteville family which he did not think at all to be their due. On many occasions his wife had spoken as though her sister had married into a House of peculiar nobility,— because, forsooth, Lord Persiflage was in the Cabinet, and was supposed to have made a figure in politics. The Marquis was not at all disposed to regard the Earl as in any way bigger than was he himself. He could have paid all the Earl's debts,—which the Earl certainly could not do himself,—and never have felt it. The social gatherings at Castle Hautboy were much more numerous than any at Trafford, but the guests at Castle Hautboy were often people whom the Marquis would never have entertained. His wife pined for the social influence which her sister was supposed to possess, but he felt no sympathy with his wife in that respect.

"I deny it," said the father, rising from his chair, and scowling at his wife as he stood leaning upon the table. " They have not disgraced themselves."

"I say they have." Her ladyship made her assertion boldly, having come into the room prepared for battle, and determined if possible to be victor. " Has not

Fanny disgraced herself in having engaged herself to a low fellow, the scum of the earth, without saying anything even to you about it ? "

" No ! " shouted the Marquis, who was resolved to contradict his wife in anything she might say.

" Then I know nothing of what becomes a young woman," continued the Marchioness. " And does not Hampstead associate with all manner of low people ? "

" No, never."

" Is not this George Roden a low person ? Does he ever live with young men or with ladies of his own rank ? "

" And yet you're angry with him because he goes to Castle Hautboy ! Though, no doubt, he may meet people there quite unfit for society."

" That is not true," said the Marchioness. " My brother-in-law entertains the best company in Europe."

" He did do so when he had my son and my daughter under his roof."

" Hampstead does not belong to a single club in London," said the step-mother.

" So much the better," said the father, " as far as I know anything about the clubs. Hautboy lost fourteen hundred pounds the other day at the Pandemonium ; and where did the money come from to save him from being expelled ? "

" That's a very old story," said the Marchioness, who knew that her husband and Hampstead between them had supplied the money to save the young lad from disgrace.

"And yet you throw it in my teeth that Hampstead doesn't belong to any club! There isn't a club in London he couldn't get into to-morrow, if he were to put his name down."

"I wish he'd try at the Carlton," said her ladyship, whose father and brother, and all her cousins, belonged to that aristocratic and exclusive political association.

"I should disown him," said the still Liberal Marquis;—"that is to say, of course he'll do nothing of the kind. But to declare that a young man has disgraced himself because he doesn't care for club life, is absurd;—and coming from you as his stepmother is wicked." As he said this he bobbed his head at her, looking into her face as though he should say to her, "Now you have my true opinion about yourself." At this moment there came a gentle knock at the door, and Mr. Greenwood put in his head. "I am busy," said the Marquis very angrily. Then the unhappy chaplain retired abashed to his own rooms, which were also on the ground floor, beyond that in which his patron was now sitting.

"My lord," said his wife, towering in her passion, "if you call me wicked in regard to your children, I will not continue to live under the same roof with you."

"Then you may go away."

"I have endeavoured to do my duty by your children, and a very hard time I've had of it. If you think that your daughter is now conducting herself with propriety, I can only wash my hands of her."

"Wash your hands," he said.

"Very well. Of course I must suffer deeply, because the shadow of the disgrace must fall more or less upon my own darlings."

"Bother the darlings," said the Marquis.

"They're your own children, my lord; your own children."

"Of course they are. Why shouldn't they be my own children? They are doing very well, and will get quite as good treatment as younger brothers ought to have."

"I don't believe you care for them the least in the world," said the Marchioness.

"That is not true. You know I care for them."

"You said 'bother the darlings' when I spoke of them." Here the poor mother sobbed, almost overcome by the contumely of the expression used towards her own offspring.

"You drive a man to say anything. Now look here. I will not have Hampstead and Fanny abused in my presence. If there be anything wrong I must suffer more than you, because they are my children. You have made it impossible for her to live here——"

"I haven't made it impossible for her to live

here. I have only done my duty by her. Ask Mr.
Greenwood."

"D—— Mr. Greenwood!" said the Marquis. He
certainly did say the word at full length, as far as it
can be said to have length, and with all the emphasis
of which it was capable. He certainly did say it,
though when the circumstance was afterwards not
unfrequently thrown in his teeth, he would forget it
and deny it. Her ladyship heard the word very
plainly, and at once stalked out of the room, thereby
showing that her feminine feelings had received a
wrench which made it impossible for her any longer to
endure the presence of such a foul-mouthed monster.
Up to that moment she had been anything but the
victor; but the vulgarity of the curse had restored to
her much of her prestige, so that she was able to leave
the battlefield as one retiring with all his forces in
proper order. He had "bothered" his own children,
and "damned" his own chaplain!

The Marquis sat awhile thinking alone, and then
pulled a string by which communication was made
between his room and that in which the clergyman
sat. It was not a vulgar bell, which would have
been injurious to the reverence and dignity of a
clerical friend, as savouring of a menial's task work,
nor was it a pipe for oral communication, which is
undignified, as requiring a man to stoop and put his
mouth to it,—but an arrangement by which a light tap
was made against the wall so that the inhabitant of

the room might know that he was wanted without any
process derogatory to his self-respect. The chaplain
obeyed the summons, and, lightly knocking at the door,
again stood before the lord. He found the Marquis
standing upon the hearth-rug, by which, as he well
knew, it was signified that he was not intended to sit
down. "Mr. Greenwood," said the Marquis, in a tone
of voice which was intended to be peculiarly mild, but
which at the same time was felt to be menacing, "I do
not mean at the present moment to have any conversation with you on the subject to which it is necessary
that I should allude, and as I shall not ask for your
presence for above a minute or two, I will not detain
you by getting you to sit down. If I can induce you
to listen to me without replying to me it will, I think,
be better for both of us."

"Certainly, my lord."

"I will not have you speak to me respecting Lady
Frances."

"When have I done so?" asked the chaplain
plaintively.

"Nor will I have you speak to Lady Kingsbury
about her step-daughter." Then he was silent, and
seemed to imply, by what he had said before, that the
clergyman should now leave the room. The first order
given had been very simple. It was one which the
Marquis certainly had a right to exact, and with which
Mr. Greenwood felt that he would be bound to comply.
But the other was altogether of a different nature. He

was in the habit of constant conversation with Lady
Kingsbury as to Lady Frances. Twice, three times,
four times a day her ladyship, who in her present
condition had no other confidant, would open out her
sorrow to him on this terrible subject. Was he to tell
her that he had been forbidden by his employer to
continue this practice, or was he to continue it in
opposition to the Marquis's wishes? He would have
been willing enough to do as he was bidden, but that
he saw that he would be driven to quarrel with the
lord or the lady. The lord, no doubt, could turn him
out of the house, but the lady could make the house
too hot to hold him. The lord was a just man, though
unreasonable, and would probably not turn him out without compensation; but the lady was a violent woman,
who if she were angered would remember nothing of
justice. Thinking of all this he stood distracted and
vacillating before his patron. "I expect you," said the
Marquis, "to comply with my wishes,—or to leave me."

"To leave Trafford?" asked the poor man.

"Yes; to leave Trafford; to do that or to comply
with my wishes on a matter as to which my wishes are
certainly entitled to consideration. Which is it to be,
Mr. Greenwood?"

"Of course, I will do as you bid me." Then the
Marquis bowed graciously as he still stood with his
back to the fire, and Mr. Greenwood left the room.

Mr. Greenwood knew well that this was only the
beginning of his troubles. When he made the promise

he was quite sure that he would be unable to keep it.
The only prospect open to him was that of breaking
the promise and keeping the Marquis in ignorance of
his doing so. It would be out of his power not to follow
any lead in conversation which the Marchioness might
give him. But it might be possible to make the
Marchioness understand that her husband must be
kept in the dark as to any confidence between them.
For, in truth, many secrets were now discussed between
them, as to which it was impossible that her ladyship
should be got to hold her tongue. It had come to be
received as a family doctrine between them that Lord
Hampstead's removal to a better world was a thing
devoutly to be wished. It is astonishing how quickly,
though how gradually, ideas of such a nature will be
developed when entertainment has once been given to
them. The Devil makes himself at home with great
rapidity when the hall door has been opened to him.
A month or two back, before her ladyship went to
Königsgraaf, she certainly would not have ventured to
express a direct wish for the young man's death,
however frequently her thoughts might have travelled
in that direction. And certainly in those days, though
they were yet not many weeks since, Mr. Greenwood
would have been much shocked had any such suggestion been made to him as that which was now quite
commonly entertained between them. The pity of it,
the pity of it, the pity of it! It was thus the heart-
broken mother put the matter, reconciling to herself

her own wishes by that which she thought to be a duty
to her own children. It was not that she and Mr.
Greenwood had between them any scheme by which
Lord Hampstead might cease to be in the way.
Murder certainly had not come into their thoughts.
But the pity of it; the pity of it! As Lord Hampstead
was in all respects unfit for that high position which, if
he lived, he would be called upon to fill, so was her
boy, her Lord Frederic, made to adorn it by all good
gifts. He was noble-looking, gracious, and aristocratic
from the crown of his little head to the soles of his
little feet. No more glorious heir to a title made
happy the heart of any British mother,—if only he
were the heir. And why should it be denied to her, a
noble scion of the great House of Montressor, to be the
mother of none but younger sons? The more her
mind dwelt upon it, the more completely did the
iniquity of her wishes fade out of sight, and her
ambition appear to be no more than the natural
anxiety of a mother for her child. Mr. Greenwood had
no such excuses to offer to himself; but with him, too,
the Devil having once made his entrance soon found
himself comfortably at home. Of meditating Lord
Hampstead's murder he declared to himself that he
had no idea. His conscience was quite clear to him in
that respect. What was it to him who might inherit
the title and the property of the Traffords? He was
simply discussing with a silly woman a circumstance
which no words of theirs could do aught either to cause

or to prevent. It soon seemed to him to be natural
that she should wish it, and natural also that he should
seem to sympathize with her who was his best friend.
The Marquis, he was sure, was gradually dropping him.
Where was he to look for maintenance, but to his own
remaining friend? The Marquis would probably give
him something were he dismissed;—but that something would go but a short way towards supporting
him comfortably for the rest of his life. There was a
certain living in the gift of the Marquis, the Rectory
of Appleslocombe in Somersetshire, which would
exactly suit Mr. Greenwood's needs. The incumbent
was a very old man, now known to be bed-ridden.
It was 800*l.* a year. There would be ample for himself and for a curate. Mr. Greenwood had spoken to
the Marquis on the subject;—but had been told,
with some expression of civil regret, that he was considered to be too old for new duties. The Marchioness
had talked to him frequently of Appleslocombe;—but
what was the use of that? If the Marquis himself
were to die, and then the Rector, there would be a
chance for him,—on condition that Lord Hampstead
were also out of the way. But Mr. Greenwood, as
he thought of it, shook his head at the barren prospect. His sympathies no doubt were on the side of
the lady. The Marquis was treating him ill. Lord
Hampstead was a disgrace to his order. Lady Frances
was worse even than her brother. It would be a good
thing that Lord Frederic should be the heir. But

all this had nothing to do with murder,—or even with
meditation of murder. If the Lord should choose to
take the young man it would be well ; that was all.

On the same afternoon, an hour or two after he
had made his promise to the Marquis, Lady Kingsbury
sent for him. She always did send for him to drink
tea with her at five o'clock. It was so regular that
the servant would simply announce that tea was ready
in her ladyship's room up-stairs. " Have you seen his
lordship to-day ? " she asked.

" Yes ;—I have seen him."

" Since he told you in that rude way to leave the
room ? "

" Yes, he called me after that."

" Well ? "

" He bade me not talk about Lady Frances."

" I dare say not. He does not wish to hear her
name spoken. I can understand that."

" He does not wish me to mention her to you."

" Not to me ? Is my mouth to be stopped ? I
shall say respecting her whatever I think fit. I dare
say, indeed ! "

" It was to my talking that he referred."

" He cannot stop people's mouths. It is all nonsense.
He should have kept her at Königsgraaf, and locked
her up till she had changed her mind."

" He wanted me to promise that I would not speak
of her to your ladyship."

" And what did you say ? " He shrugged his

shoulders, and drank his tea. She shook her head and bit her lips. She would not hold her tongue, be he ever so angry. " I almost wish that she would marry the man, so that the matter might be settled. I don't suppose he would ever mention her name then himself. Has she gone back to Hendon yet ? "

" I don't know, my lady."

" This is his punishment for having run counter to his uncle's wishes and his uncle's principles. You cannot touch pitch and not be defiled." The pitch, as Mr. Greenwood very well understood, was the first Marchioness. " Did he say anything about Hampstead ? "

" Not a word."

" I suppose we are not to talk about him either ! Unfortunate young man ! I wonder whether he feels himself how thoroughly he is destroying the family."

" I should think he must."

" Those sort of men are so selfish that they never think of any one else. It does not occur to him what Frederic might be if he were not in the way. Nothing annoys me so much as when he pretends to be fond of the children."

" I suppose he won't come any more now."

" Nothing will keep him away,—unless he were to die." Mr. Greenwood shook his head sadly. " They say he rides hard."

" I don't know." There was something in the suggestion which at the moment made the clergyman almost monosyllabic.

" Or his yacht might go down with him."

" He •never yachts at this time of the year," said the clergyman, feeling comfort in the security thus assured.

"I suppose not. Bad weeds never ʼget cut off. But yet it is astonishing how many elder sons have been — taken away, during the last quarter of a century."

" A great many."

" There never could have been one who could be better spared," said the stepmother.

" Yes ;—he might be spared."

" If you only think of the advantage to the family ! It will be ruined if he comes to the title. And my Fred would be such an honour to the name ! There is nothing to be done, of course." That was the first word that had ever been spoken in that direction, and that word was allowed to pass without any reply having been made to it, though it had been uttered almost in a question.

CHAPTER XIX.

LADY AMALDINA'S LOVER.

TRAFFORD PARK was in Shropshire. Llwddythlw, the Welsh seat of the Duke of Merioneth, was in the next county;—one of the seats that is, for the Duke had mansions in many counties. Here at this period of the year it suited Lord Llwddythlw to live,—not for any special gratification of his own, but because North Wales was supposed to require his presence. He looked to the Quarter Sessions, to the Roads, to the Lunatic Asylum, and to the Conservative Interests generally of that part of Great Britain. That he should spend Christmas at Llwddythlw was a thing of course. In January he went into Durham; February to Somersetshire. In this way he parcelled himself out about the kingdom, remaining in London of course from the first to the last of the Parliamentary Session. It was, we may say emphatically, a most useful life, but in which there was no recreation and very little excitement. It was not wonderful that he should be unable to find time to get married. As he could not get as far as Castle Hautboy,—

partly, perhaps, because he did not especially like the omnium-gatherum mode of living which prevailed there,—it had been arranged that he should give up two days early in December to meet the lady of his love under her aunt's roof at Trafford Park. Lady Amaldina and he were both to arrive there on Wednesday, December 3rd, and remain till the Tuesday morning. There had not been any special term arranged as to the young lady's visit, as her time was not of much consequence; but it had been explained minutely that the lover must reach Denbigh by the 5.45 train, so as to be able to visit certain institutions in the town before a public dinner which was to be held in the Conservative interest at seven. Lord Llwddythlw had comfort in thinking that he could utilize his two days' idleness at Trafford in composing and studying the speech on the present state of affairs, which, though to be uttered at Denbigh, would, no doubt, appear in all the London newspapers on the following morning.

As it was to be altogether a lover's meeting, no company was to be invited. Mr. Greenwood would, of course, be there. To make up something of a dinner-party, the Mayor of Shrewsbury was asked for the first evening, with his wife. The Mayor was a strong conservative politician, and Lord Llwddythlw would therefore be glad to meet him. For the next day's dinner the clergyman of the parish, with his wife and daughter, were secured. The chief drawback to these festive arrangements consisted in the fact that both Lady Amaldina and her lover arrived on the day of the bitter quarrel between the Marquis and his wife.

Perhaps, however, the coming of guests is the best relief which can be afforded for the misery of such domestic feuds. After such words as had been spoken Lord and Lady Trafford could hardly have sat down comfortably to dinner, with no one between them but Mr. Greenwood. In such case there could not have been much conversation. But now the Marquis could come bustling into the drawing-room to welcome his wife's niece before dinner without any reference to the discomforts of the morning. Almost at the same moment Lord Llwddythlw made his appearance, having arrived at the latest possible moment, and having dressed himself in ten minutes. As there was no one present but the family, Lady Amaldina kissed her future husband,—as she might have kissed her grandfather,—and his lordship received the salutation as any stern, undemonstrative grandfather might have done. Then Mr. Greenwood entered, with the Mayor and his wife, and the party was complete. The Marquis took Lady Amaldina out to dinner and her lover sat next to her. The Mayor and his wife were on the other side of the table, and Mr. Greenwood was between them. The soup had not been handed round before Lord Llwddythlw was deep in a question as to the comparative merits of the Shropshire and

Welsh Lunatic asylums. From that moment till the
time at which the gentlemen went to the ladies in
the drawing-room the conversation was altogether of
a practical nature. As soon as the ladies had left
the table roads and asylums gave way to general
politics,—as to which the Marquis and Mr. Greenwood
allowed the Conservatives to have pretty much their
own way. In the drawing-room conversation became
rather heavy, till, at a few minutes after ten, the
Mayor, observing that he had a drive before him,
retired for the night. The Marchioness with Lady
Amaldina followed quickly; and within five minutes
the Welsh lord, having muttered something as to the
writing of letters, was within the seclusion of his own
bedroom. Not a word of love had been spoken, but
Lady Amaldina was satisfied. On her toilet-table
she found a little parcel addressed to her by his lordship containing a locket with her monogram, " A. L.,"
in diamonds. The hour of midnight was long passed
before his lordship had reduced to words the first
half of those promises of constitutional safety which
he intended to make to the Conservatives of Denbigh.
Not much was seen of Lord Llwddythlw after breakfast
on the following morning, so determined was he to
do justice to the noble cause which he had in hand.
After lunch a little expedition was arranged for the
two lovers, and the busy politician allowed himself
to be sent out for a short drive with no other companion than his future bride. Had he been quite

intimate with her he would have given her the manuscript of his speech, and occupied himself by saying
it to her as a lesson which he had learnt. As he could
not do this he recapitulated to her all his engagements,
as though excusing his own slowness as to matrimony,
and declared that what with the property and what
with Parliament, he never knew whether he was
standing on his head or his heels. But when he
paused he had done nothing towards naming a certain
day, so that Lady Amaldina found herself obliged to
take the matter into her own hands. "When then
do you think it will be?" she asked. He put his hand
up and rubbed his head under his hat as though the
subject were very distressing to him. "I would not
for worlds, you know, think that I was in your
way," she said, with just a tone of reproach in her
voice.

He was in truth sincerely attached to her;—much
more so than it was in the compass of her nature to
be to him. If he could have had her for his wife
without any trouble of bridal preparations, or of subsequent honeymooning, he would most willingly have
begun from this moment. It was incumbent on him
to be married, and he had quite made up his mind
that this was the sort of wife that he required. But
now he was sadly put about by that tone of reproach.
"I wish to goodness," he said, "that I had been
born a younger brother, or just anybody else than
I am."

"Why on earth should you wish that?"

"Because I am so bothered. Of course, you don't understand it."

"I do understand," said Amaldina;—"but there must, you know, be some end to all that. I suppose the Parliament and the Lunatic Asylums will go on just the same always."

"No doubt,—no doubt."

"If so, there is no reason why any day should ever be fixed. People are beginning to think that it must be off, because it has been talked of so long."

"I hope it will never be off."

"I know the Prince said the other day that he had expected——. But it does not signify what he expected." Lord Llwddythlw had also heard the story of what the Prince had said that he expected, and he scratched his head again with vexation. It had been reported that the Prince had declared that he had hoped to be asked to be godfather long ago. Lady Amaldina had probably heard some other version of the story. "What I mean is that everybody was surprised that it should be so long postponed, but that they now begin to think it is abandoned altogether."

"Shall we say June next?" said the ecstatic lover. Lady Amaldina thought that June would do very well. "But there will be the Town's Education Improvement Bill," said his lordship, again scratching his head.

"I thought all the towns had been educated long ago." He looked at her with feelings of a double sorrow;—sorrow that she should have known so little, sorrow that she should be treated so badly. "I think we will put it off altogether," she said angrily.

"No, no, no," he exclaimed. "Would August do? I certainly have promised to be at Inverness to open the New Docks."

"That's nonsense," she said. "What can the Docks want with you to open them?"

"My father, you know," he said, "has a very great interest in the city. I think I'll get David to do it." Lord David was his brother, also a Member of Parliament, and a busy man, as were all the Powell family; but one who liked a little recreation among the moors when the fatigue of the House of Commons were over.

"Of course he could do it," said Lady Amaldina. "He got himself married ten years ago."

"I'll ask him, but he'll be very angry. He always says that he oughtn't to be made to do an elder brother's work."

"Then I may tell mamma?" His lordship again rubbed his head, but did it this time in a manner that was conceived to signify assent. The lady pressed his arm gently, and the visit to Trafford, as far as she was concerned, was supposed to have been a success. She gave him another little squeeze as they got out of the carriage, and he went away sadly to learn the rest of his speech, thinking how sweet it might be " To do as others use ; Play with the tangles of Neæra's hair, Or sport with Amaryllis in the shade."

But there was a worse interruption for Lord Llwddythlw than this which he had now undergone. At about five, when he was making the peroration of his speech quite secure in his memory, a message came to him from the Marchioness, saying that she would be much obliged to him if he would give her five minutes in her own room. Perhaps he would be kind enough to drink a cup of tea with her. This message was brought by her ladyship's own maid, and could be regarded only as a command. But Lord Llwddythlw wanted no tea, cared not at all for Lady Kingsbury, and was very anxious as to his speech. He almost cursed the fidgety fretfulness of women as he slipped the manuscript into his letter-case, and followed the girl along the passages.

"This is so kind of you," she said. He gave himself the usual rub of vexation as he bowed his head, but said nothing. She saw the state of his mind, but was determined to persevere. Though he was a man plain to look at, he was known to be the very pillar and support of his order. No man in England was so wedded to the Conservative cause,—to that cause which depends for its success on the maintenance of those social institutions by which Great Britain has become the first among the nations. No one believed as did Lord Llwddythlw in keeping the different classes in their own places,—each place requiring honour, truth, and industry. The Marchioness understood something of his character in that respect. Who therefore would be so ready to see the bitterness of her own injuries, to sympathize with her as to the unfitness of that son and daughter who had no blood relationship to herself, to perceive how infinitely better it would be for the "order" that her own little Lord Frederic should be allowed to succeed and to assist in keeping the institutions of Great Britain in their proper position? She had become absolutely dead to the fact that by any allusion to the probability of such a succession she was expressing a wish for the untimely death of one for whose welfare she was bound to be solicitous. She had lost, by constant dwelling on the subject, her power of seeing how the idea would strike the feelings of another person. Here was a man peculiarly blessed in the world, a man at the very top of his "order," one who would be closely connected with herself, and on whom at some future time she might be able to lean as on a strong staff. Therefore she determined to trust her sorrows into his ears.

"Won't you have a cup of tea?"

"I never take any at this time of the day."

"Perhaps a cup of coffee?"

"Nothing before dinner, thank you."

"You were not at Castle Hautboy when Hampstead and his sister were there?"

" I have not been at Castle Hautboy since the spring."

"Did you not think it very odd that they should have been asked ? "

" No, indeed ! Why odd ? "

"You know the story;—do you not ? As one about to be so nearly connected with the family, you ought to know it. Lady Frances has made a most unfortunate engagement, to a young man altogether beneath her,— to a Post Office clerk ! "

" I did hear something of that."

" She behaved shockingly here, and was then taken away by her brother. I have been forced to divorce myself from her altogether." Lord Llwddythlw rubbed his head; but on this occasion Lady Kingsbury mis-interpreted the cause of his vexation. He was troubled at being made to listen to this story. She conceived that he was disgusted by the wickedness of Lady Frances. "After that I think my sister was very wrong to have her at Castle Hautboy. No countenance ought to be shown to a young woman who can behave so abominably." He could only rub his head. "Do you not think that such marriages are most injurious to the best interests of society ? "

" I certainly think that young ladies should marry in their own rank."

" So much depends upon it,—does it not, Lord Llwddythlw ? All the future blood of our head families ! My own opinion is that nothing could be too severe for such conduct."

"Will severity prevent it ?"

"Nothing else can. My own impression is that a father in such case should be allowed to confine his daughter. But then the Marquis is so weak."

"The country would not stand it for a moment."

"So much the worse for the country," said her ladyship, holding up her hands. "But the brother is if possible worse than the sister."

"Hampstead ?"

"He utterly hates all idea of an aristocracy."

"That is absurd."

"Most absurd," said the Marchioness, feeling herself to be encouraged;—"most absurd, and abominable, and wicked. He is quite a revolutionist."

"Not that, I think," said his lordship, who knew pretty well the nature of Hampstead's political feelings.

"Indeed he is. Why, he encourages his sister! He would not mind her marrying a shoeblack if only he could debase his own family. Think what I must feel, I, with my darling boys!"

"Is not he kind to them ?"

"I would prefer that he should never see them!"

"I don't see that at all," said the angry lord.

But she altogether misunderstood him. "When I think of what he is, and to what he will reduce the whole family should he live, I cannot bear to see him touch them. Think of the blood of the Traffords, of the blood of the Mountressors, of the blood of the Hautevilles;——think of your own blood, which is now to be connected with theirs, and that all this is to be defiled because this man chooses to bring about a disreputable, disgusting marriage with the expressed purpose of degrading us all."

"I beg your pardon, Lady Kingsbury; I shall be in no way degraded."

"Think of us; think of my children."

"Nor will they. It may be a misfortune, but will be no degradation. Honour can only be impaired by that which is dishonourable. I wish that Lady Frances had given her heart elsewhere, but I feel sure that the name of her family is safe in her hands. As for Hampstead, he is a young man for whose convictions I have no sympathy,—but I am sure that he is a gentleman."

"I would that he were dead," said Lady Kingsbury in her wrath.

"Lady Kingsbury!"

"I would that he were dead!"

"I can only say," said Lord Llwddythlw, rising from his chair, "that you have made your confidence most unfortunately. Lord Hampstead is a young nobleman whom I should be proud to call my friend. A man's politics are his own. His honour, his integrity, and even his conduct belong in a measure to his family. I do not think that his father, or his brothers, or, if I may say so, his stepmother, will ever have occasion to blush for anything that he may do." With this he bowed to the Marchioness, and stalked out of the room with a grand manner, which those who saw him shuffling his feet in the House of Commons would hardly have thought belonged to him.

The dinner on that day was very quiet, and Lady Kingsbury retired to bed earlier even than usual. The conversation at the dinner was dull, and turned mostly on Church subjects. Mr. Greenwood endeavoured to be sprightly, and the parson, and the parson's wife, and the parson's daughter were uncomfortable. Lord Llwddythlw was almost dumb. Lady Amaldina, having settled the one matter of interest to her, was simply contented. On the next morning her lover took his departure by an earlier train than he had intended. It was, he said, necessary that he should look into some matters at Denbigh before he made his speech. He contrived to get a compartment to himself, and there he practised his lesson till he felt that further practice would only confuse him.

" You had Fanny at the Castle the other day," Lady Kingsbury said the next morning to her niece.

" Mamma thought it would be good-natured to ask them both."

" They did not deserve it. Their conduct has been such that I am forced to say that they deserve nothing from my family. Did she speak about this marriage of hers ? "

" She did mention it."

" Well ! "

" Oh, there was nothing. Of course there was much

more to say about mine. She was saying that she would be glad to be a bridesmaid."

"Pray don't have her."

"Why not, aunt?"

"I could not possibly be there if you did. I have been compelled to divorce her from my heart."

"Poor Fanny!"

"But she was not ashamed of what she is doing?"

"I should say not. She is not one of those that are ever ashamed."

"No, no. Nothing would make her ashamed. All ideas of propriety she has banished from her,—as though they didn't exist. I expect to hear that she disregards marriage altogether."

"Aunt Clara!"

"What can you expect from doctrines such as those which she and her brother share? Thank God, you have never been in the way of hearing of such things. It breaks my heart when I think of what my own darlings will be sure to hear some of these days,— should their half-brother and half-sister still be left alive. But, Amaldina, pray do not have her for one of your bridesmaids." Lady Amaldina, remembering that her cousin was very handsome, and also that there might be a difficulty in making up the twenty titled virgins, gave her aunt no promise.

CHAPTER XX.

THE SCHEME IS SUCCESSFUL.

WHEN the matter was mentioned to George Roden by his mother he could see no reason why she should not dine at Hendon Hall. He himself was glad to have an opportunity of getting over that roughness of feeling which had certainly existed between him and his friend when they parted with each other on the road. As to his mother, it would be well that she should so far return to the usages of the world as to dine at the house of her son's friend. "It is only going back to what you used to be," he said.

"You know nothing of what I used to be," she replied, almost angrily.

"I ask no questions, and have endeavoured so to train myself that I should care but little about it. But I knew it was so." Then after a pause he went back to the current of his thoughts. "Had my father been a prince I think that I should take no pride in it."

"It is well to have been born a gentleman," she said.

"It is well to be a gentleman, and if the good things

which are generally attendant on high birth will help
a man in reaching noble feelings and grand resolves,
so it may be that to have been well born will be an
assistance. But if a man derogates from his birth,—as
so many do,—then it is a crime."

"All that has to be taken for granted, George."

"But it is not taken for granted. Though the man
himself be knave, and fool, and coward, he is supposed
to be ennobled because the blood of the Howards run
in his veins. And worse again : though he has gifts
of nobility beyond compare he can hardly dare to
stand upright before lords and dukes because of his
inferiority."

"That is all going away."

"Would that it could be made to go a little faster.
It may be helped in its going. It may be that in
these days the progress shall be accelerated. But
you will let me write to Hampstead and say that
you will come." She assented, and so that part of
the little dinner-party was arranged.

After that she herself contrived to see the Quaker
one evening on his return home. "Yes," said Mr. Fay;
"I have heard thy proposition from Marion. Why
should the young lord desire such a one as I am to sit
at his table ? "

"He is George's intimate friend.

"That thy son should choose his friend well, I surely
believe, because I see him to be a prudent and wise
young man, who does not devote himself over-much

to riotous amusements." George did occasionally go to a theatre, thereby offending the Quaker's judgment, justifying the "overmuch," and losing his claim to a full measure of praise. "Therefore I will not quarrel with him that he has chosen his friend from among the great ones of the earth. But like to like is a good motto. I fancy that the weary draught-horse, such as I am, should not stable himself with hunters and racers."

"This young man affects the society of such as yourself and George, rather than that of others nobly born as himself."

"I do not know that he shows his wisdom the more."

"You should give him credit at any rate for good endeavours."

"It is not for me to judge him one way or the other. Did he ask that Marion should also go to his house?"

"Certainly. Why should not the child see something of the world that may amuse her?"

"Little good· can come to my Marion from such amusements, Mrs. Roden; but something, perhaps, of harm. Wilt thou say that such recreation must necessarily be of service to a girl born to perform the hard duties of a strict life?"

"I would trust Marion in anything," said Mrs. Roden, eagerly.

"So would I; so would I. She hath ever been a good girl."

" But do you not distrust her if you shut her up, and are afraid to allow her even to sit at table in a strange house ? "

" I have never forbidden her to sit at thy table," said the Quaker.

" And you should let her go specially as a kindness to me. For my son's sake I have promised to be there, and it would be a comfort to me to have another woman with me."

" Then you will hardly need me," said Mr. Fay, not without a touch of jealousy.

" He specially pressed his request that you would come. It is among such as you that he would wish to make himself known. Moreover, if Marion is to be there, you, I am sure, will choose to accompany her. Would you not wish to see how the child bears herself on such an occasion ? "

" On all occasions, at all places, at all hours, I would wish to have my child with me. There is nothing else left to me in all the world on which my eye can rest with pleasure. But I doubt whether it may be for her good." Then he took his departure, leaving the matter still undecided, speaking of it with words which seemed to imply that he must ultimately refuse, but impressing Mrs. Roden with a conviction that he would at last accept the invitation.

" Doest thou wish it thyself ? " he said to his daughter before retiring to rest that night.

" If you will go, father, I should like it."

"Why shouldst thou like it? What doest thou expect? Is it because the young man is a lord, and that there will be something of the gilded grandeur of the grand ones of the earth to be seen about his house and his table?"

"It is not for that, father."

"Or is it because he is young and comely, and can say soft things as such youths are wont to say, because he will smell sweetly of scents and lavender, because his hand will be soft to the touch, with rings on his fingers, and jewels perhaps on his bosom like a woman?"

"No, father; it is not for that."

"The delicacies which he will give thee to eat and to drink; the sweetmeats and rich food cannot be much to one nurtured as thou hast been."

"Certainly not, father; they can be nothing to me."

"Then why is it that thou wouldst go to his house?"

"It is that I may hear you, father, speak among men."

"Nay," said he, laughing, "thou mayst hear me better speak among men at King's Court in the City. There I can hold my own well enough, but with these young men over their wine, I shall have but little to say, I fancy. If thou hast nothing to gain but to hear thy old father talk, the time and money will be surely thrown away."

"I would hear him talk, father."

" The young lord ? "

" Yes ; the young lord. He is bright and clever, and, coming from another world than our world, can tell me things that I do not know."

" Can he tell thee aught that is good ? "

" From what I hear of him from our friend he will tell me, I think, naught that is bad. You will be there to hear, and to arrest his words if they be evil. But I think him to be one from whose mouth no guile or folly will be heard."

" Who art thou, my child, that thou shouldst be able to judge whether words of guile are likely to come from a young man's lips ? " But this he said smiling and pressing her hand while he seemed to rebuke her.

" Nay, father; I do not judge. I only say that I think it might be so. They are not surely all false and wicked. But if you wish it otherwise I will not utter another syllable to urge the request."

" We will go, Marion. Thy friend urged that it is not good that thou shouldst always be shut up with me alone. And, though I may distrust the young lord as not knowing him, my confidence in thee is such that I think that nothing will ever shake it." And so it was settled that they should all go. He would send to a livery stable and hire a carriage for this unusual occasion. There should be no need for the young lord to send them home. Though he did not know, as he said, much of the ways of the

outside world, it was hardly the custom for the host
to supply carriages as well as viands. When he dined,
as he did annually, with the elder Mr. Pogson, Mr.
Pogson sent him home in no carriage. He would sit
at the lord's table, but he would go and come as did
other men.

On the Friday named the two ladies and the two
men arrived at Hendon Hall in something more
than good time. Hampstead hopped and skipped
about as though he were delighted as a boy might
have been at their coming. It may be possible that
there was something of guile even in this, and that
he had calculated that he might thus best create
quickly that intimacy with the Quaker and his
daughter which he felt to be necessary for his full
enjoyment of the evening. If the Quaker himself
expected much of that gilding of which he had spoken
he was certainly disappointed. The garniture of
Hendon Hall had always been simple, and now had
assumed less even of aristocratic finery than it used
to show when prepared for the use of the Marchioness.
"I'm glad you've come in time," said he, "because
you can get comfortably warm before dinner." Then
he fluttered about round Mrs. Roden, paying her
attention much rather than Marion Fay,—still with
some guile, as knowing that he might thus best
prepare for the coming of future good things. "I
suppose you found it awfully cold" he said.

"I do not know that we were awed, my lord,"

said the Quaker. "But the winter has certainly set
in with some severity."

"Oh, father!" said Marion, rebuking him.

"Everything is awful now," said Hampstead, laughing. "Of course the word is absurd, but one gets in
the way of using it because other people do."

"Nay, my lord, I crave pardon if I seemed to
criticize thy language. Being somewhat used to a
sterner manner of speaking, I took the word in its
stricter sense."

"It is but slang from a girl's school, after all," said
Roden.

"Now, Master George, I am not going to bear
correction from you," said Hampstead, "though I put
up with it from your elders. Miss Fay, when you
were at school did they talk slang?"

"Where I was at school, Lord Hampstead," Marion
answered, "we were kept in strict leading-strings.
Fancy, father, what Miss Watson would have said if
we had used any word in a sense not used in a
dictionary."

"Miss Watson was a sensible woman, my dear, and
understood well, and performed faithfully, the duties
which she had undertaken. I do not know that as
much can be said of all those who keep fashionable
seminaries for young ladies at the West End."

"Miss Watson had a red face, and a big cap, and
spectacles;—had she not?" said Hampstead, appealing
to Marion Fay.

"Miss Watson," said Mrs. Roden, "whom I remember to have seen once when Marion was at school with her, was a very little woman, with bright eyes, who wore her own hair, and always looked as though she had come out of a bandbox."

"She was absolutely true to her ideas of life, as a Quaker should be," said Mr. Fay, "and I only hope that Marion will follow her example. As to language, it is, I think, convenient that to a certain extent our mode of speech should consort with our mode of living. You would not expect to hear from a pulpit the phrases which belong to a racecourse, nor would the expressions which are decorous, perhaps, in aristocratic drawing-rooms befit the humble parlours of clerks and artisans."

"I never will say that anything is awful again," said Lord Hampstead, as he gave his arm to Mrs. Roden, and took her in to dinner.

"I hope he will not be angry with father," whispered Marion Fay to George Roden, as they walked across the hall together.

"Not in the least. Nothing of that kind could anger him. If your father were to cringe or to flatter him then he would be disgusted."

"Father would never do that," said Marion, with confidence.

The dinner went off very pleasantly, Hampstead and Roden taking between them the weight of the conversation. The Quaker was perhaps a little frightened by the asperity of his own first remark, and ate his good things almost in silence. Marion was quite contented to listen, as she had told her father was her purpose; but it was perhaps to the young lord's words that she gave attention rather than to those of his friends'. His voice was pleasant to her ears. There was a certain graciousness in his words, as to which she did not suppose that their softness was specially intended for her hearing. Who does not know the way in which a man may set himself at work to gain admission into a woman's heart without addressing hardly a word to herself? And who has not noted the sympathy with which the woman has unconsciously accepted the homage? That pressing of the hand, that squeezing of the arm, that glancing of the eyes, which are common among lovers, are generally the developed consequences of former indications which have had their full effect, even though they were hardly understood, and could not have been acknowledged, at the time. But Marion did, perhaps, feel that there was something of worship even in the way in which her host looked towards her with rapid glances from minute to minute, as though to see that if not with words, at any rate with thoughts, she was taking her share in the conversation which was certainly intended for her delight. The Quaker in the mean time ate his dinner very silently. He was conscious of having shown himself somewhat of a prig about that slang phrase, and was repenting himself.

Mrs. Roden every now and then would put in a word in answer rather to her son than to the host, but she was aware of those electric sparks which, from Lord Hampstead's end of the wire, were being directed every moment against Marion Fay's heart.

"Now just for the fashion of the thing you must sit here for a quarter of an hour, while we are supposed to be drinking our wine." This was said by Lord Hampstead when he took the two ladies into the drawing-room after dinner.

"Don't hurry yourselves," said Mrs. Roden. "Marion and I are old friends, and will get on very well."

"Oh yes," said Marion. "It will be pleasure enough to me just to sit here and look around me." Then Hampstead knelt down between them, pretending to doctor up the fire, which certainly required no doctoring. They were standing, one on one side and the other on the other, looking down upon him.

"You are spoiling that fire, Lord Hampstead," said Mrs. Roden.

"Coals were made to be poked. I feel sure of that. Do take the poker and give them one blow. That will make you at home in the house for ever, you know." Then he handed the implement to Marion. She could hardly do other than take it in her hand. She took it, blushed up to the roots of her hair, paused a moment, and then gave the one blow to the coals that had been required of her. "Thanks," said he, nodding at her as he still knelt at her feet and took the poker

from her; " thanks. Now you are free of Hendon
Hall for ever. I wouldn't have any one but a friend
poke my fire." Upon that he got up and walked
slowly out of the room.

" Oh, Mrs. Roden," said Marion, " I wish I hadn't
done it."

" It doesn't matter. It was only a joke."

" Of course it was a joke ! but I wish I hadn't done
it. It seemed at the moment that I should look to
be cross if I didn't do as he bade me. But when he
had said that about being at home——! Oh, Mrs.
Roden, I wish I had not done it."

" He will know that it was nothing, my dear. He
is good-humoured and playful, and likes the feeling
of making us feel that we are not strangers." But
Marion knew that Lord Hampstead would not take
it as meaning nothing. Though she could see no more
than his back as he walked out of the room, she knew
that he was glowing with triumph.

" Now, Mr. Fay, here is port if you like, but I
recommend you to stick to the claret."

" I have pretty well done all the sticking, my lord,
of which I am competent," said the Quaker. " A
little wine goes a long way with me, as I am not
much used to it."

" Wine maketh glad the heart of man," said Roden.

"True enough, Mr. Roden. But I doubt whether
it be good that a man's heart should be much gladdened.
Gladness and sorrow counterbalance each other too

T 2

surely. An even serenity is best fitted to human life, if it can be reached."

" A level road without hills," said Hampstead. " They say that horses are soonest tired by such travelling."

" They would hardly tell you so themselves if they could give their experience after a long day's journey." Then there was a pause, but Mr. Fay continued to speak. " My lord, I fear I misbehaved myself in reference to that word 'awful' which fell by chance from thy mouth."

" Oh, dear no ; nothing of the kind."

" I was bethinking me that I was among the young men in our court in Great Broad Street, who will indulge sometimes in a manner of language not befitting their occupation at the time, or perhaps their station in life. I am wont then to remind them that words during business hours should be used in their strict sense. But, my lord, if you will take a farm horse from his plough you cannot expect from him that he should prance upon the green."

" It is because I think that there should be more mixing between what you call plough horses and animals used simply for play, that I have been so proud to make you welcome here. I hope it may not be by many the last time that you will act as a living dictionary for me. If you won't have any more wine we will go to them in the drawing-room."

Mrs. Roden very soon declared it necessary that they should start back to Holloway. Hampstead himself

did not attempt to delay them. The words that had
absolutely passed between him and Marion had hardly
been more than those which have been here set down,
but yet he felt that he had accomplished not only
with satisfaction but with some glory to himself the
purpose for which he had specially invited his guests.
His scheme had been carried out with perfect success.
After the manner in which Marion had obeyed his
behest about the fire, he was sure that he was justified
in regarding her as a friend.

CHAPTER XXI.

WHAT THEY ALL THOUGHT AS THEY WENT HOME.

LORD HAMPSTEAD had come to the door to help
them into the carriage. "Lord Hampstead," said
Mrs. Roden, "you will catch your death of cold.
It is freezing, and you have nothing on your
head."

"I am quite indifferent about those things," he said,
as for a moment he held Marion's hand while he
helped her into the carriage.

"Do go in," she whispered. Her lips as she spoke
were close to his ear,—but that simply came from the
position in which chance had placed her. Her hand
was still in his,—but that, too, was the accident of the
situation. But there is, I think, an involuntary
tendency among women to make more than necessary
use of assistance when the person tendering it has
made himself really welcome. Marion had certainly
no such intention. Had the idea come to her at the
moment she would have shrank from his touch. It
was only when his fingers were withdrawn, when the
feeling of the warmth of this proximity had passed

away, that she became aware that he had been so close
to her, and that now they were separated.

Then her father entered the carriage, and Roden.

"Good-night, my lord," said the Quaker. "I have
passed my evening very pleasantly. I doubt whether
I may not feel the less disposed for my day's work
to-morrow."

"Not at all, Mr. Fay; not at all. You will be like
a giant refreshed. There is nothing like a little
friendly conversation for bracing up the mind. I hope
it will not be long before you come and try it again."
Then the carriage was driven off, and Lord Hampstead
went in to warm himself before the fire which Marion
Fay had poked.

He had not intended to fall in love with her. Was
there ever a young man who, when he first found a
girl to be pleasant to him, has intended to fall in love
with her? Girls will intend to fall in love, or, more
frequently perhaps, to avoid it; but men in such
matters rarely have a purpose. Lord Hampstead had
found her, as he thought, to be an admirable specimen
of excellence in that class of mankind which his convictions and theories induced him to extol. He thought
that good could be done by mixing the racers and
plough-horses,—and as regarded the present experiment, Marion Fay was a plough-horse. No doubt he
would not have made this special attempt had she not
pleased his eye, and his ear, and his senses generally.
He certainly was not a philosopher to whom in his

search after wisdom an old man such as Zachary Fay
could make himself as acceptable as his daughter. It
may be acknowledged of him that he was susceptible
to female influences. But it had not at first occurred
to him that it would be a good thing to fall in love
with Marion Fay. Why should he not be on friendly
terms with an excellent and lovely girl without loving
her? Such had been his ideas after first meeting
Marion at Mrs. Roden's house. Then he had determined that friends could not become friends without
seeing each other, and he had concocted his scheme
without being aware of the feelings which she had
excited. The scheme had been carried out; he had
had his dinner-party; Marion Fay had poked his fire;
there had been one little pressure of the hand as he
helped her into the carriage, one little whispered word,
which had it not been whispered would have been as
nothing; one moment of consciousness that his lips
were close to her cheek; and then he returned to
the warmth of his fire, quite conscious that he was
in love.

What was to come of it? When he had argued
both with his sister and with Roden that their
marriage would be unsuitable because of their difference in social position, and had justified his opinion by
declaring it to be impossible that any two persons
could, by their own doing, break through the conventions of the world without ultimate damage to
themselves and to others, he had silently acknowledged

to himself that he also was bound by the law which he was teaching. That such conventions should gradually cease to be, would be good; but no man is strong enough to make a new law for his own governing at the spur of the moment;—and certainly no woman. The existing distances between man and man were radically bad. This was the very gist of his doctrine; but the instant abolition of such distances had been proved by many experiments to be a vain dream, and the diminution of them must be gradual and slow. That such diminution would go on till the distances should ultimately disappear in some future millennium was to him a certainty. The distances were being diminished by the increasing wisdom and philanthropy of mankind. To him, born to high rank and great wealth, it had been given to do more perhaps than another. In surrendering there is more efficacy, as there is also more grace, than in seizing. What of his grandeur he might surrender without injury to others to whom he was bound, he would surrender. Of what exact nature or kind should be the woman whom it might please him to select as his wife, he had formed no accurate idea; but he would endeavour so to marry that he would make no step down in the world that might be offensive to his family, but would yet satisfy his own convictions by drawing himself somewhat away from aristocratic blood. His father had done the same when choosing his first wife, and the happiness of his choice would have been perfect had not death interfered. Actuated by such reasoning as this, he had endeavoured in a mild way to separate his sister from her lover, thinking that they who were in love should be bound by the arguments which seemed good to him, who was not in love. But now he also was in love, and the arguments as they applied to himself fell into shreds and tatters as he sat gazing at his fire, holding the poker in his hand.

Had there ever been anything more graceful than the mock violence with which she had pretended to strike heartily at the coals ?—had there ever anything been more lovely than that mingled glance of doubt, of fear, and of friendliness with which she had looked into his face as she did it ? She had quite understood his feeling when he made his little request. There had been heart enough in her, spirit enough, intelligence enough, to tell her at once the purport of his demand. Or rather she had not seen it all at once, but had only understood when her hand had gone too far to be withdrawn that something of love as well as friendship had been intended. Before long she should know how much of love had been intended ! Whether his purpose was or was not compatible with the wisdom of his theory as to a gradual diminution of distances, his heart had gone too far now for any retracting. As he sat there he at once began to teach himself that the arguments he had used were only good in reference to high-born females, and that they need not necessarily affect himself. Whomever he might marry he would

raise to his own rank. For his rank he did not care
a straw himself. It was of the prejudices of others he
was thinking when he assured himself that Marion
would make as good a Countess and as good a
Marchioness as any lady in the land. In regard to his
sister it was otherwise. She must follow the rank of
her husband. It might be that the sores which she
would cause to many by becoming the wife of a Post
Office clerk ought to be avoided. But there need
be no sores in regard to his marriage with Marion
Fay.

His present reasoning was, no doubt, bad, but such
as it was it was allowed to prevail absolutely. It did
not even occur to him that he would make an attempt
to enfranchise himself from Marion's charms. Whatever might occur, whatever details there might be
which would require his attention in regard to his
father or others of the family, everything must give
way to his present passion. She had poked his fire,
and she must be made to sit at his hearth for the
remainder of their joint existence. She must be made
to -sit there if he could so plead his cause that his
love should prevail with her. As to the Quaker father,
he thought altogether well of him too,—an industrious,
useful, intelligent man, of whose quaint manners and
manly bearing he would not be ashamed in any society.
She, too, was a Quaker, but that to him was little or
nothing. He also had his religious convictions, but
they were not of a nature to be affronted or shocked

by those of any one who believed that the increasing
civilization of the world had come from Christ's teaching. The simple, earnest purity of the girl's faith
would be an attraction to him rather than otherwise.
Indeed, there was nothing in his Marion, as he saw
her, that was not conducive to feminine excellence.

His Marion! How many words had he spoken to
her? How many thoughts had he extracted from her?
How many of her daily doings had he ever witnessed?
But what did it matter? It is not the girl that the
man loves, but the image which imagination has built
up for him to fill the outside covering which has pleased
his senses. He was quite as sure that the Ten Com-
mandments were as safe in Marion's hands as though
she were already a saint, canonized for the perfection
of all virtues. He was quite ready to take that for
granted; and having so convinced himself, was now
only anxious as to the means by which he might make
this priceless pearl his own.

There must be some other scheme. He sat, thinking
of this, cudgelling his brains for some contrivance by
which he and Marion Fay might be brought together
again with the least possible delay. His idea of a
dinner-party had succeeded beyond all hope. But he
could not have another dinner-party next week. Nor
could he bring together the guests whom he had to-
day entertained after his sister's return. He was
bound not to admit George Roden to his house as long
as she should be with him. Without George he could

hardly hope that Mrs. Roden would come to him, and without Mrs. Roden how could he entice the Quaker and his daughter? His sister would be with him on the following day, and would, no doubt, be willing to assist him with Marion if it were possible. But the giving of such assistance on her part would tacitly demand assistance also from him in her difficulties. Such assistance, he knew, he could not give, having pledged himself to his father in regard to George Roden. He could at the present moment devise no other scheme than the very simple one of going to Mrs. Roden, and declaring his love for the girl.

* * * * * * *

The four guests in the carriage were silent throughout their drive home. They all had thoughts of their own sufficient to occupy them. George Roden told himself that this, for a long day, must be his last visit to Hendon Hall. He knew that Lady Frances would arrive on the morrow, and that then his presence was forbidden. He had refused to make any promise as to his assured absence, not caring to subject himself to an absolute bond; but he was quite aware that he was bound in honour not to enter the house in which he could not be made welcome. He felt himself to be safe, with a great security. The girl whom he loved would certainly be true. He was not impatient, as was Hampstead. He did not trouble his mind with schemes which were to be brought to bear within the next few days. He could bide his time, comforting himself with his faith. But still a lover can hardly be satisfied with the world unless he can see some point in his heaven from which light may be expected to break through the clouds. He could not see the point from which the light might be expected.

The Quaker was asking himself many questions. Had he done well to take his girl to this young nobleman's house? Had he done well to take himself there? It had been as it were a sudden disruption in the settled purposes of his life. What had he or his girl to do with lords? And yet he had been pleased. Courtesy always flatters, and flattery is always pleasant. A certain sense of softness had been grateful to him. There came upon him a painful question,—as there does on so many of us, when for a time we make a successful struggle against the world's allurements,— whether in abandoning the delights of life we do in truth get any compensation for them. Would it not after all be better to do as others use? Phœbus as he touches our trembling ear encourages us but with a faint voice. It had been very pleasant,—the soft chairs, the quiet attendance, the well-cooked dinner, the good wines, the bright glasses, the white linen,— and pleasanter than all that silvery tone of conversation to which he was so little accustomed either in King's Court or Paradise Row. Marion indeed was always gentle to him as a dove cooing; but he was aware of himself that he was not gentle in return. Stern truth, expressed shortly in strong language, was

the staple of his conversation at home. He had declared to himself all through his life that stern truth
and strong language were better for mankind than soft
phrases. But in his own parlour in Paradise Row he
had rarely seen his Marion bright as she had been at
this lord's table. Was it good for his Marion that she
should be encouraged to such brightness; and if so, had
he been cruel to her to suffuse her entire life with a
colour so dark as to admit of no light? Why had her
beauty shone so brightly in the lord's presence? He
too knew something of love, and had it always present
to his mind that the time would come when his
Marion's heart would be given to some stranger. He
did not think, he would not think, that the stranger
had now come;—but would it be well that his girl's
future should be affected even as was his own? He
argued the points much within himself, and told himself
that it could not be well.

Mrs. Roden had read it nearly all,—though she
could not quite read the simple honesty of the young
lord's purpose. The symptoms of love had been plain
enough to her eyes, and she had soon told herself that
she had done wrong in taking the girl to the young
lord's house. She had seen that Hampstead had
admired Marion, but she had not dreamed that it
would be carried to such a length as this. But when
he had knelt on the rug between them, leaning just
a little towards the girl, and had looked up into the
girl's face, smiling at his own little joke, but with his

face full of love;—then she had known. And when Marion had whispered the one word, with her little fingers lingering within the young lord's touch, then she had known. It was not the young lord only who had given way to the softness of the moment. If evil had been done, she had done it; and it seemed as though evil had certainly been done. If much evil had been done, how could she forgive herself?

And what were Marion's thoughts? Did she feel that an evil had been done, an evil for which there could never be a cure found? She would have so assured herself, had she as yet become aware of the full power and depth and mortal nature of the wound she had received. For such a wound, for such a hurt, there is but one cure, and of that she certainly would have entertained no hope. But, as it will sometimes be that a man shall in his flesh receive a fatal injury, of which he shall for awhile think that only some bruise has pained him, some scratch annoyed him; that a little time, with ointment and a plaister, will give him back his body as sound as ever; but then after a short space it becomes known to him that a deadly gangrene is affecting his very life; so will it be with a girl's heart. She did not yet,—not yet,— tell herself that half-a-dozen gentle words, that two or three soft glances, that a touch of a hand, the mere presence of a youth whose comeliness was endearing to the eye, had mastered and subdued all that there was of Marion Fay. But it was so. Not for a moment did her mind run away, as they were taken homewards, from the object of her unconscious idolatry. Had she behaved ill?—that was her regret! He had been so gracious;—that was her joy! Then there came a pang from the wound, though it was not as yet a pang as of death. What right had such a one as she to receive even an idle word of compliment from a man such as was Lord Hampstead? What could he be to her, or she to him? He had his high mission to complete, his great duties to perform, and doubtless would find some noble lady as a fit mother for his children. He had come across her path for a moment, and she could not but remember him for ever! There was something of an idea present to her that love would now be beyond her reach. But the pain necessarily attached to such an idea had not as yet reached her. There came something of a regret that fortune had placed her so utterly beyond his notice;—but she was sure of this, sure of this, that if the chance were offered to her, she would not mar his greatness by accepting the priceless boon of his love. But why,—why had he been so tender to her? Then she thought of what were the ways of men, and of what she had heard of them. It had been bad for her to go abroad thus with her poor foolish softness, with her girl's untried tenderness,—that thus she should be affected by the first chance smile that had been thrown to her by one of those petted darlings of Fortune! And then she was brought round to that same resolution which was

at the moment forming itself in her father's mind;—
that it would have been better for her had she not
allowed herself to be taken to Hendon Hall.   Then
they were in Paradise Row, and were put down at
their separate doors with but few words of farewell to
each other.

"They have just come home," said Clara Demijohn,
rushing into her mother's bedroom.   "You'll find it is
quite true.   They have been dining with the lord!"

CHAPTER XXII.

AGAIN AT TRAFFORD.

THE meeting between Hampstead and his sister was affectionate and, upon the whole, satisfactory, though it was necessary that a few words should be spoken which could hardly be pleasant in themselves. "I had a dinner-party here last night," he said laughing, desirous of telling her something of George Roden,—and something also of Marion Fay.

"Who were the guests?"

"Roden was here." Then there was silence. She was glad that her lover had been one of the guests, but she was not as yet moved to say anything respecting him. "And his mother."

"I am sure I shall like his mother," said Lady Frances.

"I have mentioned it," continued her brother, speaking with unusual care, "because, in compliance with the agreement I made at Trafford, I cannot ask him here again at present."

"I am sorry that I should be in your way, John."

"You are not in my way, as I think you know.

U 2

Let us say no more than that at present. Then I had a singular old Quaker, named Zachary Fay, an earnest, honest, but humble man, who blew me up instantly for talking slang."

"Where did you pick him up?"

"He comes out of the City," he said, not wishing to refer again to Paradise Row and the neighbourhood of the Rodens,—"and he brought his daughter."

"A young lady?"

"Certainly a young lady."

"Ah, but young,—and beautiful?"

"Young,—and beautiful."

"Now you are laughing. I suppose she is some strong-minded, rather repulsive, middle-aged woman."

"As to the strength of her mind, I have not seen enough to constitute myself a judge," said Hampstead, almost with a tone of offence. "Why you should imagine her to be repulsive because she is a Quaker, or why middle-aged, I do not understand. She is not repulsive to me."

"Oh, John, I am so sorry! Now I know that you have found some divine beauty."

"We sometimes entertain angels unawares. I thought that I had done so when she took her departure."

"Are you in earnest?"

"I am quite in earnest as to the angel. Now I have to consult you as to a project." It may be remembered that Hampstead had spoken to his father

as to the expediency of giving up his horses if he
found that his means were not sufficient to keep up
Hendon Hall, his yacht, and his hunting establishment in Northamptonshire. The Marquis, without
saying a word to his son, had settled that matter,
and Gorse Hall, with its stables, was continued. The
proposition now made to Lady Frances was that she
should go down with him and remain there for a week
or two till she should find the place too dull. He
had intended to fix an almost immediate day; but
now he was debarred from this by his determination
to see Marion yet once again before he took himself
altogether beyond the reach of Holloway. The plan,
therefore, though it was fixed as far as his own intention went and the assent of Lady Frances, was
left undefined as to time. The more he thought of
Holloway, and the difficulties of approaching Paradise
Row, the more convinced he became that his only
mode of approaching Marion must be through Mrs.
Roden. He had taken two or three days to consider
what would be the most appropriate manner of going
through this operation, when on a sudden he was
arrested by a letter from his father, begging his
presence down at Trafford. The Marquis was ill, and
was anxious to see his son. The letter in which the
request was made was sad and plaintive throughout.
He was hardly able to write, Lord Kingsbury said,
because he was so unwell; but he had no one to
write for him. Mr. Greenwood had made himself so

disagreeable that he could no longer employ him for
such purposes. "Your stepmother is causing me much
vexation, which I do not think that I deserve from
her." He then added that it would be necessary for
him to have his lawyer down at Trafford, but that
he wished to see Hampstead first in order that they
might settle as to certain arrangements which were
required in regard to the disposition of the property.
There were some things which Hampstead could not
fail to perceive from this letter. He was sure that
his father was alarmed as to his own condition, or
he would not have thought of sending for the lawyer
to Trafford. He had hitherto always been glad to
seize an opportunity of running up to London when
any matter of business had seemed to justify the
journey. Then it occurred to his son that his father
had rarely or ever spoken or written to him of his
"stepmother." In certain moods the Marquis had been
wont to call his wife either the Marchioness or Lady
Kingsbury. When in good humour he had generally
spoken of her to his son as "your mother." The
injurious though strictly legal name now given to her
was a certain index of abiding wrath. But things
must have been very bad with the Marquis at Trafford
when he had utterly discarded the services of Mr.
Greenwood,—services to which he had been used for
a time to which the memory of his son did not go
back. Hampstead of course obeyed his father's injunctions, and went down to Trafford instantly, leaving

his sister alone at Hendon Hall. He found the Marquis not in bed indeed, but confined to his own sitting-room, and to a very small bed-chamber which had been fitted up for him close to it. Mr. Greenwood had been anxious to give up his own rooms as being more spacious; but the offer had been peremptorily and almost indignantly refused. The Marquis had been unwilling to accept anything like a courtesy from Mr. Greenwood. Should he make up his mind to turn Mr. Greenwood out of the house,—and he had almost made up his mind to do so,—then he could do what he pleased with Mr. Greenwood's rooms. But he wasn't going to accept the loan of chambers in his own house as a favour from Mr. Greenwood.

Hampstead on arriving at the house saw the Marchioness for a moment before he went to his father. "I cannot tell how he is," said Lady Kingsbury, speaking in evident dudgeon. "He will hardly let me go near him. Doctor Spicer seems to think that we need not be alarmed. He shuts himself up in those gloomy rooms down-stairs. Of course it would be better for him to be off the ground floor, where he would have more light and air. But he has become so obstinate, that I do not know how to deal with him."

"He has always liked to live in the room next to Mr. Greenwood's."

"He has taken an absolute hatred to Mr. Greenwood. You had better not mention the poor old gentleman's name to him. Shut up as I am here, I have no one else to speak a word to, and for that reason, I suppose, he wishes to get rid of him. He is absolutely talking of sending the man away after having had him with him for nearly thirty years." In answer to all this Hampstead said almost nothing. He knew his step-mother, and was aware that he could do no service by telling her what he might find it to be his duty to say to his father as to Mr. Greenwood, or on any other subject. He did not hate his stepmother,—as she hated him. But he regarded her as one to whom it was quite useless to speak seriously as to the affairs of the family. He knew her to be prejudiced, ignorant, and falsely proud,—but he did not suppose her to be either wicked or cruel.

His father began almost instantly about Mr. Green-wood, so that it would have been quite impossible for him to follow Lady Kingsbury's advice on that matter had he been ever so well minded. "Of course I'm ill," he said; "I suffer so much from sickness and dyspepsia that I can eat nothing. Doctor Spicer seems to think that I should get better if I did not worry myself; but there are so many things to worry me. The conduct of that man is abominable."

"What man, sir?" asked Hampstead,—who knew, however, very well what was coming.

"That clergyman," said Lord Kingsbury, pointing in the direction of Mr. Greenwood's room.

"He does not come to you, sir, unless you send for him?"

"I haven't seen him for the last five days, and I don't care if I never see him again."

"How has he offended you, sir?"

"I gave him my express injunctions that he should not speak of your sister either to me or the Marchioness. He gave me his solemn promise, and I know very well that they are talking about her every hour of the day."

"Perhaps that is not his fault."

"Yes, it is. A man needn't talk to a woman unless he likes. It is downright impudence on his part. Your stepmother comes to me every day, and never leaves me without abusing Fanny."

"That is why I thought it better that Fanny should come to me."

"And then, when I argue with her, she always tells me what Mr. Greenwood says about it. Who cares about Mr. Greenwood? What business has Mr. Greenwood to interfere in my family? He does not know how to behave himself, and he shall go."

"He has been here a great many years, sir," said Hampstead, pleading for the old man.

"Too many," said the Marquis. "When you've had a man about you so long as that, he is sure to take liberties."

"You must provide for him, sir, if he goes."

"I have thought of that. He must have something, of course. He has had three hundred a-year for the last ten years, and has had everything found for him down to his washing and his cab fares. For five-and-twenty years he has never paid for a bed or a meal out of his own pocket. What has he done with his money? He ought to be a rich man for his degree."

"What a man does with his money is, I suppose, no concern to those who pay it. It is supposed to have been earned, and there is an end of it as far as they are concerned."

"He shall have a thousand pounds," said the Marquis.

"That would hardly be liberal. I would think twice before I dismissed him, sir."

"I have thought a dozen times."

"I would let him remain," said Hampstead, "if only because he's a comfort to Lady Kingsbury. What does it matter though he does talk of Fanny? Were he to go she would talk to somebody else who might be perhaps less fit to hear her, and he would, of course, talk to everybody."

"Why has he not obeyed me?" demanded the Marquis, angrily. "It is I who have employed him. I have been his patron, and now he turns against me." Thus the Marquis went on till his strength would not suffice for any further talking. Hampstead found himself quite unable to bring him to any other subject on that day. He was sore with the injury done him in that he was not allowed to be the master in his own house.

On the next morning Hampstead heard from Dr. Spicer that his father was in a state of health very

far from satisfactory. The doctor recommended that
he should be taken away from Trafford, and at last
wont so far as to say that his advice extended to
separating his patient from Lady Kingsbury. " It is,
of course, a very disagreeable subject," said the doctor,
"for a medical man to meddle with; but, my lord,
the truth is that Lady Kingsbury frets him. I don't,
of course, care to hear what it is, but there is something
wrong." Lord Hampstead, who knew very well what
it was, did not attempt to contradict him. When,
however, he spoke to his father of the expediency of
change of air, the Marquis told him that he would rather
die at Trafford than elsewhere.

That his father was really thinking of his death
was only too apparent from all that was said and
done. As to those matters of business, they were soon
settled between them. There was, at any rate, that
comfort to the poor man that there was no probability
of any difference between him and his heir as to the
property or as to money. Half-an-hour settled all
that. Then came the time which had been arranged
for Hampstead's return to his sister. But before he
went there were conversations between him and Mr.
Greenwood, between him and his stepmother, and
between him and his father, to which, for the sake of
our story, it may be as well to refer.

"I think your father is ill-treating me," said Mr.
Greenwood. Mr. Greenwood had allowed himself to
be talked into a thorough contempt and dislike for

the young lord ; so that he had almost brought himself
to believe in those predictions as to the young lord's
death in which Lady Kingsbury was always indulging.
As a consequence of this, he now spoke in a voice
very different from those obsequious tones which he
had before been accustomed to use when he had
regarded Lord Hampstead as his young patron.

"I am sure my father would never do that," said
Hampstead, angrily.

"It looks very like it. I have devoted all the best
of my life to his service, and he now talks of dismissing
me as though I were no better than a servant."

"Whatever he does, he will, I am sure, have adequate
cause for doing."

"I have done nothing but my duty. It is out of
the question that a man in my position should submit
to orders as to what he is to talk about and what not.
It is natural that Lady Kingsbury should come to me
in her troubles."

"If you will take my advice," said Lord Hampstead,
in that tone of voice which always produces in the
mind of the listener a determination that the special
advice offered shall not be taken, "you will comply
with my father's wishes while it suits you to live in
his house. If you cannot do that, it would become
you, I think, to leave it." In every word of this there
was a rebuke ; and Mr. Greenwood, who did not like
being rebuked, remembered it.

"Of course I am nobody in this house now," said

the Marchioness in her last interview with her stepson.
It is of no use to argue with an angry woman, and in
answer to this Hampstead made some gentle murmur
which was intended neither to assent or to dispute the
proposition made to him. "Because I ventured to
disapprove of Mr. Roden as a husband for your sister
I have been shut up here, and not allowed to speak to
any one."

"Fanny has left the house, so that she may no longer
cause you annoyance by her presence."

"She has left the house in order that she may
be near the abominable lover with whom you have
furnished her."

"This is not true," said Hampstead, who was moved
beyond his control by the double falseness of the
accusation.

"Of course you can be insolent to me, and tell
me that I speak falsehoods. It is part of your new
creed that you should be neither respectful to a parent,
nor civil to a lady."

"I beg your pardon, Lady Kingsbury,"—he had
never called her Lady Kingsbury before,—"if I have
been disrespectful or uncivil, but your statements were
very hard to bear. Fanny's engagement with Mr.
Roden has not even received my sanction. Much less
was it arranged or encouraged by me. She has not
gone to Hendon Hall to be near Mr. Roden, with whom
she had undertaken to hold no communication as long
as she remains there with me. Both for my own sake

and for hers I am bound to repudiate the accusation."
Then he went without further adieu, leaving with her
a conviction that she had been treated with the greatest
contumely by her husband's rebellious heir.

Nothing could be sadder than the last words which
the Marquis spoke to his son. "I don't suppose,
Hampstead, that we shall ever meet again in this
world."

"Oh, father!"

"I don't think Mr. Spicer knows how bad I am."

"Will you have Sir James down from London?"

"No Sir James can do me any good, I fear. It is
ill ministering to a mind diseased."

"Why, sir, should you have a mind diseased? With
few men can things be said to be more prosperous than
with you. Surely this affair of Fanny's is not of such
a nature as to make you feel that all things are bitter
round you."

"It is not that."

"What then? I hope I have not been a cause of
grief to you?"

"No, my boy;—no. It irks me sometimes to think
that I should have trained you to ideas which you have
taken up too violently. But it is not that."

"My mother——?"

"She has set her heart against me,—against you and
Fanny. I feel that a division has been made between
my two families. Why should my daughter be expelled
from my own house? Why should I not be able to

have you here, except as an enemy in the camp? Why am I to have that man take up arms against me, whom I have fed in idleness all his life?"

"I would not let him trouble my thoughts."

"When you are old and weak you will find it hard to banish thoughts that trouble you. As to going, where am I to go to?"

"Come to Hendon."

"And leave her here with him, so that all the world shall say that I am running away from my own wife? Hendon is your house now, and this is mine;—and here I must stay till my time has come."

This was very sad, not as indicating the state of his father's health, as to which he was more disposed to take the doctor's opinion than that of the patient but as showing the infirmity of his father's mind. He had been aware of a certain weakness in his father's character,—a desire not so much for ruling as for seeming to rule all that were around him. The Marquis had wished to be thought a despot even when he had delighted in submitting himself to the stronger mind of his first wife. Now he felt the chains that were imposed upon him, so that they galled him when he could not throw them off. All this was very sad to Hampstead; but it did not make him think that his father's health had in truth been seriously affected.

VOLUME II

MARION FAY.

CHAPTER I.

THE IRREPRESSIBLE CROCKER.

HAMPSTEAD remained nearly a fortnight down at
Trafford, returning to Hendon only a few days before
Christmas. Crocker, the Post Office clerk, came back
to his duties at the same time, but, as was the custom
with him, stole a day more than belonged to him, and
thus incurred the frowns of Mr. Jerringham and the
heavy wrath of the great Æolus. The Æoluses of the
Civil Service are necessarily much exercised in their
minds by such irregularities. To them personally it
matters not at all whether one or another young man
may be neglectful. It may be known to such a one
that a Crocker may be missed from his seat without
any great injury,—possibly with no injury at all,—to
the Queen's service. There are Crockers whom it
would be better to pay for their absence than their

presence. This Æolus thought it was so with this
Crocker. Then why not dismiss Crocker, and thus
save the waste of public money? But there is a
necessity,—almost a necessity,—that the Crockers of
the world should live. They have mothers, or perhaps
even wives, with backs to be clothed and stomachs to
be fed, or perhaps with hearts to be broken. There is,
at any rate, a dislike to proceed to the ultimate resort
of what may be called the capital punishment of the
Civil Service. To threaten, to frown, to scold, to make
a young man's life a burden to him, are all within the
compass of an official Æolus. You would think occasionally that such a one was resolved to turn half the
clerks in his office out into the streets,—so loud are the
threats. In regard to individuals he often is resolved
to do so at the very next fault. But when the time
comes his heart misgives him. Even an Æolus is
subject to mercy, and at last his conscience becomes
so callous to his first imperative duty of protecting the
public service, that it grows to be a settled thing with
him, that though a man's life is to be made a burden
to him, the man is not to be actually dismissed. But
there are men to whom you cannot make their life a
burden,—men upon whom no frowns, no scoldings, no
threats operate at all; and men unfortunately sharp
enough to perceive what is that ultimate decision to
which their Æolus had been brought. Such a one was
our Crocker, who cared very little for the blusterings.
On this occasion he had remained away for the sake of

THE IRREPRESSIBLE CROCKER.

having an additional day with the Braeside Harriers, and when he pleaded a bilious headache no one believed him for an instant. It was in vain for Æolus to tell him that a man subject to health so precarious was altogether unfitted for the Civil Service. Crocker had known beforehand exactly what was going to be said to him, and had discounted it at its exact worth. Even in the presence of Mr. Jerningham he spoke openly of the day's hunting, knowing that Mr. Jerningham would prefer his own ease to the trouble of renewed complaint. "If you would sit at your desk now that you have come back, and go on with your docketing, instead of making everybody else idle, it would be a great deal better," said Mr. Jerningham.

"Then my horse took the wall in a fly, and old Amblethwaite crept over afterwards," continued Crocker, standing with his back to the fire, utterly disregarding Mr. Jerningham's admonitions.

On his first entrance into the room Crocker had shaken hands with Mr. Jerningham, then with Bobbin and Geraghty, and at last he came to Roden, with whom he would willingly have struck up terms of affectionate friendship had it been possible for him to do so. He had resolved that it should be so, but when the moment came his courage a little failed him. He had made himself very offensive to Roden at their last interview, and could see at a glance that Roden remembered it. As far as his own feelings were concerned such "tiffs," as he called them, went for nothing. He

had, indeed, no feelings, and was accustomed to say
that he liked the system of give and take,—meaning
that he liked being impudent to others, and did not
care how impudent others might be to him. This
toughness and insolence are as sharp as needles to
others who do not possess the same gifts. Roden had
learned to detest the presence of the young man, to
be sore when he was even spoken to, and yet did not
know how to put him down. You may have a fierce
bull shut up. You may muzzle a dog that will bite.
You may shoot a horse that you cannot cure of biting
and tearing. But you cannot bring yourself to spend a
morning in hunting a bug or killing a flea. Crocker
had made himself a serious annoyance even to Lord
Hampstead, though their presence together had only
been for a very short time. But Roden had to pass his
life at the same desk with the odious companion.
Absolutely to cut him, to let it be known all through
the office that they two did not speak, was to make too
much of the matter. But yet it was essentially necessary for his peace that some step should be taken to
save himself from the man's insolence. On the present
occasion he nodded his head to Crocker, being careful
not to lay the pen down from his fingers. "Ain't you
going to give us your hand, old fellow?" said Crocker,
putting on his best show of courage.

"I don't know that I am," said Roden. "Perhaps
some of these days you may learn to make yourself less
disagreeable."

"I'm sure I've always meant to be very friendly, especially with you," said Crocker; "but it is so hard to get what one says taken in the proper sense."

After this not a word was spoken between the two all the morning. This happened on a Saturday,—Saturday, the 20th of December, on which day Hampstead was to return to his own house. Punctually at one Crocker left his desk, and with a comic bow of mock courtesy to Mr. Jerningham, stuck his hat on the side of his head, and left the office. His mind, as he took himself home to his lodgings, was full of Roden's demeanour towards him. Since he had become assured that his brother clerk was engaged to marry Lady Frances Trafford, he was quite determined to cultivate an enduring and affectionate friendship. But what steps should he take to recover the ground which he had lost? It occurred to him now that while he was in Cumberland he had established quite an intimacy with Lord Hampstead, and he thought that it would be well to use Lord Hampstead's acknowledged good-nature for recovering the ground which he had lost with his brother clerk.

*　　　*　　　*　　　*　　　*　　　*

At about three o'clock that afternoon, when Lady Frances was beginning to think that the time of her brother's arrival was near at hand, the servant came into the drawing-room, and told her that a gentleman had called, and was desirous of seeing her. "What gentleman?" asked Lady Frances. "Has he sent his name?"

"No, my lady; but he says,—he says that he is a clerk from the Post Office." Lady Frances was at the moment so dismayed that she did not know what answer to give. There could be but one Post Office clerk who should be anxious to see her, and she had felt from the tone of the servant's voice that he had known that it was her lover who had called. Everybody knew that the Post Office clerk was her lover. Some immediate answer was necessary. She quite understood the pledge that her brother had made on her behalf; and, though she had not herself made any actual promise, she felt that she was bound not to receive George Roden. But yet she could not bring herself to turn him away from the door, and so to let the servant suppose that she was ashamed to see him to whom she had given the promise of her hand. "You had better show the gentleman in," she said at last, with a voice that almost trembled. A moment afterwards the door was opened, and Mr. Crocker entered the room!

She had endeavoured in the minute which had been allowed her to study the manner in which she should receive her lover. As she heard the approaching footsteps, she prepared herself. She had just risen from her seat, nearly risen, when the strange man appeared. It has to be acknowledged that she was grievously disappointed, although she had told herself that Roden ought not to have come to her. What woman is there will not forgive her lover for coming, even though he certainly should not have come? What woman is there will fail to receive a stranger with hard looks when a stranger shall appear to her instead of an expected lover? "Sir?" she said, standing as he walked up the room and made a low bow to her as he took his position before her.

Crocker was dressed up to the eyes, and wore yellow kid gloves. "Lady Frances," he said, "I am Mr. Crocker, Mr. Samuel Crocker, of the General Post Office. You may not perhaps have heard of me from my friend, Mr. Roden?"

"No, indeed, sir."

"You might have done so, as we sit in the same room and at the same desk. Or you may remember meeting me at dinner at your uncle's castle in Cumberland."

"Is anything, — anything the matter with Mr. Roden?"

"Not in the least, my lady. I had the pleasure of leaving him in very good health about two hours since. There is nothing at all to occasion your ladyship the slightest uneasiness." A dark frown came across her brow as she heard the man talk thus freely of her interest in George Roden's condition. She no doubt had betrayed her own secret as far as there was a secret; but she was not on that account the less angry because he had forced her to do so.

"Has Mr. Roden sent you as a messenger?" she asked.

"No, my lady; no. That would not be at all probable. I am sure he would very much rather come with any message of his own." At this he sniggered most offensively. "I called with a hope of seeing your brother, Lord Hampstead, with whom I may take the liberty of saying that I have a slight acquaintance."

"Lord Hampstead is not at home."

"So the servant told me. Then it occurred to me that as I had come all the way down from London for a certain purpose, to ask a little favour from his lordship, and as I was not fortunate enough to find his lordship at home, I might ask the same from your ladyship."

"There can be nothing that I can do for you, sir."

"You can do it, my lady, much better than any one else in the world. You can be more powerful in this matter even than his lordship."

"What can it be?" asked Lady Frances.

"If your ladyship will allow me I will sit down, as the story I have to tell is somewhat particular." It was impossible to refuse him the use of a chair, and she could therefore only bow as he seated himself. "I and George Roden, my lady, have known each other intimately for these ever so many years." Again she bowed her head. "And I may say that we used to be quite pals. When two men sit at the same desk together they ought to be thick as thieves. See what a cat and dog life it is else! Don't you think so, my lady?"

"I know nothing of office life. As I don't think that

I can help you, perhaps you wouldn't mind — going
away ? "

" Oh, my lady, you must hear me to the end, because
you are just the person who can help me. Of course
as you two are situated he would do anything you were
to bid him. Now he has taken it into his head to be
very huffy with me."

" Indeed I can do nothing in the matter," she said, in
a tone of deep distress.

" If you would only just tell him that I have never
meant to offend him ! I am sure I don't know what it
is that has come up. It may be that I said a word in
joke about Lord Hampstead, only that there really
could not have been anything in that. Nobody could
have a more profound respect for his lordship's qualities
than I have, and I may say the same for your ladyship
most sincerely. I have always thought it a great
feather in Roden's cap that he should be so closely
connected,—more than closely, I may say,—with your
noble family."

What on earth was she to do with a man who would
go on talking to her, making at every moment insolent
allusions to the most cherished secret of her heart !
" I must beg you to go away and leave me, sir," she
said. " My brother will be here almost immediately."

This had escaped from her with a vain idea that the
man would receive it as a threat,—that he would think
probably that her brother would turn him out of the
house for his insolence. In this she was altogether

mistaken. He had no idea that he was insolent.
"Then perhaps you will allow me to wait for his
lordship," he said.

"Oh dear, no! He may come or he may not.
You really cannot wait. You ought not to have come
at all."

"But for the sake of peace, my lady! One word
from your fair lips——." Lady Frances could endure
it no longer. She got up from her seat and walked
out of the room, leaving Mr. Crocker planted in his
chair. In the hall she found one of the servants, whom
she told to "take that man to the front door at once."
The servant did as he was bid, and Crocker was ushered
out of the house without any feeling on his part that
he had misbehaved himself.

Crocker had hardly got beyond the grounds when
Hampstead did in truth return. The first words spoken
between him and his sister of course referred to their
father's health. "He is unhappy rather than ill," said
Hampstead.

"Is it about me?" she asked.

"No; not at all about you in the first instance."

"What does that mean?"

"It is not because of you; but from what others say
about you."

"Mamma?" she asked.

"Yes; and Mr. Greenwood."

"Does he interfere?"

"I am afraid he does;—not directly with my father,

but through her ladyship, who daily tells my father
what the stupid old man says. Lady Kingsbury is
most irrational and harassing. I have always thought
her to be silly, but now I cannot keep myself from
feeling that she misbehaves herself grievously. She
does everything she can to add to his annoyance."

"That is very bad."

"It is bad. He can turn Mr. Greenwood out of the
house if Mr. Greenwood becomes unbearable. But he
cannot turn his wife out."

"Could he not come here?"

"I am afraid not,—without bringing her too. She
has taken it into her stupid head that you and I are
disgracing the family. As for me, she seems to think
that I am actually robbing her own boys of their
rights. I would do anything for them, or even for her,
if I could comfort her; but she is determined to look
upon us as enemies. My father says that it will worry
him into his grave."

"Poor papa!"

"We can run away, but he can not. I became very
angry when I was there, both with her ladyship and
that pestilential old clergyman, and told them both
pretty much what I thought. I have the comfort
of knowing that I have two bitter enemies in the
house."

"Can they hurt you?"

"Not in the least,—except in this, that they can
teach those little boys to regard me as an enemy. I

would fain have had my brothers left to me. Mr. Greenwood, and I must now say her ladyship also, are nothing to me."

It was not till after dinner that the story was told about Crocker. " Think what I must have felt when I was told that a clerk from the Post Office wanted to see me ! "

" And then that brute Crocker was shown in ? " asked Hampstead.

" Do you really know him ? "

" Know him ! I should rather think so. Don't you remember him at Castle Hautboy ? "

" Not in the least. But he told me that he had been there."

" He never would leave me. He absolutely drove me out of the country because he would follow me about when we were hunting. He insulted me so grievously that I had to turn tail and run away from him. What did he want of me ? "

" To intercede for him with George Roden."

" He is an abominable man, irrepressible, so thick-skinned that you cannot possibly get at him so as to hurt him. It is of no use telling him to keep his distance, for he does not in the least know what you mean. I do not doubt that he has left the house with a conviction that he has gained a sincere friend in you."

*   *   *   *   *   *

It was now more than a fortnight since Marion Fay had dined at Hendon, and Hampstead felt that unless he could succeed in carrying on the attack which he had commenced, any little beginning of a friendship which he had made with the Quaker would be obliterated by the length of time. If she thought about him at all, she must think that he was very indifferent to let so long a time pass by without any struggle on his part to see her again. There had been no word of love spoken. He had been sure of that. But still there had been something of affectionate intercourse which she could not have failed to recognize. What must she think of him if he allowed that to pass away without any renewal, without an attempt at carrying it further? When she had bade him go in out of the cold there had been something in her voice which had made him feel that she was in truth anxious for him. Now more than a fortnight had gone, and there had been no renewal! "Fanny," he said, "how would it be if we were to ask those Quakers to dine here on Christmas Day?"

"It would be odd, wouldn't it, as they are strangers, and dined here so lately?"

"People like that do not stand on ceremony at all. I don't see why they shouldn't come. I could say that you want to make their acquaintance."

"Would you ask them alone?"

In that he felt that the great difficulty lay. The Fays would hardly come without Mrs. Roden, and the Rodens could not be asked. "One doesn't always ask the same people to meet each other."

"It would be very odd, and I don't think they'd come," said Lady Frances, gravely. Then after a pause she went on. "I fear, John, that there is more in it than mere dinner company."

"Certainly there is," he said boldly;—"much more in it."

"You are not in love with the Quaker's daughter?"

"I rather think I am. When I have seen her three or four times more, I shall be able to find out. You may be sure of this, that I mean to see her three or four times more, and at any rate one of the times must be before I go down to Gorse Hall." Then of course she knew the whole truth. He did, however, give up the idea as to the Christmas dinner-party, having arrived at the belief, after turning the matter over in his mind, that Zachary Fay would not bring his daughter again so soon.

CHAPTER II.

MRS. RODEN'S ELOQUENCE.

ON Sunday Hampstead was nervous and fidgety. He had at one time thought that it would be the very day for him to go to Holloway. He would be sure to find Mrs. Roden at home after church, and then, if he could carry things to the necessary length, he might also see Zachary Fay. But on consideration it appeared to him that Sunday would not suit his purpose. George Roden would be there, and would be sadly in the way. And the Quaker himself would be in the way, as it would be necessary that he should have some preliminary interview with Marion before anything could be serviceably said to her father. He was driven, therefore, to postpone his visit. Nor would Monday do, as he knew enough of the manners of Paradise Row to be aware that on Monday Mrs. Vincent would certainly be there. It would be his object, if things could be made to go pleasantly, first to see Mrs. Roden for a few minutes, and then to spend as much of the afternoon as might be possible with Marion Fay. He therefore fixed on the Tuesday for his purpose, and having

telegraphed about the country for his horses, groom,
and other appurtenances, he went down to Leighton
on the Monday, and consoled himself with a day's
hunting with the staghounds.

On his return his sister spoke to him very seriously
as to her own affairs. "Is not this almost silly, John,
about Mr. Roden not coming here ?"

"Not silly at all, according to my ideas."

"All the world knows that we are engaged. The
very servants have heard of it. That horrid young
man who came from the Post Office was aware of
it."

"What has all that to do with it ?"

"If it has been made public in that way, what can
be the object of keeping us apart ? Mamma no doubt
told her sister, and Lady Persiflage has published it
everywhere. Her daughter is going to marry a duke,
and it has crowned her triumph to let it be known that
I am going to marry only a Post Office clerk. I don't
begrudge her that in the least. But as they have
talked about it so much, they ought, at any rate, to let
me have my Post Office clerk."

"I have nothing to say about it one way or the
other," said Hampstead. "I say nothing about it, at
any rate now."

"What do you mean by that, John ?"

"When I saw how miserable you were at Trafford I
did my best to bring you away. But I could only
bring you here on an express stipulation that you

should not meet George Roden while you were in my house. If you can get my father's consent to your meeting him, then that part of the contract will be over."

" I don't think I made any promise."

" I understand it so."

" I said nothing to papa on the subject,—and I do not remember that I made any promise to you. I am sure I did not."

" I promised for you." To this she was silent. " Are you going to ask him to come here ?"

" Certainly not. But if he did come, how could I refuse to see him ? I thought that he was here on Saturday, and I told Richard to admit him. I could not send him away from the door."

" I do not think he will come unless he is asked," said Hampstead. Then the conversation was over.

On the following day, at two o'clock, Lord Hampstead again started for Holloway. On this occasion he drove over, and left his trap and servant at the "Duchess of Edinburgh." He was so well known in the neighbourhood now as hardly to be able to hope to enter on the domains of Paradise Row without being recognized. He felt that it was hard that his motions should be watched, telling himself that it was one of the evils belonging to an hereditary nobility; but he must accept this mischief as he did others, and he walked up the street trying to look as though he didn't know that his

motions were being watched first from Number Fifteen
as he passed it, and then from Number Ten opposite, as
he stood at Mrs. Roden's door.

Mrs. Roden was at home, and received him, of course,
with her most gracious smile; but her heart sank
within her as she saw him, for she felt sure that he had
come in pursuit of Marion Fay. "It is very kind of
you to call," she said. "I had heard from George that
you had gone down into the country since we had the
pleasure of dining with you."

"Yes; my father has been unwell, and I had to stay
with him a few days or I should have been here sooner.
You got home all of you quite well?"

"Oh, yes."

"Miss Fay did not catch cold?"

"Not at all;—though I fear she is hardly strong."

"She is not ill, I hope?"

"Oh, no; not that. But she lives here very quietly,
and I doubt whether the excitement of going out is
good for her."

"There was not much excitement at Hendon Hall, I
think," he said, laughing.

"Not for you, but for her perhaps. In appreciating
our own condition we are so apt to forget what is the
condition of others! To Marion Fay it was a strange
event to have to dine at your house,—and strange also
to receive little courtesies such as yours. It is hard
for you to conceive how strongly the nature of such
a girl may be effected by novelties. I have almost

regretted, Lord Hampstead, that I should have consented to take her there."

"Has she said anything?"

"Oh, no; there was nothing for her to say. You are not to suppose that any harm has been done."

"What harm could have been done?" he asked. Of what nature was the harm of which Mrs. Roden was speaking? Could it be that Marion had made any sign of altered feelings; had declared in any way her liking or disliking; had given outward testimony of thoughts which would have been pleasant to him,—or perhaps unpleasant,—had he known them?

"No harm, of course," said Mrs. Roden;—"only to a nature such as hers all excitement is evil."

"I cannot believe that," he said, after a pause. "Now and then in the lives of all of us there must come moments of excitement which cannot be all evil. What would Marion say if I were to tell her that I loved her?"

"I hope you will not do that, my lord."

"Why should you hope so? What right have you to hope so? If I do love her, is it not proper that I should tell her?"

"But it would not be proper that you should love her."

"There, Mrs. Roden, I take the liberty of declaring that you are altogether in the wrong, and that you speak without due consideration."

"Do I, my lord?"

" I think so. Why am I not to be allowed the
ordinary privilege of a man,—that of declaring my
passion to a woman when I meet one who seems in all
things to fulfil the image of perfection which I have
formed for myself,—when I see a girl that I fancy
I can love ? "

" Ah, there is the worst ! It is only a fancy."

" I will not be accused in that way without defending
myself. Let it be fancy or what not, I love Marion
Fay, and I have come here to tell her so. If I can
make any impression on her I shall come again and
tell her father so. I am here now because I think that
you can help me. If you will not, I shall go on without
your help."

" What can I do ? "

" Go to her with me now, at once. You say that
excitement is bad for her. The excitement will be
less if you will come with me to her house."

Then there was a long pause in the conversation,
during which Mrs. Roden was endeavouring to determine what might be her duty at this moment. She
certainly did not think that it would be well that Lord
Hampstead, the eldest son of the Marquis of Kingsbury
should marry Marion Fay. She was quite sure that
she had all the world with her there. Were any one
to know that she had assisted in arranging such a
marriage, that any one would certainly condemn her.
That would assuredly be the case, not only with the
young lord's family, not only with others of the young

lord's order, but with all the educated world of Great
Britain. How could it be that such a one as Marion
Fay should be a fitting wife for such a one as Lord
Hampstead ? Marion Fay had undoubtedly great gifts
of her own. She was beautiful, intelligent, sweet-
minded, and possessed of natural delicacy,—so much
so that to Mrs. Roden herself she had become as dear
almost as a daughter; but it was impossible that she
should have either the education or the manners fit for
the wife of a great English peer. Though her manners
might be good and her education excellent, they were
not those required for that special position. And then
there was cause for other fears. Marion's mother and
brothers and sisters had all died young. The girl
herself had hitherto seemed to escape the scourge
under which they perished. But occasionally there
would rise to her cheeks a bright colour, which for the
moment would cause Mrs. Roden's heart to sink within
her. Occasionally there would be heard from her not
a cough, but that little preparation for coughing which
has become so painfully familiar to the ears of those
whose fate it has been to see their beloved ones gradually fade from presumed health. She had already
found herself constrained to say a word or two to the
old Quaker, not telling him that she feared any coming
evil, but hinting that change of air would certainly be
beneficial to such a one as Marion. Acting under this
impulse, he had taken her during the inclemency of the
past spring to the Isle of Wight. She was minded

gradually to go on with this counsel, so as if possible
to induce the father to send his girl out of London
for some considerable portion of the year. If this
were so, how could she possibly encourage Lord
Hampstead in his desire to make Marion his wife ?

And then, as to the girl herself, could it be for her
happiness that she should be thus lifted into a strange
world, a world that would be hard and ungracious to
her, and in which it might be only too probable that
the young lord should see her defects when it would be
too late for either of them to remedy the evil that had
been done ? She had thought something of all this
before, having recognized the possibility of such a step
as this after what she had seen at Hendon Hall. She
had told herself that it would be well at any rate to
discourage any such idea in Marion's heart, and had
spoken jokingly of the gallantry of men of rank.
Marion had smiled sweetly as she had listened to her
friend's words, and had at once said that such manners
were at any rate pretty and becoming in one so placed
as Lord Hampstead. There had been something in
this to make Mrs. Roden almost fear that her words
had been taken as intending too much,—that Marion
had accepted them as a caution against danger. Not
for worlds would she have induced the girl to think
that any danger was apprehended. But now the danger
had come, and it behoved Mrs. Roden if possible to
prevent the evil. "Will you come across with me
now ? " said Hampstead, having sat silent in his chair

while these thoughts were passing through the lady's mind.

"I think not, my lord."

"Why not, Mrs. Roden? Will it not be better than that I should go alone?"

"I hope you will not go at all."

"I shall go,—certainly. I consider myself bound by all laws of honesty to tell her what she has done to me. She can then judge what may be best for herself."

"Do not go at any rate to-day, Lord Hampstead. Let me beg at least as much as that of you. Consider the importance of the step you will be taking."

"I have thought of it," said he.

"Marion is as good as gold."

"I know she is."

"Marion, I say, is as good as gold; but is it likely that any girl should remain untouched and undazzled by such an offer as you can make her?"

"Touched I hope she may be. As for dazzled,—I do not believe in it in the least. There are eyes which no false lights can dazzle."

"But if she were touched, as would no doubt be the case," said Mrs. Roden, "could it be well that you with such duties before you should marry the daughter of Zachary Fay? Listen to me a moment," she continued, as he attempted to interrupt her. "I know what you would say, and I sympathize with much of it; but it cannot be well for society that classes should be mixed together suddenly and roughly."

"What roughness would there be?" he asked.

"As lords and ladies are at present, as dukes are, and duchesses, and such like, there would be a roughness to them in having Marion Fay presented to them as one of themselves. Lords have married low-born girls, I know, and the wives have been contented with a position which has almost been denied to them, or only grudgingly accorded. I have known something of that, my lord, and have felt—at any rate I have seen —its bitterness. Marion Fay would fade and sink to nothing if she were subjected to such contumely. To be Marion Fay is enough for her. To be your wife, and not to be thought fit to be your wife, would not be half enough."

"She shall be thought fit."

"You can make her Lady Hampstead, and demand that she shall be received at Court. You can deck her with diamonds, and cause her to be seated high in honour according to your own rank. But could you induce your father's wife to smile on her?" In answer to this he was dumb. "Do you think she would be contented if your father's wife were to frown on her?"

"My father's wife is not everybody."

"She would necessarily be much to your wife. Take a week, my lord, or a month, and think upon it. She expects nothing from you yet, and it is still in your power to save her from unhappiness."

"I would make her happy, Mrs. Roden."

"Think about it;—think about it."

"And I would make myself happy also. You count my feelings as being nothing in the matter."

"Nothing as compared with hers. You see how plainly I deal with you. Let me say that for a time your heart will be sore;—that you do in truth love this girl so as to feel that she is necessary to your happiness. Do you not know that if she were placed beyond your reach you would recover from that sting? The duties of the world would still be open to you. Being a man, you would still have before you many years for recovery before your youth had departed from you. Of course you would find some other woman, and be happy with her. For her, if she came to shipwreck in this venture, there would be no other chance."

"I would make this chance enough for her."

"So you think; but if you will look abroad you will see that the perils to her happiness which I have attempted to describe are not vain. I can say no more, my lord, but can only beg that you will take some little time to think of it before you put the thing out of your own reach. If she had once accepted your love I know that you would never go back."

"Never."

"Therefore think again while there is time." He slowly dragged himself up from his chair, and left her almost without a word at parting. She had persuaded him—to take another week. It was not that he doubted in the least his own purpose, but he did not know how to gainsay her as to this small request. In that frame

of mind which is common to young men when they do
not get all that they want, angry, disappointed, and
foiled, he went down-stairs, and opened the front door,—
and there on the very steps he met Marion Fay.

"Marion," he said, pouring all the tenderness of his
heart into his voice.

"My lord?"

"Come in, Marion,—for one moment." Then she
followed him into the little passage, and there they
stood. "I had come over to ask you how you are
after our little party."

"I am quite well;—and you?"

"I have been away with my father, or I should have
come sooner."

"Nay;—it was not necessary that you should trouble
yourself."

"It is necessary;—it is necessary; or I should be
troubled very much. I am troubled." She stood there
looking down on the ground as though she were biding
her time, but she did not speak to him. "She would
not come with me," he said, pointing up the stairs on
which Mrs. Roden was now standing. "She has told
me that it is bad that I should come; but I will come
one day soon." He was almost beside himself with
love as he was speaking. The girl was so completely
after his own heart as he stood there close to her, filled
with her influences, that he was unable to restrain
himself.

"Come up, Marion dear," said Mrs. Roden, speaking

from the landing. "It is hardly fair to keep Lord Hampstead standing in the passage."

"It is most unfair," said Marion. "Good day, my lord."

"I will stand here till you come down to me, unless you will speak to me again. I will not be turned out while you are here. Marion; you are all the world to me. I love you with my whole, whole heart. I had come here, dear, to tell you so;—but she has delayed me. She made me promise that I would not come again for a week, as though weeks or years could change me? Say one word to me, Marion. One word shall suffice now, and then I will go. Marion, can you love me?"

"Come to me, Marion, come to me," said Mrs. Roden. "Do not answer him now."

"No," said Marion, looking up, and laying her hand gently on the sleeve of his coat. "I will not answer him now. It is too sudden. I must think of words to answer such a speech. Lord Hampstead, I will go to her now."

"But I shall hear from you."

"You shall come to me again, and I will tell you."

"To-morrow?"

"Nay; but give me a day or two. On Friday I will be ready with my answer."

"You will give me your hand, Marion." She gave it to him, and he covered it with kisses. "Only have this in your mind, fixed as fate, that no man ever loved a woman more truly than I love you. No man was ever more determined to carry out his purpose. I am in your hands. Think if you cannot dare to trust yourself into mine." Then he left her, and went back to the "Duchess of Edinburgh," not thinking much of the eyes which might be looking at him.

CHAPTER III.

MARION'S VIEWS ABOUT MARRIAGE.

WHEN Lord Hampstead shut the door behind him, Marion went slowly up the stairs to Mrs. Roden, who had returned to her drawing-room. When she entered, her friend was standing near the door, with anxiety plainly written on her face,—with almost more than anxiety. She took Marion by the hand and, kissing her, led her to the sofa. "I would have stopped him if I could," she said.

"Why should you have stopped him?"

"Such things should be considered more."

"He had made it too late for considering to be of service. I knew, I almost knew, that he would come."

"You did?"

"I can tell myself now that I did, though I could not say it even to myself before." There was a smile on her face as she spoke, and, though her colour was heightened, there was none of that peculiar flush which Mrs. Roden so greatly feared to see. Nor was there any special excitement in her manner. There was no look either of awe or of triumph. She seemed to take it as a matter of course, quite as much at least as any Lady Amaldina could have done, who might have been justified by her position in expecting that some young noble eldest son would fling himself at her feet.

"And are you ready with your answer?" Marion turned her eyes towards her friend, but made no immediate reply. "My darling girl,—for you in truth are very dear to me,—much thought should be given to such an appeal as that before any answer is made."

"I have thought."

"And are you ready?"

"I think so. Dear Mrs. Roden, do not look at me like that. If I do not say more to tell you immediately it is because I am not perhaps quite sure;—not sure, at any rate, of the reasons I may have to give. I will come to you to-morrow, and then I will tell you."

There was room then at any rate for hope! If the girl had not quite resolved to grasp at the high destiny offered to her, it was still her friend's duty to say something that might influence her.

"Marion, dear!"

"Say all that you think, Mrs. Roden. Surely you know that I know that whatever may come from you will come in love. I have no mother, and to whom can I go better than to you to fill a mother's place?"

"Dear Marion, it is thus I feel towards you. What I would say to you I would say to my own child. There are great differences in the ranks of men."

"I have felt that."

"And though I do in my honest belief think that the best and honestest of God's creatures are not always to be found among so-called nobles, yet I think that a certain great respect should be paid to those whom chance has raised to high places."

"Do I not respect him?"

"I hope so. But perhaps you may not show it best by loving him."

"As to that, it is a matter in which one can, perhaps, hardly control oneself. If asked for love it will come from you like water from a fountain. Unless it be so, then it cannot come at all."

"That surely is a dangerous doctrine for a young woman."

"Young women, I think, are compassed by many dangers," said Marion; "and I know but one way of meeting them."

"What way is that, dear?"

"I will tell you, if I can find how to tell it, to-morrow."

"There is one point, Marion, on which I feel myself bound to warn you, as I endeavoured also to warn him. To him my words seemed to have availed nothing; but you, I think, are more reasonable. Unequal marriages never make happy either the one side or the other."

"I hope I may do nothing to make him unhappy."

"Unhappy for a moment you must make him;—for a month, perhaps, or for a year; though it were for years, what would that be to his whole life?"

"For years?" said Marion. "No, not for years. Would it be more than for days, do you think?"

"I cannot tell what may be the nature of the young man's heart;—nor can you. But as to that, it cannot be your duty to take much thought. Of his lasting welfare you are bound to think."

"Oh, yes; of that certainly;— of that above all things."

"I mean as to this world. Of what may come afterwards to one so little known we here can hardly dare to speak,—or even to think. But a girl, when she has been asked to marry a man, is bound to think of his welfare in this life."

"I cannot but think of his eternal welfare also," said Marion.

"Unequal marriages are always unhappy," said Mrs. Roden, repeating her great argument.

"Always?"

"I fear so. Could you be happy if his great friends, his father, and his stepmother, and all those high-born lords and ladies who are connected with him,—could you be happy if they frowned on you?"

"What would their frowns be to me? If he smiled I should be happy. If the world were light and bright to him, it would certainly be light and bright to me."

"I thought so once, Marion. I argued with myself once just as you are arguing now."

"Nay, Mrs. Roden, I am hardly arguing."

"It was just so that I spoke to myself, saying that the joy which I took in a man's love would certainly be enough for my happiness. But oh, alas! I fell to the ground. I will tell you now more of myself than I have told any one for many a year, more even than I have told George. I will tell you because I know that I can trust your faith."

"Yes; you can trust me," said Marion.

"I also married greatly; greatly, as the world's honours are concerned. In mere rank I stood as a girl higher perhaps than you do now. But I was lifted out of my own degree, and in accepting the name which my husband gave me I assured myself that I would do honour to it, at any rate by my conduct. I did it no dishonour;—but my marriage was most unfortunate."

"Was he good?" asked Marion.

"He was weak. Are you sure that Lord Hampstead is strong? He was fickle-hearted. Can you be sure that Lord Hampstead will be constant amidst the charms of others whose manners will be more like his own than yours can be?"

"I think he would be constant," said Marion.

"Because you are ready to worship him who has condescended to step down from his high pedestal and worship you. Is it not so?"

"It may be that it is so," said Marion.

"Ah, yes, my child. It may be that it is so. And then, think of what may follow,—not only for him, but for you also; not only for you, but for him also. Broken hearts, crushed ambitions, hopes all dead, personal dislikes, and perhaps hatred."

" Not hatred; not hatred."

"I lived to be hated;—and why not another?" Then she was silent, and Marion rising from her seat kissed her, and went away to her home.

She had very much to think of. Though she had declared that she had almost expected this offer from her lover, still it could not be that the Quaker girl, the daughter of Zachary Fay, Messrs. Poyson and Littlebird's clerk, should not be astounded by having such an offer from such a suitor as Lord Hampstead. But in truth the glory of the thing was not very much to her. It was something, no doubt. It must be something to a girl to find that her own personal charms have sufficed to lure down from his lofty perch the topmost bird of them all. That Marion was open to some such weakness may be acknowledged of her. But of the coronet, of the diamonds, of the lofty title, and high seats, of the castle, and the parks, and well-arranged equipages, of the rich dresses, of the obsequious servants, and fawning world that would be gathered around her, it may be said that she thought not at all. She had in her short life seen one man who had pleased her ear and her eye, and had touched her heart; and that one man had instantly declared himself to be all her own. That made her bosom glow with some feeling of triumph!

That same evening she abruptly told the whole story to her father. "Father," she said, "Lord Hampstead was here to-day."

"Here, in this house?"

"Not in this house. But I met him at our friend's, whom I went to see, as is my custom almost daily."

"I am glad he came not here," said the Quaker.

"Why should you be glad?" To this the Quaker made no answer.

"His purpose was to have come here. It was to see me that he came."

"To see thee?"

"Father, the young lord has asked me to be his wife."

"Asked thee to be his wife!"

"Yes, indeed. Have you not often heard that young men may be infatuated? It has chanced that I have been the Cinderella for his eyes."

"But thou art no princess, child."

"And, therefore, am unfit to mate with this prince. I could not answer him at once, father. It was too sudden for me to find the words. And the place was hardly fitting. But I have found them now."

"What words, my child?"

"I will tell him with all respect and deference,— nay, I will tell him with some love, for I do love him, —that it will become him to look for his wife elsewhere."

"Marion," said the Quaker, who was somewhat

D 2

moved by those things which had altogether failed
with the girl herself; "Marion, must it be so?"

"Father, it must certainly be so."

"And yet thou lovest him?"

"Though I were dying for his love it must be so."

"Why, my child, why? As far as I saw the young
man he is good and gracious, of great promise, and like
to be true-hearted."

"Good, and gracious, and true-hearted! Oh, yes!
And would you have it that I should bring such a one
as that to sorrow,—perhaps to disgrace?"

"Why to sorrow? Why to disgrace? Wouldst
thou be more likely to disgrace a husband than one
of those painted Jezebels who know no worship but
that of their faded beauty? Thou hast not answered
him, Marion?"

"No, father. He is to come on Friday for my
answer."

"Think of it yet again, my child. Three days are no
time for considering a matter of such moment. Bid
him leave you for ten days further."

"I am ready now," said Marion.

"And yet thou lovest him! That is not true to
nature, Marion. I would not bid thee take a man's
hand because he is rich and great if thou couldst not
give him thy heart in return. I would not have thee
break any law of God or man for the glitter of gold
or tinsel of rank. But the good things of this world,
if they be come by honestly, are good. And the love

of an honest man, if thou lovest him thyself in return, is not of the less worth because he stands high in wealth and in honour."

"Shall I think nothing of him, father?"

"Yea, verily; it will be thy duty to think of him, almost exclusively of him,—when thou shalt be his wife."

"Then, father, shall I never think of him."

"Wilt thou pay no heed to my words, so as to crave from him further time for thought?"

"Not a moment. Father, you must not be angry with your child for this. My own feelings tell me true. My own heart, and my own heart alone, can dictate to me what I shall say to him. There are reasons——"

"What reasons?"

"There are reasons why my mother's daughter should not marry this man." Then there came a cloud across his brow, and he looked at her as though almost over-come by his anger. It seemed as though he strove to speak; but he sat for a while in silence. Then rising from his chair he left the room, and did not see her again that night.

This was on a Tuesday, on the Wednesday he did not speak to her on the subject. The Thursday was Christmas Day, and she went to church with Mrs. Roden. Nor did he on that day allude to the matter; but on the evening she made to him a little request. "To-morrow, father, is a holiday, is it not, in the City?"

"So they tell me. I hate such tom-fooleries. When

I was young a man might be allowed to earn his bread
on all lawful days of the week. Now he is expected to
spend the wages he cannot earn in drinking and shows."

"Father, you must leave me here alone after our
dinner. He will come for his answer."

"And you will give it?"

"Certainly, father, certainly. Do not question me
further, for it must be as I told you." Then he left
her as he had done before; but he did not urge her
with any repetition of his request.

This was what occurred between Marion and her
father; but on the Wednesday she had gone to Mrs.
Roden as she had promised, and there explained her
purpose more fully than she had before been able to do.
"I have come, you see," she said, smiling. "I might
have told you all at once, for I have changed nothing
of my mind since first he spoke to me all so suddenly
in the passage down-stairs."

"Are you so sure of yourself?"

"Quite sure;—quite sure. Do you think I would
hurt him?"

"No, no. You would not, I know, do so willingly."

"And yet I must hurt him a little. I hope it will
hurt him just a little." Mrs. Roden stared at her.
"Oh, if I could make him understand it all! If I
could bid him be a man, so that it should wound him
only for a short time."

"What wound!"

"Did you think that I could take him, I, the daughter

of a City clerk, to go and sit in his halls, and shame him before all the world, because he had thought fit to make me his wife? Never!"

"Marion, Marion!"

"Because he has made a mistake which has honoured me, shall I mistake also, so as to dishonour him? Because he has not seen the distance, shall I be blind to it? He would have given himself up for me. Shall I not be able to make a sacrifice? To such a one as I am to sacrifice myself is all that I can do in the world."

"Is it such a sacrifice?"

"Could it be that I should not love him? When such a one comes, casting his pearls about, throwing sweet odours through the air, whispering words which are soft-sounding as music in the heavens, whispering them to me, casting them at me, turning on me the laughing glances of his young eyes, how could I help to love him? Do you remember when for a moment he knelt almost at my feet, and told me that I was his friend, and spoke to me of his hearth? Did you think that that did not move me?"

"So soon, my child;—so soon?"

"In a moment. Is it not so that it is done always?"

"Hearts are harder than that, Marion."

"Mine, I think, was so soft just then that the half of his sweet things would have ravished it from my bosom. But I feel for myself that there are two parts in me. Though the one can melt away, and pass altogether from my control, can gush like water that runs out and cannot be checked, the other has something in it of hard substance which can stand against blows, even from him."

"What is that something, Marion?"

"Nay, I cannot name it. I think it be another heart, of finer substance, or it may be it is woman's pride, which will suffer all things rather than hurt the one it loves. I know myself. No words from him,— no desire to see his joy, as he would be joyful, if I told him that I could give him all he asks,—no longing for all his love could do for me, shall move me one tittle. He shall tell himself to his dying day that the Quaker girl, because she loved him, was true to his interests."

"My child;—my child!" said Mrs. Roden, taking Marion in her arms.

"Do you think that I do not know,—that I have forgotten? Was it nothing to me to see my—mother die, and her little ones? Do I not know that I am not, as others are, free to wed, not a lord like that, but even one of my own standing? Mrs. Roden, if I can live till my poor father shall have gone before me, so that he may not be left alone when the weakness of age shall have come upon him,—then,—then I shall be satisfied to follow them. No dream of loving had ever crossed my mind. He has come, and without my mind, the dream has been dreamed. I think that my lot will be happier so, than if I had passed away without any feeling such as that I have now. Perhaps he will not marry till I am gone."

"Would that hurt you so sorely?"

"It ought not. It shall not. It will be well that he should marry, and I will not wish to cause him evil. He will have gone away, and I shall hardly know of it. Perhaps they will not tell me." Mrs. Roden could only embrace her, sobbing, wiping her eyes with piteousness. "But I will not begrudge aught of the sacrifice," she continued. "There is nothing, I think, sweeter than to deny oneself all things for love. What are our lessons for but to teach us that? Shall I not do unto him as it would be well for me that some such girl should do for my sake if I were such as he?"

"Oh, Marion, you have got the better part."

"And yet,—and yet——. I would that he should feel a little because he cannot have the toy that has pleased his eye. What was it that he saw in me, do you think?" As she asked the question she cheered up wonderfully.

"The beauty of your brow and eyes,—the softness of your woman's voice."

"Nay, but I think it was my Quaker dress. His eye, perhaps, likes things all of a colour. I had, too, new gloves and a new frock when he saw me. How well I remember his coming,—how he would glance round at me till I hardly knew whether I was glad that he should observe me so much, — or offended at his persistence. I think that I was glad, though I told myself that he should not have glanced at me so often. And then, when he asked us to go down to his house I

did long,—I did long,—to win father's consent to the
journey.   Had he not gone——"

"Do not think of it, Marion."

"That I will not promise;—but I will not talk of it.
Now, dear Mrs. Roden, let all then be as though it had
never been.   I do not mean to mope, or to neglect my
work, because a young lord has crossed my path and
told me that he loves me.   I must send him from me,
and then I will be just as I have been always."   Having made this promise she went away, leaving Mrs.
Roden much more flurried by the interview than was
she herself.   When the Friday came, holiday as it was,
the Quaker took himself off to the City after dinner,
without another word as to his daughter's lover.

CHAPTER IV.

LORD HAMPSTEAD IS IMPATIENT.

HAMPSTEAD, when he was sent away from Paradise Row, and bade to wait till Friday for an answer, was disappointed, almost cross, and unreasonable in his feelings towards Mrs. Roden. To Mrs. Roden altogether he attributed it that Marion had deferred her reply. Whether the delay thus enjoined told well or ill for his hopes he could not bring himself to determine. As he drove himself home his mind was swayed now in one direction and now in the other. Unless she loved him somewhat, unless she thought it possible that she should love him, she would hardly have asked for time to think of it all. And yet, had she really have loved him, why should she have asked for time ? He had done for her all that a man could do for a girl, and if she loved him she should not have tormented him by foolish delays, —by coying her love !

It should be said on his behalf that he attributed to himself no preponderance of excellence, either on the score of his money or his rank. He was able so to honour the girl as to think of her that such things

would go for nothing with her. It was not that he had
put his coronet at her feet, but his heart. It was of
that he thought when he reminded himself of all that
he had done for her, and told himself angrily that she
should not have tormented him. He was as arrogant
and impatient of disappointment as any young lord of
them all,—but it was not, however, because he was a
lord that he thought that Marion's heart was due
to him.

"I have been over to Holloway," he said to his sister,
almost as soon as he had returned.

Out of the full heart the mouth speaks. "Have you
seen George?" asked Lady Frances.

"No; I did not go to see him. He, of course, would
be at his office during the day. I went about my own
business."

"You need not be so savage with me, John. What
was your own business at Holloway?"

"I went to ask Marion Fay to be my wife."

"You did?"

"Yes; I did. Why should I not? It seems the
fashion for us all now to marry just those we fancy
best."

"And why not? Have I gainsaid you? If this
Quaker's daughter be good and honest, and fair to
look at——"

"That she is fair to look at I can say certainly.
That she is good I believe thoroughly. That she is
honest, at any rate to me, I cannot say as yet."

" Not honest ? "

"She will not steal or pick a pocket, if you mean that."

" What is it, John ? Why do you speak of her in this way ? "

" Because I have chosen to tell you. Having made up my mind to do this thing, I would not keep it secret as though I were ashamed of it. How can I say that she is honest till she has answered me honestly ? "

" What answer has she made you ? " she asked.

" None ;—as yet ! She has told me to come again another day."

" I like her better for that."

" Why should you like her better ? Just because you're a woman, and think that shilly-shallying and pretending not to know your own mind, and keeping a fellow in suspense, is becoming. I am not going to change my mind about Marion ; but I do think that mock hesitation is unnecessary, and in some degree dishonest."

"Must it necessarily be mock hesitation ? Ought she not to be sure of herself that she can love you ? "

"Certainly ; or that she should not love me. I am not such a puppy as to suppose that she is to throw herself into my arms just because I ask her. But I think that she must have known something of herself so as to have been able to tell me either to hope or not to hope. She was as calm as a Minister in the House of Commons answering a question ; and she told me to wait till Friday just as those fellows do when they have to find out from the clerks in the office what it is they ought to say."

"You will go again on Friday?" she asked.

"Of course I must. It is not likely that she should come to me. And then if she says that she'd rather not, I must come home once more with my tail between my legs."

"I do not think she will say that."

"How can you tell?"

"It is the nature of a girl, I think," said Lady Frances, "to doubt a little when she thinks that she can love, but not to doubt at all when she feels that she cannot. She may be persuaded afterwards to change her mind, but at first she is certain enough."

"I call that shilly-shally."

"Not at all. The girl I'm speaking of is honest throughout. And Miss Fay will have been honest should she accept you now. It is not often that such a one as you, John, can ask a girl in vain."

"That is mean," he said, angrily. "That is imputing falseness, and greed, and dishonour to the girl I love. If she has liked some fellow clerk in her father's office better than she likes me, shall she accept me merely because I am my father's son?"

"It was not that of which I was thinking. A man may have personal gifts which will certainly prevail with a girl young and unsullied by the world, as I suppose is your Marion Fay."

"Bosh," he said, laughing. "As far as personal gifts are concerned, one fellow is pretty nearly the same as another. A girl has to be good-looking. A man has got to have something to buy bread and cheese with. After that it is all a mere matter of liking and disliking —unless, indeed, people are dishonest, which they very often are."

Up to this period of his life Lord Hampstead had never met any girl whom he had thought it desirable to make his wife. It was now two years since the present Marchioness had endeavoured to arrange an alliance between him and her own niece, Lady Amaldina Haute ville. This, though but two years had passed since, seemed to him to have occurred at a distant period of his life. Very much had occurred to him during those two years. His political creed had been strengthened by the convictions of others, especially by those of George Roden, till it had included those advanced opinions which have been described. He had annoyed, and then dismayed, his father by his continued refusal to go into Parliament. He had taken to himself ways of living of his own, which gave to him the manners and appearance of more advanced age. At that period, two years since, his stepmother still conceived high hopes of him, even though he would occasionally utter in her presence opinions which seemed to be terrible. He was then not of age, and there would be time enough for a woman of her tact and intellect to cure all those follies. The best way of curing them, she

thought, would be by arranging a marriage between the
heir to the Marquisate and the daughter of so distinguished a conservative Peer as her brother-in-law, Lord
Persiflage. Having this high object in view, she opened
the matter with diplomatic caution to her sister. Lady
Persiflage had at that moment begun to regard Lord
Llwddythlw as a possible son-in-law, but was alive
to the fact that Lord Hampstead possessed some
superior advantages. It was possible that her girl
should really love such a one as Lord Hampstead,—
hardly possible that there should be anything romantic
in a marriage with the heir of the Duke of Merioneth.
As far as wealth and rank went there was enough in
both competitors. She whispered therefore to her girl
the name of the younger aspirant,—aspirant as he
might be hoped to be,—and the girl was not opposed
to the idea. Only let there be no falling to the ground
between two stools; no starving for want of fodder
between two bundles of hay! Lord Llwddythlw had
already begun to give symptoms. No doubt he was
bald ; no doubt he was pre-occupied with Parliament
and the county. There was no doubt that his wife
would have to encounter that touch of ridicule which a
young girl incurs when she marries a man altogether
removed beyond the world of romance. But dukes are
scarce, and the man of business was known to be a man
of high honour. There would be no gambling, no
difficulties, no possible question of a want of money.
And then his politics were the grandest known in

England,—those of an old Tory willing always to work
for his party without desiring any of those rewards
which the "party" wishes to divide among as select a
number as possible. What Lord Hampstead might
turn out to be, there was as yet no knowing. He
had already declared himself to be a Radical. He was
fond of hunting, and it was quite on the cards that he
should take to Newmarket. Then, too, his father might
live for five-and-twenty years, whereas the Duke of
Merioneth was already nearly eighty. But Hampstead
was as beautiful as a young Phœbus, and the pair would
instantly become famous if only from their good looks
alone. The chance was given to Lady Amaldina, but
only given on the understanding that she must make
very quick work of her time.

Hampstead was coaxed down to Castle Hautboy for a
month in September, with an idea that the young
lovers might be as romantic as they pleased among the
Lakes. Some little romance there was; but at the end
of the first week Amaldina wisely told her mother that
the thing wouldn't do. She would always be glad to
regard Lord Hampstead as a cousin, but as to anything
else, there must be an end of it. "I shall some day
give up my title and abandon the property to Freddy.
I shall then go to the United States, and do the best
I can there to earn my own bread." This little speech,
made by the proposed lover to the girl he was expected
to marry, opened Lady Amaldina's eyes to the danger
of her situation. Lord Llwddythlw was induced to

spend two days in the following month at Castle
Hautboy, and then the arrangements for the Welsh
alliance were completed.

From that time forth a feeling of ill-will on the part
of Lady Kingsbury towards her stepson had grown and
become strong from month to month. She had not at
first conceived any idea that her Lord Frederic ought
to come to the throne. That had come gradually when
she perceived, or thought that she perceived, that
Hampstead would hardly make a marriage properly
aristocratic. Hitherto no tidings of any proposed
marriage had reached her ears. She lived at last it
daily fear, as any marriage would be the almost sure
forerunner of a little Lord Highgate. If something
might happen,—something which she had taught herself to regard as beneficent and fitting rather than fatal
—something which might ensure to her little Lord
Frederic those prospects which he had almost a right
to expect, then in spite of all her sufferings Heaven
would have done something for her for which she might
be thankful. " What will her ladyship say when she
hears of my maid Marion ? " said Hampstead to her
sister on the Christmas Day before his further visit
to Holloway.

" Will it matter much ? " asked Lady Frances.

" I think my feelings towards her are softer than
yours. She is silly, arrogant, harsh, and insolent to my
father, and altogether unprincipled in her expectations
and ambitions."

"What a character you give her," said his sister.

"But nevertheless I feel for her to such an extent that I almost think I ought to abolish myself."

"I cannot say that I feel for her."

"It is all for her son that she wants it; and I agree with her in thinking that Freddy will be better fitted than I am for the position in question. I am determined to marry Marion if I can get her; but all the Traffords, unless it be yourself, will be broken-hearted at such a marriage. If once I have a son of my own the matter will be hopeless. If I were to call myself Snooks, and refused to take a shilling from the property, I should do them no good. Marion's boy would be just as much in their way as I am."

"What a way of looking at it."

"How my stepmother will hate her! A Quaker's daughter! A clerk at Pogson and Littlebird's! Living at Paradise Row! Can't you see her! Is it not hard upon her that we should both go to Paradise Row?" Lady Frances could not keep herself from laughing. "You can't do her any permanent injury, because you are only a girl; but I think she will poison me. It will end in her getting Mr. Greenwood to give me some broth."

"John, you are too terrible."

"If I could be on the jury afterwards, I would certainly acquit them both on the ground of extreme provocation."

Early on the following morning he was in a fidget,

having fixed no hour for his visit to Holloway. It was
not likely that she should be out or engaged, but he
determined not to go till after lunch. All employment
was out of the question, and he was rather a trouble to
his sister; but in the course of the morning there came
a letter which did for a while occupy his thoughts. The
envelope was addressed in a hand he did not know, and
was absurdly addressed to the

"RIGHT HONOURABLE,

"THE LORD HAMPSTEAD."

"I wonder who this ass is," said he, tearing it open.
The ass was Samuel Crocker, and the letter was as
follows;—

" Heathcote Street,
" Mecklenburg Square,
" Christmas Day, 18—.

"MY DEAR LORD HAMPSTEAD,

          "I hope I may be excused for addressing your
lordship in this familiar manner. I take occasion of
this happy day to write to your lordship on a message
of peace. Since I had the honour of meeting you at
your noble uncle's mansion, Castle Hautboy, I have
considered it one of the greatest delights of my life
to be able to boast of your acquaintance. You will not,
I am sure, forget that we have been fellow sportsmen,
and that we rode together on that celebrated run
when we killed our fox in the field just over Airey
Force. I shall never forget the occasion, or how
well your lordship went over our rough country. To

my mind there is no bond of union so strong as that of sport.

'Up strikes little Davy with his musical horn.'

" I am sure you will remember that, my lord, and the beautiful song to which it belongs. I remember, too, how, as we were riding home after the run, your lordsh'p was talking all the way about our mutual friend, George Roden.

" He is a man for whom I have a most sincere regard, both as being an excellent public servant, and as a friend of your lordship's. It is quite a pleasure to see the way in which he devotes himself to the service,—as I do also. When you have taken the Queen's shilling you ought to earn it. Those are my principles, my lord. We have a couple of young fellows there whose only object it is to get through the day and eat their lunches. I always tell them that official hours ain't their own. I suppose they'll understand me some day.

" But as I was saying to your lordship about George Roden, there has something come up which I don't quite understand, which seems to have turned him against me. Nothing has ever given me so much pleasure as when I heard of his prospects as to a certain matter—which your lordship will know what I mean. Nothing could be more flattering than the way I've wished him joy ever so many times. So I do also your lordship and her ladyship, because he is a most respectable young man, though his station in life isn't so high as some people's. But a clerk in H. M. S. has always been taken for a gentleman which I am proud to think is my position as well as his.

"But, as I was saying to your lordship, something seems to have gone against him as to our mutual friendship. He sits there opposite and won't speak a word to me, except just to answer a question, and that hardly civil. He is as sweet as sugar to those fellows who ain't at the same desk with him as I am,—or I should think it was his future prospects were making him upsetting. Couldn't your lordship do something to make things up between us again,—especially on this festive occasion? I'm sure your lordship will remember how pleasant we were together at Castle Hautboy, and at the hunt, and especially as we were riding home together on that day. I did take the liberty of calling at Hendon Hall, when her ladyship was kind enough to see me. Of course there was a delicacy in speaking to her ladyship about Mr. Roden, which nobody could understand better than I do; but I think she made me something of a promise that she would say a word when a proper time might come.

"It could only have been a joke of mine; and I do joke sometimes, as your lordship may have observed. But I shouldn't think Roden would be the man to be mortally offended by anything of that sort. Anyway, I will leave the matter in your lordship's hands, merely remarking that,—as your lordship may remember,—

'Blessed are the peace-makers, for theirs is the King-dom of Heaven.'

> "I have the honour to be,
> "My dear Lord Hampstead,
> "Your lordship's most obedient,
> "Very humble servant,
> "SAMUEL CROCKER."

Fretful and impatient as he was on that morning, it was impossible for Hampstead not to laugh at this letter. He showed it to his sister, who, in spite of her annoyance, was constrained to laugh also. "I shall tell George to take him to his bosom at once," said he.

"Why should George be bothered with him?"

"Because George can't help himself. They sit at the same desk together, as Crocker has not forgotten to tell me a dozen times. When a man perseveres in this way, and is thick-skinned enough to bear all rebuffs, there is nothing he will not accomplish. I have no doubt he will be riding my horses in Leicestershire before the season is over." An answer, however, was written to him in the following words ;—

> "DEAR MR. CROCKER,
> "I am afraid I cannot interfere with Mr. Roden, who doesn't like to be dictated to in such matters.
> "Yours truly,
> "HAMPSTEAD."

"There," said he; "I do not think he can take that letter as a mark of friendship."

In this way the morning was passed till the time came for the start to Holloway. Lady Frances, standing at the hall door as he got into his trap, saw that the fashion of his face was unusually serious.

CHAPTER V.

THE QUAKER'S ELOQUENCE.

WHEN the Friday morning came in Paradise Row
both father and daughter, at No. 17, were full of thought
as they came down to breakfast. To each of them it
was a day laden with importance. The father's mind
had been full of the matter ever since the news had
been told to him. He had received Marion's positive
assurance that such a marriage was altogether impossible with something of impatience till she had used
that argument as to her own health, which was so
powerful with her. On hearing that he had said
nothing, but had gone away. Nor had he spoken a
word on the subject since. But his mind had been
full of it. He had lost his wife,—and all his little
ones, as she had said; but he had declared to himself
with strong confidence that this child was to be spared
to him. He was a man whose confidence was un-
bounded in things as to which he had resolved. It
was as though he had determined, in spite of Fate, in
spite of God, that his Marion should live. And she
had grown up under his eyes, if not robust, by no

means a weak creature. She did her work about the
house, and never complained. In his eyes she was
very beautiful; but he saw nothing in her colour
which was not to him a sign of health. He told
himself that it was nothing that she, having seen so
many die in her own family, should condemn herself;
but for himself he repudiated the idea, and declared
to himself that she should not become an early victim.
So thinking, he exercised his mind constantly during
those few days in considering whether there was any
adequate cause for the refusal which Marion had
determined to give this man.

He, in truth, was terribly anxious that this grand
stroke of fortune should be acknowledged and accepted.
He wanted nothing from the young lord himself,—
except, perhaps, that he might be the young lord's
father-in-law. But he did want it all, long for it all,
pant for it all, on behalf of his girl. If all these good
things came in his girl's way because of her beauty,
her grace, and her merit, why should they not be
accepted? Others not only accepted these things for
their daughters, but hunted for them, cheated for them,
did all mean things in searching for them,—and had
their tricks and their lies regarded by the world quite
as a matter of course,—because it was natural that parents
should be anxious for their children. He had not
hunted. He had not cheated. The thing had come
in his girl's way. The man had found her to be the
most lovely, the most attractive, the most loveable

among all whom he had seen. And was this glory to
be thrown away because she had filled her mind with
false fears? Though she were to die, must not the
man take his chance with her, as do other husbands
in marrying other wives?

He had been thinking of this, and of nothing but
this, during the days which had intervened since Lord
Hampstead had been in Paradise Row. He had not
said a word to his daughter,—had indeed not dared to
say a word to her, so abhorrent to him was the idea of
discussing with her the probabilities of her own living
or dying. And he was doubtful, too, whether any
words coming from him at the present might not
strengthen her in her resolution. If the man really
loved her he might prevail. His words would be
stronger to overcome her than any that could be spoken
by her father. And then, too, if he really loved her,
the one repulse would not send him back for ever. It
might, perhaps, be better that any arguments from her
father should be postponed till she should have heard
her lover's arguments. But his mind was so filled with
the whole matter that he could not bring himself to
assure himself certainly that his decision was the best.
Though he was one who rarely needed counsel from
others, on this occasion he did need it, and now it was
his purpose to ask counsel of Mrs. Roden before the
moment should have come which might be fatal to
his hopes.

As this was the day immediately following Christmas,

there was no business for him in the City. In order
that the weary holiday might be quicker consumed,
they breakfasted at No. 17 an hour later than was
usual. After breakfast he got through the morning as
well as he could with his newspaper, and some record
of stocks and prices which he had brought with him
from the City. So he remained, fretful, doing nothing,
pretending to read, but with his mind fixed upon the
one subject, till it was twelve o'clock, at which hour he
had determined to make his visit. At half-past one
they were to dine, each of them having calculated,
without, however, a word having been spoken, that
Lord Hampstead would certainly not come till the
ceremony of dinner would be over. Though the matter
was so vitally important to both of them, not a word
concerning it was spoken.

At twelve o'clock he took up his hat, and walked
out. "You will be back punctually for dinner, father?"
she asked. He made his promise simply by nodding
his head, and then left the room. Five minutes afterwards he was closeted with Mrs. Roden in her drawing-
room. Having conceived the difficulty of leading up
to the subject gradually, he broke into it at once.
"Marion has told thee that this young man will be
here to-day?" She simply assented. "Hast thou
advised her as to what she should say?"

"She has not seemed to want advice."

"How should a girl not want advice in so great a
matter?"

"How, indeed? But yet she has needed none."

"Has she told thee," he asked, "what it is in her mind to do?"

"I think so."

"Has she said that she would refuse the man?"

"Yes; that certainly was her purpose."

"And given the reasons?" he said, almost trembling as he asked the question.

"Yes, she gave her reasons."

"And didst thou agree with her?" Before she could reply to this Mrs. Roden felt herself compelled to pause. When she thought of that one strongest reason, fully as she agreed with it, she was unable to tell the father of the girl that she did so. She sat looking at him, wanting words with which she might express her full concurrence with Marion without plunging a dagger into the other's heart. "Then thou didst agree with her?" There was something terrible in the intensity and slowness of the words as he repeated the question.

"On the whole I did," she said. "I think that unequal marriages are rarely happy."

"That was all?" he asked. Then when she was again silent, he made the demand which was so important to him. "Did she say aught of her health in discussing all this with thee?"

"She did, Mr. Fay."

"And thou?"

"It was a subject, my friend, on which I could not speak to her. All that was said came from her. Her mind was so fully made up, as I have said before, no advice from me could avàil anything. With some people it is easy to see that whether you agree with them or differ from them it is impossible to turn them."

" But to me thou canst say whether thou hast agreed with her. Yes; I know well that the subject is one difficult to talk of in a father's hearing. But there are things which should be talked of, though the heart should break." After another pause he continued; "Is there, thinkest thou, sufficient cause in the girl's health to bid her sever herself from these delights of life and customary habits which the Lord has intended for His creatures?" At every separate question he paused, but when she was silent he went on with other questions. "Is there that in her looks, is there that in her present condition of life, which make it needful for thee, her friend, or for me, her father, to treat her as though she were already condemned by the hand of the Lord to an early grave?" Then, again, looking almost fiercely into her face, he went on with his examination, " That is what thou art doing."

" Not I ;—not I."

" Yes, thou, my friend ; thou, with all thy woman's softness in thy heart! It is what I shall do, unless I bring myself to tell her that her fears are vain. To me she has said that that is her reason. It is not that she cannot love the man. Has she not said as much to thee?"

" Yes; truly."

"And art thou not assenting to it unless thou tell'st her that her fancies are not only vain, but wrong? Though thou hast not spoken the word, has not thy silence assented as fully as words could do? Answer me at any rate to that."

"It is so," she said.

"Is it then necessary to condemn her? Art thou justified in thine own thoughts in bidding her regard herself as one doomed?" Again there was a pause. What was she to say? "Thou art aware that in our poor household she does all that the strictest economy would demand from an active mother of a family? She is never idle. If she suffers I do not see it. She takes her food, if not with strong appetite, yet regularly. She is upright, and walks with no languor. No doctor comes near her. If like others she requires change of air and scene, what can give her such chance as this marriage? Hast thou not heard that for girls of feeble health marriage itself will strengthen them? Is she such that thou as her friend must bid her know that she must perish like a blighted flower? Must I bid her to hem and stitch her own winding-sheet? It comes to that if no word be said to her to turn her from this belief. She has seen them all die,—one after another, — one after another, till the idea of death, of death for herself as well as for them, has gotten hold of her. And yet it will be the case that one in a family shall escape. I have asked among those who know, and I have found that it is so. The Lord does

not strike them all, always.   But if she thinks that she
is stricken then she will fall.   If she goes forth to meet
Death on the path, Death will come half way to
encounter her.   Dost thou believe of me that it
is because the man is a noble lord that I desire this
marriage ? "

"Oh no, Mr. Fay."

"He will take my child away from me.   She will
then be but little to me.   What want I with lords, who
for the few days of active life that are left to me would
not change my City stool for any seat that any lord can
give me ?   But I shall know that she has had her
chance in the world, and has not been unnecessarily
doomed—to an early grave ! "

"What would you have me do ? "

" Go to her, and tell her that she should look forward,
with trust in God, to such a state of health as· He may
vouchsafe to give her.   Her thoughts are mostly with
her God.   Bid her not shorten His mercies.   Bid her
not to tell herself that she can examine His purposes.
Bid her do in this as her nature bids her, and, if she
can love this man, give herself into his arms and leave
the rest to the Lord."

"But he will be there at once."

"If he be there, what harm ?   Thou canst go when
he comes to the door.   I shall go to her now, and we
shall dine together, and then at once I will leave her.
When you see me pass the window then thou canst
take thine occasion."   So saying, without waiting

for a promise, he left her and went back to his own house.

And Marion's heart had been full of many thoughts that morning,—some of them so trifling in their object, that she herself would wonder at herself because that they should occupy her. How should she be dressed to receive her lover ? In what words first should she speak to him,—and in what sort ? Should she let any sign of love escape from her ? Her resolution as to her great purpose was so fixed that there was no need for further thought on that matter. It was on the little things that she was intent. How far might she indulge herself in allowing some tenderness to escape her ? How best might she save him from any great pain, and yet show him that she was proud that he had loved her ? In what dress she might receive him, in that would she sit at table with her father. It was Christmas time, and the occasion would justify whatever of feminine smartness her wardrobe possessed. As she brought out from its recess the rich silk frock, still all but new, in which he had first seen her, she told herself that she would probably have worn it for her father's sake, had no lover been coming. On the day before, the Christmas Day, she had worn it at church. And the shoes with the pretty buckles, and the sober but yet handsome morsel of lace which was made for her throat,—and which she had not been ashamed to wear at that memorable dinner,—they were all brought out. It was Christmas, and her father's presence would

surely have justified them all! And would she not
wish to leave in her lover's eyes the memory of whatever prettiness she might have possessed? They were
all produced. But when the moment came for arraying
herself they were all restored to their homes. She
would be the simple Quaker girl as she was to be found
there on Monday, on Tuesday, and on Wednesday. It
would be better that he should know how little there
was for him to lose.

Zachary Fay ate his dinner almost without a word.
She, though she smiled on him and tried to look
contented, found it almost impossible to speak. She
uttered some little phrases which she intended to be
peculiar to the period of the year; but she felt that
her father's mind was intent on what was coming, and
she discontinued her efforts. She found it hardly
possible to guess at the frame of his mind, so silent had
he been since first he had yielded to her when she
assured him of her purpose. But she had assured him,
and he could not doubt her purpose. If he were
unhappy for the moment it was needful that he should
be unhappy. There could be no change, and therefore
it was well that he should be silent. He had hardly
swallowed his dinner when he rose from his chair, and,
bringing in his hat from the passage, spoke a word to
her before he departed. "I am going into the City,
Marion," he said. "I know it is well that I should be
absent this afternoon. I shall return to tea. God bless
thee, my child."

Marion, rising from her chair, kissed his lips and cheeks, and accompanied him to the door. "It will be all well, my father," she said;. "it will be all well, and your child will be happy."

About half-an-hour afterwards there came a knock at the door, and Marion for a moment thought that her lover was already there. But it was Mrs. Roden who came up to her in the drawing-room. "Am I in the way, Marion?" she asked. "I will be gone in a minute; but perhaps I can say a word first."

"Why should you be in the way?"

"He is coming."

"Yes, I suppose so. He said that he would come. But what if he come? You and he are old friends."

"I would not be here to interrupt him. I will escape when we hear the knock. Oh, Marion!"

"What is it, Mrs. Roden? You are sad, and something troubles you?"

"Yes, indeed. There is something which troubles me sorely. This lover of yours?"

"It is fixed, dear friend; fixed as fate. It does not trouble me. It shall not trouble me. Why should it be a trouble? Suppose I had never seen him!"

"But you have seen him, my child."

"Yes, indeed; and whether that be for good or evil, either to him or to me, it must be accepted. Nothing now can alter that. But I think, indeed, that it is a blessing. It will be something to me to remember that such a one as he has loved me. And for him——"

"I would speak now of you, Marion."

" I am contented."

"It may be, Marion, that in this concerning your health you should be altogether wrong."

" How wrong ? "

"What right have you or I to say that the Lord has determined to shorten your days."

" Who has said so ? "

"It is on that theory that you are acting."

"No ;—not on that; not on that alone. Were I as strong as are other girls,—as the very strongest,—I would do the same. Has my father been with you ? "

" Yes, he has."

"My poor father ! But it is of no avail. It would be wrong, and I will not do it. If I am to die, I must die. If I am to live, let me live. I shall not die certainly because I have resolved to send this fine lover away. However weak Marion Fay may be, she is strong enough not to pine for that."

" If there be no need ? "

"No need ? What was it you said of unequal marriages ? What was the story that you told me of your own ? If I love this man, of whom am I to think the most ? Could it be possible that I should be to him what a wife ought to be to her husband ? Could I stand nobly on his hearth-rug, and make his great guests welcome ? Should I be such a one that every day he should bless the kind fortune which had given him such a woman to help him to rule his house ?

How could I go from the littleness of these chambers to walk through his halls without showing that I knew myself to be an intruder? And yet I should be so proud that I should resent the looks of all who told me by their faces that I was so. He has done wrong in allowing himself to love me. He has done wrong in yielding to his passion, and telling me of his love. I will be wiser and nobler than he. If the Lord will help me, if my Saviour will be on my side, I will not do wrong. I did not think that you, Mrs. Roden, would turn against me."

"Turn against thee, Marion? I to turn against thee!"

"You should strengthen me."

"It seems to me that you want no strength from others. It is for your poor father that I would say a word."

"I would not have father believe that my health has aught to do with it. You know,—you know what right I have to think that I am fit to marry and to hope to be the mother of children. It needs not that he should know. Let it suffice for him to be told that I am not equal to this greatness. A word escaped me in speaking to him, and I repent myself that I so spoke to him. But tell him,—and tell him truly,—that were my days fixed here for the next fifty years, were I sure of the rudest health, I would not carry my birth, my manners, my habits into that young lord's house. How long would it be, Mrs. Roden, before he saw some little trick

that would displease him? Some word would be
wrongly spoken, some garment would be ill-folded, some
awkward movement would tell the tale,—and then he
would feel that he had done wrong to marry the
Quaker's daughter. All the virtues under the sun
cannot bolster up love so as to stand the battery of one
touch of disgust. Tell my father that, and tell him
that I have done well. Then you can tell him also,
that, if God shall so choose it, I shall live a strong old
maid for many years, to think night and day of his
goodness to me,—of his great love."

Mrs. Roden, as she had come across from her own
house, had known that her mission would fail. To
persuade another against one's own belief is difficult in
any case, but to persuade Marion Fay on such a matter
as this was a task beyond the eloquence of man or
woman. She had made up her mind that she must fail
utterly when the knock came at the door. She took
the girl in her arms and kissed her without further
attempt. She would not even bid her think of it once
again, as might have been so easy at parting. "I will
go into your room while he passes," she said. As she
did so Lord Hampstead's voice was heard at the door.

CHAPTER VI.

MARION'S OBSTINACY.

LORD HAMPSTEAD drove himself very fast from Hendon Hall to the "Duchess of Edinburgh" at Holloway, and then, jumping out of his trap, left it without saying a word to his servant, and walked quickly up Paradise Row till he came to No. **17.** There, without pausing a moment, he knocked sharply at the door. Going on such a business as this, he did not care who saw him. There was an idea present to him that he would be doing honour to Marion Fay if he made it known to all the world of Holloway that he had come there to ask her to be his wife. It was this feeling which had made him declare his purpose to his sister, and which restrained him from any concealment as to his going and coming.

Marion was standing alone in the middle of the room, with her two hands clasped together, but with a smile on her face. She had considered much as to this moment, determining even the very words that she would use. The words probably were forgotten, but the purpose was all there. He had resolved upon nothing, had considered nothing,—except that she should be made to understand that, because of his exceeding love, he required her to come to him as his wife. "Marion," he said, "Marion, you know why I am here!" And he advanced to her, as though he would at once have taken her in his arms.

"Yes, my lord, I know."

"You know that I love you. I think, surely, that never love was stronger than mine. If you can love me say but the one word, and you will make me absolutely happy. To have you for my wife is all that the world can give me now. Why do you go from me? Is it to tell me that you cannot love me, Marion? Do not say that, or I think my heart will break."

She could not say that, but as he paused for her answer it was necessary that she should say something. And the first word spoken must tell the whole truth, even though it might be that the word must be repeated often before he could be got to believe that it was an earnest word. "My lord," she began.

"Oh, I do hate that form of address. My name is John. Because of certain conventional arrangements the outside people call me Lord Hampstead."

"It is because I can be to you no more than one of the outside people that I call you—my lord."

"Marion!"

"Only one of the outside people;—no more, though my gratitude to you, my appreciation, my friendship for you may be ever so strong. My father's daughter must be just one of the outside people to Lord Hampstead,—and no more."

"Why so? Why do you say it? Why do you torment me? Why do you banish me at once, and tell me that I must go home a wretched, miserable man? Why?—why?—why?

"Because, my lord——"

"I can give a reason,—a good reason,—a reason which I cannot oppose, though it must be fatal to me unless I can remove it; a reason to which I must succumb if necessary, but to which, Marion, I will not succumb at once. If you say that you cannot love me that will be a reason."

If it were necessary that she should tell him a lie, she must do so. It would have been pleasant if she could have made him understand that she would be content to love him on condition that he would be content to leave her. That she should continue to love him, and that he should cease to love her,— unless, perhaps, just a little,——that had been a scheme for the future which had recommended itself to her. There should be a something left which should give a romance to her life, but which should leave him free in all things. It had been a dream, in which she had much trusted, but which, while she listened to the violence of his words, she acknowledged to herself to be almost impossible. She must tell the lie;—but at the moment it seemed to her that there might be a middle course. "I dare not love you," she said.

"Dare not love me, Marion? Who hinders you? Who tells you that you may not? Is it your father?"

"No, my lord, no."

"It is Mrs. Roden."

"No, my lord. This is a matter in which I could obey no friend, no father. I have had to ask myself, and I have told myself that I do not dare to love above my station in live."

"I am to have that bugbear again between me and my happiness?"

"Between that and your immediate wishes;—yes. Is it not so in all things? If I,—even I,—had set my heart upon some one below me, would not you, as my friend, have bade me conquer the feeling?"

"I have set my heart on one whom in the things of the world I regard as my equal,—in all other things as infinitely my superior."

"The compliment is very sweet to me, but I have trained myself to resist sweetness. It may not be, Lord Hampstead. It may not be. You do not know as yet how obstinate such a girl as I may become when she has to think of another's welfare,—and a little, perhaps, of her own."

"Are you afraid of me?"

"Yes."

"That I should not love you?"

"Even of that. When you should come to see in me that which is not lovable you would cease to love me. You would be good to me because your nature is good; kind to me because your nature is kind. You would not ill-treat me because you are gentle, noble, and forgiving. But that would not suffice for me. I should see it in your eye, despite yourself,—and hear it in your voice, even though you tried to hide it by occasional softness. I should eat my own heart½ when I came to see that you despised your Quaker wife."

"All that is nonsense, Marion."

"My lord !"

"Say the word at once if it has to be said,—so that I may know what it is that I have to contend with· For you my heart is so full of love that it seems to be impossible that I should live without you. If there could be any sympathy I should at once be happy. If there be none, say so."

"There is none."

"No spark of sympathy in you for me,—for one who loves you so truly ?" When the question was put to her in that guise she could not quite tell so monstrous a lie as would be needed for an answer fit for her purpose. "This is a matter, Marion, in which a man has a right to demand an answer,—to demand a true answer."

"Lord Hampstead, it may be that you should perplex me sorely. It may be that you should drive me away from you, and beg you never to trouble me any further. It may be that you should force me to remain dumb before you, because that I cannot reply to you in proper words. But you will never alter my purpose. If you think well of Marion Fay, take her word when she gives it you. I can never become your lordship's wife."

" Never ? "

" Never !   Certainly never ! "

" Have you told me why ;—all the reason why ? "

" I have told you enough, Lord Hampstead."

" By heavens, no ! You have not answered me the one question that I have asked you. You have not given me the only reason which I would take,——even for a while. Can you love me, Marion ? "

" If you loved me you would spare me," she said. Then feeling that such words utterly betrayed her, she recovered herself, and went to work with what best eloquence was at her command to cheat him out of the direct answer which he required. " I think," she said, " you do not understand the workings of a girl's heart in such a matter. She does not dare to ask herself about her love, when she knows that loving would avail her nothing. For what purpose should I inquire into myself when the object of such inquiry has already been obtained ? Why should I trouble myself to know whether this thing would be a gain to me or not, when I am well aware that I can never have the gain ? "

" Marion, I think you love me." She looked at him and tried to smile, — tried to utter some half-joking word ; and then as she felt that she could no longer repress her tears, she turned her face from him, and made no attempt at a reply. " Marion," he said again, " I think that you love me."

" If you loved me, my lord, you would not torture me." She had seated herself now on the sofa, turning

her face away from him over her shoulder so that she
might in some degree hide her tears. He sat himself
at her side, and for a moment or two got possession of
her hand.

"Marion," he said, pleading his case with all the
strength of words which was at his command, "you
know, do you not, that no moment of life can be of
more importance to me than this?"

"Is it so, my lord?"

"None can be so important. I am striving to get
her for my companion in life, who to me is the sweetest
of all human beings. To touch you as I do now is a
joy to me, even though you have made my heart so
sad." At the moment she struggled to get her hand
away from him, but the struggle was not at first successful. "You answer me with arguments which are
to me of no avail at all. They are, to my thinking,
simply a repetition of prejudices to which I have been
all my life opposed. You will not be angry because I
say so?"

"Oh, no, my lord," she said; "not angry. I am not
angry, but indeed you must not hold me." With that
she extricated her hand, which he allowed to pass from
his grasp as he continued his address to her.

"As to all that, I have my opinion and you have
yours. Can it be right that you should hold to your
own and sacrifice me who have thought so much of
what it is I want myself,—if in truth you love me?
Let your opinion stand against mine, and neutralize it.

Let mine stand against yours, and in that we shall be equal. Then after that let love be lord of all. If you love me, Marion, I think that I have a right to demand that you shall be my wife."

There was something in this which she did not know how to answer;—but she did know, she was quite sure, that no word of his, no tenderness either on his part or on her own, would induce her to yield an inch. It was her duty to sacrifice herself for him,—for reasons which were quite apparent to herself,—and she would do it. The fortress of her inner purpose was safe, although he had succeeded in breaking down the bulwark by which it had been her purpose to guard it. He had claimed her love, and she had not been strong enough to deny the claim. Let the bulwark go. She was bad at lying. Let her lie as she might, he had wit enough to see through it. She would not take the trouble to deny her love should he persist in saying that it had been accorded to him. But surely she might succeed at last in making him understand that, whether she loved him or no, she would not marry him. "I certainly shall never be your wife," she said.

"And that is all?"

"What more, my lord?"

"You can let me go, and never wish me to return?"

"I can, my lord. Your return would only be a trouble to you, and a pain to me. Another time do not turn your eyes too often on a young woman because her face may chance to please you. It is well that you should marry. Go and seek a wife, with judgment, among your own people. When you have done that, then you may return and tell Marion Fay that you have done well by following her advice."

"I will come again, and again, and again, and I will tell Marion Fay that her counsels are unnatural and impossible. I will teach her to know that the man who loves her can seek no other wife;—that no other mode of living is possible to him than one in which he and Marion Fay shall be joined together. I think I shall persuade her at last that such is the case. I think she will come to know that all her cold prudence and worldly would-be wisdom can be of no avail to separate those who love each other. I think that when she finds that her lover so loves her that he cannot live without her, she will abandon those fears as to his future fickleness, and trust herself to one of whose truth she will have assured herself." Then he took her hand, and kneeling at her knee, he kissed it before she was powerful enough to withdraw it. And so he left her, without another word, and mounting on his vehicle, drove himself home without having exchanged a single word at Holloway with any one save Marion Fay.

She, when she was left alone, threw herself at full length on the sofa and burst into an ecstacy of tears. Trust herself to him! Yes, indeed. She would trust herself to him entirely, only in order that she might have the joy, for one hour, of confessing her love to him openly, let the consequences to herself afterwards be what they might ! As to that future injury to her pride of which she had spoken both to her father and also to her friend,—of which she had said so much to herself in discussing this matter with her own heart—as to that he had convinced her. It did not become her in any way to think of herself in this matter. He certainly would be able to twist her as he would if she could stand upon no surer rock than her fears for her own happiness. One kiss from him would be payment for it all. But all his love, all his sweetness, all his truth, all his eloquence should avail nothing with her towards overcoming that spirit of self-sacrifice by which she was dominated. Though he should extort from her all her secret, that would be her strength. Though she should have to tell him of her failing health,—her certainly failing health,—though even that should be necessary, she certainly would not be won from her purpose. It might be sweet, she thought, to make him in all respects her friend of friends ; to tell him everything ; to keep no fear, no doubt, no aspiration a secret from him. " Love you, oh my dearest, thou very pearl of my heart, love you indeed ! Oh, yes. Do you not know that not even for an instant could I hide my love ? Are you not aware, did you not see at the moment, that when you first knelt at my feet, my heart had flown to you without an effort on my part to arrest it ? But now, my beloved one, now we understand each other. Now there need be no reproaches between us. Now there need be no speaking of distrust. I am all yours,—only it is not fit, as you know, dearest, that the poor Quaker girl should become your wife. Now that we both understand that, why should we be sad? Why should we mourn?" Why should she not succeed in bringing things to such a pass as this; and if so, why should life be unhappy either to him or to her?

Thus she was thinking of it till she had almost brought herself to a state of bliss, when her father returned to her. "Father," she said, getting up and embracing his arm as he stood, "it is all over."

"What is over?" asked the Quaker.

"He has been here."

"Well, Marion; and what has he said?"

"What he said it is hardly for me to tell you. What I said,——I would you could know it all without my repeating a word of it."

"Has he gone away contented?"

"Nay, not that, father. I hardly expected that. I hardly hoped for that. Had he been quite contented perhaps I might not have been so."

"Why should you not have both been made happy?" asked the father.

"It may be that we shall be so. It may be that he shall understand."

"Thou hast not taken his offer then?"

"Oh, no! No, father, no. I can never accept his offer. If that be in your mind put it forth. You shall never see your Marion the wife of any man, whether of that young lord or of another more fitted to her. No

one ever shall be allowed to speak to me as he has
spoken."

"Why dost thou make thyself different from other
girls?" he said, angrily.

"Oh, father, father!"

"It is romance and false sentiment, than which
nothing is more odious to me. There is no reason why
thou shouldst be different from others. The Lord has
not marked thee out as different from other girls, either
in His pleasure or His displeasure. It is wrong for
thee to think it of thyself." She looked up piteously
into his face, but said not a word. "It is thy duty to
take thyself from His hands as He has made thee; and
to give way to no vain ecstatic terrors. If, as I gather
from thy words, this young man be dear to thee, and if,
as I gather from this second coming of his, thou art
dear to him, then I as thy father tell thee that thy
duty calls thee to him. It is not that he is a
lord."

"Oh, no, father."

"It is not, I say, that he is a lord, or that he is rich,
or that he is comely to the eyes, that I would have
thee go to him as his wife. It is because thou and he
love each other, as it is the ordinance of the Lord
Almighty that men and women should do. Marriage is
honourable, and I, thy father, would fain see thee married.
I believe the young man to be good and true. I could
give thee to him, lord though he be, with a trusting
heart, and think that in so disposing of my child I had

done well for her. Think of this, Marion, if it be not already too late." All this he had said standing, so that he was able to leave the room without the ceremony of rising from his chair. Without giving her a moment for reply, having his hand on the lock of the door as he uttered the last words of his counsel to her, he marched off, leaving her alone.

It may be doubted whether at the moment she could have found words for reply, so full was her heart with the feelings that were crowded there. But she was well aware that all her father's words could go for nothing. Of only one thing was she sure,—that no counsel, no eloquence, no love would ever induce her to become the wife of Lord Hampstead.

CHAPTER VII.

MRS. DEMIJOHN'S PARTY.

" MRS. DEMIJOHN presents her compliments to Mr.
Crocker, and begs the honour of his company to tea at
nine o'clock on Wednesday, 31st of December, to see
the New Year in.

" R.I.V.P. (Do come, C. D.)

" 10, Paradise Row, Holloway.

" 29th December, 18—."

This note was delivered to Crocker on his arrival at
his office on the morning of Saturday, the 27th.

It must be explained that Crocker had lately made
the acquaintance of Miss Clara Demijohn without any
very formal introduction.   Crocker, with that determination which marked his character, in pursuit of the one
present purport of his mind to effect a friendly reconciliation with George Roden, had taken himself down
to Holloway, and had called at No. 11, thinking that
he might induce his friend's mother to act on his behalf
in a matter appertaining to peace and charity.   Mrs.
Roden had unhappily been from home, but he had had
the good fortune to encounter Miss Demijohn.   Perhaps

it was that she had seen him going in and out of the
house, and had associated him with the great mystery
of the young nobleman; perhaps she had been simply
attracted by the easy air with which he cocked his hat
and swung his gloves;—or, perhaps it was simply
chance. But so it was that in the gloom of the evening
she met him just round the corner opposite to the
"Duchess of Edinburgh," and the happy acquaintance
was commenced. No doubt, as in all such cases, it was
the gentleman who spoke first. Let us, at any rate,
hope so for the sake of Paradise Row generally. Be that
as it may, before many minutes were over she had
explained to him that Mrs. Roden had gone out in
a cab soon after dinner, and that probably something
was up at Wimbledon, as Mrs. Roden never went anywhere else, and this was not the day of the week on
which her visits to Mrs. Vincent were generally made.
Crocker, who was simplicity itself, soon gave her various
details as to his own character and position in life. He,
too, was a clerk in the Post Office, and was George
Roden's particular friend. "Oh, yes; he knew all
about Lord Hampstead, and was, he might say, intimately acquainted with his lordship. He had been in
the habit of meeting his lordship at Castle Hautboy,
the seat of his friend, Lord Persiflage, and had often
ridden with his lordship in the hunting-field. He knew
all about Lady Frances and the engagement, and had
had the pleasure of making the acquaintance of her
ladyship. He had been corresponding lately with Lord

Hampstead on the subject. No;—he had not as yet heard anything of Marion Fay, the Quaker's daughter. Then Clara had something to say on her side. She quite understood that if she expected to be communicated with, she also must communicate; and moreover, young Mr. Crocker was by his age, appearance, and sex, just such a one as prompted her to be communicative without loss of self-respect. What was the good of telling things to Mrs. Duffer, who was only an old widow without any friends, and with very small means of existence? She had communicated her secrets to Mrs. Duffer simply from want of a better pair of ears into which she could pour them. But here was one in telling secrets to whom she could take delight, and who had secrets of his own to give in return. It is not to be supposed that the friendship which arose grew from the incidents of one meeting only. On that first evening Crocker could not leave the fair one without making arrangements for a further interview, and so the matter grew. The intimacy between them was already of three days' standing when the letter of invitation above given reached Crocker's hands. To tell the very truth, the proposed party was made up chiefly for Crocker's sake. What is the good of having a young man if you cannot show him to your friends?

"Crocker!" said Mrs. Demijohn to her niece; "where did you pick up Crocker?"

"What questions you do ask, aunt! Pick him up, indeed!"

"So you have——; picked him up, as you're always a doing with young men. Only you never know how to keep 'em when you've got 'em."

"I declare, aunt, your vulgarity is unbearable."

"I'm not going to have any Crocker in my house," said the old woman, "unless I know where he comes from. Perhaps he's a counter-skipper. He may be a ticket-of-leave man for all you know."

"Aunt Jemima, you're so provoking that I sometimes think I shall have to leave you."

"Where will you go to, my dear?"

To this question, which had often been asked before, Clara thought it unnecessary to make any answer; but returned at once to the inquiries which were not unnaturally made by the lady who stood to her in the place of a mother. "Mr. Crocker, Aunt Jemima, is a clerk in the Post Office, who sits at the same desk with George Roden, and is intimately acquainted both with Lord Hampstead and with Lady Frances Trafford. He used to be George Roden's bosom friend; but there has lately been some little tiff between the young men, which would be so pleasant if we could make it up. You have got to a speaking acquaintance with Mrs. Roden, and perhaps if you will ask them they'll come. I am sure Marion Fay will come, because you always get your money from Pogson and Littlebird. I wish I had the cheek to ask Lord Hampstead." Having heard all this, the old lady consented to receive our sporting friend from the Post Office,

and also assented to the other invitations, which were
given.

Crocker, of course, sent his compliments, and expressed the great pleasure he would have in "seeing
the New Year in" in company with Mrs. Demijohn.
As the old lady was much afflicted with rheumatism,
the proposition as coming from her would have been
indiscreet had she not known that her niece on such
occasions was well able to act as her deputy. Mrs.
Roden also promised to come, and with difficulty persuaded her son that it would be gracious on his part
to be so far civil to his neighbours. Had he known
that Crocker also would be there he certainly would
not have yielded; but Crocker, when at the office, kept
the secret of his engagement to himself. The Quaker
also and Marion Fay were to be there. Mr. Fay and
Mrs. Demijohn had long known each other in regard to
matters of business, and he, for the sake of Messrs.
Pogson and Littlebird's firm, could not refuse to drink
a cup of tea at their client's house. A junior clerk
from the same counting-house, one Daniel Tribbledale
by name, with whom Clara had made acquaintance at
King's Court some two years since, was also to be of
the party. Mr. Tribbledale had at one time, among all
Clara's young men, been the favourite. But circumstances had occurred which had somewhat lessened her
goodwill towards him. Mr. Littlebird had quarrelled
with him, and he had been refused promotion. It was
generally supposed at the present time in the neigh-

bourhood of Old Broad Street that Daniel Tribbledale
was languishing for the love of Clara Demijohn. Mrs.
Duffer, of course, was to be there, and so the list of
friends for the festive occasion was completed,

Mrs. Duffer was the first to come. Her aid, indeed,
was required for the cutting up of the cakes and
arrangements of the cups and saucers. The Quaker
and his daughter were next, appearing exactly at nine
o'clock,—to do which he protested to be the best sign
of good manners that could be shown. "If they want
me at ten, why do they ask me at nine?" demanded
the Quaker. Marion was forced to give way, though
she was by no means anxious to spend a long evening
in company with Mrs. Demijohn. As to that seeing of
the New Year in, it was quite out of the question for
the Quaker or for his daughter. The company altogether came early. The only touch of fashion evinced
on this occasion was shown by Mr. Crocker. The
Rodens, with Mr. Tribbledale at their heels, appeared
not long after Mr. Fay, and then the demolition of the
Sally Lunns was commenced. "I declare I think he
means to deceive us," whispered Clara to her friend,
Mrs. Duffer, when all the good tea had been consumed
before the young man appeared. "I don't suppose he
cares much for tea," said Mrs. Duffer; "they don't
now-a-days." "It isn't just for the tea that a man is
expected to come," said Clara, indignantly. It was
now nearly ten, and she could not but feel that the
evening was going heavily. Tribbledale had said one

tender word to her; but she had snubbed him, expecting Crocker to be there almost at once, and he had retired silent into a corner. George Roden had altogether declined to make himself agreeable—to her; but as he was an engaged man, and engaged to a lady of rank, much could not be expected of him. Mrs. Roden and the Quaker and Mrs. Demijohn did manage to keep up something of conversation. Roden from time to time said a few words to Marion. Clara, who was repenting herself of her hardness to young Tribbledale, was forced to put up with Mrs. Duffer. When suddenly there came a thundering knock at the door, and Mr. Crocker was announced by the maid, who had been duly instructed beforehand as to all peculiarities in the names of the guests.

There was a little stir, as there always is when a solitary guest comes in much after the appointed time. Of course there was rebuke,—suppressed rebuke from Mrs. Demijohn, mild rebuke from Mrs. Duffer, a very outburst of rebuke from Clara. But Crocker was up to the occasion. "Upon my word, ladies, I had no help for it. I was dining with a few friends in the City, and I couldn't get away earlier. If my own ideas of happiness had been consulted I should have been here an hour ago. Ah, Roden, how are you? Though I know you live in the same street, I didn't think of meeting you." Roden gave him a nod, but did not vouchsafe him a word. "How's his lordship? I told you, didn't I, that I had heard from him the other day?" Crocker had

mentioned more than once at his office the fact that he
had received a letter from Lord Hampstead.

"I don't often see him, and very rarely hear from
him," said Roden, without turning away from Marion
to whom he was at the moment speaking.

"If all our young noblemen were like Hampstead,"
said Crocker, who had told the truth in declaring that
he had been dining, "England would be a very different
sort of place from what it is. The most affable young
lord that ever sat in the House of Peers." Then he
turned himself towards Marion Fay, at whose identity
he made a guess. He was anxious at once to claim
her as a mutual friend, as connected with himself by
her connection with the lord in question. But as he
could find no immediate excuse for introducing himself,
he only winked at her.

"Are you acquainted with Mr. Tribbledale, Mr.
Crocker?" asked Clara.

"Never had the pleasure as yet," said Crocker.
Then the introduction was effected. "In the Civil
Service?" asked Crocker. Tribbledale blushed, and of
necessity repudiated the honour. "I thought, perhaps,
you were in the Customs. You have something of the
H.M.S. cut about you." Tribbledale acknowledged the
compliment with a bow. "I think the Service is the best
thing a man can do with himself," continued Crocker.

"It is genteel," said Mrs. Duffer.

"And the hours so pleasant," said Clara. "Bank
clerks have always to be there by nine."

"Is a young man to be afraid of that?" asked the Quaker, indignantly. "Ten till four, with one hour for the newspapers and another for lunch. See the consequence. I never knew a young man yet from a public office who understood the meaning of a day's work."

"I think that is a little hard," said Roden. "If a man really works, six hours continuously is as much as he can do with any good to his employers or himself."

"Well done, Roden," said Crocker. "Stick up for Her Majesty's shop." Roden turned himself more round than before, and continued to address himself to Marion.

"Our employers wouldn't think much of us," said the Quaker, "if we didn't do better for them than that in private offices. I say that the Civil Service destroys a young man, and teaches him to think that the bread of idleness is sweet. As far as I can see, nothing is so destructive of individual energy as what is called public money. If Daniel Tribbledale would bestir himself he might do very well in the world without envying any young man his seat either at the Custom House or the Post Office." Mr. Fay had spoken so seriously that they all declined to carry that subject further. Mrs. Demijohn and Mrs. Duffer murmured their agreement, thinking it civil to do so, as the Quaker was a guest. Tribbledale sat silent in his corner, awestruck at the idea of having given rise to the conversation. Crocker winked at Mrs. Demijohn, and thrust his hands into his pockets as much as to say that he could get the

better of the Quaker altogether if he chose to exercise
his powers of wit and argument.

Soon after this Mr. Fay rose to take his daughter
away. "But," said Clara, with affected indignation,
"you are to see the Old Year out and the New
Year in."

"I have seen enough of the one," said Mr. Fay, "and
shall see enough of the other if I live to be as near its
close as I am to its birth."

"But there are refreshments coming up," said Mrs.
Demijohn.

"I have refreshed myself sufficiently with thy tea,
madam. I rarely take anything stronger before retiring
to my rest. Come, Marion, thou requirest to be at
no form of welcoming the New Year. Thou, too,
wilt be better in thy bed, as thy duties call upon thee
to be early." So saying, the Quaker bowed formally to
each person present, and took his daughter out with
him under his arm. Mrs. Roden and her son escaped
almost at the same moment, and Mrs. Demijohn, having
waited to take what she called just a thimbleful of hot
toddy, went also to her rest.

"Here's a pretty way of seeing the New Year in,"
said Clara, laughing.

"We are quite enough of us for the purpose," said
Crocker, "unless we also are expected to go away."
But as he spoke he mixed a tumbler of brandy and
water, which he divided among two smaller glasses,
handing them to the two ladies present.

"I declare," said Mrs. Duffer, "I never do anything of the kind,—almost never."

"On such an occasion as this everybody does it," said Crocker.

"I hope Mr. Tribbledale will join us," said Clara. Then the bashful clerk came out of his corner, and seating himself at the table prepared to do as he was bid. He made his toddy very weak, not because he disliked brandy, but guided by an innate spirit of modesty which prevented him always from going more than halfway when he was in company.

Then the evening became very pleasant. "You are quite sure that he is really engaged to her ladyship?" asked Clara.

"I wish I were as certainly engaged to you," replied the polite Crocker.

"What nonsense you do talk, Mr. Crocker;—and before other people too. But you think he is?"

"I am sure of it. Both Hampstead and she have told me so much themselves out of their own mouths."

"My!" exclaimed Mrs. Duffer.

"And here's her brother engaged to Marion Fay," said Clara. Crocker declared that as to this he was by no means so well assured. Lord Hampstead in spite of their intimacy had told him nothing about it. "But it is so, Mr. Crocker, as sure as ever you are sitting there. He has been coming here after her over and over again, and was closeted with her only last Friday

for hours. It was a holiday, but that sly old Quaker
went out of the way, so as to leave them together.
That Mrs. Roden, though she's as stiff as buckram,
knows all about it. To the best of my belief she got
it all up. Marion Fay is with her every day. It's my
belief there's something we don't understand yet. She's
got a hold of them young people, and means to do
just what she likes with 'em." Crocker, however, could
not agree to this. He had heard of Lord Hampstead's
peculiar politics, and was assured that the young lord
was only carrying out his peculiar principles in select-
ing Marion Fay for himself and devoting his sister to
George Roden.

"Not that I like that kind of thing, if you ask me,"
said Crocker. "I'm very fond of Hampstead, and I've
always found Lady Frances to be a pleasant and affable
lady. I've no cause to speak other than civil of both
of them. But when a man has been born a lord,
and a lady a lady——. A lady of that kind, Miss
Demijohn."

"Oh, exactly;—titled you mean, Mr. Crocker?"

"Quite high among the nobs, you know. Hampstead
will be a Marquis some of these days, which is next to
a Duke."

"And do you know him,—yourself?" asked Tribbledale with a voice of awe.

"Oh, yes," said Crocker.

"To speak to him when you see him?"

"I had a long correspondence with him about a

week ago about a matter which interested both of us
"very much."

"And how does he address you?" asked Clara,—also
with something of awe.

"'Dear Crocker;'—just that. I always say 'My
dear Lord Hampstead,' in return. I look upon 'Dear
Hampstead,' as a little vulgar, you know, and I always
think that one ought to be particular in these matters.
But, as I was saying, when it comes to marriage, people
ought to be true to themselves. Now if I was a
Marquis,—I don't know what I mightn't do if I saw
you, you know, Clara." "Clara" pouted, but did not
appear to have been offended either by the compliment
or by the familiarity. "But under any other circumstances less forcible I would stick to my order."

"So would I," said Mrs. Duffer. "Marquises ought
to marry marquises, and dukes dukes."

"There it is!" said Clara, "and now we must drink
its health, and I hope we may be all married to them.
we like best before it comes round again." This had
reference to the little clock on the mantelpiece, the
hands of which had just crept round to twelve o'clock."

"I wish we might," said Crocker, "and have a baby
in the cradle too."

"Go away," said Clara.

"That would be quick," said Mrs. Duffer. "What
do you say, Mr. Tribbledale?"

"Where my heart's fixed," said Tribbledale, who was
just becoming warm with the brandy-and-water, "there

ain't no hope for this year, nor yet for the one after."
Whereupon Crocker remarked that " care killed a cat."

"You just put on your coat and hat, and take me
across to my lodgings.   See if I don't give you a
chance," said Mrs. Duffer, who was also becoming somewhat merry under the influences of the moment.   But
she knew that it was her duty to do something for her
young hostess, and, true woman as she was, thought
that this was the best way of doing it.   Tribbledale did
as he was bid, though he was obliged thus to leave his
lady-love and her new admirer together.   "Do you
really mean it?" said Clara, when she and Crocker
were alone.

"Of course I do,—honest," said Crocker.

"Then you may," said Clara, turning her face to
him.

CHAPTER VIII.

NEW YEAR'S DAY.

CROCKER had by no means as yet got through his
evening. Having dined with his friends in the City,
and "drank tea" with the lady of his love, he was
disposed to proceed, if not to pleasanter delights, at any
rate to those which might be more hilarious. Every
Londoner, from Holloway up to Gower Street, in which
he lived, would be seeing the New Year in,—and
beyond Gower Street down in Holborn, and from
thence all across to the Strand, especially in the neighbourhood of Covent Garden and the theatres, there
would be a whole world of happy revellers engaged in
the same way. On such a night as this there could
certainly be no need of going to bed soon after twelve
for such a one as Samuel Crocker. In Paradise Row
he again encountered Tribbledale, and suggested to
that young man that they should first have a glass of
something at the "Duchess" and then proceed to more
exalted realms in a hansom. "I did think of walking
there this fine starlight night," said Tribbledale, mindful
of the small stipend at which his services were at

present valued by Pogson and Littlebird. But Crocker soon got the better of all this. "I'll stand Sammy for this occasion," said he. "The New Year comes in only once in twelve months." Then Tribbledale went into "The Duchess," and after that was as indifferent, while his money lasted him, as was Crocker himself. "I've loved that girl for three years," said Tribbledale, as soon as they had left "The Duchess" and were again in the open air.

It was a beautiful night, and Crocker thought that they might as well walk a little way. It was pleasant under the bright stars to hear of the love adventures of his new friend, especially as he himself was now the happy hero. "For three years?" he asked.

"Indeed I have, Crocker." That glass of hot whiskey-and-water, though it enhanced the melancholy tenderness of the young man, robbed him of his bashfulness, and loosened the strings of his tongue. "For three years! And there was a time when she worshipped the very stool on which I sat at the office. I don't like to boast."

"You have to be short, sharp, and decisive if you mean to get a girl like that to travel with you."

"I should have taken the ball at the hop, Crocker; that's what I ought to have done. But I see it all now. She's as fickle as she is fair;—fickler, perhaps, if anything."

"Come, Tribbledale; I ain't going to let you abuse her, you know."

"I don't want to abuse her. God knows I love her too well in spite of all. It's your turn now. I can see that. There's a great many of them have had their turns."

"Were there now?" asked Crocker anxiously.

"There was Pollocky;—him at the Highbury Gas Works. He came after me. It was because of him she dropped me."

"Was that going on for a marriage?"

"Right ahead, I used to think. Pollocky is a widower with five children."

"Oh Lord!"

"But he's the head of all the gas, and has four hundred a year. It wasn't love as carried her on with him. I could see that. She wouldn't go and meet him anywhere about the City, as she did me. I suppose Pollocky is fifty, if he's a day."

"And she dropped him also?"

"Or else it was he." On receipt of this information Crocker whistled. "It was something about money," continued Tribbledale. "The old woman wouldn't part."

"There is money I suppose?"

"The old woman has a lot."

"And isn't the niece to have it?" asked Crocker.

"No doubt she will; because there never was a pair more loving. But the old lady will keep it herself as long as she is here." Then there entered an idea into Crocker's head that if he could manage to make Clara his own, he might have power enough to manage the aunt as well as the niece. They had a little more whiskey-and-water at the Angel at Islington before they got into the cab which was to take them down to the Paphian Music-Hall, and after that Tribbledale passed from the realm of partial fact to that of perfect poetry. "He would never," he said, "abandon Clara Demijohn, though he should live to an age beyond that of any known patriarch. He quite knew all that there was against him. Crocker he thought might probably prevail. He rather hoped that Crocker might prevail;—for why should not so good a fellow be made happy, seeing how utterly impossible it was that he, Daniel Tribbledale, should ever reach that perfect bliss in dreaming of which he passed his miserable existence. But as to one thing he had quite made up his mind. The day that saw Clara Demijohn a bride would most undoubtedly be the last of his existence.

"Oh, no, damme; you won't," said Crocker turning round upon him in the cab.

"I shall!" said Tribbledale with emphasis. "And I've made up my mind how to do it too. They've caged up the Monument, and you're so looked after on the Duke of York's, that there isn't a chance. But there's nothing to prevent you from taking a header at the Whispering Gallery of Saint Paul's. You'd be more talked of that way, and the vergers would be sure to show the stains made on the stones below. 'It was here young Tribbledale fell,—a clerk at Pogson and

Littlebird's, who dashed out his brains for love on the
very day as Clara Demijohn got herself married.' I'm
of that disposition, Crocker, as I'd do anything for love;
—anything." Crocker was obliged to reply that he
trusted he might never be the cause of such a fatal
attempt at glory; but he went on to explain that in
the pursuit of love a man could not in any degree give
way to friendship. Even though numberless lovers
might fall from the Whispering Gallery in a confused
heap of mangled bodies, he must still tread the path
which was open to him. These were his principles,
and he could not abandon them even for the sake of
Tribbledale. "Nor would I have you," shouted Tribbledale, leaning out over the door of the cab. "I would
not delay you not for a day, not for an hour. Were
to-morrow to be your bridal morning it would find me
prepared. My only request to you is that a boy might
be called Daniel after me. You might tell her it was
an uncle or grandfather. She would never think that
in her own child was perpetuated a monument of poor
Daniel Tribbledale." Crocker, as he jumped out of the
cab with a light step in front of the Paphian Hall,
promised that in this particular he would attend to the
wishes of his friend.

The performances at the Paphian Hall on that festive
occasion need not be described here with accuracy.
The New Year had been seen well in with music,
dancing, and wine. The seeing of it in was continued
yet for an hour, till an indulgent policeman was forced

to interfere. It is believed that on the final ejection
of our two friends, the forlorn lover, kept steady, no
doubt, by the weight of his woe, did find his way home
to his own lodgings. The exultant Crocker was less
fortunate, and passed his night without the accommo-
dation of sheets and blankets somewhere in the neighbourhood of Bow Street. The fact is important to us,
as it threatened to have considerable effect upon our
friend's position at his office. Having been locked up
in a cell during the night, and kept in durance till he
was brought on the following morning before a magistrate, he could not well be in his room at ten o'clock.
Indeed when he did escape from the hands of the
Philistines, at about two in the day, sick, unwashed
and unfed, he thought it better to remain away altogether for that day. The great sin of total absence
would be better than making an appearance before Mr.
Jerningham in his present tell-tale condition. He well
knew his own strength and his own weakness. All
power of repartee would be gone from him for the day.
Mr. Jerningham would domineer over him, and Æolus,
should the violent god be pleased to send for him,
would at once annihilate him. So he sneaked home to
Gower Street, took a hair of the dog that bit him, and
then got the old woman who looked after him to make
him some tea and to fry a bit of bacon for him. In
this ignominious way he passed New Year's Day,—at
least so much of it as was left to him after the
occurrences which have been described.

But on the next morning the great weight of his
troubles fell upon him heavily. In his very heart of
hearts he was afraid of Æolus. In spite of his "brum-
magem" courage the wrath of the violent god was
tremendous to him. He knew what it was to stand
with his hand on the lock of the door and tremble
before he dared to enter the room. There was something in the frown of the god which was terrible to
him. There was something worse in the god's smile.
He remembered how he had once been unable to move
himself out of the room when the god had told him
that he need not remain at the office, but might go home
and amuse himself just as he pleased. Nothing crushes
a young man so much as an assurance that his presence
can be dispensed with without loss to any one. Though
Crocker had often felt the mercies of Æolus, and had
told himself again and again that the god never did in
truth lift up his hand for final irrevocable punishment,
still he trembled as he anticipated the dread encounter.

When the morning came, and while he was yet in
his bed, he struggled to bethink himself of some
strategy by which he might evade the evil hour. Could
he have been sent for suddenly into Cumberland?
But in this case he would of course have telegraphed
to the Post Office on the preceding day. Could he
have been taken ill with a fit,—so as to make his
absence absolutely necessary, say for an entire week?
He well knew that they had a doctor at the Post Office,
a crafty, far-seeing, obdurate man, who would be with

him at once and would show him no mercy. He had
tried these schemes all round, and had found that there
were none left with which Æolus was not better acquainted than was he himself. There was nothing for
it but to go and bear the brunt.

Exactly at ten o'clock he entered the room, hung his
hat up on the accustomed peg, and took his seat on the
accustomed chair before any one spoke a word to him.
Roden on the opposite seat took no notice of him.
"Bedad, he's here anyhow this morning," whispered
Geraghty to Bobbin, very audibly. "Mr. Crocker," said
Mr. Jerningham, "you were absent throughout the
entire day yesterday. Have you any account to give
of yourself?" There was certainly falsehood implied
in this question, as Mr. Jerningham knew very well
what had become of Crocker. Crocker's misadventure
at the police office had found its way into the newspapers, and had been discussed by Æolus with Mr.
Jerningham. I am afraid that Mr. Jerningham must
have intended to tempt the culprit into some false
excuse.

"I was horribly ill," said Crocker, without stopping
the pen with which he was making entries in the big
book before him. This no doubt was true, and so far
the trap had been avoided.

"What made you ill, Mr. Crocker?"

"Headache."

"It seems to me, Mr. Crocker, you're more subject to
such attacks as these than any young man in the office."

"I always was as a baby," said Crocker, resuming something of his courage. Could it be possible that Æolus should not have heard of the day's absence?

"There is ill-health of so aggravated a nature," said Mr. Jerningham, "as to make the sufferer altogether unfit for the Civil Service."

"I'm happy to say I'm growing out of them gradually," said Crocker. Then Geraghty got up from his chair and whispered the whole truth into the sufferer's ears. "It was all in the *Pall Mall* yesterday, and Æolus knew it before he went away." A sick qualm came upon the poor fellow as though it were a repetition of yesterday's sufferings. But still it was necessary that he should say something. "New Year's Day comes only once a year, I suppose."

"It was only a few weeks since that you remained a day behind your time when you were on leave. But Sir Boreas has taken the matter up, and I have nothing to say to it. No doubt Sir Boreas will send for you." Sir Boreas Bodkin was that great Civil servant in the General Post Office whom men were wont to call Æolus.

It was a wretched morning for poor Crocker. He was not sent for till one o'clock, just at the moment when he was going to eat his lunch! That horrid sickness, the combined result of the dinner in the City, of Mrs. Demijohn's brandy, and of the many whiskies which followed, still clung to him. The mutton-chop and porter which he had promised himself would have relieved him; but now he was obliged to appear before the god in all his weakness. Without a word he followed a messenger who had summoned him, with his tail only too visibly between his legs. Æolus was writing a note when he was ushered into the room, and did not condescend to arrest himself in the progress merely because Crocker was present. Æolus well knew the effect on a sinner of having to stand silent and all alone in the presence of an offended deity.

"So, Mr. Crocker," said Æolus at last, looking up from his completed work; "no doubt you saw the Old Year out on Wednesday night." The jokes of the god were infinitely worse to bear than his most furious blasts. "Like some other great men," continued Æolus, "you have contrived to have your festivities chronicled in the newspapers." Crocker found it impossible to utter a word. "You have probably seen the *Pall Mall* of yesterday, and the *Standard* of this morning?"

"I haven't looked at the newspaper, sir, since——"

"Since the festive occasion," suggested Æolus.

"Oh, Sir Boreas——"

"Well, Mr. Crocker; what is it that you have to say for yourself?"

"I did dine with a few friends."

"And kept it up tolerably late, I should think."

"And then afterwards went to a tea-party," said Crocker.

"A tea-party!"

"It was not all tea," said Crocker, with a whine.

"I should think not. There was a good deal besides tea, I should say." Then the god left off to smile, and the blasts began to blow. "Now, Mr. Crocker, I should like to know what you think of yourself. After having read the accounts of your appearance before the magistrate in two newspapers, I suppose I may take it for granted that you were abominably drunk out in the streets on Wednesday night." It is very hard for a young man to have to admit under any circumstances that he has been abominably drunk out in the streets; —so that Crocker stood dumb before his accuser. "I choose to have an answer, sir. I must either have your own acknowledgment, or must have an official account from tne police magistrate."

"I had taken something, sir."

"Were you drunk? If you will not answer me you had better go, and I shall know how to deal with you." Crocker thought that he had perhaps better go and leave the god to deal with him. He remained quite silent. "Your personal habits would be nothing to me, sir," continued Æolus, "if you were able to do your work and did not bring disgrace on the department. But you neglect the office. You are unable to do your work. And you do bring disgrace on the department. How long is it since you remained away a day before?"

"I was detained down in Cumberland for one day, after my leave of absence."

"Detained in Cumberland! I never tell a gentleman, Mr. Crocker, that I do not believe him,—never. If it comes to that with a gentleman, he must go." This was hard to bear; but yet Crocker was aware that he had told a fib on that occasion in reference to the day's hunting. Then Sir Boreas took up his pen and again had recourse to his paper, as though the interview was over. Crocker remained standing, not quite knowing what he was expected to do. "It's of no use your remaining there," said Sir Boreas. Whereupon Crocker retired, and, with his tail still between his legs, returned to his own desk. Soon afterwards Mr. Jerningham was sent for, and came back with an intimation that Mr. Crocker's services were no longer required, at any rate for that day. When the matter had been properly represented to the Postmaster-General, a letter would be written to him. The impression made on the minds of Bobbin and Geraghty was that poor Crocker would certainly be dismissed on this occasion. Roden, too, thought that it was now over with the unfortunate young man, as far as the Queen's service was concerned, and could not abstain from shaking hands with the unhappy wretch as he bade them all a melancholy good-bye. "Good afternoon," said Mr. Jerningham to him severely, not condescending to shake hands with him at all.

But Mr. Jerningham heard the last words which the

god had spoken on the subject, and was not therefore
called upon to be specially soft-hearted. " I never
saw a poor devil look so sick in my life," Æolus had
said.

" He must have been very bad, Sir Boreas."

Æolus was fond of a good dinner himself, and had a
sympathy for convivial offences.   Indeed for all offences
he had a sympathy.   No man less prone to punish ever
lived.   But what is a man to do with inveterate
offenders ?   Æolus would tear his hair sometimes in
dismay because he knew that he was retaining in
the service men whom he would have been bound
to get rid of had he done his duty.   " You had better
tell him to go home," said Æolus,—" for to-day, you
know."

" And what then, Sir Boreas ? "

" I suppose he'll sleep it off by to-morrow.   Have a
letter written to him, — to frighten him, you know.
After all, New Year's Day only does come once a year."
Mr. Jerningham, having thus received instructions,
went back to his room and dismissed Crocker in the
way we have seen.   As soon as Crocker's back was
turned Roden was desired to write the letter.

" Sir,

          " Your conduct in absenting yourself without
leave from the office yesterday is of such a nature as to
make it necessary for me to inform you, that should it
be repeated I shall have no alternative but to bring

your name under the serious consideration of my Lord
the Postmaster-General.

"I am, sir,

"Your obedient servant,

(Signed)   "BOREAS BODKIN."

In the same envelope was a short note from one of
his brother clerks.

"DEAR CROCKER,

"You had better be here sharp at ten to-morrow.
Mr. Jerningham bids me tell you.

"Yours truly,

"BART. BOBBIN."

Thus Crocker got through his troubles on this
occasion.

CHAPTER IX.

MISS DEMIJOHN'S INGENUITY.

ON the day on which Crocker was going through his purgatory at the Post Office, a letter reached Lady Kingsbury at Trafford Park, which added much to the troubles and annoyances felt by different members of the family there. It was an anonymous letter, and the reader,—who in regard to such mysteries should never be kept a moment in ignorance,—may as well be told at once that the letter was written by that enterprising young lady, Miss Demijohn. The letter was written on New Year's Day, after the party,—perhaps in consequence of the party, as the rash doings of some of the younger members of the Trafford family were made specially obvious to Miss Demijohn by what was said on that occasion. The letter ran as follows:

"MY LADY MARCHIONESS—

"I conceive it to be my duty as a well-wisher of the family to inform you that your stepson, Lord Hampstead, has become entangled in what I think to be a dangerous way with a young woman living in a neighbouring street to this." The "neighbouring" street was of course a stroke of cunning on the part of Miss Demijohn. "She lives at No. 17, Paradise Row, Holloway, and her name is Marion Fay. She is daughter to an old Quaker, who is clerk to Pogson and Littlebird, King's Court, Great Broad Street, and isn't of course in any position to entertain such hopes as these. He may have a little money saved, but what's that to the likes of your ladyship and his lordship the Marquis? Some think she is pretty. I don't. Now I don't like such cunning ways. Of what I tell your ladyship there isn't any manner of doubt. His lordship was there for hours the other day, and the girl is going about as proud as a peacock.

"It's what I call a regular Paradise Row conspiracy, and though the Quaker has lent himself to it, he ain't at the bottom. Next door but two to the Fays there is a Mrs. Roden living, who has got a son, a stuck-up fellow and a clerk in the Post Office. I believe there isn't a bit of doubt but he has been and got himself engaged to another of your ladyship's noble family. As to that, all Holloway is talking of it. I don't believe there is a 'bus driver up and down the road as doesn't know it. It's my belief that Mrs. Roden is the doing of it all! She has taken Marion Fay by the hand just as though she were her own, and now she has got the young lord and the young lady right into her mashes. If none of 'em isn't married yet it won't be long so unless somebody interferes. If you don't believe me do

you send to the 'Duchess of Edinburgh' at the corner,
and you'll find that they know all about it.

" Now, my Lady Marchioness, I've thought it my
duty to tell you all this because I don't like to see
a noble family put upon. There isn't nothing for
me to get out of it myself. But I do it just as one of
the family's well-wishers. Therefore I sign myself your
very respectful,

                                      " A WELL-WISHER."

The young lady had told her story completely as
far as her object was concerned, which was simply
that of making mischief. But the business of anonymous letter-writing was one not new to her hand.
It is easy, and offers considerable excitement to
the minds of those whose time hangs heavy on their
hands.

The Marchioness, though she would probably have
declared beforehand that anonymous letters were of
all things the most contemptible, nevertheless read
this more than once with a great deal of care. And
she believed it altogether. As to Lady Frances, of
course she knew the allegations to be true. Seeing
that the writer was so well acquainted with the facts as
to Lady Frances, why should she be less well-informed
in reference to Lord Hampstead ? Such a marriage
as this with the Quaker girl was exactly the sort of
match which Hampstead would be pleased to make
Then she was especially annoyed by the publicity of

the whole affair. That Holloway and the drivers of
the omnibuses, and the "Duchess of Edinburgh" should
know all the secrets of her husband's family,—should
be able to discuss the disgrace to which "her own
darlings" would be subjected, was terrible to her. But
perhaps the sting that went sharpest to her heart was
that which came from the fact that Lord Hampstead
was about to be married at all. Let the wife be a
Quaker or what not, let her be as low as any woman
that could be found within the sound of Bow Bells,
still, if the marriage ceremony were once pronounced
over them, that woman's son would become Lord
Highgate, and would be heir to all the wealth and all
the titles of the Marquis of Kingsbury,—to the
absolute exclusion of the eldest-born of her own
darlings.

She had had her hopes in the impracticability of
Lord Hampstead. Such men as that, she had told
herself, were likely to keep themselves altogether free
of marriage. He would not improbably, she thought,
entertain some abominable but not unlucky idea that
marriage in itself was an absurdity. At any rate, there
was hope as long as he could be kept unmarried. Were
he to marry and then have a son, even though he broke
his neck out hunting next day, no good would come of
it. In this condition of mind she thought it well to
show the letter to Mr. Greenwood before she read it
to her husband. Lord Kingsbury was still very ill,—so
ill as to have given rise to much apprehension; but

still it would be necessary to discuss this letter with
him, ill as he might be. Only it should be first
discussed with Mr. Greenwood.

Mr. Greenwood's face became flatter, and his jaw
longer, and his eyes more like gooseberries as he read
the letter. He had gradually trained himself to say
and to hear all manner of evil things about Lady
Frances in the presence of the Marchioness. He had
too accustomed himself to speak of Lord Hampstead
as a great obstacle which it would be well if the Lord
would think proper to take out of the way. He had
also so far followed the lead of his patroness as to be
deep if not loud in his denunciations of the folly of the
Marquis. The Marquis had sent him word that he
had better look out for a new home, and without
naming an especial day for his dismissal, had given
him to understand that it would not be convenient to
receive him again in the house in Park Lane. But
the Marquis had been ill when he had thus expressed
his displeasure,—and was now worse. It might be
that the Marquis himself would never again visit
Park Lane. As no positive limit had been fixed for
Mr. Greenwood's departure from Trafford Park, there
he remained,—and there he intended to remain for
the present. As he folded up the letter carefully after
reading it slowly, he only shook his head.

" Is it true, I wonder ? " asked the Marchioness.

" There is no reason why it should not be."

" That's just what I say to myself. We know it is

true about Fanny. Of course there's that Mr. Roden,
and the Mrs. Roden. When the writer knows so much,
there is reason to believe the rest."

"A great many people do tell a great many lies," said
Mr. Greenwood.

"I suppose there is such a person as this Quaker,—
and that there is such a girl?"

"Quite likely."

"If so, why shouldn't Hampstead fall in love with
her? Of course he's always going to the street because
of his friend Roden."

"Not a doubt, Lady Kingsbury."

"What ought we to do?" To this question Mr.
Greenwood was not prepared with an immediate
answer. If Lord Hampstead chose to get himself
married to a Quaker's daughter, how could it be
helped? "His father would hardly have any influence
over him now." Mr. Greenwood shook his head.
"And yet he must be told." Mr. Greenwood nodded
his head. "Perhaps something might be done about
the property."

"He wouldn't care two straws about settlements,"
said Mr. Greenwood.

"He doesn't care about anything he ought to. If
I were to write and ask him, would he tell the truth
about this marriage?"

"He wouldn't tell the truth about anything," said
Mr. Greenwood.

The Marchioness passed this by, though she knew

it at the moment to be calumny. But she was not
unwilling to hear calumny against Lord Hampstead.
"There used to be ways," she said, "in which a
marriage of that kind could be put on óne side
afterwards."

"You must put it on one side before, now-a-days, if
you mean to do it at all," said the clergyman.

"But how?—how?"

"If he could be got out of the way."

"How out of the way?"

"Well;—that's what I don't know. Suppose he
could be made to go out yachting, and she be married
to somebody else when he's at sea!" Lady Kingsbury
felt that her friend was but little good at a stratagem.
But she felt also that she was not very good herself.
She could wish; but wishing in such matters is very
vain. She had right on her side. She was quite
confident as to that. There could be no doubt but
that "gods and men" would desire to see her little
Lord Frederic succeed to the Marquisate rather than
this infidel Republican. If this wretched Radical
could be kept from marrying there would evidently
be room for hope, because there was the fact,—proved
by the incontestable evidence of Burke's Peerage,—that
younger sons did so often succeed. But if another
heir were to be born, then, as far as she was aware,
Burke's Peerage promised her nothing. "It's a pity
he shouldn't break his neck out hunting," said Mr.
Greenwood.

"Even that wouldn't be much if he were to be married first," said the Marchioness.

Every day she went to her husband for half-an-hour before her lunch, at which time the nurse who attended him during the day was accustomed to go to her dinner. He had had a physician down from London since his son had visited him, and the physician had told the Marchioness that though there was not apparently any immediate danger, still the symptoms were such as almost to preclude a hope of ultimate recovery. When this opinion had been pronounced there had arisen between the Marchioness and the chaplain a discussion as to whether Lord Hampstead should be once again summoned. The Marquis himself had expressed no such wish. A bulletin of a certain fashion had been sent three or four times a week to Hendon Hall purporting to express the doctor's opinion of the health of their noble patient; but the bulletin had not been scrupulously true. Neither of the two conspirators had wished to have Lord Hampstead at Trafford Park. Lady Kingsbury was anxious to make the separation complete between her own darlings and their brother, and Mr. Greenwood remembered, down to every tittle of a word and tone, the insolence of the rebuke which he had received from the heir. But if Lord Kingsbury were really to be dying, then they would hardly dare to keep his son in ignorance.

"I've got something I'd better show you," she said, as she seated herself by her husband's sofa. Then she

proceeded to read to him the letter, without telling him
as she did so that it was anonymous. When he had
heard the first paragraph he demanded to know the
name of the writer. "I'd better read it all first," said
the Marchioness. And she did read it all to the end,
closing it, however, without mentioning the final "Well-
Wisher." "Of course it's anonymous," she said, as she
held the letter in her hand.

"Then I don't believe a word of it," said the Marquis.

"Very likely not; but yet it sounds true."

"I don't think it sounds true at all. Why should
it be true? There is nothing so wicked as anonymous
letters."

"If it isn't true about Hampstead it's true at any
rate of Fanny. That man comes from Holloway, and
Paradise Row and the 'Duchess of Edinburgh.' Where
Fanny goes for her lover, Hampstead is likely to follow.
'Birds of a feather flock together.'"

"I won't have you speak of my children in that way,"
said the sick lord.

"What can I do? Is it not true about Fanny? If
you wish it, I will write to Hampstead and ask him all
about it." In order to escape from the misery of the
moment he assented to this proposition. The letter
being anonymous had to his thinking been disgraceful,
and therefore he had disbelieved it. And having
induced himself to disbelieve the statements made, he
had been drawn into expressing,—or at any rate to
acknowledging by his silence,—a conviction that such a

marriage as that proposed with Marion Fay would be very base. Her ladyship felt therefore that if Lord Hampstead could be got to acknowledge the engagement, something would have been done towards establishing a quarrel between the father and the son.

"Has that man gone yet?" he asked as his wife rose to leave the room.

"Has what man gone?"

"Mr. Greenwood."

"Gone? How should he have gone? It has never been expected that he should go by this time. I don't see why he should go at all. He was told that you would not again require his services up in London. As far as I know, that is all that has been said about going." The poor man turned himself on his sofa angrily, but did not at the moment give any further instructions as to the chaplain's departure.

"He wants to know why you have not gone," Lady Kingsbury said to the clergyman that afternoon.

"Where am I to go to?" whined the unfortunate one. "Does he mean to say that I am to be turned out into the road at a moment's notice because I can't approve of what Lady Frances is doing? I haven't had any orders as to going. If I am to go I suppose he will make some arrangement first." Lady Kingsbury said what she could to comfort him, and explained that there was no necessity for his immediate departure. Perhaps the Marquis might not think of it again for another

week or two ; and there was no knowing in what condition they might find themselves.

Her ladyship's letter to her stepson was as follows ;
and by return of post her stepson's answer came ;—

"MY DEAR HAMPSTEAD,—

        "Tidings have reached your father that you
have engaged yourself to marry a girl, the daughter of a
Quaker named Fay, living at No. 17, Paradise Row. He,
the Quaker, is represented as being a clerk in a counting-house in the City. Of the girl your father has heard
nothing, but can only imagine that she should be such
as her position would make probable. He desires me
to ask you whether there is any truth in the statement.
You will observe that I express no opinion myself
whether it be true or false, whether proper or improper.
After your conduct the other day I should not think of
interfering myself; but your father wishes me to ask
for his information.

                        "Yours truly,
                                "CLARA KINGSBURY."

Hampstead's answer was very short, but quite sufficient for the purpose ;—

"MY DEAR LADY KINGSBURY,

        "I am not engaged to marry Miss Fay,—as
yet. I think that I may be some day soon.

                        "Yours affectionately,
                                "HAMPSTEAD."

By the same post he wrote a letter to his father, and
that shall also be shown to the reader.

"MY DEAR FATHER,—

"I have received a letter from Lady Kingsbury, asking me as to a report of an engagement between me and a young lady named Marion Fay. I am
sorry that her writing should be evidence that you are
hardly yet strong enough to write yourself. I trust
that it may not long be so.

"Would you wish to see me again at Trafford? I
do not like to go there without the expression of a
wish from you; but I hold myself in readiness to start
whenever you may desire it. I had hoped from the
last accounts that you were becoming stronger.

"I do not know how you may have heard anything
of Marion Fay. Had I engaged myself to her, or to
any other young lady, I should have told you at once.
I do not know whether a young man is supposed to
declare his own failures in such matters, when he has
failed,—even to his father. But, as I am ashamed of
nothing in the matter, I will avow that I have asked
the youug lady to be my wife, but she has as yet
declined. I shall ask her again, and still hope to
succeed.

"She is the daughter of a Mr. Fay who, as Lady
Kingsbury says, is a Quaker, and is a clerk in a house
in the City. As he is in all respects a good man,
standing high for probity and honour among those who

know him, I cannot think that there is any drawback.
She, I think, has all the qualities which I would wish
to find in the woman whom I might hope to make my
wife. They live at No. 17, Paradise Row, Holloway.
Lady Kingsbury, indeed, is right in all her details.

"Pray let me have a line, if not from yourself, at any
rate dictated by you, to say how you are.

"Your affectionate son,

"HAMPSTEAD."

It was impossible to keep the letter from Lady
Kingsbury. It thus became a recognized fact by the
Marquis, by the Marchioness, and by Mr. Greenwood,
that Hampstead was going to marry the Quaker's
daughter. As to that pretence of a refusal, it went
for nothing, even with the father. Was it probable
that a Quaker's daughter, the daughter of a merchant's
clerk out of the City, should refuse to become a Marchioness ? The sick man was obliged to express anger,
having been already made to treat the report as in-
credible because of the disgrace which would accompany
it, if true. Had he been left to himself he would have
endeavoured to think as little about it as possible.
Not to quarrel with his two eldest children was the
wish that was now strongest at his heart. But his
wife recalled the matter to him at each of the two
daily visits which she made. "What can I do ?" he
was driven to ask on the third morning.

"Mr. Greenwood suggests——," began his wife, not

intending to irritate him, having really forgotten at the moment that no suggestion coming from Mr. Greenwood could be welcome to him.

"D—— Mr. Greenwood," he shouted, lifting himself up erect from the pillows on his sofa. The Marchioness was in truth so startled by the violence of his movement, and by the rage expressed on his haggard face, that she jumped from her chair with unexpected surprise. "I desire," said the Marquis, "that that man shall leave the house by the end of this month."

CHAPTER X.

KING'S COURT, OLD BROAD STREET.

HAMPSTEAD received the letter from Lady Kingsbury, and answered it on Saturday, the 3rd of January,
having at that time taken no active steps in regard to
Marion Fay after the rejection of his suit on the day
following Christmas. Eight days had thus elapsed, and
he had done nothing. He had done nothing, though
there was not an hour in the day in which he was not
confirming his own resolve to do something by which
he might make Marion Fay his own. He felt that he
could hardly go to the girl again immediately after the
expression of her resolution. At first he thought that
he would write to her, and did sit down to the table
for that purpose; but as he strove to produce words
which might move her, he told himself that the words
which he might speak would be better. Then he rode
half way to Holloway, with the object of asking aid
from Mrs. Roden; but he returned without completing
his purpose, telling himself that any such aid, even if
it could be obtained, would avail him nothing. In such
a contest, if a man cannot succeed by his own doing,

surely he will not do so by the assistance of any one
else; and thus he was in doubt.

After having written to Lady Kingsbury and his
father he reflected that, in his father's state of health,
he ought to go again to Trafford Park. If it were only
for a day or for an hour he ought to see his father. He
knew that he was not wanted by his stepmother. He
knew also that no desire to see him had reached him
from the Marquis. He was afraid that the Marquis
himself did not wish to see him. It was almost impossible for him to take his sister to the house unless
an especial demand for her attendance was made; and
he could not very well leave her alone for any lengthened
period. Nevertheless he determined to make a rapid
run into Shropshire, with the intention of returning the
following day, unless he found the state of his father's
health so bad as to make it expedient that he should
remain. He intended to hunt on the Monday and the
Tuesday, travelling from London to Leighton and back.
But he would leave London by the night mail train
from Paddington on Wednesday evening so as to reach
Trafford Park House on the following morning between
four and five. It was a journey which he had often
made before in the same manner, and to which the
servants at Trafford were well accustomed. Even at
that time in the morning he would walk to the Park
from the station, which was four miles distant, leaving
his luggage, if he had any, to be sent for on the following morning; but he would usually travel without

luggage, having all things necessary for his use in his own room at Trafford.

It had hitherto been his custom to acquaint his sister with his manœuvres on these occasions, having never been free in his correspondence with his stepmother. He had written or telegraphed to Lady Frances, and she had quite understood that his instructions, whatever they might be, were to be obeyed. But Lady Frances was no longer a resident at Trafford Park, and he therefore telegraphed to the old butler, who had been a servant in the family from a period previous to his own birth. This telegram he sent on the Monday, as follows ; — "Shall be at Trafford Thursday morning, 4.30 A.M. Will walk over. Let Dick be up. Have room ready. Tell my father." He fixed Wednesday night for his journey, having made up his mind to devote a portion of the Wednesday morning to the business which he had on hand in reference to Marion Fay.

It was not the proper thing, he thought, to go to a girl's father for permission to ask the girl to be his wife, before the girl had herself assented ; but the circumstances in this case were peculiar. It had seemed to him that Marion's only reason for rejecting him was based on disparity in their social condition,—which to his thinking was the worst reason that could be given. It might be that the reason had sprung from some absurd idea originating with the Quaker father ; or it might be that the Quaker father would altogether

disapprove of any such reason. At any rate he would
be glad to know whether the old man was for him or
against him. And with the object of ascertaining this,
he determined that he would pay a visit to the office
in King's Court on the Wednesday morning. He could
not endure the thought of leaving London,—it might
be for much more than the one day intended,—without
making some effort in regard to the object which was
nearest his heart.

Early in the day he walked into Messrs. Pogson and
Littlebird's office, and saw Mr. Tribbledale seated on
a high stool behind a huge desk, which nearly filled
up the whole place. He was rather struck by the
smallness and meanness of Messrs. Pogson and Littlebird's premises, which, from a certain nobility belonging
to the Quaker's appearance, he would have thought
to be spacious and important. It is impossible not to
connect ideas after this fashion. Pogson and Littlebird
themselves carried in their own names no flavour of
commercial grandeur. Had they been only known to
Hampstead by their name, any small mercantile retreat
at the top of the meanest alley in the City might
have sufficed for them. But there was something in
the demeanour of Zachary Fay which seemed to give
promise of one of those palaces of trade which are now
being erected in every street and lane devoted in the
City to business. Nothing could be less palatial than
Pogson and Littlebird's counting-house. Hampstead
had entered it from a little court, which it seemed to

share with one other equally unimportant tenement
opposite to it, by a narrow low passage. Here he saw
two doors only, through one of which he passed, as it
was open, having noticed that the word "Private" was
written on the other. Here he found himself face to
face with Tribbledale and with a little boy who sat at
Tribbledale's right hand on a stool equally high. Of
these two, as far as he could see, consisted the establishment of Messrs. Pogson and Littlebird. "Could I
see Mr. Fay?" asked Hampstead.

"Business?" suggested Tribbledale.

"Not exactly. That is to say, my business is private."

Then there appeared a face looking at him over a
screen about five feet and a-half high, which divided off
from the small apartment a much smaller apartment,
having, as Hampstead now regarded it, the appearance
of a cage. In this cage, small as it was, there was a
desk, and there were two chairs; and here Zachary Fay
carried on the business of his life, and transacted most
of those affairs appertaining to Messrs. Pogson and
Littlebird which could be performed in an office.
Messrs. Pogson and Littlebird themselves, though they
had a room of their own, to which that door marked
"Private" belonged, were generally supposed to be
walking on 'Change as British merchants should do, or
making purchases of whole ships' cargos in the Docks,
or discounting bills, the least of which would probably
represent £10,000. The face which looked over the
barrier of the cage at Lord Hampstead was of course

that of Zachary Fay. "Lord Hampstead!" he said, with surprise.

"Oh, Mr. Fay, how do you do? I have something I want to say to you. Could you spare me, five minutes?"

The Quaker opened the door of the cage and asked Lord Hampstead to walk in. Tribbledale, who had heard and recognized the name, stared hard at the young nobleman,—at his friend Crocker's noble friend, at the lord of whom it had been asserted positively that he was engaged to marry Mr. Fay's daughter. The boy, too, having heard that the visitor was a lord, stared also. Hampstead did as he was bid, but remembering that the inhabitant of the cage had at once heard what had been said in the office, felt that it would be impossible for him to carry on his conversation about Marion without other protection from the ears of the world. "It is a little private what I have to say," remarked Hampstead.

The Quaker looked towards the private room. "Old Mr. Pogson is there," whispered Tribbledale. "I heard him come in·a quarter of an hour ago."

"Perhaps thou wouldst not mind walking up and down the yard," said the Quaker. Hampstead of course walked out, but on looking about him found that the court was very small for the communication which he had to make. Space would be required, so that he might not be troubled by turning when he was in the midst of his eloquence. "Half-a-dozen steps would carry him the whole length of King's Court; and who could tell his love-story in a walk limited to six steps?

"Perhaps we might go out into the street?" he suggested.

"Certainly, my lord," said the Quaker. "Tribbledale, should any one call before I return, and be unable to wait for five minutes, I shall be found outside the court, not above fifty yards either to the right or to the left." Hampstead, thus limited to a course not exceeding a hundred yards in one of the most crowded thoroughfares of the City, began the execution of his difficult task.

"Mr. Fay," he said, "are you aware of what has passed between me and your daughter Marion?"

"Hardly, my lord."

"Has she told you nothing of it?"

"Yea, my lord; she has in truth told me much. She has told me no doubt all that it behoves a father to hear from a daughter in such circumstances. I live on such terms with my Marion that there are not many secrets kept by either of us from the other."

"Then you do know?"

"I know that your lordship tendered to her your hand,—honestly, nobly, and truly, as I take it."

"With perfect honesty and perfect truth most certainly."

"And I know also that she declined the honour thus offered her."

"She did."

"Is this you, Zachary? How are you this morning?" This came from a stout, short, red-faced man, who stopped them, standing in the middle of the pavement.

"Well, I thank thee, Mr. Gruby. At this moment I am particularly engaged. That is Jonathan Gruby," said the Quaker to his companion as soon as the stout man had walked on; "one of the busiest men in the City. You have heard probably of Gruby and Inderwald."

Hampstead had never heard of Gruby and Inderwald, and wished that the stout man had been minding his business at that moment. "But as to Miss Fay," he said, endeavouring to continue to tell his love-story.

"Yes, as to Marion. I hardly do know what passed between you two, not having heard the reasons she gave thee."

"No reasons at all;—nothing worth speaking of between persons who know anything of the world."

"Did she tell thee that she did not love thee, my lord?—because that to my thinking would be reason enough."

"Nothing of the kind. I don't mean to boast, but I don't see why she should not like me well enough."

"Nor in sooth do I either."

"What, Zachary; you walking about at this busy time of the day?"

"I am walking about, Sir Thomas. It is not customary with me, but I am walking about." Then he turned on his heel, moved almost to dudgeon by the interruption, and walked the other way. "Sir Thomas

Bolster, my lord; a very busy sort of gentleman, but
one who has done well in the world.—Nor in sooth do
I either; but this is a matter in which a young maiden
must decide for herself. I shall not bid her not to
love thee, but I cannot bid her to do so."

"It isn't that, Mr. Fay. Of course I have no right
to pretend to any regard from her. But as to that
there has been no question."

"What did she say to thee?"

"Some trash about rank."

"Nay, my lord, it is not trash. I cannot hear thee
speak so of thine own order without contradiction."

"Am I to be like a king in the old days, who was
forced to marry any ugly old princess that might be
found for him, even though she were odious to him?
I will have nothing to do with rank on such terms.
I claim the right to please myself, as do other men,
and I come to you as father to the young lady to ask
from you your assistance in winning her to be my
wife." At this moment up came Tribbledale running
from the office.

"There is Cooke there," said Tribbledale, with much
emphasis in his voice, as though Cooke's was a very
serious affair; "from Pollock and Austen's."

"Is not Mr. Pogson within?"

"He went out just after you. Cooke says that
it's most important that he should see some one
immediately."

"Tell him that he must wait yet five minutes longer,"

said Zachary Fay, frowning. Tribbledale, awestruck as he bethought himself how great were the affairs of Pollock and Austen, retreated back hurriedly to the court.

"You know what I mean, Mr. Fay," continued Lord Hampstead.

"I know well what thou meanest, my lord. I think I know what thou meanest. Thou meanest to offer to my girl not only high rank and great wealth, but, which should be of infinitely more value to her, the heart and the hand of an honest man. I believe thee to be an honest man, my lord."

"In this matter, Mr. Fay, at any rate, I am."

"In all matters as I believe; and how should I, being such a one as I am, not be willing to give my girl to such a suitor as thee? And what is it now?" he shrieked in his anger, as the little boy off the high stool came rushing to him.

"Mr. Pogson has just come back, Mr. Fay, and he says that he can't find those letters from Pollock and Austen anywhere about the place. He wants them immediately, because he can't tell the prices named without seeing them."

"Lord Hampstead," said the Quaker, almost white with rage, "I must pray thee to excuse me for five minutes." Hampstead promised that he would confine himself to the same uninteresting plot of ground till the Quaker should return to him, and then reflected that there were certain reasons upon which he had not

calculated against falling in love with the daughter of a
City clerk.

"We will go a little further afield," said the Quaker,
when he returned, "so that we may not be troubled
again by those imbeciles in the court. It is little,
however, that I have to say to thee further. Thou hast
my leave."

"I am glad of that."

"And all my sympathies. But, my lord, I suppose I
had better tell the truth."

"Oh, certainly."

"My girl fears that her health may fail her."

"Her health!"

"It is that as I think. She has not said so to me
openly; but I think it is that. Her mother died early,
—and her brothers and her sisters. It is a sad tale,
my lord."

"But need that hinder her?"

"I think not, my lord. But it must be for thee to
judge. As far as I know she is as fit to become a man's
wife as are other girls. Her health has not failed her.
She is not robust, but she does her work in looking
after my household, such as it is, well and punctually.
I think that her mind is pervaded with vain terrors.
Now I have told thee all, placing full confidence in thee
as in an honest man. There is my house. Thou art
welcome to go there if it seemeth thee good, and to deal
with Marion in this matter as thy love and thy judgment may direct thee." Having said this he returned

hurriedly to King's Court as though he feared that
Tribbledale or the boy might again find him out.

So far Hampstead had succeeded; but he was much
troubled in his mind by what he had heard as to
Marion's health. Not that it occurred to him for a
moment that such a marriage as he contemplated would
be undesirable because his Marion might become ill.
He was too thoroughly in love to entertain such an
idea. Nor is it one which can find ready entrance into
the mind of a young man who sees a girl blooming with
the freshness and beauty of youth. It would have
seemed to him, had he thought about it at all, that
Marion's health was perfect. But he was afraid of her
obstinacy, and he felt that this objection might be more
binding on her than that which she put forward in
reference to his rank. He went back, therefore, to
Hendon Hall only half-satisfied, — sometimes elated,
but sometimes depressed. He would, however, go and
discuss the matter with her at full length as soon as
he should have returned from Shropshire. He would
remain there only for one day,—though it might be
necessary for him to repeat the journey almost immediately,—so that no time might be lost in using his
eloquence upon Marion. After what had passed
between him and the Quaker, he thought that he was
almost justified in assuring himself that the girl did in
truth love him.

" Give my father my kindest love," said Lady Frances,
as her brother was about to start for the train.

"Of course I will."

"And tell him that I will start at a moment's notice whenever he may wish to see me."

"In such case of course I should take you."

"And be courteous to her if you can."

"I doubt whether she will allow me. If she abuses you or insults me I must answer her."

"I wouldn't."

"You would be more ready than I am. One cannot but answer her because she expects to hear something said in return. I shall keep out of her way as much as possible. I shall have my breakfast brought to me in my own room to-morrow, and shall then remain with my father as much as possible. If I leave him at all I shall get a walk. There will only be the dinner. As to one thing I have quite made up my mind. Nothing shall drive me into having any words with Mr. Greenwood ;—unless, indeed, my father were to ask me to speak to him."

CHAPTER XI.

MR. GREENWOOD BECOMES AMBITIOUS.

MR. GREENWOOD was still anxious as to the health of
the Rector of Appleslocombe. There might be even
yet a hope for him ; but his chance, he thought, would
be better with the present Marquis—ill-disposed towards him as the Marquis was—than with the heir.
The Marquis was weary of him, and anxious to get
rid of him,—was acting very meanly to him, as Mr.
Greenwood thought, having offered him £1000 as a
final payment for a whole life's attention. The Marquis, who had ever been a liberal man, had now,
perhaps on his death-bed, become unjust, harsh, and
cruel. But he was weak and forgetful, and might
possibly be willing to save his money and get rid of
the nuisance of the whole affair by surrendering the
living. This was Mr. Greenwood's reading of the
circumstances as they at present existed. But the
Marquis could not dispose of the living while the
Rector was still alive ; nor could he even promise it,
to any good effect, without his son's assent. That
Lord Hampstead would neither himself so bestow his

patronage or allow it to be so bestowed, Mr. Greenwood
was very sure. There had been that between him and
Lord Hampstead which convinced him that the young
man was more hostile to him even than the father.
The Marquis, as Mr. Greenwood thought, had insulted
him of late;—but Lord Hampstead, young as he was,
had also been insolent; and what was worse, he had
insulted Lord Hampstead. There had been something
in the young lord's eye which had assured him of the
young lord's contempt as well as dislike. If anything
could be done about the living it must be done by
the Marquis. The Marquis was very ill; but it was
still probable that the old rector should die first. He
had been given to understand that the old rector
could hardly live many weeks.

Mr. Greenwood understood but little of the young
lord's character. The Marquis, no doubt, he knew well,
having lived with him for many years. When he
supposed his patron to be fretful and irascible because
of his infirmities, but to be by nature forgiving, unreasonable, and weak, he drew an easy portrait, which
was like the person portrayed. But in attributing
revenge, or harshness, or pride of power to Lord
Hampstead he was altogether wrong. As regarded
Appleslocombe and other parishes, the patronage of
which would some day belong to him, Lord Hampstead had long since made up his mind that he would
have nothing to do with them, feeling himself unfit
to appoint clergymen to ministrations in a Church to

which he did not consider himself to belong. All that
he would leave to the Bishop, thinking that the Bishop
must know more about it than himself. Was his
father, however, to make any request to him with
reference to Appleslocombe especially, he would no
doubt regard the living as bestowed before his father's
death. But of all this Mr. Greenwood could understand
nothing. He felt, however, that as the Marquis had
given him cause for anger, so had the young lord
given him cause for hatred as well as anger.

Daily, almost hourly, these matters were discussed
between Lady Kingsbury and the chaplain. There had
come to be strong sympathy between them as far as
sympathy can exist where the feelings are much stronger
on the one side than on the other. The mother of the
" darlings " had allowed herself to inveigh very bitterly
against her husband's children by his former marriage,
and at first had been received only half way by her
confidential friend. But of late her confidential friend
had become more animated and more bitter than herself, and had almost startled her by the boldness of his
denunciations. She in her passion had allowed herself
more than once to express a wish that her stepson——
were dead. She had hardly in truth meant as much as
she implied, — or meaning it had hardly thought of
what she meant. But the chaplain taking the words
from her lips, had repeated them till she was almost
terrified by their iniquity and horror. He had no
darlings to justify him ! No great injury had been

done to him by an unkind fortune ! Great as were the
sin of Lord Hampstead and his sister, they could bring
no disgrace upon him ! And yet there was a settled
purpose of hatred in his words which frightened her,
though she could not bring herself to oppose them.
She in her rage had declared that it would be well that
Lord Hampstead should break his neck out hunting or
go down in his yacht at sea; and she had been gratified
to find that her friend had sanctioned her ill-wishes.
But when Mr. Greenwood spoke as though something
might possibly be done to further those wishes, then
she almost repented herself.

She had been induced to say that if any power should
come to her of bestowing the living of Appleslocombe
she would bestow it on Mr. Greenwood. Were Lord
Hampstead to die before the Marquis, and were the
Marquis to die before the old rector, such power would
belong to her during the minority of her eldest son.
There had, therefore, been some meaning in the
promise ; and the clergyman had referred to it more
than once or twice. "It is most improbable, you know,
Mr. Greenwood," she had said very seriously. He had
replied as seriously that such improbabilities were of
frequent occurrence. "If it should happen I will do
so," she had answered. But after that she had never
of her own accord referred to the probability of Lord
Hampstead's death.

From day to day there grew upon her a feeling
that she had subjected herself to domination, almost to

tyranny from Mr. Greenwood. The man whom she had known intimately during her entire married life now appeared to assume different proportions and almost a different character. He would still stand before her with his flabby hands hanging listlessly by his side, and with eyes apparently full of hesitation, and would seem to tremble as though he feared the effect of his own words; but still the words that fell from him were felt to be bonds from which she could not escape. When he looked at her from his lack-lustre eyes, fixing them upon her for minutes together, till the minutes seemed to be hours, she became afraid. She did not confess to herself that she had fallen into his power; nor did she realize the fact that it was so; but without realizing it she was dominated, so that she also began to think that it would be well that the chaplain should be made to leave Trafford Park. He, however, continued to discuss with her all family matters as though his services were indispensable to her; and she was unable to answer him in such a way as to reject his confidences.

The telegram reached the butler as to Hampstead's coming on the Monday, and was, of course, communicated at once to Lord Kingsbury. The Marquis, who was now confined to his bed, expressed himself as greatly gratified, and himself told the news to his wife. She, however, had already heard it, as had also the chaplain. It quickly went through the whole household, in which among the servants there existed an

opinion that Lord Hampstead ought to have been again
sent for some days since. The Doctor had hinted as
much to the Marchioness, and had said so plainly to the
butler. Mr. Greenwood had expressed to her ladyship
his belief that the Marquis had no desire to see his son,
and that the son certainly had no wish to pay another
visit to Trafford. "He cares more about the Quaker's
daughter than anything else," he had said,—"about her
and his hunting. He and his sister consider themselves
as separated from the whole of the family. I should
leave them alone if I were you." Then she had said a
faint word to her husband, and had extracted from
him something that was supposed to be the expression
of a wish that Lord Hampstead should not be disturbed. Now Lord Hampstead was coming without
any invitation.

"Going to walk over, is he, in the middle of the
night?" said Mr. Greenwood, preparing to discuss the
matter with the Marchioness. There was something of
scorn in his voice, as though he were taking upon
himself to laugh at Lord Hampstead for having chosen
this way of reaching his father's house.

"He often does that," said the Marchioness.

"It's an odd way of coming into a sick house,—to
disturb it in the middle of the night." Mr. Greenwood,
as he spoke, stood looking at her ladyship severely.

"How am I to help it? I don't suppose anybody
will be disturbed at all. He'll come round to the side
door, and one of the servants will be up to let him

in. He always does things differently from anybody else."

"One would have thought that when his father was dying——"

"Don't say that, Mr. Greenwood. There's nothing to make you say that. The Marquis is very ill, but nobody has said that he's so bad as that." Mr. Greenwood shook his head, but did not move from the position in which he was standing. "I suppose that on this occasion Hampstead is doing what is right."

"I doubt whether he ever does what is right. I am only thinking that if anything should happen to the Marquis, how very bad it would be for you and the young lords."

"Won't you sit down, Mr. Greenwood?" said the Marchioness, to whom the presence of the standing chaplain had become almost intolerable.

The man sat down,—not comfortably in his chair, but hardly more than on the edge of it, so as still to have that air of restraint which had annoyed his companion. "As I was saying, if anything should happen to my lord it would be very sad for your ladyship and for Lord Frederick, and Lord Augustus, and Lord Gregory."

"We are all in the hands of God," said her ladyship, piously.

"Yes;—we are all in the hands of God. But it is the Lord's intention that we should all look out for ourselves, and do the best we can to avoid injustice, and cruelty, and,—and—robbery."

"I do not think there will be any robbery, Mr. Greenwood."

"Would it not be robbery if you and their little lordships should be turned at once out of this house?"

"It would be his own;—Lord Hampstead's,—of course. I should have Slocombe Abbey in Somersetshire. As far as a house goes, I should like it better than this. Of course it is much smaller;—but what comfort do I ever have out of a house like this?"

"That's true enough. But why?"

"There is no good in talking about it, Mr. Greenwood."

"I cannot help talking about it. It is because Lady Frances has broken up the family by allowing herself to be engaged to a young man beneath her own station in life." Here he shook his head, as he always did when he spoke of Lady Frances. "As for Lord Hampstead, I look upon it as a national misfortune that he should outlive his father."

"What can we do?"

"Well, my lady; it is hard to say. What will my feelings be, should anything happen to the Marquis, and should I be left to the tender mercies of his eldest son? I should have no claim upon Lord Hampstead for a shilling. As he is an infidel, of course he would not want a chaplain. Indeed I could not reconcile it to my conscience to remain with him. I should be cast out penniless, having devoted all my life, as I may say, to his lordship's service."

"He has offered you a thousand pounds."

"A thousand pounds, for the labours of a whole life! And what assurance shall I have of that? I don't suppose he has ever dreamed of putting it into his will. And if he has, what will a thousand pounds do for me? You can go to Slocombe Abbey. But the rectory, which was as good as promised, will be closed against me." The Marchioness knew that this was a falsehood, but did not dare to tell him so. The living had been talked about between them till it was assumed that he had a right to it. "If the young man were out of the way," he continued, "there would be some chance for me."

"I cannot put him out of the way," said the Marchioness.

"And some chance for Lord Frederic and his brothers."

"You need not tell me of that, Mr. Greenwood."

"But one has to look the truth in the face. It is for your sake that I have been anxious,—rather than my own. You must own that." She would not own anything of the kind. "I suppose there was no doubt about the first marriage?"

"None at all," said the Marchioness, terrified.

"Though it was thought very odd at the time. It ought to be looked to, I think. No stone ought to be left unturned."

"There is nothing to be hoped for in that direction, Mr. Greenwood."

"It ought to be looked to;—that's all. Only think what it will be if he marries, and has a son before anything is—is settled."

To this Lady Kingsbury made no answer; and after a pause Mr. Greenwood turned to his own grievances. "I shall make bold," he said, "to see the Marquis once again before Lord Hampstead comes down. He cannot but acknowledge that I have a great right to be anxious. I do not suppose that any promise would be sacred in his son's eyes, but I must do the best I can." To this her ladyship would make no answer, and they parted, not in the best humour with each other.

That was on the Monday. On the Tuesday Mr. Greenwood, having asked to be allowed an interview, crept slowly into the sick man's room. "I hope your lordship find yourself better this morning?" The sick man turned in his bed, and only made some feeble grunt in reply. "I hear that Lord Hampstead is coming down to-morrow, my lord."

"Why should he not come?" There must have been something in the tone of Mr. Greenwood's voice which had grated against the sick man's ears, or he would not have answered so sulkily.

"Oh, no, my lord. I did not mean to say that there was any reason why his lordship should not come. Perhaps it might have been better had he come earlier."

" It wouldn't have been at all better."

" I only just meant to make the remark, my lord; there was nothing in it."

" Nothing at all," said the sick man. " Was there anything else you wished to say, Mr. Greenwood ? "

The nurse all this time was sitting in the room, which the chaplain felt to be uncomfortable. " Could we be alone for a few minutes, my lord ? " he asked.

" I don't think we could," said the sick man.

" There are a few points which are of so much importance to me, Lord Kingsbury."

" I ain't well enough to talk business, and I won't do it. Mr. Roberts will be here to-morrow, and you can see him."

Mr. Roberts was a man of business, or agent to the property, who lived at Shrewsbury, and whom Mr. Greenwood especially disliked. Mr. Greenwood being a clergyman was, of course, supposed to be a gentleman, and regarded Mr. Roberts as being much beneath himself. It was not customary for Mr. Roberts to dine at the house, and he was therefore regarded by the chaplain as being hardly more than an upper servant. It was therefore very grievous to him to be told that he must discuss his own private affairs and make his renewed request as to the living through Mr. Roberts. It was evidently intended that he should have no opportunity of discussing his private affairs. Whatever the Marquis might offer him he must take; and that, as far as he could see, without any power of

redress on his side. If Mr. Roberts were to offer him
a thousand pounds, he could only accept the cheque
and depart with it from Trafford Park, shaking off from
his feet the dust which such ingratitude would forbid
him to carry with him.

He was in the habit of walking daily for an hour
before sunset, moving very slowly up and down the
driest of the roads near the house, generally with his
hands clasped behind his back, believing that in doing
so he was consulting his health, and maintaining that
bodily vigour which might be necessary to him for the
performance of the parochial duties at Appleslocombe.
Now when he had left the bed-room of the Marquis he
went out of the front door, and proceeded on his walk
at a somewhat quicker pace than usual. He was full of
wrath, and his passion gave some alacrity to his movements. He was of course incensed against the Marquis;
but his anger burnt hottest against Lord Hampstead.
In this he was altogether unreasonable, for Lord Hampstead had said nothing and done nothing that could
injure his position. Lord Hampstead disliked him and,
perhaps, despised him, but had been anxious that the
Marquis should be liberal in the mode of severing a
connection which had lasted so long. But to Mr.
Greenwood himself it was manifest that all his troubles
came from the iniquities of his patron's two elder
children; and he remembered at every moment that
Lord Hampstead had insulted him when they were
both together. He was certainly not a man to forgive

an enemy, or to lose any opportunity for revenge which
might come in his way.

Certainly it would be good if the young man could
be got to break his neck out hunting;—or good if the
yacht could be made to founder, or go to pieces on a
rock, or come to any other fatal maritime misfortune.
But these were accidents which he personally could
have no power to produce. Such wishing was infantine,
and fit only for a weak woman, such as the Marchioness. If anything were to be done it must be
done by some great endeavour; and the endeavour must
come from himself. Then he reflected how far the
Marchioness would certainly be in his power, if both
the Marquis and his eldest son were dead. He did
believe that he had obtained great influence over her.
That she should rebel against him was of course on
the cards. But he was aware that within the last
month, since the date, indeed, at which the Marquis
had threatened to turn him out of the house, he had
made considerable progress in imposing himself upon
her as a master. He gave himself in this respect much
more credit than was in truth due to him. Lady
Kingsbury, though she had learnt to fear him, had not
so subjected herself to his influence as not to be able to
throw him off should a time come at which it might be
essential to her comfort to do so. But he had misread
the symptoms, and had misread also the fretfulness
of her impatience. He now assured himself that if
anything could be done he might rely entirely on her

support. After all that she had said to him, it would be impossible that she should throw him over. Thinking of all this, and thinking also how expedient it was that something should be done, he returned to the house when he had taken the exact amount of exercise which he supposed necessary for his health.

CHAPTER XII.

LIKE THE POOR CAT I' THE ADAGE.

WISHING will do nothing. If a man has sufficient cause for action he should act. "Letting I dare not wait upon I would, Like the poor cat i' the adage," never can produce results. Cherries will not fall into your mouth without picking. "If it were done, when 'tis done then 'twere well it were done quickly." If grapes hang too high what is the use of thinking of them? Nevertheless,—"Where there's a will there's a way." But certainly no way will be found amidst difficulties, unless a man set himself tó work seriously to look for it. With such self-given admonitions, counsels, and tags of old quotations as these, Mr. Greenwood went to work with himself on Monday night, and came to a conclusion that if anything were to be done it must be done at once.

Then came the question—what was the thing to be done, and what at once meant? When a thing has to be done which requires a special summoning of resolution, it is too often something which ought not to be done. To virtuous deeds, if they recommend

themselves to us at all, we can generally make up our
minds more easily. It was pleasanter to Mr. Greenwood
to think of the thing as something in the future, as
something which might possibly get itself done for him
by accident, than as an act the doing of which must
fall into his own hands. Then came the " cat i' the
adage," and the " when 'tis done then 'twere well," and
the rest of it. Thursday morning, between four and
five o' clock, when it would be pitch dark, with neither
star nor moon in the heavens, when Lord Hampstead
would certainly be alone in a certain spot, unattended
and easily assailable ;—would Thursday morning be the
fittest time for any such deed as that which he had now
in truth began to contemplate ?

When the thing presented itself to him in this new
form, he recoiled from it. It cannot be said that Mr.
Greenwood was a man of any strong religious feelings.
He had been ordained early in life to a curacy, having
probably followed, in choosing his profession, the bent
given to him by his family connections, and had thus
from circumstances fallen into the household of his
present patron's uncle. From that to this he had
never performed a service in a church, and his domestic
services as chaplain had very soon become nothing.
The old Lord Kingsbury had died very soon afterwards,
and Mr. Greenwood's services had been continued
rather as private secretary and librarian than as
domestic chaplain. He had been crafty, willing, and,
though anxious, he had been able to conceal his anxiety

in that respect, and ready to obey when he found it necessary. In this manner he had come to his present condition of life, and had but few of the manners or feelings of a clergyman about him. He was quite willing to take a living if it should come in his way,— but to take it with a purpose that the duties should be chiefly performed by a curate. He was not a religious man; but when he came to look the matter in the face, not on that account could he regard himself as a possible murderer without terrible doubts.

As he thought of it his first and prevailing fear did not come from the ignominious punishment which is attached to, and which generally attends, the crime. He has been described as a man flabby in appearance, as one who seemed to tremble in his shoes when called upon for any special words, as one who might be supposed to be devoid of strong physical daring. But the true character of the man was opposed to his outward bearing. Courage is a virtue of too high a nature to be included among his gifts; but he had that command of his own nerves, that free action of blood round his heart, that personal audacity coming from self-confidence, which is often taken to represent courage. Given the fact that he wanted an enemy out of the way, he could go to work to prepare to put him out of the way without exaggerated dread of the consequences as far as this world is concerned. He trusted much in himself, and thought it possible that he could so look through all the concomitant incidents

of such an act as that he contemplated without allowing
one to escape him which might lead to detection. He
could so look at the matter, he thought, as to be sure
whether this or the other plot might or might not
be safe. It might be that no safe plot were possible,
and that the attempt must therefore be abandoned.
These, at any rate, were not the dangers which made
him creep about in dismay at his own intentions.

There were other dangers of which he could not
shake off the dread. Whether he had any clear hope
as to eternal bliss in another life, it may be doubted.
He probably drove from his mind thoughts on the
subject, not caring to investigate his own belief. It
is the practice of many to have their minds utterly
callous in that respect. To suppose that such men
think this or think the other as to future rewards
and punishments is to give them credit for a condition
of mind to which they have never risen. Such a one
was probably Mr. Greenwood; but nevertheless he
feared something when this idea respecting Lord
Hampstead presented itself to him. It was as is
some boggy-bo to a child, some half-belief in a spectre
to a nervous woman, some dread of undefined evil
to an imaginative but melancholy man. He did not
think that by meditating such a deed, by hardening
his heart to the necessary resolution, by steeling himself up to its perpetration, he would bring himself
into a condition unfitted for a life of bliss. His
thoughts did not take any such direction. But though

there might be no punishment in this world,—even
though there were to be no other world in which
punishment could come,—still something of evil would
surely fall upon him. The conviction f of the world
since the days of Cain have all gone in that direction.
It was thus that he allowed himself to be cowed, and
to be made to declare to himself again and again that
the project must be abandoned.

But "the cat i' the adage" succeeded so far on
the Tuesday in getting the better of his scruples,
that he absolutely did form a plot. He did not as
yet quite see his way to that security which would
be indispensable;—but he did form a plot. Then
came the bitter reflection that what he would do
would be done for the benefit of others rather than
his own. What would Lord Frederic know of his
benefactor when he should come to the throne—as
in such case he would do—as Marquis of Kingsbury?
Lord Frederic would give him no thanks, even were
he to know it,—which of course could never be the
case. And why had not that woman assisted him,—
she who had instigated him to the doing of the deed?
"For Banquo's issue have I filed my mind," he said
to himself over and over again, not, however, in truth
thinking of the deed with any of the true remorse
to which Macbeth was a prey. The "filing of his
mind" only occurred to him because the words were
otherwise apt. Would she even be grateful when
she should tell herself, — as she surely would do, —

that the deed had been done by the partner of her
confidences ?

When he thought of the reward which was to come
to him in payment of the intended deed something like
a feeling of true conscience did arise within him.
Might it not be the case that even he, callous as he was
to most things, should find himself unable to go down
to Appleslocombe and read himself in, as the phrase
goes, as rector and pastor of the parish ? He thought
of this as he lay in his bed, and acknowledged to himself that his own audacity would probably be insufficient
to carry him through such a struggle. But still on the
morning when he rose he had not altogether rejected
the idea. The young man had scorned him and had
insulted him, and was hateful to him. But still why
should he be the Macbeth, seeing that the Lady Macbeth of the occasion was untrue to him ? In all this he
was unaware how very little his Lady Macbeth had
really meant when she had allowed herself in his
presence to express wishes as to her stepson's death.

He thought he saw his plan. The weapon was there
ready to his hand;—a weapon which he had not
bought, which could not be traced to him, which would
certainly be fatal if used with the assurance of which
he was confident. And there would be ample time for
retreat. But still as he arranged it all in his mind he
regarded it all not as a thing fixed, but as a thing which
was barely possible. It was thus that it might be done,
had the Lady Macbeth of the occasion really shown

herself competent to such a task. Why should he trouble himself on such a matter? Why should he file his mind for Banquo's issue? Yet he looked at the pistol and at the window as he prepared to go up to her ladyship's room before lunch on the Wednesday morning. It certainly could be done, he said to himself, telling himself at the same time that all that had been passing in his own mind was no more than a vague speculation. A man is apt to speculate on things which have no reality to him, till they become real.

He had assumed the practice of going to her ladyship's sitting-room up-stairs without a special summons, latterly to her ladyship's great disgust. When her quarrel had first become strong with Lady Frances she had no doubt received comfort from his support. But now she had become weary of him, and had sometimes been almost dismayed by the words he spoke to her. At half-past twelve punctually she went down to her husband's room, and it was now customary with the chaplain to visit her before she did so. She had more than once almost resolved to tell him that she preferred to be left alone during the morning. But she had not as yet assumed the courage to do this. She was aware that words had fallen from her in her anger which it was possible he might use against her, were she to subject herself to his displeasure. "Lord Hampstead will be here at half-past four—what you may call the middle of the night—to-morrow morning, Lady Kingsbury," said he, repeating an assertion which he had

already made to her two or three times. As he did so
he stood in the middle of the room, looking down upon
her with a gaze under which she had often suffered,
but which she did not in the least understand.

" Of course I know he's coming."

" Don't you think it a very improper time, with a
sick man in the house ? "

" He won't disturb his father."

" I don't know. There will be the opening and the
shutting of the door, and the servant will be going
about the passages, and there will be the bringing in of
the luggage."

" He won't have any luggage." Mr. Greenwood had
been aware of this; but it might be well that he should
affect ignorance.

" It is like everything else that he does," he said,
being anxious to induce the stepmother to speak ill of
her stepson. But the bent of her mind had been
turned. She was not conscious of the cause which had
produced the change, but she was determined to speak
no further evil of her stepchildren before Mr. Greenwood. " I suppose there is nothing to be done ? " said
Mr. Greenwood.

" What should there be to be done ? If you do
remain here I wish you would sit down, Mr. Greenwood.
You oppress me by standing up in that way in the
middle of the room."

" I do not wonder that you should be oppressed," he
said, seating himself, as was his wont, on the edge of a

chair. "I am oppressed, I know. No one ever says a word to comfort me. What am I to do if anything should happen?"

"Mr. Greenwood, what is the use of all this?"

"What would you think, Lady Kingsbury, if you had to live all the rest of your life on an income arising from a thousand pounds?"

"It isn't my fault. What's the good of your coming to me with all that? I have had nothing to do with the arrangement which Lord Kingsbury has made with you. You know very well that I do not dare even to mention your name to him, lest he should order that you should be turned out of the house."

"Turned out of the house!" he said, jumping off his chair on to his legs with an alacrity which was quite unusual to him. "Turned out of the house? —as if I were a dog! No man alive would stand such language."

"You know very well that I've always stood your friend," said the Marchioness, alarmed by the man's impetuosity.

"And you tell me that I'm to be turned out of the house."

"I only say that it would be better not to mention your name to him. I must go now, because he will be waiting for me."

"He doesn't care a straw for you; not a straw."

"Mr. Greenwood!"

"He cares only for his son and daughter;—for the

M

son and daughter of his first wife; for those two ignoble
young persons who, as you have said so often, are
altogether unworthy of their name."

"Mr. Greenwood, I cannot admit this."

"Have you not said it over and over again? Have
you not declared how good a thing it would be that
Lord Hampstead should die? You cannot go back
from all that, Lady Kingsbury."

"I must go now, Mr. Greenwood," she said, shuffling
out of the room. He had altogether frightened her,
and, as she went down-stairs, she determined that at
whatever cost she must save herself from further private
conversation with the chaplain.

Mr. Greenwood, when he was thus left alone, did not
at once leave the room. He had reseated himself, and
there he remained still gazing as though there had
been some one for him to gaze at, and still seated on
the edge of his chair as though there were some one to
see the affected humility of his position. But in truth
the gazing and the manner of sitting had become so
customary to him that they were assumed without
thought. His mind was now full of the injury done to
him by the Marchioness. She had made him her confidant; she had poured her secret thoughts into his
ears; she had done her best to inspire him with her
hatred and her desires; — and now, when she had
almost taught him to be the minister of her wishes, she
turned upon him, and upbraided him and deserted
him! Of course when he had sympathized with her as

to her ill-used darlings he had expected her to sympathize with him as to the hardships inflicted upon
him. But she cared nothing for his hardships, and was
anxious to repudiate the memory of all the hard words
which she had spoken as to her husband's children. It
should not be so! She should not escape from him in
this manner! When confidences have been made, the
persons making them must abide the consequences.
When a partnership has been formed, neither partner
has a right to retreat at once, leaving the burden of all
debts upon the other. Had not all these thoughts, and
plottings, which had been so heavy on his mind since
that telegram had come, which had been so heavy on
his soul, been her doing? Had not the idea come from
her? Had there not been an unspoken understanding
between them that in consequence of certain mutual
troubles and mutual aspirations there should be a plan
of action arranged between them? Now she was
deserting him! Well;—he thought that he could so
contrive things that she should not do so with impunity. Having considered all this he got up from his
chair and slowly walked down to his own room.

He lunched by himself, and then sat himself down
with a novel, as was his wont at that hour of the day.
There could be no man more punctual in all his daily
avocations than Mr. Greenwood. After lunch there
always came the novel; but there was seldom much of
it read. He would generally go to sleep, and would
remain so, enjoying perfect tranquillity for the best part

M 2

of an hour. Then he would go out for his constitutional walk, after which he would again take up the novel till the time came for her ladyship's tea. On this occasion he did not read at all, but neither did he at once sleep. There had been that on his mind which, even though it had not been perfected, banished sleep from him for some minutes. There was no need of any further conversation as to safety or danger. The deed, whether it would or could not have been done in the manner he had premeditated, certainly would not be done now. Certainly not now would he file his mind for Banquo's issue. But after half-an-hour of silent meditation he did sleep.

When he arose and went out for a walk he felt that his heart was light within him. He had done nothing by which he had compromised himself. He had bound himself to no deed. As he walked up and down the road he assured himself that he had never really thought of doing it. He had only speculated as to the probability,—which is so common for men to do as to performances which they had no thought of attempting. There was a great burden gone from him. Had he desired to get rid of Lord Hampstead, it was in that way that he would have done it;—and he would so have done it that he would never have been suspected of the deed. He had never intended more than that. As he returned to the house he assured himself that he had never intended anything more. And yet there was a great burden gone from him.

At five o'clock a message was brought to him that her ladyship, finding herself to be rather unwell, begged to be excused from asking him up to tea. The message was brought by the butler himself, with a suggestion that he should have tea in his own room. "I think I will, Harris," he said, "just take a cup. By-the-bye, Harris, have you seen my lord to-day?" Harris declared that he had seen his lordship, in a tone of voice which implied that he at any rate had not been banished from my lord's presence. "And how do you find him?" Harris thought that the Marquis was a little more like himself to-day than he had been for the last three days. "That's right. I am very glad to hear that. Lord Hampstead's coming to-morrow will be a great comfort to him."

"Yes, indeed," said Harris, who was quite on Lord Hampstead's side in the family quarrels. He had not been pleased with the idea of the Roden marriage, which certainly was unfortunate for the daughter of a Marquis; but he was by no means inclined to take part against the heir to the family honours.

"I wish he were coming at a little more reasonable hour in the day," said Mr. Greenwood with a smile. But Harris thought that the time of the day would do very well. It was the kind of thing which his lordship very often did, and Harris did not see any harm in it. This Harris said with his hand on the lock of the door, showing that he was not anxious for a prolonged conversation with the chaplain.

CHAPTER XIII.

LADY FRANCES SEES HER LOVER.

ON the Monday in that week,—Monday, the 5th of January, on which day Hampstead had been hunting and meditating the attack which he subsequently made on Zachary Fay, in King's Court,—Mrs. Vincent had paid a somewhat unusually long visit in Paradise Row. As the visit was always made on Monday, neither had Clara Demijohn or Mrs. Duffer been very much surprised; but still it had been observed that the brougham had been left at the Duchess of Edinburgh for an hour beyond the usual time, and a few remarks were made. " She is so punctual about her time generally," Clara had said. But Mrs. Duffer remarked that as she had exceeded the hour usually devoted to her friend's company she had probably found it quite as well to stay another. " They don't make half-hours in any of those yards, you know," said Mrs. Duffer. And so the matter had been allowed to pass as having been sufficiently explained.

But there had in truth been more than that in Mrs. Vincent's prolonged visit to her cousin. There had been much to be discussed, and the discussion led to a proposition made that evening by Mrs. Roden to her son by which the latter was much surprised. She was desirous of starting almost immediately for Italy, and was anxious that he should accompany her. If it were to be so he was quite alive to the expediency of going with her. "But what is it, mother?" he asked, when she had requested his attendance without giving the cause which rendered the journey necessary. Then she paused as though considering whether she would comply with his request, and tell him that whole secret of his life which she had hitherto concealed from him. "Of course, I will not press you," he said, "if you think that you cannot trust me."

"Oh, George, that is unkind."

"What else am I to say? Is it possible that I should start suddenly upon such a journey, or that I should see you doing so, without asking the reason why? Or can I suppose if you do not tell me, but that there is some reason why you should not trust me?"

"You know I trust you. No mother ever trusted a son more implicitly. You ought to know that. It is not a matter of trusting. There may be secrets to which a person shall be so pledged that she cannot tell them to her dearest friend. If I had made a promise would you not have me keep it?"

"Promises such as that should not be exacted, and should not be made."

"But if they have been exacted and have been

made? Do as I ask you now, and it is probable that
everything will be clear to you before we return, or at
any rate as clear to you as it is to me." After this,
with a certain spirit of reticence which was peculiar
with him, he made up his mind to do as his mother
would have him without asking further questions. He
set himself to work immediately to make the necessary
arrangements for his journey with as much apparent
satisfaction as though it were to be done on his own
behalf. It was decided that they would start on the
next Friday, travel through France and by the tunnel
of the Mont Cenis to Turin, and thence on to Milan.
Of what further there was to befall them he knew
nothing at this period.

It was necessary in the first place that he should get
leave of absence from Sir Boreas, as to which he professed himself to be in much doubt, because he had
already enjoyed the usual leave of absence allowed by
the rules of the office. But on this matter he found
Æolus to be very complaisant. "What, Italy?" said
Sir Boreas. "Very nice when you get there, I should
say, but a bad time of year for travelling. Sudden
business, eh?—To go with your mother! It is bad for
a lady to go alone. How long? You don't know?
Well! come back as soon as you can; that's all. You
couldn't take Crocker with you, could you?" For at
this time Crocker had already got into further trouble
in regard to imperfections of handwriting. He had
been promised absolution as to some complaint made

against him on condition that he could read a page of
his own manuscript. But he had altogether failed in
the attempt. Roden didn't think that he could carry
Crocker to Italy, but arranged his own affair without
that impediment.

But there was another matter which must be arranged
also. It was now six weeks since he had walked with
Lord Hampstead half-way back from Holloway to
Hendon, and had been desired by his friend not to visit
Lady Frances while she was staying at Hendon Hall.
The reader may remember that he had absolutely
refused to make any promise, and that there had consequently been some sharp words spoken between the
two friends. There might, he had then said, arise an
occasion on which he should find it impossible not to
endeavour to see the girl he loved. But hitherto,
though he had refused to submit himself to the demand
made upon him, he had complied with its spirit. At
this moment, as it seemed to him, a period had come in
which it was essential to him that he should visit her.
There had been no correspondence between them since
those Königsgraaf days in consequence of the resolutions
which she herself had made. Now, as he often told
himself, they were as completely separated as though
each had determined never again to communicate with
the other. Months had gone by since a word had
passed between them. He was a man, patient, reten-
tive, and by nature capable of enduring such a trouble
without loud complaint; but he did remember from

day to day how near they were to each other, and he did not fail to remind himself that he could hardly expect to find constancy in her unless he took some means of proving to her that he was constant himself. Thinking of all this, he determined that he would do his best to see her before he started for Italy. Should he fail to be received at Hendon Hall then he would write. But he would go to the house and make his attempt.

On Thursday morning, the day on which Hampstead arrived at Trafford Park, he went down from London, and knocking at the door asked at once for Lady Frances. Lady Frances was at home and alone;—alone altogether, having no companion with her in the house during her brother's absence. The servant who opened the door, the same who had admitted poor Crocker and had understood how much his young mistress had been dismayed when the Post Office clerk had been announced, was unwilling at once to show this other Post Office clerk into the house, although he probably understood well the difference between the two comers. "I'll go and see," he said, leaving George Roden to sit or stand in the hall as he liked best. Then the man, with a sagacity which certainly did him credit, made a roundabout journey through the house, so that the lover stationed in the hall might not know that his mistress was to be reached merely by the opening of a single door. "A gentleman in the hall?" said Lady Frances.

"Mr. Roden, my lady," said the man.

"Show him in," said Lady Frances, allowing herself just a moment for consideration,—a moment so short that she trusted that no hesitation had been visible. And yet she had doubted much. She had been very clear in explaining to her brother that she had made no promise. She had never pledged herself to any one that she would deny herself to her lover should he come to see her. She would not admit to herself that even her brother, even her father, had a right to demand from her such a pledge. But she knew what were her brother's wishes on this matter, and what were the reasons for them. She knew also how much she owed to him. But she too had suffered from that long silence. She had considered that a lover whom she never saw, and from whom she never heard, was almost as bad as no lover at all. She had beaten her feathers against her cage, as she thought of this cruel separation. She had told herself of the short distance which separated Hendon from Holloway. She perhaps had reflected that had the man been as true to her as was she to him, he would not have allowed himself to be deterred by the injunctions either of father or brother. Now, at any rate, when her lover was at the door, she could not turn him away. It had all to be thought of, but it was thought of so quickly that the order for her lover's admittance was given almost without a pause which could have been felt. Then, in half a minute, her lover was in the room with her.

Need the chronicler of such scenes declare that they were in each other's arms before a word was spoken between them? The first word that was spoken came from her. "Oh, George, how long it has been!"

"It has been long to me."

"But at last you have come?"

"Did you expect me sooner? Had you not agreed with Hampstead and your father that I was not to come?"

"Never mind. You are here now. Poor papa, you know, is very ill. Perhaps I may have to go down there. John is there now."

"Is he so ill as that?"

"John went last night. We do not quite know how ill he is. He does not write, and we doubt whether we get at the truth. I was very nearly going with him; and then, sir, you would not have seen me—at all."

"Another month, another six months, another year, would have made no difference in my assurance of your truth to me."

"That is a very pretty speech for you to make."

"Nor I think in yours for me."

"I am bound, of course, to be just as pretty as you are. But why have you come now? You shouldn't have come when John had left me all alone."

"I did not know that you were here alone."

"Or you would not have come, perhaps? But you should not have come. Why did you not ask before you came?"

"Because I should have been refused. It would have been refused; would it not?"

"Certainly it would."

"But as I wish to see you specially——"

"Why specially? I have wanted to see you always. Every day has been a special want. It should have been so with you also had you been as true as I am. There should have been no special times."

"But I am going——"

"Going! Where are you going? Not for always! You are leaving Holloway, you mean, or the Post Office." Then he explained to her that as far as he knew the journey would not be for long. He was not leaving his office, but had permission to absent himself for a time, so that he might travel with his mother as far as Milan. "Nay," said he, laughing, "why I am to do so I do not in the least know. My mother has some great Italian mystery of which she has never yet revealed to me any of the circumstances. All I know is that I was born in Italy."

"You an Italian?"

"I did not say that. There is an old saying that you need not be a horse because you were born in a stable. Nor do I quite know that I was born in Italy, though I feel sure of it. Of my father I have never known anything,—except that he was certainly a bad husband to my mother. There are circumstances which do make me almost sure that I was born in Italy; but as my mother has been unwilling to talk to me of my earliest days, I have never chosen to ask her. Now I shall perhaps know it all."

Of what else passed between them the reader need learn no details. To her the day was one of exceeding joy. A lover in China, or waging wars in Zululand or elsewhere among the distant regions, is a misfortune. A lover ought to be at hand, ready at the moment, to be kissed or scolded, to wait upon you, or, so much sweeter still, to be waited upon, just as the occasion may serve. But the lover in China is better than one in the next street or the next parish,—or only a few miles off by railway,—whom you may not see. The heart recognizes the necessity occasioned by distance with a sweet softness of tender regrets, but is hardened by mutiny, or crushed by despair in reference to stern parents or unsuitable pecuniary circumstances. Lady Frances had been enduring the sternness of parents, and had been unhappy. Now there had come a break. She had seen what he was like, and had heard his voice, and been reassured by his vows, and had enjoyed the longed-for opportunity of repeating her own. " Nothing, nothing, nothing can change me ! " How was he to be sure of that while she had no opportunity of telling him that it was so ? " No time ;—nothing that papa can say, nothing that John can do, will have any effect. As to Lady Kingsbury, of course you know that she has thrown me off altogether." It was nothing to him, he said, who might have thrown her off. Having her promise, he could bide his time. Not but that he was impatient; but that he knew that when so much was to be given to him at last, it behoved him to endure all things rather than to be faint of heart. And so they parted.

She, however, in spite of her joy, had a troubled spirit when he was gone. She had declared to her brother that she was bound by no promise as to seeing or not seeing her lover, but yet she was aware how much she owed to him, and that, though she had not promised, he had made a promise on her behalf, to her father. But for that promise she would never have been allowed to be at Hendon Hall. His brother had made all his arrangements so as to provide for her a home in which she might be free from the annoyances inflicted upon her by her stepmother; but had done so almost with a provision that she should not see George Roden. She certainly had done nothing herself to infringe that stipulation; but George Roden had come, and she had seen him. She might have refused him admittance, no doubt; but then again she thought that it would have been impossible to do so. How could she have told the man to deny her, thus professing her indifference for him in regard to whom she had so often declared that she was anxious that all the world should know that they were engaged to marry each other? It would have been impossible for her not to see him; and yet she felt that she had been treacherous to her brother, to whom she owed so much!

One thing seemed to her to be absolutely necessary.
She must write at once and tell him what had occurred.
Thinking of this she sat down and wrote so that she
might despatch her letter by that post;—and what she
wrote is here given.

"My Dear John—

"I shall be so anxious to get news from
Trafford, and to hear how you found papa. I cannot
but think that were he very ill somebody would have
let us know the truth. Though Mr. Greenwood is
cross-grained and impertinent, he would hardly have
kept us in the dark.

"Now I have a piece of news to tell you which I
hope will not make you very angry. It was not my
doing, and I do not know how I could have helped it.
Your friend, George Roden, called to-day and asked to
see me. Of course I could have refused. He was in
the hall when Richard announced him, and I suppose
I could have sent out word to say that I was not at
home. But I think you will feel that that was in
truth impossible. How is one to tell a lie to a man
when one feels towards him as I do about George? Or
how could I even let the servants think that I would
treat him so badly? Of course every one knows about
it. I want every one to know about it, so that it may
be understood that I am not in the least ashamed of
what I mean to do.

"And when you hear why he came I do not think

that you can be angry even with him. He has been called upon, for some reason, to go at once with his mother to Italy. They start for Milan to-morrow, and he does not at all know when he may return. He had to get leave at the Post Office, but that Sir Boreas whom he talks about seems to have been very good-natured about giving it. He asked him whether he would not take Mr. Crocker with him to Italy; but that of course was a joke. I suppose they do not like Mr. Crocker at the Post Office any better than you do. Why Mrs. Roden should have to go he does not understand. All he knows is that there is some Italian secret which he will hear all about before he comes home.

"Now I really do think that you cannot be surprised that he should have come to see me when he is going to take such a journey as that. What should I have thought if I had heard that he had gone without saying a word to me about it? Don't you think that that would have been most unnatural? I should have almost broken my heart when I heard that he had started.

"I do hope, therefore, that you will not be angry with either of us. But yet I feel that I may have brought you into trouble with papa. I do not care in the least for Lady Kingsbury, who has no right to interfere in the matter at all. After her conduct everything I think is over between us. But I shall be indeed sorry if papa is vexed; and shall feel it very

much if he says anything to you after all your great
kindness to me.

> "Your affectionate sister,
>
>   "FANNY."

"I have done one other thing to-day," said George
Roden, when he was explaining to his mother on
Thursday evening all the preparations he had made for
their journey.

"What other thing?" she asked, guessing accurately,
however, the nature of the thing of which he was about
to speak.

"I have seen Lady Frances Roden."

"I thought it probable that you might endeavour to
do so."

"I have done more than endeavour on this occasion.
I went down to Hendon Hall, and was shown into the
drawing-room. I am sorry for Hampstead's sake, but
it was impossible for me not to do so."

"Why sorry for his sake?" she asked.

"Because he had pledged himself to his father that
I should not do so. He clearly had no right to make
such a pledge. I could not bind myself to an assurance
by keeping which I might seem to show myself to be
indifferent. A girl may bind herself by such a promise,
but hardly a man. Had I made the promise I almost
think I must have broken it. I did not make it, and
therefore I have no sin to confess. But I fear I shall
have done him a mischief with his father."

"And what did she say, George?"

"Oh; just the old story, mother, I suppose. What she said was what I knew just as well before I went there. But yet it was necessary that I should hear what she had to say;—and as necessary I think that she should hear me."

"Quite as necessary, I am sure," said his mother kissing his forehead.

CHAPTER XIV.

MR. GREENWOOD'S FEELINGS.

ON that Wednesday night Mr. Greenwood did not
sleep much. It may be doubted whether he once
closed his eyes in slumber. He had indeed been saved
from the performance of an act which now seemed to
him to be so terrible that he could hardly believe that
he had in truth contemplated it; but yet he knew,—
he knew that it for some hours had been the purpose
of his mind to do it! He struggled to make himself
believe that it had in truth been no more than a speculation, that there had been no formed purpose, that he
had only amused himself by considering how he could
do such a deed without detection, if the deed were to
be done. He had simply been thinking over the
blunders of others, the blindness of men who had so
bungled in their business as to have left easy traces for
the eyes and intelligence of the world outside, and had
been assuring himself how much better he could manage
if the necessity of such an operation were to come upon
him. That was all. No doubt he hated Lord Hampstead,—and had cause to do so. It was thus that he

argued with himself. But his hatred had surely not carried him to the intention of murder!

There could have been no question of real murder; for why should he have troubled himself either with the danger or with the load which it would certainly have imposed on his conscience? Much as he hated Lord Hampstead, it was no business of his. It was that Lady Macbeth up-stairs, the mother of the darlings, who had really thought of murder. It was she who had spoken openly of her great desire that Lord Hampstead should cease to live. Had there been any real question of murder it would have been for her to meditate, for her to think, for her to plot;—surely not for him! Certainly, certainly he had contemplated no such deed as that, with the object of obtaining for the comfort of his old age the enjoyment of the living of Appleslocombe! He told himself now that had he in truth committed such a crime, had he carried out the plot which had formed itself in his brain only as a matter of speculation, though he might not have been detected, yet he would have been suspected; and suspicion would have been as destructive to his hopes as detection. Of course all that had been clear enough to him throughout his machinations; and therefore how could he really have intended it? He had not intended it. It had only been one of those castles in the air which the old build as well as the young,—which are no more than the "airy fabrics" of the brain!

It was thus he struggled to drive from his mind and

from his eyes the phantom of the terrible deed. But
that he did not succeed was made evident to himself by
the hot clammy drops of sweat which came out upon
his brow, by his wakefulness throughout the livelong
night, by the carefulness with which his ears watched
for the sound of the young man's coming, as though it
were necessary that he should be made assured that the
murder had in truth not been done. Before that hour
had come he found himself to be shaking even in his
bed; to be drawing the clothes around him to dispel
the icy cold, though the sweat still stood upon his
brow; to be hiding his eyes under the bed-clothes in
order that he might not see something which seemed to
be visible to him through the utmost darkness of the
chamber. At any rate he had done nothing! Let his
thoughts have been what they might, he had soiled
neither his hands nor his conscience. Though everything that he had ever done or ever thought were
known, he was free from all actual crime. She had
talked of death and thought of murder. He had only
echoed her words and her thoughts, meaning nothing,—
as a man is bound to do to a woman. Why then could
he not sleep? Why should he be hot and shiver with
cold by turns? Why should horrid phantoms perplex
him in the dark? He was sure he had never meant it.
What must be the agony of those who do mean, of
those who do execute, if such punishment as this were
awarded to one who had done no more than build a
horrid castle in the air? Did she sleep;—he wondered,

—she who had certainly done more than build a castle in the air; she who had wished and longed, and had a reason for her wishing and her longing?

At last he heard a footfall on the road, which passed but some few yards distant from his window, a quick, cheery, almost running footfall, a step full of youth and life, sounding crisp on the hard frozen ground; and he knew that the young man whom he hated had come. Though he had never thought of murdering him,—as he told himself,—yet he hated him. And then his thoughts, although in opposition to his own wishes,—which were intent upon sleep, if sleep would only come to him,—ran away to the building of other castles. How would it have been now, now at this moment, if that plan, which he had never really intended to carry out, which had only been a speculation, had been a true plan and been truly executed? How would it have been with them all now at Trafford Park? The Marchioness would have been at any rate altogether satisfied;—but what comfort would there have been in that to him? Lord Frederic would have been the heir to a grand title and to vast estates;—but how would he have been the better for that? The old lord who was lying there so sick in the next room might probably have sunk into his grave with a broken heart. The Marquis had of late been harsh to him; but there did come to him an idea at the present moment that he had for thirty years eaten the sick man's bread. And the young man would have been sent without a moment's notice to meet his final doom! Of what nature that might have been, the wretched man lying there did not dare even to make a picture in his imagination. It was a matter which he had sedulously and successfully dismissed from all his thoughts. It was of the body lying out there in the cold, not of the journey which the winged soul might make, that he unwillingly drew a picture to himself. He conceived how he himself, in the prosecution of the plan which he had formed, would have been forced to have awakened the house, and to tell of the deed, and to assist in carrying the body to what resting-place might have been found for it. There he would have had to enact a part of which he had, a few hours since, told himself that he would be capable, but in attempting which he was now sure that he would have succumbed to the difficulties of the struggle. Who would have broken the news to the father? Who would have attempted to speak the first word of vain consolation? Who would have flown to the lady's door up-stairs and have informed her that death was in the house—and have given her to understand that the eldest of her darlings was the heir? It would have been for him to do it all; for him with a spirit weighed down to the ground by that terrible burden with which the doing of such a deed would have loaded it. He would certainly have revealed himself in the struggle!

But why should he allow his mind to he perplexed with such thoughts? No such deed had been done.

There had been no murder. The young man was there now in the house, light-hearted after his walk; full of life and youthful energy. Why should he be troubled with such waking dreams as these? Must it be so with him always, for the rest of his life, only because he had considered how a thing might best be done? He heard a footstep in a distant passage, and a door closed, and then again all was silent. Was there not cause to him for joy in the young man's presence? If his speculations had been wicked, was there not time to turn for repentance,—for repentance, though there was so little for which repentance were needed? Nevertheless the night was to him so long, and the misery connected with the Trafford name so great, that he told himself that he would quit the place as soon as possible. He would take whatever money were offered to him and go. How would it have been with him had he really done the deed, when he found himself unable to sleep in the house in which he would not quite admit to himself that he had even contemplated it?

On the next morning his breakfast was brought to him in his own room, and he inquired from the servant after Lord Hampstead and his purposes. The servant thought that his lordship meant to remain on that day and the next. So he had heard Harris, the butler, say. His lordship was to see his father at eleven o'clock that morning. The household bulletin respecting the Marquis had that morning been rather more favourable than usual. The Marchioness had not yet been seen.

The doctor would probably be there by twelve. This was the news which Mr. Greenwood got from the servant who waited upon him. Could he not escape from the house during the period that the young lord would be there, without seeing the young lord? The young lord was hateful to him—more hateful than ever. He would, if possible, get himself carried into Shrewsbury, and remain there on some excuse of visiting a friend till the young lord should have returned to London. He could not tell himself why, but he felt that the sight of the young lord would be oppressive to him.

But in this he was prevented by an intimation that was given to him early in the day, before he had made preparations for his going, that Lord Hampstead wished to see him, and would wait upon him in his own room. The Marquis had expressed himself grateful to his son for coming, but did not wish to detain him at Trafford. "Of course it is very dull for you, and I think I am better."

"I am so glad of that;—but if you think that I am of any comfort to you I shall be delighted to stay. I suppose Fanny would come down if I remain here."

Then the Marquis shook his head. Fanny, he thought, had better be away. "The Marchioness and Fanny would not be happy in the house together,—unless, indeed, she has given up that young man." Hampstead could not say that she had given up the young man. "I do hope she never sees him," said the Marquis. Then

his son assured him that the two had never met since
Fanny had gone to Hendon Hall. And he was rash
enough to assure his father that there would be no such
meeting while his sister was his guest. At that moment
George Roden was standing in the drawing-room at
Hendon Hall with Lady Frances in his arms.

After that there arose a conversation between the
father and son as to Mr. Greenwood. The Marquis was
very desirous that the man who had become so objectionable to him should quit the house. "The truth is,"
said the Marquis, "that it is he who makes all the
mischief between me and your stepmother. It is he
that makes me ill. I have no comfort while he is here,
making plots against me." If they two had only known
the plot which had been made! Hampstead thought
it reasonable that the man should be sent away, if only
because his presence was disagreeable. Why should a
man be kept in the house simply to produce annoyance?
But there must be the question of compensation. He did
not think that £1000 was sufficient. Then the Marquis
was unusually difficult of persuasion in regard to money.
Hampstead thought that an annuity of £300 a year
should be settled on the poor clergyman. The Marquis
would not hear of it. The man had not performed even
the slight duties which had been required of him. The
books had not even been catalogued. To bribe a man,
such as that, by £300 a year for making himself disagreeable would be intolerable. The Marquis had
never promised him anything. He ought to have saved

his money. At last the father and son came to terms, and Hampstead sent to prepare a meeting with the chaplain.

Mr. Greenwood was standing in the middle of the room when Lord Hampstead entered it, rubbing his fat hands together. Hampstead saw no difference in the man since their last meeting, but there was a difference. Mr. Greenwood's manner was at first more submissive, as though he were afraid of his visitor; but before the interview was over he had recovered his audacity. "My father has wished me to see you," said Hampstead. Mr. Greenwood went on rubbing his hands, still standing in the middle of the room. "He seems to think it better that you should leave him."

"I don't know why he should think it better;—but, of course, I will go if he bids me." Mr. Greenwood had quite made up his mind that it would be better for him also that he should go.

"There will be no good in going into that. I think we might as well sit down, Mr. Greenwood." They did sit down, the chaplain as usual perching himself on the edge of a chair. "You have been here a great many years."

"A great many, Lord Hampstead;—nearly all my life;—before you were born, Lord Hampstead." Then, as he sat gazing, there came before his eyes the phantom of Lord Hampstead being carried into the house as a corpse while he himself was struggling beneath a portion of the weight.

"Just so; and though the Marquis cannot admit that there is any claim upon him——"

"No claim, Lord Hampstead!"

"Certainly no claim. Yet he is quite willing to do something in acknowledgment of the long connection. His lordship thinks that an annuity of £200 a year——." Mr. Greenwood shook his head, as though he would say that that certainly would not satisfy him. Hampstead had been eager to secure the full £300 for the wretched, useless man, but the Marquis had declared that he would not burden the estate with a charge so unnecessarily large. "I say," continued Hampstead, frowning, "that his lordship has desired me to say that you shall receive during your life an annuity of £200." It certainly was the fact that Lord Hampstead could frown when he was displeased, and that at such moments he would assume a look of aristocratic impatience which was at variance with his professed political theories. Mr. Greenwood again shook his head. "I do not think that I need say anything farther," continued the young lord. "That is my father's decision. He presumes that you would prefer the annuity to the immediate payment of a thousand pounds." Here the shaking of the head became more violent. "I have only in addition to ask you when it will suit you to leave Trafford Park." Lord Hampstead, when he had left his father, had determined to use his blandest manner in communicating these tidings to the chaplain. But Mr. Greenwood was odious to him. The way in which the

man stood on the floor and rubbed his hands together,
and sat on the edge of his chair, and shook his head
without speaking a word, were disgusting to him. If
the man had declared boldly his own view of what
was due to him, Hampstead would have endeavoured
to be gracious to him. As it was he was anything
but gracious, as he asked the chaplain to name the day
on which he would be prepared to leave the house.

"You mean to say that I am to be——turned out."

"It is some months since you were told that my
father no longer required your services."

"I am to be turned out,—like a dog,—after thirty
years!"

"I cannot contradict you when you say so, but I
must ask you to name a day. It is not as though the
suggestion were now made to you for the first time."
Mr. Greenwood got up from the edge of the chair, and
again stood in the middle of the room. Lord Hampstead
felt himself constrained also to stand. "Have you any
answer to make to me?"

"No; I have not," said the chaplain.

"You mean that you have not fixed upon a day?"

"I shan't go with £200 a year," said the chaplain.
"It's unreasonable; it's brutal!"

"Brutal!" shouted Lord Hampstead.

"I shan't stir till I've seen the Marquis himself.
It's out of the question that he should turn me out
in this way. How am I to live upon £200 a year? I
always understood that I was to have Appleslocombe."

"No such promise was ever made to you," said Lord Hampstead, very angrily. "No hint of such a thing has ever been made except by yourself."

"I always understood it," said Mr. Greenwood. "And I shall not leave this till I've had an opportunity of discussing the matter with the Marquis himself. I don't think the Marquis would ever have treated me in this way,—only for you, Lord Hampstead."

This was intolerable. What was he to do with the abominable man? It would be very disagreeable, the task of turning him out while the Marquis was still so ill, and yet it was not to be endured that such a man should be allowed to hold his position in the house in opposition to the will of the owner. It was, he felt, beneath him to defend himself against the charge made —or even to defend his father. "If you will not name a day, I must," said the young lord. The man remained immovable on his seat except that he continued to rub his hands. "As I can get no answer I shall have to instruct Mr. Roberts that you cannot be allowed to remain here after the last day of the month. If you have any feeling left to you you will not impose upon us so unpleasant a duty while my father is ill." With this he left the room, while Mr. Greenwood was still standing and rubbing his hands.

Two hundred pounds a year! He had better go and take it. He was quite aware of that. But how was he to live upon £200,—he who had been bedded and boarded all his life at the expense of another man, and had also

spent £300? But at the moment this was not the
thought uppermost in his mind. Would it not have
been better that he should have carried out that project
of his? Only that he had been merciful, this young lord
would not have been able to scorn him and ill-treat
him as he had done. There were no phantoms now.
Now he thought that he could have carried his share
of the corpse into the house without flinching.

CHAPTER XV.

"THAT WOULD BE DISAGREEABLE."

THINGS at Trafford on that day and on the next were very uncomfortable. No house could possibly be more so. There were four persons who, in the natural course of things, would have lived together, not one of whom would sit down to table with any other. The condition of the Marquis, of course, made it impossible that he should do so. He was confined to his room, in which he would not admit Mr. Greenwood to come near him, and where his wife's short visits did not seem to give him much satisfaction. Even with his son he was hardly at his ease, seeming to prefer the society of the nurse, with occasional visits from the doctor and Mr. Roberts. The Marchioness confined herself to her own room, in which it was her intention to prevent the inroads of Mr. Greenwood as far as it might be possible. That she should be able to exclude him altogether was more than she could hope, but much, she thought, could be done by the dint of headaches, and by a resolution never to take her food down-stairs. Lord Hampstead had declared his purpose to Harris, as well as to his

father, never again to sit down to table with Mr. Greenwood. "Where does he dine?" he asked the butler.
"Generally in the family dining-room, my lord," said
Harris. "Then give me my dinner in the breakfast
parlour." "Yes, my lord," said the butler, who at once
resolved to regard Mr. Greenwood as an enemy of the
family. In this manner Mr. Greenwood gave no trouble,
as he had his meat sent to him in his own sitting-room.
But all this made the house very uncomfortable.

In the afternoon Mr. Roberts came over from
Shrewsbury, and saw Lord Hampstead. "I knew he
would make himself disagreeable, my lord," said Mr.
Roberts.

"How did you know it?"

"Things creep out. He had made himself disagreeable to his lordship for some months past; and then we
heard that he was talking of Appleslocombe as though
he were certain to be sent there."

"My father never thought of it."

"I didn't think he did. Mr. Greenwood is the idlest
human being that ever lived, and how could he have
performed the duties of a parish?"

"He asked my father once, and my father flatly
refused him."

"Perhaps her ladyship——," suggested Mr. Roberts,
with some hesitation.

"At any rate he is not to have Appleslocombe, and
he must be made to go. How is it to be done?" Mr.
Roberts raised his eyebrows. "I suppose there must

be some means of turning an objectionable resident out
of a house."

"The police, of course, could carry him out—with a
magistrate's order. He would have to be treated like
any other vagrant."

"That would be disagreeable."

"Very disagreeable, my lord," said Mr. Roberts.
"My lord should be saved from that if possible."

"How if we gave him nothing to eat?" said Lord
Hampstead.

"That would be possible; but it would be troublesome. What if he resolved to remain and be starved?
It would be seeing which would hold out the longer.
I don't think my lord would have the heart to keep
him twenty-four hours without food. We must try
and save my lord from what is disagreeable as much as
we can." Lord Hampstead was in accord as to this,
but did not quite see his way how to effect it. There
were still, however, more than three weeks to run
before the day fixed for the chaplain's exit, and Mr.
Roberts suggested that it might in that time be fully
brought home to the man that his £200 a year would
depend on his going. "Perhaps you'd better leave him
to me, my lord," said Mr. Roberts; "and I shall deal
with him better when you're not here."

When the time came for afternoon tea Mr. Greenwood, perceiving that no invitation came to him from
the Marchioness, sent a note up to her asking for the
favour of an interview. "He had a few words to say,

and would be much obliged to her if she would allow
him to come to her." On receiving this she pondered
for some time before she could make up her mind as
to what answer she should give. She would have been
most anxious to do as she had already heard that Lord
Hampstead had done, and decline to meet him at all.
She could not analyze her own feelings about the
man, but had come during the last few days to hold
him in horror. It was as though something of the
spirit of the murderer had shown itself to her in her
eyes. She had talked glibly, wickedly, horribly of the
death of the man who had seemed to stand in her
way. She had certainly wished for it. She had taught
herself to think, by some ultra-feminine lack of logic,
that she had really been injured in that her own
eldest boy had not been born heir to his father's titles.
She had found it necessary to have some recipient for
her griefs. Her own sister, Lady Persiflage, had given
her no comfort, and then she had sought for and
had received encouragement from her husband's chaplain. But in talking of Lord Hampstead's death
she had formed no plan. She had only declared in
strong language that if, by the hand of Providence,
such a thing should be done, it would be to her a
happy chance. She had spoken out where another
more prudent than she would perhaps only have
wished. But this man had taken up her words with
an apparently serious purpose which had frightened
her; and then, as though he had been the recipient

of some guilty secret, he had laid aside the respect
which had been usual to him, and had assumed a
familiarity of co-partnership which had annoyed and
perplexed her. She did not quite understand it all,
but was conscious of a strong desire to be rid of him.
But she did not dare quite as yet to let him know
that such was her purpose, and she therefore sent her
maid down to him with a message. "Mr. Greenwood
wants to see me," she said to the woman. "Will you
tell him with my compliments that I am not very well,
and that I must beg him not to stay long."

"Lord Hampstead has been a' quarrelling with Mr.
Greenwood, my lady,—this very morning," said the
maid.

"Quarrelling, Walker?"

"Yes, my lady. There has been ever so much about
it. My lord says as he won't sit down to dinner with
Mr. Greenwood on no account, and Mr. Roberts has
been here, all about it. He's to be turned away."

"Who is to be turned away?"

"Mr. Greenwood, my lady. Lord Hampstead has
been about it all the morning. It's for that my lord
the Marquis has sent for him, and nobody's to speak
to him till he's packed up everything, and taken himself
right away out of the house."

"Who has told you all that, Walker?" Walker, however, would not betray her informant. She answered
that it was being talked of by everybody down-stairs,
and she repeated it now only because she thought it

proper that "my lady" should be informed of what
was going on. "My lady" was not sorry to have
received the information even from her maid, as it
might assist her in her conversation with the chaplain.

On this occasion Mr. Greenwood sat down without
being asked. "I am sorry to hear that you are so
unwell, Lady Kingsbury."

"I have got one of my usual headaches;—only it's
rather worse than usual."

"I have something to say which I am sure you will
not be surprised that I should wish to tell you. I have
been grossly insulted by Lord Hampstead."

"What can I do?"

"Well;—something ought to be done."

"I cannot make myself answerable for Lord Hampstead, Mr. Greenwood."

"No; of course not. He is a young man for whom
no one would make himself answerable. He is head-
strong, violent, and most uncourteous. He has told me
very rudely that I must leave the house by the end of
the month."

"I suppose the Marquis had told him."

"I don't believe it. Of course the Marquis is ill, and
I could bear much from him. But I won't put up with
it from Lord Hampstead."

"What can I do?"

"Well;—after what has passed between us, Lady
Kingsbury,——" He paused, and looked at her as he
made this appeal. She compressed her lips and

collected herself, and prepared for the fight which she felt was coming. He saw it all, and prepared himself also. "After what has passed between us, Lady Kingsbury," he said, repeating his words, "I think you ought to be on my side."

"I don't think anything of the kind. I don't know what you mean about sides. If the Marquis says you're to go, I can't keep you."

"I'll tell you what I've done, Lady Kingsbury. I have refused to stir out of this house till I've been allowed to discuss the matter with his lordship; and I think you ought to give me your countenance. I'm sure I've always been true to you. When you have unburdened your troubles to my ears I have always been sympathetic. When you have told me what a trouble this young man has been to you, have not I always,—always,—always taken your part against him ?" He almost longed to tell her that he had formed a plan for ridding her altogether of the obnoxious young man; but he could not find the words in which to do this. "Of course I have felt that I might depend upon you for assistance and countenance in this house."

"Mr. Greenwood," she said, "I really cannot talk to you about these things. My head is aching very badly, and I must ask you to go."

"And that is to be all?"

"Don't you hear me tell you that I cannot interfere?" Still he kept that horrid position of his upon the chair, staring at her with his large, open, lustreless eyes.

"Mr. Greenwood, I must ask you to leave me. As a gentleman you must comply with my request."

"Oh," he said; "very well! Then I am to know that after thirty years' faithful service all the family has turned against me. I shall take care——" But he paused, remembering that were he to speak a word too much, he might put in jeopardy the annuity which had been promised him; and at last he left the room.

Of Mr. Greenwood no one saw anything more that day, nor did Lord Hampstead encounter him again before he returned to London. Hampstead had arranged to stay at Trafford during the following day, and then to return to London, again using the night mail train. But on the next morning a new trouble fell upon him. He received his sister's letter, and learned that George Roden had been with her at Hendon Hall. He had certainly pledged himself that there should be no such meeting, and had foolishly renewed this pledge only yesterday. When he read the letter he was vexed, chiefly with himself. The arguments which she had used as to Roden's coming, and also those by which she had excused herself for receiving him, did seem to him to be reasonable. When the man was going on such a journey it was natural that he should wish to see the girl he loved; and natural that she should wish to see him. And he was well aware that neither of them had pledged themselves. It was he only who had given a pledge, and that as to the conduct of others who had refused to support him in it. Now his pledge had been

broken, and he felt himself called upon to tell his
father of what had occurred. "After all that I told
you yesterday," he said, "George Roden and Fanny
have met each other." Then he attempted to make
the best excuse he could for this breach of the promise
which he had made.

"What's the good?" said the Marquis. "They can't
marry each other. I wouldn't give her a shilling if she
were to do such a thing without my sanction." Hampstead knew very well that, in spite of this, his father
had made by his will ample provision for his sister, and
that it was very improbable that any alteration in this
respect would be made, let his sister's disobedience be
what it might. But the Marquis seemed hardly to be
so much affected as he had expected by these tidings.
"Whatever you do," said the Marquis, "don't let her
ladyship know it. She would be sure to come down to
me and say it was all my fault; and then she would
tell me what Mr. Greenwood thought about it." The
poor man did not know how little likely it was that she
would ever again throw Mr. Greenwood in his teeth.

Lord Hampstead had not as yet even seen his stepmother, but had thought it no more than decent to send
her word that he would wait upon her before he left the
house. All domestic troubles he knew to be bad. For
his stepmother's sake, and for that of his sister and little
brothers, he would avoid as far as might be possible
any open rupture. He therefore went to the Marchioness
before he ate his dinner. "My father is much better,"

he said; but his stepmother only shook her head, so that there was before him the task of recommencing the conversation. " Dr. Spicer says so."

" I am not sure that Mr. Spicer knows much about it."

" He thinks so himself."

" He never tells me what he thinks. He hardly tells me anything."

" He is not strong enough for much talking."

" He will talk to Mr. Roberts by the hour together. So I hear that I am to congratulate you." This she said in a tone which was clearly intended to signify both condemnation and ridicule.

" I am not aware of it," said Hampstead with a smile.

" I suppose it is true about the Quaker lady ? "

" I can hardly tell you, not knowing what you may have heard. There can be no room for congratulation, as the lady has not accepted the offer I have made her." The Marchioness laughed incredulously,—with a little affected laugh in which the incredulity was sincere.—" I can only tell you that it is so."

" No doubt you will try again ? "

" No doubt."

" Young ladies in such circumstances are not apt to persevere in their severity. Perhaps it may be supposed that she will give way at last."

" I cannot take upon myself to answer that, Lady Kingsbury. The matter is one on which I am not particularly anxious to talk. Only as you asked me I thought it best just to tell you the facts."

"I am sure I am ever so much obliged to you. The young lady's father is——"

"The young lady's father is a clerk in a merchant's office in the City."

"So I understand,—and a Quaker?"

"And a Quaker."

"And I believe he lives at Holloway."

"Just so."

"In the same street with that young man whom Fanny has—has chosen to pick up."

"Marion Fay and her father live at No. 17, Paradise Row, Holloway; and Mrs. Roden and George Roden live at No. 10."

"Exactly. We may understand, therefore, how you became acquainted with Miss Fay."

"I don't think you can. But if you wish to know I will tell you that I first saw Miss Fay at Mrs. Roden's house."

"I suppose so."

Hampstead had begun this interview with perfect good humour; but there had gradually been growing upon him that tone of defiance which her little speeches to him had naturally produced. Scorn would always produce scorn in him, as would ridicule and satire produce the same in return. "I do not know why you should have supposed so, but such was the fact. Neither had George Roden or my sister anything to

do with it. Miss Fay is a friend of Mrs. Roden, and
Mrs. Roden introduced me to the young lady."

"I am sure we are all very much obliged to her."

"I am, at any rate,—or shall be if I succeed at
last."

"Poor fellow! It will be very piteous if you too
are thwarted in love."

"I'll say good-bye, my lady," said he, getting up to
leave her.

"You have told me nothing of Fanny."

"I do not know that I have anything to tell."

"Perhaps she also will be jilted."

"I should hardly think so."

"Because, as you tell me, she is not allowed to see
him." There was a thorough disbelief expressed in
this which annoyed him. It was as though she had
expressed her opinion that the lovers were encouraged
to meet daily in spite of the pledge which had been
given. And then the pledge had been broken; and
there would be a positive lie on his part if he were
now to leave her with the idea that they had not
met. "You must find it hard to keep them apart, as
they are so near."

"I have found it too hard, at any rate."

"Oh, you have?"

"They did meet yesterday."

"Oh, they did.   Directly your back was turned?"

"He was going abroad, and he came; and she has
written to tell me of it.   I say nothing of myself, Lady

Kingsbury; but I do not think you can understand how true she can be,—and he also."

"That is your idea of truth."

"That is my idea of truth, Lady Kingsbury; which, as I said before, I am afraid I cannot explain to you. I have never meant to deceive you; nor have they."

"I thought a promise was a promise," she said. Then he left her, condescending to make no further reply. On that night he went back to London, with a sad feeling at his heart that his journey down to Trafford had done no good to any one. He had, however, escaped a danger of which he had known nothing.

CHAPTER XVI.

"I DO."

LORD HAMPSTEAD did not reach his house till nearly six on the following morning, and, having been travelling two nights out of three, allowed himself the indulgence of having his breakfast in bed. While he was so engaged his sister came to him, very penitent for her fault, but ready to defend herself should he be too severe to her. "Of course I am very sorry because of what you had said. But I don't know how I am to help myself. It would have looked so very strange."

"It was unfortunate—that's all."

"Was it so very unfortunate, John?"

"Of course I had to tell them down there."

"Was papa angry?"

"He only said that if you chose to make such a fool of yourself, he would do nothing for you—in the way of money."

"George does not think of that in the least."

"People must eat, you know."

"Ah; that would make no difference either to him

or to me. We must wait, that's all. I do not think it would make me unhappy to wait till I died, if he only were content to wait also. But was papa so very angry?"

"He wasn't so very angry,—only angry. I was obliged to tell him; but I said as little to him as possible because he is ill. Somebody else made herself disagreeable."

"Did you tell her?"

"I was determined to tell her;—so that she should not turn round upon me afterwards and say that I had deceived her. I had made a promise to my father."

"Oh, John, I am so sorry."

"There is no use in crying after spilt milk. A promise to my father she would of course take as a promise to her, and it would have been flung in my face."

"She will do so now."

"Oh, yes;—but I can fight the battle better, having told her everything."

"Was she disagreeable?"

"Abominable! She mixed you up with Marion Fay, and really showed more readiness than I gave her credit for in what she said. Of course she got the better of me. She could call me a liar and a fool to my face, and I could not retaliate. But there's a row in the house which makes everything wretched there."

"Another row?"

"You are forgotten in this new row,—and so am I. George Roden and Marion Fay are nothing in comparison with poor Mr. Greenwood. He has been committing horrible offences, and is to be turned out. He swears he won't go, and my father is determined he shall. Mr. Roberts has been called in, and there is a question whether Harris shall not put him on gradually diminished rations till he be starved into surrender. He's to have £200 a year if he goes, but he says that it is not enough for him."

"Would it be much?"

"Considering that he likes to have everything of the very best I do not think it would. He would probably have to go to prison or else hang himself."

"Won't it be rather hard upon him?"

"I think it will. I don't know what it is that makes the governor so hard to him. I begged and prayed for another hundred a year as though he were the dearest friend I had in the world; but I couldn't turn the governor an inch. I don't think I ever disliked any one so much in the world as I do Mr. Greenwood."

"Not Mr. Crocker?" she asked.

"Poor Crocker! I love Crocker, in comparison. There is a delightful pachydermatousness about Crocker which is almost heroic. But I hate Mr. Greenwood, if it be in my nature to hate any one. It is not only that he insults me, but he looks at me as though he would take me by the throat and strangle me if he could. But still I will add the other hundred a year out of my own pocket, because I think he is being treated hardly. Only I must do it on the sly."

" But Lady Kingsbury is still fond of him ?"

" I rather think not. I fancy he has made himself too free with her, and has offended her. However, there he is shut up all alone, and swearing that he won't stir out of the house till something better is done for him."

There were two matters now on Lord Hampstead's mind to which he gave his attention, the latter of which, however, was much the more prominent in his thoughts. He was anxious to take his sister down to Gorse Hall, and there remain for the rest of the hunting season, making such short runs up to Holloway as he might from time to time find to be necessary. No man can have a string of hunters idle through the winter without feeling himself to be guilty of an unpardonable waste of property. A customer at an eating-house will sometimes be seen to devour the last fragments of what has been brought to him, because he does not like to abandon that for which he must pay. So it is with the man who hunts. It is not perhaps that he wants to hunt. There are other employments in life which would at the moment be more to his taste. It is his conscience which prompts him,—the feeling that he cannot forgive himself for intolerable extravagance if he does not use the articles with which he has provided himself. You can neglect your billiard-table, your books, or even your wine-cellar,—because they eat nothing. But your horses soon eat their heads off their own shoulders if you pass weeks without getting on their backs. Hampstead had endeavoured to mitigate for himself this feeling of improvidence by running up and down to Aylesbury; but the saving in this respect was not sufficient for his conscience, and he was therefore determined to balance the expenditure of the year by a regular performance of his duties at Gorse Hall. But the other matter was still more important to him. He must see Marion Fay before he went into Northamptonshire, and then he would learn how soon he might run up with the prospect of seeing her again. The distance of Gorse Hall and the duty of hunting would admit of certain visits to Holloway. " I think I shall go to Gorse Hall to-morrow," he said to his sister as soon as he had come down from his room.

"All right; I shall be ready. Hendon Hall or Gorse Hall,—or any other Hall, will be the same to me now." Whereby she probably intended to signify that as George Roden was on his way to Italy all parts of England were indifferent to her.

"But I am not quite certain," said he.

"What makes the doubt ? "

"Holloway, you know, has not been altogether deserted. The sun no doubt has set in Paradise Row, but the moon remains." At this she could only laugh, while he prepared himself for his excursion to Holloway.

He had received the Quaker's permission to push his
suit with Marion, but he did not flatter himself that
this would avail him much. He felt that there was a
strength in Marion which, as it would have made her
strong against her father had she given away her heart
without his sanction, so would it be but little moved
by any permission coming from him. And there was
present to the lover's mind a feeling of fear which had
been generated by the Quaker's words as to Marion's
health. Till he had heard something of that story of
the mother and her little ones, it had not occurred to
him that the girl herself was wanting in any gift of
physical well-being. She was beautiful in his eyes, and
he had thought of nothing further. Now an idea had
been put into his head which, though he could hardly
realize it, was most painful to him. He had puzzled
himself before. Her manner to him had been so soft,
so tender, so almost loving, that he could not but hope,
could hardly not think, that she loved him. That,
loving him, she should persist in refusing him because
of her condition of life, seemed to him to be unnatural.
He had, at any rate, been confident that, were there
nothing else, he could overcome that objection. Her
heart, if it were really given to him, would not be able
to support itself in its opposition to him upon such a
ground of severance as that. He thought that he could
talk her out of so absurd an argument. But in that
other argument there might be something that she
would cling to with persistency.

But the Quaker himself had declared that there was
nothing in it. "As far as I know," the Quaker had
said, "she is as fit to become a man's wife as any other
girl." He surely must have known had there been
any real cause. Girls are so apt to take fancies into
their heads, and then will sometimes become so obstinate in their fancies! In this way Hampstead discussed
the matter with himself, and had been discussing it
ever since he had walked up and down Broad Street
with the Quaker. But if she pleaded her health, he
had what her own father had said to use as an argument with which to convince her. If she spoke again
of his rank, he thought that on that matter his love
might be strong enough as an argument against her,—
or perhaps her own.

He found no trouble in making his way into her
presence. She had heard of his visit to King's Court,
and knew that he would come. She had three things
which she had to tell him, and she would tell them all
very plainly if all should be necessary. The first was
that love must have nothing to do in this matter,—but
only duty. The second, which she feared to be somewhat weak,—which she almost thought would not of
itself have been strong enough,—was that objection as
to her condition in life which she had urged to him
before. She declared to herself that it would be strong
enough both for him, and for her, if they would only
guide themselves by prudence. But the third,—that
should be a rock to her if it were necessary; a cruel

rock on which she must be shipwrecked, but against
which his bark should surely not be dashed to atoms.
If he would not leave her in peace without it she would
tell him that she was fit to be no man's wife.

If it came to that, then she must confess her own
love. She acknowledged to herself that it must be so.
There could not be between them the tenderness necessary for the telling of such a tale without love, without
acknowledged love. It would be better that it should
not be so. If he would go and leave her to dream of
him,—there might be a satisfaction even in that to
sustain her during what was left to her of life. She
would struggle that it should be so. But if his love
were too strong, then must he know it all. She had
learned from her father something of what had passed
at that interview in the City, and was therefore ready
to receive her lover when he came. " Marion," he said,
"you expected me to come to you again?"

"Certainly I did."

"Of course I have come. I have had to go to my
father, or I should have been here sooner. You know
that I shall come again and again till you will say a
word to me that shall comfort me."

"I knew that you would come again, because you
were with father in the City."

"I went to ask his leave,—and I got it."

"It was hardly necessary for you, my lord, to take
that trouble."

"But I thought it was. When a man wishes to take

a girl away from her own home, and make her the mistress of his, it is customary that he shall ask for her father's permission."

"It would have been so, had you looked higher,—as you should have done."

"It was so in regard to any girl that I should wish to make my wife. Whatever respect a man can pay to any woman, that is due to my Marion." She looked at him, and with the glance of her eye went all the love of her heart. How could she say those words to him, full of reason and prudence and wisdom, if he spoke to her like this? "Answer me honestly. Do you not know that if you were the daughter of the proudest lord living in England you would not be held by me as deserving other usage than that which I think to be your privilege now?"

"I only meant that father could not but feel that you were honouring him."

"I will not speak of honour as between him and me or between me and you. With me and your father honesty was concerned. He has believed me, and has accepted me as his son-in-law. With us, Marion, with us two, all alone as we are here together, all in all to each other as I hope we are to be, only love can be brought in question. Marion, Marion!" Then he threw himself on his knees before her, and embraced her as she was sitting.

"No, my lord; no; it must not be." But now he had both her hands in his, and was looking into her face. Now was the time to speak of duty,—and to speak with some strength, if what she might say was to have any avail.

"It shall not be so, my lord." Then she did regain her hands, and struggled up from the sofa on to her feet. "I, too, believe in your honesty. I am sure of it, as I am of my own. But you do not understand me. Think of me as though I were your sister."

"As my sister?"

"What would you have your sister do if a man came to her then, whom she knew that she could never marry? Would you have her submit to his embrace because she knew him to be honest?"

"Not unless she loved him."

"It would have nothing to do with it, Lord Hampstead."

"Nothing, Marion!"

"Nothing, my lord. You will think that I am giving myself airs if I speak of my duty."

"Your father has allowed me to come."

"I owe him duty, no doubt. Had he bade me never to see you, I hope that that would have sufficed. But there are other duties than that,—a duty even higher than that."

"What duty, Marion?"

"That which I owe to you. If I had promised to be your wife——"

"Do promise it."

"Had I so promised, should I not then have been bound to think first of your happiness?"

"You would have accomplished it, at any rate."

"Though I cannot be your wife I do not owe it you the less to think of it,—seeing all that you are willing to do for me,—and I will think of it. I am grateful to you."

"Do you love me?"

"Let me speak, Lord Hampstead. It is not civil in you to interrupt me in that way. I am thoroughly grateful, and I will not show my gratitude by doing that which I know would ruin you."

"Do you love me?"

"Not if I loved you with all my heart,——" and she spread out her arms as though to assure herself how she did love him with all her very soul,—"would I for that be brought even to think of doing the thing that you ask me."

"Marion!"

"No,—no. We are utterly unfit for each other." She had made her first declaration as to duty, and now she was going on as to that second profession which she intended should be, if possible, the last. "You are as high as blood and wealth and great friends can make you. I am nothing. You have called me a lady."

"If God ever made one, you are she."

"He has made me better. He has made me a woman. But others would not call me a lady. I cannot talk as they do, sit as they do, act as they do,—even think as they do. I know myself, and I will not presume to make myself the wife of such a man as you."

As she said this there came a flush across her face, and
a fire in her eye, and, as though conquered by her own
emotion, she sank again upon the sofa.

"Do you love me, Marion?"

"I do," she said, standing once more erect upon her
feet. "There shall be no shadow of a lie between us.
I do love you, Lord Hampstead. I will have nothing
to make me blush in my own esteem when I think of
you. How should it be other than that a girl such as I
should love such a one as you when you ask me with
words so sweet!"

"Then, Marion, you shall be my own."

"Oh, yes, I must now be yours,—while I am alive.
You have so far conquered me." As he attempted to
take her in his arms she retreated from him; but so
gently that her very gentleness repressed him. "If
never loving another is to be yours,—if to pray for you
night and day as the dearest one of all, is to be yours,—
if to remind myself every hour that all my thoughts are
due to you, if to think of you so that I may console
myself with knowing that one so high and so good has
condescended to regard me,—if that is to be yours,—
then I am yours; then shall I surely be yours while I
live. But it must be only with my thoughts, only with
my prayers, only with all my heart."

"Marion, Marion!" Now again he was on his knees
before her, but hardly touching her.

"It is your fault, Lord Hampstead," she said, trying
to smile. "All this is your doing, because you

would not let a poor girl say simply what she had to say."

"Nothing of it shall be true,—except that you love me. That is all that I can remember. That I will repeat to you daily till you have put your hand in mine, and call yourself my wife."

"That I will never do," she exclaimed, once again standing. "As God hears me now I will never say it. It would be wrong,—and I will never say it." In thus protesting she put forth her little hands clenched fast, and then came again the flush across her brow, and her eyes for a moment seemed to wander, and then, failing in strength to carry her through it all, she fell back senseless on the sofa.

Lord Hampstead, finding that he alone could do nothing to aid her, was forced to ring the bell, and to give her over to the care of the woman, who did not cease to pray him to depart. "I can't do nothing, my lord, while you stand over her that way."

CHAPTER XVII.

AT GORSE HALL.

HAMPSTEAD, when he was turned out into Paradise Row, walked once or twice up the street, thinking what he might best do next, regardless of the eyes at No. 10 and No. 15;—knowing that No. 11 was absent, where alone he could have found assistance had the inhabitant been there. As far as he could remember he had never seen a woman faint before. The way in which she had fallen through from his arms on to the sofa when he had tried to sustain her, had been dreadful to him; and almost more dreadful the idea that the stout old woman with whom he had left her should be more powerful than he to help her. He walked once or twice up and down, thinking what he had best now do, while Clara Demijohn was lost in wonder as to what could have happened at No. 17. It was quite intelligible to her that the lover should come in the father's absence and be entertained,—for a whole afternoon if it might be so; though she was scandalized by the audacity of the girl who had required no screen of darkness under the protection of which

her lover's presence might be hidden from the inquiries
of neighbours. All that, however, would have been
intelligible. There is so much honour in having a lord
to court one that perhaps it is well to have him seen.
But why was the lord walking up and down the street
with that demented air?

It was now four o'clock, and Hampstead had heard
the Quaker say that he never left his office till five.
It would take him nearly an hour to come down in
an omnibus from the City. Nevertheless Hampstead
could not go till he had spoken to Marion's father.
There was the "Duchess of Edinburgh," and he could
no doubt find shelter there. But to get through two
hours at the "Duchess of Edinburgh" would, he
thought, be beyond his powers. To consume the time
with walking might be better. He started off, therefore,
and tramped along the road till he came nearly to
Finchley, and then back again. It was dark as he
returned, and he fancied that he could wait about
without being perceived. "There he is again," said
Clara, who had in the mean time gone over to Mrs.
Duffer. "What can it all mean?"

"It's my belief he's quarrelled with her," said Mrs.
Duffer.

"Then he'd never wander about the place in that
way. There's old Zachary just come round the corner.
Now we shall see what he does."

"Fainted, has she?" said Zachary, as they walked
together up to the house. "I never knew my girl do

that before. Some of them can faint just as they please; but that's not the way with Marion." Hampstead protested that there had been no affectation on this occasion; that Marion had been so ill as to frighten him, and that, though he had gone out of the house at the woman's bidding, he had found it impossible to leave the neighbourhood till he should have learnt something as to her condition. " Thou shalt hear all I can tell thee, my friend," said the Quaker, as they entered the house together.

Hampstead was shown into the little parlour, while the Quaker went up to inquire after the state of his daughter. " No; thou canst not well see her," said he, returning, " as she has taken herself to her bed. That she should have been excited by what passed between you is no more than natural. I cannot tell thee now when thou mayst come again; but I will write thee word from my office to-morrow." Upon this Lord Hampstead would have promised to call himself at King's Court on the next day, had not the Quaker declared himself in favour of writing rather than of speaking. The post, he said, was very punctual; and on the next evening his lordship would certainly receive tidings as to Marion.

" Of course I cannot say what we can do about Gorse Hall till I hear from Mr. Fay," said Hampstead to his sister when he reached home. "Everything must depend on Marion Fay." That his sister should have packed all her things in vain seemed to him to be nothing while Marion's health was in question; but when the Quaker's letter arrived the matter was at once settled. They would start for Gorse Hall on the following day, the Quaker's letter having been as follows;—

"MY LORD,—

"I trust I may be justified in telling thee that there is not much to ail my girl. She was up to-day, and about the house before I left her, and assured me with many protestations that I need not take any special steps for her comfort or recovery. Nor indeed could I see in her face anything which could cause me to do so. Of course I mentioned thy name to her, and it was natural that the colour should come and go over her cheeks as I did so. I think she partly told me what had passed between you two, but only in part. As to the future, when I spoke of it, she told me that there was no need of any arrangement, as everything had been said that needed speech. But I guess that such is not thy reading of the matter; and that after what has passed between thee and me I am bound to offer to thee an opportunity of seeing her again shouldst thou wish to do so. But this must not be at once. It will certainly be better for her and, may be, for thee also that she should rest awhile before she be again asked to see thee. I would suggest, therefore, that thou shouldst leave her to her own thoughts for some weeks to come. If thou will'st write to me

and name a day some time early in March I will
endeavour to bring her round so far as to see thee
when thou comest.

> " I am, my lord,
>> " Thy very faithful friend,
>>> " ZACHARY FAY."

It cannot be said that Lord Hampstead was by any
means satisfied with the arrangement which had been
made for him, but he was forced to acknowledge to
himself that he could not do better than accede to it.
He could of course write to the Quaker, and write also
to Marion; but he could not well show himself in
Paradise Row before the time fixed, unless unexpected
circumstances should arise. He did send three loving
words to Marion—" his own, own, dearest Marion," and
sent them under cover to her father, to whom he wrote,
saying that he would be guided by the Quaker's
counsels. " I will write to you on the first of March,"
he said, " but I do trust that if in the mean time anything should happen,—if, for instance, Marion should
be ill,—you will tell me at once as being one as much
concerned in her health as you are yourself."

He was nervous and ill-at-ease, but not thoroughly
unhappy. She had told him how dear he was to her,
and he would not have been a man had he not been
gratified. And there had been no word of objection
raised on any matter beyond that one absurd objection
as to which he thought himself entitled to demand that

his wishes should be allowed to prevail. She had been
very determined; how absolutely determined he was
not probably himself aware. She had, however, made
him understand that her conviction was very strong.
But this had been as to a point on which he did not
doubt that he was right, and as to which her own father
was altogether on his side. After hearing the strong
protestation of her affection he could not think that she
would be finally obdurate when the reasons for her
obduracy were so utterly valueless. But still there
were vague fears about her health. Why had she
fainted and fallen through his arms? Whence had
come that peculiar brightness of complexion which
would have charmed him had it not frightened him?
A dim dread of something that was not intelligible to
him pervaded him, and robbed him of a portion of the
triumph which had come to him from her avowal.

  *   *   *   *   *   *

As the days went on at Gorse Hall his triumph
became stronger than his fears, and the time did not
pass unpleasantly with him. Young Lord Hautboy
came to hunt with him, bringing his sister Lady Amaldina, and after a few days Vivian found them. The
conduct of Lady Frances in reference to George Roden
was no doubt very much blamed, but the disgrace did
not loom so large in the eyes of Lady Persiflage as in
those of her sister the Marchioness. Amaldina was,
therefore, suffered to amuse herself, even as the guest
of her wicked friend;—even though the host were

himself nearly equally wicked. It suited young Hautboy very well to have free stables for his horses, and occasionally an extra mount when his own two steeds were insufficient for the necessary amount of hunting to be performed. Vivian, who had the liberal allowance of a private secretary to a Cabinet Minister to fall back upon, had three horses of his own. So that among them they got a great deal of hunting,—in which Lady Amaldina would have taken a conspicuous part had not Lord Llwddythlw entertained strong opinions as to the expediency of ladies riding to hounds. "He is so absurdly strict, you know," she said to Lady Frances.

"I think he is quite right," said the other. "I don't believe in girls trying to do all the things that men do."

"But what is the difference in jumping just over a hedge or two? I call it downright tyranny. Would you do anything Mr. Roden told you?"

"Anything on earth,—except jump over the hedges. But our temptations are not likely to be in that way."

"I think it very hard because I almost never see Llwddythlw."

"But you will when you are married."

"I don't believe I shall;—unless I go and look at him from behind the grating in the House of Commons You know we have settled upon August."

"I had not heard it."

"Oh yes. I nailed him at last. But then I had to get David. You don't know David?"

"No special modern David."

" Our David is not very modern. He is Lord David
Powell, and my brother that is to be. I had to persuade
him to do something instead of his brother, and I had
to swear that we couldn't ever be married unless he
would consent. I suppose Mr. Roden could get married
any day he pleased." Nevertheless Lady Amaldina
was better than nobody to make the hours pass when
the men are away hunting.

But at last there came a grand day, on which the
man of business was to come out hunting himself.
Lord Llwddythlw had come into the neighbourhood,
and was determined to have a day's pleasure. Gorse
Hall was full, and Hautboy, though his sister was very
eager in beseeching him, refused to give way to his
future magnificent brother-in-law. "Do him all the
good in the world," said Hautboy, "to put up at the
pot-house. He'll find out all about whiskey and beer
and gin, and know exactly how many beds the landlady
makes up." Lord Llwddythlw, therefore, slept at a
neighbouring hotel, and no doubt did turn his spare
moments to some profit.

Lord Llwddythlw was a man who had always horses,
though he very rarely hunted; who had guns, though
he never fired them; and fishing-rods, though nobody
knew where they were. He kept up a great establishment, regretting nothing in regard to it except the
necessity of being sometimes present at the festivities
for which it was used. On the present occasion he had
been enticed into Northamptonshire no doubt with the

purpose of laying some first bricks, or opening some completed institution, or eating some dinner,—on any one of which occasions he would be able to tell the neighbours something as to the constitution of their country. Then the presence of his lady-love seemed to make this a fitting occasion for, perhaps, the one day's sport of the year. He came to Gorse Hall to breakfast, and then rode to the meet along with the open carriage in which the two ladies were sitting. "Llwddythlw," said his lady-love, "I do hope you mean to ride."

"Being on horseback, Amy, I shall have no other alternative."

Lady Amaldina turned round to her friend, as though to ask whether she had ever seen such an absurd creature in her life. "You know what I mean by riding, Llwddythlw," she said.

"I suppose I do. You want me to break my neck."

"Oh, heavens! Indeed I don't."

"Or, perhaps, only to see me in a ditch."

"I can't have that pleasure," she said, "because you won't allow me to hunt."

"I have taken upon myself no such liberty as even to ask you not to do so. I have only suggested that tumbling into ditches, however salutary it may be for middle-aged gentlemen like myself, is not a becoming amusement for young ladies."

"Llwddythlw," said Hautboy, coming up to his future brother-in-law, "that's a tidy animal of yours."

"I don't quite know what tidy means as applied to a

horse, my boy; but if it's complimentary, I am much obliged to you."

"It means that I should like to have the riding of him for the rest of the season."

"But what shall I do for myself if you take my tidy horse ?"

"You'll be up in Parliament, or down at Quarter Sessions, or doing your duty somewhere like a Briton."

"I hope I may do my duty not the less because I intend to keep the tidy horse myself. When I am quite sure that I shall not want him any more, then I'll let you know."

There was the usual trotting about from covert to covert, and the usual absence of foxes. The misery of sportsmen on these days is sometimes so great that we wonder that any man, having experienced the bitterness of hunting disappointment, should ever go out again. On such occasions the huntsman is declared among private friends to be of no use whatever. The master is an absolute muff. All honour as to preserving has been banished from the country. The gamekeepers destroy the foxes. The owners of coverts encourage them. "Things have come to such a pass," says Walker to Watson, "that I mean to give it up. There's no good keeping horses for this sort of thing." All this is very sad, and the only consolation comes from the evident delight of those who take pleasure in trotting about without having to incur the labour and peril of riding to hounds.

At two o'clock on this day the ladies went home, having been driven about as long as the coachmen had thought it good for their horses. The men of course went on, knowing that they could not in honour liberate themselves from the toil of the day till the last covert shall have been drawn at half-past three o'clock. It is certainly true as to hunting that there are so many hours in which the spirit is vexed by a sense of failure, that the joy when it does come should be very great to compensate the evils endured. It is not simply that foxes will not dwell in every spinney, or break as soon as found, or always run when they do break. These are the minor pangs. But when the fox is found, and will break, and does run, when the scent suffices, and the hounds do their duty, when the best country which the Shires afford is open to you, when your best horse is under you, when your nerves are even somewhat above the usual mark,—even then there is so much of failure! You are on the wrong side of the wood, and getting a bad start are never with them for a yard; or your horse, good as he is, won't have that bit of water; or you lose your stirrup-leather, or your way; or you don't see the hounds turn, and you go astray with others as blind as yourself; or, perhaps, when there comes the run of the season, on that very day you have taken a liberty with your chosen employment, and have lain in bed. Look back upon your hunting lives, brother sportsmen, and think how few and how far between the perfect days have been.

In spite of all that was gone this was one of those perfect days to those who had the pleasure afterwards of remembering it. "Taking it all in all, I think that Lord Llwddythlw had the best of it from first to last," said Vivian, when they were again talking of it in the drawing-room after they had come in from their wine.

"To think that you should be such a hero!" said Lady Amaldina, much gratified. "I didn't believe you would take so much trouble about such a thing."

"It was what Hautboy called the tidiness of the horse."

"By George, yes; I wish you'd lend him to me. I got my brute in between two rails, and it took me half-an-hour to smash a way through. I never saw anything of it after that." Poor Hautboy almost cried as he gave this account of his own misfortune.

"You were the only fellow I saw try them after Crasher," said Vivian. "Crasher came on his head, and I should think he must be there still. I don't know where Hampstead got through."

"I never know where I've been," said Hampstead, who had, in truth, led the way over the double rails which had so confounded Crasher and had so perplexed Hautboy. But when a man is too forward to be seen, he is always supposed to be somewhere behind.

Then there was an opinion expressed by Walker that Tolleyboy, the huntsman, had on that special occasion stuck very well to his hounds, to which Watson gave his cordial assent. Walker and Watson had both been asked to dinner, and during the day had been heard to express to each other all that adverse criticism as to the affairs of the hunt in general which appeared a few lines back. Walker and Watson were very good fellows, popular in the hunt, and of all men the most unlikely to give it up.

When that run was talked about afterwards, as it often was, it was always admitted that Lord Llwddythlw had been the hero of the day. But no one ever heard him talk of it. Such a trifle was altogether beneath his notice.

CHAPTER XVIII.

POOR WALKER.

THAT famous run took place towards the end of February, at which time Hampstead was counting all the hours till he should again be allowed to show himself in Paradise Row. He had in the mean time written one little letter to the Quaker's daughter;—

"·DEAREST MARION,—I only write because I cannot keep myself quiet without telling you how well I love you. Pray do not believe that because I am away I think of you less. I am to see you, I hope, on Monday, the 2nd of March. If you would write me but one word to say that you will be glad to see me !

"Always your own,

"H."

She showed this to her father, and the sly old Quaker told her that it would not be courteous in her not to send some word of reply. As the young lord, he said, had been permitted by him, her father, to pay his addresses to her, so much was due to him. Why

should his girl lose this grand match ? Why should his
daughter not become a happy and a glorious wife, seeing
that her beauty and her grace had entirely won this
young lord's heart ? " MY LORD," she wrote back to him,
—" I shall be happy to see you when you come, whatever
day may suit you. But, alas ! I can only say what I have
said.—Yet I am thine, MARION." She had intended
not to be tender, and yet she had thought herself bound
to tell him that all that she had said before was true.

It was after this that Lord Llwddythlw distinguished
himself, so much so that Walker and Watson did
nothing but talk about him all the next day. " It's
those quiet fellows that make the best finish after all ! "
said Walker, who had managed to get altogether to
the bottom of his horse during the run, and had hardly
seen the end of it quite as a man wishes to see it.

The day but one after this, the last Friday in
February, was to be the last of Hampstead's hunting,
at any rate until after his proposed visit to Holloway.
He, and Lady Frances with him, intended to return to
London on the next day, and then, as far as he was
concerned, the future loomed before him as a great
doubt. Had Marion been the highest lady in the land,
and had he from his position and rank been hardly
entitled to ask for her love, he could not have been
more anxious, more thoughtful, or occasionally more
down-hearted. But this latter feeling would give way
to joy when he remembered the words with which she
had declared her love. No assurance could have been

more perfect, or more devoted. She had coyed him
nothing as far as words are concerned, and he never
for a moment doubted but that her full words had
come from a full heart. "But alas! I can only say
what I have said." That of course had been intended
to remove all hope. But if she loved him as she said
she did, would he not be able to teach her that everything should be made to give way to love? It was
thus that his mind was filled, as day after day he
prepared himself for his hunting, and day after day did
his best in keeping to the hounds.

Then came that last day in February as to which
all those around him expressed themselves to be full
of hope. Gimberley Green was certainly the most
popular meet in the country, and at Gimberley Green
the hounds were to meet on this occasion. It was
known that men were coming from the Pytchley and
the Cottesmore, so that everybody was supposed to be
anxious to do his best. Hautboy was very much on
the alert, and had succeeded in borrowing for the
occasion Hampstead's best horse. Even Vivian, who
was not given to much outward enthusiasm, had had
consultations with his groom as to which of two he
had better ride first. Sometimes there does come a
day on which rivalry seems to be especially keen, when
a sense of striving to excel and going ahead of others
seems to instigate minds which are not always ambitious.
Watson and Walker were on this occasion very much
exercised, and had in the sweet confidences of close

friendship agreed with themselves that certain heroes who were coming from one of the neighbouring hunts should not be allowed to carry off the honours of the day.

On this occasion they both breakfasted at Gorse Hall, which was not uncommon with them, as the hotel, —or pot-house, as Hautboy called it,—was hardly more than a hundred yards distant. Walker was peculiarly exuberant, and had not been long in the house before he confided to Hautboy in a whisper their joint intention that "those fellows" were not to be allowed to have it all their own way. "Suppose you don't find after all, Mr. Walker," said Lady Amaldina, as the gentlemen got up from breakfast, and loaded themselves with sandwiches, cigar-cases, and sherry-flasks.

"I won't believe anything so horrible," said Walker.

"I should cut the concern," said Watson, "and take to stagging in Surrey." This was supposed to be the bitterest piece of satire that could be uttered in regard to the halcyon country in which their operations were carried on.

"Tolleyboy will see to that," said Walker. "We haven't had a blank yet, and I don't think he'll disgrace himself on such a day as this." Then they all started, in great glee, on their hacks, their hunters having been already sent on to Gimberley Green.

The main part of the story of that day's sport, as far as we're concerned with it, got itself told so early in the

day that readers need not be kept long waiting for the
details. Tolleyboy soon relieved these impetuous riders
from all dangers as to a blank. At the first covert
drawn a fox was found immediately, and without any of
those delays, so perplexing to some and so comforting
to others, made away for some distant home of his own.
It is, perhaps, on such occasions as these that riders are
subjected to the worst perils of the hunting field.
There comes a sudden rush, when men have not cooled
themselves down by the process of riding here and
there and going through the usual preliminary prefaces
to a run. They are collected in crowds, and the horses
are more impatient even than their riders. No one on
that occasion could have been more impatient than
Walker,—unless it was the steed upon which Walker
was mounted. There was a crowd of men standing in a
lane at the corner of the covert,—of men who had only
that moment reached the spot,—when at about thirty
yards from them a fox crossed the lane, and two or
three leading hounds close at his brush. One or two
of the strangers from the enemy's country occupied a
position close to, or rather in the very entrance of, a
little hunting gate which led out of the lane into the
field opposite. Between the lane and the field there
was a fence which was not "rideable!" As is the
custom with lanes, the roadway had been so cut down
that there was a bank altogether precipitous about
three feet high, and on that a hedge of trees and stakes
and roots which had also been cut almost into the

consistency of a wall. The gate was the only place,—
into which these enemies had thrust themselves, and in
the possession of which they did not choose to hurry
themselves, asserting as they kept their places that it
would be well to give the fox a minute. The assertion
in the interests of hunting might have been true. A
sportsman who could at such a moment have kept his
blood perfectly cool, might have remembered his duties
well enough to have abstained from pressing into the
field in order that the fox might have his fair chance.
Hampstead, however, who was next to the enemies, was
not that cool hero, and bade the strangers move on, not
failing to thrust his horse against their horses. Next
to him, and a little to the left, was the unfortunate
Walker. To his patriotic spirit it was intolerable that
any stranger should be in that field before one of their
own hunt. What he himself attempted, what he wished
to do, or whether any clear intention was formed in his
mind, no one ever knew. But to the astonishment of
all who saw it the horse got himself half-turned round
towards the fence, and attempted to take it in a stand.
The eager animal did get himself up amidst the thick
wood on the top of the bank, and then fell headlong
over, having entangled his feet among the boughs.
Had his rider sat loosely he would probably have got
clear of his horse. But as it was they came down
together, and unfortunately the horse was uppermost.
Just as it happened Lord Hampstead made his way
through the gate, and was the first who dismounted to

give assistance to his friend. In two or three minutes
there was a crowd round, with a doctor in the midst of
it, and a rumour was going about that the man had
been killed. In the mean time the enemies were riding
well to the hounds, with Tolleyboy but a few yards
behind them, Tolleyboy having judiciously remembered
a spot at which he could make his way out of the covert
into field without either passing through the gate or
over the fence.

The reader may as well know at once that Walker
was not killed. He was not killed, though he was so
crushed and mauled with broken ribs and collar-bone,
so knocked out of breath and stunned and mangled and
squeezed, so pummelled and pounded and generally
misused, that he did not come to himself for many
hours, and could never after remember anything of that
day's performances after eating his breakfast at Gorse
Hall. It was a week before tidings went through the
Shires that he was likely to live at all, and even then it
was asserted that he had been so altogether smashed
that he would never again use any of his limbs. On
the morning after the hunt his widowed mother and
only sister were down with him at the hotel, and there
they remained till they were able to carry him away to
his own house. "Won't I?" was almost the first
intelligible word he said when his mother suggested to
him, her only son, that now at least he would promise
to abandon that desperate amusement, and would never
go hunting any more. It may be said in praise of

British surgery generally that Walker was out again on
the first of the following November.

But Walker with his misfortunes and his heroism and
his recovery would have been nothing to us had it been
known from the first to all the field that Walker had
been the victim. The accident happened between
eleven and twelve,—probably not much before twelve.
But the tidings of it were sent up by telegraph from
some neighbouring station to London in time to be
inserted in one of the afternoon newspapers of that
day; and the tidings as sent informed the public that
Lord Hampstead while hunting that morning had fallen
with his horse at the corner of Gimberly Green, that
the animal had fallen on him,—and that he had been
crushed to ·death. Had the false information been
given in regard to Walker it might probably have
excited so little attention that the world would have
known nothing about it till it learned that the poor
fellow had not been killed. But, having been given as
to a young nobleman, everybody had heard of it before
dinner-time that evening. Lord Persiflage knew it in
the House of Lords, and Lord Llwddythlw had heard
it in the House of Commons. There was not a club
which had not declared poor Hampstead to be an
excellent fellow, although he was a little mad. The
Montressors had already congratulated themselves on
the good fortune of little Lord Frederic; and the
speedy death of the Marquis was prophesied, as men
and women were quite sure that he would not be able

in his present condition to bear the loss of his eldest
son. The news was telegraphed down to Trafford Park
by the family lawyer,—with an intimation, however,
that, as the accident had been so recent, no absolute
credence should yet be given as to its fatal result.
" Bad fall probably," said the lawyer in his telegram,
" but I don't believe the rest. Will send again when I
hear the truth." At nine o'clock that evening the truth
was known in London, and before midnight the poor
Marquis had been relieved from his terrible affliction.
But for three hours it had been supposed at Trafford
Park that Lord Frederic had become the heir to his
father's title and his father's property.

Close inquiry was afterwards made as to the person
by whom this false intelligence had been sent to the
newspaper, but nothing certain was ever asserted
respecting it. That a general rumour had prevailed
for a time among many who were out that Lord Hampstead had been the victim, was found to have been the
case. He had been congratulated by scores of men who
had heard that he had fallen. When Tolleyboy was
breaking up the fox, and wondering why so few men
had ridden through the hunt with him, he was told that
Lord Hampstead had been killed, and had dropped his
bloody knife out of his hands. But no one would own
as to having sent the telegram. Suspicion attached
itself to an attorney from Kettering who had been seen
in the early part of the day, but it could not be traced
home to him. Official inquiry was made; but as it was

not known who sent the message, or to what address,
or from what post town, or even the wording of the
message, official information was not forthcoming. It
is probable that Sir Boreas at the Post Office did not
think it proper to tell everybody all that he knew. It
was admitted that a great injury had been done to the
poor Marquis, but it was argued on the other side that
the injury had been quickly removed.

There had, however, been three or four hours at
Trafford Park, during which feelings had been excited
which afterwards gave rise to bitter disappointment.
The message had come to Mr. Greenwood, of whose
estrangement from the family the London solicitor had
not been as yet made aware. He had been forced to
send the tidings into the sick man's room by Harris,
the butler, but he had himself carried it up to the Marchioness. "I am obliged to come," he said, as though
apologizing when she looked at him with angry eyes
because of his intrusion. "There has been an accident."
He was standing, as he always stood, with his hands
hanging down by his side. But there was a painful
look in his eyes more than she had usually read
there.

"What accident—what accident, Mr. Greenwood?
Why do you not tell me?" Her heart ran away at
once to the little beds in which her darlings were
already lying in the next room.

"It is a telegram from London."

From London—a telegram! Then her boys were

safe. "Why do you not tell me instead of standing
there ? "

"Lord Hampstead——"

"Lord Hampstead ! What has he done ?. Is he
married ? "

"He will never be married." Then she shook in
every limb, and clenched her hands, and stood with
open mouth, not daring to question him. "He has had
a fall, Lady Kingsbury."

" A fall ! "

"The horse has crushed him."

"Crushed him ! "

"I used to say it would be so, you know. And now
it has come to pass."

" Is he——? "

"Dead ? Yes, Lady Kingsbury, he is—dead." Then
he gave her the telegram to read. She struggled to
read it, but the words were too vague ; or her eyes too
dim. "Harris has gone in with the tidings. I had
better read the telegram, I suppose, but I thought
you'd like to see it. I told you how it would be, Lady
Kingsbury ; and now it has come to pass." He stood
standing a minute or two longer, but as she sat hiding
her face, and unable to speak, he left the room without
absolutely asking her to thank him for his news.

As soon as he was gone she crept slowly into the
room in which her three boys were sleeping. A door
from her own chamber opened into it, and then another
into that in which one of the nurses slept. She leaned

over them and kissed them all; but she knelt at that
on which Lord Frederic lay, and woke him with her
warm embraces. "Oh, mamma, don't," said the boy.
Then he shook himself, and sat up in his bed. "Mamma,
when is Jack coming?" he said. Let her train them
as she would, they would always ask for Jack. "Go
to sleep, my darling, my darling, my darling!" she said,
kissing him again and again. "Trafford," she said,
whispering to herself, as she went back to her own
room, trying the sound of the title he would have
to use. It had been all arranged in her own mind
how it was to be, if such a thing should happen.

"Go down," she said to her maid soon afterwards,
"and ask Mrs. Crawley whether his Lordship would
wish to see me." Mrs. Crawley was the nurse. But
the maid brought back word that "My Lord" did not
wish to see "My Lady." For three hours he lay
stupefied in his sorrow; and for three hours she sat
alone, almost in the dark. We may doubt whether it
was all triumph. Her darling had got what she
believed to be his due; but the memory that she had
longed for it,—almost prayed for it,—must have dulled
her joy.

There was no such regret with Mr. Greenwood. It
seemed to him that Fortune, Fate, Providence, or what
not, had only done its duty. He believed that he had
in truth foreseen and foretold the death of the pernicious
young man. But would the young man's death be
now of any service to him? Was it not too late? Had

they not all quarrelled with him? Nevertheless he had been avenged.

So it was at Trafford Park for three hours. Then there came a postboy galloping on horseback, and the truth was known. Lady Kingsbury went again to her children, but this time she did not kiss them. A gleam of glory had come there and had passed away;—but yet there was something of relief.

Why had he allowed himself to be so cowed on that morning? That was Mr. Greenwood's thought.

The poor Marquis fell into a slumber almost immediately, and on the next morning had almost forgotten that the first telegram had come.

CHAPTER XIX.

FALSE TIDINGS.

BUT there was another household which the false tidings of Lord Hampstead's death reached that same night. The feelings excited at Trafford had been very keen,—parental agony, maternal hope, disappointment, and revenge; but in that other household there was suffering quite as great. Mr. Fay himself did not devote much time during the day either to the morning or the evening newspapers. Had he been alone at Messrs. Pogson and Littlebird's he would have heard nothing of the false tidings. But sitting in his inner room, Mr. Pogson read the third edition of the *Evening Advertiser*, and then saw the statement, given with many details. "We," said the statement, "have sent over to the office of our contemporary, and have corroborated the facts." Then the story was repeated. Pushing his way through a gate at Gimberley Green, Lord Hampstead's horse had tumbled down, and all the field had ridden over him. He had been picked up dead, and his body had been carried home to Gorse Hall. Now Lord Hampstead's name had become

familiar in King's Court. Tribbledale had told how
the young lord had become enamoured of Zachary Fay's
daughter, and was ready to marry her at a moment's
notice. The tale had been repeated to old Littlebird
by young Littlebird, and at last even to Mr. Pogson
himself. There had been, of course, much doubt in
King's Court as to the very improbable story. But
some inquiries had been made, and there was now a
general belief in its truth. When Mr. Pogson read the
account of the sad tragedy he paused a moment to
think what he would do, then opened his door and
called for Zachary Fay. They who had known the
Quaker long always called him Zachary, or Friend
Zachary, or Zachary Fay. "My friend," said Mr.
Pogson, "have you read this yet?" and he handed him
the paper.

"I never have much time for the newspaper till I
get home at night," said the clerk, taking the sheet
that was offered him.

"You had better read it, perhaps, as I have heard
your name mentioned, I know not how properly, with
that of the young lord. Then the Quaker, bringing
his spectacles down from his forehead over his eyes,
slowly read the paragraph. As he did so Mr. Pogson
looked at him carefully. But the Quaker showed
very little emotion by his face. "Does it concern you,
Zachary?"

"I know the young man, Mr. Pogson. Though he
be much out of my own rank, circumstances have

brought him to my notice. I shall be grieved if this be true. With thy permission, Mr. Pogson, I will lock up my desk and return home at once." To this Mr. Pogson of course assented, recommending the Quaker to put the newspaper into his pocket.

Zachary Fay, as he walked to the spot where he was wont to find the omnibus, considered much as to what he might best do when he reached home. Should he tell the sad tidings to his girl, or should he leave her to hear it when further time should have confirmed the truth. To Zachary himself it seemed too probable that it should be true. Hunting to him, in his absolute ignorance of what hunting meant, seemed to be an occupation so full of danger that the wonder was that the hunting world had not already been exterminated. And then there was present to him a feeling, as there is to so many of us, that the grand thing which Fortune seemed to offer him was too good to be true. It could hardly be that he should live to see his daughter the mother of a future British peer! He had tried to school himself not to wish it, telling himself that such wishes were vain, and such longings wicked; he had said much to himself as to the dangers of rank and titles and wealth for those who were not born to them. He had said something also of that family tragedy which had robbed his own life of most of its joys, and which seemed to have laid so heavy a burden on his girl's spirit. Going backwards and forwards morning and evening to his work, he had endeavoured to make his

own heart acknowledge that the marriage was not
desirable; but he had failed;—and had endeavoured
to reconcile the failure to his conscience by telling
himself falsely that he as a father had been anxious
only for the welfare of his child. Now he felt the blow
terribly on her account, feeling sure that his girl's
heart had been given to the young man; but he felt
it also on his own. It might be, nevertheless, that the
report would prove untrue. Had the matter been one
in which he was not himself so deeply interested, he
would certainly have believed it to be untrue, he being
a man by his nature not prone to easy belief. It
would, however, be wiser, he said to himself as he left
the omnibus at the "Duchess of Edinburgh," to say
nothing as yet to Marion. Then he put the paper
carefully into his breast coat pocket, and considered
how he might best hide his feelings as to the sad
news. But all this was in vain. The story had already
found its way down to Paradise Row. Mrs. Demijohn
was as greedy of news as her neighbours, and would
generally send round the corner for a halfpenny evening
journal. On this occasion she did so, and within two
minutes of the time in which the paper had been put
into her hands exclaimed to her niece almost with
ecstasy, "Clara, what do you think? That young lord
who comes here to see Marion Fay has gone and got
himself killed out hunting."

"Lord Hampstead!" shouted Clara. "Got himself
killed! Laws, aunt, I can't believe it!" In her tone,

also, there was something almost of exultation. The
glory that had been supposed to be awaiting Marion
Fay was almost too much for the endurance of any
neighbour. Since it had become an ascertained fact
that Lord Hampstead had admired the girl, Marion's
popularity in the Row had certainly decreased. Mrs.
Duffer believed her no longer to be handsome; Clara
had always thought her to be pert; Mrs. Demijohn had
expressed her opinion that the man was an idiot; and
the landlady at the "Duchess of Edinburgh" had
wittily asserted that "young marquises were not to be
caught with chaff." There was no doubt a sense of
relief in Clara Demijohn's mind when she heard that
this special young marquis had been trampled to death
in the hunting field, and carried home a corpse.

"I must go and tell the poor girl," said Clara,
immediately.

"Leave it alone," said the old woman. "There will
be plenty to tell her, let alone you." But such occasions occur so rarely that it does not do not to take
advantage of them. In ordinary life events are so
unfrequent, and when they do arrive they give such
a flavour of salt to hours which are generally tedious,
that sudden misfortunes come as godsends,—almost
even when they happen to ourselves. Even a funeral
gives a tasteful break to the monotony of our usual
occupations, and small-pox in the next street is a
gratifying excitement. Clara soon got possession of
the newspaper, and with it in her hand ran across the

street to No. 17. Miss Fay was at home, and in a minute or two came down to Miss Demijohn in the parlour.

It was only during the minute or two that Clara began to think how she should break the tidings to her friend, or in any way to realize the fact that the "tidings" would require breaking. She had rushed across the street with the important paper in her hand, proud of the fact that she had something great to tell. But during that minute or two it did occur to her that a choice of words was needed for such an occasion. "Oh, Miss Fay," she said, "have you heard?"

"Heard what?" asked Marion.

"I do not know how to tell you, it is so terrible! I have only just seen it in the newspaper, and have thought it best to run over and let you know."

"Has anything happened to my father?" asked the girl.

"It isn't your father. This is almost more dreadful, because he is so young." Then that bright pink hue spread itself over Marion's face; but she stood speechless with her features almost hardened by the resolution which she had already formed within her not to betray the feelings of her heart before this other girl. The news, let it be what it might, must be of him! There was no one else "so young," of whom it was probable that this young woman would speak to her after this fashion. She stood silent, motionless, conveying nothing of her feelings by her face,—unless one might have

read something from the deep flush of her complexion.
"I don't know how to say it," said Clara Demijohn.
"There; you had better take the paper and read for
yourself. It's in the last column but one near the
bottom. 'Fatal Accident in the Field!' You'll
see it."

Marion took the paper, and read the words through
without faltering or moving a limb. Why would not
the cruel young woman go and leave her to her
sorrow? Why did she stand there looking at her, as
though desirous to probe to the bottom the sad secret
of her bosom? She kept her eyes still fixed upon the
paper, not knowing where else to turn them,—for she
would not look into her tormentor's face for pity.
"Ain't it sad?" said Clara Demijohn.

Then there came a deep sigh. "Sad," she said,
repeating the word; "sad! Yes, it's sad. I think, if
you don't mind, I'll ask you to leave me now. Oh, yes;
there's the newspaper."

"Perhaps you'd like to keep it for your father."
Here Marion shook her head. "Then I'll take it back
to aunt. She's hardly looked at it yet. When she
came to the paragraph, of course, she read it out; and
I wouldn't let her have any peace till she gave it me to
bring over."

"I wish you'd leave me," said Marion Fay.

Then with a look of mingled surprise and anger she
left the room, and returned across the street to No. 10.
"She doesn't seem to me to care a straw about it," said

the niece to her aunt; "but she got up just as highty tighty as usual and asked me to go away."

When the Quaker came to the door, and opened it with his latch-key, Marion was in the passage ready to receive him. Till she had heard the sound of the lock she had not moved from the room, hardly from the position, in which the other girl had left her. She had sunk into a chair which had been ready for her, and there she had remained thinking over it. "Father," she said, laying her hand upon his arm as she went to meet him, and looking up into his face;—"father?"

"My child!"

"Have you heard any tidings in the City?"

"Have you heard any, Marion?"

"Is it true then?" she said, seizing both his arms as though to support her.

"Who knows? Who can say that it be true till further tidings shall come? Come in, Marion. It is not well that we should discuss it here."

"Is it true? Oh, father;—oh, father; it will kill me."

"Nay, Marion, not that. After all, the lad was little more than a stranger to thee."

"A stranger?"

"How many weeks is it since first thou saw'st him? And how often? But two or three times. I am sorry for him;—if it be true; if it be true! I liked him well."

"But I have loved him."

" Nay, Marion, nay; thou shouldst moderate thyself."

" I will not moderate myself." Then she disengaged herself from his arm. "I loved him,—with all my heart, and all my strength; nay, with my whole soul. If it be so as that paper says, then I must die too. Oh, father, is it true, think you?"

He paused a while before he answered, examining himself what it might be best that he should say as to her welfare. As for himself, he hardly knew what he believed. These papers were always in search of paragraphs, and would put in the false and true alike,—the false perhaps the sooner, so as to please the taste of their readers. But if it were true, then how bad would it be to give her false hopes! "There need be no ground to despair," he said, "till we shall hear again in the morning."

" I know he is dead."

" Not so, Marion. Thou canst know nothing. If thou wilt bear thyself like a strong-hearted girl, as thou art, I will do this for thee. I will go across to the young lord's house at Hendon at once, and inquire there as to his safety. They will surely know if aught of ill has happened to their master."

So it was done. The poor old man, after his long day's labour, without waiting for his evening meal, taking only a crust with him in his pocket, got into a cab on that cold November evening, and had himself driven by suburban streets and lanes to Hendon Hall. Here the servants were much surprised and startled by the inquiries made. They had heard nothing. Lord Hampstead and his sister were expected home on the following day. Dinner was to be prepared for them, and fires had already been lighted in the rooms. "Dead!" "Killed out hunting!" "Trodden to death in the field!" Not a word of it had reached Hendon Hall. Nevertheless the housekeeper, when the paragraph was shown to her, believed every word of it. And the servants believed it. Thus the poor Quaker returned home with but very little comfort.

Marion's condition during that night was very sad, though she struggled to bear up against her sorrow in compliance with her father's instructions. There was almost nothing said as she sat by him while he ate his supper. On the next morning, too, she rose to give him his breakfast, having fallen asleep through weariness a hundred times during the night, to wake again within a minute or two to the full sense of her sorrow. "Shall I know soon?" she said as he left the house.

"Surely some one will know," he said; "and I will send thee word."

But as he left the house the real facts had already been made known at the "Duchess of Edinburgh." One of the morning papers had a full, circumstantial, and fairly true account of the whole matter. "It was not his lordship at all," said the good-natured landlady, coming out to him as he passed the door.

"Not Lord Hampstead?"

"Not at all."

" He was not killed ? "

" It wasn't him as was hurt, Mr. Fay. It was another of them young men—one Mr. Walker; only son of Watson, Walker, and Warren. And whether he be dead or alive nobody knows; but they do say there wasn't a whole bone left in his body. It's all here, and I was a-going to bring it you. I suppose Miss Fay did take it badly ? "

" I knew the young man," said the Quaker, hurrying back to his own house with the paper,—anxious if possible not to declare to the neighbourhood that the young lord was in truth a suitor for his daughter's hand. " And I thank thee, Mrs. Grimley, for thy care. The suddenness of it all frightened my poor girl."

" That'll comfort her up," said Mrs. Grimley cheerily. " From all we hear, Mr. Fay, she do have reason to be anxious for this young lord. I hope he'll be spared to her, Mr. Fay, and show himself a true man."

Then the Quaker returned with his news,—which was accepted by him and by them all as trustworthy. " Now my girl will be happy again ? "

" Yes, father."

" But my child has told the truth to her old father at last."

" Had I told you any untruth ? "

" No, indeed, Marion."

" I said that I am not fit to be his wife, and I am not. Nothing is changed in all that. But when I heard that he was——. But, father, we will not talk of it now. How good you have been to me, I shall never forget,—and how tender!"

"Who should be soft-hearted if not a father?"

"They are not all like you. But you have been always good and gentle to your girl. How good and how gentle we cannot always see;—can we? But I have seen it now, father."

As he went into the City, about an hour after his proper time, he allowed his heart to rejoice at the future prospects of his girl. He did now believe that there would be a marriage between her and her noble lover. She had declared her love to him,—to him, her father, and after that she would surely do as they would have her. Something had reached even his ears of the coyness of girls, and it was not displeasing to him that his girl had not been at once ready to give herself with her easy promise to her lover. How strong she had looked, even in the midst of her sufferings, on the previous evening! That she should be weaker this morning, less able to restrain her tears, more prone to tremble as he spoke to her, was but natural. The shock of the grief will often come after the sorrow is over. He knew that, and told himself that there need be nothing,—need not at least be much,—to fear.

But it was not so with Marion as she lay all the morning convulsed almost with the violence of her emotions. Her own weakness was palpable to herself, as she struggled to regain her breath, struggled to repress her sobs, struggled to move about the house, and be as might be any other girl. "Better just lie thee down till thy father return, and leave me to bustle through the work," said the old Quaker woman who had lived with them through all their troubles. Then Marion yielded, and laid herself on the bed till the hour had come in which her father might be expected.

CHAPTER XX.

NEVER, NEVER, TO COME AGAIN.

THE trouble to Hampstead occasioned by the accident was considerable, as was also for the first twenty-four hours his anxiety and that of his sister as to the young man's fate. He got back to Gorse Hall early in the day, as there was no more hunting after the killing of that first fox. There had been a consultation as to the young man, and it had been held to be best to have him taken to the inn at which he had been living, as there would be room there for any of his friends who might come to look after him. But during the whole of that day inquiries were made at Gorse Hall after Lord Hampstead himself, so general had been the belief that he was the victim. From all the towns around, from Peterborough, Oundle, Stilton, and Thrapstone, there came mounted messengers, with expressions of hope and condolence as to the young lord's broken bones.

And then the condition of their poor neighbour was so critical that they found it to be impossible to leave Gorse Hall on the next day, as they had intended. He

had become intimate with them, and had breakfasted at
Gorse Hall on that very morning. In one way Hampstead felt that he was responsible, as, had he not been
in the way, poor Walker's horse would have been next to
the gate, and would not have attempted the impossible
jump. They were compelled to put off the journey till the
Monday. "Will go by the 9.30 train," said Hampstead in
his telegram, who, in spite of poor Walker's mangled
body, was still determined to see Marion on that day. On
the Saturday morning it became known to him and his
sister that the false report had been in the London newspapers, and then they had found themselves compelled
to send telegrams to every one who knew them, to the
Marquis, and to the lawyer in London, to Mr. Roberts,
and to the housekeeper at Hendon Hall. Telegrams
were also sent by Lady Amaldina to Lady Persiflage,
and especially to Lord Llwddythlw. Vivian sent others
to the Civil Service generally. Hautboy was very eager
to let everybody know the truth at the Pandemonium.
Never before had so many telegrams been sent from the
little office at Gimberley. But there was one for which
Hampstead demanded priority, writing it himself, and
himself giving it into the hands of the despatching
young lady, the daughter of the Gimberley grocer, who
no doubt understood the occasion perfectly.

"To Marion Fay, 17, Paradise Row, Holloway.
"It was not I who was hurt. Shall be at No. 17 by
three on Monday."

" I wonder whether they heard it down at Trafford," said Lady Amaldina to Lady Frances. On this subject they were informed before the day was over, as a long message came from Mr. Roberts in compliance with the instructions from the Marquis. " Because if they did what a terrible disappointment my aunt will have to bear."

" Do not say anything so horrible," said Lady Frances.

" I always look upon Aunt Clara as though she were not quite in her right senses about her own children. She thinks a great injury is done her because her son is not the heir. Now for a moment she will have believed that it was so." This, however, was a view of the matter which Lady Frances found herself unable to discuss.

" He's going to get well after all," said Hautboy that evening, just before dinner. He had been running over to the inn every hour to ask after the condition of poor Walker. At first the tidings had been gloomy enough. The doctor had only been able to say that he needn't die because of his broken bones. Then late in the afternoon there arrived a surgeon from London who gave something of a stronger hope. The young man's consciousness had come back to him, and he had expressed an appreciation for brandy and water. It was this fact which had seemed so promising to young Lord Hautboy. On the Saturday there came Mrs. Walker and Miss Walker, and before the Sunday

evening it was told how the patient had signified his
intention of hunting again on the first possible opportunity. " I always knew he was a brick," said Hautboy,
as he repeated the story, "because he always would
ride at everything."

"I don't think he'll ever ride again at the fence just
out of Gimberley Wood," said Lord Hampstead. They
were all able to start on the Monday morning without
serious concern, as the accounts from the injured man's
bed-room were still satisfactory. That he had broken
three ribs, a collar-bone, and an arm seemed to be
accounted as nothing. Nor was there much made of
the scalp wound on his head, which had come from a
kick the horse gave him in the struggle. As his brains
were still there, that did not much matter. His cheek
had been cut open by a stake on which he fell, but the
scar, it was thought, would only add to his glories. It
was the pressure of the horse which had fallen across
his body which the doctors feared. But Hautboy very
rightly argued that there couldn't be much danger,
seeing that he had recovered his taste for brandy and
water. "If it wasn't for that," said Hautboy, "I don't
think I'd have gone away and left him."

Lord Hampstead found, when he reached home on
the Monday morning, that his troubles were not yet
over. The housekeeper came out and wept, almost
with her arms round his neck. The groom, and the
footman, and the gardener, even the cowboy himself,
flocked about him, telling stories of the terrible

condition in which they had been left after the coming of
the Quaker on the Friday evening. " I didn't never
think I'd ever see my lord again," said the cook solemnly.
" I didn't a'most hope it," said the housemaid, " after
hearing the Quaker gentleman read it all out of the
newspaper." Lord Hampstead shook hands with them
all, and laughed at the misfortune of the false telegram,
and endeavoured to be well pleased with everything,
but it occurred to him to think what must have been
the condition of Mr. Fay's house that night, when he
had come across from Holloway through the darkness
and rain to find out for his girl what might be the
truth or falsehood of the report which had reached
him.

At 3.0 punctually he was in Paradise Row. Perhaps
it was not unnatural that even then his advent should
create emotion. As he turned down from the main
road the very potboy from " The Duchess " rushed up
to him, and congratulated h'm on his escape. " I have
had nothing to escape," said Lord Hampstead trying
to pass on. But Mrs. Grimley saw him, and came out
to him. " Oh, my lord, we are so thankful ;—indeed,
we are.

" You are very good, ma'am," said the lord.

" And now, Lord 'Ampstead, mind and be true to
that dear young lady who was well-nigh heart-broke
when she heard as it were you who was smashed up."

He was hurrying on finding it impossible to make any
reply to this, when Miss Demijohn, seeing that Mrs.

Grimley had been bold enough to address the noble visitor to their humble street, remembering how much she had personally done in the matter, having her mind full of the important fact that she had been the first to give information on the subject to the Row generally, thinking that no such appropriate occasion as this would ever again occur for making personal acquaintance with the lord, rushed out from her own house, and seized the young man's hand before he was able to defend himself. "My lord," she said, "my lord, we were all so depressed when we heard of it."

"Were you, indeed?"

"All the Row was depressed, my lord. But I was the first who knew it. It was I who communicated the sad tidings to Miss Fay. It was, indeed, my lord. I saw it in the *Evening Tell-Tale,* and went across with the paper at once."

"That was very good of you."

"Thank'ee, my lord. And, therefore, seeing you and knowing you,—for we all know you now in Paradise Row——"

"Do you now?"

"Every one of us, my lord. Therefore I thought I'd just make bold to come out and introduce myself. Here's Mrs. Duffer. I hope you'll let me introduce you to Mrs. Duffer of No. 17. Mrs. Duffer, Lord Hampstead. And oh, my lord, it will be such an honour to the Row if anything of that kind should happen."

Lord Hampstead, having with his best grace gone through the ceremony of shaking hands with Mrs. Duffer, who had come up to him and Clara just at the step of the Quaker's house, was at last allowed to knock at the door. Miss Fay would be with him in a minute, said the old woman as she showed him into the sitting-room up-stairs.

Marion, as soon as she heard the knock, ran for a moment to her own bed-room. Was it not much to her that he was with her again, not only alive, but uninjured, that she should again hear his voice, and see the light of his countenance, and become aware once more of a certain almost heavenly glory which seemed to surround her when she was in his presence? She was aware that on such occasions she felt herself to be lifted out of her ordinary prosaic life, and to be for a time floating, as it were, in some upper air; among the clouds, indeed;—alas, yes; but among clouds which were silver-lined; in a heaven which could never be her own, but in which she could dwell, though it were but for an hour or two, in ecstasy,—if only he would allow her to do so without troubling her with further prayer. Then there came across her a thought that if only she could so begin this interview with him that it might seem to be an occasion of special joy,—as though it were a thanksgiving because he had come back to her safe,—she might, at any rate for this day, avoid words from him which might drive her again to refuse his great request. He already knew that she

loved him, must know of what value to her must be
his life, must understand how this had come at first
a terrible, crushing, killing sorrow, and then a relief
which by the excess of its joy must have been almost
too much for her. Could she not let all that be a
thing acknowledged between them, which might be
spoken of as between dearest friends, without any
allusion for the present to that request which could
never be granted?

But he, as he waited there a minute or two, was
minded to make quite another use of the interview.
He was burning to take her in his arms as his own,
to press his lips to hers and know that she returned
his caress, to have the one word spoken which would
alone suffice to satisfy the dominating spirit of the man
within him. Had she acceded to his request, then
his demand would have been that she should at once
become his wife, and he would not have rested at
peace till he had reduced her months to weeks. He
desired to have it all his own way. He had drawn
her into his presence as soon almost as he had seen
her. He had forced upon her his love. He had
driven her to give him her heart, and to acknowledge
that it was so. Of course he must go on with his
triumph over her. She must be his altogether, from
the crown of her head to the soles of her feet,—and
that without delay. His hunting and his yacht, his
politics and his friendships, were nothing to him
without Marion Fay. When she came into the room,

his heart was in sympathy with her, but by no means his mind.

"My lord," she said, letting her hand lie willingly between the pressure of his two, "you may guess what we suffered when we heard the report, and how we felt when we learnt the truth."

"You got my telegram? I sent it as soon as I began to understand how foolish the people had been."

"Oh yes, my lord. It was so good of you!"

"Marion, will you do something for me?"

"What shall I do, my lord?"

"Don't call me, 'my lord.'"

"But it is proper."

"It is most improper, and abominable, and unnatural."

"Lord Hampstead!"

"I hate it. You and I can understand each other, at any rate."

"I hope so."

"I hate it from everybody. I can't tell the servants not to do it. They wouldn't understand me. But from you! It seems always as though you were laughing at me."

"Laugh at you!"

"You may if you like it. What is it you may not do with me? If it were really a joke, if you were quizzing, I shouldn't mind it." He held her hand the whole time, and she did not attempt to withdraw it.

What did her hand signify? If she could only so manage with him on that day that he should be satisfied to be happy, and not trouble her with any request. "Marion," he said, drawing her towards him.

"Sit down, my lord. Well. I won't. You shan't be called my lord to-day, because I am so happy to see you;—because you have had so great an escape."

"But I didn't have any escape."

If only she could keep him in this way! If he would only talk to her about anything but his passion! "It seemed to me so, of course. Father was broken-hearted about it. He was as bad as I. Think of father going down without his tea to Hendon Hall, and driving the poor people there all out of their wits."

"Everybody was out of his wits."

"I was," she said, bobbing her head at him. She was just so far from him, she thought, as to be safe from any impetuous movement. "And Hannah was nearly as bad." Hannah was the old woman. "You may imagine we had a wretched night of it."

"And all about nothing," said he, falling into her mood in the moment. "But think of poor Walker."

"Yes, indeed! I suppose he has friends, too, who loved him, as—as some people love you. But he is not going to die?"

"I hope not. Who is that young woman opposite who rushed out to me in the street? She says she brought you the news first."

"Miss Demijohn."

" Is she a friend of yours ? "

" No," said Marion, blushing as she spoke the word very firmly.

" I am rather glad of that, because I didn't fall in love with her. She introduced me to ever so many of the neighbours. The landlady of the public-house was one, I think."

" I am afraid they have offended you among them."

" Not in the least. I never take offence except when I think people mean it. But now, Marion, say one word to me."

" I have said many words. Have I not said nice words ? "

" Every word out of your mouth is like music to me. But there is one word which I am dying to hear."

" What word ? " she said. She knew that she should not have asked the question, but it was so necessary for her to put off the evil if it were only for a moment.

" It is whatever word you may choose to use when you speak to me as my wife. My mother used to call me John; the children call me Jack; my friends call me Hampstead. Invent something sweet for yourself. I always call you Marion because I love the sound so dearly."

" Every one calls me Marion."

" No ! I never did so till I had told myself that, if possible, you should be my own. Do you remember when you poked the fire for me at Hendon Hall ? "

"I do;—I do. It was wrong of me; was it not;— when I hardly knew you?"

"It was beyond measure good of you; but I did not dare to call you Marion then, though I knew your name as well as I do now, Marion! I have it here, written all round my heart." What could she say to a man who spoke to her after this fashion? It was as though an angel from heaven were courting her! If only she could have gone on listening so that nothing further should come of it! "Find some name for me, and tell me that it shall be written round your heart."

"Indeed it is. You know it is, Lord Hampstead."

"But what name?"

"Your friend;—your friend of friends."

"It will not do. It is cold."

"Then it is untrue to her from whom it comes. Do you think that my friendship is cold for you?"

She had turned towards him, and was sitting before him with her face looking into his, with her hands clasped as though in assurance of her truth;—when suddenly he had her in his arms and had pressed his lips to hers. In a moment she was standing in the middle of the room. Though he was strong, her strength was sufficient for her. "My lord!" she exclaimed.

"Ah, you are angry with me?"

"My lord, my lord,—I did not think you would treat me like that."

"But, Marion; do you not love me?"

"Have I not told you that I do? Have I not been true and honest to you? Do you not know it all?" But in truth he did not know it all. "And now I must bid you never, never to come again."

"But I shall come. I will come. I will come always. You will not cease to love me?"

"No;—not that—I cannot do that. But you must not come. You have done that which makes me ashamed of myself." At that moment the door was opened, and Mrs. Roden came into the room.

CHAPTER XXI.

DI CRINOLA.

THE reader must submit to have himself carried back some weeks,—to those days early in January, when Mrs. Roden called upon her son to accompany her to Italy. Indeed, he must be carried back a long way beyond that; but the time during which he need be so detained shall be short. A few pages will suffice to tell so much of the early life of this lady as will be necessary to account for her residence in Paradise Row.

Mary Roden, the lady whom we have known as Mrs. Roden, was left an orphan at the age of fifteen, her mother having died when she was little more than an infant. Her father was an Irish clergyman with no means of his own but what he secured from a small living; but his wife had inherited money amounting to about eight thousand pounds, and this had descended to Mary when her father died. The girl was then taken in charge by a cousin of her own, a lady ten years her senior who had lately married, and whom we have since met as Mrs. Vincent, living at Wimbledon. Mr. Vincent had been well connected and well-to-do in the world,

and till he died the household in which Mary Roden
had been brought up had been luxurious as well as
comfortable. Nor did Mr. Vincent die till after his
wife's cousin had found a husband for herself. Soon
afterwards he was gathered to his fathers, leaving to his
widow a comfortable, but not more than a comfortable,
income.

The year before his death he and his wife had gone
into Italy, rather on account of his health than for
pleasure, and had then settled themselves at Verona for
a winter,—a winter which eventually stretched itself
into nearly a year, at the close of which Mr. Vincent
died. But before that event took place Mary Roden
had become a wife.

At Verona, at first at the house of her own cousin,—
which was of course her own home,—and afterwards in
the society of the place to which the Vincents had been
made welcome,—Mary met a young man who was known
to all the world as the Duca di Crinola. No young man
more beautiful to look at, more charming in manners,
more ready in conversation, was then known in those
parts of Italy than this young nobleman. In addition
to these good gifts, he was supposed to have in his veins
the very best blood in all Europe. It was declared on
his behalf that he was related to the Bourbons and to
the Hapsburgh family. Indeed there was very little of
the best blood which Europe had produced in the last
dozen centuries of which some small proportion was not
running in his veins. He was too the eldest son of his

father, who, though he possessed the most magnificent
palace in Verona, had another equally magnificent in
Venice, in which it suited him to live with his Duchessa.
As the old nobleman did not come often to Verona, and
as the young nobleman never went to Venice, the father
and son did not see much of each other, an arrangement
which was supposed to have its own comforts, as the
young man was not disturbed in the possession of his
hotel, and as the old man was reported in Verona
generally to be arbitrary, hot-tempered, and tyrannical.
It was therefore said of the young Duke by his friends
that he was nearly as well off as though he had no
father at all.

But there were other things in the history of the
young Duke which, as they became known to the Vincents, did not seem to be altogether so charming.
Though of all the palaces in Verona that in which he
lived was by far the most beautiful to look at from the
outside, it was not supposed to be furnished in a manner
conformable to its external appearance. It was, indeed,
declared that the rooms were for the most part bare;
and the young Duke never gave the lie to these asser-
tions by throwing them open to his friends. It was
said of him also that his income was so small and so
precarious that it amounted almost to nothing, that the
cross old Duke at Venice never allowed him a shilling,
and that he had done everything in his power to destroy
the hopes of a future inheritance. Nevertheless, he was
beautiful to look at in regard to his outward attire, and

could hardly have been better dressed had he been able
to pay his tailor and shirt-maker quarterly. And he
was a man of great accomplishments, who could talk
various languages, who could paint, and model, and
write sonnets, and dance to perfection. And he could
talk of virtue, and in some sort seem to believe in it,—
though he would sometimes confess of himself that
Nature had not endowed him with the strength necessary for the performance of all the good things which he
so thoroughly appreciated.

Such as he was he entirely gained the affection of
Mary Roden. It is unnecessary here to tell the efforts
that were made by Mrs. Vincent to prevent the
marriage. Had she been less austere she might,
perhaps, have prevailed with the girl. But as she
began by pointing out to her cousin the horror of
giving herself, who had been born and bred a Protestant, to a Roman Catholic,—and also of bestowing
her English money upon an Italian,—all that she said
was without effect. The state of Mr. Vincent's health
made it impossible for them to move, or Mary might
perhaps have been carried back to England. When
she was told that the man was poor, she declared that
there was so much the more reason why her money
should be given to relieve the wants of the man she
loved. It ended in their being married, and all that
Mr. Vincent was able to accomplish was to see that
the marriage ceremony should be performed after the
fashion both of the Church of England and of the

Church of Rome. Mary at the time was more than twenty-one, and was thus able, with all the romance of girlhood, to pour her eight thousand pounds into the open hands of her thrice-noble and thrice-beautiful lover.

The Duchino with his young Duchessina went their way rejoicing, and left poor Mr. Vincent to die at Verona. Twelve months afterwards the widow had settled herself at the house at Wimbledon, from which she had in latter years paid her weekly visits to Paradise Row, and tidings had come from the young wife which were not altogether satisfactory. The news, indeed, which declared that a young little Duke had been born to her was accompanied by expressions of joy which the other surrounding incidents of her life were not permitted at the moment altogether to embitter. Her baby, her well-born beautiful baby, was for a few months allowed to be a joy to her, even though things were otherwise very sorrowful. But things were very sorrowful. The old Duke and the old Duchess would not acknowledge her. Then she learned that the quarrel between the father and son had been carried to such a pitch that no hope of reconciliation remained. Whatever was left of family property was gone as far as any inheritance on the part of the elder son was concerned. He had himself assisted in making over to a second brother all right that he possessed in the property belonging to the family. Then tidings of horror accumulated itself upon her and her baby.

Then came tidings that her husband had been already
married when he first met her,—which tidings did not
reach her till he had left her alone, somewhere up
among the Lakes, for an intended absence of three
days. After that day she never saw him again. The
next she heard of him was from Italy, from whence he
wrote to her to tell her that she was an angel, and that
he, devil as he was, was not fit to appear in her
presence. Other things had occurred during the
fifteen months in which they had lived together to
make her believe at any rate the truth of this last
statement. It was not that she ceased to love him,
but that she knew that he was not fit to be loved.
When a woman is bad a man can generally get quit of
her from his heartstrings;—but a woman has no such
remedy. She can continue to love the dishonoured one
without dishonour to herself,—and does so.

Among other misfortunes was the loss of all her
money. There she was, in the little villa on the side
of the lake, with no income,—and with statements
floating about her that she had not, and never had had,
a husband. It might well be that after that she should
caution Marion Fay as to the imprudence of an exalted
marriage. But there came to her assistance, if not
friendship and love, in the midst of her misfortunes.
Her brother-in-law,—if she had a husband or a brother-
in-law,—came to her from the old Duke with terms of
surrender; and there came also a man of business, a
lawyer, from Venice, to make good the terms if they

should be accepted. Though money was very scarce
with the family, or the power of raising money, still
such was the feeling of the old nobleman in her misfortunes that the entire sum which had been given up
to his eldest son should be restored to trustees for her
use and for the benefit of her baby, on condition that
she should leave Italy, and consent to drop the title of
the Di Crinola family. As to that question of a former
marriage, the old lawyer declared that he was unable to
give any certain information. The reprobate had no
doubt gone through some form of a ceremony with a
girl of low birth at Venice. It very probably was not a
marriage. The young Duchino, the brother, declared
his belief that there had been no such marriage. But
she, should she cling to the name, could not make her
title good to it without obtaining proofs which they had
not been able to find. No doubt she could call herself
Duchess. Had she means at command she might
probably cause herself to be received as such. But no
property would thus be affected,—nor would it rob him,
the younger son, of his right to call himself also by the
title. The offer made to her was not ungenerous. The
family owed her nothing, but were willing to sacrifice
nearly half of all they had with the object of restoring
to her the money of which the profligate had robbed
her,—which he had been enabled to take from her by
her own folly and credulity. In this terrible emergency
of her life, Mrs. Vincent sent over to her a solicitor
from London, between whom and the Italian man of

business a bargain was struck. The young wife undertook to drop her husband's name, and to drop it also on
behalf of her boy. Then the eight thousand pounds
was repaid, and Mrs. Roden, as she afterwards called
herself, went back to Wimbledon and to England with
her baby.

So far the life of George Roden's mother had been
most unfortunate. After that, for a period of sixteen
years time went with her, if not altogether happily, at
least quietly and comfortably. Then there came a
subject of disruption. George Roden took upon himself
to have opinions of his own; and would not hold his
peace in the presence of Mrs. Vincent, to whom those
opinions were most unacceptable. And they were the
more unacceptable because the mother's tone of mind
had always taken something of the bent which appeared
so strongly afterwards in her son. George at any rate
could not be induced to be silent; nor,—which was
worse,—could he after reaching his twentieth year be
made to go to church with that regularity which was
necessary for the elder lady's peace of mind. He at this
time had achieved for himself a place in the office ruled
over by our friend Sir Boreas, and had in this way
become so much of a man as to be entitled to judge for
himself. In this way there had been no quarrel between
Mrs. Vincent and Mrs. Roden, but there had come a
condition of things in which it had been thought
expedient that they should live apart. Mrs. Roden had
therefore taken for herself a house in Paradise Row,

and those weekly inter-visitings had been commenced between her and her cousin.

Such had been the story of Mrs. Roden's life, till tidings were received in England that her husband was dead. The information had been sent to Mrs. Vincent by the younger son of the late old Duke, who was now a nobleman well known in the political life of his own country. He had stated that, to the best of his belief, his brother's first union had not been a legal marriage. He thought it right, he had said, to make this statement, and to say that as far as he was concerned he was willing to withdraw that compact upon which his father had insisted. If his sister-in-law wished to call herself by the name and title of Di Crinola, she might do so. Or if the young man of whom he spoke as his nephew wished to be known as Duca di Crinola he would raise no objection. But it must be remembered that he had nothing to offer to his relative but the barren tender of the name. He himself had succeeded to but very little, and that which he possessed had not been taken from his brother.

Then there were sundry meetings between Mrs. Vincent and Mrs. Roden, at which it was decided that Mrs. Roden should go to Italy with her son. Her brother-in-law had been courteous to her, and had offered to receive her if she would come. Should she wish to use the name of Di Crinola, he had promised that she should be called by it in his house; so that the world around might know that she was recognized

by him and his wife and children. She determined
that she would at any rate make the journey, and that
she would take her son with her.

George Roden had hitherto learnt nothing of his
father or his family. In the many consultations held
between his mother and Mrs. Vincent it had been
decided that it would be better to keep him in the
dark. Why fill his young imagination with the glory
of a great title in order that he might learn at last, as
might too probably be the case, that he had no right to
the name,—no right to consider himself even to be his
father's son ? She, by her folly,—so she herself acknowledged,—had done all that was possible to annihilate
herself as a woman. There was no name which she
could give to her son as certainly as her own. This,
which had been hers before she had been allured into
a mock marriage, would at any rate not be disputed.
And thus he had been kept in ignorance of his mother's
story. Of course he had asked. It was no more than
natural that he should ask. But when told that it was
for his mother's comfort that he should ask no more, he
had assented with that reticence which was peculiar to
him. Then chance had thrown him into friendship
with the young English nobleman, and the love of
Lady Frances Trafford had followed.

His mother, when he consented to accompany her,
had almost promised him that all mysteries should be
cleared up between them before their return. In the
train, before they reached Paris, a question was asked

and an answer given which served to tell much of the truth. As they came down to breakfast that morning, early in the dark January morning, he observed that his mother was dressed in deep mourning. It had always been her custom to wear black raiment. He could not remember that he had ever seen on her a coloured dress, or even a bright ribbon. And she was not now dressed quite as is a widow immediately on the death of her husband. It was now a quarter of a century since she had seen the man who had so ill-used her. According to the account which she had received, it was twelve months at least since he had died in one of the Grecian islands. The full weeds of a mourning widow would ill have befitted her condition of mind, or her immediate purpose. But yet there was a speciality of blackness in her garments which told him that she had dressed herself with a purpose as of mourning. "Mother," he said to her in the train, "you are in mourning,—as for a friend?" Then when she paused he asked again, "May I not be told for whom it is done? Am I not right in saying that it is so?"

"It is so, George."

"For whom then?"

They two were alone in the carriage, and why should his question not be answered now? But it had come to pass that there was a horror to her in mentioning the name of his father to him. "George," she said, "it is more than twenty-five years since I saw your father."

"Is he dead——only now?"

"It is only now,—only the other day,—that I have heard of his death."

"Why should not I also be in black?"

"I had not thought of it. But you never saw him since he had you in his arms as a baby. You cannot mourn for him in heart."

"Do you?"

"It is hard to say for what we mourn sometimes. Of course I loved him once. There is still present to me a memory of what I loved,—of the man who won my heart by such gifts as belonged to him; and for that I mourn. He was beautiful and clever, and he charmed me. It is hard to say sometimes for what we mourn."

"Was he a foreigner, mother?"

"Yes, George. He was an Italian. You shall know it all soon now. But do not you mourn. To you no memories are left. Were it not for the necessity of the present moment, no idea of a father should ever be presented to you." She vouchsafed to tell him no more at that moment, and he pressed her with no further questions.

END OF VOL. II.

VOLUME III

MARION FAY.

CHAPTER I.

"I WILL COME BACK AS I WENT."

WHILE Lord Hampstead's party were at Gorse Hall, some weeks before poor Walker's accident, there came a letter from George Roden to Lady Frances, and she, when she reached Hendon Hall, found a second. Both these letters, or parts of them, shall be here given, as they will tell all that need be added to what is already known of the story of the man, and will explain to the reader the cause and manner of action which he adopted.

"*Rome,*
"*January* 30*th,* 18—

"DEAREST FANNY,—

"I wonder whether it will seem as odd to you to receive a letter from me written at Rome as it is to me to write it. Our letters hitherto have

been very few in number, and have only declared that
in spite of obstacles we shall always love each other.
I have never before had anything in truth to tell you;
but now I have so much that I do not know how to
begin or how to go on with it. But it must be written,
as there is much that will interest you as my dearest
friend, and much also that will concern yourself should
you ever become my wife. It may be that a point
will arise as to which you and your friends,—your
father, for instance, and your brother,—will feel yourselves entitled to have a voice in deciding. It may
be quite possible that your judgment, or, at any rate,
that of your friends, may differ from my own. Should
it be so I cannot say that I shall be prepared to yield ;
but I will, at any rate, enable you to submit the case to
them with all fairness.

"I have told you more than once how little I have
known of my own family,—that I have known indeed
nothing. My mother has seemed to me to be perversely
determined not to tell me all that which I will acknowledge I have thought that I ought to know. But with
equal perversity I have refrained from asking questions
on a subject of which I think I should have been told
everything without questioning. And I am a man
not curious by nature as to the past. I am more
anxious as to what I may do myself than as to what
others of my family may have done before me.

"When, however, my mother asked me to go with her
to Italy, it was manifest that her journey had reference

to her former life. I knew from circumstances which
could not be hidden from me,—from her knowledge,
for instance, of Italian, and from some relics which
remained to her of her former life,—that she had
lived for some period in this country. As my place
of birth had never been mentioned to me, I could
not but guess that I had been born in Italy, and
when I found that I was going there I felt certain
that I must learn some portion of the story of which
I had been kept in ignorance. Now I have learnt
it all as far as my poor mother knows it herself; and
as it will concern you to know it too, I must endeavour
to explain to you all the details. Dearest Fanny, I
do trust that when you have heard them you will
think neither worse of me on that account,—nor better.
It is as to the latter that I am really in fear. I wish
to believe that no chance attribute could make me
stand higher in your esteem than I have come to
stand already by my own personal character."

Then he told her,—not, perhaps, quite so fully as
the reader has heard it told in the last chapter,—the
story of his mother's marriage and of his own birth.
Before they had reached Rome, where the Duca di
Crinola at present lived, and where he was at present a
member of the Italian Cabinet, the mother had told
her son all that she knew, having throughout the
telling of the story unconsciously manifested to him
her own desire to remain in obscurity, and to bear the
name which had been hers for five-and-twenty years;

but at the same time so to manage that he should
return to England bearing the title to which by his
birth she believed him to be entitled. When in discussing this he explained to her that it would be still
necessary for him to earn his bread as a clerk in the
Post Office in spite of his high-sounding nobility, and
explained to her the absurdity of his sitting in Mr.
Jerningham's room at the desk with young Crocker,
and calling himself at the same time the Duca di
Crinola, she in her arguments exhibited a weakness
which he had hardly expected from her. She spoke
vaguely, but with an assurance of personal hope, of
Lady Frances, of Lord Hampstead, of the Marquis of
Kingsbury, and of Lord Persiflage,—as though by the
means of these noble personages the Duca di Crinola
might be able to live in idleness. Of all this Roden
could say nothing in this first letter to Lady Frances.
But it was to this that he alluded when he hoped that
she would not think better of him because of the news
which he sent her.

"At present," he wrote, continuing his letter after
the telling of the story, "we are staying with my
uncle, as I presume I am entitled to call him. He is
very gracious, as also are his wife and the young ladies
who are my cousins; but I think that he is as anxious
as I am that there should be no acknowledged branch
of the family senior to his own. He is Duca di
Crinola to all Italy, and will remain so whether I
assume the title or not. Were I to take the name,

and to remain in Italy,—which is altogether impossible,
—I should be nobody. He who has made for himself
a great position, and apparently has ample means,
would not in truth be affected. But I am sure that he
would not wish it. He is actuated by a sense of
honesty, but he certainly has no desire to be incom-
moded by relatives who would, as regards the family,
claim to be superior to himself. My dearest mother
wishes to behave well to him, wishes to sacrifice
herself; but is, I fear, above all things, anxious to
procure for her son the name and title which his
father bore.

"As for myself, you will, I think, already have
perceived that it is my desire to remain as I was when
last I saw you, and to be as ever

"Yours, most affectionately,

"GEORGE RODEN."

Lady Frances was, as may be imagined, much
startled at the receipt of this letter;—startled, and
also pleased. Though she had always declared to
herself that she was in every respect satisfied with her
lover from the Post Office, though she had been sure
that she had never wanted him to be other than he
was, still, when she heard of that fine-sounding name,
there did for a moment come upon her an idea that,
for his sake, it might be well that he should have the
possession of all that his birth had done for him. But
when she came to understand the meaning of his

words, as she did on the second or third reading of his
letter,—when she discovered what he meant by saying
that he hoped she would not think better of him by
reason of what he was telling her, when she understood
the purport of the manner in which he signed his
name, she resolved that in every respect she would
think as he thought and act as he wished her to act.
Whatever might be the name which he might be
pleased to give her, with that would she be contented,
nor would she be led by any one belonging to her
to ask him to change his purpose.

For two days she kept the letter by her unanswered,
and without speaking of it to anybody. Then she
showed it to her brother, exacting from him a promise
that he should not speak of it to any one without her
permission. " It is George's secret," she said, " and
I am sure you will see that I have no right to disclose
it. I tell you because he would do so if he were
here." Her brother was willing enough to make the
promise, which would of course be in force only till
he and Roden should see each other ; but he could
not be brought to agree with his sister as to his friend's
view of the position.

" He may have what fancies he pleases about titles,"
he said, " as may I ; but I do not think that he would
be justified in repudiating his father's name. I feel
it a burden and an absurdity to be born to be an earl
and a marquis, but I have to put up with it; and,
though my reason and political feeling on the matter

tell me that it is a burden and an absurdity, yet the
burden is easily borne, and the absurdity does not
annoy me much. There is a gratification in being
honoured by those around you, though your conscience
may be twinged that you yourself have done nothing
to deserve it. It will be so with him if he takes
his position here as an Italian nobleman."

"But he would still have to be a clerk in the Post
Office."

"Probably not."

"But how would he live?" asked Lady Frances.

"The governor, you would find, would look upon
him in a much more favourable light than he does
at present."

"That would be most unreasonable."

"Not at all. It is not unreasonable that a Marquis
of Kingsbury should be unwilling to give his daughter
to George Roden, a clerk in the Post Office,—but
that he should be willing to give her to a Duca di
Crinola."

"What has that to do with earning money?"

"The Governor would probably find an income in
one case, and not in the other. I do not quite say
that it ought to be so, but it is not unreasonable that
it should be so." Then Lady Frances said a great
deal as to that pride in her lover which would not
allow him to accept such a position as that which was
now suggested.

There was a long discussion on the subject. Her

brother explained to her how common it was for noblemen of high birth to live on means provided by their
wives' fortunes, and how uncommon it was that men
born to high titles should consent to serve as clerks
in a public office. But his common sense had no effect
upon his sister, who ended the conversation by exacting
from him a renewed assurance of secrecy. "I won't
say a word till he comes," said Hampstead; "but you
may be sure that a story like that will be all over
London before he does come."

Lady Frances of course answered her lover's letter;
but of what she said it is only necessary that the reader
should know that she promised that in all things she
would be entirely guided by his wishes.

Then came his second letter to her, dated on the
day on which poor Walker had nearly been crushed
to death. "I am so glad that you agree with me,"
he wrote. "Since my last letter to you everything
here has been decided as far as I can decide it,—or,
indeed, as far as any of us can do so. There can, I
think, be no doubt as to the legality of my mother's
marriage. My uncle is of the same opinion, and points
out to me that were I to claim my father's name no
one would attempt to dispute it. He alone could do
so,—or rather would be the person to do so if it were
done. He would make no such attempt, and would
himself present me to the King here as the Duca di
Crinola if I chose to remain and to accept the position.
But I certainly will not do so. I should in the first

place be obliged to give up my nationality. I could
not live in England bearing an Italian title, except as
an Italian. I do not know that as an Italian I should
be forced to give up my place in the Post Office.
Foreigners, I believe, are employed in the Civil Service.
But there would be an absurdity in it which to me
would be specially annoying. I could not live under
such a weight of ridicule. Nor could I live in any
position in which some meagre income might be found
for me because of my nobility. No such income would
be forthcoming here. I can imagine that your father
might make a provision for a poor son-in-law with a
grand title. He ought not to do so, according to my
ideas, but it might be possible that he should find
himself persuaded to such weakness. But I could not
accept it. I should not be above taking money with
my wife, if it happened to come in my way, provided
that I were earning an income myself to the best of
my ability. For her sake I should do what might
be best for her. But not even for your sake,—if you
wished it, as I know you do not,—could I consent to
hang about the world in idleness as an Italian duke
without a shilling of my own. Therefore, my darling,
I purpose to come back as I went,

"Your own,

"GEORGE RODEN.

"Clerk in the Post Office, and entitled to
consider myself as being on 'H.M.S.' when
at work from ten till four."

This letter reached Lady Frances at Hendon Hall
on the return of herself and her brother from Gorse
Hall. But before that time the prophecy uttered by
Lord Hampstead as to the story being all over London
had already been in part fulfilled. Vivian during their
hunting weeks at Gorse Hall had been running continually up and down from London, where his work
as private secretary to the Secretary of State had been,
of course, most constant and important. He had,
nevertheless, managed to have three days a week in
Northamptonshire, explaining to his friends in London
that he did it by sitting up all night in the country,
to his friends in the country that he sat up all night
in town. There are some achievements which are
never done in the presence of those who hear of
them. Catching salmon is one, and working all night
is another. Vivian, however, managed to do what was
required of him, and to enjoy his hunting at the
same time.

On his arrival at Gorse Hall the day before the
famous accident he had a budget of news of which
he was very full, but of which he at first spoke only
to Hampstead. He could not, at any rate, speak of
it in the presence of Lady Frances. "You have heard
this, haven't you, about George Roden?" he asked,
as soon as he could get Lord Hampstead to himself.

"Heard what about George Roden?" asked the
other, who, of course, had heard it all.

"The Italian title."

" What about an Italian title ? "

" But have you heard it ? "

" I have heard something. What have you heard ? "

" George Roden is in Italy."

" Unless he has left it. He has been there, no doubt."

" And his mother." Hampstead nodded his head. " I suppose you do know all about it ? "

" I want to know what you know. What I have heard has come to me as a secret. Your story can probably be divulged."

" I don't know that. We are apt to be pretty close as to what we hear at the Foreign Office. But this didn't come as specially private. I've had a letter from Muscati, a very good fellow in the Foreign Office there, who had in some way heard your name as connected with Roden."

" That is very likely."

" And your sisters," said Vivian in a whisper.

" That is likely too. Men talk about anything now-a-days."

" Lord Persiflage has heard direct from Italy. He is interested, of course, as being brother-in-law to Lady Kingsbury."

" But what have they heard ? "

" It seems that Roden isn't an Englishman at all."

" That will be as he likes, I take it. He has lived here as an Englishman for five-and-twenty years."

" But of course he'll prefer to be an Italian," said

Vivian. "It turns out that he is heir to one of the
oldest titles in Italy. You have heard of the Ducas
di Crinola ? "

" I have heard of them now."

" One of them is Minister of Education in the present
Cabinet, and is likely to be the Premier. But he isn't
the head of the family, and he isn't really the Duca
di Crinola. He is called so, of course. But he isn't
the head of the family. George Roden is the real Duca
di Crinola. I thought there must be something special
about the man when your sister took such a fancy
to him."

" I always thought there was something special about
him," said Hampstead ; " otherwise I should hardly
have liked him so well."

" So did I. He always seemed to be,—to me,—just
one of ourselves, you know. A fellow doesn't come out
like that unless he's somebody. You Radicals may say
what you please, but silk purses don't get made out
of sow's ears. Nobody stands up for blood less than
I do ; but, by George, it always shows itself. You
wouldn't think Crocker was heir to a dukedom."

" Upon my word, I don't know. I have a great
respect for Crocker."

" And now what's to be done ? " asked Vivian.

" How done ? "

" About Di Crinola ? Lord Persiflage says that he
can't remain in the Post Office."

" Why not ? "

" I'm afraid he doesn't come in for much ? "

" Not a shilling."

" Lord Persiflage thinks that something should be done for him. But it is so hard. It should be done in Italy, you know. I should think that they might make him extra Secretary of Legation, so as to leave him here. But then they have such a small salary ! " As the story of George Roden's birth was thus known to all the Foreign Office, it was probable that Hampstead's prophecy would be altogether fulfilled.

CHAPTER II.

TRUE TIDINGS.

THE Foreign Office, from top to bottom, was very
much moved on the occasion,—and not without cause.
The title of Di Crinola was quite historic, and had
existed for centuries.   No Duca di Crinola,—at any
rate, no respectable Duca di Crinola,—could be in
England even as a temporary visitant without being
considered as entitled to some consideration from the
Foreign Office.   The existing duke of that name, who
had lately been best known, was at present a member
of the Italian Ministry.   Had he come he would have
been entitled to great consideration.   But he, as now
appeared, was not the real Duca di Crinola.   The real
duke was an Englishman,—or an Anglicized Italian,
or an Italianized Englishman.   No one in the Foreign
Office, not even the most ancient pundit there, quite
knew what he was.   It was clear that the Foreign
Office must take some notice of the young nobleman.
But in all this was not contained more than half of
the real reasons for peculiar consideration.   This
Anglicized Italian Duca was known to be engaged

to the daughter of an English Marquis, to a lady who,
if not niece, was next door to being niece to the
Secretary of State for Foreign Affairs himself! Many
years must have passed since an individual had sprung
into notice so interesting in many different ways to all
the body of the Foreign Office!

And this personage was a clerk in the Post Office!
There had no doubt been a feeling in the Foreign
Office, if not of actual disgrace, at any rate of mingled
shame and regret, that a niece of their Secretary of
State should have engaged herself to one so low. Had
he been in the Foreign Office himself something might
have been made of him;—but a Clerk in the Post
Office! The thing had been whispered about and
talked over, till there had come up an idea that Lady
Frances should be sent away on some compulsory
foreign mission, so as to be out of the pernicious young
man's reach. But now it turned out suddenly that the
young man was the Duca di Crinola, and it was evident
to all of them that Lady Frances Trafford was justified
in her choice.

But what was to be done with the Duca? Rumours
reached the Foreign Office that the infatuated young
nobleman intended to adhere to his most unaristocratic
position. The absurdity of a clerk of the third class
in one of the branches of the Post Office, with a salary
of a hundred and seventy a year, and sitting in the
same room with Crockers and Bobbins while he would
have to be called by everybody the Duca di Crinola,

was apparent to the mind of the lowest Foreign Office official. It couldn't be so, they said to each other. Something must be done. If Government pay were necessary to him, could he not be transformed by a leap into the Elysium of their own department, where he might serve with some especial name invented for the occasion? Then there arose questions which no man could answer. Were he to be introduced into this new-fangled office proposed for him, would he come in as an Englishman or an Italian; and if as an Englishman, was it in accordance with received rules of etiquette that he should be called Duca di Crinola? Would it be possible in so special a case to get special permission from the Crown; or if not, could he be appointed to the Foreign Office as a foreigner? The special permission, though it was surrounded by so many difficulties, yet seemed to be easier and less monstrous than this latter suggestion. They understood that though he could not well be dismissed from the office which he already held, it might be difficult to appoint a foreign nobleman to the performance of duties which certainly required more than ordinary British tendencies. In this way the mind of the Foreign Office was moved, and the coming of the young duke was awaited with considerable anxiety.

The news went beyond the Foreign Office. Whether it was that the Secretary of State himself told the story to the ladies of his household, or that it reached them through private secretaries, it was certainly the case that Lady Persiflage was enabled to write a very interesting letter to her sister, and that Lady Amaldina took the occasion of congratulating her cousin and of informing her lover.

Lady Kingsbury, when she received the news, was still engaged in pointing out to her husband the iniquity of his elder children in having admitted the visit of Mr. Roden to Hendon Hall. This, she persisted in saying, had been done in direct opposition to most solemn promises made by all the parties concerned. The Marquis at the time had recovered somewhat of his strength, in consequence, as was said among the household, of the removal of Mr. Greenwood into Shrewsbury. And the Marchioness took advantage of this improved condition on the part of her husband to make him sensible of the abominable iniquity of which the young persons had been guilty. The visit had occurred two months since, but the iniquity to Lady Kingsbury's thinking still demanded express condemnation and, if possible, punishment. "A direct and premeditated falsehood on the part of them all!" said Lady Kingsbury, standing over her husband, who was recumbent on the sofa in his own room.

"No; it wasn't," said the Marquis, who found it easier to deny the whole charge than to attempt in his weakness to divide the guilt.

"My dear! When she was allowed to go to Hendon Hall, was it not done on a sacred pledge that she should not see that horrid man? Did not Hampstead repeat the promise to my own ears?"

"How could he help his coming? I wish you wouldn't trouble me about it any more."

"Then I suppose that she is to have your leave to marry the man whenever she chooses!"

Then he roused himself with whatever strength he possessed, and begged her to leave him. With much indignation she stalked out of the room, and going to her apartments found the following letter, which had just arrived from her sister;—

"My Dear Clara,—

            "As you are down in the country, I suppose the news about Fanny's 'young man' has not yet reached you."

Fanny's young man! Had Fanny been the housemaid, it was thus that they might have spoken of her lover. Could it be that "Fanny and her young man" had already got themselves married? Lady Kingsbury, when she read this, almost let the letter drop from her hand, so much was she disgusted by the manner in which her sister spoke of this most unfortunate affair.

"I heard something of it only yesterday, and the rest of the details to-day. As it has come through the Foreign Office you may be quite sure that it is true, though it is so wonderful. The young man is not George Roden at all, nor is he an Englishman. He is an Italian, and his proper name and title is Duca di Crinola." Again Lady Kingsbury allowed the letter almost to drop; but on this occasion with feelings of a very different nature. What! not George Roden! Not a miserable clerk in the English Post Office! Duca di Crinola;—a title of which she thought that she remembered to have heard as belonging to some peculiarly ancient family! It was not to be believed. And yet it came from her sister, who was usually correct in all such matters;—and came also from the Foreign Office, which she regarded as the one really trustworthy source of information as to foreign matters of an aristocratic nature. "Duca di Crinola!" she said to herself, as she went on with the reading of her letter.

"There is a long story of the marriage of his mother which I do not quite understand as yet, but it is not necessary to the facts of the case. The young man has been recognized in his own country as entitled to all the honours of his family, and must be received so by us. Persiflage says that he will be ready to present him at Court on his return as Duca di Crinola, and will ask him at once to dine in Belgrave Square. It is a most romantic story, but must be regarded by you and me as being very fortunate, as dear Fanny had certainly set her heart upon marrying the man. I am told that he inherits nothing but the bare title. Some foreign noblemen are, you know, very poor; and in this case the father, who was a '*mauvais sujet*,' contrived to

destroy whatever rights of property he had. Lord
Kingsbury probably will be able to do something for
him. Perhaps he may succeed in getting official
employment suited to his rank. At any rate we must
all of us make the best of him for Fanny's sake. It
will be better to have a Duca di Crinola among us,
even though he should not have a shilling, than a Post
Office clerk with two or three hundred a year.

"I asked Persiflage to write to Lord Kingsbury; but
he tells me that I must do it all, because he is so busy.
Were my brother-in-law well enough I think he should
come up to town to make inquiry himself and to see
the young man. If he cannot do so, he had better get
Hampstead to take him down to Trafford. Hampstead
and this young Duchino are luckily bosom friends. It
tells well for Hampstead that, after all, he did not
go so low for his associates as you thought he did.
Amaldina intends to write to Fanny to congratulate
her.

"Your affectionate sister,

"GERALDINE PERSIFLAGE."

Duca di Crinola! She could not quite believe it;—
and yet she did believe it. Nor could she be quite
sure as to herself whether she was happy in believing
it or the reverse. It had been terrible to her to think
that she should have to endure the name of being
stepmother to a clerk in the Post Office. It would not
be at all terrible to her to be stepmother to a Duca

di Crinola, even though the stepson would have no
property of his own. That little misfortune would, as
far as the feelings of society went, be swallowed up
amidst the attributes of rank. Nothing would sound
better than Duchessa or Duchessina! And, moreover,
it would be all true! This was no paltry title which
might be false, or might have been picked up, any how,
the other day. All the world would know that the
Italian Duke was the lineal representative of a magnificent family to whom this identical rank had belonged
for many years. There were strong reasons for taking
the young Duke and the young Duchess to her heart
at once.

But then there were other reasons why she should
not wish it to be true. In the first place she hated
them both. Let the man be Duca di Crinola as much
as he might, he would still have been a Post Office
clerk, and Lady Frances would have admitted his courtship having believed him at the time to have been
no more than a Post Office clerk. The sin would have
been not the less abominable in the choice of her lover,
although it might be expedient that the sin should be
forgiven. And then the girl had insulted her, and
there had been that between them which would prevent
the possibility of future love; and would it not be hard
upon her darlings if it should become necessary to carve
out from the family property a permanent income for
this Italian nobleman, and for a generation of Italian
noblemen to come; and then what a triumph would

this be for Hampstead, who, of all human beings, was the most distasteful to her.

But upon the whole she thought it would be best to accept the Duca. She must, indeed, accept him. Nothing that she could do would restore the young man to his humble desk and humble name. Nor would the Marquis be actuated by any prayer of hers in reference to the carving of the property. It would be better for her to accept the young Duke and the young Duchess, and make the best of them. If only the story should at last be shown to be true!

The duty was imposed on her of communicating the story to the Marquis; but before she did so she was surprised by a visit from Mr. Greenwood. Mr. Roberts had used no more than the violence of argument, and Mr. Greenwood had been induced to take himself to Shrewsbury on the day named for his departure. If he went he would have 200*l.* a year from the Marquis, —and 100*l.* would be added by Lord Hampstead, of which the Marquis need not know anything. Unless he went on the day fixed that 100*l.* would not be added. A good deal was said on either side, but he went. The Marquis had refused to see him. The Marchioness had bade him adieu in a most formal manner,—in a manner quite unbecoming those familiar suggestions which, he thought, had been made to him as to a specially desirable event. But he had gone, and as he went he told himself that circumstances might yet occur in the family which might be of use to him. He, too, had heard the great family news,—perhaps through some under-satellite of the Foreign Office, and he came with the idea that he would be the first to make it known at Trafford Park.

He would have asked for the Marquis, but he knew that the Marquis would not receive him. Lady Kingsbury consented to see him, and he was ushered up to the room to which he had so often made his way without any asking. "I hope you are well, Mr. Greenwood," she said. "Are you still staying in the neighbourhood?" It was, however, well known at Trafford that he was at Shrewsbury.

"Yes, Lady Kingsbury. I have not gone from the neighbourhood. I thought that perhaps you might want to see me again."

"I don't know that we need trouble you, Mr. Greenwood."

"I have come with some news respecting the family." As he said this he managed to assume the old look, and stood as though he had never moved from the place since he had last been in the room.

"Do sit down, Mr. Greenwood. What news?"

"Mr. George Roden, the clerk in the Post Office——"

But she was not going to have the tidings repeated to her by him, so as to give him any claim to gratitude for having brought them. "You mean the Duca di Crinola!"

"Oh," exclaimed Mr. Greenwood.

"I have heard all that, Mr. Greenwood."

"That the Post Office clerk is an Italian nobleman?"

"It suited the Italian nobleman for a time to be a Post Office clerk. That is what you mean."

"And Lady Frances is to be allowed——"

"Mr. Greenwood, I must ask you not to discuss Lady Frances here."

"Oh! Not to discuss her ladyship!"

"Surely you must be aware how angry the Marquis has been about it."

"Oh!" He had not seated himself, nor divested himself of that inquisitorial appearance which was so distasteful to her. "We used to discuss Lady Frances sometimes, Lady Kingsbury."

"I will not discuss her now. Let that be enough, Mr. Greenwood."

"Nor yet Lord Hampstead."

"Nor yet Lord Hampstead. I think it very wrong of you to come after all that took place. If the Marquis knew it——"

Oh! If the Marquis knew it! If the Marquis knew all, and if other people knew all! If it were known how often her ladyship had spoken, and how loud, as to the wished-for removal to a better world of his lordship's eldest son! But he could not dare to speak it out. And yet it was cruel on him! He had for some days felt her ladyship to be under his thumb, and now it seemed that she had escaped from him. "Oh! very well, Lady Kingsbury. Perhaps I had better go,—just for the present." And he went.

This served, at least, for corroboration. She did not dare to keep the secret long from her husband, and therefore, in the course of the evening, went down with her sister's letter in her hand. "What!" said the Marquis, when the story had been read to him. "What! Duca di Crinola."

"There can't be a doubt about it, my dear."

"And he a clerk in the Post Office?"

"He isn't a clerk in the Post Office now."

"I don't quite see what he will be then. It appears that he has inherited nothing."

"My sister says nothing."

"Then what's the good of his title. There is nothing so pernicious in the world as a pauper aristocracy. A clerk in the Post Office is entitled to have a wife, but a poor nobleman should at any rate let his poverty die with himself."

This was a view of the case which had not hitherto presented itself to Lady Kingsbury. When she suggested to him that the young nobleman should be asked down to Trafford, he did not seem to see that it was at all necessary. It would be much better that Fanny should come back. The young nobleman would, he supposed, live in his own country;—unless, indeed, the whole tale was a cock-and-bull story made up by Persiflage at the Foreign Office. It was just the sort of thing, he said, that Persiflage would do. He had said not a word as to carving an income out of the property for the young noble couple when she left him.

CHAPTER III.

ALL THE WORLD KNOWS IT.

THE story was in truth all over London and half
over England by the time that Lady Frances had
returned to Hendon Hall. Though Vivian had made
a Foreign Office secret of the affair at Gorse Hall,
nevertheless it had been so commonly talked about
during the last Sunday there, that Hautboy had told
it all to poor Walker and to the Walker ladies. " By
Jove, fancy ! " Hautboy had said, " to go at once from
a Post Office clerk to a duke ! It's like some of those
stories where a man goes to bed as a beggar and gets
up as a prince. I wonder whether he likes it."   Hampstead had of course discussed the matter very freely
with his sister, still expressing an opinion that a man
could not do other than take his father's name and his
father's title. Lady Frances having thus become used
to the subject was not surprised to find the following
letter from her friend Lady Amaldina when she reached,
her home :—

"My dearest Fanny,—

"I am indeed *delighted* to be able to congratulate you on the wonderful and *most romantic* story which has just been made known to us. I was never one of those who blamed you *very much* because you had given your affections to a man *so much below* you in rank. Nevertheless, we all could not but feel that it was a pity that he should be *a Post Office clerk!* Now, indeed, you have reason to be proud! I have already read up the subject, and I find that the Ducas di Crinola are supposed to have *the very best blood* in Europe. There can be no doubt that one of the family married a *Bourbon* before they came to the French throne. I could send you all the details, only I do not doubt that you have found it out for yourself already. Another married *a second cousin of that Maximilian who married Mary of Burgundy.* One of the ladies of the family is supposed to have been the wife of the younger brother of one of the Guises, though it isn't *quite* certain whether they were ever married. But that little blot, my dear, will hardly affect *you* now. Taking the name altogether, I don't think there is anything higher in all Europe. Papa says that the Di Crinolas have always been doing something in Italy in the way of politics, or rebellion, or fighting. So it isn't as though they were all washed out and no longer of any account, like some of those we read of in history. Therefore I *do* think that you must be a *very happy girl.*

"I do feel *so completely snuffed out,* because, after all, the title of Merioneth was only conferred in the time of *Charles the Second.* And though there *was* a Lord Llwddythlw before that, even he was only created by *James the First.* The Powells no doubt are a very old Welsh family, and it is supposed that there was some relationship between them and the Tudors. But what is that to be compared to the *mediæval honours* of the *great House* of *Di Crinola?*

"Papa seems to think that he will not have *much* fortune. I am one of those who do not think that a large income is at all to be compared to good birth in the way of giving *real position* in the world. Of course the Duke's estates are supposed to be *enormous,* and Llwddythlw, *even as an eldest son,* is a rich man; but as far as I can see there is nothing but trouble comes from it. If he has anything to do with a provincial town in the way of *rents* he is expected to lay the *first brick* of every church and institute about the place. If anything has to be *opened* he has to *open* it; and he is never allowed to eat his dinner without having to make *two or three speeches before and afterwards.* That's what I call a *great bore.* As far as I can see you will be always able to have your duke with you, because he will have no abominable public duties to look after.

"I suppose something will have to be *done* as to an *income.* Llwddythlw seems to think that he ought to get into Parliament. At least that is what he said

to papa the other day; for I have not seen him myself
for ever so long. He calls in the Square every Sunday
just as we have done lunch, and never remains *above
two minutes.* Last Sunday we had not heard of this
glorious news; but papa did see him one day at the
House, and that was what he said. I don't see how
he is to get into the House *if he is an Italian Duke,*
and I don't know *what* he'd get by going there. Papa
says that he might be employed in some *diplomatic*
position by his own Government; but I should think
that the Marquis could do *something for him* as he
has *so much* at his own disposition. Every acre of the
Merioneth property is settled upon,—well,—whoever
may happen to be the next heir. There will sure
to be an income. There always is. Papa says that
the young dukes are always as well off, at any rate, as
the young ravens.

"But, as I said before, what does all this signify
in comparison with BLOOD. It does make your
position, my dear, *quite another thing* from what we
had expected. You would have kept your title no
doubt; but *where* would *he* have been?

"I wonder whether you will be married now before
August. I suppose not, because it doesn't seem to be
quite certain when that *wicked papa* of his died; but I
do hope that you won't. A day at last has been fixed
for us;—the 20th of August, when, as I told you before,
Lord David is to run away *instantly* after the ceremony
so as to travel all night and *open something* the next

morning at *Aberdeen.* I mention it now, because you
will be *by far* the most *remarkable* of all my bevy of
twenty. Of course your name will have been in the
papers before that as *the* future Italian *Duchess.* That
I own will be to me a just cause of pride. I think I
have got my bevy all fixed at last, and I do *hope* that
none of them will get married before *my* day. That
has happened *so often* as to be quite *heart-breaking.* I
shall cry if I find that *you* are to be married *first.*

"Believe me to be

"Your most affectionate friend and cousin,

"AMALDINA."

She wrote also to her future husband on the same
subject;—

"DEAREST LLWDDYTHLW,—

"It was very *good* of you to come last Sunday,
but I wish you hadn't gone away just because the
Graiseburys were there. They would not have *eaten*
you, though he is a Liberal.

"I have written to Fanny Trafford to congratulate
her; because you know it is after all better than being
a mere *Post Office clerk.* That was terrible;—so bad
that one hardly knew how to mention her name in
society! When people talked about it, I really *did
feel* that I blushed all over. One can mention her
name now because people are not *supposed* to know
that he has got nothing. Nevertheless, it is very
dreadful. *What on earth are they to live on?* I have

told her about the young ravens. It was papa who said
that when he first heard of this Di Crinola affair. I suppose a girl *ought to trust in Providence* when she marries
a man without a shilling. That was what papa meant.

"Papa says that you said that he ought to go into
Parliament. But what would he *get* by-that? Perhaps
as he is in the Post Office they might make him *Postmaster-General*. Only papa says that if he were to go
into Parliament, then he could not call himself Duca
di Crinola. Altogether it seems to be *very sad*,—though
not *quite* so sad as before. It is true that one of the
Di Crinolas married a *Bourbon*, and that others of
them have married ever so many *royalties*. I think
there ought to be a law for giving such people something to live upon *out of the taxes*. How are they to
be *expected* to live upon nothing? I asked papa
whether he couldn't get it done; but he said it would
be a *money bill*, and that *you* ought to take it up.
Pray don't, for fear it should take you *all August*. I
know you wouldn't have a scruple about putting off
your own little affair, if anything of that kind *were* to
come in the way. *I believe you'd like it.*

"*Do* stop a little longer when you come on Sunday.
I have *ever so many* things to say to you. And if
you can think of anything to be done for those *poor*
Di Crinolas, anything that won't take up *all* August,—
pray do it.

"Your own,

"AMY."

One more letter shall be given; the answer, namely, to the above from the lover to his future bride;—

"DEAR AMY,—

"I'll be at the Square on Sunday by three. I will walk out if you like, but it is always raining. I have to meet five or six conservative members later on in the afternoon as to the best thing to be done as to Mr. Green's Bill for lighting London by electricity. It would suit everybody; but some of our party, I am afraid, would go with them, and the Government is very shilly-shally. I have been going into the figures, and it has taken me all the week. Otherwise I would have been to see you.

"This Di Crinola affair is quite a romance. I did not mean that he ought to go into the House by way of getting an income. If he takes up the title of course he could not do so. If he takes it, he must regard himself as an Italian. I should think him quite as respectable, earning his bread as a clerk in a public office. They tell me he's a high-spirited fellow. If he is, that is what he will do.

"Yours affectionately,

"LLWDDYTHLW."

When Lord Persiflage spoke of the matter to Baron d'Osse, the Italian Minister in London, the Baron quite acknowledged the position of the young Duca, and seemed to think that very little could be wanting to the making of the young man's fortune. "Ah, yes, your Excellency," said the Baron. "He has no great estates. Here in England you all have great estates. It is very nice to have great estates. But he has an uncle who is a great man in Rome. And he will have a wife whose uncle is a very great man in London. What more should he want?" Then the Baron bowed to the Minister of State, and the Minister of State bowed to the Baron.

But the surprise expressed and the consternation felt at the Post Office almost exceeded the feelings excited at the Foreign Office or among Lady Fanny's family and friends. Dukes and Ministers, Barons and Princes, are terms familiar to the frequenters of the Foreign Office. Ambassadors, Secretaries, and diplomatic noblemen generally, are necessarily common in the mouths of all the officials. But at the Post Office such titles still carried with them something of awe. The very fact that a man whom they had seen should be a Duke was tremendous to the minds of Bobbin and Geraghty; and when it became known to them that a fellow workman in their own room, one who had in truth been no more than themselves, would henceforth be called by so august a title, it was as though the heavens and the earth were coming together. It affected Crocker in such a way that there was for a time a doubt whether his senses were not temporarily leaving him, — so that confinement would become necessary. Of course the matter had found its way into the newspapers. It became known at the office on the last day

of February,—two days before the return of the Rodens
to London.

"Have you heard it, Mr. Jerningham?" said Crocker,
rushing into the room that morning. He was only ten
minutes after the proper time, having put himself to
the expense of a cab in his impetuous desire to be the
first to convey the great news to his fellow clerks. But
he had been forestalled in his own room by the energy
of Geraghty. The condition of mind created in Mr.
Jerningham's bosom by the story told by Geraghty
was of such a nature that he was unable to notice
Crocker's sin in reference to the ten minutes.

"Dchuca di Crinola!" shouted Geraghty in his
broadest brogue as Crocker came in; determined not
to be done out of the honour fairly achieved by him.

"By Jove, yes! A Duke," said Crocker. "A
Duke! My own especial friend! Hampstead will be
nowhere; nowhere; nowhere! Duca di Crinola! Isn't
it beautiful? By George, I can't believe it. Can you,
Mr. Jerningham?"

"I don't know what to believe," said Mr. Jerningham. "Only he was always a most steady, well-
behaved young man, and the office will have a great
loss of him."

"I suppose the Duke won't come and see us ever,"
said Bobbin. "I should like to shake hands with him
once again."

"Shake hands with him," said Crocker. "I'm sure
he won't drop out like that;—my own peculiar friend!

I don't think I ever was so fond of anybody as George Ro——, the Duca di Crinola of course I mean. By George! haven't I sat at the same table with him for the last two years! Why, it was only a night or two before he started on this remarkable tour that I spent an evening with him in private society at Holloway!" Then he got up and walked about the room impetuously, clapping his hands, altogether carried away by the warmth of his feelings.

"I think you might as well sit down to your desk, Mr. Crocker," said Mr. Jerningham.

"Oh, come, bother, Mr. Jerningham!"

"I will not be spoken to in that way, Mr. Crocker."

"Upon my word, I didn't mean anything, sir. But when one has heard such news as this, how is it possible that one should compose oneself? It's a sort of thing that never happened before,—that one's own particular friend should turn out to be the Duca di Crinola. Did anybody ever read anything like it in a novel? Wouldn't it act well? Can't I see the first meeting between myself and the Duke at the Haymarket! 'Duke,' I should say—'Duke, I congratulate you on having come to your august family title, to which no one living could do so much honour as yourself.' Bancroft should do me. Bancroft would do me to the life, and the piece should be called the *Duke's Friend*. I suppose we shall call him Duke here in England, and Duca if we happen to be in Italy together; eh, Mr. Jerningham?"

"You had better sit down, Mr. Crocker, and try to do your work."

"I can't;—upon my word I can't. The emotion is too much for me. I couldn't do it if Æolus were here himself. By the way, I wonder whether Sir Boreas has heard the news" Then he rushed off, and absolutely made his way into the room of the great potentate.

"Yes, Mr. Crocker," said Sir Boreas, "I have heard it. I read the newspapers, no doubt, as well as you do."

"But it's true, Sir Boreas?"

"I heard it spoken of two or three days ago, Mr. Crocker, and I believe it to be true."

"He was my friend, Sir Boreas; my particular friend. Isn't it a wonderful thing,—that one's particular friend should turn out to be Duca di Crinola! And he didn't know a word of it himself. I feel quite sure that he didn't know a word of it."

"I really can't say, Mr. Crocker; but as you have now expressed your wonder, perhaps you had better go back to your room and do your work."

"He pretends he knew it three days ago!" said Crocker, as he returned to his room. "I don't believe a word of it. He'd have written to me had it been known so long ago as that. I suppose he had too many things to think of, or he would have written to me."

"Go aisy, Crocker," said Geraghty.

"What do you mean by that? It's just the thing he would have done."

"I don't believe he ever wrote to you in his life," said Bobbin.

"You don't know anything about it. We were here together two years before you came into the office. Mr. Jerningham knows that we were always friends. Good heavens! Duca di Crinola! I tell you what it is, Mr. Jerningham. If it were ever so, I couldn't do anything to-day. You must let me go. There are mutual friends of ours to whom it is quite essential that I should talk it over." Then he took his hat and marched off to Holloway, and would have told the news to Miss Clara Demijohn had he succeeded in finding that young lady at home. Clara was at that moment discussing with Mrs. Duffer the wonderful fact that Mr. Walker and not Lord Hampstead had been kicked and trodden to pieces at Gimberley Green.

But even Æolus, great as he was, expressed himself with some surprise that afternoon to Mr. Jerningham as to the singular fortune which had befallen George Roden. "I believe it to be quite true, Mr. Jerningham. These wonderful things do happen sometimes."

"He won't stay with us, Sir Boreas, I suppose?"

"Not if he is Duca di Crinola. I don't think we could get on with a real duke. I don't know how it will turn out. If he chooses to remain an Englishman he can't take the title. If he chooses to take the title he must be an Italian, then he'll have nothing to live on. My belief is we shan't see him any more. I wish it had been Crocker with all my heart."

CHAPTER IV.

"IT SHALL BE DONE."

LORD HAMPSTEAD has been left standing for a long time in Marion Fay's sitting-room after the perpetration of his great offence, and Mrs. Roden has been standing there also, having come to the house almost immediately after her return home from her Italian journey. Hampstead, of course, knew most of the details of the Di Crinola romance, but Marion had as yet heard nothing of it. There had been so much for him to say to her during the interview which had been so wretchedly interrupted by his violence that he had found no time to mention to her the name either of Roden or of Di Crinola.

"You have done that which makes me ashamed of myself." These had been Marion's last words as Mrs. Roden entered the room. "I didn't know Lord Hampstead was here," said Mrs. Roden.

"Oh, Mrs. Roden, I'm so glad you are come," exclaimed Marion. This of course was taken by the lady as a kindly expression of joy that she should have returned from her journey; whereas to Hampstead it

conveyed an idea that Marion was congratulating
herself that protection had come to her from further
violence on his part. Poor Marion herself hardly knew
her own meaning,—hardly had any. She could not
even tell herself that she was angry with her lover.
It was probable that the very ecstacy of his love added
fuel to hers. If a lover so placed as were this lover,—
a lover who had come to her asking her to be his
wife, and who had been received with the warmest
assurance of her own affection for him,—if he were
not justified in taking her in his arms and kissing her,
when might a lover do so ? The ways of the world
were known to her well enough to make her feel that
it was so, even in that moment of her perturbation.
Angry with him ! How could she be angry with him ?
He had asked her, and she had declared to him that
she was not angry. Nevertheless she had been quite
in earnest when she had said that now,—after the
thing that he had done,—he must " never, never come
to her again."

She was not angry with him, but with herself she
was angry. At the moment, when she was in his arms,
she bethought herself how impossible had been the
conditions she had imposed upon him. That he should
be assured of her love, and yet not allowed to approach
her as a lover ! That he should be allowed to come
there in order that she might be delighted in looking
at him, in hearing his voice, in knowing and feeling
that she was dear to him; but that he should be kept

at arm's length because she had determined that she should not become his wife! That they should love each other dearly; but each with a different idea of love! It was her fault that he should be there in her presence at all. She had told herself that it was her duty to sacrifice herself, but she had only half carried out her duty. Should she not have kept her love to herself,—so that he might have left her, as he certainly would have done had she behaved to him coldly, and as her duty had required of her. She had longed for some sweetness which would be sweet to her though only a vain encouragement to him. She had painted for her own eyes a foolish picture, had dreamed a silly dream. She had fancied that for the little of life that was left to her she might have been allowed the delight of loving, and had been vain enough to think that her lover might be true to her and yet not suffer himself! Her sacrifice had been altogether imperfect. With herself she was angry,—not with him. Angry with him, whose very footfall was music to her ears! Angry with him, whose smile to her was as a light specially sent from heaven for her behoof! Angry with him, the very energy of whose passion thrilled her with a sense of intoxicating joy! Angry with him because she had been enabled for once,—only for once,—to feel the glory of her life, to be encircled in the warmth of his arms, to become conscious of the majesty of his strength! No,—she was not angry. But he must be made to understand,—he must be taught to acknowledge,—that he must never, never come to her again. The mind can conceive a joy so exquisite that for the enjoyment of it, though it may last but for a moment, the tranquillity, even the happiness, of years may be given in exchange. It must be so with her. It had been her own doing, and if the exchange were a bad one, she must put up with the bargain. He must never come again. Then Mrs. Roden had entered the room, and she was forced to utter whatever word of welcome might first come to her tongue.

"Yes," said Hampstead, trying to smile, as though nothing had happened which called for special seriousness of manner, "I am here. I am here, and hope to be here often and often till I shall have succeeded in taking our Marion to another home."

"No," said Marion faintly, uttering her little protest ever so gently.

"You are very constant, my lord," said Mrs. Roden.

"I suppose a man is constant to what he really loves best. But what a history you have brought back with you, Mrs. Roden! I do not know whether I am to call you Mrs. Roden."

"Certainly, my lord, you are to call me so."

"What does it mean?" asked Marion.

"You have not heard," he said. "I have not been here time enough to tell her all this, Mrs. Roden."

"You know it then, Lord Hampstead?"

"Yes, I know it;—though Roden has not condescended to write me a line. What are we to call
him?" To this Mrs. Roden made no answer on the
spur of the moment. "Of course he has written to
Fanny, and all the world knows it. It seems to have
reached the Foreign Office first, and to have been sent
down from thence to my people at Trafford. I suppose
there isn't a club in London at which it has not been
repeated a hundred times that George Roden is not
George Roden."

"Not George Roden?" asked Marion.

"No, dearest. You will show yourself terribly
ignorant if you call him so."

"What is he then, my lord?"

"Marion!"

"I beg your pardon. I will not do it again this
time. But what is he?"

"He is the Duca di Crinola."

"Duke!" said Marion.

"That's what he is, Marion."

"Have they made him that over there?"

"Somebody made one of his ancestors that ever
so many hundred years ago, when the Traffords
were——; well, I don't know what the Traffords were
doing then;—fighting somewhere, I suppose, for whatever they could get. He means to take the title, I
suppose?"

"He says not, my lord."

"He should do so."

"I think so too, Lord Hampstead. He is obstinate, you know; but, perhaps, he may consent to listen to some friend here. You will tell him."

"He had better ask others better able than I am to explain all the ins and outs of his position. He had better go to the Foreign Office and see my uncle. Where is he now?"

"He has gone to the Post Office. We reached home about noon, and he went at once. It was late yesterday when we reached Folkestone, and he let me stay there for the night."

"Has he always signed the old name?" asked Hampstead.

"Oh yes. I think he will not give it up."

"Nor his office?"

"Nor his office. As he says himself, what else will he have to live on?"

"My father might do something." Mrs. Roden shook her head. "My sister will have money, though it may probably be insufficient to furnish such an income as they will want."

"He would never live in idleness upon her money, my lord. Indeed I think I may say that he has quite resolved to drop the title as idle lumber. You perhaps know that he is not easily persuaded."

"The most obstinate fellow I ever knew in my life," said Hampstead, laughing. "And he has talked my sister over to his own views." Then he turned suddenly round to Marion, and asked her a question. "Shall I go now, dearest?" he said.

She had already told him to go,—to go, and never to return to her. But the question was put to her in such a manner that were she simply to assent to his going, she would, by doing so, assent also to his returning. For the sake of her duty to him, in order that she might carry out that self-sacrifice in the performance of which she would now be so resolute, it was necessary that he should in truth be made to understand that he was not to come back to her. But how was this to be done while Mrs. Roden was present with them? Had he not been there then she could have asked her friend to help her in her great resolution. But before the two she could say nothing of that which it was in her heart to say to both of them. "If it pleases you, my lord," she said.

"I will not be 'my lord.' Here is Roden, who is a real duke, and whose ancestors have been dukes since long before Noah, and he is allowed to be called just what he pleases, and I am to have no voice in it with my own particular and dearest friends! Nevertheless I will go, and if I don't come to-day, or the day after, I will write you the prettiest little love-letter I can invent."

"Don't," she said;—oh so weakly, so vainly;—in a manner so utterly void of that intense meaning which she was anxious to throw into her words. She was conscious of her own weakness, and acknowledged to

herself that there must be another interview, or at any
rate a letter written on each side, before he could be
made to understand her own purpose. If it must be
done by a letter, how great would be the struggle to
her in explaining herself. But perhaps even that might
be easier than the task of telling him all that she would
have to tell, while he was standing by, impetuous, impatient, perhaps almost violent, assuring her of his love,
and attempting to retain her by the pressure of his
hand.

"But I shall," he said, as he held her now for a
moment. "I am not quite sure whether I may not
have to go to Trafford; and if so there shall be the
love-letter. I feel conscious, Mrs. Roden, of being
incapable of writing a proper love-letter. 'Dearest
Marion, I am yours, and you are mine. Always believe
me ever thine.' I don't know how to go beyond that.
When a man is married, and can write about the children, or the leg of mutton, or what's to be done with
his hunters, then I dare say it becomes easy. Good-bye'
dearest. Good-bye, Mrs. Roden. I wish I could keep
on calling you Duchess in revenge for all the 'my
lordings.'" Then he left them.

There was a feeling in the mind of both of them that
he had conducted himself just as a man would do who
was in a high good-humour at having been permanently
accepted by the girl to whom he had offered his hand
Marion Fay knew that it was not so;—knew that it
never could be so. Mrs. Roden knew that it had not

been so when she had left home, now nearly two months since; and knew also that Marion had pledged herself that it should not be so. The young lord then had been too strong with his love. A feeling of regret came over her as she remembered that the reasons against such a marriage were still as strong as ever. But yet how natural that it should be so! Was it possible that such a lover as Lord Hampstead should not succeed in his love if he were constant to it himself? Sorrow must come of it,—perhaps a tragedy so bitter that she could hardly bring herself to think of it. And Marion had been so firm in her resolve that it should not be so. But yet it was natural, and she could not bring herself to express to the girl either anger or disappointment. "Is it to be?" she said, putting on her sweetest smile.

"No!" said Marion, standing up suddenly,—by no means smiling as she spoke! "It is not to be. Why do you look at me like that, Mrs. Roden? Did I not tell you before you went that it should never be so?"

"But he treats you as though he were engaged to you?"

"How can I help it? What can I do to prevent it? When I bid him go, he still comes back again, and when I tell him that I can never be his wife he will not believe me. He knows that I love him."

"You have told him that?"

"Told him! He wanted no telling. Of course he knew it. Love him! Oh, Mrs. Roden, if I could die for him, and so have done with it! And yet I would

not wish to leave my dear father. What am I to do,
Mrs. Roden?"

"But it seemed to me just now that you were so
happy with him."

"I am never happy with him;—but yet I am as
though I were in heaven."

"Marion!"

"I am never happy. I know that it cannot be, that
it will not be, as he would have it. I know that I am
letting him waste his sweetness all in vain. There
should be some one else, oh, so different from me!
There should be one like himself, beautiful, strong in
health, with hot eager blood in her veins, with a grand
name, with grand eyes and a broad brow and a noble
figure, one who, in taking his name, will give him as
much as she takes—one, above all, who will not pine
and fade before his eyes, and trouble him during her
short life with sickness and doctors and all the fading
hopes of a hopeless invalid. And yet I let him come,
and I have told him how dearly I love him. He comes
and he sees it in my eyes. And then it is so glorious
to be loved as he loves. Oh, Mrs. Roden, he kissed
me." That to Mrs. Roden did not seem to be extraordinary; but, not knowing what to say to it at the
moment, she also kissed the girl. "Then I told him
that he must go, and never come back to me again."

"Were you angry with him?"

"Angry with him! With myself I was angry. I
had given him the right to do it. How could I be

angry with him. And what does it matter;—except
for his sake? If he could only understand! If he
would only know that I am in earnest when I speak to
him! But I am weak in everything except one thing.
He will never make me say that I will be his
wife."

"My Marion! Dear Marion!"

"But father wishes it."

"Wishes you to become his wife?"

"He wishes it. Why should I not be like any
other girl, he says. How can I tell him? How
can I say that I am not like to other girls because
of my darling, my own dearest mother? And yet
he does not know it. He does not see it, though
he has seen so much. He will not see it till I am
there, on my bed, unable to come to him when he
wants me."

"There is nothing now to show him or me that you
may not live to be old as he is."

"I shall not live to be old. You know that I shall
not live to be more than young. Have any of them
lived? For my father,—for my dear father,—he must
find it out for himself. I have sometimes thought that
even yet I might last his time—that I might be with
him to the end. It might be so,—only that all this
tortures me."

"Shall I tell him;—shall I tell Lord Hampstead?"

"He must at any rate be told. He is not bound to
me as my father is. For him there need be no great

sorrow." At this Mrs. Roden shook her head. "Must it be so?"

"If he is banished from your presence he will not bear it lightly."

"Will a young man love me like that;—a young man who has so much in the world to occupy him? He has his ship, and his hounds, and his friends, and his great wealth. It is only girls, I think, who love like that."

"He must bear his sorrow as others do."

"But it shall be made as light as I can make it,—shall it not? I should have done this before. I should have done it sooner. Had he been made to go away at once, then he would not have suffered. Why would he not go when I told him? Why would he not believe me when I spoke to him? I should have heard all his words and never have answered him even with a smile. I should not have trembled when he told me that I was there, at his hearth, as a friend. But who thought then, Mrs. Roden, that this young nobleman would have really cared for the Quaker girl?"

"I saw it, Marion."

"Could you see just by looking at him that he was so different from others? Are his truth, and his loving heart, and his high honour, and his pure honesty, all written in his eyes,—to you as they are to me? But, Mrs. Roden, there shall be an end of it! Though it may kill me,—though it may for a little time half-break his heart,—it shall be done! Oh, that his dear heart

should be half-broken for me ! I will think of it, Mrs.
Roden, to-night. If writing may do it, perhaps I may
write. Or, perhaps, I may say a word that he will at
least understand. If not you shall tell him. But, Mrs.
Roden, it shall be done !"

CHAPTER V.

MARION WILL CERTAINLY HAVE HER WAY.

ON the day but one following there came a letter to Marion from Hampstead,—the love-letter which he had promised her ;—

"DEAR MARION—

"It is as I supposed. This affair about Roden has stirred them up down at Trafford amazingly. My father wants me to go to him. You know all about my sister. I suppose she will have her way now. I think the girls always do have their way. She will be left alone, and I have told her to go and see you as soon as I have gone. You should tell her that she ought to make him call himself by his father's proper name.

"In my case, dearest, it is not the girl that is to have her own way. It's the young man that is to do just as he pleases. My girl, my own one, my love, my treasure, think of it all, and ask yourself whether it is in your heart to refuse to bid me be happy. Were it not for all that you have said yourself I should not be vain enough to be happy at this

E 2

moment, as I am. But you have told me that you
love me. Ask your father, and he will tell you that,
as it is so, it is your duty to promise to be my wife.

"I may be away for a day or two,—perhaps for a
week. Write to me at Trafford,—Trafford Park,
Shrewsbury,—and say that it shall be so. I sometimes
think that you do not understand how absolutely my
heart is set upon you,—so that no pleasures are pleasant
to me, no employments useful, except in so far as I
can make them so by thinking of your love.

"Dearest, dearest Marion,

"Your own,

"HAMPSTEAD."

"Remember there must not be a word about a lord
inside the envelope. It is very bad to me when it comes
from Mrs. Roden, or from a friend such as she is; but
it simply excruciates me from you. It seems to imply
that you are determined to regard me as a stranger."

She read the letter a dozen times, pressing it to
her lips and to her bosom. She might do that at least.
He would never know how she treated this only letter
that she ever had received from him, the only letter
that she would receive. These caresses were only such
as those which came from her heart, to relieve her
solitude. It might be absurd in her to think of the
words he had spoken, and to kiss the lines which he
had written. Were she now on her deathbed that
would be permitted to her. Wherever she might lay

her head till the last day should come that letter should be always within her reach. "My girl, my own one, my love, my treasure!" How long would it last with him? Was it not her duty to hope that the words were silly words, written as young men do write, having no eagerness of purpose,—just playing with the toy of the moment? Could it be that she should wish them to be true, knowing, as she did, that his girl, his love, his treasure, as he called her, could never be given up to him? And yet she did believe them to be true, knew them to be true, and took an exceeding joy in the assurance. It was as though the beauty and excellence of their truth atoned to her for all else that was troublous to her in the condition of her life. She had not lived in vain. Her life now could never be a vain and empty space of time, as it had been consecrated and ennobled and blessed by such a love as this. And yet she must make the suffering to him as light as possible. Though there might be an ecstasy of joy to her in knowing that. she was loved, there could be nothing akin to that in him. He wanted his treasure, and she could only tell him that he might never have it. "Think of it all, and ask yourself whether it is in your heart to refuse to bid me be happy." It was in her heart to do it. Though it might break her heart she would do it. It was the one thing to do which was her paramount duty. "You have told me that you love me." Truly she had told him so, and certainly she would never recall her words. If he ever

thought of her in future years when she should long
have been at her rest,—and she thought that now and
again he would think of her, even when that noble
bride should be sitting at his table,—he should always
remember that she had given him her whole heart.
He had bade her write to him at Trafford. She would
obey him at once in that; but she would tell him that
she could not obey him in aught else. "Tell me that
it shall be so," he had said to her with his sweet,
imperious, manly words. There had been something
of command about him always, which had helped to
make him so perfect in her eyes. "You do not understand," he said, "how absolutely my heart is set upon
you." Did he understand, she wondered, how absolutely her heart had been set upon him ? "No pleasures
are pleasant to me, no employment useful, unless I can
make them so by thinking of your love!" It was
right that he as a man,—and such a man,—should
have pleasures and employments, and it was sweet to
her to be told that they could be gilded by the remembrance of her smiles. But for her, from the moment in
which she had known him, there could be no pleasure
but to think of him, no serious employment but to
resolve how best she might do her duty to him.

It was not till the next morning that she took up
her pen to begin her all-important letter. Though her
resolution had been so firmly made, yet there had been
much need for thinking before she could sit down to
form the sentences. For a while she had told herself

that it would be well first to consult her father; but
before her father had returned to her she had remembered that nothing which he could say would induce
her in the least to alter her purpose. His wishes had
been made known to her; but he had failed altogether
to understand the nature of the duty she had imposed
upon herself. Thus she let that day pass by, although
she knew that the writing of the letter would be an affair
of much time to her. She could not take her sheet of
paper, and scribble off warm words of love as he had
done. To ask, or to give, in a matter of love must
surely, she thought, be easy enough. But to have
given and then to refuse—that was the difficulty.
There was so much to say of moment both to herself
and to him, or rather so much to signify, that it was
not at one sitting, or with a single copy, that this letter
could be written. He must be assured, no doubt, of
her love; but he must be made to understand,—quite
to understand, that her love could be of no avail to
him. And how was she to obey him as to her mode
of addressing him? "It simply excruciates me from
you," he had said, thus debarring her from that only
appellation which would certainly be the easiest, and
which seemed to her the only one becoming. At last
the letter, when written, ran as follows;—

"How I am to begin my letter I do not know, as
you have forbidden me to use the only words which
would come naturally. But I love you too well to

displease you in so small a matter. My poor letter
must therefore go to you without any such beginning
as is usual. Indeed, I love you with all my heart. I
told you that before, and I will not shame myself by
saying that it was untrue. But I told you also before
that I could not be your wife. Dearest love, I can only
say again what I said before. Dearly as I love you I
cannot become your wife. You bid me to think of it all,
and to ask myself whether it is in my heart to refuse
to bid you to be happy. It is not in my heart to let
you do that which certainly would make you unhappy.

"There are two reasons for this. Of the first, though
it is quite sufficient, I know that you will make nothing.
When I tell you that you ought not to choose such a
one as me for your wife because my manners of life
have not fitted me for such a position, then you sometimes laugh at me, and sometimes are half angry,—with
that fine way you have of commanding those that are
about you. But not the less am I sure that I am right.
I do believe that of all human beings poor Marion Fay
is the dearest to you. When you tell me of your love
and your treasure I do not for a moment doubt that it
is all true. And were I to be your wife, your honour
and your honesty would force you to be good to me.
But when you found that I was not as are other grand
ladies, then I think you would be disappointed. I
should know it by every line of your dear face, and
when I saw it there I should be broken-hearted.

"But this is not all. If there were nothing further,

I think I should give way because I am only a weak girl; and your words, my own, own love, would get the better of me. But there is another thing. It is hard for me to tell, and why should you be troubled with it? But I think if I tell it you out and out, so as to make you understand the truth, then you will be convinced. Mrs. Roden could tell you the same. My dear, dear father could tell you also; only that he will not allow himself to believe, because of his love for the only child that remains to him. My mother died; and all my brothers and sisters have died. And I also shall die young.

"Is not that enough? I know that it will be enough. Knowing that it will be enough, may I not speak out to you, and tell you all my heart? Will you not let me do so, as though it had been understood between us, that though we can never be more to each other than we are, yet we may be allowed to love each other? Oh, my dearest, my only dearest, just for this once I have found the words in which I may address you. I cannot comfort you as I can myself, because you are a man, and cannot find comfort in sadness and disappointment, as a girl may do. A man thinks that he should win for himself all that he wants. For a girl, I think it is sufficient for her to feel that, as far as she herself is concerned, that would have been given to her which she most desires, had not Fortune been unkind. You, dearest, cannot have what you want, because you have come to poor Marion Fay with all the glory and sweetness of your love. You must suffer for a while. I, who would so willingly give my life to serve you, must tell you that it will be so. But as you are a man, pluck up your heart, and tell yourself that it shall only be for a time. The shorter the better, and the stronger you will show yourself in overcoming the evil that oppresses you. And remember this. Should Marion Fay live to know that you had brought a bride home to your house, as it will be your duty to do, it will be a comfort to her to feel that the evil she has done has been cured.

"MARION."

"I cannot tell you how proud I should be to see your sister if she will condescend to come and see me. Or would it not be better that I should go over to Hendon Hall? I could manage it without trouble. Do not you write about it, but ask her to send me one word."

Such was the letter when it was at last finished and despatched. As soon as it was gone,—dropped irrevocably by her own hand into the pillar letter-box which stood at the corner opposite to the public-house,—she told her father what she had done. "And why?" he said crossly. "I do not understand thee. Thou art flighty and fickle, and knowest not thy own mind."

"Yes, father; I have known my own mind always in this matter. It was not fitting."

"If he thinks it fitting, why shouldst thou object?"

"I am not fit, father, to be the wife of a great noble-man. Nor can I trust my own health." This she said with a courage and firmness which seemed to silence him,—looking at him as though by her looks she forbade him to urge the matter further. Then she put her arms round him and kissed him. "Will it not be better, father, that you and I shall remain together till the last?"

"Nothing can be better for me that will not also be best for thee."

"For me it will be best. Father, let it be so, and let this young man be no more thought of between us." In that she asked more than could be granted to her; but for some days Lord Hampstead's name was not mentioned between them.

Two days afterwards Lady Frances came to her. "Let me look at you," said Marion, when the other girl had taken her in her arms and kissed her. "I like to look at you, to see whether you are like him. To my eyes he is so beautiful."

"More so than I am."

"You are a—lady, and he is a man. But you are like him, and very beautiful. You, too, have a lover, living close to us?"

"Well, yes. I suppose I must own it."

"Why should you not own it? It is good to be loved and to love. And he has become a great noble-man,—like your brother."

"No, Marion; he is not that.—May I call you Marion?"

"Why not? He called me Marion almost at once."

"Did he so?"

"Just as though it were a thing of course. But I noticed it. It was not when he bade me poke the fire, but the next time. Did he tell you about the fire?"

"No, indeed."

"A man does not tell of such things, I think; but a girl remembers them. It is so good of you to come. You know—do you not?

"Know what?"

"That I,—and your brother,—have settled everything at last?" The smile of pleasant good humour passed away from the face of Lady Frances, but at the moment she made no reply. "It is well that you should know. He knows now, I am sure. After what I said in my letter he will not contradict me again." Lady Frances shook her head. "I have told him that while I live he of all the world must be dearest to me. But that will be all."

"Why should you—not live?"

"Lady Frances——"

"Nay, call me Fanny."

"You shall be Fanny if you will let me tell you. Oh! I do so wish that you would understand it all, and make me tell you nothing further. But you must know,—you must know that it cannot be as your brother has wished. If it were only less known,—if he would consent and you would consent,—then I think that I could be happy. What is it after all,—the few years that we may have to live here? Shall we not meet again, and shall we not love each other then?"

"I hope so."

"If you can really hope it, then why should we not be happy? But how could I hope it if, with my eyes open, I were to bring a great misfortune upon him? If I did him an evil here, could I hope that he would love me in Heaven, when he would know all the secrets of my heart? But if he shall say to himself that I denied myself,—for his sake; that I refused to be taken into his arms because it would be bad for him, then, though there may be some one dearer, then shall not I also be dear to him?" The other girl could only cling to her and embrace her. "When he shall have strong boys round his hearth,—the hearth he spoke of as though it were almost mine,—and little girls with pink cheeks and bonny brows, and shall know, as he will then, what I might have done for him, will he not pray for me, and tell me in his prayers that when we shall meet hereafter I shall still be dear to him? And when she knows it all, she who shall lie on his breast, shall I not be dear also to her?"

"Oh, my sister!"

"He will tell her. I think he will tell her,—because of his truth, his honour, and his manliness."

Lady Frances, before she left the house, had been made to understand that her brother could not have his way in the matter which was so near his heart, and that the Quaker's daughter would certainly have hers.

CHAPTER VI.

"BUT HE IS;—HE IS."

GEORGE RODEN had come to a decision as to his
title, and had told every one concerned that he meant
to be as he always had been,—George Roden, a clerk in
the Post Office. When spoken to, on this side and the
other, as to the propriety,—or rather impropriety,—of
his decision, he had smiled for the most part, and had
said but little, but had been very confident in himself.
To none of the arguments used against him would he
yield in the least. As to his mother's fame, he said, no
one had doubted, and no one would doubt it for a
moment. His mother's name had been settled by herself, and she had borne it for a quarter of a century.
She had not herself thought of changing it. For her
to blaze out into the world as a Duchess,—it would be
contrary to her feelings, to her taste, and to her comfort!
She would have no means of maintaining the title,—
and would be reduced to the necessity of still living in
Paradise Row, with the simple addition of an absurd
nickname. As to that, no question had been raised.
It was only for him that she required the new appellation.

As for herself, the whole thing had been settled at once by her own good judgment.

As for himself, he said, the arguments were still stronger against the absurd use of the grand title. It was imperative on him to earn his bread, and his only means of doing so was by doing his work as a clerk in the Post Office. Everybody admitted that it would not be becoming that a Duke should be a clerk in the Post Office. It would be so unbecoming, he declared, that he doubted whether any man could be found brave enough to go through the world with such a fool's cap on his head. At any rate he had no such courage. Moreover, no Englishman, as he had been told, could at his own will and pleasure call himself by a foreign title. It was his pleasure to be an Englishman. He had always been an Englishman. As an inhabitant of Holloway he had voted for two Radical members for the Borough of Islington. He would not stultify his own proceedings, and declare that everything which he had done was wrong. It was thus that he argued the matter; and, as it seemed, no one could take upon himself to prove that he was an Italian, or to prove that he was a Duke.

But, though he seemed to be, if not logical, at any rate rational, the world generally did not agree with him. Wherever he was encountered there seemed to be an opinion that he ought to assume whatever name and whatever rights belonged to his father. Even at the Post Office the world was against him.

"I don't quite know why you couldn't do it," said Sir Boreas, when Roden put it to him whether it would be practicable that a young man calling himself Duca di Crinola should take his place as a clerk in Mr. Jerningham's room. It may be remembered that Sir Boreas had himself expressed some difficulty in the matter. He had told Mr. Jerningham that he did not think that they could get on very well with a real Duke among them. It was thus that the matter had at first struck him. But he was a brave man, and, when he came to look at it all round, he did not see that there would be any impossibility. It would be a nine days' wonder, no doubt. But the man would be there just the same,— the Post Office clerk inside the Duke. The work would be done, and after a little time even he would become used to having a Duke among his subordinates. As to whether the Duke were a foreigner or an English-man,—that, he declared, would not matter in the least, as far as the Post Office was concerned. "I really don't see why you shouldn't try it," said Sir Boreas.

"The absurdity would be so great that it would crush me, sir. I shouldn't be worth my salt," said Roden.

"That's a kind of thing that wears itself out very quickly. You would feel odd at first,—and so would the other men, and the messengers. I should feel a little odd when I asked some one to send the Duca di Crinola to me, for we are not in the habit of sending for Dukes. But there is nothing that you can't get used to. If your father had been a Prince I don't think I should break down under it after the first month."

"What good would it do me, Sir Boreas?"

"I think it would do you good. It is difficult to explain the good, — particularly to a man who is so violently opposed as you to all ideas of rank. But——."

"You mean that I should get promoted quicker because of my title?"

"I think it probable that the Civil Service generally would find itself able to do something more for a good officer with a high name than for a good officer without one."

"Then, Sir Boreas, the Civil Service ought to be ashamed of itself."

"Perhaps so;—but such would be the fact. Somebody would interfere to prevent the anomaly of the Duca di Crinola sitting at the same table with Mr. Crocker. I will not dispute it with you,—whether it ought to be so;—but, if it be probable, there is no reason why you should not take advantage of your good fortune, if you have capacity and courage enough to act up to it. Of course what we all want in life is success. If a chance comes in your way I don't see why you should fling it away." This was the wisdom of Sir Boreas; but Roden would not take advantage of it. He thanked the great man for his kindness and sympathy, but declined to reconsider his decision.

In the outer office,—in the room, for instance, in

which Mr. Jerningham sat with Crocker and Bobbin
and Geraghty, the feeling was very much stronger in
favour of the title, and was expressed in stronger
language. Crocker could not contain himself when he
heard that there was a doubt upon the subject. On
Roden's first arrival at the office Crocker almost flung
himself into his friend's arms, with just a single
exclamation. "Duca, Duca, Duca!" he had said, and
had then fallen back into his own seat overcome by
his emotions. Roden had passed this by without
remark. It was very distasteful to him, and disgusting.
He would fain have been able to sit down at his own
desk, and go on with his own work, without any special
notice of the occasion, other than the ordinary greeting
occasioned by his return. It was distressing to him
that anything should have been known about his father
and his father's title. But that it should be known was
natural. The world had heard of it. The world had
put it into the newspapers, and the world had talked
about it. Of course Mr. Jerningham also would talk of
it, and the two younger clerks,—and Crocker. Crocker
would of course talk of it louder than any one else.
That was to be expected. A certain amount of misconduct was to be expected from Crocker, and must be
forgiven. Therefore he passed over the ecstatic and
almost hysterical repetition of the title which his father
had borne, hoping that Crocker might be overcome by
the effort, and be tranquil. But Crocker was not so
easily overcome. He did sit for a moment or two on

his seat with his mouth open; but he was only preparing himself for his great demonstration.

"We are very glad to see you again,—sir," said Mr. Jerningham; not at first quite knowing how it would become him to address his fellow-clerk.

"Thank you, Mr. Jerningham. I have got back again safe."

"I am sure we are all delighted to hear—what we have heard," said Mr. Jerningham cautiously.

"By George, yes," said Bobbin. "I suppose it's true; isn't it? Such a beautiful name!"

"There are so many things are true, and so many are false, that I don't quite know how to answer you," said Roden.

"But you are——?" asked Geraghty; and then he stopped, not quite daring to trust himself with the grand title.

"No;—that's just what I'm not," replied the other.

"But he is," shouted Crocker, jumping from his seat. "He is! He is! It's quite true. He is Duca di Crinola. Of course we'll call him so, Mr. Jerningham; —eh?"

"I am sure I don't know," said Mr. Jerningham with great caution.

"You'll allow me to know my own name," said Roden.

"No! no!" continued Crocker. "It's all very well for your modesty, but it's a kind of thing which your friends can't stand. We are quite sure that you're the

Duca." There was something in the Italian title which
was peculiarly soothing to Crocker's ears. " A man has
to be called by what he is, not by what he chooses. If
the Duke of Middlesex called himself Mr. Smith, he'd
be Duke all the same;—wouldn't he, Mr. Jerningham ?
All the world would call him Duke. So it must be
with you. I wouldn't call your Grace Mr. —— ; you
know what I mean, but I won't pronounce it ever
again;—not for ever so much." Roden's brow became
very black as he found himself subjected to the effects
of the man's folly. " I call upon the whole office,"
continued Crocker, " for the sake of its own honour, to
give our dear and highly-esteemed friend his proper
name on all occasions. Here's to the health of the
Duca di Crinola !" Just at that moment Crocker's
lunch had been brought in, consisting of bread and
cheese and a pint of stout. The pewter pot was put to
his mouth and the toast was drank to the honour and
glory of the drinker's noble friend with no feeling of
intended ridicule. It was a grand thing to Crocker to
have been brought into contact with a man possessed
of so noble a title. In his heart of hearts he reverenced
"The Duca." He would willingly have stayed there
till six or seven o'clock and have done all the Duca's
work for him,—because the Duca was a Duca. He
would not have done it satisfactorily, because it was not
in his nature to do any work well, but he would have
done it as well as he did his own. He hated work; but
he would have sooner worked all night than see a Duca

do it,—so great was his reverence for the aristocracy generally.

"Mr. Crocker," said Mr. Jerningham severely, "you are making yourself a nuisance. You generally do."

"A nuisance!"

"Yes; a nuisance. When you see that a gentleman doesn't wish a thing, you oughtn't to do it."

"But when a man's name is his name!"

"Never mind. When he doesn't wish it, you oughtn't to do it!"

"If it's a man's own real name!"

"Never mind," said Mr. Jerningham.

"If it shoots a gintleman to be incognito, why isn't he to do as he plaises?" asked Geraghty.

"If the Duke of Middlesex did call himself Mr. Smith," said Bobbin, "any gentleman that was a gentleman would fall in with his views." Crocker, not conquered, but for the moment silenced, seated himself in a dudgeon at his desk. It might do very well for poor fellows, weak creatures like Jerningham, Bobbin, and Geraghty, thus to be done out of their prey;—but he would not be cheated in that way. The Duca di Crinola should be Duca di Crinola as far as he, Crocker, could make his voice heard; and all that heard him should know that the Duca was his own old peculiar friend.

In Paradise Row the world was decidedly against Roden; and not only were the Demijohns and Duffers against him, but also his own mother and her friend

Mrs. Vincent. On the first Monday after Mrs. Roden's return Mrs. Vincent came to the Row as usual,—on this occasion to welcome her cousin, and to hear all the news of the family as it had been at last brought back from Italy. There was a great deal to be told. Many things had been brought to light which had had their commencement in Mrs. Vincent's days. There was something of the continuation of a mild triumph for her in every word that was spoken. She had been against the Di Crinola marriage, when it had been first discussed more than a quarter of a century ago. She had never believed in the Duca di Crinola, and her want of faith had been altogether justified. She did not, after all those years, bear hardly on her friend,—but there was still that well-known tone of gentle censure and of gentle self-applause. "I told you so," said the elder crow to the younger crow. When does the old crow cease to remind the younger crow that it was so? "A sad, sad story," said Mrs. Vincent, shaking her head.

"All our stories I suppose have much in them that is sad. I have got my son, and no mother can have more reason to be proud of a son." Mrs. Vincent shook her head. "I say it is so," repeated the mother; "and having such a son, I will not admit that it has all been sad."

"I wish he were more ready to perform his religious duties," said Mrs. Vincent.

"We cannot all agree about everything. I do not know that that need be brought up now."

"It is a matter that should be brought up every hour and every day, Mary,—if the bringing of it up is to do any good."

But it was not on this matter that Mrs. Roden now wished to get assistance from her cousin ;—certainly not with any present view towards the amelioration of her son's religious faith. That might come afterwards perhaps. But it was her present object to induce her cousin to agree with her, that her son should permit himself to be called by his father's title. "But you think he should take his father's name?" she asked. Mrs. Vincent shook her head and tried to look wise. The question was one on which her feelings were very much divided. It was of course proper that the son should be called by his father's name. All the proprieties of the world, as known to Mrs. Vincent, declared that it should be so. She was a woman, too, who by no means despised rank, and who considered that much reverence was due to those who were privileged to carry titles. Dukes and lords were certainly very great in her estimation, and even the humblest knight was respected by her, as having been in some degree lifted above the community by the will of his Sovereign. And though she was always in some degree hostile to George Roden, because of the liberties he took in regard to certain religious matters, yet she was good enough and kind enough to wish well to her own cousin. Had there been a question in regard to an English title she certainly would not have shaken her head. But as to this outlandish Italian title, she had her doubts. It did not seem to her to be right that an Englishman should be called a Duca. If it had been Baron, or even Count, the name would have been less offensive. And then to her mind hereditary titles, as she had known them, had been recommended by hereditary possessions. There was something to her almost irreligious in the idea of a Duke without an acre. She could therefore only again shake her head. " He has as much right to it," continued Mrs. Roden, " as has the eldest son of the greatest peer in England."

" I dare say he has, my dear, but———."

" But what ? "

" I dare say you're right, only—; only it's not just like an English peer, you know."

" The privilege of succession is the same."

" He never could sit in the House of Lords, my dear."

" Of course not. He would assume only what is his own. Why should he be ashamed to take an Italian title any more than his friend Lord Hampstead is to take an English one? It is not as though it would prevent his living here. Many foreign noblemen live in England."

" I suppose he could live here," said Mrs. Vincent as though she were making a great admission. " I don't think that there would be any law to turn him out of the country."

" Nor out of the Post Office, if he chooses to remain there," said Mrs. Roden.

"I don't know how that may be."

"Even if they did, I should prefer that it should be so. According to my thinking, no man should fling away a privilege that is his own, or should be ashamed of assuming a nobility that belongs to him. If not for his own sake, he should do it for the sake of his children. He at any rate has nothing to be ashamed of in the name. It belonged to his father and to his grandfather, and to his ancestors through many generations. Think how men fight for a title in this country; how they struggle for it when there is a doubt as to who may properly have inherited it! Here there is no doubt. Here there need be no struggle." Convinced by the weight of this argument Mrs. Vincent gave in her adhesion, and at last expressed an opinion that her cousin should at once call himself by his father's name.

CHAPTER VII.

THE GREAT QUESTION.

NEITHER were the arguments of Mrs. Roden nor the adhesion of Mrs. Vincent of any power in persuading George Roden. He answered his mother gently, kindly, but very firmly. Had anything, he said, been necessary to strengthen his own feeling, it would have been found in his mother's determination to keep his old name. "Surely, mother, if I may say so without disrespect, what is sauce for the goose is sauce for the gander." At this the mother smiled, kissing her son to show that the argument had been taken in good part. "In this matter," he continued, "we certainly are in a boat together. If I am a Duke you would be a Duchess. If I am doomed to make an ape of myself at the Post Office, you must be equally ridiculous in Paradise Row, —unless you are prepared to go back to Italy and live your life there."

"And you?"

"I could not live there. How could I earn my bread there? How could I pass my days so as to be in any degree useful? What could be more mean?

My uncle, though he has been civil, and to a certain
degree generous, would be specially anxious not to see
me in public life. You and I together would have just
means enough for existence. I should be doomed to
walk about the streets of some third-rate Italian town,
and call myself by my grand name. Would a life like
that satisfy your ambition on my behalf?" Then she
thought of the girl who was in love with him, of the
friends whom he had made for himself, of the character
which belonged to him, and she was driven to confess
that, by whatever name he might be called, he must
continue to live an Englishman's life, and to live in
England. Nevertheless, she told herself that the title
would not be abolished, because it might be in abeyance.
She might, she thought, still live to hear her son
called by the name of which she herself had been proud
till she had become thoroughly ashamed of the husband
who had given it to her.

But there were others besides Crocker and Mrs.
Vincent, and his mother and Sir Boreas, who were
much interested by George Roden's condition. Mrs.
Roden returned home on the 2nd of March, and, as
may be remembered, the tidings respecting her son had
reached England before she came. By the end of the
month many persons were much exercised as to the
young man's future name, and some people of high
rank had not only discussed the subject at great length,
but had written numerous letters concerning it. It was
manifest to Lady Persiflage that no further attempt

should now be made to throw obstacles in the way of
Lady Frances and her lover. Lady Persiflage had never
believed in the obstacles from the first. "Of course
they'll marry," she had said to her one daughter, who
was now almost as good as married herself, and equally
trustworthy. "When a girl is determined like that, of
course nothing will stop her. My sister shouldn't have
let her meet the young man at first." But this had
been said before the young man had turned out to be
an Italian Duke. Since the news had come Lady
Persiflage had been very eager in recommending her
sister to discontinue the opposition. "Make the most
of him," she had said in one of her letters. "It is all
that can be done now. It is a fine name, and though
Italian titles do not count like ours, yet, when they are
as good as this, they go for a good deal. There are real
records of the Di Crinola family, and there is no manner
of doubt but that he is the head of them. Take him
by the hand, and have him down at Trafford if Kingsbury is well enough. They tell me he is quite present-
able, with a good figure and all that;—by no means a
young man who will stand shivering in a room because
he doesn't know how to utter a word. Had he been
like that Fanny would never have set her heart upon
him. Persiflage has been talking about him, and he
says that something will be sure to turn up if he is
brought forward properly, and is not ashamed of his
family name. Persiflage will do whatever he can, but
that can only be if you will open your arms to him."

Lady Kingsbury did feel that she was called upon to
undergo a terrible revulsion of sentiment. Opening
her arms to the Duca di Crinola might be possible to
her. But how was she to open her arms to Lady
Frances Trafford ? The man whom she had seen but
once might appear before her with his new title as a
young nobleman of whose antecedents she was not
bound to remember anything. She might seem to
regard him as a new arrival, a noble suitor for her
stepdaughter's hand, of whom she had not before heard.
But how was she to receive Fanny Trafford, the girl
whom she had locked up at Königsgraaf, whose letters
she had stopped as they came from the Post Office ?
Nevertheless she consented,—as far at least as her sister
was concerned. " I shall never like Fanny," she had
said, " because she is so sly." Girls are always called
sly by their friends who want to abuse them. " But of
course I will have them both here, as you think it will
be best. What they are to live upon Heaven only
knows. But of course that will be no concern of
mine."

As a first result of this Lady Persiflage asked George
Roden down to Castle Hautboy for the Easter holidays.
There was a difficulty about this. How was he to be
addressed ? Hampstead was consulted, and he, though
he was not much in heart just then for the arrangement
of such a matter, advised that for the present his
friend's old name should be used. Lady Persiflage
therefore wrote to—George Roden, Esq., at the General

Post Office. In this letter it was signified that Lord
Persiflage was very anxious to make the acquaintance
of—Mr. Roden. Lady Persiflage was also very anxious.
Lady Persiflage explained that she was aware of,—Well!
Lady Frances Trafford was to be at Castle Hautboy,
and that she thought might act as an inducement to
——Mr. Roden. The letter was very cleverly managed.
Though it never once mentioned the grand title it
made allusions which implied that the real rank of the
Post Office clerk was well known to every one at Castle
Hautboy. And though nothing of course was said as
to any possible relations between Lord Persiflage as a
member of the British Cabinet and the clerk's uncle as
a member of the Italian Cabinet, nevertheless as to
this also there were allusions which were intelligible.
This letter was altogether very gracious,—such a one
as few young men would be able to resist coming from
such a person as Lady Persiflage. But the special offer
which prevailed with our Post Office clerk was no
doubt the promise of the presence of Fanny Trafford.
In all the rest, gracious as the words were, there was
nothing but trouble for him. It was clear enough to
him that Lady Persiflage was on the same side as
Crocker. Lady Persiflage would no doubt prefer a
Duca di Crinola to a Post Office clerk for Lady Frances.
And he could see also that the Secretary of State for
Foreign Affairs was on the same side. The Secretary
of State would not have expressed a special desire to
see him, the Post Office clerk, at Castle Hautboy, and

have, as it were, welcomed him to the possession of his brother-in-law's daughter, had nothing been told of the Duca di Crinola. He heard as much from Lord Hampstead, who advised him to go to Castle Hautboy, and make himself acquainted with Fanny's family friends. It was all manifest. And as it was all being done in opposition to his own firm resolution, he would not have gone,—but that the temptation was too great for him. Fanny Trafford would be there,—and he was quite open to the charm of the offer which was almost being made to him of Lady Fanny's hand. He arranged the matter at the office, and wrote to Lady Persiflage accepting the invitation.

"So you're going to Castle Hautboy?" said Crocker to him. Crocker was in torments at the time. He had been made to understand that he would be doing quite wrong in calling the Duca "Your Grace." Roden, if a Duke at all, could be only an Italian Duke—and not on that account "Your Grace." This had been explained by Bobbin, and had disturbed him. The title "Duca" was still open to him; but he feared Roden's wrath if he should use it too freely.

"How do you know?" asked Roden.

"I have been there myself, you know;—and am in the habit of hearing from Castle Hautboy." His father was agent on the property, and of course he heard tidings, if not from his father, at any rate from his sisters.

"Yes; I am going to Castle Hautboy."

"Hampstead will be there probably. I met Hampstead there. A man in Lord Persiflage's position will, of course, be delighted to welcome the—the—Duca di Crinola." He shrank as though he feared that Roden would strike him—but he uttered the words.

"Of course, if you choose to annoy me, I cannot well help myself," said Roden as he left the room.

On his first arrival at the Castle things were allowed to go quietly with him. Every one called him "Mr. Roden." Lady Persiflage received him very graciously. Lady Frances was in the house, and her name was mentioned to him with the whispered intimacy which on such occasions indicates the triumph of the man's position. She made no allusion either to his rank or to his office, but treated him just as she might have done any other suitor,—which was exactly what he wanted. Lord Llwddythlw had come down for his Easter holidays of two days, and was very civil to him. Lady Amaldina was delighted to make his acquaintance, and within three minutes was calling upon him to promise that he would not get himself married before August in consideration for her bevy. "If I was to lose Fanny now," she said, "I really think I should give it up altogether." Then before dinner he was allowed to find himself alone with Fanny, and for the first time in his life felt that his engagement was an acknowledged thing.

All this was made very pleasant to him by the occasional use of his proper name. He had been almost

ashamed of himself because of the embarrassment which
his supposed title had occasioned him. He felt that he
had thought of the matter more than it was worth.
The annoyances of Crocker had been abominable to
him. It was not likely that he should encounter a
second Crocker, but still he dreaded he hardly knew
what. It certainly was not probable that these people
at Castle Hautboy should call him by a name he had
never used without consulting him. But still he had
dreaded something, and was gratified that the trouble
seemed to pass by him easily. Lady Persiflage and
Lady Amaldina had both used his legitimate name,
and Lord Llwddythlw had called him nothing at
all. If he could only be allowed to go away just as he
had come, without an allusion from any one to the
Di Crinola family, then he should think that the people
at Castle Hautboy were very well-bred. But he feared
that this was almost too much to hope. He did not
see Lord Persiflage till a moment before dinner, when
he specially remarked that he was introduced as Mr.
Roden. "Very glad to see you, Mr. Roden. I hope
you're fond of scenery. We're supposed to have the
finest view in England from the top of the tower. I
have no doubt my daughter will show it you. I can't
say that I ever saw it myself. Beautiful scenery is all
very well when you are travelling, but nobody ever
cares for it at home." Thus Lord Persiflage had done
his courtesy to the stranger, and the conversation
became general, as though the stranger were a stranger

no longer. When Roden found that he was allowed to give his arm to Lady Frances, and go out and eat his dinner quietly and comfortably without any reference to the peculiarity of his position, he thought that perhaps no further troubles were in store for him.

The whole of the next day was devoted to the charms of love and scenery. The spring weather was delightful, and Roden was allowed to ramble about where he pleased with Lady Frances. Every one about the place regarded him as an accepted and recognized lover. As he had never been in truth accepted by one of the family except by the girl herself;—as the Marquis had not condescended even to see him when he had come, but had sent Mr. Greenwood to reject him scornfully; as the Marchioness had treated him as below contempt; as even his own friend Lord Hampstead had declared that the difficulties would be insuperable, this sudden cessation of all impediments did seem to be delightfully miraculous. Assent on the part of Lord and Lady Persiflage would, he understood, be quite as serviceable as that of Lord and Lady Kingsbury. Something had occurred which, in the eyes of all the family, had lifted him up as it were out of the gutter and placed him on a grand pedestal. There could be no doubt as to this something. It was all done because he was supposed to be an Italian nobleman. And yet he was not an Italian nobleman; nor would he allow any one to call him so, as far as it might be in his power to prevent it.

His visit was limited to two entire days. One was

passed amidst all the sweets of love-making. With the
pleasures of that no allusions were allowed to interfere.
On the following morning he found himself alone with
Lord Persiflage after breakfast. "Delighted to have
had you down here, you know," began his lordship. To
this Roden simply bowed. "I haven't the pleasure of
knowing your uncle personally, but there isn't a man in
Europe for whom I have a higher respect." Again
Roden bowed. "I've heard all about this romance of
yours from D'Ossi. You know D'Ossi?" Roden
declared that he had not the honour of knowing the
Italian Minister. "Ah; well, you must know D'Ossi,
of course. I won't say whether he's your countryman
or not, but you must know him. He is your uncle's
particular friend."

"It's only by accident that I know my uncle, or even
learnt that he was my uncle."

"Just so. But the accident has taken place, and the
result fortunately remains. Of course you must take
your own name."

"I shall keep the name I have, Lord Persiflage."

"You will find it to be quite impossible. The Queen
will not allow it." Upon hearing this Roden opened
his eyes; but the Secretary of State for Foreign Affairs
looked him full in the face as though to assure him
that, though he had never heard of such a thing before,
such, in fact, was the truth. "Of course there will be
difficulties. I'm not prepared at the present moment
to advise how this should be done. Perhaps you had

better wait till Her Majesty has signified her pleasure to receive you as the Duca di Crinola. When she has done so you will have no alternative."

" No alternative as to what I may call myself ? "

"None in the least, I should say. I am thinking now in a great measure as to the welfare of my own relative, Lady Frances. Something will have to be done. I don't quite see my way as yet; but something, no doubt, will be done. The Duca di Crinola will, I have no doubt, find fitting employment." Then a little bell was rung, and Vivian, the private secretary, came into the room. Vivian and Roden knew each other, and a few pleasant words were spoken; but Roden found himself obliged to take his departure without making any further protests in regard to Her Majesty's assumed wishes.

About five o'clock that evening he was invited into a little sitting-room belonging to Lady Persiflage upstairs. "Haven't I been very good to you ? " she said, laughing.

"Very good, indeed. Nothing could be so good as inviting me down here to Castle Hautboy."

"That was done for Fanny's sake. But have I said one word to you about your terrible name ? "

"No, indeed; and now, Lady Persiflage, pray go on and be good to the end."

"Yes," she said, "I will be good to the end,—before all the people down-stairs. I haven't said a word of it even to Fanny. Fanny is an angel."

" According to my thinking."

" That's of course. But even an angel likes to have
her proper rank. You mustn't allow yourself to suppose that even Fanny Trafford is indifferent to titles.
There are things that a man may expect a girl to do
for him, but there are things which cannot be expected,
let her be ever so much in love. Fanny Trafford has
got to become Duchess of Crinola."

" I am afraid that that is more than I can do for
her."

" My dear Mr. Roden, it must be done. I cannot let
you go away from here without making you understand
that, as a man engaged to be married, you cannot drop
your title. Did you intend to remain single, I cannot
say how far your peculiar notions might enable you to
prevail; but as you mean to marry, she, too, will have
rights. I put it to you whether it would be honest on
your part to ask her to abandon the rank which she
will be entitled to expect from you. Just you think of
it, Mr. Roden. And now I won't trouble you any more
upon the subject."

Not a word more was said on the subject at Castle
Hautboy, and on the next day he returned to the Post
Office.

CHAPTER VIII.

"I CANNOT COMPEL HER.'

ABOUT the middle of April Lord and Lady Kingsbury came up to London. From day to day and week
to week he had declared that he would never again be
able to move out of his room; and had gone on making
up his mind to die immediately, till people around him
began to think that he was not going to die at all. He
was, however, at last persuaded that he might at any
rate as well die in London as at Trafford, and, therefore,
allowed himself to be carried up to Park Lane. The
condition of his own health was, of course, given to him
for the reason of this movement. At this peculiar
period of the year, it would be better for him, they said,
to be near his London doctor. No doubt the Marquis
believed that it was so. When a man is ill nothing is
so important to him as his own illness. But it may be
a question whether the anxiety felt by the Marchioness
as to other affairs of the family generally had not an
effect with her in inducing her to persuade her husband.
The Marquis had given a modified assent to his
daughter's marriage; and she, in a manner still more

modified, had withdrawn her opposition. Permission
had been given to Fanny to marry the Duca di Crinola.
This had been given without any reference to money,
but had certainly implied a promise of a certain amount
of income from the bride's father. How else would it
be possible that they should live? The letter had been
written to Lady Frances by her stepmother at the
dictation of the Marquis. But the words absolutely
dictated had not perhaps been religiously followed.
The father had intended to be soft and affectionate,
merely expressing his gratification that his girl's lover
should turn out to be the Duca di Crinola. Out of this
the Marchioness had made a stipulation. The lover
should be received as a lover, on condition that he bore
the name and title. Lady Persiflage had told her sister
that as a matter of course the name would be taken.
"A man always takes his father's name as a matter of
course," Lady Persiflage had said. She believed that
the man's absurd notions would be overcome by con-
tinual social pressure. Whether the social pressure
would or would not prevail, the man would certainly
marry the girl. There could, therefore, be no better
course than that of trusting to social pressure. Lady
Persiflage was quite clear as to her course. But the
Marchioness, though yielding to her sister in much, still
thought that a bargain should be made. It had been
suggested that she should invite "the young man"
down to Trafford. Roden was usually called "the
young man" at present in these family conclaves. She

had thought that it would be better to see him up in
London. Lady Frances would come to them in Park
Lane, and then the young man should be invited. The
Marchioness would send her compliments to the "Duca
di Crinola." Nothing on earth should induce her to
write the name of Roden,—unless it might happily come
to pass that the engagement should be broken.

Hampstead at this time was still living at Hendon.
His sister remained with him till the Marchioness came
up to town about the middle of April, but no one else
except George Roden saw much of him. Since Roden's
return from Italy his visits to Hendon Hall had been
tacitly permitted. The Kingsbury and Persiflage world
had taken upon itself to presume that the young man
was the Duca di Crinola, and, so presuming, had in
truth withdrawn all impediments. Lady Frances had
written to her father in answer to the letter which had
reached her from the Marchioness in his name, and had
declared that Mr. Roden was Mr. Roden, and would
remain Mr. Roden. She had explained his reasons at
great length, but had probably made them anything
but intelligible to her father. He, however, had simply
concealed the letter when he had half-read it. He
would not incur the further trouble of explaining this
to his wife, and had allowed the matter to go on,
although the stipulation made was absolutely repudiated by the parties who were to have been bound
by it.

For Roden and Lady Frances this was no doubt very

pleasant. Even Lady Amaldina Hauteville with her
bevy was not more thoroughly engaged to her aristocratic lover than was Lady Frances to this precarious
Italian nobleman. But the brother in these days was
by no means as happy as his sister. There had been a
terrible scene between him and Lady Frances after his
return from Trafford. He came back with Marion's
letter in his pocket,—with every word contained in it
clear in his memory; but still, still doubting as to the
necessity of obeying Marion's orders. She had declared,
with whatever force of words she had known how to
use, that the marriage which he proposed to himself
was impossible. She had told him so more than once
before, and the telling had availed nothing. Her first
assertion that she could not become his wife had
hardly served to moderate in the least the joy which
he had felt from the assurances of her affections. It
had meant nothing to him. When she had spoken to
him simply of their differences of rank he had thrown
the arguments under his feet, and had trampled upon
them with his masterful imperious determination. His
whole life and energy were devoted to the crushing of
arguments used towards him by those who were daily
telling him that he was severed from other men by the
peculiarities of his rank. He certainly would not be
severed from this one woman whom he loved by any
such peculiarity. Fortifying his heart by these reflec-
tions, he had declared to himself that the timid doubtings of the girl should go for nothing. As she loved

him he would of course be strong enough to conquer all
such doubtings. He would take her up in his arms
and carry her away, and simply tell her that she had
got to do it. He had a conviction that a girl when
once she had confessed that she loved a man, belonged
to the man, and was bound to obey him. To watch
over her, to worship her, to hover round her, so that no
wind should be allowed to blow too strongly on her, to
teach her that she was the one treasure in the world
that could be of real value to him,—but at the same
time to make a property of her, so that she should be
altogether his own,—that had been his idea of the bond
which should unite him and Marion Fay together.
As she took a joy in his love it could not be but that
she would come to his call at last.

She too had perceived something of this,—so much,
that it had become necessary to her to tell him the
whole truth. Those minor reasons, though even they
should have been strong enough, were not, she found,
powerful with him. She tried it, and acknowledged to
herself that she failed. The man was too wilful for her
guidance,—too strong for the arguments by which she
had hoped to control him. Then it had been necessary
to tell him all the truth. This she had done at last
with very few words. " My mother died; and all my
brothers and sisters have died. And I also shall die
young." Very simple, this had been; but, ah, powerful
as it was simple ! In it there had been a hard assertion
of facts too strong even for his masterful nature. He

could not say, even to himself, that it was not so,—that
it should not be so. It might be that she might be
spared where others had not been spared. That risk,
of course, he was prepared to run. Without turning it
much in his thoughts, without venturing to think of
the results or to make a calculation, he was prepared to
tell her that she too must leave all that in the hand of
God, and run her chance as do all human mortal beings.
He certainly would so argue the matter with her. But
he could not tell her that there was no ground for fear.
He could not say that though her mother had died, and
though her little brothers and sisters had died, there
was yet no cause for fear. And he felt that should she
persist in her resolution there would be a potency about
her which it might well be that he should fail to
dominate. If we can live, let us live together; and if
we must die, let us die,—as nearly together as may be.
That we should come together is the one thing absolutely essential; and then let us make our way through
our troubles as best we may under the hands of Fate.
This was what he would now say to her. But he knew
that he could not say it with that bright look and those
imperious tones which had heretofore almost prevailed
with her. Not replying to Marion's letter by any written
answer, but resolving that the words which would be
necessary might best be spoken, he came back to
Hendon. Oh how softly they should be spoken! With
his arm round her waist he would tell her that still it
should be for better or for worse. "I will say nothing

of what may happen except this ;—that whatever may befall us we will take it and bear it together." With such words whispered into her ear, would he endeavour to make her understand that though it might all be true, still would her duty be the same.

But when he reached his house, intending to go on almost at once to Holloway, he was stopped by a note from the Quaker.

"My dear young friend," said the note from the Quaker, "I am desired by Marion to tell thee that we have thought it better that she should go for a few weeks to the seaside. I have taken her to Pegwell Bay, whence I can run up daily to my work in the City. After that thou last saw her she was somewhat unwell, —not ill, indeed, but flurried, as was natural, by the interview. And I have taken her down to the seaside in compliance with medical advice. She bids me, however, to tell thee that there is no cause for alarm. It will, however, be better, for a time at least, that she should not be called upon to encounter the excitement of meeting thee.

"Thy very faithful friend,

"Zachary Fay."

This made him nervous, and for the moment almost wretched. It was his desire at first to rush off to Pegwell Bay and learn for himself what might be the truth of her condition. But on consideration he felt that he did not dare to do so in opposition to the

Quaker's injunction. His arrival there among the strangers of the little watering-place would of course flurry her. He was obliged to abandon that idea, and content himself with a resolve to see the Quaker in the City on the next morning. But the words spoken to him afterwards by his sister were heavier to bear than the Quaker's letter. "Dear John," she had said, "you must give it up."

"I will never give it up," he had answered. And as he spoke there came across his brows an angry look of determination.

"Dear John!"

"What right have you to tell me to give it up? What would you say to me if I were to declare that George Roden should be given up?"

"If there were the same cause!"

"What do you know of any cause?"

"Dear, dearest brother."

"You are taking a part against me. You can be obstinate. I am not more likely to give a thing up than you are yourself."

"It is her health."

"Is she the first young woman that was ever married without being as strong as a milkmaid? Why should you take upon yourself to condemn her?"

"It is not I. It is Marion herself. You told me to go to her, and of course she spoke to me."

He paused a moment, and then in a hoarse, low voice

asked a question. " What did she say to you when you
spoke to her ? "

" Oh, John !—I doubt I can hardly tell you what she
said. But you know what she said. Did she not write
and tell you that because of her health it cannot be as
you would have it."

" And would you have me yield, because for my sake
she is afraid ? If George Roden were not strong would
you throw him over and go away ? "

" It is a hard matter to discuss, John."

" But it has to be discussed. It has at any rate to
be thought of. I don't think that a woman has a right
to take the matter into her own hands, and say that as
a certainty God Almighty has condemned her to an
early death. These things must be left to Providence,
or Chance, or Fate, as you may call it."

" But if she has her own convictions—? "

" She must not be left to her own convictions. It is
just that. She must not be allowed to sacrifice herself
to a fantastic idea."

" You will never prevail with her," said his sister, taking
him by the arm, and looking up piteously into his face.

" I shall not prevail ? Do you say that certainly I
shall not prevail ? " She was still holding his arm, and
still looking up into his face, and now she answered
him by slightly shaking her head. " Why should you
speak so positively ? "

" She could say things to me which she could hardly
say to you."

"What was it then?"

"She could say things to me which I can hardly repeat to you. Oh, John, believe me,—believe me. It must be abandoned. Marion Fay will never be your wife." He shook himself free from her hand, and frowned sternly at her. "Do you think I would not have her for my sister, if it were possible? Do you not believe that I too can love her? Who can help loving her?"

He knew, of course, that as the shoe pinched him it could not pinch her. What were any other love or any other sadness as compared to his love or to his sadness? It was to him as though the sun were suddenly taken out of his heaven, as though the light of day were destroyed for ever from before his eyes,—or rather as though a threat were being made that the sun should be taken from his heaven and the light from his eyes,—a threat under which it might be necessary that he should succumb. "Marion, Marion, Marion," he said to himself again and again, walking up and down between the lodge and the hall door. Whether well or ill, whether living or dying, she surely must be his! "Marion!" And then he was ashamed of himself, as he felt rather than heard that he had absolutely shouted her name aloud.

On the following day he was with the Quaker in London, walking up and down Old Broad Street in front of the entrance leading up to Pogson and Littlebird's. "My dear friend," said the Quaker, "I do not say that it shall never be so. It is in the hands of the Almighty." Hampstead shook his head impatiently. "You do not doubt the power of the Almighty to watch over His creatures?"

"I think that if a man wants a thing he must work for it."

The Quaker looked him hard in the face. "In the ordinary needs of life, my young lord, the maxim is a good one."

"It is good for everything. You tell me of the Almighty. Will the Almighty give me the girl I love if I sit still and hold my peace? Must I not work for that as for anything else?"

"What can I do, Lord Hampstead?"

"Agree with me that it will be better for her to run her chance. Say as I do that it cannot be right that she should condemn herself. If you,—you her father,— will bid her, then she will do it."

"I do not know."

"You can try with her;—if you think it right. You are her father."

"Yes,—I am her father."

"And she is obedient to you. You do not think that she should——? Eh?"

"How am I to say? What am I to say else than that it is in God's hands? I am an old man who have suffered much. All have been taken from me;—all but she. How can I think of thy trouble when my own is so heavy?"

"It is of her that we should think."

"I cannot comfort her; I cannot control her. I will not even attempt to persuade her. She is all that I have. If I did think for a moment that I should like to see my child become the wife of one so high as thou art, that folly has been crushed out of me. To have my child alive would be enough for me now, let alone titles, and high places, and noble palaces."

"Who has thought of them?"

"I did. Not she,—my angel; my white one!" Hampstead shook his head and clenched his fist, shaking it, in utter disregard of the passers by, as the hot, fast tears streamed down his face. Could it be necessary that her name should be mentioned even in connection with feelings such as those which the Quaker owned.

"Thou and I, my lord," continued Zachary Fay, "are in sore trouble about this maiden. I believe that thy love is, as mine, true, honest, and thorough. For her sake I wish I could give her to thee,—because of thy truth and honesty; not because of thy wealth and titles. But she is not mine to give. She is her own,— and will bestow her hand or refuse to do so as her own sense of what is best for thee may direct her. I will say no word to persuade her one way or the other." So speaking the Quaker strode quickly up the gateway, and Lord Hampstead was left to make his way back out of the City as best he might.

CHAPTER IX.

IN PARK LANE.

On Monday, the 20th of April, Lady Frances returned to her father's roof. The winter had certainly not been a happy time for her. Early in the autumn she had been taken off to the German castle in great disgrace because of her plebeian lover, and had, ever since, been living under so dark a cloud, as to have been considered unfit for the companionship of those little darlings, the young lords, her half-brothers. She had had her way no doubt, never having for a moment wavered in her constancy to the Post Office clerk ; but she had been assured incessantly by all her friends that her marriage with the man was impossible, and had no doubt suffered under the conviction that her friends were hostile to her. Now she might be happy. Now she was to be taken back to her father's house. Now she was to keep her lover, and not be held to have been disgraced at all. No doubt in this there was great triumph.

But her triumph had been due altogether to an accident ;—to what her father graciously called a

romance, while her stepmother described it less civilly
as a "marvellous coincidence, for which she ought to
thank her stars on her bended knees." The accident,
—or coincidence or romance as it might be called,—
was, of course, her lover's title. Of this she was by no
means proud, and would not at all thank her stars for
it on her bended knees. Though she was happy in
her lover's presence, her happiness was clouded by the
feeling that she was imposing upon her father. She
had been allowed to ask her lover to dine at Kingsbury
House because her lover was supposed to be the Duca
di Crinola. But the invitation had been sent under an
envelope addressed to George Roden, Esq., General
Post Office. No one had yet ventured to inscribe the
Duke's name and title on the back of a letter. The
Marchioness was assured by her sister that it would all
come right, and had, therefore, submitted to have the
young man asked to come and eat his dinner under the
same roof with her darlings. But she did not quite
trust her sister, and felt that after all it might become
her imperative duty to gather her children together in
her bosom, and fly with them from contact with the
Post Office clerk,—the Post Office clerk who would not
become a Duke. The Marquis himself was only anxious
that everything should be made to be easy. He had,
while at Trafford, been so tormented by Mr. Greenwood
and his wife that he longed for nothing so much as a
reconciliation with his daughter. He was told on very
good authority,—on the authority of no less a person

than the Secretary of State,—that this young man was the Duca di Crinola. There had been a romance, a very interesting romance; but the fact remained. The Post Office clerk was no longer George Roden, and would, he was assured, soon cease to be a Post Office clerk. The young man was in truth an Italian nobleman of the highest order, and as such was entitled to marry the daughter of an English nobleman. If it should turn out that he had been misinformed, that would not be his fault.

So it was when George Roden came to dine at Kingsbury House. He himself at this moment was not altogether happy. The last words which Lady Persiflage had said to him at Castle Hautboy had disturbed him. "Would it be honest on your part," Lady Persiflage had asked him, "to ask her to abandon the rank which she will be entitled to expect from you?" He had not put the matter to himself in that light before. Lady Frances was entitled to as much consideration in the matter as was himself. The rank would be as much hers as his. And yet he couldn't do it. Not even for her sake could he walk into the Post Office and call himself the Duca di Crinola. Not even for her sake could he consent to live an idle, useless life as an Italian nobleman. Love was very strong with him, but with it there was a sense of duty and manliness which would make it impossible for him to submit himself to such thraldom. In doing it he would have to throw over all the strong convictions of his life. And yet he was about

to sit as a guest at Lord Kingsbury's table, because
Lord Kingsbury would believe him to be an Italian
nobleman. He was not, therefore, altogether happy
when he knocked at the Marquis's door.

Hampstead had refused to join the party. He was
not at present in a condition to join any social gathering. But, omitting him, a family party had been
collected. Lord and Lady Persiflage were there, with
Lady Amaldina and her betrothed. The Persiflages
had taken the matter up very strongly, so that they
may have been said to have become George Roden's
special patrons or protectors. Lord Persiflage, who
was seldom much in earnest about anything, had
determined that the Duca di Crinola should be recognized, and was supposed already to have spoken a
word on the subject in a very high quarter indeed.
Vivian, the Private Secretary, was there. The poor
Marquis himself was considered unable to come down
into the dining-room, but did receive his proposed son-
in-law up-stairs. They had not met since the unfortunate visit made by the Post Office clerk to Hendon
Hall, when no one had as yet dreamed of his iniquity;
nor had the Marchioness seen him since the terrible
sound of that feminine Christian name had wounded
her ears. The other persons assembled had in a
measure become intimate with him. Lord Llwddythlw
had walked round Castle Hautboy and discussed with
him the statistics of telegraphy. Lady Amaldina had
been confidential with him as to her own wedding.

Both Lord and Lady Persiflage had given him in a very friendly manner their ideas as to his name and position. Vivian and he had become intimate personal friends. They could, all of them, accept him with open arms when he was shown into the drawing-room, except Lady Kingsbury herself. " No ; I am not very well just at present," said the Marquis from his recumbent position as he languidly stretched out his hand. " You won't see me down at dinner. God knows whether anybody will ever see me down at dinner again."

" Not see you down at dinner ! " said Lord Persiflage. " In another month you will be talking treason in Pall Mall as you have done all your life."

" I wish you had made Hampstead come with you, Mr. ——" But the Marquis stopped himself, having been instructed that he was not on any account to call the young man Mr. Roden. " He was here this morn-ing, but seemed to be in great trouble about something. He ought to come and take his place at the bottom of the table, seeing how ill I am ;—but he won't."

Lady Kingsbury waited until her husband had done his grumbling before she attempted the disagreeable task which was before her. It was very disagreeable. She was a bad hypocrite. There are women who have a special gift of hiding their dislikings from the objects of them, when occasion requires. They can smile and be soft, with bitter enmity in their hearts, to suit the circumstances of the moment. And as they do so, their faces will overcome their hearts, and their enmity will

give way to their smiles. They will become almost
friendly because they look friendly. They will cease to
hate because hatred is no longer convenient. But the
Marchioness was too rigid and too sincere for this. She
could command neither her features nor her feelings.
It was evident from the moment the young man entered
the room, that she would be unable to greet him even
with common courtesy. She hated him, and she had told
every one there that she hated him. "How do you
do?" she said, just touching his hand as soon as he was
released from her husband's couch. She, too, had been
specially warned by her sister that she must not call
the young man by any name. If she could have
addressed him by his title, her manner might perhaps
have been less austere.

"I am much obliged to you by allowing me to come
here," said Roden, looking her full in the face, and
making his little speech in such a manner as to be
audible to all the room. It was as though he had
declared aloud his intention of accepting this permission
as conveying much more than a mere invitation to
dinner. Her face became harder and more austere than
ever. Then finding that she had nothing more to say
to him she seated herself and held her peace.

Only that Lady Persiflage was very unlike her sister,
the moment would have been awkward for them all.
Poor Fanny, who was sitting with her hand within her
father's, could not find a word to say on the occasion.
Lord Persiflage, turning round upon his heel, made a

grimace to his Private Secretary. Llwddythlw would
willingly have said something pleasant on the occasion
had he been sufficiently ready. As it was he stood still,
with his hands in his trousers pockets and his eyes fixed
on the wall opposite. According to his idea the Marchioness was misbehaving herself. "Dear Aunt Clara,"
said Lady Amaldina, trying to say something that might
dissipate the horror of the moment, "have you heard
that old Sir Gregory Tollbar is to marry Letitia Tar-
barrel at last?" But it was Lady Persiflage who really
came to the rescue. "Of course we're all very glad to
see you," she said. "You'll find that if you'll be nice
to us, we'll all be as nice as possible to you. Won't we,
Lord Llwddythlw?"

"As far as I am concerned," said the busy Member
of Parliament, "I shall be delighted to make the
acquaintance of Mr. Roden." A slight frown, a shade
of regret, passed over the face of Lady Persiflage as she
heard the name. A darker and bitterer cloud settled
itself on Lady Kingsbury's brow. Lord Kingsbury
rolled himself uneasily on his couch. Lady Amaldina
slightly pinched her lover's arm. Lord Persiflage was
almost heard to whistle. Vivian tried to look as if
it didn't signify. "I am very much obliged to you
for your courtesy, Lord Llwddythlw," said George
Roden. To have called him by his name was the
greatest favour that could have been done to him
at that moment. Then the door was opened and
dinner announced.

"Time and the hour run through the roughest day."
In this way that dinner at Kingsbury House did come
to an end at last. There was a weight of ill-humour
about Lady Kingsbury on this special occasion against
which even Lady Persiflage found it impossible to
prevail. Roden, whose courage rose to the occasion,
did make a gallant effort to talk to Lady Frances, who
sat next to him. But the circumstances were hard
upon him. Everybody else in the room was closely
connected with everybody else. Had he been graciously
accepted by the mistress of the house, he could have
fallen readily enough into the intimacies which would
then have been opened to him. But as it was he was
forced to struggle against the stream, and so to struggle
as to seem not to struggle. At last, however, time and
the hour had done its work, and the ladies went up to
the drawing-room.

"Lord Llwddythlw called him Mr. Roden!" This
was said by the Marchioness in a tone of bitter reproach
as soon as the drawing-room door was closed.

"I was so sorry," said Lady Amaldina.

"It does not signify in the least," said Lady Persiflage.
"It cannot be expected that a man should drop his old
name and take a new one all in a moment."

"He will never drop his old name and take the new
one," said Lady Frances.

"There now," said the Marchioness. "What do you
think of that, Geraldine?"

"My dear Fanny," said Lady Persiflage, without a

touch of ill-nature in her tone, "how can you tell what a young man will do?"

"I don't think it right to deceive Mamma," said Fanny. "I know him well enough to be quite sure that he will not take the title, as he has no property to support it. He has talked it over with me again and again, and I agree with him altogether."

"Upon my word, Fanny, I didn't think that you would be so foolish," said her aunt. "This is a kind of thing in which a girl should not interfere at all. It must be arranged between the young man's uncle in Italy, and—and the proper authorities here. It must depend very much upon——." Here Lady Persiflage reduced her words to the very lowest whisper. "Your uncle has told me all about it, and of course he must know better than any one else. It's a kind of thing that must be settled for a man by,—by—by those who know how to settle it. A man can't be this or that just as he pleases."

"Of course not," said Lady Amaldina.

"A man has to take the name, my dear, which he inherits. I could not call myself Mrs. Jones any more than Mrs. Jones can call herself Lady Persiflage. If he is the Duca di Crinola he must be the Duca di Crinola."

"But he won't be Duca di Crinola," said Lady Frances.

"There now!" said the Marchioness.

"If you will only let the matter be settled by those

who understand it, and not talk about it just at present,
it would be so much better."

" You heard what Lord Llwddythlw called him,"
said the Marchioness.

" Llwddythlw always was an oaf," said Amaldina.

" He meant to be gracious," said Fanny; "and I am
much obliged to him."

" And as to what you were saying, Fanny, as to
having nothing to support the title, a foreign title in
that way is not like one here at home. Here it must
be supported."

" He would never consent to be burdened with a
great name without any means," said Fanny.

" There are cases in which a great name will help
a man to get means. Whatever he calls himself, I
suppose he will have to live, and maintain a wife."

" He has his salary as a clerk in the Post Office,"
said Fanny very boldly. Amaldina shook her head
sadly. The Marchioness clasped her hands together
and raised her eyes to the ceiling with a look of supplication. Were not her darlings to be preserved from
such contamination ?

" He can do better than that, my dear," exclaimed
Lady Persiflage; "and, if you are to be his wife, I
am sure that you will not stand in the way of his
promotion. His own Government and ours between
them will be able to do something for him as Duca
di Crinola, whereas nothing could be done for George
Roden."

"The English Government is his Government," said Fanny indignantly.

"One would almost suppose that you want to destroy all his prospects," said Lady Persiflage, who was at last hardly able to restrain her anger.

"I believe she does," said the Marchioness.

In the mean time the conversation was carried on below stairs, if with less vigour, yet perhaps with more judgment. Lord Persiflage spoke of Roden's Italian uncle as a man possessing intellectual gifts and political importance of the highest order. Roden could not deny that the Italian Cabinet Minister was his uncle, and was thus driven to acknowledge the family, and almost to acknowledge the country. "From what I hear," said Lord Persiflage, "I suppose you would not wish to reside permanently in Italy, as an Italian?"

"Certainly not," said Roden.

"There is no reason why you should. I can imagine that you should have become too confirmed an Englishman to take kindly to Italian public life as a career. You could hardly do so except as a follower of your uncle, which perhaps would not suit you."

"It would be impossible."

"Just so. D'Ossi was saying to me this morning that he thought as much. But there is no reason why a career should not be open to you here as well as there;—not political perhaps, but official."

" It is the only career that at present is open to me."

" There might be difficulty about Parliament certainly. My advice to you is not to be in a hurry to decide upon anything for a month or two. You will find that things will shake down into their places." Not a word was said about the name or title. When the gentlemen went up-stairs there had been no brilliancy of conversation, but neither were there any positive difficulties to be incurred. Not a word further was said in reference to "George Roden" or to the "Duca di Crinola."

CHAPTER X.

AFTER ALL HE ISN'T.

Six weeks passed by, and nothing special had yet
been done to arrange George Roden's affairs for him
in the manner suggested by Lady Persiflage. "It's a
kind of thing that must be settled for a man by, by,
by—those who know how to settle it." That had been
her counsel when she was advocating delay. No doubt
"things" often do arrange themselves better than men
or women can arrange them. Objections which were
at first very strong gradually fade away. Ideas which
were out of the question become possible. Time
quickly renders words and names and even days
habitual to us. In this Lady Persiflage had not been
unwise. It was quite probable that a young man
should become used to a grand name quicker than he
had himself expected. But nothing had as yet been
done in the right direction when the 1st of June had
come.

Attempts had been made towards increasing the
young man's self-importance, of which he himself had
been hardly aware. Lord Persiflage had seen Sir

Boreas Bodkin, and Vivian had seen the private
secretary of the Postmaster-General. As the first
result of these interviews our clerk was put to sit in
a room by himself, and called upon to manage some
separate branch of business in which he was free from
contact with the Crockers and Bobbins of the Department. It might, it was thought, be possible to call
a man a Duke who sat in a separate room, even though
he were still a clerk. But, as Sir Boreas had observed,
there were places to be given away, Secretaryships,
Inspectorships, Surveyorships, and suchlike, into one of
which the Duke, if he would consent to be a Duke,
might be installed before long. The primary measure
of putting him into a room by himself had already
been carried out. Then a step was taken, of which
George Roden had ground to complain. There was a
certain Club in London called the Foreigners, made up
half of Englishmen and half of men of other nations,
which was supposed to stand very high in the world of
fashion. Nearly every member was possessed of either
grand titles before his name, or of grand letters after it.
Something was said by Vivian to George Roden as to
this club. But no actual suggestion was made, and
certainly no assent was given. Nevertheless the name
of the Duca di Crinola was put down in the Candidate
Book, as proposed by Baron d'Ossi and seconded by
Lord Persiflage. There it was, so that all the world
would declare that the young "Duca" was the "Duca."
Otherwise the name would not have been inserted

there by the Italian Minister and British Secretary of
State. Whereas George Roden himself knew nothing
about it. In this way attempts were made to carry
out that line of action which Lady Persiflage had
recommended.

Letters, too, were delivered to Roden, addressed to
the Duca di Crinola, both at Holloway and at the Post
Office. No doubt he refused them when they came.
No doubt they generally consisted of tradesmen's
circulars, and were probably occasioned by manœuvres
of which Lady Persiflage herself was guilty. But they
had the effect of spreading abroad the fact that George
Roden was George Roden no longer, but was the Duca
di Crinola. "There's letters coming for the Duker
every day," said the landlady of the Duchess to Mrs.
Duffer of Paradise Row. "I see them myself. I
shan't stand on any p's and q's. I shall call him Duker
to his face." Paradise Row determined generally to
call him Duker to his face, and did so frequently, to his
great annoyance.

Even his mother began to think that his refusal
would be in vain. "I don't see how you're to stand
out against it, George. Of course if it wasn't so you'd
have to stand out against it; but as it is the fact——"

"It is no more a fact with me than with you," he
said angrily.

"Nobody dreams of giving me a title. If all the
world agrees, you will have to yield."

Sir Boreas was as urgent. He had always been

very friendly with the young clerk, and had now become particularly intimate with him. "Of course, my dear fellow," he said, "I shall be guided entirely by yourself."

"Thank you, sir."

"If you tell me you're George Roden, George Roden you'll be to me. But I think you're wrong. And I think moreover that the good sense of the world will prevail against you. As far as I understand anything of the theory of titles, this title belongs to you. The world never insists on calling a man a Lord or a Count for nothing. There's too much jealousy for that. But when a thing is so, people choose that it shall be so."

All this troubled him, though it did not shake his convictions. But it made him think again and again of what Lady Persiflage had said to him down at Castle Hautboy. "Will it be honest on your part to ask her to abandon the rank which she will be entitled to expect from you?" If all the world conspired to tell him that he was entitled to take this name, then the girl whom he intended to marry would certainly be justified in claiming it. It undoubtedly was the fact that titles such as these were dear to men,—and specially dear to women. As to this girl, who was so true to him, was he justified in supposing that she would be different from others, simply because she was true to him? He had asked her to come down as it were from the high pedestal of her own rank, and to submit herself to his lowly lot. She had consented, and there never had been to him a moment of remorse in thinking that he was about to injure her. But as Chance had brought it about in this way, as Fortune had seemed determined to give back to her that of which he would have deprived her, was it right that he should stand in the way of Fortune? Would it be honest on his part to ask her to abandon these fine names which Chance was putting in her way?

That it might be so, should he be pleased to accept what was offered to him, did become manifest to him. It was within his power to call himself and to have himself called by this new name. It was not only the party of the Crockers. Others now were urgent in persuading him. The matter had become so far customary to him as to make him feel that if he would simply put the name on his card, and cause it to be inserted in the Directories, and write a line to the officials saying that for the future he would wish to be so designated, the thing would be done. He had met Baron D'Ossi, and the Baron had acknowledged that an Englishman could not be converted into an Italian Duke without his own consent,—but had used very strong arguments to show that in this case the Englishman ought to give his consent. The Baron had expressed his own opinion that the Signorina would be very much ill-used indeed if she were not allowed to take her place among the Duchessinas. His own personal feelings were in no degree mitigated. To be a Post Office clerk, living at Holloway, with a few hundreds a-year to spend,—and yet to be known all over the world as the claimant of a magnificently grand title! It seemed as though a cruel fate had determined to crush him with a terrible punishment because of his specially democratic views! That he of all the world should be selected to be a Duke in opposition to his own wishes! How often had he been heard to declare that all hereditary titles were, of their very nature, absurd! And yet he was to be forced to become a penniless hereditary Duke!

Nevertheless he would not rob her whom he hoped to make his wife of that which would of right belong to her. "Fanny," he said to her one day, "you cannot conceive how many people are troubling me about this title."

"I know they are troubling me. But I would not mind any of them;—only for papa."

"Is he very anxious about it?"

"I am afraid he is."

"Have I ever told you what your aunt said to me just before I left Castle Hautboy?"

"Lady Persiflage, you mean. She is not my aunt, you know."

"She is more anxious than your father, and certainly uses the only strong argument I have heard."

"Has she persuaded you?"

"I cannot say that; but she has done something towards persuading me. She has made me half think that it may be my duty."

"Then I suppose you will take the name," she said.

"It shall depend entirely upon you. And yet I ought not to ask you. I ought to do as these people bid me without even troubling you for an expression of your wish. I do believe that when you become my wife, you will have as complete a right to the title as has Lady Kingsbury to hers. Shall it be so?"

"No," she said.

"It shall not?"

"Certainly, no; if it be left to me."

"Why do you answer in that way when all your friends desire it?"

"Because I believe that there is one friend who does not desire it. If you can say that you wish it on your own account, of course I will yield. Otherwise all that my friends may say on the matter can have no effect on me. When I accepted the offer which you made me, I gave up all idea of rank. I had my reasons, which I thought to be strong enough. At any rate I did so, and now because of this accident I will not be weak enough to go back. As to what Lady Persiflage says about me, do not believe a word of it. You certainly will not make me happy by bestowing on me a name which you do not wish me to bear, and which will be distasteful to yourself."

After this there was no longer any hesitation on Roden's part, though his friends, including Lord Persiflage, the Baron, Sir Boreas, and Crocker, were as active in their endeavours as ever. For some days he had doubted, but now he doubted no longer. They might address to him what letters they would, they might call him by what nickname they pleased, they might write him down in what book they chose, he would still keep the name of George Roden, as she had protested that she was satisfied with it.

It was through Sir Boreas that he learnt that his name had been written down in the club Candidate Book as " Duca di Crinola." Sir Boreas was not a member of the club, but had heard what had been done, probably at some club of which he was a member. "I am glad to hear that you are coming up at the Foreigners," said Æolus.

" But I am not."

" I was told last night that Baron D'Ossi had put your name down as Duca di Crinola." Then Roden discovered the whole truth,—how the Baron had proposed him and the Foreign Secretary had seconded him, without even going through the ceremony of asking him. " Upon my word I understood that you wished it," Vivian said to him. Upon this the following note was written to the Foreign Secretary.

" Mr. Roden presents his compliments to Lord Persiflage, and begs to explain that there has been a misunderstanding about the Foreigners' Club. Mr. Roden feels very much the honour that has been done him, and is much obliged to Lord Persiflage; but as he feels himself not entitled to the honour of belonging

to the club, he will be glad that his name should be
taken off. Mr. Roden takes the opportunity of assuring
Lord Persiflage that he does not and never will claim
the name which he understands to have been inscribed
in the club books."

"He's a confounded ass," said Lord Persiflage to the
Baron as he did as he was bid at the club. The Baron
shrugged his shoulders, as though acknowledging that
his young fellow-nobleman certainly was an ass. "There
are men, Baron, whom you can't help, let you struggle
ever so much. This man has had stuff enough in him
to win for himself a very pretty girl with a good fortune
and high rank, and yet he is such a fool that he won't
let me put him altogether on his legs when the opportunity comes!"

Not long after this Roden called at the house in
Park Lane, and asked to see the Marquis. As he
passed through the hall he met Mr. Greenwood coming
very slowly down the stairs. The last time he had met
the gentleman had been in that very house when the
gentleman had received him on behalf of the Marquis.
The Marquis had not condescended to see him, but had
deputed his chaplain to give him whatever ignominious
answer might be necessary to his audacious demand for
the hand of Lady Frances. On that occasion Mr.
Greenwood had been very imperious. Mr. Greenwood
had taken upon himself almost the manners of the
master of the house. Mr. Greenwood had crowed as

though the dunghill had been his own. George Roden even then had not been abashed, having been able to remember through the interview that the young lady was on his side; but he had certainly been severely treated. He had wondered at the moment that such a man as Lord Kingsbury should confide so much of his family matters to such a man as Mr. Greenwood. Since then he had heard something of Mr. Greenwood's latter history from Lady Frances. Lady Frances had joined with her brother in disliking Mr. Greenwood, and all that Hampstead had said to her had been passed on to her lover. Since that last interview the position of the two men had been changed. The chaplain had been turned out of the establishment, and George Roden had been almost accepted into it as a son-in-law. As they met on the foot of the staircase, it was necessary that there should be some greeting. The Post Office clerk bowed very graciously, but Mr. Greenwood barely acknowledged the salutation. "There," said he to himself, as he passed on, "that's the young man that's done all the mischief. It's because such as he are allowed to make their way in among noblemen and gentlemen that England is going to the dogs." Nevertheless, when Mr. Greenwood had first consented to be an inmate of the present Lord Kingsbury's house, Lord Kingsbury had, in spite of his Order, entertained very liberal views.

The Marquis was not in a good humour when Roden was shown into his room. He had been troubled by his late chaplain, and he was not able to bear such troubles easily. Mr. Greenwood had said words to him which had vexed him sorely, and these words had in part referred to his daughter and his daughter's lover. "No, I'm not very well," he said in answer to Roden's inquiries. " I don't think I ever shall be better. What is it about now ? "

" I have come, my lord," said Roden, " because I do not like to be here in your house under a false pretence."

" A false pretence ? What false pretence ? I hate false pretences."

" So do I."

" What do you mean by a false pretence now ? "

" I fear that they have told you, Lord Kingsbury, that should you give me your daughter as my wife, you will give her to the Duca di Crinola." The Marquis, who was sitting in his arm-chair, shook his head from side to side, and moved his hands uneasily, but made no immediate reply. " I cannot quite tell, my lord, what your own ideas are, because we have never discussed the subject."

" I don't want to discuss it just at present," said the Marquis.

" But it is right that you should know that I do not claim the title, and never shall claim it. Others have done so on my behalf, but with no authority from me. I have no means to support the rank in the country to which it belongs; nor as an Englishman am I entitled to assume it here."

"I don't know that you're an Englishman," said the Marquis. "People tell me that you're an Italian."

"I have been brought up as an Englishman, and have lived as one for five-and-twenty years. I think it would be difficult now to rob me of my rights. Nobody, I fancy, will try. I am, and shall be, George Roden, as I always have been. I should not, of course, trouble you with the matter were it not that I am a suitor for your daughter's hand. Am I right in supposing that I have been accepted here by you in that light?" This was a question which the Marquis was not prepared to answer at the moment. No doubt the young man had been accepted. Lady Frances had been allowed to go down to Castle Hautboy to meet him as her lover. All the family had been collected to welcome him at the London mansion. The newspapers had been full of mysterious paragraphs in which the future happy bridegroom was sometimes spoken of as an Italian Duke and sometimes as an English Post Office clerk. "Of course he must marry her now," the Marquis had said to his wife, with much anger. "It's all your sister's doings," he had said to her again. He had in a soft moment given his affectionate blessing to his daughter in special reference to her engagement. He knew that he couldn't go back from it now, and had it been possible, would have been most unwilling to give his wife such a triumph. But yet he was not prepared to accept the Post Office clerk simply as a Post Office clerk. "I am sorry to trouble you at this moment, Lord Kingsbury, if you are not well."

"I ain't well at all. I am very far from well. If you don't mind I'd rather not talk about it just at present. When I can see Hampstead, then, perhaps, things can be settled." As there was nothing further to be said George Roden took his leave.

CHAPTER XI.

"OF COURSE THERE WAS A BITTERNESS."

IT was not surprising that Lord Kingsbury should have been unhappy when Roden was shown up into his room, as Mr. Greenwood had been with him. Mr. Greenwood had called on the previous day, and had been refused admittance. He had then sent in an appeal, asking so piteously for an interview that the Marquis had been unable to repudiate it. Mr. Greenwood knew enough of letter-writing to be able to be effective on such an occasion. He had, he said, lived under the same roof with the Marquis for a quarter of a century. Though the positions of the two men in the world were so different they had lived together as friends. The Marquis throughout that long period had frequently condescended to ask the advice of his chaplain, and not unfrequently to follow it. After all this could he refuse to grant the favour of a last interview? He had found himself unable to refuse the favour. The interview had taken place, and consequently the Marquis had been very unhappy when George Roden was shown up into his room.

The Rector of Appleslocombe was dead. The interview was commenced by a communication to that effect
from Mr. Greenwood. The Marquis of course knew the
fact,—had indeed already given the living away,—had
not delayed a minute in giving it away because of some
fear which still pressed upon him in reference to Mr.
Greenwood. Nor did Mr. Greenwood expect to get
the living,—or perhaps desire it. But he wished to
have a grievance, and to be in possession of a subject on which he could begin to make his complaint. "You must have known, Mr. Greenwood,
that I never intended it for you," said the Marquis.
Mr. Greenwood, seated on the edge of his chair and
rubbing his two hands together, declared that he had
entertained hopes in that direction. "I don't know
why you should, then. I never told you so. I never
thought of it for a moment. I always meant to
put a young man into it; — comparatively young."
Mr. Greenwood shook his head and still rubbed
his hands. "I don't know that I can do anything
more for you."

"It isn't much that you have done, certainly, Lord
Kingsbury."

"I have done as much as I intend to do," said the
Marquis, rousing himself angrily. "I have explained
all that by Mr. Roberts."

"Two hundred a year after a quarter of a century!"
Mr. Greenwood had in truth been put into possession
of three hundred a year; but as one hundred of this

came from Lord Hampstead it was not necessary to mention the little addition.

"It is very wrong,—your pressing your way in here and talking to me about it at all."

"After having expected the living for so many years!"

"You had no right to expect it. I didn't promise it. I never thought of it for a moment. When you asked me I told you that it was out of the question. I never heard of such impertinence in all my life. I must ask you to go away and leave me, Mr. Greenwood." But Mr. Greenwood was not disposed to go away just yet. He had come there for a purpose, and he intended to go on with it. He was clearly resolved not to be frightened by the Marquis. He got up from his chair and stood looking at the Marquis, still rubbing his hands, till the sick man was almost frightened by the persistency of his silence. "What is it, Mr. Greenwood, that makes you stand thus? Do you not hear me tell you that I have got nothing more to say to you?"

"Yes, my lord; I hear what you say?"

"Then why don't you go away? I won't have you stand there staring like that." He still shook his head. "Why do you stand there and shake your head?"

"It must be told, my lord."

"What must be told?"

"The Marchioness!"

"What do you mean, sir? What have you got to say?"

"Would you wish to send for her ladyship?"

"No; I wouldn't. I won't send for her ladyship at all. What has her ladyship got to do with it?"

"She promised."

"Promised what?"

"Promised the living! She undertook that I should have Appleslocombe the moment it became vacant."

"I don't believe a word of it."

"She did. I don't think that her ladyship will deny it." It might have been so, certainly; and had there been no chance of truth in the statement he would hardly have been so ready to send for Lady Kingsbury. But had she done so the promise would amount to nothing. Though he was sick and wretched and weak, and in some matters afraid of his wife, there had been no moment of his life in which he would have given way to her on such a subject as this. "She promised it me,—for a purpose."

"A purpose!"

"For a purpose, my lord."

"What purpose?" Mr. Greenwood went on staring and shaking his head and rubbing his hands, till the Marquis, awestruck and almost frightened, put out his hand towards the bell. But he thought of it again. He remembered himself that he had nothing to fear. If the man had anything to say about the Marchioness it might perhaps be better said without the presence of servants. "If you mean to say anything, say it. If not,—go. If you do neither one nor the other very quickly, I shall have you turned out of the house."

"Turned out of the house?"

"Certainly. If you have any threat to make, you had better make it in writing. You can write to my lawyers, or to me, or to Lord Hampstead, or to Mr. Roberts."

"It isn't a threat. It is only a statement. She promised it me,—for a purpose."

"I don't know what you mean by a purpose, Mr. Greenwood. I don't believe Lady Kingsbury made any such promise; but if she did it wasn't hers to promise. I don't believe it; but had she promised I should not be bound by it."

"Not if you have not given it away?"

"I have given it away, Mr. Greenwood."

"Then I must suggest——"

"Suggest what!"

"Compensation, my lord. It will only be fair. You ask her ladyship. Her ladyship cannot intend that I should be turned out of your lordship's house with only two hundred a year, after what has passed between me and her ladyship."

"What passed?" said the Marquis, absolutely rousing himself so as to stand erect before the other man.

"I had rather, my lord, you should hear it from her ladyship."

"What passed?"

"There was all that about Lady Frances."

"What about Lady Frances?"

"Of course I was employed to do all that I could to prevent the marriage. You employed me yourself, my lord. It was you sent me down to see the young man, and explain to him how impertinent he was. It isn't my fault, Lord Kingsbury, if things have got themselves changed since then."

"You think you ought to make a demand upon me because as my Chaplain you were asked to see a gentleman who called here on a delicate matter?"

"It isn't that I am thinking about. If it had been only that I should have said nothing. You asked me what it was about, and I was obliged to remind you of one thing. What took place between me and her ladyship was, of course, much more particular; but it all began with your lordship. If you hadn't commissioned me I don't suppose her ladyship would ever have spoken to me about Lady Frances."

"What is it all? Sit down;—won't you?—and tell it all like a man if you have got anything to tell." The Marquis, fatigued with his exertion, was forced to go back to his chair. Mr. Greenwood also sat down,— but whether or no like a man may be doubted. "Remember this, Mr. Greenwood, it does not become a gentleman to repeat what has been said to him in confidence,—especially not to repeat it to him or to them from whom it was intended to be kept secret. And it does not become a Christian to endeavour to make ill-blood between a husband and his wife. Now,

if you have got anything to say, say it." Mr. Greenwood shook his head. "If you have got nothing to
say, go away. I tell you fairly that I don't want
to have you here. You have begun something like a
threat, and if you choose to go on with it, you may.
I am not afraid to hear you, but you must say it
or go."

Mr. Greenwood again shook his head. "I suppose
you won't deny that her ladyship honoured me with a
very close confidence."

"I don't know anything about it."

"Your lordship didn't know that her ladyship down
at Trafford used to be talking to me pretty freely about
Lord Hampstead and Lady Frances?"

"If you have got anything to say, say it," screamed
the Marquis.

"Of course his lordship and her ladyship are not her
ladyship's own children."

"What has that got to do with it?"

"Of course there was a bitterness."

"What is that to you? I will hear nothing from
you about Lady Kingsbury, unless you have to tell me
of some claim to be made upon her. If there has been
money promised you, and she acknowledges it, it shall
be paid. Has there been any such promise?"

Mr. Greenwood found it very difficult,—nay, quite
impossible,—to say in accurate language that which he
was desirous of explaining by dark hints. There had,
he thought, been something of a compact between

K

himself and the Marchioness. The Marchioness had
desired something which she ought not to have desired,
and had called upon the Chaplain for more than his
sympathy. The Chaplain had been willing to give her
more than his sympathy,—had at one time been almost
willing to give her very much more. He might possibly, as he now felt, have misinterpreted her wishes.
But he had certainly heard from her language so strong,
in reference to her husband's children, that he had been
justified in considering that it was intended to be secret.
As a consequence of this he had been compelled to
choose between the Marquis and the Marchioness. By
becoming the confidential friend of the one he had
necessarily become the enemy of the other. Then, as a
further consequence, he was turned out of the house,—
and, as he declared to himself, utterly ruined. Now in
this there had certainly been much hardship, and who
was to compensate him if not the Marquis?

There certainly had been some talk about Appleslocombe during those moments of hot passion in which
Lady Kingsbury had allowed herself to say such evil
things of Lady Frances and Lord Hampstead. Whether
any absolute promise had been given she would probably not now remember. There certainly had been a
moment in which she had thought that her husband's life
might possibly pass away before that of the old rector;
and reference may have been made to the fact that
had her own darling been the heir, the gift of the

living would then have fallen into her own hands. Mr.
Greenwood had probably thought more of some possible
compensation for the living than of the living itself.
He had no doubt endeavoured to frighten her ladyship
into thinking that some mysterious debt was due to
him, if not for services actually rendered, at any rate
for extraordinary confidences. But before he had forced
upon her the acknowledgment of the debt, he was
turned out of the house! Now this he felt to be hard.

What were two hundred a-year as a pension for a
gentleman after such a life-long service? Was it to
be endured that he should have listened for so many
years to all the abominable politics of the Marquis,
and to the anger and disappointment of the Marchioness, that he should have been so closely connected,
and for so many years, with luxury, wealth, and rank,
and then arrive at so poor an evening of his day?
As he thought of this he felt the more ashamed of
his misfortune, because he believed himself to be in
all respects a stronger man than the Marquis. He had
flattered himself that he could lead the Marquis, and
had thought that he had been fairly successful in doing
so. His life had been idle, luxurious, and full of
comfort. The Marquis had allowed him to do pretty
well what he pleased until in an evil hour he had taken
the side of the Marchioness in a family quarrel. Then
the Marquis, though weak in health,—almost to his
death,—had suddenly become strong in purpose, and

K 2

had turned him abruptly out of the house with a
miserable stipend hardly fit for more than a butler!
Could it be that he should put up with such usage,
and allow the Marquis to escape unscathed out of his
hand?

In this condition of mind, he had determined that he
owed it to himself to do or say something that should
frighten his lordship into a more generous final arrangement. There had been, he said to himself again and
again, such a confidence with a lady of so high a rank,
that the owner of it ought not to be allowed to languish
upon two or even upon three hundred a-year. If the
whole thing could really be explained to the Marquis,
the Marquis would probably see it himself. And to all
this was to be added the fact that no harm had been
done. The Marchioness owed him very much for having
wished to assist her in getting rid of an heir that was
disagreeable to her. The Marquis owed him more for
not having done it. And they both owed him very
much in that he had never said a word of it all to
anybody else. He had thought that he might be
clever enough to make the Marquis understand something of this without actually explaining it. That some
mysterious promise had been made, and that, as the
promise could not be kept, some compensation should
be awarded,—this was what he had desired to bring
home to the mind of the Marquis. He had betrayed
no confidence. He intended to betray none. He was

very anxious that the Marquis should be aware, that as he, Mr. Greenwood, was a gentleman, all confidences would be safe in his hands; but then the Marquis ought to do his part of the business, and not turn his confidential Chaplain out of the house after a quarter of a century with a beggarly annuity of two hundred a-year !

But the Marquis seemed to have acquired unusual strength of character; and Mr. Greenwood found that words were very difficult to be found. He had declared that there had been "a bitterness," and beyond that he could not go. It was impossible to hint that her lady-ship had wished to have Lord Hampstead—removed. The horrid thoughts of a few days had become so vague to himself that he doubted whether there had been any real intention as to the young lord's removal even in his own mind. There was nothing more that he could say than this,—that during the period of this close intimacy her ladyship had promised to him the living of Apple-slocombe, and that, as that promise could not be kept, some compensation should be made to him. "Was any sum of money named ?" asked the Marquis.

"Nothing of the kind. Her ladyship thought that I ought to have the living."

"You can't have it; and there's an end of it."

"And you think that nothing should be done for me ?"

"I think that nothing should be done for you more than has been done."

"Very well. I am not going to tell secrets that have been intrusted to me as a gentleman, even though I am so badly used by those who have confided them to me. Her ladyship is safe with me. Because I sympathized with her ladyship your lordship turned me out of the house."

"No; I didn't."

"Should I have been treated like this had I not taken her ladyship's part? I am too noble to betray a secret, or, no doubt, I could compel your lordship to behave to me in a very different manner. Yes, my lord, I am quite ready to go now. I have made my appeal, and I have made it in vain. I have no wish to call upon her ladyship. As a gentleman I am bound to give her ladyship no unnecessary trouble."

While this last speech was going on a servant had come into the room, and had told the Marquis that the "Duca di Crinola" was desirous of seeing him. The servants in the establishment were of course anxious to recognize Lady Frances' lover as an Italian Duke. The Marquis would probably have made some excuse for not receiving the lover at this moment, had he not felt that he might in this way best insure the immediate retreat of Mr. Greenwood. Mr. Greenwood went, and Roden was summoned to Lord Kingsbury's presence; but the meeting took place under circumstances which naturally made the Marquis incapable of entering at the moment with much spirit on the great "Duca" question.

CHAPTER XII.

LORD HAMPSTEAD AGAIN WITH MRS. RODEN.

WEEKS had passed by since Lord Hampstead had
walked up and down Broad Street with Mr. Fay,—
weeks which were to him a period of terrible woe. His
passion for Marion had so seized upon him, that it had
in all respects changed his life. The sorrow of her
alleged ill-health had fallen upon him before the
hunting had been over, but from that moment he had
altogether forgotten his horses. The time had now
come in which he was wont to be. on board his yacht,
but of his yacht he took no notice whatever. "I can
tell you nothing about it as yet," he said in the only
line which he wrote to his skipper in answer to piteous
applications made to him. None of those who were
near and dear to him knew how he passed his time.
His sister left him and went up to the house in
London, and he felt that her going was a relief to him.
He would not even admit his friend Roden to come
to him in his trouble. He spent his days all alone
at Hendon, occasionally going across to Holloway in

order that he might talk of his sorrow to Mrs. Roden.
Midsummer had come upon him before he again saw
the Quaker. Marion's father had left a feeling almost
of hostility in his mind in consequence of that conversation in Broad Street. "I no longer want anything on
your behalf," the Quaker had seemed to say. "I care
nothing now for your name, or your happiness. I am
anxious only for my child, and as I am told that it will
be better that you should not see her, you must stay
away." That the father should be anxious for his
daughter was natural enough. Lord Hampstead could
not quarrel with Zachary Fay. But he taught himself
to think that their interests were at variance with each
other. As for Marion, whether she were ill or whether
she were well, he would have had her altogether to
himself.

Gradually there had come upon him the conviction
that there was a real barrier existing between himself
and the thing that he desired. To Marion's own words,
while they had been spoken only to himself, he had
given no absolute credit. He had been able to declare
to her that her fears were vain, and that whether she
were weak or whether she were strong, it was her duty
to come to him. When they two had been together
his arguments and assurances had convinced at any
rate himself. The love which he had seen in her eyes
and had heard from her lips had been so sweet to him,
that their savour had overcome whatever strength her

words possessed. But these protestations, these assurances that no marriage could be possible, when they
reached him second-hand, as they had done through his
sister and through the Quaker, almost crushed him.
He did not dare to tell them that he would fain marry
the girl though she were dying,—that he would accept
any chance or no chance, if he might only be allowed
to hold her in his arms, and tell her that she was all
his own. There had come a blow, he would say to
himself, again and again, as he walked about the
grounds at Hendon, there had come a blow, a fatal
blow, a blow from which there could be no recovery,—
but, still, it should, it ought, to be borne together. He
would not admit to himself that because of this verdict
there ought to be a separation between them two. It
might be that the verdict had been uttered by a Judge
against whom there could be no appeal; but even the
Judge should not be allowed to say that Marion Fay
was not his own. Let her come and die in his arms
if she must die. Let her come and have what of life
there might be left to her, warmed and comforted and
perhaps extended by his love. It seemed to him to
be certainly a fact, that because of his great love, and
of hers, she did already belong to him; and yet he was
told that he might not see her;—that it would be
better that she should not be disturbed by his presence,
—as though he were no more than a stranger to her.
Every day he almost resolved to disregard them, and

go down to the little cottage in which she was living.
But then he remembered the warnings which were
given to him, and was aware that he had in truth no
right to intrude upon the Quaker's household. It is
not to be supposed that during this time he had no
intercourse with Marion. At first there came to be
a few lines, written perhaps once a week from her, in
answer to many lines written by him; but by degrees
the feeling of awe which at first attached itself to the
act of writing to him wore off, and she did not let a
day pass without sending him some little record of
herself and her doings. It had come to be quite
understood by the Quaker that Marion was to do
exactly as she pleased with her lover. No one dreamed
of hinting to her that this correspondence was improper
or injurious. Had she herself expressed a wish to see
him, neither would the Quaker nor Mrs. Roden have
made strong objection. To whatever might have been
her wish or her decision they would have acceded. It
was by her word that the marriage had been declared
to be impossible. It was in obedience to her that he
was to keep aloof. She had failed to prevail with her
own soft words, and had therefore been driven to use
the authority of others.

But at this period, though she did become weaker
and weaker from day to day, and though the doctor's
attendance was constant at the cottage, Marion herself
was hardly unhappy. She grieved indeed for his grief;

but, only for that, there would have been triumph and joy to her rather than grief. The daily writing of these little notes was a privilege to her and a happiness, of which she had hitherto known nothing. To have a lover, and such a lover, was a delight to her, a delight to which there was now hardly any drawback, as there was nothing now of which she need be afraid. To have him with her as other girls may have their lovers, she knew was impossible to her. But to read his words, and to write loving words to him, to talk to him of his future life, and bid him think of her, his poor Marion, without allowing his great manly heart to be filled too full with vain memories, was in truth happiness to her. "Why should you want to come?" she said. "It is infinitely better that you should not come. We understand it all now, and acknowledge what it is that the Lord has done for us. It would not have been good for me to be your wife. It would not have been good for you to have become my husband. But it will I think be good for me to have loved you; and if you will learn to think of it as I do, it will not have been bad for you. It has given a beauty to my life," she said, "which makes me feel that I ought to be contented to die early. If I could have had a choice I would have chosen it so."

But these teachings from her had no effect whatever upon him. It was her idea that she would pass away, and that there would remain with him no more than a

fair sweet shade which would have but little effect
upon his future life beyond that of creating for him
occasionally a gentle melancholy. It could not be,
she thought, that for a man such as he,—for one so
powerful and so great,—such a memory should cause a
lasting sorrow. But with him, to his thinking, to his
feeling, the lasting biting sorrow was there already.
There could be no other love, no other marriage, no
other Marion. He had heard that his stepmother was
anxious for her boy. The way should be open for the
child. It did seem to him that a life, long continued,
would be impossible to him when Marion should have
been taken away from him.

"Oh yes;—he's there again," said Miss Demijohn to
her aunt. "He comes mostly on Tuesdays, Thursdays,
and Saturdays. What he can be coming about is more
than I can guess. Crocker says it's all true love.
Crocker says that the Duca says——"

"Bother the Duca," exclaimed the old woman. "I
don't believe that Crocker and George Roden ever
exchange a word together."

"Why shouldn't they exchange words, and they fast
friends of five years' standing? Crocker says as Lord
Hampstead is to be at Lady Amaldina's wedding in
August. His lordship has promised. And Crocker
thinks——"

"I don't believe very much about Crocker, my young
woman. You had better look to yourself, or, perhaps,

you'll find when you have got yourself married that Crocker has not got a roof to cover you."

Lord Hampstead had walked over to Paradise Row, and was seated with Mrs. Roden when this little squabble was going on. "You don't think that I ought to let things remain as they are," he said to Mrs. Roden. To all such questions Mrs. Roden found it very difficult to make any reply. She did in truth think that they ought to be allowed to remain as they were,—or rather that some severance should be made more decided even than that which now existed. Putting aside her own ideas, she was quite sure that Marion would not consent to a marriage. And, as it was so, and must be so, it was better, she thought, that the young people should see no more of each other. This writing of daily letters,—what good could it do to either of them? To her indeed, to Marion, with her fixed purpose, and settled religious convictions, and almost certain fate, little evil might be done. But to Lord Hampstead the result would be, and was, terribly pernicious. He was sacrificing himself, not only as Mrs. Roden thought for the present moment, but for many years perhaps,—perhaps for his future life,—to a hopeless passion. A cloud was falling upon him which might too probably darken his whole career. From the day on which she had unfortunately taken Marion to Hendon Hall, she had never ceased to regret the acquaintance which she had caused. To her thinking

the whole affair had been unfortunate. Between
people so divided there should have been no intimacy,
and yet this intimacy had been due to her. "It is
impossible that I should not see her," continued Lord
Hampstead. "I will see her."

"If you would see her, and then make up your mind
to part with her,—that I think would be good."

"To see her, and say farewell to her for ever?"

"Yes, my lord."

"Certainly not. That I will never do. If it should
come to pass that she must go from me for ever, I
would have her in my arms to the very last!"

"At such a moment, my lord, those whom nature
has given to her for her friends——"

"Has not nature given me too for her friend? Can
any friend love her more truly than I do? Those
should be with us when we die to whom our life is of
most importance. Is there any one to whom her life
can be half as much as it is to me? The husband is
the dearest to his wife. When I look upon her as
going from me for ever, then may I not say that she is
the same to me as my wife."

"Why,—why,—why?"

"I know what you mean, Mrs. Roden. What is the
use of asking 'why' when the thing is done? Could I
make it so now, as though I had never seen her?
Could I if I would? Would I if I could? What
is the good of thinking of antecedents which are

impossible ? She has become my treasure. Whether
past and fleeting, or likely to last me for my life, she is
my treasure. Can I make a change because you ask
why,—and why,—and why? Why did I ever come
here? Why did I know your son? Why have I got
a something here within me which kills me when I
think that I shall be separated from her, and yet crowns
me with glory when I feel that she has loved me.
If she must leave me, I have to bear it. What I shall
do, where I shall go, whether I shall stand or fall, I do
not pretend to say. A man does not know, himself, of
what stuff he is made, till he has been tried. But
whatever may be my lot, it cannot be altered by any
care or custody now. She is my own, and I will not be
separated from her. If she were dead, I should know
that she was gone. She would have left me, and I
could not help myself. As yet she is living, and may
live, and I will be with her. I must go to her there,
or she must come here to me. If he will permit it
I will take some home for myself close to hers. What
will it matter now, though every one should know it?
Let them all know it. Should she live she will
become mine. If she must go,—what will the world
know but that I have lost her who was to have been
my wife?"

Even Mrs. Roden had not the heart to tell him that
he had seen Marion for the last time. It would have
been useless to tell him so, for he would not have

obeyed the behest contained in such an assertion.
Ideas of prudence and ideas of health had restrained
him hitherto,—but he had been restrained only for a
time. No one had dared suggest to him that he should
never again see his Marion. "I suppose that we must
ask Mr. Fay," she replied. She was herself more
powerful than the Quaker, as she was well aware; but
it had become necessary to her to say something.

"Mr. Fay has less to say to it even than I have,"
said Hampstead. "My belief is that Marion herself is
the only one among us who is strong. If it were not
that she is determined, he would yield and you would
yield."

"Who can know as she knows?" said Mrs. Roden.
"Which among us is so likely to be guided by what is
right? Which is so pure, and honest, and loving?
Her conscience tells her what is best."

"I am not sure of that," said he. "Her conscience
may fill her as well as another with fears that are
unnecessary. I cannot think that a girl should be
encouraged by those around her to doom herself after
this fashion. Who has a right to say that God has
determined that she shall die early?" Mrs. Roden
shook her head. "I am not going to teach others what
religion demands, but to me it seems that we should
leave these things in God's hands. That she may
doubt as to herself may be natural enough, but others
should not have encouraged her."

"You mean me, my lord?"

"You must not be angry with me, Mrs. Roden. The matter to me is so vital that I have to say what I think about it. It does seem to me that I am kept away from her, whereas, by all the ties which can bind a man and a woman together, I ought to be with her. Forms and ceremonies seem to sink to nothing, when I think of all she is to me, and remember that I am told that she is soon to be taken away from me."

"How would it be if she had a mother?"

"Why should her mother refuse my love for her daughter? But she has no mother. She has a father who has accepted me. I do believe that had the matter been left wholly to him, Marion would now be my wife."

"I was away, my lord, in Italy."

"I will not be so harsh to such a friend as you, as to say that I wish you had remained there; but I feel,—I cannot but feel——"

"My lord, I think the truth is that you hardly know how strong in such a matter as this our Marion herself can be. Neither have I nor has her father prevailed upon her. I can go back now, and tell you without breach of confidence all that passed between her and me. When first your name was discussed between us; when first I saw that you seemed to make much of her——"

"Make much of her!" exclaimed Hampstead, angrily.

"Yes; make much of her! When first I thought that you were becoming fond of her."

"You speak as though there had been some idle dallying. Did I not worship her? Did I not pour out my whole heart into her lap from the first moment in which I saw her? Did I hide it even from you? Was there any pretence, any falsehood?"

"No, indeed."

"Do not say that I made much of her. The phrase is vile. When she told me that she loved me, she made much of me."

"When first you showed us that you loved her," she continued, "I feared that it would not be for good."

"Why should it not be for good?"

"I will not speak of that now, but I thought so. I thought so, and I told my thoughts to Marion."

"You did?"

"I did;—and I think that in doing so, I did no more than my duty to a motherless girl. Of the reasons which I gave to her I will say nothing now. Her reasons were so much stronger, that mine were altogether unavailing. Her resolutions were built on so firm a rock, that they needed no persuasions of mine to strengthen them. I had ever known Marion to be pure, unselfish, and almost perfect. But I had never before seen how high she could rise, how certainly she could soar above all weakness and temptation. To her there was never a moment of doubt. She knew from the very first that it could not be so."

"It shall be so," he said, jumping up from his chair, and flinging up his arms.

"It was not I who persuaded her, or her father. Even you cannot persuade her. Having convinced herself that were she to marry you, she would injure you, not all her own passionate love will induce her to accept the infinite delight of yielding to you. What may be best for you;—that is present to her mind, and nothing else. On that her heart is fixed, and so clear is her judgment respecting it, that she will not allow the words of any other to operate on her for a moment. Marion Fay, Lord Hampstead, is infinitely too great to have been persuaded in any degree by me."

*   *   *   *   *   *

Nevertheless Mrs. Roden did allow herself to say that in her opinion the lover should be allowed to see his mistress. She herself would go to Pegwell Bay, and endeavour to bring Marion back to Holloway. That Lord Hampstead should himself go down and spend his long hours at the little seaside place did not seem to her to be fitting. But she promised that she would do her best to arrange at any rate another meeting in Paradise Row.

CHAPTER XIII.

LORD HAMPSTEAD AGAIN WITH MARION.

THE Quaker had become as weak as water in his
daughter's hands.   To whatever she might have desired
he would have given his assent. He went daily up
from Pegwell Bay to Pogson and Littlebird's, but even
then he was an altered man. It had been said there
for a few days that his daughter was to become the
wife of the eldest son of the Marquis of Kingsbury,
and then it had been said that there could be no such
marriage—because of Marion's health. The glory while
it lasted he had borne meekly, but with a certain
anxious satisfaction. The pride of his life had been in
Marion, and this young lord's choice had justified his
pride. But the glory had been very fleeting. And
now it was understood through all Pogson and Littlebird's that their senior clerk had been crushed, not by
the loss of his noble son-in-law, but by the cause which
produced the loss. Under these circumstances poor
Zachary Fay had hardly any will of his own, except to
do that which his daughter suggested to him. When

she told him that she would wish to go up to London
for a few days, he assented as a matter of course. And
when she explained that she wished to do so in order
that she might see Lord Hampstead, he only shook his
head sadly, and was silent.

"Of course I will come as you wish it," Marion had
said in her letter to her lover. "What would I not do
that you wish,—except when you wish things that you
know you ought not? Mrs. Roden says that I am to
go up to be lectured. You mustn't be very hard upon
me. I don't think you ought to ask me to do things
which you know,—which you know that I cannot do.
Oh, my lover! oh, my love! would that it were all
over, and that you were free!"

In answer to this, and to other letters of the kind, he
wrote to her long argumentative epistles, in which he
strove to repress the assurances of his love, in order
that he might convince her the better by the strength
of his reasoning. He spoke to her of the will of God,
and of the wickedness of which she would be guilty if
she took upon herself to foretell the doings of Providence. He said much of the actual bond by which
they had tied themselves together in declaring their
mutual love. He endeavoured to explain to her that
she could not be justified in settling such a question
for herself without reference to the opinion of those
who must know the world better than she did. Had
the words of a short ceremony been spoken, she would

have been bound to obey him as her husband. Was
she not equally bound now, already, to acknowledge
his superiority,—and if not by him, was it not her
manifest duty to be guided by her father? Then at
the end of four carefully-written, well-stuffed pages,
there would come two or three words of burning love.
"My Marion, my self, my very heart!" It need hardly
be said that as the well-stuffed pages went for nothing
with Marion,—had not the least effect towards convincing
her, so were the few words the very food on which she
lived. There was no absurdity in the language of love
that was not to her a gem so brilliant that it deserved
to be garnered in the very treasure house of her
memory! All those long useless sermons were preserved because they had been made rich and rare by
the expression of his passion.

She understood him, and valued him at the proper
rate, and measured him correctly in everything. He
was so true, she knew him to be so true, that even his
superlatives could not be other than true! But as for
his reasoning, she knew that that came also from his
passion. She could not argue the matter out with him,
but he was wrong in it all. She was not bound to
listen to any other voice but that of her own conscience.
She was bound not to subject him to the sorrows which
would attend him were he to become her husband.
She could not tell how weak or how strong might be
his nature in bearing the burden of the grief which

would certainly fall upon him at her death. She had heard, and had in part seen, that time does always mitigate the weight of that burden. Perhaps it might be best that she should go at once, so that no prolonged period of his future career should be injured by his waiting. She had begun to think that he would be unable to look for another wife while she lived. By degrees there came upon her the full conviction of the steadfastness, nay, of the stubbornness, of his heart. She had been told that men were not usually like that. When first he had become sweet to her, she had not thought that he would have been like that. Was it not almost unmanly,—or rather was it not womanly? And yet he,—strong and masterful as he was,—could he have aught of a woman's weakness about him? Could she have dreamed that it would bo so from the first, she thought that from the very first she could have abstained.

"Of course I shall be at home on Tuesday at two. Am I not at home every day at all hours? Mrs. Roden shall not be there as you do not wish it, though Mrs. Roden has always been your friend. Of course I shall be alone. Papa is always in the City. Good to you! Of course I shall be good to you! How can I be bad to the one being that I love better than all the world? I am always thinking of you; but I do wish that you would not think so much of me. A man should not think so much of a girl,—only just at his spare moments.

I did not think that it would be like that when I told
you that you might love me."

All that Tuesday morning, before he left home, he
was not only thinking of her, but trying to marshal in
order what arguments he might use,—so as to convince
her at last.   He did not at all understand how utterly
fruitless his arguments had been with her.   When Mrs.
Roden had told him of Marion's strength he had only
in part believed her.   In all matters concerning the
moment Marion was weak and womanly before him.
When he told her that this or the other thing was proper
and becoming, she took it as Gospel because it came
from him.   There was something of the old awe even
when she looked up into his face.   Because he was
a great nobleman, and because she was the Quaker's
daughter, there was still, in spite of their perfect love,
something of superiority, something of inferiority of
position.   It was natural that he should command,—
natural that she should obey.   How could it be then
that she should not at last obey him in this great thing
which was so necessary to him ?   And yet hitherto
he had never gone near to prevailing with her.   Of
course he marshalled all his arguments.

Gentle and timid as she was, she had made up her
mind to everything, even down to the very greeting
with which she would receive him.   His first warm
kiss had shocked her.   She had thought of it since,
and had told herself that no harm could come to

her from such tokens of affection,—that it would be
unnatural were she to refuse it to him. Let it pass by
as an incident that should mean nothing. To hang
upon his neck and to feel and to know that she was
his very own,—that might not be given to her. To
hear his words of love and to answer him with words as
warm,—that could be allowed to her. As for the rest,
it would be better that she should let it so pass by
that there need be as little of contention as possible on
a matter so trivial.

When he came into the room he took her at once,
passive and unresisting, into his arms. "Marion," he
said. "Marion! Do you say that you are ill? You
are as bright as a rose."

"Rose leaves soon fall. But we will not talk about
that. Why go to such a subject?"

"It cannot be helped." He still held her by the
waist, and now again he kissed her. There was
something in her passive submission which made him
think at the moment that she had at last determined
to yield to him altogether. "Marion, Marion," he
said, still holding her in his embrace, "you will be
persuaded by me? You will be mine now?"

Gradually,—very gently,—she contrived to extricate
herself. There must be no more of it, or his passion
would become too strong for her. "Sit down, dearest,"
she said. "You flurry me by all this. It is not good
that I should be flurried."

"I will be quiet, tame, motionless, if you will only say the one word to me. Make me understand that we are not to be parted, and I will ask for nothing else."

"Parted! No, I do not think that we shall be parted."

"Say that the day shall come when we may really be joined together; when——"

"No, dear; no; I cannot say that. I cannot alter anything that I have said before. I cannot make things other than they are. Here we are, we two, loving each other with all our hearts, and yet it may not be. My dear, dear lord!" She had never even yet learned another name for him than this. "Sometimes I ask myself whether it has been my fault." She was now sitting, and he was standing over her, but still holding her by the hand.

"There has been no fault. Why should either have been in fault?"

"When there is so great a misfortune there must generally have been a fault. But I do not think there has been any here. Do not misunderstand me, dear. The misfortune is not with me. I do not know that the Lord could have sent me a greater blessing than to have been loved by you,—were it not that your trouble, your grief, your complainings rob me of my joy."

"Then do not rob me," he said.

"Out of two evils you must choose the least. You have heard of that, have you not?"

"There need be no evil;—no such evil as this."
Then he dropped her hand, and stood apart from her
while he listened to her, or else walked up and down
the room, throwing at her now and again a quick angry
word, as she went on striving to make clear to him the
ideas as they came to her mind.

"I do not know how I could have done otherwise,"
she said, "when you would make it so certain to me
that you loved me. I suppose it might have been
possible for me to go away, and not to say a word in
answer."

"That is nonsense,—sheer nonsense," he said.

"I could not tell you an untruth. I tried it once,
but the words would not come at my bidding. Had I
not spoken them, you would read the truth in my eyes.
What then could I have done? And yet there was
not a moment in which J have not known that it must
be as it is."

"It need not be; it need not be. It should not be."

"Yes, dear, it must be. As it is so why not let us
have the sweet of it as far as it will go? Can you
not take a joy in thinking that you have given an
inexpressible brightness to your poor Marion's days;
that you have thrown over her a heavenly light which
would be all glorious to her if she did not see that you
were covered by a cloud? If I thought that you
could hold up your head with manly strength, and
accept this little gift of my love, just for what it is

worth,—just for what it is worth,—then I think I could be happy to the end."

"What would you have me do? Can a man love and not love?"

"I almost think he can. I almost think that men do. I would not have you not love me. I would not lose my light and my glory altogether. But I would have your love to be of such a nature that it should not conquer you. I would have you remember your name and your family——"

"I care nothing for my name. As far as I am concerned, my name is gone."

"Oh, my lord!"

"You have determined that my name shall go no further."

"That is unmanly, Lord Hampstead. Because a poor weak girl such as I am cannot do all that you wish, are you to throw away your strength and your youth, and all the high hopes which ought to be before you? Would you say that it were well in another if you heard that he had thrown up everything, surrendered all his duties, because of his love for some girl infinitely beneath him in the world's esteem?"

"There is no question of above and beneath. I will not have it. As to that, at any rate we are on a par."

"A man and a girl can never be on a par. You have a great career, and you declare that it shall go for nothing because I cannot be your wife."

"Can I help myself if I am broken-hearted? You can help me."

"No, Lord Hampstead; it is there that you are wrong. It is there that you must allow me to say that I have the clearer knowledge. With an effort on your part the thing may be done."

"What effort? What effort? Can I teach myself to forget that I have ever seen you?"

"No, indeed; you cannot forget. But you may resolve that, remembering me, you should remember me only for what I am worth. You should not buy your memories at too high a price."

"What is it that you would have me do?"

"I would have you seek another wife."

"Marion!"

"I would have you seek another wife. If not instantly, I would have you instantly resolve to do so."

"It would not hurt you to feel that I loved another?"

"I think not. I have tried myself, and now I think that it would not hurt me. There was a time in which I owned to myself that it would be very bitter, and then I told myself, that I hoped,—that I hoped that you would wait. But now, I have acknowledged to myself the vanity and selfishness of such a wish. If I really love you am I not bound to want what may be best for you?"

"You think that possible?" he said, standing over her, and looking down upon her. "Judging from your own heart do you think that you could do that if outward circumstances made it convenient?"

"No, no, no."

"Why should you suppose me to be harder-hearted than yourself, more callous, more like a beast of the fields?"

"More like a man is what I would have you."

"I have listened to you, Marion, and now you may listen to me. Your distinctions as to men and women are all vain. There are those, men and women both, who can love and do love, and there are those who neither do nor can. Whether it be for good or evil,— we can, you and I, and we do. It would be impossible to think of giving yourself to another?"

"That is certainly true."

"It is the same with me, — and will ever be so. Whether you live or die, I can have no other wife than Marion Fay. As to that I have a right to expect that you shall believe me. Whether I have a wife or not you must decide."

"Oh, dearest, do not kill me."

"It has to be so. If you can be firm so can I. As to my name and my family, it matters nothing. Could I be allowed to look forward and think that you would sit at my hearth, and that some child that should be my child should lie in your arms, then I could look forward to what you call a career. Not that he might be the last of a hundred Traffords, not that he might be an Earl or a Marquis like his forefathers, not that he might some day live to be a wealthy peer, would I have it so,—but because he would be yours and mine." Now she got up, and threw her arms around him, and stood leaning on him as he spoke. "I can look forward to that and think of a career. If that cannot be, the rest of it must provide for itself. There are others who can look after the Traffords,—and who will do so whether it be necessary or not. To have gone a little out of the beaten path, to have escaped some of the traditional absurdities, would have been something to me. To have let the world see how noble a Countess I could find for it—that would have satisfied me. And I had succeeded. I had found one that would really have graced the name. If it is not to be so,—why then let the name and family go on in the old beaten track. I shall not make another venture. I have made my choice, and it is to come to this."

"You must wait, dear;—you must wait. I had not thought it would be like this; but you must wait."

"What God may have in store for me, who can tell. You have told me your mind, Marion; and now I trust that you will understand mine. I do not accept your decision, but you will accept mine. Think of it all, and when you see me again in a day or two, then see whether you will not be able to join your lot to mine and make the best of it." Upon this he kissed her again, and left her without another word.

CHAPTER XIV.

CROCKER'S DISTRESS.

WHEN Midsummer came Paradise Row was alive
with various interests.   There was no one there who
did not know something of the sad story of Marion Fay
and her love.   It was impossible that such a one as
Lord Hampstead should make repeated visits to the
street without notice.   When Marion returned home
from Pegwell Bay, even the potboy at The Duchess
of Edinburgh knew why she had come, and Clara
Demijohn professed to be able to tell all that passed
at the interview next day.   And there was the great
"Duca" matter;—so that Paradise Row generally
conceived itself to be concerned on all questions of
nobility, both Foreign and British.   There were the
Ducaites and the anti-Ducaites.   The Demijohn faction
generally, as being under the influence of Crocker,
were of opinion that George Roden being a Duke
could not rid himself of his ducal nature, and they
were loud in their expression of the propriety of calling
the Duke Duke whether he wished it or no.   But

Mrs. Grimley at The Duchess was warm on the other side. George Roden, according to her lights, being a clerk in the Post Office, must certainly be a Briton, and being a Briton, and therefore free, was entitled to call himself whatever he pleased. She was generally presumed to enunciate a properly constitutional theory in the matter, and, as she was a leading personage in the neighbourhood, the Duca was for the most part called by his old name; but there were contests, and on one occasion blows had been struck. All this helped to keep life alive in the Row.

But there had arisen another source of intense interest. Samuel Crocker was now regularly engaged to marry Miss Demijohn. There had been many difficulties before this could be arranged. Crocker not unnaturally wished that a portion of the enormous wealth which rumour attributed to Mrs. Demijohn should be made over to the bride on her marriage. But the discussions which had taken place between him and the old lady on the matter had been stormy and unsuccessful. "It's a sort of thing that one doesn't understand at all, you know," Crocker had said to Mrs. Grimley, giving the landlady to understand that he was not going to part with his own possession of himself without adequate consideration. Mrs. Grimley had comforted the young man by reminding him that the old lady was much given to hot brandy and water, and that she could not "take her money with her where she was going."

Crocker had at last contented himself with an assurance
that there should be a breakfast and a trousseau which
was to cost £100. With the promise of this and the
hope of what brandy-and-water might do for him, he
had given in, and the match was made. Had there
been no more than this in the matter the Row would
not have been much stirred by it. The Row was so
full of earls, marquises, and dukes that Crocker's love
would have awakened no more than a passing attention,
but for a concomitant incident which was touching in
its nature, and interesting in its development. Daniel
Tribbledale, junior clerk at Pogson and Littlebird's, had
fought a battle with his passion for Clara Demijohn
like a man; but, manly though the battle had been,
Love had prevailed over him. He had at last found
it impossible to give up the girl of his heart, and he
had declared his intention of "punching Crocker's
head" should he ever find him in the neighbourhood
of the Row. With the object of doing this he fre-
quented the Row constantly from ten in the evening
till two in the morning, and spent a great deal more
money than he ought to have done at The Duchess.
He would occasionally knock at No. 10, and boldly ask
to be allowed to see Miss Clara. On one or two of
these occasions he had seen her, and tears had flown in
great quantities. He had thrown himself at her feet,
and she had assured him that it was in vain. He
had fallen back at Pogson and Littlebird's to £120

a year, and there was no prospect of an increase. Moreover the betrothment with Crocker was complete. Clara had begged him to leave the vicinity of Holloway. Nothing, he had sworn, should divorce him from Paradise Row. Should that breakfast ever be given; should these hated nuptials ever take place; he would be heard of. It was in vain that Clara had threatened to die on the threshold of the church if anything rash were done. He was determined, and Clara, no doubt, was interested in the persistency of his affection. It was, however, specially worthy of remark that Crocker and Tribbledale never did meet in Paradise Row.

Monday, 13th of July, was the day fixed for the marriage, and lodgings for the happy pair had been taken at Islington. It had been hoped that room might have been made for them at No. 10; but the old lady, fearing the interference of a new inmate, had preferred the horrors of solitude to the combined presence of her niece and her niece's husband. She had, however, given a clock and a small harmonium to grace the furnished sitting-room;—so that things might be said to stand on a sound and pleasant footing. Gradually, however, it came to be thought both by the old and the young lady, that Crocker was becoming too eager on that great question of the Duca. When he declared that no earthly consideration should induce him to call his friend by any name short of that noble title which he was entitled to use, he was asked a

M 2

question or two as to his practice at the office. For it had come round to Paradise Row that Crocker was giving offence at the office by his persistency. "When I speak of him I always call him the 'Duca,'" said Crocker, gallantly, "and when I meet him I always address him as Duca. No doubt it may for a while create a little coolness, but he will recognize at last the truth of the spirit which actuates me. He is 'the Duca.'"

"If you go on doing what they tell you not to do," said the old woman, "they'll dismiss you." Crocker had simply smiled ineffably. Not Æolus himself would dismiss him for a loyal adherence to the constitutional usages of European Courts.

Crocker was in truth making himself thoroughly disagreeable at the Post Office. Sir Boreas had had his own view as to Roden's title, and had been anxious to assist Lord Persiflage in forcing the clerk to accept his nobility. But when he had found that Roden was determined, he had given way. No order had been given on the subject. It was a matter which hardly admitted of an order. But it was understood that as Mr. Roden wished to be Mr. Roden, he was to be Mr. Roden. It was declared that good taste required that he should be addressed as he chose to be addressed. When, therefore, Crocker persisted it was felt that Crocker was a bore. When Crocker declared to Roden personally that his conscience would not allow him to encounter a man whom he believed to be a nobleman without calling him by his title, the office generally felt that Crocker was an ass. Æolus was known to have expressed himself as very angry, and was said to have declared that the man must be dismissed sooner or later. This had been reported to Crocker. "Sir Boreas can't dismiss me for calling a nobleman by his right name," Crocker had replied indignantly. The clerks had acknowledged among themselves that this might be true, but had remarked that there were different ways of hanging a dog. If Æolus was desirous of hanging Crocker, Crocker would certainly find him the rope before long. There was a little bet made between Bobbin and Geraghty that the office would know Crocker no longer before the end of the year.

Alas, alas;—just before the time fixed for the poor fellow's marriage, during the first week of July, there came to our Æolus not only an opportunity for dismissing poor Crocker, but an occasion on which, by the consent of all, it was admitted to be impossible that he should not do so, and the knowledge of the sin committed came upon Sir Boreas at a moment of great exasperation caused by another source. "Sir Boreas," Crocker had said, coming into the great man's room, "I hope you will do me the honour of being present at my wedding breakfast." The suggestion was an unpardonable impertinence. "I am asking no one else in the Department except the Duca," said Crocker.

With what special flea in his ear Crocker was made to leave the room instantly cannot be reported; but the reader may be quite sure that neither did Æolus nor the Duca accept the invitation. It was on that very afternoon that Mr. Jerningham, with the assistance of one of the messengers, discovered that Crocker had— actually torn up a bundle of official papers!

Among many official sins of which Crocker was often guilty was that of "delaying papers." Letters had to be written, or more probably copies made, and Crocker would postpone the required work from day to day. Papers would get themselves locked up, and sometimes it would not be practicable to trace them. There were those in the Department who said that Crocker was not always trustworthy in his statements, and there had come up lately a case in which the unhappy one was supposed to have hidden a bundle of papers of which he denied having ever had the custody. Then arose a tumult of anger among those who would be supposed to have had the papers if Crocker did not have them, and a violent search was instituted. Then it was discovered that he had absolutely—destroyed the official documents! They referred to the reiterated complaints of a fidgety old gentleman who for years past had been accusing the Department of every imaginable iniquity. According to this irritable old gentleman, a diabolical ingenuity had been exercised in preventing him from receiving a single letter through a long series of years.

This was a new crime. Wicked things were often done, but anything so wicked as this had never before been perpetrated in the Department. The minds of the senior clerks were terribly moved, and the young men were agitated by a delicious awe. Crocker was felt to be abominable; but heroic also,—and original. It might be that a new opening for great things had been invented.

The fidgety old gentleman had never a leg to stand upon,—not a stump; but now it was almost impossible that he should not be made to know that all his letters of complaint had been made away with! Of course Crocker must be dismissed. He was at once suspended, and called upon for his written explanation. "And I am to be married next week!" he said weeping to Mr. Jerningham. Æolus had refused to see him, and Mr. Jerningham, when thus appealed to, only shook his head. What could a Mr. Jerningham say to a man who had torn up official papers on the eve of his marriage? Had he laid violent hands on his bride, but preserved the papers, his condition, to Mr. Jerningham's thinking, would have been more wholesome.

It was never known who first carried the tidings to Paradise Row. There were those who said that Tribbledale was acquainted with a friend of Bobbin, and that he made it all known to Clara in an anonymous letter. There were others who traced a friendship between the potboy at The Duchess and a son of one of the messengers. It was at any rate known at No. 10. Crocker was summoned to an interview with the old woman; and the match was then and there declared to be broken off. "What are your intentions, sir, as to supporting that young woman?" Mrs. Demijohn demanded with all the severity of which she was capable. Crocker was so broken-hearted that he had not a word to say for himself. He did not dare to suggest that perhaps he might not be dismissed. He admitted the destruction of the papers. "I never cared for him again when I saw him so knocked out of time by an old woman," said Clara afterwards.

"What am I to do about the lodgings?" asked Crocker weeping.

"Tear 'em up," said Mrs. Demijohn. "Tear 'em up. Only send back the clock and the harmonium."

Crocker in his despair looked about everywhere for assistance. It might be that Æolus would be softer-hearted than Clara Demijohn. He wrote to Lord Persiflage, giving him a very full account of the affair. The papers, he said, had in fact been actually torn by accident. He was afraid of "the Duca," or he would have applied to him. "The Duca," no doubt had been his most intimate friend,— so he still declared,—but in such an emergency he did not know how to address "the Duca." But he bethought himself of Lord Hampstead, of that hunting acquaintance, with whom his intercourse had been so pleasant and so genial, and he made a journey down Hendon. Lord Hampstead at this time was living there all alone. Marion Fay had been taken back to Pegwell Bay, and her lover was at the old house holding intercourse almost with no one. His heart just now was very heavy with him. He had begun to believe that Marion would in truth never become his wife. He had begun to think that she would really die, and that he would never have had the sad satisfaction of calling her his own. All lightness and brightness had gone from him, all the joy which he used to take in argument, all the eagerness of his character,—unless the hungry craving of unsatisfied love could still be called an eagerness.

He was in this condition when Crocker was brought out to him in the garden where he was walking. "Mr. Crocker," he said, standing still in the pathway and looking into the man's face.

"Yes, my lord; it's me. I am Crocker. You remember me, my lord, down in Cumberland?"

"I remember you,—at Castle Hautboy."

"And out hunting, my lord,—when we had that pleasant ride home from Airey Force."

"What can I do for you now?"

"I always do think, my lord, that there is nothing like sport to cement affection. I don't know how you feel about it, my lord."

"If there is anything to be said—perhaps you will say it."

"And there's another bond, my lord. We have both
been looking for the partners of our joys in Paradise
Row."

"If you have anything to say, say it."

"And as for your friend, my lord, the,—the——.
You know whom I mean. If I have given any offence
it has only been because I've thought that as the title
was certainly theirs, a young lady who shall be name-
less ought to have the advantage of it. I've only done
it because of my consideration for the family."

"What have you come here for, Mr. Crocker? I am
not just now disposed to converse,—on, I may say, any
subject. If there be anything——"

"Indeed, there is. Oh, my lord, they are going to
dismiss me! For the sake of Paradise Row, my lord,
pray, pray, interfere on my behalf." Then he told the
whole story about the papers, merely explaining that
they had been torn in accident. "Sir Boreas is angry
with me because I have thought it right to call—you
know whom—by his title, and now I am to be dismissed
just when I was about to take that beautiful and accomplished young lady to the hymeneal altar. Only
think if you and Miss Fay was to be divided in the
same way!"

With much lengthened explanation, which was, however, altogether ineffectual, Lord Hampstead had to
make his visitor understand that there was no ground
on which he could even justify a request. "But a

letter! You could write a letter. A letter from your lordship would do so much." Lord Hampstead shook his head. "If you were just to say that you had known me intimately down in Cumberland! Of course I am not taking upon myself to say it was so,—but to save a poor fellow on the eve of his marriage!"

"I will write a letter," said Lord Hampstead, thinking of it, turning over in his mind his own idea of what marriage would be to him. "I cannot say that we have been intimate friends, because it would not be true."

"No;—no; no! Of course not that."

"But I will write a letter to Sir Boreas. I cannot conceive that it should have any effect. It ought to have none."

"It will, my lord."

"I will write, and will say that your father is connected with my uncle, and that your condition in regard to your marriage may perhaps be accepted as a ground for clemency. Good day to you." Not very quickly, but with profuse thanks and the shedding of some tears, poor Crocker took his leave. He had not been long gone before the following letter was written;—

"SIR,

"Though I have not the honour of any acquaintance with you, I take the liberty of writing to you as to the condition of one of the clerks in your office. I am perfectly aware that should I receive a reprimand from your hands, I shall have deserved it by my unjustifiable interference.

" Mr. Crocker represents to me that he is to be dismissed because of some act of which you as his superior officer highly disapprove. He asks me to appeal to you on his behalf because we have been acquainted with each other. His father is agent to my uncle Lord Persiflage, and we have met at my uncle's house. I do not dare to put this forward as a plea for mercy. But I understand that Mr. Crocker is about to be married almost immediately, and, perhaps, you will feel with me that a period in a man's life which should beyond all others be one of satisfaction, of joy, and of perfect contentment, may be regarded with a feeling of mercy which would be prejudicial if used more generally.

" Your faithful servant,

" HAMPSTEAD."

When he wrote those words as to the period of joy and satisfaction his own heart was sore, sore, sore almost to breaking. There could never be such joy, never be such satisfaction for him.

CHAPTER XV.

"DISMISSAL.   B. B."

By return of post Lord Hampstead received the following answer to his letter ;—

"My dear Lord Hampstead,—

"Mr. Crocker's case is *a very bad one ;* but the Postmaster General shall see your appeal, and his lordship will, I am sure, sympathize with your humanity —as do I also.   I cannot take upon myself to say what his lordship will think it right to do, and it will be better, therefore, that you should abstain for the present from communicating with Mr. Crocker.

"I am,

"Your lordship's very faithful servant,

"Boreas Bodkin."

Any excuse was sufficient to our Æolus to save him from the horror of dismissing a man. He knew well that Crocker, as a public servant, was not worth his salt. Sir Boreas was blessed,— or cursed,— with a conscience, but the stings of his conscience, though they were painful, did not hurt him so much as those of his feelings. He had owned to himself on this occasion that Crocker must go. Crocker was in every way distasteful to him. He was not only untrustworthy and incapable, but audacious also, and occasionally impudent. He was a clerk of whom he had repeatedly said that it would be much better to pay him his salary and let him have perpetual leave of absence, than keep him even if there were no salary to be paid. Now there had come a case on which it was agreed by all the office that the man must go. Destroy a bundle of official papers! Mr. Jerningham had been heard to declare that the law was in fault in not having provided that a man should be at once sent to Newgate for doing such a thing. "The stupid old fool's letters weren't really worth anything," Sir Boreas had said, as though attempting to palliate the crime! Mr. Jerningham had only shaken his head. What else could he do? It was not for him to dispute any matter with Sir Boreas. But to his thinking the old gentle-man's letters had become precious documents, priceless records, as soon as they had once been bound by the red tape of the Government, and enveloped by the security of an official pigeon-hole. To stay away with-out leave,—to be drunk,—to be obstinately idle,—to be impudent, were great official sins; but Mr. Jerningham was used to them, and knew that as they had often occurred before, so would they re-occur. Clerks are mortal men, and will be idle, will be reckless, will sometimes get into disreputable rows. A little added severity, Mr. Jerningham thought, would improve his branch of the department, but, knowing the nature of men, the nature especially of Sir Boreas, he could make excuses. Here, however, was a case in which no superior Civil Servant could entertain a doubt. And yet Sir Boreas palliated even this crime! Mr. Jerningham shook his head, and Sir Boreas shoved on one side, so as to avoid for a day the pain of thinking about them, the new bundle of papers which had already formed itself on the great Crocker case. If some one would tear up that, what a blessing it would be!

In this way there was delay, during which Crocker was not allowed to show his face at the office, and during this delay Clara Demijohn became quite confirmed in her determination to throw over her engagement. Tribbledale with his £120 would be much better than Crocker with nothing. And then it was agreed generally in Paradise Row that there was something romantic in Tribbledale's constancy. Tribbledale was in the Row every day,—or perhaps rather every night;—seeking counsel from Mrs. Grimley, and comforting himself with hot gin-and-water. Mrs. Grimley was good-natured, and impartial to both the young men. She liked customers, and she liked marriages generally. " If he ain't got no income of course he's out of the running," Mrs. Grimley said to Tribbledale, greatly comforting the young man's heart. " You go in and win," said Mrs. Grimley, indicating by that her opinion that the ardent suitor would probably be successful if he urged his love at the present moment. " Strike while the iron is hot," she said, alluding probably to the heat to which Clara's anger would be warmed by the feeling that the other lover had lost his situation just when he was most bound to be careful in maintaining it.

Tribbledale went in and pleaded his case. It is probable that just at this time Clara herself was made acquainted with Tribbledale's frequent visits to The Duchess, and though she may not have been pleased with the special rendezvous selected, she was gratified by the devotion shown. When Mrs. Grimley advised Tribbledale to "go in and win," she was, perhaps, in Clara's confidence. When a girl has told all her friends that she is going to be married, and has already expended a considerable portion of the sum of money allowed for her wedding garments, she cannot sink back into the simple position of an unengaged young woman without pangs of conscience and qualms of remorse. Paradise Row knew that her young man was to be dismissed from his office, and condoled with her frequently and most unpleasantly. Mrs. Duffer was so unbearable in the matter that the two ladies had

quarrelled dreadfully. Clara from the first moment
of her engagement with Crocker had been proud of
the second string to her bow, and now perceived that
the time had come in which it might be conveniently
used.

It was near eleven when Tribbledale knocked at the
door of No. 10, but nevertheless Clara was up, as was
also the servant girl, who opened the door for the sake
of discretion. " Oh, Daniel, what hours you do keep ! "
said Clara, when the young gentleman was shown into
the parlour. " What on earth brings you here at such
a time as this ? "

Tribbledale was never slow to declare that he was
brought thither by the overwhelming ardour of his
passion. His love for Clara was so old a story, and had
been told so often, that the repeating of it required
no circumlocution. Had he chanced to meet her in
the High Street on a Sunday morning, he would have
begun with it at once. " Clara," he said, " will you
have me ? I know that that other scoundrel is a
ruined man."

" Oh, Daniel, you shouldn't hit those as are down."

" Hasn't he been hitting me all the time that I was
down ? Hasn't he triumphed ? Haven't you been in
his arms ? "

" Laws ; no."

" And wasn't that hitting me when I was down, do
you think ? "

"It never did you any harm."

"Oh, Clara;—if you knew the nature of my love you'd understand the harm. Every time he has pressed your lips I have heard it, though I was in King's Head Court all the time."

"That must be a crammer, Daniel."

"I did;—not with the ears of my head, but with the fibres of my breast."

"Oh;—ah. But, Daniel, you and Sam used to be such friends at the first go off."

"Go off of what?"

"When he first took to coming after me. You remember the tea-party, when Marion Fay was here."

"I tried it on just then;—I did. I thought that, maybe, I might come not to care about it so much."

"I'm sure you acted it very well."

"And I thought that perhaps it might be the best way of touching that cold heart of yours."

"Cold! I don't know as my heart is colder than anybody else's heart."

"Would that you would make it warm once more for me."

"Poor Sam!" said Clara, putting her handkerchief up to her eyes.

"Why is he any poorer than me? I was first. At any rate I was before him."

"I don't know anything about firsts or lasts," said

Clara, as the ghosts of various Banquos flitted before her eyes.

" And as for him, what right has he to think of any girl ? He's a poor mean creature, without the means of getting so much as a bed for a wife to lie on. He used to talk so proud of Her Majesty's Civil Service. Her Majesty's Civil Service has sent him away packing."

" Not yet, Daniel."

" They have. I've made it my business to find out, and Sir Boreas Bodkin has written the order to-day. ' Dismissal—B. B.' I know those who have seen the very words written in the punishment book of the Post Office."

" Poor Sam ! "

" Destroying papers of the utmost importance about Her Majesty's Mail Service ! What else was he to expect ? And now he's penniless."

" A hundred and twenty isn't so very much, Daniel."

" Mr. Fay was saying only the other day that if I was married and settled they'd make it better for me."

" You're too fond of The Duchess, Daniel."

" No, Clara — no; I deny that. You ask Mrs. Grimley why it is I come to The Duchess so often. It isn't for anything that I take there."

" Oh; I didn't know. Young men when they frequent those places generally do take something."

" If I had a little home of my own with the girl I love on the other side of the fireplace, and perhaps a baby in her arms——" Tribbledale as he said this looked at her with all his eyes.

"Laws, Daniel; what things you do say!"

"I should never go then to any Duchess, or any Marquess of Granby, or to any Angel." These were public-houses so named, all standing thick together in the neighbourhood of Paradise Row. "I should not want to go anywhere then,—except where that young woman and that baby were to be found."

"Daniel, you was always fine at poetry."

"Try me, if it isn't real prose. The proof of the pudding's in the eating. You come and try." By this time Clara was in his arms, and the re-engagement was as good as made. Crocker was no doubt dismissed,—or if not dismissed had shown himself to be unworthy. What could be expected of a husband who could tear up a bundle of Her Majesty's Mail papers? And then Daniel Tribbledale had exhibited a romantic constancy which certainly deserved to be rewarded. Clara understood that the gin-and-water had been consumed night after night for her sake. And there were the lodgings and the clock and the harmonium ready for the occasion. "I suppose it had better be so, Daniel, as you wish it so much."

"Wish it! I have always wished it. I wouldn't change places now with Mr. Pogson himself."

"He married his third wife three years ago!"

"I mean in regard to the whole box and dice of it.

I'd rather have my Clara with £120, than be Pogson
and Littlebird with all the profits." This gratifying
assurance was rewarded, and then, considerably after
midnight, the triumphant lover took his leave.

Early on the following afternoon Crocker was in
Paradise Row. He had been again with Lord Hampstead, and had succeeded in worming out of the good-
natured nobleman something of the information contained in the letter from Sir Boreas. The matter was
to be left to the Postmaster-General. Now there was
an idea in the office that when a case was left to his
lordship, his lordship never proceeded to extremities.
Kings are bound to pardon if they allow themselves
to be personally concerned as to punishment. There
was something of the same feeling in regard to official
discipline. As a fact the letter from Sir Boreas had
been altogether false. He had known, poor man, that
he must at last take the duty of deciding upon himself,
and had used the name of the great chief simply as a
mode of escape for the moment. But Crocker had felt
that the mere statement indicated pardon. The very
delay indicated pardon. Relying upon these indications
he went to Paradise Row, dressed in his best frock coat,
with gloves in his hand, to declare to his love that the
lodgings need not be abandoned, and that the clock
and harmonium might be preserved.

"But you've been dismissed !" said Clara.

"Never ! never !"

"It has been written in the book! 'Dismissal—B. B.!' I know the eyes that have seen it."

"That's not the way they do it at all," said Crocker, who was altogether confused.

"It has been written in the book, Sam; and I know that they never go back from that."

"Who wrote it? Nothing has been written. There isn't a book;—not at least like that. Tribbledale has invented it."

"Oh, Sam, why did you tear those papers;—Her Majesty's Mail papers? What else was there to expect? 'Dismissal—B. B.;' Why did you do it,—and you engaged to a young woman? No;—don't come nigh to me. How is a young woman to go and get herself married to a young man, and he with nothing to support her? It isn't to be thought of. When I heard those words, 'Dismissal—B. B.,' I thought my very heart would sink within me."

"It's nothing of the kind," said Crocker.

"What's nothing of the kind?"

"I ain't dismissed at all."

"Oh, Sam; how dare you?"

"I tell you I ain't. He's written a letter to Lord Hampstead, who has always been my friend. Hampstead wasn't going to see me treated after that fashion. Hampstead wrote, and then Æolus wrote,—that's Sir Boreas,—and I've seen the letter,—that is, Hampstead told me what there is in it; and I ain't to be dismissed

at all. When I heard the good news the first thing I
did was to come as fast as my legs would carry me, and
tell the girl of my heart."

Clara did not quite believe him; but then neither
had she quite believed Tribbledale, when he had announced the dismissal with the terrible corroboration
of the great man's initials. But the crime committed
seemed to her to be so great that she could not understand that Crocker should be allowed to remain after
the perpetration of it. Crocker's salary was £150;
and, balancing the two young men together as she had
often done, though she liked the poetry of Tribbledale,
she did on the whole prefer the swagger and audacity
of Crocker. Her Majesty's Civil Service, too, had its
charms for her. The Post Office was altogether superior
to Pogson and Littlebird's. Pogson and Littlebird's
hours were 9 to 5. Those of Her Majesty's Service
were much more genteel;—10 namely to 4. But what
might not a man do who had shown the nature of his
disposition by tearing up official papers? And then,
though the accidents of the occasion had enveloped
her in difficulties on both sides, it seemed to her that,
at the present moment, the lesser difficulties would be
encountered by adhering to Tribbledale. She could
excuse herself with Crocker. Paradise Row had already
declared that the match with Crocker must be broken
off. Crocker had indeed been told that the match was
to be broken off. When Tribbledale had come to her

overnight she had felt herself to be a free woman. When she had given way to the voice of the charmer, when she had sunk into his arms, softened by that domestic picture which he had painted, no pricks of conscience had disturbed her happiness. Whether the "Dismissal—B. B." had or had not yet been written, it was sure to come. She was as free to "wed another" as was Venice when her Doge was deposed. She could throw herself back upon the iniquity of the torn papers were Crocker to complain. But should she now return to her Crocker, how could she excuse herself with Tribble- dale? "It is all over between you and me, Sam," she said with her handkerchief up to her eyes.

"All over! Why should it be all over?"

"You was told it was all over."

"That was when all the Row said that I was to be dismissed. There was something in it,——then; though, perhaps, a girl might have waited till a fellow had got up upon his legs again."

"Waiting ain't so pleasant, Mr. Crocker, when a girl has to look after herself."

"But I ain't dismissed at all, and there needn't be any waiting. I thought that you would be suffering as well as me, and so I came right away to you, all at once."

"So I have suffered, Sam. No one knows what I have suffered."

"But it'll come all right now?" Clara shook her

head. "You don't mean that Tribbledale's been and talked you over already?"

"I knew Mr. Tribbledale before ever I saw you, Sam."

"How often have I heard you call him a poor mean skunk?"

"Never, Crocker; never. Such a word never passed my lips."

"Something very like it then."

"I may have said he wanted sperrit. I may have said so, though I disremember it. But if I did,—what of that?"

"You despised him."

"No, Crocker. What I despise is a man as goes and tears up Her Majesty's Mail papers. Tribbledale never tore up anything at Pogson and Littlebird's,— except what was to be tore. Tribbledale was never turned out for nigh a fortnight, so that he couldn't go and show his face in King's Head Court. Tribbledale never made hisself hated by everybody." That unknown abominable word which Crocker had put into her mouth had roused all the woman within her, so that she was enabled to fight her battle with a courage which would not have come to her aid had he been more prudent.

"Who hates me?"

"Mr. Jerningham does, and Roden, and Sir Boreas, and Bobbin." She had learned all their names. "How

can they help hating a man that tears up the mail
papers! And I hate you."

"Clara!"

"I do. What business had you to say I used that
nasty word? I never do use them words. I wouldn't
even so much as look at a man who'd demean himself
to put such words as them into my mouth. So I tell
you what it is, Mr. Crocker; you may just go away. I
am going to become Daniel Tribbledale's wife, and it
isn't becoming in you to stand here talking to a young
woman that is engaged to another young man."

"And this is to be the end of it?"

"If you please, Mr. Crocker."

"Well!"

"If ever you feel inclined to speak your mind to
another young woman, and you carry it as far as we
did, and you wishes to hold on to her, don't you go and
tear Her Majesty's Mail papers. And when she tells
you a bit of her mind, as I did just now, don't you go
and put nasty words into her mouth. Now, if you
please, you may just as well send over that clock and
that harmonium to Daniel Tribbledale, Esq., King's
Head Court, Great Broad Street." So saying she left
him, and congratulated herself on having terminated
the interview without much unpleasantness.

Crocker, as he shook the dust off his feet upon
leaving Paradise Row, began to ask himself whether he
might not upon the whole congratulate himself as to

the end to which that piece of business had been
brought. When he had first resolved to offer his hand
to the young lady, he had certainly imagined that that
hand would not be empty. Clara was no doubt " a fine
girl," but not quite so young as she was once. And she
had a temper of her own. Matrimony, too, was often
followed by many troubles. Paradise Row would no
doubt utter jeers, but he need not go there to hear
them. He was not quite sure but that the tearing of
the papers would in the long run be beneficial to him.

CHAPTER XVI.

PEGWELL BAY.

JULY had come and nearly gone before Lord Hampstead again saw Marion Fay. He had promised not
to go to Pegwell Bay,—hardly understanding why such
a promise had been exacted from him, but still acceding
to it when it had been suggested to him by Mrs. Roden,
at the request, as she said, of the Quaker. It was
understood that Marion would soon return to Holloway,
and that on that account the serenity of Pegwell Bay
need not be disturbed by the coming of so great a
man as Lord Hampstead. Hampstead had of course
ridiculed the reason, but had complied with the
request,—with the promise, however, that Marion
should return early in the summer. But the summer
weeks had passed by, and Marion did not return.

Letters passed between them daily in which Marion
attempted always to be cheerful. Though she had as
yet invented no familiar name for her noble lover, yet
she had grown into familiarity with him, and was no
longer afraid of his nobility. " You oughtn't to stay

there," she said, "wasting your life and doing nothing, because of a sick girl. You've got your yacht, and are letting all the summer weather go by." In answer to this he wrote to her, saying that he had sold his yacht. "Could you have gone with me, I would have kept it," he wrote. "Would you go with me I would have another ready for you, before you would be ready. I will make no assurance as to my future life. I cannot even guess what may become of me. It may be that I shall come to live on board some ship so that I may be all alone. But with my heart as it is now I cannot bear the references which others make to me about empty pleasures." At the same time he sold his horses, but he said nothing to her as to that.

Gradually he did acknowledge to himself that it was her doom to die early,—almost acknowledged to himself that she was dying. Nevertheless he still thought that it would have been fit that they should be married. "If I knew that she were my own even on her deathbed," he once said to Mrs. Roden, "there would be a comfort to me in it." He was so eager in this that Mrs. Roden was almost convinced. The Quaker was willing that it should be so,—but willing also that it should not be so. He would not even try to persuade his girl as to anything. It was his doom to see her go, and he, having realized that, could not bring himself to use a word in opposition to her word. But Marion herself was sternly determined against the suggestion. It was

unfitting, she said, and would be wicked. It was not
the meaning of marriage. She could not bring herself
to disturb the last thoughts of her life, not only by the
empty assumption of a grand name, but by the sounding
of that name in her ears from the eager lips of those
around her. "I will be your love to the.end," she said,
"your own Marion. But I will not be made a Countess,
only in order that a vain name may be carved over my
grave." "God has provided a bitter cup for your lips,
my love," she wrote again, "in having put it into your
head to love one whom you must lose so soon. And
mine is bitter because yours is bitter. But we cannot
rid ourselves of the bitterness by pretences. Would
it make your heart light to see me dressed up for a
bridal ceremony, knowing, as you would know, that it
was all for nothing ? My lord, my love, let us take it
as God has provided it. It is only because you grieve
that I grieve;—for you and my poor father. If you
could only bring yourself to be reconciled, then it would
be so much to me to have had you to love me in my
last moments,—to love me and to be loved."

He could not but accept her decision. Her father
and Mrs. Roden accepted it, and he was forced to do
so also. He acknowledged to himself now that there
was no appeal from it. Her very weakness gave her
a strength which dominated him. There was an end
of all his arguments and his strong phrases. He was
aware that they had been of no service to him,—that

her soft words had been stronger than all his reasonings. But not on that account did he cease to wish that it might be as he had once wished, since he had first acknowledged to himself his love. "Of course I will not drive her," he said to Mrs. Roden, when that lady urged upon him the propriety of abstaining from a renewal of his request. "Had I any power of driving her, as you say, I would not do so. I think it would be better. That is all. Of course it must be as she shall decide."

"It would be a comfort to her to think that you and she thought alike about all things," said Mrs. Roden.

"There are points on which I cannot alter my convictions even for her comfort," he answered. "She bids me love some other woman. Can I comfort her by doing that? She bids me seek another wife. Can I do that;—or say that I will do it at some future time? It would comfort her to know that I have no wound,—that I am not lame and sick and sore and weary. It would comfort her to know that my heart is not broken. How am I to do that for her?"

"No;"—said Mrs. Roden—"no."

"There is no comfort. Her imagination paints for her some future bliss, which shall not be so far away as to be made dim by distance,—in enjoying which we two shall be together, as we are here, with our hands free to grasp each other, and our lips free to kiss;—a heaven, but still a heaven of this world, in which we can

hang upon each other's necks and be warm to each
other's hearts. That is to be, to her, the reward of her
innocence, and in the ecstacy of her faith she believes
in it, as though it were here. I do think,—I do think,
—that if I told her that it should be so, that I trusted
to renew my gaze upon her beauty after a few short
years, then she would be happy entirely. It would be
for an eternity, and without the fear of separation."

"Then why not profess as she does?"

"A lie? As I know her truth when she tells me her
creed, so would she know my falsehood, and the lie
would be vain."

"Is there then to be no future world, Lord Hampstead?"

"Who has said so? Certainly not I. I cannot
conceive that I shall perish altogether. I do not think
that if, while I am here, I can tame the selfishness of
self, I shall reach a step upwards in that world which
shall come next after this. As to happiness, I do not
venture to think much of it. If I can only be somewhat nobler,—somewhat more like the Christ whom we
worship,—that will be enough without happiness. If
there be truth in this story, He was not happy. Why
should I look for happiness,—unless it be when the
struggle of many worlds shall have altogether purified
my spirit? But thinking like that,—believing like
that,—how can I enter into the sweet Epicurean
Paradise which that child has prepared for herself?"

" Is it no better than that ? "

" What can be better, what can be purer,—if only it
be true ? And though it be false to me, it may be true
to her. It is for my sake that she dreams of her
Paradise,—that my wounds may be made whole, that
my heart may be cured. Christ's lesson has been so
learned by her that no further learning seems necessary.
I fancy sometimes that I can see the platform raised
just one step above the ground on which I stand,—and
look into the higher world to which I am ascending.
It may be that it is given to her to look up the one
rung of the ladder by mounting which she shall find
herself enveloped in the full glory of perfection."

In conversations such as these Mrs. Roden was confounded by the depth of the man's love. It became
impossible to bid him not be of a broken heart, or even
to allude to those fresh hopes which Time would bring.
He spoke to her often of his future life, always speaking of a life from which Marion would have been withdrawn by death, and did so with a cold, passionless
assurance which showed her that he had almost resolved
as to the future. He would see all lands that were to
be seen, and converse with all people. The social
condition of God's creatures at large should be his
study. The task would be endless, and, as he said, an
endless task hardly admits of absolute misery. " If I
die there will be an end of it. If I live till old age
shall have made me powerless to carry on my work,

time will then probably have done something to dim the feeling." " I think," he said again;—" I feel that could I but remember her as my wife——"

" It is impossible," said Mrs. Roden.

" But if it were so! It would be no more than a thin threadbare cloak over a woman's shivering shoulders. It is not much against the cold; but it would be very cruel to take that little from her." She looked at him with her eyes flooded with tears, but she could only shake her head in sign that it was impossible.

At last, just at the end of July, there came a request that he would go down to Pegwell Bay. "It is so long since we have seen each other," she wrote, " and, perhaps, it is better that you should come than that I should go. The doctor is fidgety, and says so. But my darling will be good to me;—will he not? When I have seen a tear in your eyes it has gone near to crush me. That a woman, or even a man, should weep at some unexpected tidings of woe is natural. But who cries for spilt milk? Tell me that God's hand, though it be heavy to you, shall be borne with reverence and obedience and love."

He did not tell her this, but he resolved that if possible she should see no tears. As for that cheerfulness, that reconciliation to his fate which she desired, he knew it to be impossible. He almost brought himself to believe as he travelled down to Pegwell Bay that it would be better that they should not meet. To

thank the Lord for all His mercies was in her mind.
To complain with all the bitterness of his heart of the
cruelty with which he was treated was in his. He had
told Mrs. Roden that according to his creed there would
be a better world to come for him if he could succeed
in taming the selfishness of self. But he told himself
now that the struggle to do so had hitherto been vain.
There had been but the one thing which had ever been
to him supremely desirable. He had gone through the
years of his early life forming some Utopian ideas,—
dreaming of some perfection in politics, in philanthropy,
in social reform, and the like,—something by devoting
himself to which he could make his life a joy to himself.
Then this girl had come across him, and there had
suddenly sprung up within him a love so strong that all
these other things faded into littlenesses. They should
not be discarded. Work would be wanted for his life,
and for hers. But here he had found the true salt by
which all his work would be vivified and preserved and
made holy and happy and glorious. There had come a
something to him that was all that he wanted it to be.
And now the something was fading from him,—was
already all but gone. In such a state how should he
tame the selfishness of self? He abandoned the
attempt, and told himself that difficulties had been
prepared for him greater than any of which he had
dreamed when he had hoped that that taming might be
within his power. He could not even spare her in his

selfishness.   He declared to himself that it was so, and
almost owned that it would be better that he should
not go to her.

"Yes," she said, when he sat down beside her on her
sofa, at an open window looking out on the little bay,
"put your hand on mine, dear, and leave it there.   To
have you with me, to feel the little breeze, and to see
you and to touch you is absolute happiness."

"Why did you so often tell me not to come ? "

"Ah, why ?   But I know why it was, my lord."
There was something half of tenderness, half pleasantry
in the mode of address, and now he had ceased to rebel
against it.

"Why should I not come if it be a joy to you ? "

"You must not be angry now."

"Certainly not angry."

"We have got through all that,—you and I have
for ourselves ;—but there is a sort of unseemliness
in your coming down here to see a poor Quaker's
daughter."

"Marion ! "

"But there is.   We had got through all that in
Paradise Row.   Paradise Row had become used to you,
and I could bear it.   But here—— They will all be
sure to know who you are."

"Who cares ? "

"That Marion Fay should have a lover would of
itself make a stir in this little place ;—but that she

should have a lord for her lover! One doesn't want to
be looked at as a miracle."

"The follies of others should not ruffle you and me."

"That's very well, dear;—but what if one is ruffled?
But I won't be ruffled, and you shall come. When I
thought that I should go again to our own house, then
I thought we might perhaps dispense with the ruffling;
—that was all."

There was a something in these words which he
could not stand,—which he could not bear and repress
that tear which, as she had said, would go near to
crush her if she saw it. Had she not plainly intimated
her conviction that she would never again return to
her old home? Here, here in this very spot, the doom
was to come, and to come quickly. He got up and
walked across the room, and stood a little behind her,
where she could not see his face.

"Do not leave me," she said. "I told you to stay
and let your hand rest on mine." Then he returned,
and laying his hand once again upon her lap turned his
face away from her. "Bear it," she said. "Bear it."
His hand quivered where it lay as he shook his head.
"Call upon your courage and bear it."

"I cannot bear it," he said, rising suddenly from his
chair, and hurrying out of the room. He went out of
the room and from the house, on to the little terrace
which ran in front of the sea. But his escape was of
no use to him; he could not leave her. He had come

out without his hat, and he could not stand there in
the sun to be stared at. "I am a coward," he said,
going back to her and resuming his chair. "I own it.
Let there be no more said about it. When a trouble
comes to me, it conquers me. Little troubles I think
I could bear. If it had been all else in all the world,—
if it had been my life before my life was your life, I
think that no one would have seen me blench. But
now I find that when I am really tried, I fail."

"It is in God's hands, dearest."

"Yes;—it is in God's hands. There is some power,
no doubt, that makes you strong in spirit, but frail in
body; while I am strong to live but weak of heart.
But how will that help me?"

"Oh, Lord Hampstead, I do so wish you had never
seen me."

"You should not say that, Marion; you shall not
think it. I am ungrateful; because, were it given me
to have it all back again, I would not sell what I have
had of you, though the possession has been so limited,
for all other imaginable treasures. I will bear it. Oh,
my love, I will bear it. Do not say again that you
wish you had not seen me."

"For myself, dear,—for myself——"

"Do not say it for me. I will struggle to make a
joy of it, a joy in some degree, though my heart bleeds
at the widowhood that is coming on it. I will build up
for myself a memory in which there shall be much to

satisfy me. I shall have been loved by her to have
possessed whose love has been and shall be a glory
to me."

"Loved indeed, my darling."

"Though there might have been such a heaven of
joy, even that shall be counted as much. It shall be
to me during my future life as though when wandering
through the green fields in some long-past day, I had
met a bright angel from another world; and the angel
had stopped to speak to me, and had surrounded me
with her glorious wings, and had given me of her
heavenly light, and had spoken to me with the music
of the spheres, and I had thought that she would stay
with me for ever. But there had come a noise of the
drums and a sound of the trumpets, and she had flown
away from me up to her own abode. To have been so
favoured, though it had been but for an hour, should
suffice for a man's life. I will bear it, though it be in
solitude."

"No, darling; not in solitude."

"It will be best so for me. The light and the music
and the azure of the wings will so remain with me the
purer and the brighter. Oh,—if it had been! But I
will bear it. No ear shall again hear a sound of complaint. Not yours even, my darling, my own, mine for
so short a time, but yet my very own for ever and ever."
Then he fell on his knees beside her, and hid his face
in her dress, while the fingers of both her hands rambled

through his hair. "You are going," he said, when he rose up to his feet, "you are going whither I cannot go."

"You will come; you will come to me."

"You are going now, now soon, and I doubt not that you are going to joys inexpressible. I cannot go till some chance may take me. If it be given to you in that further world to see those and to think of those whom you have left below, then, if my heart be true to your heart, keep your heart true to mine. If I can fancy that, if I can believe that it is so, then shall I have that angel with me, and though my eyes may not see the tints, my ears will hear the music;—and though the glory be not palpable as is the light of heaven, there will be an inner glory in which my soul will be sanctified." After that there were not many words spoken between them, though he remained there till he was disturbed by the Quaker's coming. Part of the time she slept with her hand in his, and when awake she was contented to feel his touch as he folded the scarf close round her neck and straightened the shawl which lay across her feet, and now and again stroked her hair and put it back behind her ears as it strayed upon her forehead. Ever and again she would murmur a word or two of love as she revelled in the perception of his solicitude. What was there for her to regret, for her to whom was given the luxury of such love? Was not a month of it more than a whole life without it? Then, when the father came, Hampstead took his leave.

As he kissed her lips, something seemed to tell him
that it would be for the last time. It was not good,
the Quaker had said, that she should be disturbed.
Yes; he could come again; but not quite yet.

At the very moment when the Quaker so spoke she
was pressing her lips to his. "God keep you and take
you, my darling," she whispered to him, "and bring
you to me in heaven." She noticed not at all at the
moment the warm tears that were running on to her
own face; nor did the Quaker seem to notice it when
Lord Hampstead left the house without saying to him
a word of farewell.

CHAPTER XVII.

LADY AMALDINA'S WEDDING.

THE time came round for Lady Amaldina's marriage, than which nothing more august, nothing more aristocratic, nothing more truly savouring of the hymeneal altar, had ever been known or was ever to be known in the neighbourhood of Hanover Square. For it was at last decided that the marriage should take place in London before any of the aristocratic assistants at the ceremony should have been whirled away into autumnal spaces. Lord Llwddythlw himself knew but very little about it,—except this, that nothing would induce him so to hurry on the ceremony as to interfere with his Parliamentary duties. A day in August had been mentioned in special reference to Parliament. He was willing to abide by that, or to go to the sacrifice at any earlier day of which Parliament would admit. Parliament was to sit for the last time on Wednesday, 12th August, and the marriage was fixed for the 13th. Lady Amaldina had prayed for the concession of a week. Readers will not imagine that she based her prayers on

the impatience of love. Nor could a week be of much
significance in reference to that protracted and dangerous
delay to which the match had certainly been subjected.
But the bevy might escape. How were twenty young
ladies to be kept together in the month of August
when all the young men were rushing off to Scotland?
Others were not wedded to their duties as was Lord
Llwddythlw. Lady Amaldina knew well how completely Parliament became a mere affair of Govern-
mental necessities during the first weeks of August.
" I should have thought that just on this one occasion
you might have managed it," she said to him, trying to
mingle a tone of love with the sarcasm which at such a
crisis was natural to her. He simply reminded her of
the promise which he had made to her in the spring.
He thought it best not to break through arrangements
which had been fixed. When she told him of one very
slippery member of the bevy, — slippery, not as to
character, but in reference to the movements of her
family, — he suggested that no one would know the
difference if only nineteen were to be clustered round
the bride's train. "Don't you know that they must
be in pairs?" "Will not nine pairs suffice?" he
asked. "And thus make one of them an enemy for
ever by telling her that I wish to dispense with her
services !"

But it was of no use. "Dispense with them altogether," he said, looking her full in the face. "The

twenty will not quarrel with you. My object is to
marry you, and I don't care twopence for the bridesmaids." There was something so near to a compliment
in this, that she was obliged to accept it. And she
had, too, begun to perceive that Lord Llwddythlw was
a man not easily made to change his mind. She was
quite prepared for this in reference to her future life.
A woman, she thought, might be saved much trouble
by having a husband whom she was bound to obey.
But in this matter of her marriage ceremony,—this last
affair in which she might be presumed to act as a free
woman,—she did think it hard that she might not be
allowed to have her own way. The bridegroom, however, was firm. If Thursday, the 13th, did not suit her,
he would be quite ready on Thursday, the 20th.
"There wouldn't be one of them left in London," said
Lady Amaldina. "What on earth do you think that
they are to do with themselves?"

But all the bevy were true to her. Lady Amelia
Beaudesert was a difficulty. Her mother insisted on
going to a far-away Bavarian lake on which she had
a villa;—but Lady Amelia at the last moment surrendered the villa rather than break up the bevy, and
consented to remain with a grumpy old aunt in Essex
till an opportunity should offer. It may be presumed,
therefore, that it was taken to be a great thing to be
one of the bevy. It is, no doubt, a pleasant thing for a
girl to have it asserted in all the newspapers that she

is, by acknowledgment, one of the twenty most beautiful unmarried ladies in Great Britain.

Lady Frances was of course one of the bevy. But there was a member of the family,—a connection rather,—whom no eloquence could induce to show himself either in the church or at the breakfast. This was Lord Hampstead. His sister came to him and assured him that he ought to be there. "Sorrows," she said, "that have declared themselves before the world are held as sufficient excuse; but a man should not be hindered from his duties by secret grief."

"I make no secret of it. I do not talk about my private affairs. I do not send a town-crier to Charing Cross to tell the passers-by that I am in trouble. But I care not whether men know or not that I am unfitted for joining in such festivities. My presence is not wanted for their marriage."

"It will be odd."

"Let it be odd. I most certainly shall not be there." But he remembered the occasion, and showed that he did so by sending to the bride the handsomest of all the gems which graced her exhibition of presents, short of the tremendous set of diamonds which had come from the Duke of Merioneth.

This collection was supposed to be the most gorgeous thing that had ever as yet been arranged in London. It would certainly not be too much to say that the wealth of precious toys brought together would, if sold at its cost price, have made an ample fortune for a young newly-married couple. The families were noble and wealthy, and the richness of the wedding presents was natural. It might perhaps have been better had not the value of the whole been stated in one of the newspapers of the day. Who was responsible for the valuation was never known, but it seemed to indicate that the costliness of the gifts was more thought of than the affection of the givers; and it was undoubtedly true that, in high circles and among the clubs, the cost of the collection was much discussed. The diamonds were known to a stone, and Hampstead's rubies were spoken of almost as freely as though they were being exhibited in public. Lord Llwddythlw when he heard of all this muttered to his maiden sister a wish that a gnome would come in the night and run away with everything. He felt himself degraded by the publicity given to his future wife's ornaments. But the gnome did not come, and the young men from Messrs. Bijou and Carcanet were allowed to arrange the tables and shelves for the exhibition.

The breakfast was to take place at the Foreign Office, at which the bride's father was for the time being the chief occupant. Lord Persiflage had not at first been willing that it should be so, thinking that his own more modest house might suffice for the marriage of his own daughter. But grander counsels had been allowed to prevail. With whom the idea first arose Lord Persiflage never knew. It might probably have been with some of the bevy, who had felt that an ordinary drawing-room would hardly suffice for so magnificent an array of toilets. Perhaps the thought had first occurred to Messrs. Bijou and Carcanet, who had foreseen the glory of spreading out all that wealth in the magnificent saloon intended for the welcoming of ambassadors. But it travelled from Lady Amaldina to her mother, and was passed on from Lady Persiflage to her husband. "Of course the Ambassadors will all be there," the Countess had said, "and, therefore, it will be a public occasion." "I wish we could be married at Llanfihangel," Lord Llwddythlw said to his bride. Now Llanfihangel church was a very small edifice, with a thatched roof, among the mountains in North Wales, with which Lady Amaldina had been made acquainted when visiting the Duchess, her future mother-in-law. But Llwddythlw was not to have his way in everything, and the preparations at the Foreign Office were continued.

The beautifully embossed invitations were sent about among a large circle of noble and aristocratic friends. All the Ambassadors and all the Ministers, with all their wives and daughters, were, of course, asked. As the breakfast was to be given in the great Banqueting Hall at the Foreign Office it was necessary that the guests should be many. It is sometimes well in a matter of festivals to be saved from extravagance by

the modest size of one's rooms. Lord Persiflage told
his wife that his daughter's marriage would ruin him.
In answer to this she reminded him that Llwddythlw
had asked for no fortune. Lord Llwddythlw was one
of those men who prefer giving to taking. He had a
feeling that a husband should supply all that was
wanted, and that a wife should owe everything to the
man she marries. The feeling is uncommon just at
present,—except with the millions who neither have
nor expect other money than what they earn. If you
are told that the daughter of an old man who has
earned his own bread is about to marry a young man
in the same condition of life, it is spoken of as a
misfortune. But Lord Llwddythlw was old-fashioned,
and had the means of acting in accordance with his
prejudices. Let the marriage be ever so gorgeous, it
would not cost the dowry which an Earl's daughter
might have expected. That was the argument used
by Lady Persiflage, and it seemed to have been
effectual.

As the day drew near it was observed that the
bridegroom became more sombre and silent even than
usual. He never left the House of Commons as long
as it was open to him as a refuge. His Saturdays and
his Sundays and his Wednesdays he filled up with
work so various and unceasing that there was no time
left for those pretty little attentions which a girl about
to be married naturally expects. He did call, perhaps,

every other day at his bride's house, but never remained
there above two minutes. "I am afraid he is not
happy," the Countess said to her daughter.

"Oh, yes, mamma, he is."

"Then why does he go on like that?"

"Oh, mamma, you do not know him."

"Do you?"

"I think so. My belief is that there isn't a man in
London so anxious to be married as Llwddythlw."

"I am glad of that."

"He has lost so much time that he knows it ought
to be got through and done with without further delay.
If he could only go to sleep and wake up a married
man of three months' standing, he would be quite
happy. If it could be administered under chloroform
it would be so much better! It is the doing of the
thing, and the being talked about and looked at, that
is so odious to him."

"Then why not have had it done quietly, my dear?"

"Because there are follies, mamma, to which a
woman should never give way. I will not have myself
made humdrum. If I had been going to marry a
handsome young man so as to have a spice of romance
out of it all, I would have cared nothing about the
bridesmaids and the presents. The man then would
have stood for everything. Llwddythlw is not young,
and is not handsome."

"But he is thoroughly noble."

"Quite so. He's as good as gold. He will always be somebody in people's eyes because he's great and grand and trustworthy all round. But I want to be somebody in people's eyes, too, mamma. I'm all very well to look at, but nothing particular. I'm papa's daughter, which is something,—but not enough. I mean to begin and be magnificent. He understands it all, and I don't think he'll oppose me when once this exhibition day is over. I've thought all about it, and I think that I know what I'm doing."

At any rate, she had her way, and thoroughly enjoyed the task she had on hand. When she had talked of a possible romance with a handsome young lover she had not quite known herself. She might have made the attempt, but it would have been a failure. She could fall in love with a Master of Ravenswood in a novel, but would have given herself by preference,— after due consideration,—to the richer, though less poetical, suitor. Of good sterling gifts she did know the value, and was therefore contented with her lot. But this business of being married, with all the most extravagant appurtenances of the hymeneal altar, was to her taste.

That picture in one of the illustrated papers which professed to give the hymeneal altar at St. George's, with the Bishop and the Dean and two Queen's Chaplains officiating, and the bride and the bridegroom in all their glory, with a Royal Duke and a Royal

Duchess looking on, with all the Stars and all the Garters from our own and other Courts, and especially with the bevy of twenty, standing in ten distinct pairs, and each from a portrait, was manifestly a work of the imagination. I was there, and to tell the truth, it was rather a huddled matter. The spaces did not seem to admit of majestic grouping, and as three of these chief personages had the gout, the sticks of these lame gentlemen were to my eyes very conspicuous. The bevy had not room enough, and the ladies in the crush seemed to feel the intense heat. Something had made the Bishop cross. I am told that Lady Amaldina had determined not to be hurried, while the Bishop was due at an afternoon meeting at three. The artist, in creating the special work of art, had soared boldly into the ideal. In depicting the buffet of presents and the bridal feast, he may probably have been more accurate. I was not myself present. The youthful appearance of the bridegroom as he rose to make his speech may probably be attributed to a poetic license, permissible, nay laudable, nay necessary on such an occasion. The buffet of presents no doubt was all there; though it may be doubted whether the contributions from Royalty were in truth so conspicuous as they were made to appear. There were speeches spoken by two or three Foreign Ministers, and one by the bride's father. But the speech which has created most remark was from the bridegroom. "I hope we may be as happy as your kind wishes would have us," said he;—and then he sat down. It was declared afterwards that these were the only words which passed his lips on the occasion. To those who congratulated him he merely gave his hand and bowed, and yet he looked to be neither fluttered nor ill at ease. We know how a brave man will sit and have his tooth taken out, without a sign of pain on his brow,—trusting to the relief which is to come to him. So it was with Lord Llwddythlw. It might, perhaps, have saved pain if, as Lady Amaldina had said, chloroform could have been used.

"Well, my dear, it is done at last," Lady Persiflage said to her daughter, when the bride was taken into some chamber for the readjustment of her dress.

"Yes, mamma, it is done now."

"And are you happy?"

"Certainly I am. I have got what I wanted."

"And you can love him?" Coming from Lady Persiflage this did seem to be romantic; but she had been stirred up to some serious thoughts as she remembered that she was now surrendering to a husband the girl whom she had made, whom she had tutored, whom she had prepared either for the good or for the evil performance of the duties of life.

"Oh, yes, mamma," said Lady Amaldina. It is so often the case that the pupils are able to exceed the teaching of their tutors! It was so in this case. The mother, as she saw her girl given up to a silent middle-

aged unattractive man, had her misgivings; but not so
the daughter herself. She had looked at it all round,
and had resolved that she could do her duty—under
certain stipulations which she thought would be accorded
to her. "He has more to say for himself than you
think;—only he won't trouble himself to make asser-
tions. And if he is not very much in love, he likes
me better than anybody else, which goes a long way."
Her mother blessed her, and led her away into a room
where she joined her husband in order that she might
be then taken down to the carriage.

The bride herself had not quite understood what was
to take place, and was surprised to find herself quite
alone for a moment with her husband. "My wife," he
said; "now kiss me."

She ran into his arms and put up her face to him.
"I thought you were going to forget that," she said, as
he held her for a moment with his arm round her
waist.

"I could not dare," he said, "to handle all that
gorgeous drapery of lace. You were dressed up then
for an exhibition. You look now as my wife ought to
look."

"It had to be done, Llwddythlw."

"I make no complaint, dearest. I only say that I
like you better as you are, as a girl to kiss, and to
embrace, and to talk to, and to make my own." Then
she curtsied to him prettily, and kissed him again; and

after that they walked out arm-in-arm down to the carriage.

There were many carriages drawn up within the quadrangle of which the Foreign Office forms a part, but the carriage which was to take the bride and the bridegroom away was allowed a door to itself,—at any rate till such time as they should have been taken away. An effort had been made to keep the public out of the quadrangle; but as the duties of the four Secretaries of State could not be suspended, and as the great gates are supposed to make a public thoroughfare, this could only be done to a certain extent. The crowd, no doubt, was thicker out in Downing Street, but there were very many standing within the square. Among these there was one, beautifully arrayed in frock coat and yellow gloves, almost as though he himself was prepared for his own wedding. When Lord Llwddythlw brought Lady Amaldina out from the building and handed her into the carriage, and when the husband and wife had seated themselves, the well-dressed individual raised his hat from his head, and greeted them. "Long life and happiness to the bride of Castle Hautboy!" said he at the top of his voice. Lady Amaldina could not but see the man, and, recognizing him, she bowed.

It was Crocker,—the irrepressible Crocker. He had been also in the church. The narrator and he had managed to find standing room in a back pew under one of the galleries. Now would he be able to say with perfect truth that he had been at the wedding, and had received a parting salute from the bride; whom he had known through so many years of her infancy. He probably did believe that he was entitled to count the future Duchess of Merioneth among his intimate friends.

CHAPTER XVIII.

CROCKER'S TALE.

A THING difficult to get is the thing mostly prized, not the thing that is valuable. Two or three additional Kimberley mines found somewhere among the otherwise uninteresting plains of South Africa would bring down the price of diamonds amazingly. It could hardly have been the beauty, or the wit, or the accomplishments of Clara Demijohn which caused Mr. Tribbledale to triumph so loudly and with so genuine an exultation, telling all Broad Street of his success, when he had succeeded in winning the bride who had once promised herself to Crocker. Were it not that she had all but slipped through his fingers he would never surely have thought her to be worthy of such a pæan. Had she come to his first whistle he might have been contented enough,—as are other ordinary young men with their ordinary young women. He would probably have risen to no enthusiasm of passion. But as things had gone he was as another Paris who had torn a Helen from her Menelaus,—only in this case an honest Paris, with a

correct Helen, and from a Menelaus who had not as yet
made good his claim. But the subject was worthy of
another Iliad, to be followed by another Æneid. By
his bow and his spear he had torn her from the arms
of a usurping lover, and now made her all his own.
Another man would have fainted and abandoned the
contest, when rejected as he had been. But he had
continued the fight, even when lying low on the dust of
the arena. He had nailed his flag to the mast when
all his rigging had been cut away;—and at last he had
won the battle. Of course his Clara was doubly dear
to him, having been made his own after such difficulties
as these.

"I'm not one of those who easily give way in an
affair of the heart," he said to Mr. Littlebird, the junior
partner in the firm, when he told that gentleman of his
engagement.

"So I perceive, Mr. Tribbledale."

"When a man has set his affection on a young lady,
—that is, his real affection,—he ought to stick to it,—or
die." Mr. Littlebird, who was the happy father of three
or four married and marriageable daughters, opened his
eyes with surprise. The young men who had come
after his young ladies had been pressing enough, but
they had not died. "Or die!" repeated Tribbledale.
"It is what I should have done. Had she become Mrs.
Crocker, I should never again have been seen in the
Court,"—"the Court" was the little alley in which

Pogson and Littlebird's office was held,—"unless they had brought my dead body here to be identified." He was quite successful in his enthusiasm. Though Mr. Littlebird laughed when he told the story to Mr. Pogson, not the less did they agree to raise his salary to £160 on and from the day of his marriage.

"Yes, Mr. Fay," he said to the poor old Quaker, who had lately been so broken by his sorrow as hardly to be as much master of Tribbledale as he used to be, "I have no doubt I shall be steady now. If anything can make a young man steady it is—success in love."

"I hope thou wilt be happy, Mr. Tribbledale."

"I shall be happy enough now. My heart will be more in the business,—what there isn't of it at any rate with that dear creature in our mutual home at Islington. It was lucky about his having taken those lodgings, because Clara had got as it were used to them. And there are one or two things, such as a clock and the like, which need not be moved. If anything ever should happen to you, Mr. Fay, Pogson and Littlebird will find me quite up to the business."

"Something will happen some day, no doubt," said the Quaker.

On one occasion Lord Hampstead was in the Court having a word to say to Marion's father, or, perhaps, a word to hear. "I'm sure you'll excuse me, my lord," said Tribbledale, following him out of the office.

"Oh, yes," said Hampstead, with a smile,—for he

had been there often enough to have made some acquaintance with the junior clerk. "If there be anything I can do for you, I will do it willingly."

"Only just to congratulate me, my lord. You have heard of—Crocker?" Lord Hampstead owned that he had heard of Crocker. "He has been interfering with me in the tenderest of parts." Lord Hampstead looked serious. "There is a young woman"—the poor victim frowned, he knew not why; but remitted his frown and smiled again; "who had promised herself to me. Then that rude assailant came and upset all my joy." Here, as the narrator paused, Lord Hampstead owned to himself that he could not deny the truth of the description. "Perhaps," continued Tribbledale,— "perhaps you have seen Clara Demijohn." Lord Hampstead could not remember having been so fortunate. "Because I am aware that your steps have wandered in the way of Paradise Row." Then there came the frown again,—and then the smile. "Well; —perhaps it may be that a more perfect form of feminine beauty may be ascribed to another." This was intended as a compliment, more civil than true, paid to Marion Fay on Lord Hampstead's behalf. "But for a combination of chastity and tenderness I don't think you can easily beat Clara Demijohn." Lord Hampstead bowed, as showing his readiness to believe such a statement coming from so good a judge. "For awhile the interloper prevailed. Interlopers do prevail;

—such is the female heart. But the true rock shows itself always at last. She is the true rock on which I have built the castle of my happiness."

"Then I may congratulate you, Mr. Tribbledale."

"Yes;—and not only that, my lord. But Crocker is nowhere. You must own that there is a triumph in that. There was a time! Oh! how I felt it. There was a time when he triumphed; when he talked of 'my Clara,' as though I hadn't a chance. He's up a tree now, my lord. I thought I'd just tell you as you are so friendly, coming among us, here, my lord!" Lord Hampstead again congratulated him, and expressed a hope that he might be allowed to send the bride a small present.

"Oh, my lord," said Tribbledale, "it shall go with the clock and the harmonium, and shall be the proudest moment of my life."

When Miss Demijohn heard that the salary of Pogson and Littlebird's clerk,—she called it "Dan's screw" in speaking of the matter to her aunt,—had been raised to £160 per annum, she felt that there could be no excuse for a further change. Up to that moment it had seemed to her that Tribbledale had obtained his triumph by a deceit which it still might be her duty to frustrate. He had declared positively that those fatal words had been actually written in the book, "Dismissal—B. B." But she had learned that the words had not been written as yet. All is fair in

love and war. She was not in the least angry with
Tribbledale because of his little ruse. A lie told in
such a cause was a merit. But not on that account
need she be led away by it from her own most advantageous course. In spite of the little quarrel which
had sprung up between herself and Crocker, Crocker,
still belonging to Her Majesty's Civil Service, must be
better than Tribbledale. But when she found that
Tribbledale's statement as to the £160 was true, and
when she bethought herself that Crocker would probably be dismissed sooner or later, then she determined
to be firm. As to the £160, old Mrs. Demijohn herself
went to the office, and learned the truth from Zachary
Fay. " I think he is a good young man," said the
Quaker, " and he will do very well if he will cease to
think quite so much of himself." To this Mrs. Demijohn remarked that half-a-dozen babies might probably
cure that fault.

So the matter was settled, and it came to pass that
Daniel Tribbledale and Clara Demijohn were married
at Holloway on that very Thursday which saw completed the alliance which had been so long arranged
between the noble houses of Powell and De Hauteville.
There were two letters written on the occasion which
shall be given here as showing the willingness to forget
and forgive which marked the characters of the two
persons. A day or two before the marriage the
following invitation was sent ;—

"DEAR SAM,—

"I hope you will quite forget what is past, at any rate what was unpleasant, and come to our wedding on Thursday. There is to be a little breakfast here afterwards, and I am sure that Dan will be very happy to shake your hand. I have asked him, and he says that as he is to be the bridegroom he would be proud to have you as best man.

"Your old sincere friend,

"CLARA DEMIJOHN,—for the present."

The answer was as follows :—

"DEAR CLARA,—

"There's no malice in me. Since our little tiff I have been thinking that, after all, I'm not the man for matrimony. To sip the honey from many flowers is, perhaps, after all my line of life. I should have been happy to be Dan Tribbledale's bottle-holder, but that there is another affair coming off which I must attend. Our Lady Amaldina is to be married, and I must be there. Our families have been connected, as you know, for a great many years, and I could not forgive myself if I did not see her turned off. No other consideration would have prevented me from accepting your very kind invitation.

"Your loving old friend,

"SAM CROCKER."

There did come a pang of regret across Clara's
heart, as she read this as to the connection of the
families. Of course Crocker was lying. Of course it
was an empty boast. But there was a savour of
aristocracy even in the capability of telling such a lie.
Had she made Crocker her husband she also would
have been able to drag Castle Hautboy into her daily
conversations with Mrs. Duffer.

At the time of these weddings, the month of August,
Æolus had not even yet come to a positive and actual
decision as to Crocker's fate. Crocker had been
suspended;—by which act he had been temporarily
expelled from the office, so that his time was all
his own to do what he pleased with it. Whether
when suspended he would receive his salary, no one
knew as a certainty. The presumption was that a
man suspended would be dismissed,—unless he could
succeed in explaining away or diminishing the sin of
which he had been supposed to be guilty. Æolus
himself could suspend, but it required an act on the
part of the senior officer to dismiss,—or even to deprive
the sinner of any part of his official emoluments.
There had been no explanation possible. No diminishing of the sin had been attempted. It was
acknowledged on all sides that Crocker had,—as
Miss Demijohn properly described it,—destroyed Her
Majesty's Mail papers. In order that unpardonable
delay and idleness might not be traced home to him,

he had torn into fragments a bundle of official documents. His character was so well known that no one
doubted his dismissal. Mr. Jerningham had spoken of
it as a thing accomplished. Bobbin and Geraghty had
been congratulated on their rise in the department.
"Dismissal—B. B." had been recorded, if not in any
official book, at any rate in all official minds. But
B. B. himself had as yet decided nothing. When
Crocker attended Lady Amaldina's wedding in his best
coat and gloves he was still under suspension; but
trusting to the conviction that after so long a reprieve
capital punishment would not be carried out.

Sir Boreas Bodkin had shoved the papers on one
side, and, since that, nothing further had been said on
the matter. Weeks had passed, but no decision had
been made public. Sir Boreas was a man whom the
subordinates nearest to him did not like to remind
as to any such duty as this. When a case was "shoved
on one side" it was known to be something unpalate-
able. And yet, as Mr. Jerningham whispered to
George Roden, it was a thing that ought to be settled.
"He can't come back, you know," he said.

"I dare say he will," said the Duca.

"Impossible! I look upon it as impossible!" This
Mr. Jerningham said very seriously.

"There are some people, you know," rejoined the
other, "whose bark is so much worse than their bite."

"I know there are, Mr. Roden, and Sir Boreas is

perhaps one of them; but there are cases in which to pardon the thing done seems to be perfectly impossible. This is one of them. If papers are to be destroyed with impunity, what is to become of the Department? I for one should not know how to go on with my duties. Tearing up papers! Good Heavens! When I think of it I doubt whether I am standing on my head or my heels."

This was very strong language for Mr. Jerningham, who was not accustomed to find fault with the proceedings of his superiors. He went about the office all these weeks with a visage of woe and the air of a man conscious that some great evil was at hand. Sir Boreas had observed it, and knew well why that visage was so long. Nevertheless when his eyes fell on that bundle of papers,—on the Crocker bundle of papers,—he only pushed it a little further out of sight than it was before.

Who does not know how odious a letter will become by being shoved on one side day after day? Answer it at the moment, and it will be nothing. Put it away unread, or at least undigested, for a day, and it at once begins to assume ugly proportions. When you have been weak enough to let it lie on your desk, or worse again, hidden in your breast-pocket, for a week or ten days, it will have become an enemy so strong and so odious that you will not dare to attack it. It throws a gloom over all your joys. It makes you cross to your wife, severe to the cook, and critical to your own wine-cellar. It becomes the Black Care which sits behind you when you go out a riding. You have neglected a duty, and have put yourself in the power of perhaps some vulgar snarler. You think of destroying it and denying it, dishonestly and falsely,—as Crocker did the mail papers. And yet you must bear yourself all the time as though there were no load lying near your heart. So it was with our Æolus and the Crocker papers. The papers had become a great bundle. The unfortunate man had been called upon for an explanation, and had written a blundering long letter on a huge sheet of foolscap paper,—which Sir Boreas had not read, and did not mean to read. Large fragments of the torn "mail papers" had been found, and were all there. Mr. Jerningham had written a well-worded lengthy report,—which never certainly would be read. There were former documents in which the existence of the papers had been denied. Altogether the bundle was big and unholy and distasteful. Those who knew our Æolus well were sure that he would never even undo the tape by which the bundle was tied. But something must be done. One month's pay-day had already passed since the suspension, and the next was at hand. "Can anything be settled about Mr. Crocker?" asked Mr. Jerningham, one day about the end of August. Sir Boreas had already sent his family to a little place he had in the West of Ireland, and was postponing his holiday because of this horrid matter. Mr. Jerningham could never go away till Æolus went. Sir Boreas knew all this, and was thoroughly ashamed of himself. "Just speak to me about it to-morrow and we'll settle the matter," he said, in his blandest voice. Mr. Jerningham retreated from the room frowning. According to his thinking there ought to be nothing to settle. "D—— the fellow," said Sir Boreas, as soon as the door was closed; and he gave the papers another shove which sent them off the huge table on to the floor. Whether it was Mr. Jerningham or Crocker who was damned, he hardly knew himself. Then he was forced to stoop to the humility of picking up the bundle.

That afternoon he roused himself. About three o'clock he sent, not for Mr. Jerningham, but for the Duca. When Roden entered the room the bundle was before him, but not opened. "Can you send for this man and get him here to-day?" he asked. The Duca promised that he would do his best. "I can't bring myself to recommend his dismissal," he said. The Duca only smiled. "The poor fellow is just going to be married, you know." The Duca smiled again. Living in Paradise Row himself, he knew that the lady, *née* Clara Demijohn, was already the happy wife of Mr. Tribbledale. But he knew also that after so long an interval Crocker could not well be dismissed, and he was not ill-natured enough to rob his chief of so

good an excuse. He left the room, therefore, declaring that he would cause Crocker to be summoned
immediately.

Crocker was summoned, and came. Had Sir Boreas
made up his mind briefly to dismiss the man, or briefly
to forgive him, the interview would have been unnecessary. As things now were the man could not
certainly be dismissed. Sir Boreas was aware of that.
Nor could he be pardoned without further notice.
Crocker entered the room with that mingling of the
bully and the coward in his appearance which is
generally the result when a man who is overawed
attempts to show that he is not afraid. Sir Boreas
passed his fingers through the hairs on each side of
his head, frowned hard, and, blowing through his
nostrils, became at once the Æolus that he had been
named ;

> Assumes the god,
> Affects to nod,
> And seems to shake the spheres.

" Mr. Crocker," said the god, laying his hand on the
bundle of papers still tied up in a lump. Then he
paused and blew the wrath out of his nostrils.

"Sir Boreas, no one can be more sorry for an accident
than I am for that."

" An accident ! "

" Well, Sir Boreas ; I am afraid I shall not make you
understand it all."

" I don't think you will."

" The first paper I did tear up by accident, thinking it was something done with."

" Then you thought you might as well send the others after it."

" One or two were torn by accident. Then——"

" Well!"

" I hope you'll look it over this time, Sir Boreas."

" I have done nothing but look it over, as you call it, since you came into the Department. You've been a disgrace to the office. You're of no use whatsoever. You give more trouble than all the other clerks put together. I'm sick of hearing your name."

" If you'll try me again I'll turn over a new leaf, Sir Boreas."

" I don't believe it for a moment. They tell me you're just going to be married." Crocker was silent. Could he be expected to cut the ground from under his own feet at such a moment? "For the young lady's sake, I don't like turning you adrift on the world at such a time. I only wish that she had a more secure basis for her happiness."

" She'll be all right," said Crocker. He will probably be thought to have been justified in carrying on the delusion at such a crisis of his life.

" But you must take my assurance of this," said Æolus, looking more like the god of storms, " that no

wife or baby,—no joy or trouble,—shall save you again
if you again deserve dismissal." Crocker with his most
affable smile thanked Sir Boreas and withdrew. It
was said afterwards that Sir Boreas had seen and read
that smile on Roden's face, had put two and two
together in regard to him, and had become sure that
there was to be no marriage. But, had he lost that
excuse, where should he find another?

CHAPTER XIX.

"MY MARION."

THE blow came very suddenly at last. About the middle of September the spirit of Marion Fay flitted away from all its earthly joys and all its earthly troubles. Lord Hampstead saw her alive for the last time at that interview which was described a few pages back. Whenever he proposed to go down again to Pegwell Bay some objection was made, either by the Quaker or by Mrs. Roden on the Quaker's behalf. The doctor, it was alleged, had declared that such visits were injurious to his patient,—or perhaps it was that Marion had herself said that she was unable to bear the excitement. There was, no doubt, some truth in this. And Marion had seen that though she herself could enjoy the boundless love which her lover tendered to her, telling herself that though it was only for a while, it was very sweet to have it so, yet for him these meetings were full of agony. But in addition to this there was, I think, a jealousy on the part of Zachary Fay as to his daughter. When there was still a question whether the young lord should be his son-in-law, he had been willing to give way and to subordinate himself, even though his girl were the one thing left to him in all the world. While there was an idea that she should be married, there had accompanied that idea a hope, almost an expectation, that she might live. But when it was brought home to him as a fact that her marriage was out of the question because her life was waning, then unconsciously there grew up in his heart a feeling that the young lord ought not to rob him of what was left. Had Marion insisted, he would have yielded. Had Mrs. Roden told him that it was cruel to separate them, he would have groaned and given way. As it was, he simply leaned to that view of the matter which gave him the greatest preponderance with his own child. It may be that she saw it too, and would not wound him by asking for her lover's presence.

About the middle of September she died, having written to Hampstead the very day before her death. Her letters lately had become but a few words each, which Mrs. Roden would put into an envelope and send to their destination. He wrote daily, assuring her that he would not leave his home for a day in order that he might go to her instantly when she would send for him. To the last she never gave up the idea of seeing him again;—but at last the little light flickered out quicker than had been expected.

Mrs. Roden was at Pegwell Bay when the end came,

and to her fell the duty of making it known to Lord
Hampstead. She went up to town immediately, leaving
the Quaker in the desolate cottage, and sent down a
note from Holloway to Hendon Hall. "I must see you
as soon as possible. Shall I go to you, or will you come
to me?" When she wrote the words she was sure that
he would understand their purport, and yet it was
easier to write so than to tell the cruel truth plainly.
The note was sent down by a messenger, but Lord
Hampstead in person was the answer.

There was no need of any telling. When he stood
before her dressed from head to foot in black, she took
him by the two hands and looked into his face. "It is
all over for her," he said,—"the trouble and the anguish,
and the sense of long dull days to come. My Marion!
How infinitely she has the best of it! How glad I
ought to be that it is so."

"You must wait, Lord Hampstead," she said.

"Pray, pray, let me have no consolation. Waiting in
the sense you mean there will be none. For the one
relief which will finally come to me I must of course
wait. Did she say any word that you would wish to
tell me?"

"Many, many."

"Were they for my ears?"

"What other words should she have spoken to me?
They were prayers for your health."

"My health needs not her prayers."

" Prayers for your soul's health."

" Such praying will be efficacious there,—or would
be were anything needed to make her fit for those
angels among whom she has gone. For me they
can do nothing,—unless ıt be that in knowing how
much she loved me I may strive to be as she
was."

" And for your happiness."

" Psha ! " he exclaimed.

" You must let me do her commission, Lord Hampstead. I was to bid you remember that God in His
goodness has ordained that the dead after awhile shall
be remembered only with a softened sorrow. I was to
tell you that as a man you should give your thoughts
to other things. It is not from myself ;—it is from
her."

" She did not know. She did not understand. As
regards good and evil she was, to my eyes, perfect ;—
perfect as she was in beauty, in grace, and feminine
tenderness. But the character of others she had not
learned to read. But I need not trouble you as to that,
Mrs. Roden. You have been good to her as though
you were her mother, and I will love you for it while **I**
live." Then he was going away ; but he turned again
to ask some question as to the funeral. Might he do
it. Mrs. Roden shook her head. " But I shall be
there ? " To this she assented, but explained to him
that Zachary Fay would admit of no interference with

that which he considered to be his own privilege and his own duty.

Lord Hampstead had driven himself over from Hendon Hall, and had driven fast. When he left Mrs. Roden's house the groom was driving the dog-cart up and down Paradise Row, waiting for his master. But the master walked on out of the Row, forgetting altogether the horse and the cart and the man, not knowing whither he was going.

The blow had come, and though it had been fully expected, though he had known well that it was coming, it struck him now as hard, almost harder than if it had not been expected. It seemed to himself that he was unable to endure his sorrow now because he had been already weakened by such a load of sorrow. Because he had grieved so much, he could not now bear this further grief. As he walked on he beat his hands about, unconscious that he was in the midst of men and women who were gazing at him in the streets. There was nothing left to him,—nothing, nothing, nothing! He felt that if he could rid himself of his titles, rid himself of his wealth, rid himself of the very clothes upon his back, it would be better for him, so that he might not seem to himself to think that comfort could be found in externals. "Marion," he said, over and over again, in little whispered words, but loud enough for his own ears to hear the sound. And then he uttered phrases which were almost fantastic in their

woe, but which declared what was and had been the
condition of his mind towards her since she had become
so inexpressibly dear to him. "My wife," he said, "my
own one! Mother of my children. My woman; my
countess; my princess. They should have seen. They
should have acknowledged. They should have known
whom it was that I had brought among them;—of
what nature should be the woman whom a man should
set in a high place. I had made my choice;—and then
that it should come to this!" "There is no good to be
done," he said again. "It all turns to ashes and to
dust. The low things of the world are those which
prevail." "Oh, Marion, that I could be with you!
Though it were to be nowhere,—though the great story
should have no pathetic ending, though the last long
eternal chapter should be a blank, — still to have
wandered away with you would have been something."
As soon as he reached his house he walked straight
into the drawing-room, and having carefully closed the
door, he took the poker in his hand and held it clasped
there as something precious. "It is the only thing of
mine," he said, "that she has touched. Even then I
swore to myself that this hearth should be her hearth,
that here we would sit together, and be one flesh and
one bone." Then surreptitiously he took the bit of iron
away with him, and hid it among his treasures,—to the
subsequent dismay of the housemaid.

There came to him a summons from the Quaker to

the funeral, and on the day named, without saying a
word to any one, he took the train and went down to
Pegwell Bay. From the moment on which the messenger had come from Mrs. Roden he had dressed
himself in black, and he now made no difference in
his garments. Poor Zachary said but little to him;
but that little was very bitter. "It has been so with
all of them," he said. "They have all been taken.
The Lord cannot strike me again now." Of the
highly-born stranger's grief, or of the cause which
brought him there, he had not a word to say; nor did
Lord Hampstead speak of his own sorrow. "I sympathize and condole with you," he said to the old man.
The Quaker shook his head, and after that there was
silence between them till they parted. To the few
others who were there Lord Hampstead did not address
himself, nor did they to him. From the grave, when
the clod of earth had been thrown on it, he walked
slowly away, without a sign on his face of that agony
which was rending his heart. There was a carriage
there to take him to the railway, but he only shook
his head when he was invited to enter it. He walked
off and wandered about for hours, till he thought that
the graveyard would be deserted. Then he returned,
and when he found himself alone he stood over the
newly heaped-up soil. "Marion," he said to himself
over and over again, whispering as he stood there.
"Marion,—Marion; my wife; my woman." As he

stood by the grave side, one came softly stealing up to him, and laid a hand upon his shoulder. He turned round quickly, and saw that it was the bereaved father. "Mr. Fay," he said, "we have both lost the only thing that either of us valued."

"What is it to thee, who are young, and hardly knew her twelve months since?"

"Months make no difference, I think."

"But old age, my lord, and childishness, and solitude——"

"I, too, am alone."

"She was my daughter, my own. Thou hadst seen a pretty face, and that was all. She had remained with me when those others died. Had thou not come——"

"Did my coming kill her, Mr. Fay?"

"I do not say that. Thou hast been good to her, and I would not say a hard word to thee."

"I did think that nothing could have added to my sorrow."

"No, my lord; no, no. She would have died. She was her dear mother's child, and she was doomed. Go away, and be thankful that thou, too, hast not become the father of children born only to perish in your sight. I will not say an unkind word, but I would wish to have my girl's grave to myself." Upon this Lord Hampstead walked off, and went back to his own home, hardly knowing how he reached it.

It was a month after this that he returned to the

churchyard, and might have been seen sitting on the
small stone slab which the Quaker had already caused
to be laid over the grave. It was a fine October evening, and the sombre gloom of the hours was already
darkening everything around. He had crept into the
enclosure silently, almost slily, so as to insure himself
that his presence should not be noted; and now, made
confident by the coming darkness, he had seated himself on the stone. During the long hours that he sat
there no word was formed within his lips, but he
surrendered himself entirely to thoughts of what his
life might have been had she been spared to him. He
had come there for a purpose, the very opposite of
that; but how often does it come to pass that we are
unable to drive our thoughts into that channel in
which we wish them to flow? He had thought much
of her last words, and was minded to attempt to do
something as she would have had him do it;—not
that he might enjoy his life, but that he might make
it useful. But as he sat there, he could not think of
the real future,—not of the future as it might be made
to take this or that form by his own efforts; but of
the future as it would have been had she been with
him, of the glorious, bright, beautiful future which her
love, her goodness, her beauty, her tenderness would
have illuminated.

Till he had seen her his heart had never been
struck. Ideas, sufficiently pleasant in themselves,

though tinged with a certain irony and sarcasm, had
been frequent with him as to his future career. He
would leave that building up of a future family of
Marquises,—if future Marquises there were to be,—to
one of those young darlings whose bringing-up would
manifestly fit them for the work. For himself he
would perhaps philosophize, perhaps do something that
might be of service,—would indulge at any rate his
own views as to humanity;—but he would not burden
himself with a Countess and a nursery full of young
lords and ladies. He had often said to Roden, had
often said to Vivian, that her ladyship, his stepmother,
need not trouble herself. He certainly would not be
guilty of making either a Countess or a Marchioness.
They, of course, had laughed at him, and had bid him
bide his time. He had bided his time,—as they had
said,—and Marion Fay had been the result.

Yes;—life would have been worth the having if
Marion Fay had remained to him. It was thus he
communed with himself as he sat there on the tomb.
From the moment in which he had first seen her
in Mrs. Roden's house he had felt that things were
changed with him. There had come a vision before
him which filled him full of delight. As he learned to
know the tones of her voice, and the motion of her
limbs, and to succumb to the feminine charms with
which she enveloped him, all the world was brightened
up to his view. Here there was no pretence of special

blood, no assumption of fantastic titles, no claim to
superiority because of fathers and mothers who were in
themselves by no means superior to their neighbours.
And yet there had been all the grace, all the loveliness,
all the tenderness, without which his senses would not
have been captivated. He had never known his want;
—but he had in truth wanted one who should be at
all points a lady, and yet not insist on a right to be
so esteemed on the strength of inherited privileges.
Chance, good fortune, providence had sent her to him,
—or more probably the eternal fitness of things, as he
had allowed himself to argue when things had fallen
out so well to his liking. Then there had arisen
difficulties, which had seemed to him to be vain and
absurd,—though they would not allow themselves to be
at once swept away. They had talked to him of his
station and of hers, making that an obstacle which to
him had been a strong argument in favour of her love.
Against this he had done battle with the resolute
purpose which a man has who is sure of his cause.
He would have none of their sophistries, none of their
fears, none of their old-fashioned absurdities. Did she
love him? Was her heart to him as was his to her?
That was the one question on which it must all
depend. As he thought of it all, sitting there on
the tombstone, he put out his arm as though to fold
her form to his bosom when he thought of the moment
in which he became sure that it was so. There had

been no doubt of the full-flowing current of her love. Then he had aroused himself, and had shaken his mane like a lion, and had sworn aloud that this vain obstacle should be no obstacle, even though it was pleaded by herself. Nature had been strong enough within him to assure him that he would overcome the obstacle.

And he had overcome it,—or was overcoming it,— when that other barrier gradually presented itself, and loomed day by day terribly large before his affrighted eyes. Even to that he would not yield,—not only as regarded her but himself also. Had there been no such barrier, the possession of Marion would have been to him an assurance of perfect bliss which the prospect of far-distant death would not have effected. When he began to perceive that her condition was not as that of other young women, he became aware of a great danger, —of a danger to himself as well as to her, to himself rather than to her. This increased rather than diminished his desire for the possession. As the ardent rider will be more intent to take the fence when it looms before him large and difficult, so with him the resolution to make Marion his wife became the stronger when he knew that there were reasons of prudence, reasons of caution, reasons of worldly wisdom, why he should not do so. It had become a religion to him that she should be his one. Then gradually her strength had become known to him, and slowly he was made aware that he must bow to her decision. All that he wanted in all the world he must not have,—not that the love which he craved was wanting, but because she knew that her own doom was fixed.

She had bade him retrick his beams, and take the light and the splendour of his sun elsewhere. The light and the splendour of his sun had all passed from him. She had absorbed them altogether. He, while he had been boasting to himself of his power and his manliness, in that he would certainly overcome all the barriers, had found himself to be weak as water in her hands. She, in her soft feminine tones, had told him what duty had required of her, and, as she had said so she had done. Then he had stood on one side, and had remained looking on, till she had—gone away and left him. She had never been his. It had not been allowed to him even to write his name, as belonging also to her, on the gravestone.

But she had loved him. There was nothing in it all but this to which his mind could revert with any feeling of satisfaction. She had certainly loved him. If such love might be continued between a disembodied spirit and one still upon the earth,—if there were any spirit capable of love after that divorce between the soul and the body,—her love certainly would still be true to him. Most assuredly his should be true to her. Whatever he might do towards obeying her in striving to form some manly purpose for his life, he would never ask another woman to be his wife, he would never look for other love. The black coat should be laid aside as soon as might be, so that the world around him should not have cause for remark; but the mourning should never be taken from his heart.

Then, when the darkness of night had quite come upon him, he arose from his seat, and flinging himself on his knees, stretched his arms wildly across the grave. "Marion," he said; "Marion; oh, Marion, will you hear me? Though gone from me, art thou not mine?" He looked up into the night, and there, before his eyes, was her figure, beautiful as ever, with all her loveliness of half-developed form, with her soft hair upon her shoulders; and her eyes beamed on him, and a heavenly smile came across her face, and her lips moved as though she would encourage him. "My Marion;—my wife!"

Very late that night the servants heard him as he opened the door and walked across the hall, and made his way up to his own room.

CHAPTER XX.

MR. GREENWOOD'S LAST BATTLE.

DURING the whole of that long summer nothing was
absolutely arranged as to Roden and Lady Frances,
though it was known to all London, and to a great
many persons outside of London, that they were
certainly to become man and wife. The summer was
very long to Lord and Lady Trafford because of the
necessity incumbent on them of remaining through the
last dregs of the season on account of Lady Amaldina's
marriage. Had Lady Amaldina thrown herself away
on another Roden the aunt would have no doubt gone
to the country; but her niece had done her duty in
life with so much propriety and success that it would
have been indecent to desert her. Lady Kingsbury
therefore remained in Park Lane, and was driven to
endure frequently the sight of the Post Office clerk.

For George Roden was admitted to the house even
though it was at last acknowledged that he must be
George Roden, and nothing more. And it was found
also that he must be a Post Office clerk, and nothing

more. Lord Persiflage, on whom Lady Kingsbury
chiefly depended for seeing that her own darlings
should not be disgraced by being made brothers-in-law
to anything so low as a clerk in the Post Office, was
angry at last, and declared that it was impossible to
help a man who would not help himself. "It is no
use trying to pick a man up who will lie in the
gutter." It was thus he spoke of Roden in his anger;
and then the Marchioness would wring her hands and
abuse her stepdaughter. Lord Persiflage did think
that something might be done for the young man if
the young man would only allow himself to be called a
Duke. But the young man would not allow it, and
Lord Persiflage did not see what could be done.
Nevertheless there was a general idea abroad in the
world that something would be done. Even the
mysterious savour of high rank which attached itself to
the young man would do something for him.

It may be remembered that the Marquis himself,
when first the fact had come to his ears that his
daughter loved the young man, had been almost as
ferociously angry as his wife. He had assented to the
carrying of her away to the Saxon castle. He had
frowned upon her. He had been a party to the
expelling her from his own house. But gradually his
heart had become softened towards her; in his illness
he had repented of his harshness; he had not borne
her continued absence easily, and had of late looked

about for an excuse for accepting her lover. When the man was discovered to be a Duke, though it was only an Italian Duke, of course he accepted him. Now his wife told him daily that Roden was not a Duke, because he would not accept his Dukedom,—and ought therefore again to be rejected. Lord Persiflage had declared that nothing could be done for him, and therefore he ought to be rejected. But the Marquis clung to his daughter. As the man was absolutely a Duke, according to the laws of all the Heralds, and all the Courts, and all the tables of precedency and usages of peerage in Christendom, he could not de-grade himself even by any motion of his own. He was the eldest and the legitimate son of the last Duca di Crinola,—so the Marquis said,—and as such was a fitting aspirant for the hand of the daughter of an English peer. "But he hasn't got a shilling," said Lady Kingsbury weeping. The Marquis felt that it was within his own power to produce some remedy for this evil, but he did not care to say as much to his wife, who was tender on that point in regard to the interest of her three darlings. Roden continued his visits to Park Lane very frequently all through the summer, and had already arranged for an autumn visit to Castle Hautboy,—in spite of that angry word spoken by Lord Persiflage. Everybody knew he was to marry Lady Frances. But when the season was over, and all the world had flitted from London, nothing was settled.

Lady Kingsbury was of course very unhappy during
all this time ; but there was a source of misery deeper,
more pressing, more crushing than even the Post Office
clerk. Mr. Greenwood, the late chaplain, had, during his
last interview with the Marquis, expressed some noble
sentiments. He would betray nothing that had been
said to him in confidence. He would do nothing that
could annoy the Marchioness, because the Marchioness
was a lady, and as such, entitled to all courtesy from
him as a gentleman. There were grounds no doubt on
which he could found a claim, but he would not insist
on them, as his doing so would be distasteful to her
ladyship. He felt that he was being ill-treated, almost
robbed ; but he would put up with that rather than say
a word which would come against his own conscience as
a gentleman. With these high assurances he took his
leave of the Marquis as though he intended to put up
with the beggarly stipend of £200 a year which the
Marquis had promised him. Perhaps that had been his
intention ;—but before two days were over he had
remembered that though it might be base to tell her
ladyship's secrets, the penny-post was still open to him.

It certainly was the case that Lady Kingsbury had
spoken to him with strong hopes of the death of the
heir to the title. Mr. Greenwood, in discussing the
matter with himself, went beyond that, and declared to
himself that she had done so with expectation as well
as hope. Fearful words had been said. So he assured

himself. He thanked his God that nothing had come
of it. Only for him something,—he assured himself,—
would have come of it. The whisperings in that
up-stairs sitting-room at Trafford had been dreadful.
He had divulged nothing. He had held his tongue,—
like a gentleman. But ought he not to be paid for
holding his tongue? There are so many who act
honestly from noble motives, and then feel that their
honesty should be rewarded by all those gains which
dishonesty might have procured for them! About a
fortnight after the visit which Mr. Greenwood made to
the Marquis he did write a letter to the Marchioness.
" I am not anxious," he said, " to do more than remind
your ladyship of those peculiarly confidential discussions
which took place between yourself and me at Trafford
during the last winter; but I think you will acknowledge that they were of a nature to make me feel that I
should not be discarded like an old glove. If you would
tell his lordship that something should be done for me,
something would be done." Her ladyship when she
received this was very much frightened. She remembered
the expressions she had allowed herself to use, and did
say a hesitating, halting word to her husband, suggest-
ing that Mr. Greenwood's pension should be increased.
The Marquis turned upon her in anger. " Did you ever
promise him anything?" he asked. No;—she had
promised him nothing. "I am giving him more than
he deserves, and will do no more," said the Marquis.

There was something in his voice which forbade her to speak another word.

Mr. Greenwood's letter having remained for ten days without an answer, there came another. " I cannot but think that you will acknowledge my right to expect an answer," he said, "considering the many years through which I have enjoyed the privilege of your ladyship's friendship, and the *very confidential terms* on which we have been used to discuss matters of the highest interest to us both." The "matters" had no doubt been the probability of the accession to the title of her own son through the demise of his elder brother! She understood now all her own folly, and something of her own wickedness. To this second appeal she wrote a short answer, having laid awake over it one entire night.

"DEAR MR. GREENWOOD—I have spoken to the Marquis, and he will do nothing.

　　　　　　　　　　"Yours truly,
　　　　　　　　　　　　" C. KINGSBURY."

This she did without saying a word to her husband.

Then, after the interval of a few days, there came a third letter.

"MY DEAR LADY KINGSBURY,—

　　　　　　"I cannot allow myself to think that this should be the end of it all, after so many years of social

intimacy and confidential intercourse. Can you yourself imagine the condition of a gentleman of my age
reduced after a life of ease and comfort to exist on a
miserable pension of £200 a year? It simply means
death,—death! Have I not a right to expect something better after the devotion of a life?

"Who has known as well as I the stumbling-blocks
to your ladyship's ambition which have been found in
the existences of Lord Hampstead and Lady Frances
Trafford? I have sympathized with you no doubt,—
partly because of their peculiarities, partly from sincere
affection for your ladyship. It cannot surely be that
your ladyship should now treat me as an enemy because
I could do no more than sympathize!

"Dig I cannot. To beg I am ashamed. You will
hardly wish that I should perish from want. I have
not as yet been driven to open out my sad case to any
one but yourself. Do not force me to it,—for the sake
of those darling children for whose welfare I have ever
been so anxious.

"Believe me to be,

"Your ladyship's most devoted and faithful friend,

"THOMAS GREENWOOD."

This epistle so frightened her that she began to
consider how she might best collect together a sufficient
sum of money to satisfy the man. She did succeed in
sending him a note for £50. But this he was too wary

to take. He returned it, saying that he could not,
though steeped in poverty, accept chance eleemosynary
aid. What he required,—and had he thought a right
to ask,—was an increase to the fixed stipend allowed
him. He must, he thought, again force himself upon
the presence of the Marquis, and explain the nature of
the demand more explicitly.

Upon this Lady Kingsbury showed all the letters to
her husband. "What does he mean by stumbling-
blocks?" asked the Marquis in his wrath. Then there
was a scene which was sad enough. She had to confess
that she had spoken very freely to the chaplain respecting her step-children. "Freely! What does freely
mean? Do you want them out of the way?" What a
question for a husband to have to ask his wife! But
she had a door by which she could partly escape. It
was not that she had wanted them out of the way, but
that she had been so horrified by what she had thought
to be their very improper ideas as to their own rank of
life. Those marriages which they had intended had
caused her to speak as she had done to the chaplain.
When alone at Trafford she had no doubt opened her
mind to the clergyman. She rested a great deal on the
undoubted fact that Mr. Greenwood was a clergyman.
Hampstead and Fanny had been stumbling-blocks to
her ambition because she had desired to see them
married properly into proper families. She probably
thought that she was telling the truth as she said all

this. It was at any rate accepted as truth, and she was condoned. As to Hampstead, it was known by this time that that marriage could never take place ; and as to Lady Frances, the Marchioness was driven, in her present misery, to confess, that as the Duca was in truth a Duca, his family must be held to be proper.

But the Marquis sent for Mr. Cumming, his London solicitor, and put all the letters into his hand,—with such explanation as he thought necessary to give. Mr. Cumming at first recommended that the pension should be altogether stopped ; but to this the Marquis did not consent. " It would not suit me that he should starve," said the Marquis. " But if he continues to write to her ladyship something must be done."

"Threatening letters to extort money ! " said the lawyer confidently. " I can have him before a magistrate to-morrow, my lord, if it be thought well." It was, however, felt to be expedient that Mr. Cumming should in the first case send for Mr. Greenwood, and explain to that gentleman the nature of the law.

Mr. Cumming no doubt felt himself that it would be well that Mr. Greenwood should not starve, and well also that application should not be made to the magistrate, unless as a last resort. He, too, asked himself what was meant by "stumbling-blocks." Mr. Greenwood was a greedy rascal, descending to the lowest depth of villany with the view of making money out of the fears of a silly woman. But the silly woman, the lawyer thought, must have been almost worse than silly. It seemed natural to Mr. Cumming that a stepmother should be anxious for the worldly welfare of her own children;—not unnatural, perhaps, that she should be so anxious as to have a feeling at her heart amounting almost to a wish that "chance" should remove the obstacle. Chance, as Mr. Cumming was aware, could in such a case mean only—death. Mr. Cumming, when he put this in plain terms to himself, felt it to be very horrid; but there might be a doubt whether such a feeling would be criminal, if backed up by no deed and expressed by no word. But here it seemed that words had been spoken. Mr. Greenwood had probably invented that particular phrase, but would hardly have invented it unless something had been said to justify it. It was his business, however, to crush Mr. Greenwood, and not to expose her ladyship. He wrote a very civil note to Mr. Greenwood. Would Mr. Greenwood do him the kindness to call in Bedford Row at such or such an hour,—or indeed at any other hour that might suit him. Mr. Greenwood thinking much of it, and resolving in his mind that any increase to his pension might probably be made through Mr. Cumming, did as he was bid, and waited upon the lawyer.

Mr. Cumming, when the clergyman was shown in, was seated with the letters before him,—the various letters which Mr. Greenwood had written to Lady Kingsbury,—folded out one over another, so that the visitor's eye might see them and feel their presence; but he did not intend to use them unless of necessity. "Mr. Greenwood," he said, "I learn that you are discontented with the amount of a retiring allowance which the Marquis of Kingsbury has made you on leaving his service."

"I am, Mr. Cumming; certainly I am.—£200 a year is not——"

"Let us call it £300, Mr. Greenwood."

"Well, yes; Lord Hampstead did say something——"

"And has paid something. Let us call it £300. Not that the amount matters. The Marquis and Lord Hampstead are determined not to increase it."

"Determined!"

"Quite determined that under no circumstances will they increase it. They may find it necessary to stop it."

"Is this a threat?"

"Certainly it is a threat,—as far as it goes. There is another threat which I may have to make for the sake of coercing you; but I do not wish to use it if I can do without it."

"Her ladyship knows that I am ill-treated in this matter. She sent me £50 and I returned it. It was not in that way that I wished to be paid for my services."

"It was well for you that you did. But for that I could not certainly have asked you to come and see me here."

" You could not ? "

" No ;—I could not. You will probably understand what I mean." Here Mr. Cumming laid his hands upon the letters, but made no other allusion to them. " A very few words more will, I think, settle all that there is to be arranged between us. The Marquis, from certain reasons of humanity,—with which I for one hardly sympathize in this case,—is most unwilling to stop, or even to lessen, the ample pension which is paid to you."

" Ample ;—after a whole lifetime ! "

" But he will do so if you write any further letters to any member of his family."

" That is tyranny, Mr. Cumming."

" Very well. Then is the Marquis a tyrant. But he will go further than that in his tyranny. If it be necessary to defend either himself or any of his family from further annoyance, he will do so by criminal proceedings. You are probably aware that the doing this would be very disagreeable to the Marquis. Undoubtedly it would. To such a man as Lord Kingsbury it is a great trouble to have his own name, or worse, that of others of his family, brought into a Police Court. But, if necessary, it will be done. I do not ask you for any assurance, Mr. Greenwood, because it may be well that you should take a little time to think of it. But unless you are willing to lose your income, and to be taken before a police magistrate for endeavouring to extort money by threatening letters, you had better hold your hand."

"I have never threatened."

"Good morning, Mr. Greenwood."

"Mr. Cumming, I have threatened no one."

"Good morning, Mr. Greenwood." Then the discarded chaplain took his leave, failing to find the words with which he could satisfactorily express his sense of the injury which had been done him.

Before that day was over he had made up his mind to take his £300 a year and be silent. The Marquis, he now found, was not so infirm as he had thought, nor the Marchioness quite so full of fears. He must give it up, and take his pittance. But in doing so he continued to assure himself that he was greatly injured, and did not cease to accuse Lord Kingsbury of sordid parsimony in refusing to reward adequately one whose services to the family had been so faithful and long-enduring.

It may, however, be understood that in the midst of troubles such as these Lady Kingsbury did not pass a pleasant summer.

CHAPTER XXI.

THE REGISTRAR OF STATE RECORDS.

ALTHOUGH Lord Persiflage had seemed to be very angry with the recusant Duke, and had made that uncivil speech about the gutter, still he was quite willing that George Roden should be asked down to Castle Hautboy. "Of course we must do something for him," he said to his wife; "but I hate scrupulous men. I don't blame him at all for making such a girl as Fanny fall in love with him. If I were a Post Office clerk I'd do the same if I could."

"Not you. You wouldn't have given yourself the trouble."

"But when I had done it I wouldn't have given her friends more trouble than was necessary. I should have known that they would have had to drag me up somewhere. I should have looked for that. But I shouldn't have made myself difficult when chance gave a helping hand. Why shouldn't he have taken his title?"

"Of course we all wish he would."

"Fanny is as bad as he is. She has caught some of Hampstead's levelling ideas and encourages the young man. It was all Kingsbury's fault from the first. He began the world wrong, and now he cannot get himself right again. A radical aristocrat is a contradiction in terms. It is very well that there should be Radicals. It would be a stupid do-nothing world without them. But a man can't be oil and vinegar at the same time." This was the expression made by Lord Persiflage of his general ideas on politics in reference to George Roden and his connection with the Trafford family; but not the less was George Roden asked down to Castle Hautboy. Lady Frances was not to be thrown over because she had made a fool of herself,—nor was George Roden to be left out in the cold, belonging as he did now to Lady Frances. Lord Persiflage never approved very much of anybody,—but he never threw anybody over.

It was soon after the funeral of Marion Fay that Roden went down to Cumberland. During the last two months of Marion's illness Hampstead and Roden had been very often together. Not that they had lived together, as Hampstead had declared himself unable to bear continued society. His hours had been passed alone. But there had not been many days in which the friends had not seen each other for a few minutes. It had become a habit with Hampstead to ride over to Paradise Row when Roden had returned from the

office.   At first Mrs. Roden also had been there;—but
latterly she had spent her time altogether at Pegwell
Bay.   Nevertheless Lord Hampstead would come, and
would say a few words, and would then ride home
again.   When all was over at Pegwell Bay, when the
funeral was at hand, and during the few days of absolutely prostrating grief which followed it, nothing was
seen of him;—but on the evening before his friend's
journey down to Castle Hautboy he again appeared
in the Row.   On this occasion he walked over, and his
friend returned with him a part of the way.   "You
must do something with yourself," Roden said to him.

"I see no need of doing anything special.   How
many men do nothing with themselves!"

"Men either work or play."

"I do not think I shall play much."

"Not for a time certainly.   You used to play; but
I can imagine that the power of doing so will have
deserted you."

"I shan't hunt, if you mean that."

"I do not mean that at all," said Roden;—"but
that you should do something.   There must be some
occupation, or life will be insupportable."

"It is insupportable," said the young man looking
away, so that his countenance should not be seen.

"But it must be supported.   Let the load be ever
so heavy, it must be carried.   You would not destroy
yourself?"

"No;"—said the other slowly; "no. I would not do that. If any one would do it for me!"

"No one will do it for you. Not to have some plan of active life, some defined labour by which the weariness of the time may be conquered, would be a weakness and a cowardice next door to that of suicide."

"Roden," said the lord, "your severity is brutal."

"The question is whether it be true. You shall call it what you like,—or call me what you like; but can you contradict what I say? Do you not feel that it is your duty as a man to apply what intellect you have, and what strength, to some purpose?"

Then, by degrees, Lord Hampstead did explain the purpose he had before him. He intended to have a yacht built, and start alone, and cruise about the face of the world. He would take books with him, and study the peoples and the countries which he visited.

"Alone?" asked Roden.

"Yes, alone;—as far as a man may be alone with a crew and a captain around him. I shall make acquaintances as I go, and shall be able to bear them as such. They will know nothing of my secret wound. Had I you with me,—you and my sister let us suppose, —or Vivian, or any one from here who had known me, I could not even struggle to raise my head."

"It would wear off."

"I will go alone; and if occasion offers I will make fresh acquaintances. I will begin another life which

shall have no connection with the old one,—except that
which will be continued by the thread of my own
memory. No one shall be near me who may even
think of her name when my own ways and manners
are called in question." He went on to explain that he
would set himself to work at once. The ship must be
built, and the crew collected, and the stores prepared.
He thought that in this way he might find employment
for himself till the spring. In the spring, if all was
ready, he would start. Till that time came he would
live at Hendon Hall,—still alone. He so far relented,
however, as to say that if his sister was married before
he began his wanderings he would be present at her
marriage.

Early in the course of the evening he had explained
to Roden that his father and he had conjointly
arranged to give Lady Frances £40,000 on her wedding.
" Can that be necessary ? " asked Roden.

" You must live ; and as you have gone into a nest
with the drones, you must live in some sort as the
drones do."

" I hope I shall never be a drone."

" You cannot touch pitch and not be defiled. You'll
be expected to wear gloves and drink fine wine,—or, at
any rate, to give it to your friends. Your wife will
have to ride in a coach. If she don't people will point
at her, and think she's a pauper, because she has
a handle to her name. They talk of the upper ten

thousand. It is as hard to get out from among them as it is to get in among them. Though you have been wonderfully stout about the Italian title, you'll find that it will stick to you." Then it was explained that the money, which was to be given, would in no wise interfere with the "darlings." Whatever was to be added to the fortune which would naturally have belonged to Lady Frances, would come not from her father but from her brother.

When Roden arrived at Castle Hautboy Lord Persiflage was there, though he remained but for a day. He was due to be with the Queen for a month,—a duty which was evidently much to his taste, though he affected to frown over it as a hardship. "I am sorry, Roden," he said, "that I should be obliged to leave you and everybody else;—but a Government hack, you know, has to be a Government hack." This was rather strong from a Secretary of State to a Clerk in the Post Office; but Roden had to let it pass lest he should give an opening to some remark on his own repudiated rank. "I shall be back before you are gone, I hope, and then perhaps we may arrange something." The only thing that Roden wished to arrange was a day for his own wedding, as to which, as far as he knew, Lord Persiflage could have nothing to say.

"I don't think you ought to be sorry," Lady Frances said to her lover as they were wandering about on the mountains. He had endeavoured to explain to her that this large income which was now promised to him rather impeded than assisted the scheme of life which he had suggested to himself.

"Not sorry,—but disappointed, if you know the difference."

"Not exactly."

"I had wanted to feel that I should earn my wife's bread."

"So you shall. If a man works honestly for his living, I don't think he need inquire too curiously what proportion of it may come from his own labour or from some other source. If I had had nothing we should have done very well without the coach,—as poor Hampstead calls it. But if the coach is there I don't see why we shouldn't ride in it."

"I should like to earn the coach too," said Roden.

"This, sir, will be a lesson serviceable in teaching you that you are not to be allowed to have your own way in everything."

An additional leave of absence for a month had been accorded to Roden. He had already been absent during a considerable time in the spring of the year, and in the ordinary course of events would not have been entitled to this prolonged indulgence. But there were reasons deemed to be sufficient. He was going to meet a Cabinet Minister. He was engaged to marry the daughter of a Marquis. And it was known that he was not simply George Roden, but in truth the

Duca di Crinola. He had suffered some qualms of conscience as to the favour to be thus shown him, but had quieted them by the idea that when a man is in love something special ought to be done for him. He remained, therefore, till the Foreign Secretary returned from his royal service, and had by that time fixed the period of his marriage. It was to take place in the cold comfortless month of March. It would be a great thing, he had said, to have Hampstead present at it, and it was Hampstead's intention to start on his long travels early in April. " I don't see why people shouldn't be married in cold weather as well as in hot," said Vivian. "Brides need not go about always in muslin."

When Lord Persiflage returned to Castle Hautboy, he had his plan ready arranged for relieving his future half-nephew-in-law,—if there be such a relationship,— from the ignominy of the Post Office. "I have Her Majesty's permission," he said to Roden, "to offer you the position of Registrar of State Records to the Foreign Office."

"Registrar of State Records to the Foreign Office!"

"Fifteen hundred a year," said his lordship, going off at once to this one point of true vital importance. "I am bound to say that I think I could have done better for you had you consented to bear the title, which is as completely your own, as is that mine by which I am called."

"Don't let us go back to that, my lord."

" Oh no ;—certainly not. Only this ; if you could be brought to think better of it,—if Fanny could be induced to make you think better of it,—the office now offered to you would, I think, be more .comfortable to you."

" How so ? "

"I can hardly explain, but it would. There is no reason on earth why it should not be held by an Italian. We had an Italian for many years librarian at the Museum. And as an Italian you would of course be entitled to call yourself by your hereditary title."

" I shall never be other than an Englishman."

"Very well. One man may lead a horse to water, but a thousand cannot make him drink. I only tell you what would be the case. The title would no doubt give a prestige to the new office. It is exactly that kind of work which would fall readily into the hands of a foreigner of high rank. One cannot explain these things, but it is so. The £1500 a year would more probably become £2000 if you submitted to be called by your own proper name." Everybody knew that Lord Persiflage understood the Civil Service of his country perfectly. He was a man who never worked very hard himself, or expected those under him to do so; but he liked common sense, and hated scruples, and he considered it to be a man's duty to take care of himself,—of himself first of all, and then, perhaps, afterwards, of the Service.

Neither did Roden nor did Lady Frances give way a

bit the more for this. They were persistent in clinging to their old comparatively humble English name. Lady Frances would be Lady Frances to the end, but she would be no more than Lady Frances Roden. And George Roden would be George Roden, whether a clerk in the Post Office or Registrar of State Records to the Foreign Office. So much the next new bride declared with great energy to the last new bride who had just returned from her short wedding tour, having been hurried home so that her husband might be able to lay the first stone of the new bridge to be built over the Menai Straits. Lady Llwddythlw, with all the composed manners of a steady matron, was at Castle Hautboy, and used all her powers of persuasion. " Never mind, my dear, what he says," Lady Llwddythlw urged. " What you should think of is what will be good for him. He would be somebody,—almost as good as an Under Secretary of State,—with a title. He would get to be considered among the big official swells. There is so much in a name! Of course, you've got your rank. But you ought to insist on it for his sake."

Lady Frances did not give way in the least, nor did any one venture to call the Duca by his title, formally or openly. But, as Lord Hampstead had said, " it stuck to him." The women when they were alone with him would call him Duca, joking with him; and it was out of the question that he should be angry with them for

their jokes. He became aware that behind his back he
was always spoken of as The Duke, and that this was
not done with any idea of laughing at him. The people
around him believed that he was a Duke and ought to
be called a Duke. Of course it was in joke that Lady
Llwddythlw always called Lady Frances Duchessina
when they were together, because Lady Frances had
certainly not as yet acquired her right to the name;
but it all tended to the same point. He became aware
that the very servants around him understood it. They
did not call him "your grace" or "my Lord," or make
spoken allusion to his rank; but they looked it. All
that obsequiousness due to an hereditary nobleman,
which is dear to the domestic heart, was paid to him.
He found himself called upon by Lady Persiflage to go
into the dining-room out of his proper place. There
was a fair excuse for this while the party was small,
and confined to few beyond the family, as it was
expected that the two declared lovers should sit
together. But when this had been done with a larger
party he expostulated with his hostess. "My dear
Mr. Roden," she said,—"I suppose I must call you so."

"It's my name at any rate."

"There are certain points on which, as far as I
can see, a man may be allowed to have his way,—and
certain points on which he may not."

"As to his own name——"

"Yes; on the matter of your name. I do not see

my way how to get the better of you just at present, though on account of my near connection with Fanny I am very anxious to do so. But as to the fact of your rank, there it is. Whenever I see you,—and I hope I shall see you very often,—I shall always suppose that I see an Italian nobleman of the first class, and shall treat you so." He shrugged his shoulders, feeling that he had nothing else to do. " If I were to find myself in the society of some man calling himself by a title to which I knew that he had no right,—I should probably call him by no name; but I should be very careful not to treat him as a nobleman, knowing that he had no right to be so treated. What can I do in your case but just reverse the position ? "

He never went back to the Post Office,—of course. What should a Registrar of State Records to the Foreign Office do in so humble an establishment ? He never went back for the purposes of work. He called to bid farewell to Sir Boreas, Mr. Jerningham, Crocker, and others with whom he had served. " I did not think we should see much more of you," said Sir Boreas, laughing.

"I intended to live and die with you," said Roden.

"We don't have dukes; or at any rate we don't keep them. Like to like is a motto which I always find true. When I heard that you were living with a young lord, and were going to marry the daughter of a marquis, and had a title of your own which you could use as soon as you pleased, I knew that I should lose you." Then he added in a little whisper, "You couldn't get Crocker made a duke, could you,—or a Registrar of Records?"

Mr. Jerningham was full of smiles and bows, pervaded thoroughly by a feeling that he was bidding farewell to an august nobleman, though, for negative reasons, he was not to be allowed to gratify his tongue by naming the august name. Crocker was a little shy; —but he plucked up his courage at last. "I shall always know what I know, you know," he said, as he shook hands with the friend to whom he had been so much attached. Bobbin and Geraghty made no allusions to the title, but they, too, as they were severally greeted, were evidently under the influence of the nobility of their late brother clerk.

The marriage was duly solemnized when March came in the parish church of Trafford. There was nothing grand,—no even distant imitation of Lady Amaldina's glorious cavalcade. Hampstead did come down, and endeavoured for the occasion to fit himself for the joy of the day. His ship was ready for him, and he intended to start now in a week or two. As it happened that the House was not sitting, Lord Llwddythlw, at the instigation of his wife, was present. "One good turn deserves another," Lady Llwddythlw had said to him. And the darlings were there in all their glory, loud, beautiful, and unruly. Lady Kingsbury was of course present; but was too much in abeyance to be able to arouse even a sign of displeasure. Since that reference to the "stumbling blocks" had reached her husband, and since those fears with which Mr. Greenwood had filled her, she had been awed into quiescence.

The bridegroom was of course married under the simple name of George Roden,—and we must part with him under that name; but it is the belief of the present chronicler that the aristocratic element will prevail, and that the time will come soon in which the Registrar of State Records to the Foreign Office will be known in the purlieus of Downing Street as the Duca di Crinola.

THE END.